THE QUEST

Wilbur Smith was born in Central Africa in 1933. He was educated at Michaelhouse and Rhodes University. He became a full-time writer in 1964 after the successful publication of *When the Lion Feeds*, and has since written over thirty novels, all meticulously researched on his numerous expeditions world-wide. His books are now translated into twenty-six languages.

'Wilbur Smith's swashbuckling novels of Africa – the bodices rip and the blood flows. You can get lost in them and misplace all of August'
Stephen King

WILBUR SMITH

THE QUEST

PAN BOOKS

First published 2007 by Macmillan

This edition published 2008 by Pan Books
an imprint of Pan Macmillan Ltd
Pan Macmillan, 20 New Wharf Road, London N1 9RR
Basingstoke and Oxford
Associated companies throughout the world
www.panmacmillan.com

ISBN 978-0-330-41272-8

3 5 7 9 8 6 4 2

A CIP catalogue record for this book is available from
the British Library.

Typeset by SetSystems Ltd, Saffron Walden, Essex
Printed and bound in Great Britain by
Mackays of Chatham plc, Chatham, Kent

Visit **www.panmacmillan.com** to read more about all our books
and to buy them. You will also find features, author interviews and
news of any author events, and you can sign up for e-newsletters
so that you're always first to hear about our new releases.

This book is for my wife

MOKHINISO

Beautiful, loving, loyal and true;
There is no one in the world but you.

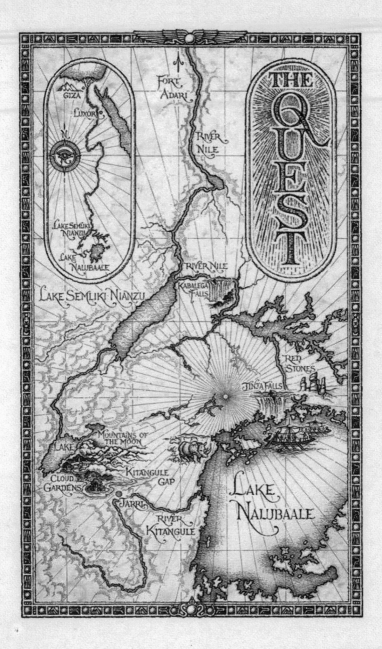

Two lonely figures came down from the high mountains. They were dressed in travel-worn furs and leather helmets with ear-flaps strapped beneath their chins against the cold. Their beards were untrimmed and their faces weatherbeaten. They carried all their meagre possessions upon their backs. It had taken a hard and daunting journey to reach this spot. Although he led, Meren had no inkling where they were, neither was he sure why they had come so far. Only the old man who followed close behind him knew that, and he had not yet chosen to enlighten Meren.

Since leaving Egypt they had crossed seas and lakes and many mighty rivers; they had traversed vast plains and forests. They had encountered strange and dangerous animals and even stranger and more dangerous men. Then they had entered the mountains, a prodigious chaos of snowy peaks and gaping gorges, where the thin air was hard to breathe. Their horses had died in the cold and Meren had lost the tip of one finger, burned black and rotting by the crackling frosts. Fortunately it was not the finger of his sword hand, nor one of those that released the arrow from his great bow.

Meren stopped on the brink of the last sheer cliff. The old man came up beside him. His fur coat was made from the skin of a snow tiger that Meren had slain with a single arrow as it sprang upon him. Standing shoulder to shoulder, they looked down on a foreign land of rivers and dense green jungles.

'Five years,' Meren said. 'Five years we have been upon the road. Is this the end of the journey, Magus?'

'Ha, good Meren, surely it has not been that long?' Taita asked, and his eyes sparkled teasingly under frost-white brows.

In reply Meren unslung his sword scabbard from his back and displayed the lines of notches scratched in the leather. 'I have recorded every day, should you wish to count them,' he assured him. He had followed Taita and protected him for more than half his own lifetime, but he was still never entirely certain whether the other was serious or merely jesting with him. 'But you have not answered my question, revered Magus. Have we reached the end of our journey?'

'Nay, we have not.' Taita shook his head. 'But take comfort, for at least we have made a good beginning.' Now he took the lead and set out along a narrow ledge that angled down across the face of the cliff.

Meren gazed after him for a few moments, then his bluff, handsome features creased into a grin of rueful resignation. 'Will the old devil never stop?' he asked the mountains, slung his scabbard on his back and followed him.

At the bottom of the cliff they came round a buttress of white quartz rock and a voice piped out of the sky, 'Welcome, travellers! I have waited a long time for your coming.'

They stopped in surprise and looked up at the ledge above them. On it sat a childlike figure, a boy who seemed no older than eleven years. It was odd that they had not noticed him before for he was in full view: the high bright sunlight picked him out and reflected off the shining quartz that surrounded him with a radiant nimbus, which pained the eyes.

'I have been sent to guide you to the temple of Saraswati, the goddess of wisdom and regeneration,' said the child, and his voice was mellifluous.

'You speak the Egyptian language!' Meren blurted in astonishment.

The boy turned the fatuous remark with a smile. He had the brown face of a mischievous monkey, but his smile was so winsome that Meren could not help but return it.

'My name is Ganga. I am the messenger. Come! There is still some way to go.' He stood, and his thick braid of black hair dangled over one bare shoulder. Even in the cold he wore only a loincloth. His smooth bare torso was a dark chestnut colour, yet he carried on his back a hump like that of a camel, grotesque and shocking. He saw their expressions and smiled again. 'You will grow accustomed to it, as I have,' he said. He jumped down from the shelf and reached up to take Taita's hand. 'This way.'

For the next two days Ganga led them through thick bamboo forest. The track took many twists and turns and without him they would have lost it a hundred times. As they descended, the air grew warmer and they were able at last to shed their furs and go on bareheaded. Taita's locks were thin, straight and silvery. Meren's were dense, dark and curling. On the second day they came to the end of the bamboo forests and followed the path into thick jungle with galleries that met overhead and blotted out the sunlight. The air was warm and heavy with the scent of damp earth and rotting plants. Birds of bright plumage flashed over their heads, small monkeys chattered and gibbered on the top branches and brilliantly coloured butterflies hovered over the flowering vines.

With dramatic suddenness the jungle ended and they came out into an open plain that extended about a league to the opposite wall of the jungle. In the centre of this clearing stood a mighty edifice. The towers, turrets and terraces were built from butter-yellow stone blocks, and the entire complex was surrounded by a high wall of the same stone. The decorative statues and panels that covered the exterior depicted a riot of naked men and voluptuous women.

'What those statues are playing at would startle the horses,' Meren said, in a censorious tone, although his eyes glittered.

'Methinks you would have made a fine model for the sculptors,' Taita suggested. Every conceivable conjunction of human bodies was carved into the yellow stone. 'Surely there is nothing shown on those walls that is new to you?'

'On the contrary, I could learn much,' Meren admitted. 'I had not even dreamed the half of it.'

'The Temple of Knowledge and Regeneration,' Ganga reminded them. 'Here, the act of procreation is regarded as both sacred and beautiful.'

'Meren has long held the same view,' Taita remarked drily. Now the path beneath their feet was paved and they followed it to the gateway in the outer wall of the temple. The massive teak gates stood open.

'Go through!' Ganga urged. 'You are expected by the *apsaras*.'

'*Apsaras*?' Meren asked.

'The temple maidens,' Ganga explained.

They went through the gateway, and then even Taita blinked with surprise, for they found themselves in a marvellous garden. The smooth green lawns were studded with clumps of flowering shrubs and fruit trees, many of which were already in full bearing, the plump fruits ripening lusciously. Even Taita, who was a learned herbalist and horticulturist, did not recognize some of the exotic species. The flower-beds were a splendour of dazzling colours. Near the gateway three young women were seated on the lawn. When they saw the travellers they sprang up and ran lightly to meet them. Laughing and dancing with excitement, they kissed and embraced both Taita and Meren. The first *apsara* was slim, golden-haired and lovely. She, too, appeared girlish, for her creamy skin was unblemished. 'Hail and well met! I am Astrata,' she said.

The second *apsara* had dark hair and slanted eyes. Her skin was as translucent as beeswax and polished, like ivory carved by a master craftsman. She was magnificent in the full bloom of womanhood. 'I am Wu Lu,' she said, stroking Meren's muscled arm admiringly, 'and you are beautiful.'

'I am Tansid,' said the third *apsara*, who was tall and statuesque. Her eyes were a startling turquoise green, her hair was flaming auburn, and her teeth were white and perfect. When she kissed Taita her breath was as perfumed as any of the flowers in the garden. 'You are welcome,' Tansid told him. 'We were waiting for you. Kashyap and Samana told us you were coming. They sent us to meet you. You bring us joy.'

With one arm round Wu Lu, Meren looked back at the gateway. 'Where has Ganga gone?' he asked.

'Ganga never was,' Taita told him. 'He is a forest sprite, and now that his task has been completed he has gone back into the other world.' Meren accepted this. Having lived so long with the Magus, he was no longer surprised by even the most bizarre and magical phenomena.

The *apsaras* took them into the temple. After the bright hot sunlight of the garden the high halls were cool and dim, the air scented by the incense-burners that stood before golden images of the goddess Saraswati. Priests and priestesses in flowing saffron robes worshipped before them, while more *apsaras* flitted through the shadows like butterflies. Some came to kiss and hug the strangers. They stroked Meren's arms and chest, and fondled Taita's silver beard.

At last Wu Lu, Tansid and Astrata took the two by the hand and led them down a long gallery, into the living quarters of the temple. In the refectory the women served them bowls of stewed vegetables and cups of sweet red wine. They had been on meagre rations for so long that even Taita ate hungrily. When they were replete, Tansid took Taita to the chamber that had been set aside for him. She helped him undress and made him stand in a copper basin of warm water while she sponged his weary body. She was like a mother tending a child, so natural and gentle that Taita felt no embarrassment even when she ran the sponge over the ugly scar of his castration. After she had dried him, she led him to the sleeping mat and sat beside him, singing softly, until he fell into a deep, dreamless sleep.

Wu Lu and Astrata led Meren to another chamber. As Tansid had done for Taita, they bathed him, then settled him to sleep on his mat. Meren tried to keep them with him, but he was exhausted and his efforts half-hearted. They giggled and slipped away. Within moments he, too, had fallen asleep.

He slept until the light of day filtered into the chamber and woke, feeling rested and rejuvenated. His worn, soiled clothing had disappeared, replaced with a fresh, loose-fitting tunic. No sooner had he dressed than he heard sweet feminine laughter and voices approaching down the gallery outside his door. The two girls burst in upon him, carrying porcelain dishes and jugs of fruit juice. While they ate with him the *apsaras* talked to Meren in Egyptian, but between themselves they spoke a medley of languages, all of which seemed natural to them. However, each favoured what was clearly her mother tongue. Astrata's was Ionian, which explained her fine gold hair, and Wu Lu spoke with the chiming, bell-like tones of far Cathay.

When the meal was finished they took Meren out into the sunlight to where a fountain played over the waters of a deep pool. Both dropped the light garments they wore and plunged naked into the pool. When she saw that Meren was hanging back, Astrata came out of the pool to fetch him, her hair and body streaming with water. She seized him, laughing, stripped him of his tunic and dragged him to the pool. Wu Lu came to help her, and once they had him in the pool, they frolicked and splashed. Soon Meren abandoned his modesty, and became as frank and unashamed as they were. Astrata washed his hair, and marvelled at the combat scars that scored his knotted muscles.

Meren was astonished by the perfection of the two *apsaras'* bodies as they rubbed themselves against him. All the time their hands were busy beneath the surface of the water. When, between them, they had aroused him, they shrieked with delight and pulled him from the pool to a small pavilion under the trees. Piles of carpets and silken cushions lay on the stone floor, and they stretched him out on them still wet from the pool.

'Now we will worship the goddess,' Wu Lu told him.

'How do we do that?' Meren demanded.

'Have no fear. We will show you,' Astrata assured him. She pressed the full silken length of her body to his back, kissing his ears and neck from behind, her belly warmly moulded to his buttocks. Her hands reached round to caress Wu Lu, who was kissing his mouth and encircling him with her arms and legs. The two girls were consummately skilled in the arts of love. After a while it was as though the three had flowed together and been transformed into a single organism, a creature possessed of six arms, six legs and three mouths.

Like Meren, Taita woke early. Although he had been wearied by the long journey, a few hours of sleep had restored his body and spirits. The dawn light filled his chamber as he sat up on the sleeping mat, and became aware that he was not alone.

Tansid knelt beside his mat and smiled at him. 'Good morrow, Magus. I have food and drink for you. When you have fortified yourself, Kashyap and Samana are eager to meet.'

'Who are they?'

'Kashyap is our revered abbot, Samana our reverend mother. As you are, so are they both eminent magi.'

Samana was waiting for him in an arbour in the temple gardens. She was a handsome woman of indeterminate age, wearing a saffron robe. There were wings of silver in the dense hair above her ears, and her eyes were infinitely wise. After she had embraced him, she bade Taita sit beside her on the marble bench. She asked him about the journey he had made to reach the temple, and they talked for a while before she said, 'We are so glad that you have arrived in time to meet the Abbot Kashyap. He will not be with us for much longer. It was he who sent for you.'

'I knew I had been summoned to this place, but I did not know by whom.' Taita nodded. 'Why did he bring me here?'

'He will tell you himself,' Samana said. 'We will go to him now.' She stood and took his hand. They left Tansid, and Samana led him through many passages and cloisters, then up a spiral staircase that seemed endless. At last they came out in a small circular room at the top of the highest temple minaret. It was open all round with a view over the green jungles to the far parapets of snow-topped mountain ranges in the north. In the middle of the floor a soft mattress was piled with cushions, on which sat a man.

'Place yourself in front of him,' Samana whispered. 'He is almost completely deaf, and must be able to see your lips when you speak.' Taita did as she had said, then Kashyap and he regarded each other in silence for a while.

Kashyap was ancient. His eyes were pale and faded, his gums toothless. His skin was as dry and foxed as old parchment, his hair, beard and eyebrows were as pale and transparent as glass. His hands and head shook with uncontrollable tremors.

'Why have you sent for me, Magus?' Taita asked.

'Because you are of good mind.' Kashyap's voice was a whisper.

'How do you know of me?' Taita asked.

'With your esoteric power and presence, you leave a disturbance on the ether that is discernible from afar,' Kashyap explained.

'What do you want of me?'

'Nothing and everything, perhaps even your life.'

'Explain.'

'Alas! I have left it too late. The dark tiger of death is stalking me. I will be gone before the setting of the sun.'

'Is the task you have set me of moment?'

'Of the direst moment.'

'What must I do?' Taita asked.

'I had purposed to arm you for the struggle that lies ahead of you, but now I have learned from the *apsaras* that you are a eunuch. This I did not know before you came here. I cannot pass on my knowledge to you in the manner I had in mind.'

'What manner was that?' Taita asked.

'By carnal exchange.'

'Again I do not understand.'

'It would have involved sexual congress between us. Because of your injuries, that is not possible.' Taita was silent. Kashyap reached out to lay a withered, clawlike hand upon his arm. His voice was gentle when he said, 'I see by your aura that in speaking of your injuries I have offended you. For this I am sorry, but I have little time left and I must be blunt.'

Taita remained silent, so Kashyap went on: 'I have resolved to make the exchange with Samana. She is also of good mind.

Once I am gone she will impart to you that which she has garnered from me. I am sorry I have upset you.'

'The truth may be painful, but you have not been. I will do whatever you need of me.'

'Then stay with us while I pass everything I possess, the learning and wisdom of all my long life, to Samana. Later she will share it with you, and you will be armed for the sacred endeavour that is your destiny.'

Taita bowed his head in acquiescence.

Samana clapped her hands sharply and two strange *apsaras* came up the stairs, both young and lovely, one brunette, the other honey blonde. They followed Samana to the small brazier against the far wall and assisted her in brewing a bowl of sharply scented herbs over the coals. When the potion was prepared, they brought it to Kashyap. While one steadied his shaking head, the other held the bowl to his lips. He drank the potion noisily, a little dribbling down his chin, then sagged back wearily upon the mattress.

The two *apsaras* undressed him tenderly and respectfully, then poured aromatic balm from an alabaster bottle over his groin. They massaged his withered manroot gently but persistently. Kashyap groaned, muttered and rolled his head from side to side, but in the skilful hands of the *apsaras*, and under the influence of the drug, his sex swelled and engorged.

When it was fully tumescent Samana came to his mattress. She lifted the skirt of her saffron robe as high as her waist, to reveal finely sculpted legs and buttocks that were round and strong. She straddled Kashyap, then reached down to take his manroot in her hand and guide it into herself. Once they were joined in congress she let the saffron skirts drop to screen them and began to rock gently over him, whispering softly to him: 'Master, I am prepared to receive all you have to give me.'

'Willingly do I entrust it to you.' Kashyap's voice was thin and reedy. 'Use it wisely and well.' Again he rolled his head from side to side, his ancient features puckered in a dreadful rictus. Then he stiffened and groaned, his body locked in a convulsion. Neither moved again for almost an hour. Then the breath rattled out of Kashyap's throat and he collapsed on to the mattress.

Samana stifled a scream. 'He is dead,' she said, with the greatest sorrow and compassion. Gently she uncoupled from Kashyap's corpse. Kneeling beside him, she closed the lids over his pale staring eyes. Then she looked across at Taita.

'At sunset this evening we will cremate his husk. Kashyap was my patron and guide throughout my life. He was more than any father to me. Now his essence lives on within me. It has become one with my spirit soul. Forgive me, Magus, but it may be some time before I am recovered sufficiently from this harrowing experience to be of any use to you. Then I will come to you.'

That evening Taita stood, with Tansid at his side, on the small darkened balcony outside his chamber and watched the funeral pyre of the Abbot Kashyap burning in the garden of the temple below. He felt a deep sense of loss that he had not come to know the man sooner. Even during their brief acquaintance he had been aware of the affinity that had existed between them.

A soft voice spoke in the darkness, startling him out of his reverie. He turned and saw that Samana had come up to them quietly.

'Kashyap was also aware of the bond between you.' She stood at Taita's other hand. 'You, too, are a servant of the Truth. That is why he summoned you so urgently. He would have come to you if his body had been able to carry him that far. During the carnal exchange you witnessed, the last great sacrifice he made to the Truth, Kashyap passed a message to me to deliver to you. Before I do so he required me to test your faith. Tell me, Taita of Gallala, what is your creed?'

Taita thought for a while, and then he replied: 'I believe that the universe is the battleground of two mighty hosts. The first of these is the host of the gods of the Truth. The second is the host of the demons of the Lie.'

'What role can we feeble mortals play in this cataclysmic struggle?' Samana asked.

'We can devote ourselves to the Truth, or allow ourselves to be swallowed by the Lie.'

'If we choose the right-hand path of the Truth, how may we resist the dark power of the Lie?'

'By climbing the Eternal Mountain until we can see clearly the face of the Truth. Once we have achieved that we will be assimilated into the ranks of the Benevolent Immortals, who are the warriors for the Truth.'

'Is this the destiny of all men?'

'Nay! Only very few, the most worthy, will achieve that rank.'

'At the end of time will the Truth triumph over the Lie?'

'Nay! The Lie will persist, but so will the Truth. The battle rages back and forth but it is eternal.'

'Is the Truth not God?'

'Call him Ra or Ahura Maasda, Vishnu or Zeus, Woden or whatever name rings holiest in your ears, God is God, the one and alone.' Taita had made his confession of faith.

'I see from your aura that there is no vestige of the Lie in what you affirm,' Samana said quietly, and she knelt before him. 'The spirit soul of Kashyap within me is satisfied that you are indeed of the Truth. There is no check and impediment to our enterprise. Now we may proceed.'

'Explain to me what is our "enterprise", Samana.'

'In these dire times, the Lie is once more in the ascendancy. A new and menacing force has arisen that threatens all of mankind, but especially your very Egypt. The reason you have been summoned here is to be armed for your struggle against this terrible thing. I will open your Inner Eye so that you may see clearly the path you must follow.' Samana stood up and embraced him. Then she went on, 'There is little time to spare. We will begin on the morrow. But before that I must select a helper.'

'Who is there to choose from?' Taita asked.

'Your *apsara*, Tansid, has assisted me before. She knows what is required.'

'Then choose her,' Taita agreed. Samana nodded and held out a hand to Tansid. The two women embraced, then looked again to Taita.

'You must choose your own helper,' Samana said.

'Tell me what is required of him.'

'He must have the strength to stand firm, and compassion for you. You must have trust in him.'

Taita did not hesitate. 'Meren!'

'Of course,' Samana acceded.

At dawn the four ascended the foothills of the mountains, taking the path through the jungle and climbing until they reached the bamboo forest. Samana examined many of the swaying yellow bamboos before she selected a mature branch, then had Meren cut out a supple segment. He carried it back to the temple.

From the branch Samana and Tansid carefully fashioned a selection of long bamboo needles. They polished them until they were not much thicker than a human hair, but sharper and more resilient than the finest bronze.

An air of tension and expectation pervaded the serenity of the temple community. The laughter and high spirits of the *apsaras* were muted. Whenever Tansid looked at Taita it was with awe tinged with something close to pity. Samana spent most of the waiting days with him, fortifying him for the ordeal that lay ahead. They discussed many things, and Samana spoke with the voice and the wisdom of Kashyap.

At one point Taita broached a subject that had long occupied him: 'I perceive that you are a Long Liver, Samana.'

'As are you, Taita.'

'How is it that so few of us survive to an age far in excess of the rest of humanity?' he asked. 'It is beyond nature.'

'For myself, and others such as the Abbot Kashyap, it may be the manner of our existence, what we eat and drink, what we think and believe. Or perhaps that we have a purpose, a reason to continue, a spur to goad us on.'

'What of me? Although I feel I am a stripling, compared to you and the abbot, I have far surpassed the lifespan of most other men,' Taita said.

Samana smiled. 'You are of good mind. Until this time the power of your intellect has been able to triumph over the frailty of your body, but in the end we must all die, as Kashyap has.'

'You have answered my first question, but I have another. Who has chosen me?' Taita asked, but he knew that the question was doomed to remain unanswered.

Samana flashed a sweet, enigmatic smile and leant forward to place a finger on his lips. 'You have been selected,' she whispered. 'Let that suffice.' He knew that he had pushed her to the limit of her knowledge: that was as far as she could go.

They sat together and meditated, for the rest of that day and half of the night that followed, on all that had passed so far between them. Then she took him to her bed-chamber and they slept entwined, like a mother and child, until dawn filled the chamber with light. They rose and bathed together, then Samana took him to an ancient stone building in a hidden corner of the gardens that Taita had not visited before. Tansid was already there. She was busy at a marble table that stood in the centre of the large central room. When they entered she looked up at them. 'I was preparing the last of the needles,' she explained, 'but I will leave if you wish to be alone.'

'Stay, beloved Tansid,' Samana told her. 'Your presence will not disturb us.' She took Taita's hand and led him about the room. 'This building was designed by the first abbots in the beginning time. They needed good light in which to operate.' She pointed to the large open windows set high in the walls above them. 'On this marble table more than fifty generations of abbots have performed the opening of the Inner Eye. Each one was a savant, the term by which we describe the initiates, those who are able to see the aura of other humans and animals.' She pointed out to him the writing carved into the walls. 'Those are the records of all who have gone before us throughout the centuries and the millennium. Between ourselves there must stand no reservation. I will give you no false assurances – you would see through any attempt I made to deceive you before I could speak the first word. So I tell you truly that, under the tutelage of Kashyap, I attempted to open the Inner Eye four times before I was successful.'

She pointed to the most recent set of inscriptions. 'Here you can see my attempts recorded. Perhaps at first I lacked skill and dexterity. Perhaps my patients were not far enough along the right-hand path. In one instance the result was disastrous. I warn you, Taita, the risks are great.' Samana was silent for a while, ruminating. Then she went on, 'There were others before me who failed. See here!' She led him to a set of time-worn, lichen-coated inscriptions at the furthest end of the wall. 'These are so old that they are extremely difficult to decipher, but I can tell you what they record. Almost two thousand years ago a woman came to this temple. She was a survivor of an ancient people who once lived in a great city named Ilion beside the Aegean Sea. She had been the High Priestess of Apollo. She was a Long Liver, as you are. Over the centuries, since the sack and destruction of her city, she had wandered the earth, garnering wisdom and learning. The abbot at that time was named Kurma. The strange woman convinced him that she was a paragon of the Truth. In that way she induced him to open her Inner Eye. It was a success that astonished and elated him. It was only long after she had left the temple that Kurma was overtaken by doubts and misgivings. A series of terrible events occurred that made him realize she might have been an impostor, a thief, an adept of the left-hand path, a minion of the Lie. At length he discovered that she had used witchcraft to kill the one who had been originally chosen. She had assumed the murdered woman's identity and been able to cloak her true nature sufficiently to dupe him.'

'What became of this creature?'

'Generation after generation of the abbots of the goddess Saraswati have tried to trace her. But she has cloaked herself and disappeared. Perhaps by this time she is dead. That is the best we can hope for.'

'What was her name?' Taita asked.

'Here! It is inscribed.' Samana touched the writing with her fingertips, 'She called herself Eos, after the sister of the sun god. I know now that it was not her true name. But her spirit sign was the mark of a cat's paw. Here it is.'

'How many others failed?' Taita sought to divert himself from his dark forebodings.

'There were many.'

'Tell me about some from your own experience.'

Samana thought for a moment, then said, 'One in particular I remember, from when I was still a novice. His name was Wotad, a priest of the god Woden. His skin was covered with sacred blue tattoos. He was brought to this temple from the northlands across the Cold Sea. He was a man of mighty physique, but he died under the bamboo needle. Even his great strength was insufficient to survive the power that was unleashed within him by the opening. His brain burst asunder, and blood spurted from his nose and ears.' Samana sighed. 'It was a terrible death, but swift. Perhaps Wotad was luckier than some of those who preceded him. The Inner Eye can turn itself back on its owner, like a venomous serpent held by the tail. Some of the horrors it reveals are too vivid and terrible to survive.'

For the remainder of that day they were silent while Tansid busied herself at the stone table, polishing the last of the bamboo needles and arranging the surgical instruments.

At last Samana looked up at Taita and spoke softly: 'Now you know the risks that you will run. You do not have to make the attempt. The choice is yours alone.'

Taita shook his head. 'I have no choice. I know now that the choice was made for me on the day of my birth.'

That night Tansid and Meren slept in Taita's chamber. Before she blew out the lamp Tansid brought Taita a small porcelain bowl filled with a warm infusion of herbs. As soon as he had drunk it he stretched out on his mat and fell into a deep sleep. Meren rose twice in the night to listen to his breathing and to cover him when the cold air of the dawn seeped into the chamber.

When Taita awoke he found the three, Samana, Tansid and Meren, kneeling round his sleeping mat.

'Magus, are you ready?' Samana asked inscrutably.

Taita nodded, but Meren blurted out, 'Do not do this thing, Magus. Do not let them do it to you. It is evil.'

Taita took his muscular forearm and shook it sternly. 'I have chosen you for this task. I need you. Do not fail me, Meren. If I must do this alone who can say what the consequences might be? Together we can win through, as we have so often before.' Meren took a series of ragged deep breaths. 'Are you ready, Meren? Are you at my side as ever you were?'

'Forgive me, I was weak, but now I am ready, Magus,' he whispered.

Samana led them out into the brilliant sunshine of the garden, to the ancient building. At one end of the marble table lay the surgeon's instruments, and at the opposite end stood a charcoal brazier above which the heated air shimmered. Spread on the ground below the table was a sheep's fleece rug. Taita did not need to be told: he knelt in the centre of the rug, facing the table. Samana nodded at Meren; clearly, she had instructed him in his duties. He knelt behind Taita, and folded him tenderly in his arms so that he could not move.

'Close your eyes, Meren,' Samana instructed him. 'Do not watch.' She stood over them and offered a strip of leather for Taita to grip in his jaws. He refused it with a shake of his head. She knelt in front of him with a silver spoon in her right hand; with two fingers of her other hand she parted the lids of Taita's right eye. 'Always through the right eye,' she whispered, 'the side of the Truth.' She spread the lids wide. 'Hold hard, Meren!'

Meren grunted in acknowledgement and tightened his grip until it was as unyielding as a ring of bronze about his master. Samana slipped the point of the spoon under his upper eyelid and, with a firm, sure movement, eased it down behind the eyeball. Then, gently, she scooped the eye out of its socket. She let it dangle, like an egg, on to Taita's cheek, suspended on the rope of the optic nerve. The empty socket was a deep pink cave, glistening with tears. Samana handed the silver spoon to Tansid, who laid it aside and selected one of the bamboo needles. She held the point in the flame of the brazier until it scorched and hardened. It was still smoking as she handed it to Samana. With the needle in her right hand Samana lowered her head until she was staring into Taita's empty eye socket. She judged the position and angle of the optic pathway as it entered the skull.

Taita's eyelids twitched and shuddered under her fingers, blinking uncontrollably. Samana ignored them. Slowly she introduced the needle into the eye cavity until the point touched the opening of the pathway. She increased the pressure until suddenly the needle pierced the membrane and slid in alongside the nerve cord without damaging it. There was almost no resistance to its passage. Deeper and deeper it glided. When it was almost a finger's length into the frontal lobe of the brain Samana sensed rather than felt the light check as the point touched the bundle of nerve fibres from both eyes where they crossed at the optic chiasm. The bamboo point was at the portal. The next move had to be precisely executed. Although her expression remained serene, a light film of perspiration shone on Samana's unblemished skin, and her eyes narrowed. She tensed and made the final thrust. There was no reaction from Taita. She knew she had missed the minute target. She drew back the needle a fraction, realigned it, then drove it in again to the same depth, but this time she aimed a little higher.

Taita shuddered and sighed softly. Then he relaxed as he fell into oblivion. Meren had been warned to expect this, and he cupped one strong hand under Taita's chin to prevent the beloved silver head from dropping forward. Samana withdrew the needle from the eye socket as carefully as she had driven it deep. She leaned forward to examine the puncture in the lining at the back of the eye. There was no weep of blood. Before her eyes the mouth of the tiny wound closed spontaneously.

Samana made a humming sound of approbation. Then she used the spoon to ease the dangling eye back into the socket. Taita's eyelids blinked rapidly as it reseated itself. Samana reached for the linen bandage, which Tansid had soaked in a healing salve and laid ready on the marble table, then bound it around Taita's head, covering both of his eyes, and knotted it securely.

'As quickly as you are able, Meren, carry him back to his own chamber before he comes to his senses.'

Meren lifted him as though he were a sleeping infant and held his head against his sturdy shoulder. He ran with Taita back to the temple and carried him up to his room. Samana and Tansid followed them. When the two women arrived, Tansid went to the hearth, where she had left a kettle warming. She poured a bowl of the herbal infusion and brought it to Samana.

'Lift his head!' Samana ordered, and held the bowl to Taita's lips, dribbling the liquid into his mouth and massaging his throat to induce him to swallow. She made him take the contents of the bowl.

They did not have to wait long. Taita stiffened and reached up to feel the bandage that blindfolded him. His hand began to shake as though palsied. His teeth chattered, then he ground them together. The muscle in the point of his jaws bulged and Meren was terrified that he might bite off his tongue. With his thumbs he tried to prise the magus's jaws apart, but suddenly Taita's mouth flew open of its own accord and he shrieked, every muscle in his body knotted hard as cured teak. Spasm after spasm racked him. He screamed in terror and moaned with despair, then burst into gales of maniacal laughter. Just as suddenly he began to weep as though his heart was breaking. Then he screamed again and his back arched until his head touched his heels. Even Meren could not hold the frail, ancient body, which was now endowed with demonic strength.

'What possesses him?' Meren pleaded with Samana. 'Make him stop before he kills himself.'

'His Inner Eye is wide open. He has not yet learnt to control it. Images so terrible as to drive any ordinary man insane are flooding through it and overwhelming his mind. He is enduring all the suffering of mankind.' Samana, too, was panting as she tried to make Taita swallow another mouthful of the bitter drug. Taita spewed it at the ceiling of the chamber.

'This was the frenzy that killed Wotad, the northman,' Samana told Tansid. 'The images swelled his brain like an overfilled bladder of boiling oil until it could contain no more and burst asunder.' She held Taita's hands to stop him clawing at the bandage over his eyes. 'The magus is experiencing the grief of every widow and of every bereaved mother who has ever watched her firstborn die. He shares the suffering of every man or woman who was ever maimed, tortured or ravaged by disease. His soul is sickened by the cruelty of every tyrant, by the wickedness of the Lie. He is burning in the flames of sacked cities, and dying on a thousand battlefields with the vanquished. He feels the despair of every lost soul who ever lived. He is looking into the depths of hell.'

'It will kill him!' Meren was in anguish almost as intense as Taita's.

'Unless he learns to control the Inner Eye, yes, it may

indeed kill him. Hold him, do not let him harm himself.'
Taita's head was rolling so violently from side to side that his
skull thumped against the stone wall beside his bed.

Samana began to chant an invocation, in a high quavering
voice that was not her own, in a language that Meren had
never heard before. But the chanting had little effect.

Meren cradled Taita's head in his arms. Samana and Tansid
wedged themselves on each side of him, cushioning him with
their bodies, to prevent him harming himself in his wild
struggles. Tansid blew perfumed breath into his gaping mouth.
'Taita!' she called. 'Come back! Come back to us!'

'He cannot hear you,' Samana told her. She leant closer
and cupped her hands round Taita's right ear: the ear of Truth.
She whispered to him soothingly in the language of her chant.
Meren recognized its inflections: although he could not understand the meaning, he had heard Taita use it when he
conversed with other magi. It was their secret language, which
they called the Tenmass.

Taita quietened and cocked his head to one side as though
he was listening to Samana. Her voice sank lower but became
more urgent. Taita murmured a reply. Meren realized that she
was giving him instructions, helping him to shutter the Inner
Eye, to filter out the destructive images and sounds, to understand what he was experiencing and to ride the torrents of
emotion that were battering him.

They all stayed with him for the rest of that day and
through the long night that followed. By dawn Meren was
exhausted, and collapsed into sleep. The women did not
attempt to rouse him, but let him rest. His body had been
tempered by combat and hard physical endeavour, but he
could not match their spiritual stamina. Beside them, he was a
child.

Samana and Tansid stayed close to Taita. Sometimes he
seemed to sleep. At others he was restless, drifting in and out
of delirium. Behind the blindfold he seemed unable to separate
fantasy from reality. Once he sat up and hugged Tansid to him

with savage strength. 'Lostris!' he cried. 'You have returned as you promised you would. Oh, Isis and Horus, I have waited for you. I have hungered and thirsted for you all these long years. Do not leave me again.'

Tansid showed no alarm at his outburst. She stroked his long silver hair. 'Taita, you must not trouble yourself. I will remain with you as long as you still need me.' She held him tenderly, a child at her breast, until he subsided once more into insensibility. Then she looked enquiringly at Samana. 'Lostris?'

'She was once queen of Egypt,' she explained. Using her Inner Eye and the knowledge of Kashyap she was able to scry deep in Taita's mind to his memories. His abiding love of Lostris was as clear to Samana as if it were her own.

'Taita raised her from childhood. She was beautiful. Their souls were intertwined, but they could never be joined. His mutilated body lacked the manly force for him ever to be more to her than friend and protector. Nevertheless, he loved her all her life and beyond. She loved him in return. Her last words to him before she died in his arms were 'I have loved only two men in this life, and you were one. In the next life perhaps the gods will treat our love more kindly.'

Samana's voice was choked, and the women's eyes were bright with tears.

Tansid broke the silence that followed: 'Tell me all of it, Samana. There is nothing more beautiful on this earth than true love.'

'After Lostris died,' Samana said quietly, stroking the magus's head, 'Taita embalmed her. Before he laid her in her sarcophagus, he took from her head a lock of hair, which he sealed in a locket of gold.' She leaned forward and touched the Periapt of Lostris, which hung round Taita's neck on a golden chain. 'See? He wears it to this day. Still he waits for her to return to him.'

Tansid wept, and Samana shared her sorrow, but she was unable to wash it away with tears. She had travelled so much further along the Road of the Adepts that she had left such comforting human weakness behind her. Sorrow is the other face of joy. To grieve is to be human. Tansid could still weep.

By the time the great rains had passed, Taita had recovered from his ordeal and learnt to control the Inner Eye. They were all aware of the new power within him: he radiated a spiritual calm. Meren and Tansid found it comforting to be near him, not speaking but revelling in his presence.

However, Taita passed most of his waking hours with Samana. They sat day after day at the temple gates. Through their Inner Eyes they watched everyone who passed through. In their vision each human body was bathed in its own aura, a cloud of changing light that displayed to them the emotions, thoughts and character of its owner. Samana instructed Taita in the art of interpreting these signals.

When night had fallen and the others had retired to their chambers, Samana and Taita sat together in the darkest recess of the temple, surrounded by effigies of the goddess Saraswati. They talked the night away, still using the arcane Tenmass of the higher adepts that neither Meren nor the *apsaras*, not even the learned Tansid, could understand. It was as though they realized that the time of parting would soon be upon them, and that they must take full advantage of every hour that was left to them.

'You do not throw an aura?' Taita asked, during their final discussion.

'Neither do you,' Samana replied. 'No savant does. That is the certain way in which we are able to identify each other.'

'You are so much wiser than I.'

'Your hunger and capacity for wisdom far outstrip mine. Now that you have been granted the inner sight, you are entering the penultimate level of the adepts. There is only one above where you stand now, that of the Benevolent Immortal.'

'Each day I feel myself grow stronger. Each day I hear the call more clearly. It is not to be denied. I must leave you and go on.'

'Yes, your time with us here has come to an end,' Samana agreed. 'We will never meet again, Taita. Let boldness be your companion. Let the Inner Eye show you the way.'

M eren was with Astrata and Wu Lu in the pavilion beside the pool. They reached for their clothing and dressed hurriedly as Taita came towards them with a firm step, Tansid at his side. Only now did they realize the extent of the change that had come over Taita. He no longer stooped under the burden of age, but stood taller, straighter. Though his hair and beard were silver still, they seemed thicker, more lustrous. His eyes were no longer rheumy and myopic, but clear and steady. Even Meren, who was the least perceptive, could recognize these changes. He ran to Taita and prostrated himself before him, hugging his knees wordlessly. Taita lifted him up and embraced him. Then he held him at arm's length, and considered him carefully. Meren's aura was a robust orange glow like the desert dawn, the aura of an honest warrior, valiant and true. 'Fetch your weapons, good Meren, for we must go on.' For a moment Meren was rooted to the ground with dismay, but then he glanced at Astrata.

Taita studied her aura. It was as clear as the steady flame of an oil lamp, clean and uncomplicated. But suddenly he saw the flame waver, as though touched by an errant breeze. Then it steadied, as she suppressed the sorrow of parting. Meren turned from her and went into the living quarters of the temple. Minutes later he came out again, his sword belt buckled round his waist, his bow and quiver slung over his shoulder. He carried Taita's tiger-skin cloak rolled upon his back.

Taita kissed each of the women. He was fascinated by the

dancing auras of the three *apsaras*. Wu Lu was enveloped in a nimbus of silver, shot through with shimmering gold, more complex and with deeper toning than Astrata's. She was further along the Road of the Adepts.

Tansid's aura was mother-of-pearl, iridescent as a film of precious oil floating on the surface of a bowl of wine, changing colours and tones incessantly, shooting out stars of light. She possessed a noble soul and a Good Mind. Taita wondered if she would ever be called to submit herself to Samana's probing bamboo needle. He kissed her, and her aura thrilled with a brighter lustre. In the short time they had known each other they had shared many things of the spirit. She had come to love him.

'May you attain your destiny,' he whispered, as their lips parted.

'I know in my heart that you will attain yours, Magus,' she replied softly. 'I will never forget you.' Impulsively she threw her arms round his neck. 'Oh, Magus, I wish ... how I wish ...'

'I know what you wish. It would have been beautiful,' he told her gently, 'but some things are not possible.'

He turned to Meren. 'Are you ready?'

'I am ready, Magus,' Meren said. 'Lead and I will follow.'

They retraced their footsteps. They climbed into the mountains where the eternal winds wailed around the peaks, then came to the start of the great mountainous pathway and followed it towards the west. Meren recalled every twist and turn, every high pass and dangerous ford, so they wasted no time in searching for the right road, and journeyed swiftly. They came again to the windswept plains of Ecbatana where the wild horses roamed in great herds.

Taita had had an affinity with those noble animals ever since the first of them had arrived in Egypt with the invading Hyksos hordes. He had captured them from the enemy, and broken the first teams for the new chariots he had designed for the army of Pharaoh Mamose. For this service Pharaoh had awarded him the title 'Lord of Ten Thousand Chariots'. Taita's love of horses went back a long way.

They paused on their journey across the grassy plains to rest after the rigours of travel in the high mountains and to linger among the horses. As they followed the herds they came upon a rift in the bleak, featureless landscape, a concealed valley along whose course bubbled a string of natural springs, with pools of sweet clear water. The perpetual winds that scourged the exposed plains did not reach this sheltered spot, and the grass grew green and lush. There were many horses here, and Taita set up camp beside a spring to enjoy them. Meren built a hut from grass sods, and they used dried dung as fuel. There were fish in the pools and colonies of water voles, which Meren trapped while Taita searched for edible fungi and roots in the damp earth. Around their hut, close enough to discourage the horses from raiding them, Taita planted some seeds he had brought with him from the gardens at the temple of Saraswati, and raised a good crop. They ate well and rested, building up their strength for the next part of their long, hard journey.

The horses became accustomed to their presence at the springs, and soon they allowed Taita to come within a few paces of them before they tossed their manes and moved away. He assessed each animal's aura with his newly acquired Inner Eye.

Although the auras that surrounded the lower orders of animal were not as intense as those of humans, he could pick out those that were healthy and strong, and those with heart and sinew. He was also able to determine their temperament and disposition. He could distinguish between the headstrong and unruly, the mild and tractable. Over the weeks it took the plants in his garden to reach maturity, he developed a tentative relationship with five animals, all of superior intelligence, strength and amiable disposition. Three were mares with yearling foals at heel, and two were fillies, still flirting with the stallions but resisting their advances with kicks and gnashing teeth. Taita was especially attracted to one of the fillies.

This little herd was as drawn to him as he was to them. They took to sleeping close to the fence that Meren had built to protect the garden against them, which worried Meren: 'I know women, and I trust those conspiring females not at all. They are steeling their courage. One morning we will wake to find we have no garden left to us.' He spent much time strengthening his fence and patrolling it threateningly.

He was appalled when Taita picked a bag of sweet young beans, the first of the crop: instead of bringing them to the pot, he took them beyond the fence to where the little herd was watching him with interest. The filly he had chosen for himself had a creamy hide dappled with smoky grey. She allowed him to approach more closely than he had before, scissoring her ears as she listened to his endearments. At last he trespassed on her forbearance: she tossed her head and galloped away. He stopped and called after her: 'I have a gift for you, my darling. Sweets for a lovely girl.' She came up short at the sound of his voice. He held out to her a handful of beans. She swung her head back to regard him over her shoulder. She rolled her eyes until she had exposed the pink rims of her eyelids, then flared her nostrils to suck in the scent of the beans.

'Yes, you lovely creature, just smell them. How can you refuse me?'

She blew through her nostrils and nodded with indecision.

'Very well. If you don't want them, Meren will welcome them for his pot.' He turned back to the fence, but with his hand still extended. They watched each other intently. The filly took a pace towards him, and stopped again. He lifted his hand to his mouth, put a bean between his lips and chewed it with his mouth open. 'I cannot describe to you how sweet it is,' he told her, and she gave in at last. She came to him, and daintily picked the beans out of his cupped hand. Her muzzle was velvet and her breath was scented with new grass. 'What shall we call you?' Taita asked her. 'It must be a name that matches your beauty. Ah! I have one that suits you well. You shall be Windsmoke.'

Over the next weeks Taita and Meren scythed the plants. Then they winnowed the ripe beans and packed them into sacks made from the skins of water voles. They dried the plants in the sun and wind, then tied them into bundles. The horses stood in a row with their necks craned over the fence, munching the beanstalks that Taita fed them. That evening Taita gave Windsmoke a last handful, then slipped an arm round her neck and brushed out her mane with his fingers while he spoke soothingly into her ear. Then, unhurriedly, he hoisted the skirts of his tunic, threw a skinny leg over her back and sat astride her. She stood frozen with astonishment, staring at him over her shoulder with huge, glistening eyes. He nudged her with his toes and she walked away, while Meren bellowed and clapped with delight.

When they left the camp by the pools, Taita rode Windsmoke and Meren had one of the older mares. Their baggage was loaded on to the backs of the string that followed them.

In that way they returned home more swiftly than they had departed. But when they reached Gallala, they had been gone for seven years. As soon as it was known that they had reappeared, there was great rejoicing in the town. The citizens had long since given them up for dead. Every man brought his family to their home in the old ruined temple, bearing small gifts, to pay their respects. Most of the children had grown up in the time they had been away, and many had babies of their own. Taita dandled each little one and blessed them.

The news of their return was borne swiftly to the rest of Egypt by the caravan masters. Soon messengers arrived from the court at Thebes, from Pharaoh Nefer Seti and Queen Mintaka. There was little comfort in the news sent: it was the first that Taita had heard of the plagues that beset the kingdom. 'Come as soon as you are able, wise one,' Pharaoh ordered. 'We have need of you.'

'I will come to you in the new moon of Isis,' was Taita's reply. He was not being wilfully disobedient: he knew that he was not yet spiritually prepared to give counsel to his pharaoh. He sensed that the plagues were a manifestation of the greater evil of which Samana, the reverend mother, had warned him. Although he possessed the power of the Inner Eye he was not yet able to face the force of the Lie. He must study and ponder the auguries, then gather his spiritual resources. He must wait, too, for the guidance that he knew instinctively would come to him at Gallala.

But there were many disruptions and diversions. Very soon strangers began to arrive, pilgrims and supplicants begging favours, cripples and the sick seeking cures. The emissaries of kings bore rich gifts and asked for oracular and divine guidance. Taita searched their auras eagerly, hoping that one was the messenger he was expecting. Time after time he was disappointed, and he turned them away with their gifts.

'May we not keep some small tithe, Magus?' Meren begged. 'Holy as you have become, you must still eat, and your tunic is a rag. I need a new bow.'

Occasionally a visitor gave him fleeting hope, when he recognized the complexity of their aura. They were seekers after wisdom and knowledge, drawn to him by his reputation among the brotherhood of the magi. But they came to take from him: none could match his powers or offer him anything in return. Nevertheless he listened carefully to what they said, sifting and evaluating their words. Nothing was of significance, but at times a random remark, or an erroneous opinion, sent his own mind on an original tack. Through their errors he was guided to a contrary and valid conclusion. The warning that Samana and Kashyap had given him was always in his mind: a conflict ahead would require all his strength, wisdom and cunning to survive.

The caravans coming up from Egypt and going on down through the rocky wilderness to Sagafa on the Red Sea brought them regular news from Mother Egypt. When another arrived Taita sent Meren down to converse with the caravan master; they all treated Meren with deep respect for they knew he was the confidant of Taita, the renowned magus. That evening he returned from the town and reported, 'Obed Tindali, the caravan merchant, begs you to remember him in your prayers to the great god Horus. He has sent you a generous gift of the finest quality coffee beans from far-off Ethiopia, but I warn you now to steel yourself, Magus, for he has no tidings of comfort from the delta for you.'

The old man lowered his eyes to hide the shadow of fear that passed behind them. What worse news could there be than they had already received? He looked up again and spoke sternly: 'Do not try to protect me, Meren. Hold nothing back. Has the flood of the Nile commenced?'

'Not yet,' Meren replied softly, regretfully. 'Seven years now without the inundation.'

Taita's stern expression wavered. Without the rise of the waters and the rich, fertile bounty of alluvial soils they brought from the south, Egypt was given over to famine, pestilence and death.

'Magus, it grieves me deeply but there is still worse to relate,' murmured Meren. 'What little water still remains in the Nile has turned to blood.'

Taita stared at him. 'Blood?' he echoed. 'I do not understand.'

'Magus, even the shrunken pools of the river have turned dark red and they stink like the congealed blood of cadavers,' Meren said. 'Neither man nor beast can drink from them. The horses and cattle, even the goats, are perishing from thirst. Their skeletal bodies line the riverbanks.'

'Plague and affliction! Such a thing has never been dreamed

of in the history of the earth since the beginning time,' Taita whispered.

'And it is not a single plague, Magus,' Meren went on doggedly. 'From the bloody pools of the Nile have emerged great hordes of spiny toads, large and swift as dogs. Rank poison oozes from the warts that cover their hideous bodies. They eat the corpses of the dead animals. But that is not enough. The people say great Horus should forbid it, that these monsters will attack any child, or any person who is too old or feeble to defend himself. They will devour him while he still writhes and screams.' Meren paused and drew a deep breath. 'What is happening to our earth? What dreadful curse has been placed upon us, Magus?'

In all the decades they had been together, since the great battle against the usurpers, the false pharaohs, since the ascension of Nefer Seti to the double throne of Upper and Lower Egypt, Meren had been at Taita's side. He was the adopted son who could never have sprung naturally from Taita's gelded loins. Nay, Meren was more than a son: his love for the old man surpassed that of a blood tie. Now Taita was moved by his distress, although his own was as pervasive.

'Why is this happening to the land we love, to the people we love, to the king we love?' Meren pleaded.

Taita shook his head, and remained silent for a long while. Then he leant across to touch Meren's upper arm. 'The gods are angry,' he said.

'Why?' Meren insisted. The mighty warrior and stalwart companion was rendered almost childlike by his superstitious dread. 'What is the offence?'

'Since our return to Egypt I have sought the answer to that question. I have made sacrifice and I have searched the breadth and depth of the skies for some sign. The cause of their divine anger eludes me still. It is almost as though it is cloaked by some baleful presence.'

'For Pharaoh and Egypt, for all of us, you must find the answer, Magus,' Meren urged. 'But where can you still search for it?'

'It will come to me soon, Meren. This is presaged by the auguries. It will be carried by some unexpected messenger – perhaps a man or a demon, a beast or a god. Perhaps it will appear as a sign in the heavens, written in a star. But the answer will come to me here at Gallala.'

'When, Magus? Is it not already too late?'

'Perhaps this very night.'

Taita rose to his feet in a single lithe motion. Despite his great age he moved like a young man. His agility and resilience never ceased to amaze Meren, even after all the years he had spent at his side. Taita picked up his staff from the corner of the terrace and leant lightly on it as he paused at the bottom of the stairs to look up to the high tower. The villagers had built it for him. Every family in Gallala had taken part in the labour. It was a tangible sign of the love and reverence they felt for the old magus, who had opened the sweet-water spring that nourished the town, who protected them with the invisible but potent power of his magic.

Taita started up the circular staircase that wound up the outside of the tower; the treads were narrow and open to the drop, unprotected by a balustrade. He went up like an ibex, not watching his feet, the tip of his staff tapping lightly on the stones. When he reached the platform on the summit, he settled on the silken prayer rug, facing east. Meren placed a silver flask beside him, then took his place behind him, close enough to respond swiftly if Taita needed him, but not so close that he would intrude on the magus's concentration.

Taita removed the horn stopper from the flask and took a mouthful of the sharply bitter fluid. He swallowed it slowly, feeling the warmth spreading from his belly through every muscle and nerve in his body, flooding his mind with a crystalline radiance. He sighed softly and allowed the Inner Eye of his soul to open under its balmy influence.

Two nights previously the old moon had been swallowed

by the monster of night, and now the sky belonged only to the stars. Taita watched as they began to appear in order of their ranking, the brightest and most powerful leading the train. Soon they thronged the heavens in teeming multitudes, bathing the desert with a silvery luminance. Taita had studied them all his life. He had thought he knew all that there was to know and understand of them, but now, through his Inner Eye, he was developing a new understanding of the qualities and position of each in the eternal scheme of matter, and in the affairs of men and gods. There was one bright, particular star that he sought out eagerly. He knew it was nearest of all to where he sat. As soon as he saw it all his senses were exalted: that evening it seemed to hang directly above the tower.

The star had first appeared in the sky exactly ninety days after the mummification of Queen Lostris, on the night he had sealed her into her tomb. Its appearance had been miraculous. Before she died she had promised him that she would return to him, and he felt a deep conviction that the star was the fulfilment of her oath. She had never left him. For all these years her nova had been his lodestar. When he looked up at it, the desolation that had dominated his soul since her death was alleviated.

Now when he gazed at it with his Inner Eye he saw that Lostris's star was surrounded by her aura. Although it was diminutive when compared to some of the astral colossi, no other body in the heavens could match its splendour. Taita felt his love for Lostris burn steadily, undiminished, warming his soul. Suddenly his whole body stiffened with alarm and a coldness spread through his veins towards his heart.

'Magus!' Meren had sensed his change of mood. 'What ails you?' He clasped Taita's shoulder, his other hand on the hilt of his sword. Unable to speak in his distress, Taita shrugged him away, and continued to stare upwards.

In the interval since he had last laid eyes upon it, Lostris's star had swollen to several times its normal size. Its once bright and constant aura had become intermittent, the emanations fluttering as disconsolately as the torn pennant of a defeated army. Its body was distorted, bulging at each end and narrowing in the centre.

Even Meren noticed the change: 'Your star! Something has happened to it. What does this mean?' He knew how important it was to Taita.

'I cannot yet say,' Taita whispered. 'Leave me here, Meren. Go to your sleeping mat. I must have no distraction. Come for me at dawn.'

Taita kept watch until the star faded with the approach of the sun, but by the time Meren returned to lead him down from the tower, he knew that Lostris's star was moribund.

Though he was exhausted from his long night's vigil, he could not sleep. The image of the dying star filled his mind, and he was harried by dark, formless forebodings. This was the last and most awful manifestation of evil. First there had been the plagues that killed man and beast, and now this terrible malignancy, which destroyed the stars. The following night Taita did not return to the tower but went alone into the desert, seeking solace. Although Meren had been instructed not to follow his master, he did so at a distance. Of course, Taita sensed his presence and confounded him by cloaking himself in a spell of concealment. Angry, and worried for his master's safety, Meren searched for him all night. At sunrise when he hurried back to Gallala to raise a search party, he found Taita sitting alone on the terrace of the old temple.

'You disappoint me, Meren. It is unlike you to wander away and neglect your duties,' Taita chided him. 'Now do you propose to starve me? Summon the new maidservant you have employed, and let us hope her cooking is not eclipsed by her pretty face.'

He did not sleep during that day, but sat alone in the shade at the far end of the terrace. As soon as they had eaten the evening meal he climbed to the top of the tower once more. The sun was only a finger below the horizon, but he was determined not to waste a moment of the hours of darkness when the star would be revealed to him. Night came, as swiftly and stealthily as a thief. Taita strained his eyes into the east. The stars pricked through the darkling arch of the night sky, and grew brighter. Then, abruptly, the Star of Lostris appeared above his head. He was amazed that it had left its constant position in the train of the planets. Now it hung like a guttering lantern flame above the tower of Gallala.

It was no longer a star. In the few short hours since he had last laid eyes upon it, it had erupted into a fiery cloud and was blowing itself apart. Dark, ominous vapours billowed around it, lit by internal fires that were consuming it in a mighty blaze that lit the heavens above his head.

Taita waited and watched through the long hours of darkness. The maimed star did not move from its position high above his head. It was still there at sunrise, and the following night it appeared again in the same heavenly station. Night after night the star remained fixed in the sky like a mighty beacon, whose eerie light must reach to the ends of the heavens. The clouds of destruction that enveloped it swirled and eddied. The fires flared up in its centre, then died away, only to flare again in a different place.

At dawn the townsfolk came up to the ancient temple and waited for an audience with the magus in the shade of the tall columns of the hypostyle hall. When Taita descended from his tower they crowded around him, begging for an explanation of the mighty eruption of flames that hung over their city: 'O mighty Magus, does this herald another plague? Has Egypt not suffered enough? Please explain these terrible omens to us.' But he could tell them nothing for their comfort. None of his studies had prepared him for anything like the unnatural behaviour of the Star of Lostris.

The new moon waxed full and its light softened the fearful image of the burning star. When it waned, the Star of Lostris dominated the heavens once more, burning so brightly that all other stars paled into insignificance beside it. As if summoned by this beacon, a dark cloud of locusts came out of the south and descended on Gallala. They stayed for two days and devastated the irrigated fields, leaving not a single ear of dhurra corn or a leaf on the olive trees. The branches of the pomegranates bent under the weight of the swarms, then broke off. On the morning of the third day the insects rose in a vast, murmurous cloud and flew westward towards the Nile, to wreak more devastation on lands already dying from the failure of the Nile flood.

The land of Egypt quailed, and the population gave in to despair.

Then another visitor came to Gallala. He appeared during the night, but the flames of the Star of Lostris burned so brightly, like the last flare of an oil lamp before it expires, that Meren could point out the caravan to Taita when it was still a great distance away.

'Those beasts of burden are from a far-off land,' Meren remarked. The camel was not indigenous to Egypt and was still rare enough to excite his interest. 'They do not follow the caravan route but come out of the desert. All this is strange. We must be wary of them.' The foreign travellers did not waver but came directly to the temple, almost as though they were guided there. The camel drivers couched their animals, and there was the usual hubbub of a caravan setting up camp.

'Go down to them,' Taita ordered. 'Find out what you can about them.'

Meren did not return until the sun was well clear of the horizon. 'There are twenty men, all servants and retainers. They say they have travelled for many months to reach us.'

'Who is their leader? What did you learn of him?'

'I did not lay eyes on him. He has retired to rest. That is his tent in the centre of the encampment. It is of the finest wool. All his men speak of him with the greatest awe and respect.'

'What is his name?'

'I do not know. They speak of him only as the Hitama, which in their language means "exalted in learning".'

35

'What does he seek here?'

'You, Magus. He comes for you. The caravan master asked for you by name.'

Taita was only mildly surprised. 'What food have we? We must offer hospitality to this Hitama.'

'The locusts and drought have left us with little. I have some smoked fish and enough corn for a few salt cakes.'

'What of the mushrooms we collected yesterday?'

'They have turned rotten and stinking. Perhaps I can find something in the village.'

'No, do not trouble our friends. Life for them is hard enough already. We will make do with what we have.' In the end they were saved by the generosity of their visitor. The Hitama accepted their invitation to share the evening meal, but he sent Meren back with a gift of a fine fat camel. It was plain that he knew how sorely the populace was suffering from the famine. Meren slaughtered the beast and prepared a roasted shoulder. The remainder of the carcass would be enough to feed the servants of the Hitama, and most of the village population.

Taita waited for his guest on the roof of the temple. He was intrigued to discover whom he might be. His title suggested that he was one of the magi, or perhaps the abbot of some other learned sect. He had a premonition that something of great import was to be revealed to him.

Is this the messenger who was presaged by the auguries? The one for whom I have waited so long? he wondered, then stirred as he heard Meren ushering the visitor up the wide stone staircase.

'Take care with your master. The treads of the staircase are crumbling and can be dangerous,' Meren told the bearers, who at last arrived on the roof terrace. He helped them settle the curtained litter close to Taita's mat, then placed a silver bowl of pomegranate-flavoured sherbet and two drinking bowls on the low table between them. He glanced enquiringly at his own master. 'What else do you wish, Magus?'

'You may leave us now, Meren. I will call you when we are ready to eat.' Taita poured a bowl of the sherbet and placed it close to the opening in the curtains, which were still tightly drawn. 'Greetings and welcome. You bring honour to my abode,' he murmured, speaking to his unseen guest. There was no reply and he concentrated all the power of the Inner Eye on the palanquin. He was astonished not to distinguish any aura of a living person beyond the silk curtains. Though he scanned the covered space carefully he found no sign of life. It appeared blank and sterile. 'Is anybody there?' He stood quickly and crossed to the litter. 'Speak!' he demanded. 'What devilry is this?'

He jerked aside the curtain, then stepped back in surprise. A man sat cross-legged on the padded bed, facing him. He wore only a saffron loincloth. His body was skeletal, his bald head skull-like, his skin as dry and wrinkled as that shed by a serpent. His countenance was as weathered as an ancient fossil, but his expression was serene, even beautiful.

'You have no aura!' Taita exclaimed, before he could prevent the words reaching his lips.

The Hitama inclined his head slightly. 'Neither have you, Taita. None of those who have returned from the temple of Saraswati give out a detectable aura. We have left part of our humanity with Kashyap, the lamp-bearer. This deficiency enables us to recognize one another.'

Taita took a while to consider these words. The Hitama had echoed what he had been told by Samana.

'Kashyap is dead and a woman has taken his seat before the goddess. Her name is Samana. She told me there had been others. You are the first I have met.'

'Few of us are granted the gift of the Inner Eye. Even fewer of us remain. Our numbers have been reduced. There is a sinister reason for this, which I will explain to you in due time.' He made space on the mattress beside him. 'Come, sit close to me, Taita. My hearing begins to fail me, and there is much to discuss, but little time is left to us.' The visitor switched from laboured Egyptian into the arcane Tenmass of the adepts, which he spoke flawlessly. 'We must remain discreet.'

'How did you find me?' Taita asked, in the same language, as he settled beside him.

'The star led me.' The ancient seer raised his face to the eastern sky. In the time that they had been speaking together, night had fallen and the panoply of the heavens shone forth in majesty. The Star of Lostris still hung directly overhead, but it was further altered in shape and substance. It no longer had a solid centre. It had become merely a cloud of glowing gases, blowing away in a long feather on the solar winds.

'I have always been aware of my intimate connection to that star,' Taita murmured.

'With good reason,' the old man assured him mysteriously. 'Your destiny is linked to it.'

'But it is dying before our eyes.'

The old man looked at him in a way that made Taita's fingertips tingle. 'Nothing dies. What we call death is merely a change of state. She will remain with you always.'

Taita opened his mouth to say her name, 'Lostris', but the old man stopped him with a gesture.

'Do not speak her name aloud. In doing so you may betray her to those who wish you ill.'

'Is a name, then, so powerful?'

'Without one a being does not exist. Even the gods need a name. Only the Truth is nameless.'

'And the Lie,' Taita said, but the old man shook his head.

'The Lie is named Ahriman.'

'You know my name,' said Taita, 'but I am ignorant of yours.'

'I am Demeter.'

'Demeter is one of the demigods.' Taita had recognized the name at once. 'Are you that one?'

'As you can see, I am mortal.' He held up his hands and they trembled with palsy. 'I am a Long Liver, as you are, Taita. I have lived an inordinately long time. But soon I will die.

Already I am dying. In time you will follow me. Neither of us is a demigod. We are not Benevolent Immortals.'

'Demeter, you cannot leave me so soon. We have just come together,' Taita protested. 'I have searched so long to find you. There is so much I must learn from you. Surely this is why you have come to me. You did not come here to die?'

Demeter inclined his head in acquiescence. 'I shall stay as long as I am able, but I am wearied by years and sickened by the forces of the Lie.'

'We must waste not an hour of the time we have. Instruct me.' Taita spoke humbly. 'I am as a little child beside you.'

'We have already begun,' Demeter said.

'Time is a river like the one above us.' Demeter lifted his head and pointed with his chin to Oceanus, the endless river of stars that flowed from horizon to horizon across the sky above them. 'It has no beginning and no ending. There was another who came before me, as countless others came before him. He passed on this duty to me. It is a divine baton handed on from one runner to the next. Some carry it further than others. My race is almost run, for I have been shorn of much of my power. I must pass the baton to you.'

'Why to me?'

'It has been ordained. It is not for us to query or contest the decision. You must open your mind to me, Taita, to receive what I have to give you. I must caution you that it is a poisoned gift. Once you receive it you may never again know lasting peace, for you are about to shoulder all the suffering and pain of the world.'

They fell silent while Taita considered this bleak proposition. At last he sighed. 'I would refuse it if I could. Continue, Demeter, for I cannot stand against the inevitable.'

Demeter nodded. 'I have faith that you will succeed where I have failed so woefully. You are to become gatekeeper of the fortress of the Truth against the onslaughts of the minions of the Lie.'

Demeter's whispers grew bolder and took on a new urgency: 'We have spoken of gods and demigods, of adepts and Benevolent Immortals. From this I see that you already have a deep understanding of these things. But I can tell you more. Since the beginning time of the Great Chaos, the gods have been lifted up and cast down in succession. They have struggled against each other, and against the minions of the Lie. The Titans, who were the elder gods, were cast down by the Olympian gods. They, in their turn, will become enfeebled. None will trust and worship them. They will be defeated and replaced by younger deities or, if we fail, they may be superseded by the malign agents of the Lie.' He was silent for a while, but when he continued his voice was firmer: 'This rise and fall of divine dynasties is part of the natural and immutable body of laws that emerged to bring order to the Great Chaos. Those laws govern the cosmos. They order the ebb and flood of the tides. They command the succession of day and night. They order and control the wind and the storm, the volcanoes and the tidal waves, the rise and fall of empires, and the progression of days and nights. The gods are only the servants of the Truth. In the end there remain only the Truth and the Lie.' Demeter turned suddenly and glanced behind him, his expression melancholy, but resigned. 'Do you feel it, Taita? Do you hear it?'

Taita exerted all his powers, and at last he heard a faint rustling in the air around them, like the wings of vultures settling to a carrion feast. He nodded. He was too moved to speak. The sense of great evil almost overwhelmed him. He had to exert all his strength to fight it back.

'She is here with us already.' Demeter's voice sank lower, became laboured and breathless, as though his lungs were crushed by the weight of a baleful presence. 'Can you smell her?' he asked.

Taita flared his nostrils, and caught the faint reek of corruption and decay, disease and rotting flesh, the effluvium of plague and the contents of ruptured bowels. 'I sense it and smell it,' he answered.

'We are in danger,' said Demeter. He reached towards Taita. 'Join hands!' he ordered. 'We must unite our power to resist her.'

As their fingers touched an intense blue spark flashed between them. Taita resisted the impulse to jerk away his hand and break the contact. Instead he seized Demeter's hands and held them firmly. Strength flowed back and forth between them. Gradually the malign presence receded, and they could breathe freely again.

'It was inevitable,' said Demeter, with resignation. 'She has been searching for me these past centuries, ever since I escaped from her web of spells and charms. But now that you and I have come together we have created such an upheaval of psychic energy that she has been able to detect it, even at immense distance, just as a great shark can detect a shoal of sardines long before it has sight of them.' He looked sorrowfully at Taita, still holding his hands. 'She knows of you now, Taita, through me, and if not through me, she would have discovered you by some other means. The scent you leave on the wind of the cosmos is strong, and she is the ultimate predator.'

'You say "she"? Who is this female?'

'She calls herself Eos.'

'I have heard that name. A woman named Eos visited the temple of Saraswati more than fifty generations ago.'

'It is the same woman.'

'Eos is the ancient goddess of the dawn, sister of Helius, the sun,' Taita said. 'She was an insatiable nymphomaniac, but she was destroyed in the war between the Titans and the Olympians.' He shook his head. 'This cannot be the same Eos.'

'You are right, Taita. They are not the same. This Eos is the minion of the Lie. She is the consummate impostor, the usurper, the deceiver, the thief, the devourer of infants. She has stolen the identity of the old goddess. At the same time, she adopted her vices but none of her virtues.'

'Do I understand you to say that Eos has lived for fifty generations? That means she is two thousand years old,' Taita exclaimed, incredulous. 'What is she? Mortal or immortal, human or goddess?'

'In the beginning she was human. Many ages ago she was the high priestess at the temple of Apollo in Ilion. When the city was sacked by the Spartans, she escaped the pillage and assumed the name Eos, still human, but I have no words to describe what she has become.'

'Samana showed me the ancient temple inscription that recorded the visit of the woman from Ilion,' Taita said.

'She is the same. Kurma gave her the gift of the Inner Eye. He believed that she was chosen. Her powers of concealment and deceit are so powerful and persuasive that even Kurma, that great sage and savant, could not see through them.'

'If she is the embodiment of evil, surely it is our duty to seek her out and destroy her.'

Demeter smiled ruefully. 'I have devoted all my long life to that purpose, but she is as cunning as she is evil. She is as elusive as the wind. She emits no aura. She is able to protect herself with spells and wiles that far surpass my own knowledge of the occult. She lays snares to catch those who search for her. She can move with ease from one continent to another. Kurma merely enhanced her powers. Nonetheless I once succeeded in finding her.' He corrected himself: 'That is not entirely true, I did not find her. She sought me out.'

Taita leant forward eagerly. 'You know this creature? You have met her face to face? Tell me, Demeter, what is her appearance?'

'If she is threatened she can change her appearance as a chameleon does. Yet vanity is among her multitudinous vices. You cannot imagine the beauty she is able to assume. It stuns the senses, and negates reason. When she takes on this aspect no man can resist her. The sight of her reduces even the most noble soul to the level of a beast.' He fell silent, his eyes dulled with sorrow. 'Despite all my training as an adept I was not able to restrain my basest instincts. I lost the ability and the inclination to reckon consequences. For me, in that moment, nothing but her existed. I was consumed by lust. She toyed with me, like the winds of autumn with a dead leaf. To me it seemed she gave me everything, every delight contained in this earth. She gave me her body.' He groaned softly. 'Even now the memory drives me to the brink of madness. Each rise and swell, enchanted opening and fragrant cleft . . . I did not try to resist her, for no mortal man could do so.' A faint, agitated colour had risen to his wan features.

'Taita, you remarked that the original Eos was an insatiable nymphomaniac, and that is so, but this other Eos outstrips her in appetite. When she kisses, she sucks out the vital juices of her lover, as you or I might suck out the juices from a ripe orange. When she takes a man between her thighs in that exquisite but infernal coupling she draws out of him his very substance. She takes from him his soul. His substance is the ambrosia that nourishes her. She is as some monstrous vampire that feeds on human blood. She chooses only superior beings as her victims, men and women of Good Mind, servants of the Truth, a magus of illustrious reputation or a gifted seer. Once she detects her victim, she runs him down as relentlessly as a wolf harries a deer. She is omnivorous. No matter age or appearance, physical frailty or imperfection. It is not their flesh that feeds her appetites, but their souls. She devours young and old, men and women. Once she has them in her thrall, wrapped in her silken web, she draws from them their accumulated store of learning, wisdom and experience. She sucks it out through their mouths with her accursed kisses. She draws it from their loins in her loathsome embrace. She leaves only a desiccated husk.'

'I have witnessed this carnal exchange,' Taita said. 'When Kashyap reached the end of his life he passed on his wisdom and learning to Samana, whom he had chosen as his successor.'

'What you witnessed was a willing exchange. The obscene act Eos practises is a carnal invasion and conquest. She is a ravager and devourer of souls.'

For a while Taita was dumbstruck. Then he asked, 'Ancient and infirm? Whole or maimed? Man and woman? How does she couple with those who are no longer capable of union?'

'She has powers that you and I, adepts though we may be, cannot emulate or even fathom. She has developed the art of regenerating the frail flesh of her victims for a day, only to destroy them by wiping away their minds and their very substance.'

'Nevertheless, you have not answered my question, Demeter. What is she? Mortal or immortal, human or goddess? Does this rare beauty she possesses know no term? Is she not as vulnerable to the ravages of time and age as you and I?'

'My answer to your question, Taita, is that I know not. She may well be the oldest woman on earth,' Demeter spread his hands in a gesture of helplessness, 'but she seems to have discovered some power previously known only to the gods. Does that make her a goddess? I do not know. She may not be immortal, but she is certainly ageless.'

'What do you propose, Demeter? How will we trace her to her lair?'

'She has already found you. You have excited her monstrous appetites. You do not have to seek her out. She is already stalking you. She will draw you to her.'

'Demeter, I am long past any temptations and snares that even this creature can place in my path.'

'She wants you, she must have you. However, you and I together pose a threat to her.' He thought for a while about his own statement, then went on, 'She has already taken from me almost everything I can give her. She will want to rid herself of me, and isolate you, but at the same time she must see to it that no harm comes to you. Alone, you will find it almost impossible to resist her. With our combined forces we may be able to repel her, and even find a way to put her apparent immortality to the test.'

'I am glad to have you at my side,' said Taita.

Demeter did not respond at once. He studied Taita with a

strange new expression. At last he asked quietly, 'You feel no sense of dread, no premonition of disaster?'

'No. I believe that you and I can succeed,' Taita told him.

'You have considered my solemn warnings. You understand the powers against which we will pit ourselves. Yet you do not hesitate. You entertain no doubts – you, who are the wisest of men. How can you explain this?'

'I know it is inevitable. I must face her with boldness and good heart.'

'Taita, search the innermost recesses of your soul. Do you detect in yourself a sense of elation? When last did you feel so vigorous, so vital?'

Taita looked thoughtful, but did not answer.

'Taita, you must be entirely truthful with yourself. Do you feel like a warrior marching to a battle you may not survive? Or do you find in your breast another unwarranted emotion? Do you feel reckless of all consequences, like a young swain hurrying to a lovers' tryst?'

Taita remained silent but his mien changed: the light flush of his cheeks subsided and his eyes became sober. 'I am not afraid,' he said at last.

'Tell me truly. Your mind swarms with prurient images, and unconscionable yearnings, does it not?' Taita covered his eyes and clenched his jaw. Demeter went on remorselessly: 'She has already infected you with her evil. She has begun to bind you with her spells and temptations. She will twist your judgement. Soon you will begin to doubt that she is evil. She will seem to you fine, noble and as virtuous as any woman who ever lived. Soon it will seem that I am the evil one, who has poisoned your mind against her. When that happens she will have divided us and I will be destroyed. You will surrender yourself to her freely and willingly. She will have triumphed over both of us.'

Taita shook his whole body, as though to rid himself of a swarm of poisonous insects. 'Forgive me, Demeter!' he cried. 'Now that you warn me of what she is doing, I can feel the enervating weakness welling within me. I was losing control of judgement and reason. What you say is true. I find myself haunted by strange longings. Great Horus, shield me.' Taita groaned. 'I never thought to know such agony again. I thought myself long past the torments of desire.'

'The contrary emotions that assail you spring not from your wisdom and reason. They are an infection of the spirit, a poisoned arrow shot from the bow of the great witch. I was once harassed by her in the same manner. You can see the state to which I have been reduced. However, I have learnt how to survive.'

'Teach me. Help me to withstand her, Demeter.'

'I have unwittingly led Eos to you. I believed I had eluded her, but she has used me as a hunting hound to lead her to you, her next victim. But now we must stand together, as one. That is the only way we can hope to withstand her onslaughts. However, before all else, we must leave Gallala. We cannot rest long in one place. If she is uncertain of our exact whereabouts, it will be more difficult for her to focus her powers upon us. Between us we must weave a perpetual screen of concealment to cover our movements.'

'Meren!' Taita called urgently. He was swiftly at his master's side. 'How soon can we be ready to leave Gallala?'

'I will bring the horses with all haste. But where are we going, Master?'

'Thebes and Karnak,' Taita replied, and glanced at Demeter.

He nodded agreement. 'We must muster all support from every source, temporal as well as spiritual.'

'Pharaoh is the chosen of the gods, and the most powerful of men,' Taita agreed.

'And you are the chief of his favourites,' said Demeter. 'We must leave this very night, to go to him.'

Taita rode Windsmoke, and Meren followed closely on one of the other horses they had brought from the plains of Ecbatana. Demeter lay in his swaying litter, high on the back of his camel, Taita alongside him. The litter curtains were open and they could converse easily over the other soft sounds of the caravan: the creak and jingle of tack, the fall of horses' hoofs and camels' pads on the yellow sand, the low voices of the servants and guards. During the night they stopped twice to rest and water the animals. At each halt Taita and Demeter performed the spell of concealment. Their combined powers were formidable and the screen they wove seemed impervious: although they scried the silences of the night around them before they mounted and moved on, neither could detect any further sign of Eos's baleful presence.

'She has lost us for the moment, but we will always be at risk, and most vulnerable when we sleep. We should never do so at the same time,' Demeter advised.

'We will never again relax our vigilance,' Taita asserted. 'I will keep up my guard against careless mistakes. I had under-estimated our enemy, allowed Eos to take me by surprise. I am ashamed of my weakness and stupidity.'

'I am a hundred times deeper in guilt than you are,' Demeter admitted. 'I fear my powers are waning fast, Taita. I should have guided you, but I behaved like a novice. We can afford no further lapses. We must seek out the weaknesses in our enemy, and attack her there, but without exposing ourselves.'

'Despite all you have told me, my knowledge and understanding of Eos is pitifully inadequate. You must recall every detail about her that you discovered during your ordeal, no matter how trivial or seemingly insignificant,' Taita told him, 'or I am blind, while she holds every advantage.'

'You are the stronger of we two,' Demeter said, 'but you are right. Remember how swift her reaction was when you and I came together and she descried our combined forces. Within hours of our first meeting she could overlook us. From now on her attacks upon me will become more relentless and vicious. We must not rest until I have passed on to you all that I have learnt about her. We do not know how long we will be together before she kills me or drives a wedge between us. Every hour is precious.'

Taita nodded. 'Then let us begin with the most important matters. I know who she is, and where she came from. Next, I must know her whereabouts. Where is she, Demeter? Where can we find her?'

'She has hidden in numerous lairs since she escaped from the temple of Apollo, when Agamemnon and his brother, Menelaus, sacked Ilion so long ago.'

'Where did you have your fateful encounter with her?'

'On an island in the Middle Sea, which has since become the stronghold of the sea people, that nation of corsairs and pirates. At that time she lived on the slopes of a great burning mountain she named Etna, a volcano that spewed forth fire and brimstone and sent clouds of poisoned smoke to the very heavens.'

'That was long ago?'

'Centuries before either you or I was born.'

Taita chuckled drily. 'Yes, indeed, it was long ago.' His expression hardened again. 'Is it possible that Eos may still be at Etna?'

'She is no longer there,' Demeter replied, without hesitation.

'How can you be certain?'

'By the time I broke free of her, my body was shattered in health and vitality, my mind unhinged, and my psychic forces were almost dispersed by the ordeal through which she had put me. I was her prisoner for little more than a decade, but I aged a lifetime for each of those years. Nevertheless I was able to take advantage of a mighty eruption of the volcano to conceal my flight, and I had help from the priests of a small, insignificant god, whose temple lay in the valley below Etna's eastern slopes. They spirited me across the narrow straits to the mainland in a tiny boat, and led me to sanctuary in another temple of their sect, hidden in the mountains, where they placed me in the care of their brothers. Those good priests helped me to reassemble what remained of my powers, which I needed to intercept a singularly virulent spell that Eos sent after me.'

'Could you turn it back upon her?' Taita demanded. 'Were you able to wound her with her own magic?'

'She may have become complacent, because she underestimated my remaining strength and did not protect herself adequately. I aimed my return strike at her essence, which I could still see with my Inner Eye. She was close at hand. Only the narrow strait of water stood between us. My riposte flew true and hit her hard. I heard her cry of agony echo across the ether. Then she disappeared, and I believed for a while that I had destroyed her. My hosts made discreet enquiries from their brothers in the temple below the mountain of Etna. We heard from them that she had vanished, and that her former abode was deserted. I wasted no time in taking advantage of my victory. As soon as I was strong enough I left my sanctuary and travelled to the furthest ends of the earth, to the continent of ice, as far from Eos as I could go. At last I found a place where I could lie quiescent, as still as a frightened frog beneath a stone. It was as well that I did so. After a very short time, fifty years or less, I felt the resurgence of Eos, my enemy. Her powers seemed to have been mightily enhanced. The ether around me hummed with the vicious darts she hurled at random after me. She could not place me precisely, and although many of her barbs came close to where I lay, none struck home. Each day after that was one of survival while I found the one who had been ordained to succeed me. I did not make the error of responding to her attacks. Each time I sensed her closing in I moved on quietly to another hiding-place. At last I realized that there was only one place on this earth where she would never look for me again. I returned secretly to Etna, and concealed myself in the caverns that had once been her abode, and my dungeon. The echoes of her evil presence must have been so strong still that they disguised my own feeble presence. I remained hidden on the mountain, and in time I felt her interest in me fade. Her search became desultory, and at last ceased. Perhaps she believed that I had perished or that she had obliterated my powers so I no longer posed a threat. I waited in secret until the joyous day that I felt your presence stirring. When the priestess of Saraswati opened your Inner Eye, I felt the disturbance it created on the ether. Then the star you call Lostris appeared to me. I rallied my scattered resolve and followed it to you.'

After Demeter had finished Taita was silent for a time. He sat hunched on Windsmoke, swaying to her easy motion, his cloak wrapped about his head, only his eyes showing through a slit. 'So if she is not at Etna,' he said eventually, 'where is she, Demeter?'

'I have told you that I do not know.'

'You must know, even though you think you do not,' Taita contradicted him. 'How long did you abide with her? Ten years, you said?'

'Ten years,' Demeter agreed. 'Each year was an eternity.'

'Then you know her as no other living being. You have absorbed part of her: she has left traces of herself on and in you.'

'She took from me. She gave nothing,' Demeter replied.

'You took from her also, perhaps not in the same measure, but no coupling of man and woman is completely barren. You have knowledge of her still. Maybe it is so painful to you that you have hidden it even from yourself. Let me help you to retrieve it.'

Taita took on the role of inquisitor. He was ruthless, making no allowances for his victim's great age, his weaknesses and afflictions of both body and spirit. He strove to draw from him every memory he still possessed of the great witch, no matter how faint or deeply suppressed it was. Day after day he ransacked the old man's mind, and they did not break their journey. They travelled at night, to escape the savage desert sun, and camped before dawn broke. As soon as Demeter's tent had been raised, they took shelter from the sunrise and Taita resumed his questioning. Gradually he conceived strong affection and admiration for Demeter as he came to understand the full extent of the old man's suffering, the courage and fortitude he had required to survive Eos's persecutions over such a vast span. But he did not allow pity to deter him from his task.

At last it seemed there remained nothing more for Taita to learn, but he was not satisfied. Demeter's revelations seemed superficial and mundane.

'There is a spell practised by the priests of Ahura Maasda in Babylon,' he told Demeter at last. 'They can send a man into a deep trance that is close to death itself. Then they are able to direct his mind back great distances in time and space, to the very day of his birth. Every detail of his life, every word he ever spoke or heard, every voice and every face becomes clear to him.'

'Yes,' Demeter agreed. 'I have heard these matters spoken of. Are you privy to this art, Taita?'

'Do you trust me? Will you submit yourself to me?'

Demeter closed his eyes in weary resignation. 'There is nothing left within me. I am a dried-out husk from which you have sucked every drop as ravenously as the witch herself.' He wiped a clawlike hand across his face and massaged his closed eyes. Then he opened them. 'I submit myself to you. Work this spell over me, if you are able.'

Taita held up the golden Periapt before his eyes and let it swing gently on its chain. 'Concentrate on this golden star. Drive every other thought from your mind. See nothing but the star, hear nothing but my voice. You are weary to the depths of your soul, Demeter. You must sleep. Let yourself fall into sleep. Let sleep close over your head, like a soft fur blanket. Sleep, Demeter, sleep . . .'

Slowly the old man relaxed. His eyelids quivered, and were still. He lay like a corpse upon a bier, snoring softly. One of his eyelids drooped open, and behind it the eye was rolled back so that only the white showed, blind and opaque. He seemed to have sunk into a deep trance, but when Taita asked him a question he answered. His voice was blurred and weak, the tone reedy.

'Go back, Demeter, go back along the river of time.'

'Yes,' Demeter responded. 'I am rolling back the years . . . back, back, back . . .' His voice grew stronger, more vigorous.

'Where are you now?'

'I stand at the E-temen-an-ki, the Foundation of Heaven and Earth,' he replied, in a vital young voice.

Taita knew the building well: an immense structure in the centre of Babylon. The walls were of glazed bricks, in all the colours of earth and sky, shaped into a mighty pyramid. 'What do you see, Demeter?'

'I see a great open space, the very centre of the world, the axis of earth and heaven.'

'Do you see walls and high terraces?'

'There are no walls, but I see the workmen and slaves. They are as many as the ants of the earth and locusts of the sky. I hear their voices.' Then Demeter spoke in many tongues, a mighty babble of humanity. Taita recognized some of the languages he spoke, but others were obscure. Suddenly Demeter cried out in Ancient Sumerian: 'Let us build a tower whose height may reach unto heaven.'

With astonishment Taita realized that he was witnessing the laying of the foundations of the Tower of Babel. He had travelled back to the beginning time.

'Now you are journeying through the centuries. You see the E-temen-an-ki reach to its full height, and kings worshipping the gods Bel and Marduk on its summit. Come forward in time!' Taita directed him, and through Demeter's eyes, he witnessed the rise of great empires and the fall of mighty kings as Demeter described events that had been lost and forgotten in antiquity. He heard the voices of men and women who had returned to dust centuries before.

At last Demeter faltered, and his voice lost its strength. Taita laid a hand on his brow, which was as cool as a gravestone. 'Peace, Demeter,' he whispered. 'Sleep now. Leave your memories to the ages. Return to the present.'

Demeter shuddered and relaxed. He slept until sunset, then woke as naturally and calmly as though nothing unusual had occurred. He seemed refreshed and fortified. He ate the fruit

Taita brought to him with good appetite and drank the soured goat's milk, while the retainers struck camp, then loaded the tents and baggage on to the camels. When the caravan started out he was strong enough to walk a short way beside Taita.

'What memories did you extort from me while I slept?' he asked, with a smile. 'I remember nothing, so nothing it must have been.'

'You were present when the foundations of E-temen-an-ki were dug and laid,' Taita told him.

Demeter stopped short and turned to him with amazement. 'I told you that?'

In reply Taita mimicked some of the voices and languages Demeter had used in his trance. At once Demeter identified each utterance. His legs soon tired, but his enthusiasm was unaffected. He mounted his palanquin and stretched out on the mattress. Taita rode beside him, and they continued their conversation throughout the long night. At last Demeter asked a question that was central in both their minds: 'Did I speak of Eos? Were you able to uncover some hidden memory?'

Taita shook his head. 'I was careful not to alarm you. I did not broach the matter directly but allowed your memories to range freely.'

'Like a hunter with a pack of hounds,' Demeter suggested, with a sudden surprising cackle. 'Take care, Taita, that while casting for a stag you do not startle a man-devouring lioness.'

'Your memories reach so far that trying to trace Eos is like voyaging across the widest ocean in search of a particular shark among a great multitude. We might spend another lifetime before we stumble by chance upon your memories of her.'

'You must direct me to her,' Demeter said, without hesitation.

'I am fearful for your safety, perhaps even your life,' Taita demurred.

'Shall we send out the hounds again on the morrow? This time you must give them the scent of the lioness.'

They were quiet for the rest of the night, lost in their own thoughts and memories. At the first light of dawn they reached a tiny oasis and Taita called a halt among the date palms. The animals were fed and watered while the tents were erected. As soon as they were alone in the main tent, Taita asked, 'Would you like to rest a while, Demeter, before we make the next attempt? Or are you ready to begin at once?'

'I have rested all night. I am ready now.'

Taita studied the other's face. He seemed calm and his pale eyes were serene. Taita held up the Periapt of Lostris. 'Your eyes grow heavy. Let them close. You feel quiet and secure. Your limbs are heavy. You are very comfortable. You listen to my voice, and you feel sleep coming over you . . . blessed sleep . . . deep, healing sleep . . .'

Demeter dropped away more swiftly than he had on their first attempt: he was becoming increasingly susceptible to Taita's quiet suggestion.

'There is a mountain that breathes fire and smoke. Do you see it?'

For a moment Demeter was deathly still. His lips paled and quivered. Then he shook his head in wild denial. 'There is no mountain! I see no mountain!' His voice rose and cracked.

'There is a woman on the mountain,' Taita persisted, 'a beautiful woman. The most beautiful woman on earth. Do you see her, Demeter?'

Demeter began to pant like a dog, his chest pumping like the bellows of a coppersmith. Taita felt that he was losing him: Demeter was fighting the trance, trying to break out of it. He knew that this must be their last attempt for the old man was unlikely to survive another.

'Can you hear her voice, Demeter? Listen to the sweet music of her words. What is she saying to you?'

Now Demeter was wrestling with an invisible opponent, rolling about on his mattress. He drew his knees and elbows up to his chest and curled his body into a ball. Then his limbs shot out straight and his back arched. He babbled with the voices of madmen, he gibbered and giggled. He gnashed his teeth until one shattered at the back of his jaw, then spat out the shards in a mixture of blood and saliva.

'Peace, Demeter!' Panic rose in Taita, like a pot coming to the boil. 'Be still! You are safe again.'

Demeter's breathing eased, and then he spoke unexpectedly in the arcane Tenmass of the adepts. His words were strange but his tone was even more so. His voice was no longer that of an old man, but of a young woman, sweet and melodious, as musical as Taita had ever heard.

'Fire, air, water and earth, but the lord of these is fire.' Every languid inflection engraved itself into Taita's mind. He knew he would never erase the sound.

Demeter collapsed back upon the mattress. The rigidity left his body. His eyes fluttered closed. His breathing stilled, and his chest ceased heaving. Taita feared that his heart must have burst, but when he placed his ear to his ribs he heard it beating to a muted but regular rhythm. With a surge of relief he realized that Demeter had survived.

Taita let him sleep for the rest of the day. When Demeter awoke he seemed unaffected by his ordeal. Indeed, he made no reference to what had passed, and seemed to have no memory of it.

While they shared a bowl of stewed suckling goat, the two men discussed the day-to-day affairs of the caravan. They tried to estimate how far they had come from Gallala, and how soon they would reach the splendid palace of Pharaoh Nefer Seti. Taita had sent a messenger ahead to alert the king to their arrival, and they wondered how he would receive them.

'Pray to Ahura Maasda, the one true light, that no more plagues have been sent to torment that poor afflicted land,' Demeter said, then fell silent.

'Fire, air, water and earth . . .' said Taita, in a conversational tone.

'. . . but the lord of these is fire,' Demeter responded, like a schoolboy reciting a lesson by rote. His hand flew up to cover his mouth, and he stared at Taita with astonishment in his old eyes. At last he asked, shaken, 'Fire, air, water and earth, the four essential elements of creation. Why did you name them, Taita?'

'First tell me, Demeter, why you named fire as the lord of all.'

'The prayer,' Demeter whispered. 'The incantation.'

'Whose prayer? What incantation?'

Demeter turned pale as he tried to remember. 'I know not.' His voice trembled as he tried to unearth painful memories. 'I have never heard it before.'

'You have.' Now Taita spoke with the voice of the inquisitor. 'Think, Demeter! Where? Who?' Then, suddenly, Taita changed his tone again. He could mimic perfectly the voices of others. He spoke now in the heartbreakingly lovely feminine voice that Demeter had used in his trance. 'But the lord of these is fire.'

Demeter gasped and clapped his hands over his ears. 'No!' he screamed. 'When you use that voice you blaspheme. You commit loathsome sacrilege. That is the voice of the Lie, the voice of Eos, the witch!' He sank back and sobbed brokenly.

Taita waited silently for him to recover.

At last he raised his head and said, 'May Ahura Maasda have mercy on me, and forgive me my weakness. How could I have forgotten that awful utterance?'

'Demeter, you did not forget. The memory was denied to you,' Taita said gently. 'Now you must recall all of it – swiftly, before Eos intrudes once more and stifles it.'

'"But the lord of these is fire." That was the incantation with which she opened her most unholy rituals,' Demeter whispered.

'This was at Etna?'

'I knew her at no other place.'

'She exalted fire in the place of fire.' Taita was thoughtful. 'She mustered her powers in the heart of the volcano. The fire is part of her strength, but she has gone from the source of her power. Yet we know that it has been resuscitated. Do you see that you have answered our question? We know now where we must search for her.'

Demeter was evidently bewildered.

'We must look for her in the fire, in the volcano,' Taita explained.

Demeter seemed to rally his thoughts. 'Yes, I see it,' he said.

'Let us ride this horse further!' Taita exclaimed. 'The volcano possesses three of the elements: fire, earth and air. It lacks only water. Etna was beside the sea. If she has found another volcano as her lair, there must be a large body of water close at hand.'

'The sea?' asked Demeter.

'Or a great river,' Taita suggested. 'A volcano beside the sea, on an island perhaps, or near a great lake. That is where we must seek her.' He placed an arm round Demeter's shoulders and smiled at him fondly. 'So, Demeter, despite your denials, you knew all along where she is hiding.'

'I give myself little credit. It took your genius to draw it from my failing memory,' Demeter said. 'But tell me, Taita, by how little have we narrowed the area of our search? How many volcanoes are there that fit the description?' He paused, then answered his own question. 'They must be legion, and certainly they will be separated by vast tracts of land and sea. It might take years to journey to them all, and I fear I lack the strength now for such endeavour.'

'Over the centuries the brotherhood of priests in the temple of Hathor at Thebes has made an intimate study of the earth's surface. They possess detailed maps of the seas and oceans, the mountains and rivers. In my travels I gathered information that I passed on to them, so they and I are well acquainted with each other. They will provide us with a list of all the known volcanoes situated close to water. I do not believe we will have to travel to each one. You and I can combine our powers to sound each mountain from afar for the emanations of evil.'

'We will have to contain our patience and husband our resources until we reach the temple of Hathor, then. This conflict with Eos is draining to the dregs even the deep cup of your strength and fortitude. You, too, must rest, Taita,' Demeter counselled. 'You have not slept for two days, and we have barely taken the first steps on the long hard road to ferret her out.'

At this point Meren carried a bundle of perfumed desert grass into their living tent and arranged it to form a mattress. Over it he spread the tiger-skin. He knelt to remove his master's sandals and loosen the belt of his tunic, but Taita snapped at him, 'I am not a puling infant, Meren. I can undress myself.'

Meren smiled indulgently as he eased him back upon the mattress. 'We know that you are not, Magus. Strange, is it not, how often you behave like one?' Taita opened his mouth to protest, but instead gave a soft snore and, in an instant, dropped into a deep sleep.

'He has watched over me while I slept. Now I will attend him, good Meren,' Demeter said.

'That is my duty,' Meren said, still watching Taita.

'You can protect him from man and beast – no one could do that better,' Demeter said, ' – but if he is attacked through the occult, you will be helpless. Good Meren, take your bow and bring us a fat gazelle for our dinner.'

Meren hovered a little longer beside Taita, then sighed and stooped out through the flap of the tent. Demeter settled beside Taita's mattress.

T aita walked beside the seashore, along a beach bright as a snowfield against which rolled shining waters. Breezes perfumed with jasmine and lilac brushed his face and ruffled his beard. He stopped at the water's edge and the wavelets lapped his feet. He looked out across the sea, and saw the dark void beyond. He knew that he was at the very end of the earth, looking on to the chaos of eternity. He stood in the sunlight, but he gazed upon darkness, the stars floating on it like clouds of fireflies.

He searched for the Star of Lostris, but it was not there. Not even the faintest glow remained. It had come from the void, and to the void it had returned. He was assailed by a terrible sorrow, and felt himself drowning in his own loneliness. He began to turn away when, faintly, he heard singing. It was a young voice he recognized at once, although he had last heard it so long ago. His heart bounded against his ribs, a wild creature struggling to be free, as the sound drew nearer.

> 'My heart flutters up like a wounded quail
> when I see my beloved's face
> and my cheeks bloom like the dawn sky
> to the sunshine of his smile . . .'

It was the first song he had taught her, and it had always been her favourite. Eagerly he turned back to find her, for he knew that the singer could be none other than Lostris. She had been his ward, and he had been charged with her care and education soon after her natural mother had died of the river fever. He had come to love her, as he knew no man had ever loved a woman.

He shaded his eyes against the dazzle of the sunlit sea, and made out a shape upon its surface. The shape drew closer, and its outline became clearer. He saw that it was a giant golden dolphin, which swam with such speed and grace that the water curled open ahead of its snout in a creaming bow wave. A girl stood upon its back. She balanced like a skilled charioteer, leaning back against the reins of seaweed with which she controlled the elegant creature, and she smiled across at him as she sang.

Taita fell to his knees on the sand. 'Mistress!' he cried. 'Sweet Lostris!'

She was twelve again, the age at which he had first met her. She wore only a skirt of bleached linen, crisp and shining, white as the wing of an egret. The skin of her slim body was lustrous as oiled cedarwood from the mountains beyond Byblos. Her breasts were the shape of new-laid eggs, tipped with rose garnets.

'Lostris, you have returned to me. Oh, sweet Horus! Oh, merciful Isis! You have given her back to me,' he sobbed.

'I never left you, beloved Taita,' Lostris broke off from her song to say. Her expression sparkled with mischief and a childlike sense of fun. Though laughter curled her lovely lips, her eyes were soft with compassion. She glowed with womanly wisdom and understanding. 'I have never forgotten my promise to you.'

The golden dolphin slid up on to the beach, and Lostris sprang from its back to the sand in a single graceful movement. She stood with both arms extended towards him. The thick sidelock of her hair swung forward over one shoulder and dangled between her girlish breasts. Every plane and silken contour of her lovely face was graven into his mind. Her teeth sparkled like a mother-of-pearl necklace as she called, 'Come to me, Taita. Come back to me, my true love!'

Taita started towards her. He hobbled the first few steps, his legs stiff and clumsy with age. Then new strength surged through them. He raised himself on his toes and flew effortlessly over the soft white sand. He could feel his sinews taut as bowstrings, his muscles supple and resilient.

'Oh, Taita, how beautiful you are!' Lostris called. 'How swift and strong, how young, my darling.' His heart and his spirit were exalted as he knew that her words were true. He was young again, and in love.

He reached out both hands to her and she seized them in a death grip. Her fingers were cold and bony, twisted with arthritis, the skin was dry and rough.

'Help me, Taita,' she screamed, but it was no longer her voice. It was the voice of a very old man in agony. 'She has me in her coils!'

Lostris was shaking his hands with the desperation of mortal terror. Her strength was unnatural – she was crushing his fingers and he could feel the pain of bones buckling, sinews cracking. He tried to tear himself free. 'Let me go!' he shouted. 'You are not Lostris.' He was no longer young, the strength that had filled him only a moment before had evaporated. Age and dismay overwhelmed him as he felt the wondrous tapestry of his dream unravelling, ripped to tatters by the chilling gales of dreadful reality.

He found himself pinned down on the floor of the tent by an enormous weight. His chest was caving in under it. He could not breathe. His hands were still crushed. The shrill screams were close to his ear, so close he thought his eardrums might burst.

He forced his eyes open, and the last images of his dream vanished. Demeter's face was only inches above his. It was almost unrecognizable, distorted with agony, swollen and empurpled. The mouth hung open and the yellow tongue lolled out. His cries were fading into gasps and desperate wheezes.

Taita was shocked fully awake. The tent was filled with a heavy reptilian stench, and Demeter was enveloped in massive scaly coils. Only his head and one arm were free. He was still clinging with his free hand to Taita, like a drowning man. The coils were laid in perfectly symmetrical loops around him and tightened with regular muscular spasms. The scales rasped against each other as the coils clenched, crushed and constricted Demeter's frail body. The ophidian skin was patterned with a marvellous design of gold, chocolate and russet, but it was only when Taita saw the head that he knew what creature had attacked them.

'Python,' he grunted aloud. The snake's head was twice the size of his fists clenched together. Its jaws gaped wide and its fangs were fastened into Demeter's bony shoulder. Thick ropes of glistening saliva drooled from the corners of the grinning mouth – the lubricant with which it covered its prey before swallowing it whole. The small round eyes that stared at Taita were black and implacable. The coils tightened upon them-selves in another contraction. Taita found himself helpless beneath the weight of man and serpent. He looked up into Demeter's face as the man's final scream was choked into silence. Demeter was no longer able to draw breath, and his pale eyes bulged sightlessly from their sockets. Taita heard one of his ribs snap under the remorseless pressure.

Taita found enough breath to bellow, 'Meren!' He knew that Demeter was almost gone. The death grip on his hand had slackened and he was able to wrench himself free, but he was still trapped. To save Demeter he needed some weapon. He had the image of Lostris still in his mind, and his hand flew to his throat. It fastened on the gold star that hung there on its chain: the Periapt of Lostris.

'Arm me, my darling,' he whispered. The heavy metal ornament fitted snugly into his palm. He slashed at the head of the python with it. He aimed for one of its beaded eyes and the sharp metal point scored the transparent scale that covered it. The snake let out a vicious, explosive hiss. Its coiled body convulsed and twisted, but its fangs were still buried in the flesh of Demeter's shoulder. They were set back at an angle so that it could maintain a grip on its prey while it swallowed, designed by nature not to release readily. The python made a series of violent regurgitating movements as it tried to work its jaws free.

Taita struck again. He drove the sharp point of the metal star into the corner of the snake's eye, and screwed it in. The giant coils of the serpentine body sprang loose as the python released Demeter, thrashing its head from side to side until its sharp fangs were free of his flesh. Its eye was ripped open, and splattered cold oleaginous blood over both men as it reared back. With the weight off his chest Taita gasped in a shallow breath, then shoved aside Demeter's slack body as the enraged python struck at his face. He threw up his arm and the python locked its fangs into his wrist, but the hand that held the star was still free. He felt the sharp teeth grind against his wrist bone, but the pain gave him a wild new strength. He stabbed the point into the wounded eye again, and worked it deeper. The snake exploded into further paroxysms of agony as Taita tore the eye out of its skull. It freed its jaws to strike again and again, the heavy blows of its snout like those of a mailed fist. Taita rolled about on the floor of the tent, twisting and wriggling to avoid them, as he screamed for Meren. The heaving coils of the serpent, thicker than his chest, seemed to fill the entire tent.

Then Taita felt a bony spike drive deep into his thigh, and shouted again with pain. He knew what had wounded him: on each side of its genital vent, on the underside of its stubby tail, the python carried a pair of viciously hooked claws. They were used to hold the body of its mate while it plunged its long corkscrew penis into her vent and spurted into her womb. With those hooks it also gripped its prey. They acted as a fulcrum for the coils, magnifying their strength. Desperately Taita tried to tear his leg free. But the hooks were buried in his flesh, and the first slippery coil whipped round his body.

'Meren!' Taita cried again. But his voice was weaker, and the next coil enfolded him, crushing his chest. He tried to call again but the air was forced from his lungs in a rush and his ribs buckled.

Suddenly Meren appeared at the opening of the tent. For a moment he paused to take in the full import of the monstrous heaving of the serpent's dappled body. Then he leapt forward, reaching over his shoulder to draw his sword from the sheath that hung down his back. He dared not strike at the python's head for he risked injuring Taita, so he took two dancing steps to one side to alter the angle of his attack. The python's darting head was still hammering at the bodies of its victims, but its stubby tail was held erect as it drove its hooks deeper into Taita's leg. With a flick of the blade Meren hacked off the exposed portion of the snake's tail above the hooks, a section as long as Taita's leg and as thick as his thigh.

The python lashed the top half of its body as high as the tent roof. Its mouth gaped wide and its wolfish fangs gleamed as it towered above Meren. Its head wove from side to side as it watched him with its remaining eye. But the blow had severed its spinal column, and anchored it. Meren faced it with his sword lifted high. The snake swung forward and struck at his face, but Meren was ready for it. His blade whispered through the air, and the bright edge snicked cleanly through the snake's neck. The head fell clear, and the jaws snapped spasmodically as the headless carcass continued to twist. Meren kicked his way through the undulating coils and seized Taita's arm, blood spurting from the fang punctures in his wrist. He lifted Taita high above his head and carried him out of the tent.

'Demeter! You must rescue Demeter!' Taita panted. Meren ran back and hacked at the headless beast, trying to cut his way through to where Demeter lay. The other servants were at last aroused by the uproar and came running. The bravest followed Meren into the tent where they dragged the snake aside and freed Demeter. He was unconscious and bleeding copiously from the wounds in his shoulder.

Ignoring his own injuries, Taita went to work on him immediately. The old man's chest was bruised, and covered with contusions. When Taita palpated his ribs he found that at least two were cracked but his first concern was to staunch the bleeding of the shoulder wound. The pain brought Demeter round, and Taita sought to distract him as he cauterized the bites with the point of Meren's dagger heated in the flames of the brazier that burnt in a corner of the tent.

'The bite of the serpent is not venomous. That, at least, is fortunate,' he told Demeter.

'Perhaps the only thing that is.' Demeter's voice was tight with pain. 'That was no natural creature, Taita. It was sent from out of the void.'

Taita was unable to find a convincing argument to the contrary, but he did not wish to encourage the old man's gloom. 'Come, old friend,' he said. 'Nothing is so bad that brooding cannot make it worse. We are both alive. The snake might have been natural, rather than a device of Eos.'

'Have you ever heard of such a creature in Egypt before now?' Demeter asked.

'I have seen them in the lands to the south.' Taita side-stepped the question.

'Far to the south?'

'Yes, indeed,' Taita admitted. 'Beyond the Indus river in Asia, and south of where the Nile divides into two streams.'

'Always in the deep forests?' Demeter persisted. 'Never in these arid deserts? Never so massive in size?'

'As you say.' Taita capitulated.

'It was sent to kill me, not you. She does not want you dead – not yet,' Demeter said, with finality.

Taita continued his examination in silence. He was relieved to find that none of the major bones in Demeter's body were broken. He bathed the shoulder with a distillation of wine, covered the bites with a healing salve and bandaged them with strips of linen. Only then could he attend to his own injuries.

Once he had bound up his wrist, he helped Demeter to his feet and supported him as they limped out of the tent to where Meren had laid out the carcass of the gigantic python. They measured its length at fifteen full paces, without the head and the tail section; and even Meren's muscular arms were unable to encompass its girth at the thickest point. The muscles beneath the magnificently patterned skin were still twitching and trembling, although it had been dead for some time.

Taita prodded the severed head with the tip of his staff, then prised open the mouth. 'It is able to unhook the hinges of its jaws so that its mouth can open wide enough to swallow a large man with ease.'

Meren's handsome features reflected disgust. 'A foul and unholy creature. Demeter speaks truly. This is a monster from the void. I will burn the carcass to ashes.'

'You will do no such thing,' Taita told him firmly. 'The fat of such a supernatural creature has potent magical properties. If, as seems most likely, it has been conjured up by the witch, we might be able it to turn it back on her.'

'If you do not know where to find her,' Meren pointed out, 'how can you send it back to her?'

'It is her creation, a part of her. As if it were a homing pigeon, we can send it to seek her out,' Demeter explained.

Meren fidgeted uncomfortably. Even though he had been companion to the magus all these years, mysteries such as this puzzled and dismayed him.

Taita took pity on him and clasped his upper arm in a friendly grip. 'Once again I am in your debt. Without you, Demeter and I might, at this very moment, be within the gut of this creature.'

Meren's anxious expression changed to one of gratification. 'Tell me, then, what you wish me to do with it.' He kicked the twitching carcass, which was rolling itself slowly into a great ball.

'We are injured. It may be some days before we can gather our powers to work the magic. Take this offal to a place where it will not be eaten by vultures or jackals,' Taita told him. 'Later we will skin it and boil down its fat.'

Although he tried, Meren was unable to load the python on to the back of one of the camels. The animal was terrified by the stench of the carcass, and bucked, bawled and jibbed. In the end Meren and five strong men dragged it down to the horse lines and piled rocks over it to protect it from the hyenas and other scavengers.

When Meren returned he found the magi sitting on the

floor of the tent, facing each other. They had linked hands to combine their powers and cast a spell of protection and concealment round the encampment. When they had completed the intricate ceremony, Taita gave Demeter a draught of red sheppen, and soon the old man sagged into a drugged sleep.

'Leave us now, good Meren. Take your rest but stay within call,' Taita said, as he sat down beside Demeter to watch over him. But his own body betrayed him and dropped into the dark oblivion of sleep. He woke again to find Meren shaking his injured arm insistently. He sat up, groggy with sleep, and snarled. 'What ails you? Have you lost all sense and reason?'

'Come, Magus! Quickly!'

His urgent tone and stricken expression alarmed Taita and he turned anxiously to Demeter. With relief he saw that the old man was still sleeping. He scrambled to his feet. 'What is it?' he asked, but Meren was gone. Taita followed him out into the cooler air of dawn and saw him running towards the horse lines. When he caught up with him, Meren pointed wordlessly at the pile of rocks that had covered the serpent's carcass. For a moment Taita was puzzled, until he saw that the rocks had been moved aside.

'The snake has gone,' Meren blurted. 'It vanished during the night.' He pointed to a depression in the sand left by the python's heavy body. A few globules of blood had dried into black balls, but that was all that remained. Taita felt the hair at the back of his neck lift, as if touched by a cold wind. 'You have searched thoroughly?'

Meren nodded. 'We have scoured the ground for half a league around the camp. We found no sign of it.'

'Devoured by dogs or wild animals,' Taita said, but Meren shook his head.

'None of the dogs would go near it. They whined and growled and slunk away when they smelt it.'

'Hyena, vultures?'

'No bird could have moved those rocks, and a carcass that size would have fed a hundred hyenas. They would have made the night hideous with their shrieks and wails. There was no sound and there are no tracks, no spoor or drag marks.' He ran his fingers through his dense curls, then lowered his voice: 'There is no question but that Demeter was right. It has taken its head and flown away, without touching ground. It was a creature from the void.'

'An opinion not to be shared with the servants and camel drivers,' Taita warned him. 'If they suspect this, they will desert us. You must tell them that Demeter and I disposed of the body with a spell that we worked during the night.'

It was several days before Taita judged that Demeter could resume the journey, but the awkward gait of the camel that carried his palanquin aggravated the pain of his cracked ribs, and Taita had to keep him sedated with regular draughts of the red sheppen. At the same time he reduced the pace of the caravan and shortened the marching hours to avoid causing him further distress and injury.

Taita himself had recovered swiftly from the worst effects of the serpent's attack. Soon he was at ease on Windsmoke's back. Occasionally during the night marches he left Meren to attend to Demeter, while he rode ahead of the caravan. He had to be alone to study the skies. He was certain the momentous psychic events in which they were caught up must be reflected by new omens and portents among the heavenly bodies. He soon discovered that they were in evidence everywhere. The heavens blazed with the vivid trails of fire left by flocks of shooting stars and comets, more in a single night than he had seen in the previous five years. This plethora of omens was confusing and contradictory: they spelled out no clear message that he could discern. Instead there were dire warnings, promises of hope, dread threats and signs of reassurance all at the same time.

On the tenth night after the serpent's disappearance, the moon was full, an enormous luminous orb that paled the fiery tails of shooting stars, and reduced even the major planets to insignificant pricks of light. Long after midnight Taita rode out on to a barren plain he recognized. They were less than fifty leagues from the rim of the escarpment that led down to the once fertile lands of the Nile delta. He would have to turn back soon, so he reined in Windsmoke. He dismounted and found a seat on a flat rock beside the path. The mare nudged him with her muzzle so he opened the pouch that hung at his hip and absently fed her a handful of crushed dhurra meal, while he turned his full attention to the skies.

He could barely distinguish the faint cloud that was all that remained of the Star of Lostris, and felt a pang of bereavement when he realized it would soon disappear for ever. Sadly he looked back at the moon. It heralded the beginning of the planting season, a time of rejuvenation and regrowth, but without the inundation of the river no crops would be planted in the delta.

Suddenly Taita sat up straighter. He felt the chill that always preceded some dire occult event: gooseflesh prickled his arms and the hair stood up on the back of his neck. The outline of the moon was changing before his eyes. At first he thought it an illusion, a trick of the light, but within minutes a thick slice had been swallowed as though by the jaws of some dark monster. With startling rapidity the remainder of the great orb shared the same fate, and only a dark hole remained in its place. The stars reappeared but they were wan and sickly, compared to the light that had been blotted out.

All nature seemed confounded. No night bird called. The breeze dropped and was stilled. The outlines of the surrounding hills merged into the darkness. Even the grey mare was distressed: she tossed her mane and whinnied with fear. Then she reared, jerking the reins from Taita's grip, and bolted down the track along which they had come. He let her go.

Although Taita knew that no invocation or prayer would have any force with cosmic events in train, he called aloud on Ahura Maasda and all the gods of Egypt to save the moon from obliteration. Then he saw that the remains of the Star of

Lostris showed more clearly. It was just a pale smear, but he lifted the Periapt on its chain and held it towards the star. He concentrated his mind, his trained senses and the power of the Inner Eye upon it.

'Lostris!' he cried in despair. 'You who have always been the light in my heart! Use your powers to intercede with the gods who are your peers. Rekindle the moon and light the heavens again.'

Almost at once a thin sliver of light appeared where the rim of the moon had vanished. It grew in size, became curved and bright as the blade of a sword, then assumed the shape of a battleaxe. While he called upon Lostris and held aloft her Periapt, the moon returned in all its splendour and shining glory. Relief and joy flooded through him. Nevertheless, he knew that even if the moon had been restored, the warning conveyed by its eclipse remained, an omen that cancelled these more auspicious auguries.

It took him half of the remaining hours of darkness to rally after the harrowing sight of the dying moon, but at last he hoisted himself to his feet, took up his staff and struck out in search of the mare. Within a league he came up with her. She was browsing the leaves of a scrubby desert bush beside the track, and whickered a greeting when she saw him, then trotted to meet him in a show of contrition for her unconscionable behaviour. Taita mounted her and they rode back to rejoin the caravan.

The men had witnessed the swallowing of the moon, and even Meren was having difficulty controlling them. He hurried to Taita as soon as he saw him returning. 'Did you see what happened to the moon, Magus? Such a terrible omen! I feared for your very existence,' he cried. 'I give thanks to Horus that you are safe. Demeter is awake and awaits your arrival, but first will you speak to these craven dogs? They want to slink back to their kennels.'

Taita took time to reassure the men. He told them that the regeneration of the moon signalled no disaster, but instead heralded the return of the Nile inundation. His reputation was such that they were readily satisfied, and at last, quite cheerfully, they agreed to continue the journey. Taita left them and went to Demeter's tent. Over the past ten days the old man had made a heartening recovery from the mauling that the python had inflicted on him, and he was much stronger. However, he greeted Taita with a solemn mien. They sat together quietly for the rest of that night and discussed the significance of the moon's darkening.

'I have lived long enough to witness many similar occurrences,' Demeter said softly, 'but seldom have I seen such a complete obliteration.'

Taita nodded. 'Indeed, I have seen only two such disappearances before. Always they have foreshadowed some calamity – the death of great kings, the fall of beautiful and prosperous cities, famine or pestilence.'

'It was another manifestation of the dark powers of the Lie,' Demeter muttered. 'I believe that Eos flaunts her invincibility. She is trying to cow us, to drive us to despair.'

'We must linger no longer on the road, but hurry to Thebes,' Taita said.

'Above all, we must never relax our vigilance. We can expect her to unleash her next onslaught upon us at any time of day or night.' Demeter studied Taita's face seriously. 'You must forgive me if I repeat myself, but until you come to know the witch's wiles and artifices as I do, it is difficult to understand how devious they are. She is able to plant in your mind the most convincing images. She can return your earliest infant memories to you, even the images of your father and mother so vividly that you cannot doubt them.'

'In my case that will present her with some difficulty.' Taita smiled wryly. 'For I never knew either parent.'

Although the camel drivers had stepped up the pace, Taita was still consumed with impatience. The following night he left the caravan again and rode ahead, hoping to reach the escarpment of the delta and look down into his beloved Egypt after all his years of absence. His eagerness seemed infectious for Windsmoke kept up an easy canter, her flying hoofs eating the leagues until at last Taita reined her in on the rim of the escarpment. Below, the moon lit the cultivated lands with silvery radiance, and highlighted the palm groves that outlined the course of the Nile. He searched for the faintest gleam of silver waters but at this distance the riverbed was dark and sombre.

Taita dismounted and stood at the mare's head, stroking her neck and staring raptly down upon the city, the moon-white walls of the temples and palaces of Karnak. He picked out the towering walls of the Palace of Memnon on the far bank but resisted the temptation to continue down the slope, across the alluvial plain and through one of the hundred gates of Thebes.

His duty was to stay close to Demeter, not leave him to race ahead. He squatted on his haunches at the mare's head, and allowed himself to anticipate his homecoming and reunion with those he held so dear.

Pharaoh and his queen, Mintaka, held Taita in the deep affection usually reserved for a senior family member. In return he cherished an abiding love for both of them, undiminished since their childhood. Nefer's father, Pharaoh Tamose, had been murdered when Nefer was but a child, too young to succeed to the throne of Upper and Lower Egypt so a regent had been appointed. Taita had been tutor to Tamose, so it followed that his son would be placed in Taita's care until he reached manhood. Taita had seen to his formal education, had trained him as a warrior and horseman, then instructed him in the conduct of war and the direction of armies. He had taught him the duties of royalty, the lore of statecraft and diplomacy. He had made him a man. During those years a bond was forged between them, and remained unbroken.

A draught wafted up the escarpment, cool enough to make him shiver. In these hot months it was unseasonable. Instantly he was on his guard. A sudden drop in temperature often presaged an occult manifestation. Demeter's warnings still echoed in his mind.

He sat still and searched the ether. He could discern nothing sinister. Then he turned his attention to Windsmoke, who was almost as sensitive to the supernatural as he was, but she seemed relaxed and quiet. Satisfied, he rose to his feet and gathered her reins to mount her and ride back to the caravan. By now Meren would probably be calling a halt to the night march and setting up camp. Taita wanted to spend a little time in conversation with Demeter before sleep overcame him. He had not yet fully tapped the old man's treasury of wisdom and experience.

Just then Windsmoke whickered softly and pricked her ears, but she was not seriously alarmed. Taita saw that she was gazing down the slope and turned. At first he saw nothing, but he trusted the mare and he listened to the silence of the night. At last, he glimpsed a shadowy movement near the bottom of the slope. It vanished and he thought he might have been mistaken, but the mare was still alert. He waited and watched. Then he saw movement again, closer at hand and more distinct.

The dim shape of another horse and rider emerged from the darkness, following the path up the escarpment towards where he stood. The strange horse was also grey, but even paler than Windsmoke. His memory stirred: he never forgot a good horse. Even in the starlight, this one seemed familiar. He tried to think when and where he had last seen it, but the memory was so remote that he realized it must have been long ago, yet the grey paced like a four-year-old. Sharply he switched his attention to the rider upon its back – a slight figure, not a man but a boy, perhaps. Whoever he might be, he sat the grey with *élan*. There was something familiar about him, too, but, like his mount, the boy seemed too young for Taita's memory of him to be so faded. Could it be that this was the child of somebody he knew well? One of the princes of Egypt? he puzzled.

Queen Mintaka had presented Pharaoh Nefer Seti with many fine boys. All bore a strong resemblance to either their father or their mother. There was nothing ordinary about this child, and Taita could not doubt that he was of royal blood. Horse and rider drew nearer. Taita was struck by several other features. He saw that the rider wore a short chiton that left the legs bare, and they were slim, unmistakably feminine. This was a girl. Her head was covered, but as she drew closer he could make out the outline of her features beneath her head shawl.

'I know her. I know her well!' he whispered to himself. A pulse in his ears beat faster. The girl lifted a hand towards him in salutation, then thrust forward with her hips to urge the grey on. It swung into a canter, but its hoofs struck no sound from the stony path. It came up the slope towards him in eerie silence.

Too late, Taita realized that he had been lulled by a familiar appearance. He blinked rapidly to open his Inner Eye.

'They throw no aura!' he gasped, and had to place his hand on the mare's shoulder to steady himself. Neither the grey horse nor its rider was a natural creature: they came from a different dimension. Despite Demeter's warnings, he had been caught off-guard again. Swiftly he reached for the Periapt that hung at his throat, and held it in front of his face. The rider reined in and regarded him from the shadow of the shawl that covered her face. She was so close now that he could make out the glint of eyes, the soft curve of a young cheek. His memories rushed back.

Small wonder that he remembered the grey horse so well. It had been his own gift to her, chosen with care and love. He had paid for it fifty talents of silver and considered he had the best of the bargain. She had named it Gull, and it had ever been her favourite. She rode it with the grace and style Taita remembered from all those decades ago. So profound was his shock that he was unable to think clearly. He stood like a pillar of granite, holding the Periapt as a shield.

Slowly the horsewoman lifted a shapely white hand and threw back the fringe of the shawl. Taita felt the fabric of his soul ripped through as he looked upon that lovely face, each detail perfectly rendered.

It is not her. He tried to steel himself. *This is another apparition from out of the void, like the giant serpent, and perhaps as deadly.*

When he had discussed with Demeter his dream of the girl on the golden dolphin, the other man had been in no doubt whatsoever: 'Your dream was one of the ruses of the witch,' he had warned. 'You must not trust any image that feeds upon your hopes and longing. When you cast back your mind to a joyous memory, such as an old love, you open the door to Eos. She will find a way through it to reach you.'

Taita had shaken his head. 'No, Demeter, how could even Eos have conjured up such intimate detail from so long ago? Lostris's voice, the set of her eyes, the quirk of her lips when she smiled. How could Eos have copied them? Lostris has been in her sarcophagus these seventy years past. There can be no living traces of her for Eos to draw upon.'

'Eos stole from your own memories of Lostris, and gave them back to you in their most convincing, compelling form.'

'But even I had forgotten most of those details.'

'It was you who averred that we forget nothing. Every detail remains. It requires only occult skills, such as Eos possesses, to retrieve it from the vaults of your mind, as you retrieved from me my memories of Eos, her voice as she uttered the incantation to fire.'

'I cannot accept that it was not Lostris,' Taita moaned softly.

'That is because you do not want to accept it. Eos seeks to close your mind to reason. Think a moment how cunningly the image of the girl on the dolphin was woven into her evil schemes. While she lured and distracted you with false visions of a lost love, she sent her spectral serpent to destroy me. She used your dream as a distraction.'

Now, upon the escarpment of the delta, Taita was confronted with the vision again: the image of Lostris, once queen of Egypt, whose memory still ruled his heart. This time she seemed even more perfect. He felt his resolve and reason wavering, and tried desperately to check himself. But he could not prevent himself looking into Lostris's eyes. They were filled with enchanted lights, all the tears and smiles of her lifetime in their depths.

'I reject you!' he told her, in a voice as cold and stern as he could muster. 'You are not Lostris. You are not the woman I loved. You are the Great Lie. Get you hence into the darkness from which you sprang.'

At his words the sparkle in Lostris's lovely eyes was replaced by a vast sorrow. 'Darling Taita,' she called to him softly. 'I have existed without you through all the sterile and lonely years that we have been parted. Now, when you are in such mortal and spiritual danger, I have come far to be with you again. Together we can resist the evil that hovers over you.'

'You blaspheme,' he said. 'You are Eos, the Lie, and I reject you. I am protected by the Truth. You cannot reach me. You cannot harm me.'

'Oh, Taita.' Lostris's voice fell to a whisper. 'You will destroy us both. I am in peril too.' She seemed burdened by all the sorrows that had afflicted mankind since the beginning time. 'Trust me, my darling. For both our sakes you must trust me. I am none other than the Lostris you loved and who loved you. You called to me across the ether. I heeded your call and I have come to you.'

Taita felt the foundations of the earth tremble beneath his feet but he steeled himself. 'Out, cursed witch!' he cried. 'Begone, foul minion of the Lie. I reject you and all your works. Plague me no more.'

'No, Taita! You cannot do this,' she pleaded. 'We have

been given this chance, this one chance. You must not refuse it.'

'You are evil,' he told her harshly. 'You are an abomination from the void. Go back to your foul abode.'

Lostris moaned and her image receded. She faded in the same way that her star had often been eclipsed by the light of coming day. The last whisper of her voice came back to him from out of the night: 'I have tasted death once, and now I must drink the bitter cup to the dregs. Farewell, Taita, whom I loved. If only you could have loved me more.'

Then she was gone and he sank on to his knees to let the waves of remorse and loss break over his head. When he had the strength to lift his head again, the sun had risen. Already it had climbed a hand's span above the horizon. Windsmoke stood quietly beside him. She was dozing, but as soon as he stirred she threw up her head and turned her eyes on him. He was so reduced that he had to use a rock as a mounting platform to reach her back. He swayed there, almost losing his seat, as she started along the path towards the encampment.

Taita tried to order the jumble of emotions that filled his head. One salient fact emerged from his confusion: it was the manner in which Windsmoke had stood calmly, without the least sign of perturbation, during his encounter with the phantom Lostris. On every other occasion she had detected a manifestation of evil long before he had become aware of it himself. She had bolted when the moon was devoured, yet she had shown only mild interest in the wraith of Lostris and her phantom steed.

'There could not have been evil in them,' he began to convince himself. 'Did Lostris speak the truth? Did she come as my ally and friend to protect me? Have I destroyed both of us?' The pain was too much to bear. He pulled Windsmoke's head round and drove her into a full gallop back towards the delta. He checked her only when they burst out on to the rim of the escarpment, and swung down from her back on to the exact spot at which Lostris had vanished.

'Lostris!' he shouted to the sky. 'Forgive me! I was mistaken! I know now that you spoke the truth. Verily and indeed you are Lostris. Come back to me, my love! Come back!' But she was gone and the echoes mocked him: 'Come back . . . back . . . back . . .'

They were so close to the holy city of Thebes that Taita ordered Meren to continue the night march even after the sun had risen. Lit by its slanting early rays the little caravan descended the escarpment and struck out across the flat alluvial plain towards the walls of the city. The plain was desolate. No green thing grew upon it. The black earth was baked hard as brick and split with deep cracks by the furnace heat of the sun. The peasant farmers had abandoned their stricken fields and their huts stood derelict, the palm-leaf thatching falling in clumps from the rafters, the unplastered walls crumbling. The bones of the kine that had died of famine littered the fields like patches of white daisies. A whirlwind swayed and wove an erratic dance across the empty lands, spinning a column of dust and dry dhurra leaves high into the cloudless sky. The sun smote down upon the parched land like the blows of a battleaxe upon a brazen shield.

The men and animals of the caravan were as insignificant in this sullen landscape as a child's toys. They reached the river and halted involuntarily upon the bank, caught up in horrified fascination. Even Demeter dismounted from his palanquin, and hobbled down to join Taita and Meren. At this point the riverbed was four hundred yards wide. In a normal season of low Nile the mighty stream filled it from side to side, a torrent of grey, silt-laden waters, so deep and powerful that the surface was riven by shining eddies and dimpled with spinning vortices. At the season of high water the Nile could not be contained. She burst over her banks and flooded the fields. The mud and sediment dropped by her waters was so rich that they sustained three successive crops during a single growing season.

But there had been no inundation for seven years and the river was a grotesque travesty of its former mighty self. It had been reduced to a string of shallow stinking pools strung out along its bed. Their surface was stirred only by the struggles of dying fish, and the languid movements of the few surviving crocodiles. A frothy red scum covered the water, like congealing blood.

'What causes the river to bleed?' Meren asked. 'Is it a curse?'

'It seems to me that it is caused by a bloom of poisonous algae,' Taita said, and Demeter agreed.

'It is indeed algae, but I have no doubt that it is unnatural, inflicted on Egypt by the same baleful influence as stopped the flow of the waters.'

The blood-coloured pools were separated from each other by the exposed banks of black mud, which were littered with stranded rubbish and sewage from the city, roots and driftwood, the wreckage of abandoned rivercraft and the bloated carcasses of birds and animals. The only living things that frequented the open sandbanks were strange squat creatures that hopped and crawled clumsily on grotesque webbed feet over the mud. They struggled ferociously among themselves for possession of the carcasses, ripping them apart, then gulping the chunks of rotting flesh. Taita was uncertain of the creatures' nature until Meren muttered, in deep disgust, 'They are as the caravan master described them to me. Giant toads!' He hawked, then spat out the taste and stench that clogged his throat. 'Is there no end to the abominations that have descended upon Egypt?'

Taita realized then that it was the sheer size of the amphibians that had puzzled him. They were enormous. Across the back they were as wide as bush pigs, and they stood almost as tall as jackals when they raised themselves on their long back legs to their full height.

'There are human cadavers lying on the mud,' Meren exclaimed. He pointed to a tiny body that lay below them. 'There's a dead infant.'

'It seems that the citizens of Thebes are so far gone in apathy that they no longer bury their dead but cast them into the river.' Demeter shook his head sorrowfully.

As they watched, one of the toads seized the child's arm and, with a dozen shakes of its head, tore it loose from the shoulder joint. Then it threw the tiny limb high. As it dropped the toad gaped, caught and swallowed it.

All of them were sickened by the spectacle. They mounted and went on along the bank until they reached the outer walls of the city. The area outside was crowded with make-shift shelters, erected by the dispossessed peasant farmers, by the widows and orphans, by the sick and dying, and by all the other victims of the catastrophe. They huddled together under the roughly thatched roofs of the open-sided hovels. All were emaciated and apathetic. Taita saw one young mother holding her infant to shrivelled empty dugs, but the child was too weak anyway to suck, and flies crawled into its eyes and nostrils. The mother stared back at them hopelessly.

'Let me give her food for her baby.' Meren began to dismount, but Demeter stopped him.

'If you show these miserable creatures food, they will riot.'

When they rode on, Meren looked back sadly and guiltily.

'Demeter is right,' Taita told him softly. 'We cannot save a few starvelings among such multitudes. We must save the kingdom of Egypt, not a handful of her people.'

Taita and Meren picked out a camp site well away from the unfortunates. Taita called Demeter's foreman aside and pointed it out to him. 'Make certain that your master is comfortable and guard him well. Then build a fence of dried thornbush to protect the camp and keep out thieves and scavengers. Find water and fodder for the animals. Remain here until I have arranged more suitable quarters for us.'

He turned to Meren. 'I am going into the city to the palace of Pharaoh. Stay with Demeter.' He kicked his heels into the mare's flanks and headed for the main gates. The guards looked down on him from the tower as he rode through, but did not challenge him. The streets were almost deserted. The few people he saw were as pale and starving as the beggars outside the walls. They scurried away at his approach. A sickly stench hung over the city: the odour of death and suffering.

The captain of the palace guards recognized Taita, and ran to open the side gate for him, saluting respectfully as he entered the precincts. 'One of my men will take your horse to the stables, Magus. The royal grooms will care for it.'

'Is Pharaoh in residence?' Taita asked, as he dismounted.

'He is here.'

'Take me to him,' Taita ordered. The captain hurried to obey, and led him into the labyrinth of passages and halls. They passed through courtyards that had once been lovely with lawns, banks of flowers and tinkling fountains of limpid water, then on through halls and cloisters that in former times had sounded merrily to the laughter and singing of noble ladies and lords, of tumblers, troubadours and dancing slave girls. Now the rooms were deserted, the gardens were brown and dead and the fountains had run dry. The heavy silence was disturbed only by the sound of their footsteps on the stone paving.

At last they reached the antechamber of the royal audience hall. In the opposite wall there was a closed door. The captain knocked upon it with the butt of his spear, and it was opened almost immediately by a slave. Taita looked beyond him. On the floor of rose-coloured marble slabs a corpulent eunuch in a short linen skirt sat cross-legged at a low desk stacked with papyrus scrolls and writing tablets. Taita recognized him at once. He was Pharaoh's senior chamberlain. It had been on Taita's recommendation that he was selected for such an illustrious position.

'Ramram, my old friend,' Taita greeted him. Ramram jumped to his feet with surprising alacrity for such a large person, and hurried to embrace Taita. All the eunuchs in Pharaoh's service were bound by strong fraternal ties.

'Taita, you have been gone from Thebes for far too long.'
He drew Taita into his private bureau. 'Pharaoh is in council
with his generals so I cannot disturb him, but I will take you
to him the moment he is free. He would want me to do that.
However, this gives us a chance to talk. How long have you
been gone? It must be many years.'

'It is seven. Since last we met I have journeyed to strange
lands.'

'Then there is much that I must tell you about what has
befallen us in your absence. Sadly, very little is good.'

They settled down on cushions facing each other, and at
the chamberlain's bidding a slave served them bowls of sherbet
that had been cooled in earthenware jugs.

'Tell me first, how fares His Majesty?' Taita demanded
anxiously.

'I fear you will be saddened when you see him. His cares
weigh heavily upon him. Most of his days are spent in council
with his ministers, the commanders of his army and the
governors of all the nomes. He sends his envoys to every
foreign country to buy grain and food to feed the starving
population. He orders the digging of new wells to find sweet
water to replace the foul red effluent of the river.' Ramram
sighed and took a deep swig from his sherbet bowl.

'The Medes and Sumerians, the sea people, the Libyans
and all our other enemies are aware of our plight,' he continued. 'They believe our fortunes are waning, and that we
can no longer defend ourselves, so they muster their armies.
As you know, our vassal states and satraps have always grudged
the tribute they have been forced to pay Pharaoh. Many see
in our misfortunes an opportunity to break away from us, so
they enter into treasonable alliances. A multitude of foes
gathers at our borders. With our resources so grievously
depleted, Pharaoh must still find men and stores to build up
and reinforce his regiments. He stretches himself and his
empire to breaking point.'

'Any lesser monarch could not have survived these tribula-
tions,' Taita said.

'Nefer Seti is a great monarch. But he, like the rest of us lesser beings, is aware in his heart that the gods no longer smile upon Egypt. None of his efforts will succeed until he can regain their divine favour. He has ordered the priesthood in every temple throughout the land to render ceaseless prayer. He himself makes sacrifice three times a day. Although he has tried his own strength to its limit he spends half of each night, when he should be resting, in devout prayer and communion with his fellow deities.'

Tears filled the chamberlain's eyes. He wiped them away with a square of linen. 'This has been his life for the last seven years, during the failure of the mother river and the plagues that have beset us. It would have destroyed any lesser ruler. Nefer Seti is a god, but he has the heart and compassion of a man. It has changed and aged him.'

'I am indeed cast down by this news. But, tell me, how fares the queen and her children?'

'Here, too, the news is gloomy. The plagues have treated them unkindly. Queen Mintaka was struck down and lay for many weeks on the verge of death. She has now recovered, but is still much weakened. Not all of the royal children were so fortunate. Prince Khaba and his little sister Unas lie side by side in the royal mausoleum. The plague carried them away. The other children have survived, but—'

Ramram broke off as a slave entered, bowing respectfully, and whispered in the chamberlain's ear. Ramram nodded and waved him away, then turned back to Taita. 'The conclave has ended. I will go to Pharaoh and tell him of your arrival.' He hoisted himself to his feet and waddled to the back of the room. There, he touched a carved figure on the panel, which turned under his fingers. A section of the wall slid aside, and Ramram disappeared into the opening. He was not gone long before a shout of surprise and pleasure echoed from the corridor beyond the secret door. Immediately it was followed by rapid footsteps and there was another shout: 'Tata, where are you?' It was Pharaoh's nickname for him.

'Majesty, I am here.'

'You have neglected me too long,' Pharaoh accused him, as he burst through the doorway and paused to stare at Taita. 'Yes, it is truly you. I thought you might continue to flout my many summonings.'

Nefer Seti wore only open sandals below a linen skirt that covered his knees. His upper body was bare. His chest was broad and deep, his belly flat and rippling with muscle. His arms were sculpted by long practice with bow and sword. His torso was that of a warrior trained to perfection.

'Pharaoh. I salute you. I am your humble slave, as I have always been.'

Nefer Seti stepped forward and took him in a powerful embrace. 'No talk of slaves or slavery when teacher and pupil come together,' he declared. 'My heart overflows with joy to see you again.' He held him at arm's length and studied his face. 'By the grace of Horus, you have not aged a single day.'

'Nor have you, Majesty.' His tone was sincere, and Nefer Seti laughed.

'Although it is a lie, I accept your flattery as kindness to an old friend.' Nefer had set aside his formal horsehair wig, and his skin was devoid of paint, so Taita was able to study his features. Nefer's close-cropped hair was grizzled, and the crown of his skull was bald. His face was etched with the passage of time: there were deep lines at the corners of his mouth, and a cobweb of wrinkles surrounded his dark eyes, which were weary. His cheeks were hollow, and his skin had an unhealthy pallor. Taita blinked once and opened the Inner Eye; with relief he saw that Pharaoh's aura burned strongly, which betokened a brave heart and an undiminished spirit.

How old is he? Taita tried to remember. He was twelve when his father was killed, so now he must be forty-nine. The realization jolted him. An ordinary man was considered old at forty-five, and was usually dead before fifty. Ramram had told him the truth: Pharaoh was much changed.

'Has Ramram arranged lodgings for you?' Nefer Seti demanded, and looked at his chamberlain sternly over Taita's shoulder.

'I thought to allocate him one of the suites for the foreign ambassadors,' Ramram suggested.

'By no means. Taita is not a foreigner,' Nefer Seti snapped, and Taita sensed that his formerly even temper had quickened and was now more readily aroused. 'He must be lodged in the guard room at the door to my bedchamber. I want to be able to call upon him for counsel and discussion at any hour of the night.' He turned back to face Taita squarely. 'Now I must leave you. I am meeting with the Babylonian ambassador. His countrymen have tripled the price of the grain they sell us. Ramram will apprise you of all the most important matters of state. I expect to be free by midnight, and I will send for you then. You must share my dinner, though I fear you might not find it to your taste. On my orders the court enjoys the same rations as the rest of the populace.' Nefer Seti turned back to the secret doorway.

'Majesty.' Taita's tone was urgent. Nefer Seti looked back over one broad shoulder, and Taita hurried on, 'I am in company with a great and learned magus.'

'Not as powerful as you.' Nefer Seti smiled affectionately.

'Indeed, I am a child beside him. He comes to Karnak to offer aid and succour to you and your kingdom.'

'Where is this paragon now?'

'He is encamped without the city gates. Despite his learning, he is immensely aged, and feeble in body. I need to be near him.'

'Ramram, find comfortable quarters for the foreign magus in this wing of the palace.'

'Meren Cambyses is still with me as my companion and protector. I would be grateful to have him close at hand.'

'Sweet Horus, it seems I must share you with half the earth.' Nefer Seti laughed. 'But I am delighted to hear that Meren is well, and that I am to have the pleasure of his company. Ramram will find him a place. Now I must leave you.'

'Pharaoh, one more instant of your gracious presence,' Taita cut in, before he could disappear.

'You have been here but a moment, and already you have

wrung fifty favours from me. Your powers of persuasion are undimmed. What is it you still need?'

'Your permission to cross the river and pay my respects to Queen Mintaka.'

'If I refused, I would place myself in an invidious position. My queen has not lost her fire. She would treat me mercilessly.' He laughed with real affection for his wife. 'Go to her, by all means, but return here before midnight.'

As soon as Demeter was safely ensconced in the palace Taita summoned two of the royal physicians to attend him, then called Meren aside. 'I expect to return before nightfall,' he told him. 'Guard him well.'

'I should go with you, Magus. In this time of want and starvation even honest men turn in despair to brigandry to feed their families.'

'Ramram has given me an escort of guardsmen.'

It seemed strange to mount a horse, rather than a boat, to cross a river like the Nile. From the back of Windsmoke, Taita gazed towards the Palace of Memnon on the west bank and saw that many well-trodden paths led through the mudbanks between the turbid pools. They rode out along one. A monstrous toad hopped across the path in front of Taita's mare.

'Kill it!' the sergeant of the escorts snapped. A soldier couched his spear and rode down on the toad. Like a wild boar at bay, it turned ferociously to defend itself. The soldier leant forward and drove the point of his spear deep into its pulsating yellow throat. In its death throes the hideous creature clamped its jaws on the spear's shaft so the soldier had to drag it along behind his horse until it released its grip and he could pull his weapon free. He fell in beside Taita and showed him the shaft: the toad's fangs had scored the hard wood deeply.

'They are savage as wolves,' said Habari, the sergeant of the guard, a lean and scarred old warrior. 'When they first appeared, Pharaoh ordered two regiments to scour the riverbed and wipe them out. We slew them in their hundreds and then in their thousands. We piled their carcasses into windrows, but for every one we killed it seemed that another two rose from the mud to replace them. Even great Pharaoh realized that he had set us a hopeless task and now he orders that we must keep them confined to the riverbed. At times they swarm out and we must attack them again,' Habari went on. 'In their own foul manner they serve some useful purpose. They devour all the filth and carrion that is thrown into the river. The people lack the strength and energy to dig decent graves for the victims of the plague and the toads have assumed the role of undertakers.'

The horses plunged through the red slime and mud of one of the shallow pools and rode up the west bank. As soon as they came in sight of the palace the doors swung open and the gatekeeper came out to meet them.

'Hail, mighty Magus!' He saluted Taita. 'Her Majesty has word of your arrival in Thebes, and sends joyous greeting to you. She waits eagerly to welcome you.' He pointed to the palace gates. Taita looked up and saw tiny figures on top of the wall. They were women and children and Taita was uncertain which was the queen, until she waved to him. He pushed the mare, and she jumped forward and carried him through the open gates.

As he dismounted in the courtyard, Mintaka raced down the stone staircase with the grace of a girl. She had always been an athlete, a skilled charioteer and an intrepid huntress. He was delighted to see her still so lithe, until she reached up to embrace him and he saw how thin she had become. Her arms were like sticks, her features drawn and pale. Although she smiled, her dark eyes were haunted by sorrow.

'Oh, Taita, I do not know how we have done without you,' she told him, and buried her face in his beard. He stroked her head, and at his touch her gaiety evaporated. Her whole body shook with sobs. 'I thought you would never return and that Nefer and I had lost you also, as we have lost Khaba and little Unas.'

'I have been told of your bereavement. I grieve with you,' Taita murmured.

'I try to be brave. So many mothers have suffered as I have. But it is bitter to have my babies taken from me so soon.' She stood back and tried to smile again, but her eyes were welling and her lips quivered. 'Come, I want you to meet the other children. Most of them you know. Only the two youngest have never met you. They are waiting for you.'

They were lined up in two ranks. The boys in front, the princesses behind them. All were stiff with awe and respect. The smallest girl was so overcome by the stories of the great magus her siblings had told her that she dissolved into tears as soon as he looked at her. Taita picked her up and held her head against his shoulder while he whispered to her. She relaxed at once, sniffed back the tears and wrapped both arms round his neck.

'I would never have believed it if I did not remember the winning ways you have with children and animals.' Mintaka smiled at him, then called the others forward one at a time.

'I have never laid eyes on such beautiful children,' Taita told her, 'but, then, I am not surprised. They have you as their mother.'

At last Mintaka sent them away and took Taita's hand. She led him to her private apartments, where they sat beside the open window to catch the faint breeze and look out over the western hills. While she poured sherbet for him she said, 'I used to love to gaze out over the river, but no longer. The sight breaks my heart. Soon the waters will return, though. It has been prophesied.'

'By whom?' Taita asked idly, but his interest quickened when for answer she gave him a knowing, enigmatic smile, then turned the conversation to the happy times, not long past, when she was a beautiful young bride and the land was green and fruitful. Her mood lightened and she spoke animatedly. He waited for her to finish, knowing that she could not long resist returning to the mysterious prophecy.

Suddenly she dropped the reminiscences. 'Taita, do you know that our old gods have become feeble? They will soon be replaced by a new goddess with absolute power. She will restore the Nile, and rid us of the plagues that the old, effete gods have been unable to prevent.'

Taita listened respectfully. 'No, Majesty, this I did not know.'

'Oh, yes, it is certain.' Her pale features glowed with fresh colour and the years seemed to drop away. She was a girl again, suffused with joy and hope. 'But more, Taita, so much more.' She paused portentously, then went on in a rush of words, 'This goddess has the power to restore all that has been lost or taken cruelly from us, but only if we dedicate ourselves to her. If we render to her our hearts and souls, she can give back to us our youth. She can bring happiness to those who suffer and mourn. But, think on this, Taita – she even has the power to resurrect the dead.' Tears started in her eyes again, and she was so breathless with excitement that her voice shook as though she had run a long race: 'She can give me back my babies! I will be able to hold the warm, living bodies of Khaba and Unas in my arms and kiss their little faces.'

Taita could not bear to deprive her of the solace that this new hope gave her. 'These are matters almost too marvellous for us to comprehend,' he said solemnly.

'Yes, yes! It has to be explained to you by the prophet. Only then does it become clear as the brightest crystal. You cannot doubt it.'

'Who is this prophet?'

'His name is Soe.'

'Where is he to be found, Mintaka?' Taita asked.

She clapped her hands with excitement. 'Oh, Taita, this is the very best part of it,' she cried. 'He is here in my palace! I have given him sanctuary from the priests of the old gods, Osiris, Horus and Isis. They hate him for the truth he speaks. They have tried repeatedly to assassinate him. Every day he instructs me and those he chooses in the new religion. It is such a beautiful faith, Taita, that even you will be unable to resist it, but it has to be learnt in secret. Egypt is still too steeped in the worthless old superstitions. They must be eradicated before the new religion can flourish. The common people are not yet ready to accept the goddess.'

Taita nodded thoughtfully. He was filled with deep pity for her. He understood how those driven to the extremes of suffering will clutch vainly at the air as they fall. 'What is the name of this wonderful new goddess?'

'Her name is too holy to be spoken aloud by unbelievers. Only those who have taken her into their hearts and souls may utter it. Even I must complete my instruction with Soe before it is told to me.'

'When does Soe come to instruct you? I long to hear him expound these wondrous theories.'

'No, Taita,' she cried. 'You must understand that they are not theories. They are the manifest truth. Soe comes to me each morning and evening. He is the wisest and most holy man I have ever met.' Despite her bright expression, tears began to stream down her face again. She seized his hand and squeezed it. 'You will come to listen to him, promise me.'

'I am grateful to you for the trust you place in me, my beloved queen. When will it be?'

'This evening, after we have had supper,' she told him.

Taita thought for a moment. 'You say he only preaches to those he selects. What if he refuses me? I would be distraught if he did so.'

'He would never turn away anyone as wise and renowned as you, Great Magus.'

'I would not want to take that chance, my dearest Mintaka. Would it not be possible for me to listen to him without disclosing my identity just yet?'

Mintaka looked at him dubiously. 'I would not wish to deceive him,' she said at last.

'I plan no deception, Mintaka. Where do you meet him?'

'In this apartment. He sits where you now sit. On that self-same cushion.'

'Are there just the two of you?'

'No, three of my favourite ladies are with us. They have become as devoted to the goddess as I am.'

Taita was studying the layout of the room carefully, but he kept asking his questions to distract her. 'Will the goddess ever announce herself to all the peoples of Egypt, or will her religion be revealed to only those few she chooses?'

'When Nefer and I have taken her deeply into our hearts, renounced the false gods, torn down their temples and dispersed the priesthood, the goddess will come forth in glory. She will put an end to the plagues and heal all the suffering they have caused. She will order the Nile waters to flow . . .' she hesitated, then ended in a rush '. . . and give my babies back to me.'

'My precious queen. How I wish with all my heart that this will come to pass. But, tell me, has Nefer been made aware of these events?'

She sighed. 'Nefer is a wise and excellent ruler. He is a mighty warrior, a loving husband and father, but he is not a spiritual man. Soe agrees with me that we should reveal all to him only at the appropriate time, which is not yet.'

Taita nodded gravely. Pharaoh will be moved to learn, from his own beloved wife, that his grandfather and grandmother, his father and mother, not to mention the holy trinity of Osiris, Isis and Horus, are to be summarily renounced, he thought. Even he is to be stripped of his divinity. I think I know him well enough to predict that it will not happen while he lives.

That idea loosed in Taita's mind a swarm of terrifying possibilities. If Nefer Seti and his closest councillors and advisers were no longer alive to keep her in check, the prophet Soe would be left in control of a queen who would carry out his commands without question or resistance. Would she accede to the assassination of her king, her husband and the father of her children? he asked himself. The answer was clear: yes, she would, if she knew that he would be restored to her almost immediately by the nameless new goddess, along with her dead babies. Desperate people resort to desperate expedients. Aloud he asked, 'Is Soe the only prophet of this supreme goddess?'

'Soe is the chief of them all, but many of her lesser disciples are moving among the populace throughout the two kingdoms to spread the joyous tidings and prepare the way for her coming.'

'Your words have lit a blaze in my heart. I shall always be grateful to you if you allow me to listen to his testament without him being aware of me. I will have with me another magus, older and wiser than I will ever be.' He raised a finger to silence her protest. 'It is true, Mintaka. His name is Demeter. He will sit with me behind that zenana window.' He pointed to the intricately carved screen from behind which, in former times, a pharaoh's wives and concubines had given audience to foreign dignitaries without exposing their faces.

Mintaka still hesitated so Taita went on persuasively, 'You will be able to convert two influential magi to the new faith. You will please both Soe and the new goddess. She will look upon you with favour. You will be able to ask any boon of her, including the return of your children.'

'Very well, Tata. I will do your bidding. However, in return, you will not reveal to Nefer any of what I have told you today until the time is right for him to accept the goddess and renounce the old gods . . .'

'As you order, so shall it be, my queen.'

'You and your colleague Demeter must return early tomorrow morning. Come not to the main gates but to the postern. One of my hand-maidens will meet you there and lead you to this room where you can take your place behind the screen.'

'We will be here in the hour after sunrise,' Taita assured her.

As they rode out through the gates of the Palace of Memnon Taita checked the height of the afternoon sun. There remained several hours of daylight. On an impulse he ordered the sergeant of his escort not to take the direct road to Thebes, but instead to make a detour along the funereal way towards the western hills and the great royal necropolis, which was hidden in one of the rugged rock valleys. They rode past the temple in which Taita had supervised the embalming of the earthly body of his beloved Lostris. It had taken place seventy years before, but time had not dimmed the memory of that harrowing ceremony. He touched the Periapt, which contained the lock of her hair that he had snipped from her head. They climbed up through the foothills past the temple of Hathor, an impressive edifice that sat atop a pyramid of stone terraces. Taita recognized a priestess who was strolling along the bottom terrace accompanied by two of her novices, and turned aside to speak to her.

'May the divine Hathor protect you, Mother,' he greeted her, as he dismounted. Hathor was the patroness of all women, so the high priest was female.

'I had heard that you had returned from your travels, Magus.' She hurried to embrace him. 'We all hoped that you would visit us, and tell us of your adventures.'

'Indeed, I have much to relate that I hope will interest you. I have brought papyrus maps of Mesopotamia and Ecbatana, and the mountainous lands crossed by the Khorasan highway beyond Babylon.'

'Much will be new to us.' The high priestess smiled eagerly. 'Have you brought them with you?'

'Alas, no! I am on another errand and did not expect to meet you here. I left the scrolls in Thebes. However, I will bring them to you at the first opportunity.'

'That cannot be too soon,' the high priestess assured him. 'You are welcome here at any time. We are grateful for the information you have already provided. I am certain that what you have now is even more fascinating.'

'Then I will trespass upon your kindness. May I ask a favour?'

'Any favour that is mine to bestow is already yours. You have only to name it.'

'I have conceived a pressing interest in volcanoes.'

'Which ones? They are legion, and situated in many lands.'

'All those that arise close to the sea, perhaps on an island, or on the banks of a lake or a great river. I need a list, Mother.'

'That is not a burdensome request,' she assured him. 'Brother Nubank, our most senior cartographer, has always had a consuming interest in volcanoes and other subterranean sources of heat, such as thermal springs and geysers. He will be delighted to compile your list, but expect it to be over-detailed and exhaustive. Nubank is meticulous to a fault. I will set him to work on it at once.'

'How long will it take him?'

'Will you visit us in ten days' time, revered Magus?' she suggested.

Taita took his leave and rode on another league to the gates of the necropolis.

An extensive military fort guarded the entrance to the necropolis that housed the royal tombs. Each one comprised a subterranean complex of chambers that had been excavated from the solid rock. At the centre was the burial chamber in which stood the magnificent royal sarcophagus containing the mummified body of a pharaoh. Laid out around this chamber were the storerooms and depositories crammed with the greatest mass of treasure the world had ever known. It aroused the greed of every thief and grave robber in the two kingdoms, and in countries beyond their borders. They were persistent and cunning in their efforts to break into the sacred enclosure. Keeping them out required the perpetual vigilance of a small army.

Taita left his escort beside the well in the central courtyard of the fort to water the horses and refresh themselves, while he continued into the burial ground on foot. He knew the way to the tomb of Queen Lostris, as well he might: he had designed its layout and supervised its excavation. Lostris was the only one of all the queens of Egypt to be interred in this section of the cemetery, which was usually reserved for reigning pharaohs. Taita had inveigled her eldest son into granting this dispensation when he had succeeded to the throne.

He passed the site where the tomb of Pharaoh Nefer Seti was being excavated in anticipation of his departure from this world and his ascension to the next. It was thronged with stonemasons driving the main entrance passage into the rock. The rubble was carried out by chains of workers in baskets balanced on their heads. They were coated thickly with the floury white dust that hung in the air. A small group of architects and slave masters stood on the heights above, looking down on the furious activity below. The valley echoed to the ring of chisels, adzes and picks on the rock.

Unobtrusively Taita made his way up the funereal path until the valley narrowed and branched into two separate gullies. He took the left-hand fork. Within fifty paces he had turned a corner and the entrance to Lostris's tomb lay directly ahead, set into the cliff face. The entrance was surrounded by impressive granite pillars, and sealed with a wall of stone blocks, which had been plastered over, then decorated with a beautifully painted mural. Scenes from the queen's life were arranged round her cartouche: Lostris in domestic bliss with her husband and children, driving her chariot, fishing in the waters of the Nile, hunting the gazelle and the waterbirds, commanding her armies against the hordes of Hyksos invaders, leading her people in a flotilla of ships down the cataracts of the Nile and bringing them home out of exile after the final defeat of the Hyksos. It was seventy years since Taita had painted these scenes with his own hand, but the colours were still fresh.

Another mourner stood at the entrance to the tomb, swathed from head to ankles in the black robes of a priestess of the goddess Isis. She knelt quietly in an attitude of adoration facing the mural. Taita resigned himself to the delay. He turned aside and settled down to wait in the shade at the foot of the cliff. The face of Lostris in the paintings set in train a series of happy memories. It was quiet in this part of the valley: the rock walls muffled the din made by the workmen lower down. For a while he forgot the presence of the priestess at the tomb, but then she came to her feet and his attention switched back to her.

Her back was still towards him when she reached into the sleeve of her robe and brought out a small metal tool, perhaps a chisel or a knife. Then she stood on tiptoe and, to Taita's horror, tore deliberately at the mural with the point of the tool. 'What are you doing, you mad woman?' he shouted. 'That is a royal tomb you are defacing! Stop at once!'

It was as if he had not spoken. She ignored him and hacked at the face of Lostris with quick slashes of the knife. The underlying white plaster showed through the deep scoring.

Taita sprang to his feet, still yelling, 'Stop! Hear me! Your reverend mother will learn of this. I shall see that you are punished as harshly as you deserve for this sacrilege. You are calling down on yourself the wrath of the goddess . . .'

Still disdaining to glance in his direction the priestess left the entrance and, with a deliberate unhurried gait, started up the valley away from him. Beside himself with fury, Taita ran after her. He was no longer shouting but he hefted his heavy staff in his right hand. He was determined to prevent her escaping the consequences of her actions, and violence clouded his mind. At that moment he would have struck her across the back of the head, crushing her skull.

The priestess reached the point where the valley turned sharply. She stopped and looked back at him over her shoulder. Her face and hair were almost completely shrouded in a red shawl and only her eyes showed.

Taita's fury and frustration fell away, replaced by awe and wonder. The woman's gaze was level and serene, her eyes those in the portrait of the queen on the gateway to her tomb. For a moment he could neither move nor speak. When he found his voice again it was a husky croak: 'It is you!'

Her eyes glowed with a radiance that lit his heart, and although her mouth was covered by the scarf he knew she was smiling at him. She made no reply to his exclamation but nodded, then turned away and walked unhurriedly round the corner of the rock wall.

'No!' he cried wildly. 'You cannot leave me like this. Wait! Wait for me!' He dashed after her and reached the corner only seconds after she had disappeared, still reaching out to her. Then he stopped and his hand dropped to his side as the upper end of the valley opened to him. Fifty yards from where he stood, it came to a dead end, blocked by a sheer wall of grey rock too steep for even a wild goat to scale. She had vanished.

'Lostris, forgive me for rejecting you. Come back to me, my darling.' The silence of the mountains settled over him. With an effort he gathered himself and, wasting no more time in vain appeals, began to search for a crevice in the walls in which she might be hidden, or a concealed exit from the valley. He found none. He looked back the way he had come, and saw that the floor of the valley was covered with a thin layer of white sand that had been eroded from the rock. His own footprints were clearly defined, but there were no others. She had left no mark. Wearily, he turned back towards her tomb. He stood in front of the entrance and looked up at the inscription she had cut into the plaster in hieratic script: 'Six fingers point the way,' he read aloud. It made no sense. What did she mean by 'the way'? Was it a road, or was it a manner or method?

Six fingers? Were they pointing in a number of different directions or in one? Were there six separate signposts to follow? He was baffled. Again he read aloud the inscription: 'Six fingers point the way.' As he spoke the letters she had cut into the plaster began to heal, and faded before his eyes. The portrait of Lostris was undamaged. Each detail was perfectly restored. In wonderment he reached up to run his hands over it. The surface was smooth and unblemished.

He stood back and studied it. Was the smile still exactly as he had painted it or had it changed subtly? Was it tender or mocking? Was it candid or had it become enigmatic? Was it benign or was it now touched with malice? He could not be certain.

'Are you Lostris, or some wicked wraith sent to torment me?' he asked it. 'Would Lostris be so cruel? Are you offering help and guidance – or laying snares and pitfalls in my path?'

At last he turned away and went down to the fort where the escort waited for him. They mounted and set out on the return journey to Thebes.

It was dark by the time they reached the palace of Pharaoh Nefer Seti. Taita went first to Ramram.

'Pharaoh is still in conclave. He will not be able to meet you tonight as he planned. You are not to wait up for his summons. He orders you to sup with him tomorrow evening. I press you most earnestly to resort to your sleeping mat. You appear exhausted.'

He left Ramram and hurried to Demeter's chamber, where he found the old man and Meren facing each other over the *bao* board. Meren jumped to his feet with a theatrical show of relief as Taita entered. The complexities of the game were often beyond him. 'Welcome, Magus. You are just in time to save me from humiliation.'

Taita sat beside Demeter and quickly appraised his state of health and mind. 'You seem to have recovered from the rigours of the journey. Are you being well cared for?'

'I thank you for your concern, and indeed I am,' Demeter told him.

'I am delighted to hear it, for we must be up betimes on the morrow. I am taking you to the Palace of Memnon, where we will listen to one who preaches a new religion. He prophesies the coming of a new goddess who will hold dominion over all the nations of the earth.'

Demeter smiled. 'Do we not already have a plethora of gods? Enough, indeed, to last us to the end of days?'

'Ah, my friend, to us it might seem so. But according to this prophet, the old gods are to be destroyed, their temples cast down and their priests scattered to the ends of the earth.'

'I wonder if he speaks of Ahura Maasda, the one and only? If so, this is not a new religion.'

'It is not Ahura Maasda but another, more dreadful and powerful than him. She will assume human form and descend to live among us. The people will have direct access to her gracious mercy. She has the power to resurrect the dead, and to bestow immortality and perpetual happiness upon those who merit such rewards.'

'Why must we concern ourselves with such manifest nonsense, Taita?' He sounded irritable. 'We have graver matters to deal with.'

'This prophet is one of many who are moving covertly among the people and, it seems, converting great numbers of them, including Mintaka, the Queen of Egypt and wife of Pharaoh Nefer Seti.'

Demeter leant forward and his expression became grave. 'Surely Queen Mintaka has better sense than to be taken in by such nonsense?'

'When the new goddess comes, her first act will be to rid Egypt of the plagues that afflict her and heal all the suffering they have caused. Mintaka sees in her the chance to bring back from the tomb her children who died from the plague.'

'I see,' Demeter mused. 'To any mother that would be an irresistible lure. But what are the other reasons you spoke of?'

'The prophet's name is Soe.' Demeter looked mystified. 'Invert the letters of his name. Use the alphabet of the Tenmass,' Taita suggested, and Demeter's perplexity vanished.

'Eos,' he whispered. 'Your hounds have picked up the scent of the witch, Taita.'

'And we must follow it hotly to her lair.' Taita stood up. 'Compose yourself to sleep. I will send Meren to fetch you before sunrise.'

While the dawn was still a faint grey promise in the east, Habari had the horses and Demeter's camel waiting for them in the courtyard. Demeter stretched himself out in his palanquin, with Taita and Meren riding on each side of him. The escort led them down to ford the river, where they saw only one of the monstrous toads. It avoided them and they crossed to the west bank without hindrance. They circled the Palace of Memnon and came to the postern gate, where Taita and Demeter left their mounts in the care of Meren and Habari. As Mintaka had promised, one of her hand-maidens was waiting inside the gate to greet them. She led the magi through a maze of passages and tunnels until at last they stepped into a lavishly appointed room, which smelt strongly of incense and perfume. The floor was covered with silk rugs and piles of fat cushions. Richly embroidered tapestries hung on the walls. The hand-maiden crossed to the far wall and drew back the hanging that concealed a screened zenana window. Taita hurried to it and looked through the ornate tracery into the audience chamber where he had met Mintaka the previous day. It was empty. Satisfied, he went to take Demeter's arm and lead him to the window. The two settled down on the cushions. They did not have long to wait before a strange man entered the room beyond the screen.

He was of middle age, tall and spare. The heavy locks that hung to his shoulders were streaked with grey, as was his short, pointed beard. He wore the long black robes of priest-hood, the skirts embroidered with occult symbols, and at his throat hung a necklace of charms. He began to circle the room, pausing to draw aside the hangings and search behind them. He stopped in front of the zenana window and brought his face close to the screen. His features were hand-some and intelligent, but his most striking attribute was his eyes: they were those of a zealot and burned with a fanatical glare.

This is Soe, Taita thought. He was in no doubt. He took Demeter's hand and held it firmly to combine and augment their powers of concealment and protection, for they could not be certain what occult gifts the other man possessed. They stared back at him through the screen, exerting all their powers to hold the cloak of concealment around them. After a while Soe grunted, satisfied, and turned away. He went to wait by the far window, gazing out to the distant hills, which glowed like coals in the orange light of the early sun.

While he was thus distracted, Taita opened his Inner Eye. Soe was not a savant for at once his aura sprang up round him, but it was as none that he had seen before: it was inconstant, at one moment flaring strongly and at the next fading to a faint glow. Its colour shimmered brilliantly in tones of purple and vermilion, then sank away to a dull, leaden hue. Taita recognized a sharp intellect, corrupted with ruthlessness and cruelty. Soe's thoughts were confused and contradictory, but there was no doubt that he had developed considerable psychic powers.

As a group of laughing women burst into the room Soe turned quickly away from the window. They were led by Mintaka, who ran excitedly to him and embraced him with affection. Taita was taken aback: it was extraordinary behav-iour for a queen. She embraced Taita only when they were alone, not in front of her maids. He had not realized how deeply she had come under Soe's influence. While she stood with one of his arms round her shoulders, her maids came to kneel before him.

'Bless us, Holy Father,' they pleaded. 'Intercede on our behalf with the one and only goddess.'

He made a gesture of benediction over them, and they wriggled with ecstasy.

Mintaka led Soe to a pile of cushions that raised his head to a level above her own, then sat down, folding her legs sideways under her in the attitude of a young girl. She turned deliberately towards the zenana window and smiled prettily at where she knew Taita was watching. She was displaying her latest acquisition for his approval, as though Soe was an exotic bird brought from a distant country, or a precious jewel given to her by a foreign potentate. Taita was alarmed by her indiscretion, but Soe was speaking condescendingly to the maids and had not noticed this exchange. Now he turned back to Mintaka.

'Exalted Majesty, I have given much thought to the concerns you expressed when last we met. I have prayed earnestly to the goddess, and she has responded most graciously.'

Again Taita was surprised. This is no foreigner, he thought. He is an Egyptian. His use of our language is perfect. He has the accents of one who hails from Assoun in the Upper Kingdom.

Soe went on, 'These matters are of such weight and moment that they must be kept for your ears only. Dismiss your maids.' Mintaka clapped her hands. The girls jumped to their feet and scampered from the chamber like frightened mice.

'First, the matter of your husband, the Pharaoh Nefer Seti,' Soe resumed when they were alone. 'She commands me to reply to you thus.' He paused, then leant towards Mintaka and spoke in a voice that was not his own, a mellifluous feminine voice: 'In the time of my coming I shall welcome Nefer Seti into my loving embrace, and he shall come to me joyously.'

Taita was startled, but beside him Demeter started wildly. Taita reached out to calm him, although he himself was almost as agitated. Demeter was trembling. He tugged at Taita's hand.

Taita turned to him, and the old man mouthed a silent message that Taita read as clearly as if it had been shouted aloud: 'The witch! It is the voice of Eos!' It was the voice that Taita had drawn from him while he was in his trance.

'But the lord of these is fire,' he mouthed back, and spread his palms upward in full accord.

Soe was still speaking, and they turned back to listen: 'I shall raise him up to be the sovereign of all my corporeal kingdom. All the kings of all nations of earth will become his loyal satraps. In my name he will reign in eternal glory. You, my beloved Mintaka, will sit at his side.'

Mintaka burst into sobs of relief and joy. Soe smiled at her with avuncular indulgence and waited for her to recover her poise. At last she sniffed back the tears and smiled up at him. 'What of my children, my dead babies?'

'We have spoken of them already,' Soe reminded her kindly.

'Yes! But I cannot hear it too often. Please, Holy Prophet, I humbly beg you . . .'

'The goddess has commanded that they be restored to you, and that they will live out the full span of their natural lives.'

'What else has she commanded? Please tell me again.'

'When they have proved worthy of her love, she will extend to all your children the gift of eternal youth. They will never leave you.'

'I am content, Mighty Prophet of the Almighty Goddess,' Mintaka whispered. 'I submit my body and my soul completely to her will.' On her knees, she crawled to Soe. She let her tears fall on to his feet, then wiped them away with the tresses of her hair.

It was the most repugnant spectacle Taita had ever witnessed. He made a determined effort to stop himself shouting through the screen, 'He is a lackey of the Lie! Do not let him soil you with his filth.'

Mintaka called her hand-maidens, and they sat with Soe for the rest of the morning. Their conversation descended into banality for none of the girls was quick to follow his teachings. He was obliged to repeat himself in simplified language. They soon tired of this and pestered him with chatter.

'Will the goddess find me a good husband?'

'Will she give me pretty things?'

Soe treated them with remarkable forbearance and patience.

Taita realized that although it seemed he and Demeter had learnt all they could, they had no choice but to remain sitting quietly behind the zenana window. If they tried to leave their movements might alert the prophet. A little before noon Soe brought the meeting to a close with a long prayer to the goddess. Then he blessed the women again and turned back to Mintaka. 'Do you wish me to return later, Your Majesty?'

'I need to meditate on these revelations of the goddess. Please return on the morrow when we may discuss them further.' Soe bowed and withdrew.

As soon as he had gone Mintaka dismissed her handmaidens. 'Taita, are you still there?'

'I am, Your Majesty.'

She threw open the screen and demanded, 'Did I not tell you how learned and wise he is, what wonderful tidings he brings?'

'Extraordinary tidings indeed,' Taita replied.

'Is he not handsome? I trust him with all my heart. I know that what he prophesies is the divine truth, that the goddess will reveal herself to us and heal all our woes. Oh, Taita, do you believe what he tells us? Surely you must!'

Mintaka was in a religious ferment, and Taita knew that any warning he gave now would have a contrary effect. He wanted to take Demeter to a place where they might discuss what they had heard, and decide how to proceed, but he had to listen first to Mintaka's eulogy to Soe. When at last she ran out of superlatives he told her gently, 'Both Demeter and I are worn out with all this excitement. I have promised to attend Pharaoh as soon as he is free from his more pressing duties, so we must return now to Thebes to be within call. However,

I will return to you as soon as I can, and we will discuss this further, my queen.'

Reluctantly she let them go.

As soon as they had remounted and were on the road to the river, Taita and Meren took up their usual stations beside the palanquin. Then Taita and Demeter switched from Egyptian into the Tenmass so that the men of the escort could not follow their conversation.

'We have learnt much of paramount importance from Soe,' Taita began.

'Most significantly, we know that he has been in the presence of the witch,' Demeter exclaimed. 'He has heard her speak. He had her voice perfectly.'

'You know the timbre of her speech better than I do, and I do not doubt that you are right,' Taita agreed. 'There is something else that I deem important. Soe is Egyptian. His accent is from the Upper Kingdom.'

'This I did not fathom. My grasp of your tongue is not so perfect that I am able to pick up such nuances. It may indeed be a clue to the location of her present hiding-place. If we postulate that Soe has not travelled far to reach Thebes, then we should begin our search within the borders of the Two Kingdoms or, at least, in those lands immediately adjacent to them.'

'What volcanoes fall into that area?'

'There are no volcanoes or large lakes within the borders of this very Egypt. The Nile runs into the Middle Sea. That is the nearest water to the north. Etna is no more than ten days' sail. Are you certain still that Eos is not there?'

'I am.' Demeter nodded.

'Very well. What of the other great volcano in that direction, Vesuvius, on the mainland across the channel from Etna?' Taita suggested.

Demeter sucked his lower lip dubiously. 'That dog will not

hunt either,' he said, with conviction. 'After I escaped from her clutches, I hid for many years with the priests in the temple that lies fewer than thirty leagues to the north of Vesuvius. I am sure that I would have sensed her presence if she had been so close at hand, or she would have sensed mine. No, Taita, we must look elsewhere.'

'For the time being let us be guided by your instinct,' Taita said. 'On our eastern border is the Red Sea. I do not know of volcanoes in Arabia or any other land close to its shores. Do you?'

'No, I have travelled there, but I never saw or heard of any.'

'I saw two volcanoes in the land beyond the Zagreb mountains, but they are surrounded by vast plains and mountain ranges. They do not fit the description of the one we seek.'

'To the south and west of Egypt there are more vast expanses of land,' Demeter said, 'but let us consider another possibility. Might there be great rivers and lakes in the interior of Africa, and a volcano close to one?'

'I have not heard of any – but, then, no man has ventured further south than Ethiopia.'

'I have heard it told, Taita, that during the exodus from Egypt you guided Queen Lostris as far south as Qebui, the Place of the North Wind, where the Nile divides into two mighty streams.'

'That is true. From Qebui we followed the left fork of the river into the mountains of Ethiopia. The right-hand stream emerges from an endless swamp that bars further progress. No man has ever reached its southern extremity. Or if any has he has not returned to tell of it. Some say there is no limit to the swamp but that it continues, vast and forbidding, to the end of the earth.'

'Then we must rely on the priests in the temple of Hathor to supply us with further possibilities to ponder. When will they have information for us of their findings?'

'The priestess told me to return in ten days' time,' Taita reminded him.

Demeter drew aside the curtain of his palanquin and looked back towards the hills. 'We are close to the temple now. We should go there, ask the priestess for hospitality and a sleeping mat for the night. We can spend time on the morrow with her cartographers and geographers.'

'If Pharaoh summons me to his presence, his minions will not be able to find me,' Taita demurred. 'Let me see him before we leave the palace again.'

'Stop the column here,' Demeter called to Habari. 'Stop at once, I tell you.' Then he turned back to Taita. 'I do not wish to alarm you but I know now that my time with you is drawing to a close. I am haunted by dreams and dark presentiments. Despite the protection that you and Meren have given me, the witch will soon succeed in her efforts to destroy me. My remaining days are dwindling.'

Taita stared at him. Since that morning, when he had been made aware of Soe's menacing aura, he had been harried by the same premonition. He drew close to the palanquin and studied the worn old face. With a pang he saw that Demeter was right: death was close upon him. His eyes had become almost colourless and transparent, but in their depths he made out moving shadows, like the shapes of feeding sharks.

'You see it also,' Demeter said, in a flat, dull tone.

No reply was necessary. Instead Taita turned away and called to Habari, 'Turn the column. We will go to the temple of Hathor.' It was only a little more than a league distant.

They rode in silence for a while, until Demeter spoke again: 'You will travel faster without my ancient, enfeebled body to impede you.'

'You are too harsh with yourself,' Taita chided him. 'Without your help and counsel I would never have come this far.'

'I wish I could have stayed with you to the end of the hunt and been present at the kill. But it is not to be.' He was silent for a while. Then he went on, 'How to deal with Soe? One course is open to you. If Pharaoh was made aware that Soe is bewitching Mintaka, and of the traitorous thoughts he is planting in her mind, he would send his guards to seize him and you would have the chance to interrogate him under duress. I hear that the gaolers in Thebes are highly skilled in their trade. You do not shrink from the idea of torture?'

'I would not hesitate if I thought there was the smallest chance of Soe yielding to mere bodily pain. But you have seen him. The man would die willingly to protect the witch. He is so much in tune with her that she would sense his agony and its cause. She would understand that Pharaoh and Mintaka had become aware of the web she is spinning round them, which would be mortally dangerous for the royal couple.'

'That is so.' Demeter nodded.

'Furthermore, Mintaka would rush to Soe's defence and Nefer Seti would realize that she was indeed guilty of plotting against him. It would destroy their love and trust in each other. I could not do this to them.'

'Then we must hope to find the answer at the temple.'

The priests saw them from afar and sent two novices to welcome them and lead them up the ramp to the main entrance of the temple while the high priestess waited on the steps.

'I am so pleased to see you, Magus. I was about to send a messenger to Thebes to find you and tell you that Brother Nubank has worked on your request with great industry. He is ready to deliver his findings to you. But you have anticipated me.' She beamed in a motherly fashion at Taita. 'You are a thousand times welcome. The temple maidens are preparing a chamber for you in the men's quarters. You must stay with us as long as you wish. I look forward to your learned discourses.'

'You are kind and gracious, Mother. I am in company with another magus of great learning and reputation.'

'He, too, is welcome. Your retainers will be given shelter and sustenance in the grooms' quarters.'

They dismounted and, Meren supporting Demeter, entered the temple. They paused before the image of Hathor, the goddess of joy, motherhood and love, in the main hall. She was depicted in the form of an enormous piebald cow, its horns bedecked with a golden moon. The priestess offered a prayer, then summoned a novice to lead Taita and Demeter along a cloister into the priests' area of the temple. He took them to a small stone-walled cell, where rolled sleeping mats lay against the far wall with bowls of water for them to refresh themselves.

'I will return to take you to the refectory at the dinner hour. Brother Nubank will meet you there.'

Around fifty priests were already eating when they entered the refectory, but one man leapt to his feet and hurried to meet them. 'I am Nubank. You are welcome.' He was tall and lean, with cadaverous features. In these hard times there were few corpulent figures in Egypt. The meal was frugal: a bowl of pottage and a small jug of beer. The company was subdued and ate mostly in silence, with the exception of Nubank, who never stopped talking. His voice was grating and his manner pompous.

'I do not know how we will survive the morrow,' Taita said to Demeter, when they were back in their cell and settling to sleep. 'It will be a long day, listening to good Brother Nubank.'

'But his knowledge of geography is exhaustive,' Demeter pointed out.

'You employ the correct adjective, Magus.' Taita turned on his side.

The sun had not risen when a novice came to summon them to breakfast. Demeter seemed weaker, so Meren and Taita helped him gently to rise from his mat.

'Forgive me, Taita. I slept poorly.'

'The dreams?' Taita asked, in Tenmass.

'Yes. The witch is closing in on me. I cannot find strength much longer to resist her.'

Taita had also been plagued by dreams. In his, the python

had returned. Now its feral stench lingered in his nostrils and at the back of his throat. But he concealed his misgivings, and showed Demeter a confident mien. 'We still have far to travel together, you and I.'

Breakfast was a small hard dhurra loaf and another jug of weak beer. Brother Nubank resumed his monologue where it had been interrupted the night before. Fortunately the meal was soon consumed and, with some relief, they followed Nubank through the cavernous halls and cloisters to the temple library. It was a large, cool room, devoid of decoration or ornament other than the towering banks of stone shelves that covered every wall from the floor to the high ceiling; they were loaded with papyrus scrolls, of which there were several thousand.

Three novices and two senior initiates were waiting for Brother Nubank. They stood in a row, their hands clasped in front of them, a submissive attitude. They were Nubank's assistants. There was good reason for their trepidation: Nubank treated them in a hectoring manner and did not hesitate to voice his displeasure or contempt in the harshest, most insulting terms.

When Taita and Demeter were seated at the long, low central table, piled with papyrus scrolls, Nubank began his lecture. He proceeded to enumerate every volcano and every thermal phenomenon in the known world, whether or not it was situated near a large body of water. As he named each site, he sent a terrorized assistant to fetch the appropriate scroll from the shelves. In many cases this involved the ascent of a rickety ladder, while Nubank goaded them on with a string of abuse. When Taita tried tactfully to truncate this tedious procedure by referring the man to his original request, Nubank nodded blandly and continued remorselessly with his prepared recitation.

One unfortunate novice was Nubank's preferred victim. He was a misshapen creature: no part of his body seemed without fault or deformation. His shaven scalp was elongated, covered with flaking skin and a vivid rash. His brow bulged over small, close-set, pale crossed eyes. Large teeth protruded through the gap in his harelip and he dribbled when he spoke, which was not often. His chin receded so sharply that it barely existed, a large mulberry birthmark adorned his left cheek, his chest was sunken and his back mountainously hunched. His legs were thin as sticks, bowed and carried him in a sideways scuttle.

In the middle of the day a novice arrived to summon them to the refectory for the midday repast. Half starved as they were, Nubank and his assistants responded with alacrity. During the meal Taita became aware that the hunchbacked novice was making furtive attempts to catch his eye. As soon as he saw that he had Taita's attention, he stood up and hurried to the door. There, he glanced back and jerked his head to indicate that he wanted Taita to follow him.

Taita found the little fellow waiting for him on the terrace. Again the man beckoned, then vanished into the opening of a narrow passage. Taita followed, and soon found himself in one of the small temple courtyards. The walls were covered with bas-reliefs of Hathor and there was a statue of the Pharaoh Mamose. The man cowered behind it.

'Great Magus! I have something to tell you that might be of interest to you.' He prostrated himself as Taita went to him.

'Stand up,' Taita told him kindly. 'I am not the king. What is your name?' Brother Nubank had referred to the little priest only as 'you thing'.

'They call me Tiptip, for the way I walk. My grandfather was a junior physician in the court of Queen Lostris at the time of the exodus from Egypt to the land of Ethiopia. He spoke of you often. Perhaps you remember him, Magus. His name was Siton.'

'Siton?' Taita thought for a moment. 'Yes! He was a likely lad, very good at removing barbed arrowheads with the spoons. He saved the lives of many soldiers.' Tiptip grinned widely, and his harelip gaped. 'What became of your grandfather?'

'He died peacefully in his dotage, but before he went, he told many fascinating stories of your adventures in those strange southern lands. He described its peoples and wild animals. He told of the forests and mountains, and of a great swamp that stretched away for ever, to the ends of the earth.'

'They were stirring times, Tiptip.' Taita nodded encouragement. 'Go on.'

'He told how, while the main body of our people followed the left fork of the Nile into the mountains of Ethiopia, Queen Lostris despatched a legion to the right fork to discover its full extent. They set off into the great swamp under General Lord Aquer and were never seen again, but for one man of the legion. Is this true, Magus?'

'Yes, Tiptip. I remember how the queen sent out a legion.' Taita himself had recommended Aquer for the doomed command. He had been a troublemaker, stirring discontent among the people. He did not mention this now. 'It is true also that only one man returned. But he was so riddled with disease and broken by the hardship of the journey that he succumbed to fever only days after returning to us.'

'Yes! Yes!' Tiptip was so excited that he seized Taita's sleeve. 'My grandfather treated the unfortunate man. He said that during his delirium the soldier ranted about a land with mountains and enormous lakes so wide in places that the eye could not reach from one shore to the next.'

Taita's interest quickened. 'Lakes! I have not heard this before. I never laid eyes on the survivor. I was in the Ethiopian mountains, two hundred leagues distant, when he reached Qebui where he died. The report I received said that the patient was out of his mind and unable to give any coherent or reliable intelligence.' He stared at Tiptip, and opened the Inner Eye. From the other man's aura, Taita could tell that he was sincere and telling the truth as he remembered it. 'You have more to tell me, Tiptip? I think so.'

'Yes, Magus. There was a volcano,' Tiptip blurted. 'That is why I have come to you. The dying soldier rambled about a burning mountain such as none had ever seen before. After they had passed beyond the great swamps they saw it only at a great distance. He said that the smoke from its funnel stood like a perpetual cloud against the sky. Some of the legionaries took it as a warning from the dark African gods to proceed no further, but Lord Aquer declared it was a welcoming beacon and that he was determined to reach it. He ordered the march to continue. However, it was at this point, within sight of the volcano, that the soldier fell ill with the fever. He was abandoned and left for dead while his companions marched southwards. But he managed to reach a village of giant naked black people who lived on the lakeshore. They took him in. One of their shamans gave him medicine and nursed him until he had recovered sufficiently to continue his homeward journey.' In his agitation Tiptip gripped Taita's arm. 'I wanted to tell you before but Brother Nubank would not allow it. He forbade me to pester you with hearsay from seventy years ago. He said that we geographers deal only with fact. You will not tell Brother Nubank I disobeyed him? He is a good and holy man, but he can be strict.'

'You did right,' Taita reassured him, and gently dislodged the clutching fingers. Then, suddenly, he lifted Tiptip's hand to examine it more closely. 'You have six fingers!' he exclaimed.

Clearly Tiptip was mortified: he tried to hide the deformity by clenching his hand into a fist. 'The gods built my entire body awry. My head and eyes, my back and my limbs – everything about me is twisted and misformed.' His eyes filled with tears.

'But you have a good heart,' Taita consoled him. Gently, he opened the fist and spread the fingers. An additional rudimentary finger grew out of the man's palm beside the normal little finger.

'"Six fingers point the way,"' Taita whispered.

'I did not mean to point at you, Magus. I would never deliberately give offence to you in that way,' Tiptip whimpered.

'No, Tiptip, you have done me great service. Be certain of my gratitude and my friendship.'

'You will not tell Brother Nubank?'

'No. You have my oath on it.'

'The blessings of Hathor upon you, Magus. Now I must go or Brother Nubank will come to find me.' Tiptip scampered away like a crab. Taita gave him a few moments' start then made his way back to the library. He found that Demeter and Meren had preceded him, and Nubank was berating Tiptip: 'Where have you been?'

'I was in the latrine, Brother. Forgive me. I have eaten something that has upset my stomach.'

'And you have upset mine, you loathsome piece of excrement. While you were there you should have left all of yourself in the bucket.' He clouted Tiptip's birthmark. 'Now bring me the scrolls in which the islands of the eastern ocean are described.'

Taita took his place beside Demeter and said to him in Tenmass, 'Look to the little fellow's right hand.'

'He has six fingers.' Demeter exclaimed. '"Six fingers point the way!" You have learnt something from him, have you not?'

'We must follow the right branch of Mother Nile to her source. There we will find a volcano set beside a wide lake. I am certain in my heart that that is where Eos lurks.'

They left the temple of Hathor long before sunrise the next morning. Nubank bade them farewell reluctantly – he had fifty volcanoes yet to describe. It was still half dark when they reached the ford of the Nile below Thebes. Habari and Meren led the way down into the riverbed, Taita and Demeter following, but a gap had opened between the two groups. The leaders rode through the tail of one of the stinking red pools and were half-way to the far bank as Demeter's camel started across the mud. At that moment Taita became aware that a malevolent influence was focusing on them. He felt a chill in the air, the pulse in his ears pounded and his breathing was hampered. He turned quickly and looked back over his mare's rump.

A solitary figure stood on the bank they had just left. Although his dark robes merged into the shadows, Taita recognized him immediately. He opened his Inner Eye and Soe's distinctive aura appeared enveloping the man, like the flames of a bonfire. It was an angry scarlet, shot with purple and green. Taita had never seen an aura so menacing.

'Soe is here!' he called, in urgent warning to Demeter, as he lay in his palanquin, but it was too late: Soe raised an arm and pointed at the surface of the pool through which the camel was wading. Almost as though it was responding to his command, a monstrous toad launched itself from the water and, with a snap of its jaws, ripped a deep gash in the camel's back leg above the knee. The animal bawled with shock and, breaking free of its lead rein, bolted out of the pool. Instead of heading for the far bank it turned and galloped wildly along the riverbed, with Demeter's palanquin swaying and bouncing from side to side.

'Meren! Habari!' Taita shouted, as he kicked his mare into a full gallop in pursuit of the runaway camel. Meren and Habari swung their mounts round and urged them back into the riverbed to join the pursuit.

'Hold fast, Demeter!' Taita shouted. 'We are coming!' Windsmoke was flying under him, but before he caught up with Demeter the camel reached another pool and dashed into it, throwing up sheets of spray. Then the surface of the water directly in its path opened as another toad shot out. It sprang high at the head of the panic-stricken beast and clamped its jaws on the bulbous nose in a bulldog grip. It must have struck a nerve, for the front legs of the camel collapsed. Then it rolled on to its back as it thrashed its head from side to side in an attempt to break the grip of the toad's fangs. The palanquin was trapped beneath it, and its light bamboo framework was crushed into the mud under its weight.

'Demeter! We must rescue him!' Taita shouted to Meren, and urged on his mare. But before he reached the edge of the pool Demeter's head broke the surface. Somehow he had escaped from the palanquin, but he was half drowned in the mud that plastered his head, coughing and vomiting, his movements feeble and erratic.

'I am coming!' Taita shouted. 'Do not despair!' Then, suddenly, the pool was boiling with toads. They came swarming up from the bottom and fell upon Demeter, like a pack of wild dogs pulling down a gazelle. The old man's mouth was wide open as he tried to scream, but the mud choked him. The toads pulled him below the surface, and when he emerged again briefly his struggles had almost ceased. His only movements were caused by the toads below the surface, tearing off lumps of his flesh.

'I am here, Demeter!' Taita yelled despairingly. He could not take the mare among the frenzied toads for he knew they would rip into her. He reined in and slipped off her back with his staff in his hands. He started to wade into the pool, then gasped with agony as a toad sank its fangs into his leg below the surface. He thrust down at it with his staff, exerting all his physical and spiritual strength to bolster the blow. He felt the jolt as the tip struck squarely, and the creature released him. It came to the surface on its back, stunned and kicking convulsively.

'Demeter!' He could not tell the man from the toads that were devouring him alive. Man and beasts were thickly coated with shining black mud.

Suddenly two thin arms were lifted high above the teeming pack and he heard Demeter's voice. 'I am done. You must go on alone, Taita.' His voice was almost inaudible, choked by mud and the poisonous red water. And then it was snuffed out as a toad, larger than all the others, clamped its jaws into the side of his head, and pulled him under for the last time.

Taita started forward again, but Meren rode up behind him, seized him with one strong arm round his waist, lifted him out of the mud and carried him back to the bank.

'Put me down!' Taita struggled to free himself. 'We cannot leave him to those foul creatures.' But Meren would not release him.

'Magus, you are hurt. Look to your leg.' Meren tried to calm him. The blood gushed from the bite to mingle with the mud. 'Demeter is finished. I will not lose you also.' Meren held him firmly, while they watched the death struggles in the pool diminish until the surface was still once more.

'Demeter is gone,' Meren said quietly, and lowered Taita to his feet. He went to catch the grey mare and brought her to him. As he helped Taita to mount, he said softly, 'We must go, Magus. There is nothing more for us here. You must tend your injury. No doubt the toad's fangs are poisonous, and the mud is so foul that it will contaminate your flesh.'

However, Taita lingered a little longer, looking for some last sign from his ally, seeking some final contact from the ether, but there was none. When Meren leant from the back of his own mount, took hold of the mare's reins and led her away, Taita made no further protest. His leg was paining him, and he felt shocked and bereft. The old savant had gone and Taita realized how much he had come to rely on him. Now he confronted the witch alone, and the prospect filled him with dismay.

Once they were safely returned to their quarters in the palace at Thebes, Ramram sent slave girls with urns of hot water and bottles of perfumed unguents to bathe Taita and wash away the mud. When he was thoroughly cleansed two royal physicians arrived, followed by a train of assistants bearing chests filled with medicine and magical amulets. On Taita's instruction Meren met them at the door and sent them away: 'As the most skilled and learned surgeon in all of Egypt, the magus is attending to his own injury. He presents his compliments and thanks for your concern.'

Taita washed his wound with a distillate of wine. Then he numbed his leg with a self-induced trance, while Meren cauterized the deep gash with a bronze spoon heated in the flame of an oil lamp. It was one of the few medical skills that Taita had been able to teach him. When he had finished, Taita roused himself and, using long hairs from Windsmoke's tail as thread, stitched together the lips of his wound. He dressed them with ointments of his own concoction and bound them with linen bandages. By the time he had finished he was exhausted by pain and filled with sorrow at the loss of Demeter. He sank on to his mattress and closed his eyes.

He opened them when he heard a commotion at the doorway, and a familiar, authoritative voice bellowed, 'Taita, where are you? Cannot I trust you out of my sight, but that you commit some rash folly? Shame on you! You are no longer a child.' At that the Divine God on Earth, Pharaoh Nefer Seti, burst into the sickroom. His suite of lords and attendants crowded in after him.

Taita felt his spirits rise and the well of his strength begin to refill. He was not entirely alone. He smiled at Nefer Seti, and struggled up on an elbow.

'Taita, are you not ashamed of yourself? I expected to find you breathing your last. Instead you are lying at your ease, with a foolish grin on your face.'

'Majesty, it is a smile of welcome, for I am truly delighted to see you.'

Nefer Seti pushed him back gently on to the pillows, then turned to his retinue. 'My lords, you may leave me here with the magus, who is my old friend and tutor. I shall summon you when I need you.' They backed out of the chamber and Pharaoh bent to hug Taita. 'By the sweet milk from the breast of Isis, I am glad to see you safe, though I hear that your companion magus was lost. I want to hear all about it, but first let me greet Meren Cambyses.' He turned to Meren, who stood guard at the door. Meren went down on one knee before him, but Pharaoh lifted him to his feet. 'Do not abase yourself to me, companion of the Red Road.' Nefer Seti seized him in a hearty embrace. As young men they had embarked together on the ultimate test of warriorhood, the Red Road, a trial of skill in handling chariot, sword and bow. The two had been matched as a team against proven and tried veterans, who were free to employ any means, even killing, to prevent them reaching the end of the road. Together they had won through. Companions of the Red Road were brothers of the warrior blood, united for life. Until her death Meren had been betrothed to Nefer Seti's sister, the Princess Merykara, so he and Pharaoh had nearly become brothers-in-law. This reinforced the bond between them. Meren might have held high office in Thebes, but he had chosen instead to enrol himself as an apprentice to Taita.

'Has Taita been able to school you in the Mysteries? Have you become a magus as well as a mighty warrior?' Pharaoh demanded.

'Nay, Majesty. Despite the best efforts of Taita, I lacked the skills. I have never woven the simplest of spells that succeeded. A few even rebounded on my own head.' Meren made a rueful face.

'A good warrior is better than an inept sorcerer any day, old friend. Come, sit in conference with us, as was our wont in those long-ago days when we were fighting to free this very Egypt from the tyrant.'

As soon as they were seated at either side of Taita's sleeping mat, Nefer Seti became serious. 'Now, tell me of your encounter with the toads.'

Between them Taita and Meren described the death of Demeter. When they ended Nefer Seti was silent. Then he growled, 'Those animals grow bolder and more voracious every day. I am certain that it is they who have made impure and sullied what remains of the water in the river pools. I have tried every means I can think of to be rid of them, but for every one we slay two more spring up to take its place.'

'Majesty.' Taita paused for a moment before he went on. 'You must seek out the witch whose creatures they are, and destroy her. The toads and all the other plagues she heaps upon you and your kingdom will disappear with her, for she is their mistress. Then the Nile will flow again, and prosperity will return to this very Egypt.'

Nefer Seti stared at him in alarm. 'Must I infer that the plagues are not of nature?' he demanded. 'That they are created by the sorcery and witchcraft of one woman?'

'That is what I believe,' Taita assured him.

Nefer Seti sprang to his feet and strode up and down, lost in thought. At last he stopped and stared hard at Taita. 'Who is this witch? Where is she? Can she be destroyed, or is she immortal?'

'I believe she is human, Pharaoh, but her powers are formidable. She protects herself well.'

'What is her name?'

'It is Eos.'

'The goddess of the dawn?' He had been well schooled by the priests in the hierarchy of the gods, for he was a god himself. 'Did you not tell me she was human?'

'She is a human being who has usurped the goddess's name to conceal her true identity.'

'If that is so then she must have an earthly abode. Where is it, Taita?'

'Demeter and I were seeking her out, but she became aware of our intentions. First she sent a giant python to attack him but Meren and I saved him, although he came close to death. Now she has succeeded with the toads where she failed with the serpent.'

'So you do not know where I can find the witch?' Nefer Seti persisted.

'We do not know for certain, but the occult indications suggest that she lives in a volcano.'

'A volcano? Is that possible, even for a witch?' Then he laughed. 'I learnt long ago never to doubt you, Taita. But tell me, which volcano? There are many.'

'I believe that to find her we must travel to the headwater of the Nile, beyond the mighty swamps that block the river above Qebui. Her lair is near a volcano beside a great lake. Somewhere at the very end of our earth.'

'I remember you told me when I was a boy how my

grandmother, Queen Lostris, sent a legion south under Lord Aquer to find the source of the river. They disappeared into those dread swamps beyond Qebui and never came back. Has that expedition aught to do with Eos?'

'It has indeed, majesty,' Taita agreed. 'Did I not tell you that there was a lone survivor of the legionaries who returned to Qebui?'

'I do not remember that part of the tale.'

'At the time it seemed insignificant, but one man came back. He was raving and demented. The physicians thought he had been driven mad by the hardships he had endured. He died before I could speak to him. But recently I have learnt that before he died he told strange tales that were disbelieved by all who heard them so they were not reported to me. He raved about vast lakes and mountains at the end of the earth . . . and a volcano set beside the greatest of the lakes. It is from this legend that Demeter and I divined the whereabouts of the witch.' He went on to describe his meeting with the hunchback Tiptip.

Nefer Seti listened, fascinated. When Taita had finished, he thought for a while, then asked, 'Why is the volcano so important?'

In reply Taita described Demeter's captivity in the witch's lair on Etna and his escape.

'She needs the subterranean fires as a forge in which to fashion her spells. The power emitted by the immense heat and sulphurous gases enhances her powers to godlike proportions,' Taita explained.

'Why have you selected this particular volcano to examine first of all the many hundreds?' Nefer asked.

'Because it is closest to this very Egypt, and it sits upon the source of the Nile.'

'I see now that your reasoning is solid. It all fits together neatly,' Nefer Seti said. 'Seven years ago, when the Nile dried up, I remembered all that you had told me of my grandmother's expedition so I ordered another legion to march south on the same mission to reach the source and discover the cause of the river's failure. The officer I placed in command was Colonel Ah-Akhton.'

'This I did not know,' Taita said.

'Because you were not here for me to discuss it with you. You and Meren were wandering in foreign lands.' Nefer Seti's tone was a rebuke. 'You should have stayed with me.'

Taita adopted a repentant attitude. 'I did not know you had need of me, Majesty.'

'I will always have need of you.' He was readily appeased

'What news of this second expedition?' Quickly Taita seized his advantage. 'Has it returned?'

'No, it has not. Not a single man of eight hundred who marched away came back. They have vanished more completely than my grandmother's army did. Has the witch destroyed them also?'

'It is more than possible, Majesty.' He saw that Nefer Seti had already accepted the existence of the witch and did not have to be convinced or encouraged to pursue her.

'You never fail me, Tata, except when you are on a jaunt to the gods alone know where.' Nefer Seti grinned at him. 'Now I know who is mine enemy and I can move against her. Before, I was helpless to lift these terrible afflictions from my people. I was reduced to digging wells, begging food from my enemies and killing toads. Now you have made clear the solution to my problems. I must destroy the witch!'

He jumped up and continued to pace as restlessly as a caged lion. He was a man of action, eager to take to the sword. The very thought of war had lifted his spirits. Taita and Meren watched his face as the ideas came to him in floods. Every once in a while he would slap the scabbard at his side and exclaim, 'Yes! By Horus and Osiris, that is it!' At last he turned back to Taita. 'I shall lead another campaign against this Eos.'

'Pharaoh, she has already gobbled up two Egyptian armies,' Taita reminded him.

Nefer Seti sobered a little. He resumed pacing, then

stopped again. 'Very well. As Demeter did at Etna, you will work a spell of such power against her that she will fall from her mountain and burst like an overripe fruit as she hits the ground. What think you, Tata?'

'Your Majesty, do not underestimate Eos. Demeter was a mightier magus than I am. He struggled against the witch with all his powers, but in the end she destroyed him, seemingly without effort, as you might crush a tick between your finger-nails.' Taita shook his head regretfully. 'My spells are like javelins. Thrown at extreme range, they are feeble and easily deflected with a flick of her shield. If I come close enough to her, and am able to discern her whereabouts exactly, then my aim will improve. If I have her in my eye, my dart may be good enough to fly past her shield. I cannot touch her at this great distance.'

'If she is so all-powerful as to destroy Demeter, why has she not done the same to you?' He answered his own question immediately. 'Because she fears that you are stronger than she is.'

'I wish it were that simple. No, Pharaoh, it is because she has not yet struck at me with all her strength.'

Nefer Seti looked puzzled. 'But she killed Demeter, and she grinds my kingdom between the millstones of her malice. Why does she spare you?'

'She had no further use for Demeter. I told you how when he was in her clutches she sucked from him, like a great vampire, all his learning and skills. When at last he escaped she did not trouble to pursue him vigorously. He was no longer a threat to her, and had nothing more to offer. That is, until he and I united. Then her interest quickened again. Together we had become such a significant force that she was able to detect me. She does not wish to destroy me until she has sucked me dry, as she did Demeter, but she could not lure me into her snares unless she isolated me. So she struck down my ally.'

'If she wants to preserve you for her foul purposes, I will take you with my army. You will be my stalking horse. I will use you to come within striking distance, and while you distract her, both of us will attack her,' Nefer Seti proposed.

'Desperate measures, Pharaoh. Why should she allow you close enough to her when she can kill you from a distance, as she did with Demeter?'

'From what you tell me, she seeks dominion over Egypt. Very well. I will tell her that I have come to surrender myself and my land to her. I will ask to be allowed to kiss her feet in submission.'

Taita kept a grave expression, although he wanted to chuckle at this naïve suggestion. 'Sire, the witch is a savant.'

'What is that?' Nefer Seti demanded.

'With her Inner Eye she is able to scry a man's soul as readily as you read a battle plan. You would never come close to her with such anger displayed in your aura.'

'Then how do you propose to draw within range without being scried by her mysterious eye?'

'As she is, so am I a savant. I throw no aura for her to read.'

Nefer Seti was becoming angry. He had been a god long enough to resent any check or restraint. His voice rose: 'I am no longer a child for you to baffle with your esoteric cant. You are too quick to point out the flaws in my plans,' he said. 'Learned Magus, be kind and gracious enough to propose an alternative so that I may have the pleasure of treating it as you have treated mine.'

'You are the pharaoh, you are Egypt. You must not walk into the web she weaves. Your duty is here with your people, with Mintaka and your children, to protect them if I should fail.'

'You are a devious and crafty rogue, Tata. I know where this is moving. You would leave me here in Thebes, killing toads, while you and Meren set out on another adventure. Am I to be left cowering in my own harem like a woman?' he asked bitterly.

'Nay, Majesty, like a proud pharaoh on the throne, ready to defend the Two Kingdoms with your life.'

Nefer Seti placed his clenched fists on his hips and glared. 'I should not listen to your siren song. You spin a web with as strong a thread as any witch.' Then he spread his hands in a gesture of resignation. 'Sing on, Tata, and I perforce will listen.'

'You might consider giving Meren a small force to command, not more than a hundred picked warriors. They will travel fast, living off the land without recourse to a lumbering supply train. Numbers alone are no threat to the witch. She will not be concerned by a contingent of this size. As Meren projects no complex psychic aura to arouse her suspicions, she will scry him as a bluff, simple soldier. I will go with him. She will recognize me from afar, but by coming to her I am playing into her hands. In order to take from me the knowledge and power she desires, she must let me come close to her.'

Nefer Seti growled and muttered under his breath as he stamped up and down. Finally he confronted Taita again: 'It is hard for me to accept that I should not lead the expedition. However, your arguments, convoluted though they are, have swayed me from my good sense.' His glowering features cleared a little. 'Above all men in Egypt, I trust you and Meren Cambyses.' He turned to Meren. 'You shall have the rank of colonel. Choose your hundred, and I will give you my royal Hawk Seal so that you can equip them from the state armouries and remount stations anywhere in my dominions.' The Hawk Seal delegated Pharaoh's royal power to the bearer. 'I want you ready to ride with the new moon at the latest. Be guided in all things by Taita. Return safely and bring me the witch's head.'

When word got out that he was recruiting a flying column of élite cavalry, Meren was besieged by volunteers. He chose as his captains three hardy veterans, Hilto-bar-Hilto, Shabako and Tonka. None had ridden and fought with him during the civil war – they were too young for that – but their fathers had, and their grandfathers had all been companions of the Red Road.

'The warrior blood breeds true,' Meren explained to Taita. His fourth choice was Habari, whom he had come to like and trust. He offered him the command of one of his four platoons.

He mustered all four captains, confirmed their selection and questioned them closely: 'Have you a wife or woman? We travel light. There will be no place with us for camp-followers.' Traditionally Egyptian armies travelled with their women.

'I have a wife,' Habari said, 'but I will be pleased to escape from her scolding for five years, or ten, even longer if you require it, Colonel.' The other three agreed with this sensible view.

'Colonel, if we are to live off the land, then we will take our women where we find them,' said Hilto-bar-Hilto, the son of old Hilto, now long dead. He had been the Best of Ten Thousand and had worn the Gold of Praise at his throat, awarded to him by Pharaoh after the battle at Ismalia when they had overthrown the false pharaoh.

'Spoken like a true legionary.' Meren laughed. He delegated to the chosen four the selection of the troopers to fill their platoons. Within less than ten days they had assembled a hundred of the finest warriors in the entire Egyptian army. Each man was equipped, armed and sent to the remount station to pick out two chargers and a pack mule. As Pharaoh had commanded, they were ready to march from Thebes on the night of the new moon.

Two days before the departure, Taita crossed the river and rode to the Palace of Memnon to take his leave of Queen

Mintaka. He found her thinner, wan and cast down. The reason for this she confided to him within the first few minutes of their meeting.

'Oh, Tata, dear Tata. The most dreadful thing has transpired. Soe has vanished. He has gone without taking leave of me. He disappeared three days after you saw him in my audience chamber.'

Taita was not surprised. That had been the day of Demeter's gruesome death.

'I have sent messengers to find him in every possible place. Taita, I know you will be as distressed as I am. You knew and admired him. We both saw in him the salvation of Egypt. Can you not use your special powers to find him for me, and bring him back to me? Now that he has gone I will never see my dead babies again. Egypt and Nefer will remain in perpetual agony. The Nile will never flow.'

Taita did his best to console her. He could see that her health was deteriorating, and her proud spirit was on the point of breaking under the weight of her despair. He cursed Eos and her works while he did all in his power to calm Mintaka, and give her hope. 'Meren and I are setting out on an expedition beyond the southern borders. I will make it my first duty to search for and make enquiry for Soe at every point along our way. In the meantime I divine that he is alive and unharmed. Unexpected circumstances and events forced him to depart hurriedly, without taking leave of Your Majesty. However, he intends to return to Thebes at the first opportunity to continue his mission in the name of the new nameless goddess.' All of which were reasonable assumptions, Taita told himself. 'Now I must bid you farewell. I shall hold you always in my thoughts and my dutiful love.'

The Nile was no longer navigable so they took the wagon road south along the bank of the dying river. Pharaoh rode the first mile at Taita's side, belabouring him with commands and instructions. Before he turned back, he addressed the troopers of the column in an exhortation and rallying call: 'I expect each of you to do his duty,' he ended, and embraced

Taita in front of them. As he rode away, they cheered him out of sight.

Taita had planned the stages of the journey to bring them each evening to one of the many temples situated along the banks of the Nile in the Upper Kingdom. At each his reputation had preceded him. The high priest came out to offer him and his men shelter. Their welcome was sincere because Meren carried the king's Hawk Seal, which allowed him to draw additional food from the quarter-masters of the military forts that guarded each town. The priests expected their own meagre rations to be augmented by this windfall.

Each evening, after a frugal meal in the refectory, Taita retired to the inner sanctuary of the temple. Devotions and prayers had been said in these precincts for hundreds or even thousands of years. The passion of the worshippers had built spiritual fortifications that even Eos would have the greatest difficulty in penetrating. For a while he would be protected from her overlooking. He could appeal to his own gods without fear of intervention by evil wraiths sent by the witch to deceive him. He prayed to the god to whom each temple was dedicated for strength and guidance in his looming conflict with the witch. In the calm and serenity of such surroundings he could meditate and marshal his physical and spiritual strength.

The temples were the centre of each community and the repositories of learning. Although many of the priests were dull creatures, some were erudite and educated, aware of all that was happening in their nomes and in tune with the mood of their flock. They were a reliable source of information and intelligence. Taita spent hours conferring with them, interrogating them keenly. One question he put to them all: 'Have you heard of strangers moving covertly among your people, preaching a new religion?'

Each one replied that they had. 'They preach that the old gods are failing, that they are no longer able to protect this very Egypt. They preach of a new goddess who will descend among us and lift the curse from the river and the land. When she comes she will bid the plagues cease and Mother Nile once more to flood and deliver to Egypt her bounty. They tell the people that Pharaoh and his family are secret adherents of the new goddess, that soon Nefer Seti will renounce the old gods, and declare his allegiance to her.' Then, worried, they demanded, 'Tell us, great Magus, is this true? Will Pharaoh declare for the alien goddess?'

'Before that happens the stars will fall from the sky like raindrops. Pharaoh is devoted to Horus, heart and soul,' he assured them. 'But tell me, do the people hearken to these charlatans?'

'They are only human. Their children are starving and they are in the depths of despair. They will follow anyone who offers them surcease from their misery.'

'Have you met any of these preachers?'

None had. 'They are secretive and elusive,' said one. 'Although I have sent messengers to them, inviting them to explain their beliefs to me, none has come forward.'

'Have you learnt the names of any?'

'It seems they all use the same name.'

'Is it Soe?' Taita asked.

'Yes, Magus, that is the name they use. Perhaps it is a title rather than a name.'

'Are they Egyptians or foreigners? Do they speak our language as though born to it?'

'I have heard that they do and that they claim to be of our blood.'

The man he was conversing with on this occasion was Sanepi, the high priest of the temple of Khum at Iunyt, in the third nome of Upper Egypt. When Taita had heard all he had to offer on this matter, he moved on to more mundane topics: 'As an adept of the natural laws, have you tried to find some way in which to render the red waters of the river fit for human use?'

The urbane and devout man was appalled at the suggestion. 'The river is cursed. No one dare bathe in it, let alone drink it. The kine that do so waste away and die within days. The river has become the abode of gigantic carrion-eating toads, such as have never been seen before in Egypt or any other land. They defend the stinking pools ferociously, and attack anyone who approaches. I would rather die of thirst than drink that poison,' Sanepi replied, his features twisted in an expression of disgust. 'Even the temple novices believe, as I do, that the river has been desecrated by some malevolent god.'

So it was that Taita took it upon himself to conduct a series of experiments to ascertain the true nature of the red tide, and to find some method of purifying the Nile waters. Meren was pushing the column southwards at a punishing pace and he knew that, unless he could find some means of augmenting their water supply, the horses would soon die of thirst. Pharaoh's newly dug wells were situated at long intervals, and their yield was not nearly sufficient for the needs of three hundred hard-driven horses. This was the easiest stage of the journey. Above the white water of the first cataract, the river road ran thousands of leagues through hard, forbidding deserts where there were no wells. It rained there once in a hundred years and was the haunt of scorpions and wild animals such as the oryx, which could survive without surface water in the domain of the tyrannical sun. Unless he could find some reliable source of water, the expedition would perish in those scorching wastes, never to reach the confluence of the Nile, let alone its source.

At every overnight camp, Taita spent hours on his experiments, aided by four of Meren's youngest troopers who had volunteered to assist him. They were honoured to work side by side with the mighty magus: it was a tale they would tell their grandchildren. When he presided over them they had no fear of demons and curses, for all had a blind faith in Taita's ability to protect them. They laboured night after night without complaint, but even the magus's genius could find no way to sweeten the stinking waters.

Seventeen days after they had set out from Karnak they reached the large temple complex dedicated to the goddess

Hathor on the riverbank at Kom Ombo. The high priestess extended the usual warm welcome to the celebrated magus. As soon as Taita had seen his helpers put copper pots upon the fires to boil the Nile water, he left them to it and went to the inner sanctuary of the temple.

No sooner had he entered it than he became aware of a benevolent influence. He went to the image of the cow goddess, and sat cross-legged before it. Since Demeter had warned him that the images of Lostris he was receiving were almost certainly untrustworthy, conjured by the witch to deceive and confuse him, he had not dared to invoke her presence. However, in this place he felt he had the protection of Hathor, one of the most powerful goddesses in the pantheon. As patroness of all women, surely she would shield Lostris in her sanctuary.

He prepared himself mentally by reciting aloud three times the rites of approach to a deity, then opened his Inner Eye and waited quietly in the shadowy silences. Gradually the silence was broken by his own pulse beating in his ears, the harbinger of a spiritual presence drawing near to him. It grew stronger and he waited for the sensation of cold to envelop him, prepared to break off the contact at the first touch of frost in the air. The sanctuary remained quiet and pleasantly warm. His sense of security and peace increased and he drifted towards sleep. He closed his eyes and beheld a vision of limpid water, then heard a sweet, childlike voice call his name: 'Taita, I am coming to you!' He saw something flash in the depths of the water, and thought a silver fish was rising to the surface. Then he saw that he had been mistaken: it was the slim white body of a child swimming towards him. A head broke the surface, and he saw that she was a girl of about twelve. Her long sodden hair streamed down over her face and tiny breasts in a golden veil.

'I heard you call.' The laughter was a happy sound, and he laughed in sympathy. The child swam towards him, reached a white sandbank just below the surface and stood up. She was a girl: although her hips had not yet taken on feminine curves, and the outline of her ribs was all that adorned her torso, there was a tiny hairless crease between her thighs.

'Who are you?' he asked. With a toss of her head she threw back her hair to reveal her face. His heart swelled until it hampered his breathing. It was Lostris.

'Fie on you that you do not know me, for I am Fenn,' she said. The name meant Moon Fish.

'I knew you all along,' Taita told her. 'You are exactly as you were when first I met you. I could never forget your eyes. They were then and still are the greenest and prettiest in all Egypt.'

'You lie, Taita. You did not recognize me.' She stuck out a pointed pink tongue.

'I taught you not to do that.'

'Then you did not teach me very well.'

'Fenn was your baby name,' he reminded her. 'When you showed your first red moon, the priests changed it to your woman's name.'

'Daughter of the Waters.' She grimaced at him. 'I never liked it. "Lostris" sounds so silly and stuffy. I much prefer "Fenn".'

'Then Fenn you shall be,' he told her.

'I will be waiting for you,' she promised. 'I came with a gift for you, but now I must go back. They are calling me.' She dived gracefully, deep under the surface, her arms along her flanks, kicking with her slim legs to drive herself deeper. Her hair billowed behind her like a golden flag.

'Come back!' he called after her. 'You must tell me where you will wait for me.' But she was gone, and only a faint echo of laughter floated back to him.

When he woke he knew it was late for the temple lamps were guttering. He felt refreshed and exhilarated. He became aware that he was clutching something in his right hand. He opened his fist carefully and saw that he held a handful of white powder. He wondered if this was Fenn's gift. He lifted it to his nose and sniffed it cautiously.

'Lime!' he exclaimed. Every village along the river had a primitive kiln in which the peasants burned lumps of limestone to this powder. They painted the walls of their huts and granaries with it: the white coating reflected the sun's rays, and kept the interiors cooler. He was about to throw it away, but restrained himself. 'The gift of a goddess should be treated with respect.' He smiled at his folly. He folded and knotted the handful of lime into the hem of his tunic and went out.

Meren was waiting for him at the doors to the sanctuary. 'Your men have prepared the river water for you, but they have waited long for you to come to them. They are tired from the journey and need to sleep.' There was a gentle rebuke in Meren's tone. He took care of his own men. 'I hope that you do not plan to stay up all night over your stinking waterpots. I will come to fetch you before midnight, for I will not allow it.'

Taita ignored the threat and asked, 'Does Shofar have to hand the potions I prepared to treat the waters?'

Meren laughed. 'As he remarked, they stink worse than the red waters.' He led Taita to where the four pots bubbled and steamed. His helpers, who had been squatting around the fires, scrambled to their feet, thrust long poles through the handles of the pots and lifted them off the flames. Taita waited for the water to cool sufficiently, then went along the row of pots adding his potions to them. Shofar stirred each one with a wooden paddle. As he was about to treat the final pot Taita paused. 'The gift of Fenn,' he murmured, and untied the knot in the hem of his tunic. He poured the lime into the last pot. For good measure he made a pass with the golden Periapt of Lostris over the mixture, and intoned a word of power: 'Ncube!'

The four helpers exchanged an awed glance.

'Leave the pots to cool until morning,' Taita ordered, 'and go to your rest. You have done well. I thank you.'

The minute Taita stretched out on his sleeping mat he fell into a deathlike slumber, untroubled by dreams or even

Meren's snores. At dawn when they awoke Shofar was at the door with a huge grin on his face. 'Come swiftly, mighty Magus. We have something for your comfort.'

They hurried to the pots beside the cold ashes of last night's fires. Habari and the other captains stood to attention at the head of their troopers, all drawn up in review order. They beat their sword scabbards against their shields and cheered as though Taita were a victorious general taking possession of the battleground. 'Quiet!' Taita groused. 'You will split my skull.' But they cheered him all the louder.

The first three pots were filled with a nauseating black stew, but the water in the fourth was clear. He scooped out a handful and tasted it gingerly. It was not sweet, but redolent with the earthy flavour that had sustained them all since childhood: the familiar taste of Nile mud.

From then on, at each overnight camp, they boiled and limed the pots of river water, and in the mornings, before they set out, they filled the waterskins. No longer weakened by thirst, the horses recovered and the pace of the march quickened. Nine days later they reached Assoun. Ahead lay the first of the six great cataracts. They were formidable obstacles for boats, but horses could take the caravan road round them.

In the town of Assoun, Meren rested the horses and men for three days, and replenished their grain bags at the royal granary. He allowed the troopers to fortify themselves against the rigours of the next long leg of the journey by recourse to the joy-houses along the waterfront. Conscious of his new rank and responsibility, he himself greeted the blandishments and bold-eyed invitations of the local beauties with feigned indifference.

The pool below the first cataract had shrivelled to a puddle so Taita had no need of a boatman to row him to the tiny rock island on which stood the great temple of Isis. Its walls were chiselled with gigantic images of the goddess, her husband, Osiris, and Horus, her son. Windsmoke carried Taita across to it, her hoofs ringing on the rocky riverbed. All of the priests were assembled to greet him, and he spent the next three days with them.

They had little news for him of conditions in Nubia to the south. In the good times when the flood of the Nile had been reliable, strong and true there had been a large fleet of trading vessels plying the river up to Qebui, at the confluence of the two Niles. They returned with ivory, the dried meat and skins of wild animals, baulks of timber, bars of copper, and gold nuggets from the mines along the Atbara river, the principal tributary of the Nile. Now that the flood had failed and the waters that remained in the pools along the way had turned to blood, few travellers braved the dangerous road through the deserts on foot or horseback. The priests warned that the southern road and the hills along its way had become the home of criminals and outcasts.

Once again he enquired after the preachers of the false goddess. They told him that it was rumoured Soe prophets had appeared from the wastes and made their way northwards towards Karnak and the delta, but none had had contact with them.

When night fell Taita retired to the inner sanctuary of the mother goddess Isis and, under her protection, felt at ease to meditate and pray. Although he invoked his patron goddess, he received no direct response from her during the first two nights of his vigil. Nevertheless he felt stronger and better prepared to face the challenges that lay ahead on the road to Qebui and in the uncharted lands and swamps beyond. His inevitable confrontation with Eos seemed less daunting. His strengthened body and resolve might have been the result of hard riding in the company of young troopers and officers, and the spiritual disciplines he had observed since leaving Thebes, but it gave him pleasure to think that the close proximity of the goddess Lostris, or Fenn, as she now chose to be known, had armed him for the struggle.

On the last morning, as the first light of dawn roused him, he asked again for Isis's blessing and protection, and for those of any other gods who might be near. As he was about to leave the sanctuary he cast a last glance at the statue of Isis, which was hewn from a monolith of red granite. It towered to the roof and the head was shrouded in shadow, the stone eyes staring ahead implacably. He stooped to pick up his staff from beside the rug of plaited papyrus on which he had passed the night. Before he could straighten, the pulse started to beat softly in his ears, but he experienced no chill on his naked upper body. He looked up to see that the statue was gazing down at him. The eyes had come alive and glowed a luminous green. They were Fenn's eyes and their expression was as gentle as that of a mother watching an infant asleep at her breast.

'Fenn,' he whispered. 'Lostris, are you here?' The echo of her laughter came from the stone vaulting high above his head, but he could see only the dark shape of bats flitting back to their roosts.

His eyes switched back to the statue. The stone head was alive now, and it was Fenn's. 'Remember, I am waiting for you,' she whispered.

'Where will I find you? Tell me where to look,' he begged.

'Where else would you search for a moon fish?' she teased him. 'You will find me hiding among the other fishes.'

'But where are the fishes?' he pleaded. Already her living features were hardening into stone, and the brilliant eyes dulling.

'Where?' he cried. 'When?'

'Beware the prophet of darkness. He carries a knife. He also waits for you,' she whispered sadly. 'Now I must go. She will not let me stay longer.'

'Who will not let you stay? Isis or another?' To utter the name of the witch in this holy place would be sacrilege. But the statue's lips had frozen.

Hands tugged at his upper arm. He started and looked around, expecting another apparition to materialize, but he saw only the anxious face of the high priest, who said, 'Magus, what ails you? Why do you cry out?'

'It was a dream, just a foolish dream.'

'Dreams are never foolish. You of all people should know that. They are warnings and messages from the gods.'

He took his leave of the holy men, and went out to the stables. Windsmoke ran to meet him, kicking up her heels playfully, a bunch of hay stalks dangling from the corner of her mouth.

'They have been spoiling you, you fat old strumpet. Look at you now, cavorting like a foal, you with your big belly,' Taita scolded her lovingly. During their sojourn in Karnak a careless groom had let one of Pharaoh's favourite stallions reach her. Now she quietened and stood still to let him mount, then carried him to where Meren's troopers were breaking camp. When the column was ready, the men standing by their horses' heads, with the spare mounts and the pack mules on lead reins, Meren went down the ranks checking weapons and equipment, making certain that each man had his copper water-pot and a bag of lime strapped to the back of the mule.

'Mount!' he roared from the head of the column. 'Move out! Walk! Trot!' A train of weeping women followed them to the foot of the hills, where they fell back, unable to keep up with the pace that Meren set.

'Bitter the parting, but sweet the memories,' Hilto-bar-Hilto remarked, and his platoon chuckled.

'Nay, Hilto,' Meren called from the head of the column. 'The sweeter the flesh, the sweeter the memories!'

They roared with laughter and drummed on the shields with their scabbards.

'They laugh now,' Taita said drily, 'but let us see if they still laugh in the furnace of the desert.'

They looked down into the gorge of the cataract. There was no rush of angry waters. The vicious rocks, which were usually a hazard to shipping, were now exposed and dry, black as the backs of a herd of wild buffalo. At the top end, on a bluff overlooking the gorge, stood a tall granite obelisk. While the men watered their steeds and the mules, Taita and Meren climbed the cliff to the monument and stood at its foot. Taita read aloud the inscription:

'I, Queen Lostris, regent of Egypt and widow of Pharaoh Mamose, eighth of that name, mother of the crown prince Memnon, who shall rule the Two Kingdoms after me, have ordained the raising of this monument.

This is the mark and covenant of my vow to the people of this very Egypt, that I shall return to them from the wilderness whence I have been driven by the barbarian.

This stone was placed here in the first year of my rule, the nine-hundredth after the building of the great pyramid of Pharaoh Cheops.

Let this stone stand immovable as the pyramid until I make good my promise to return.'

As the memories flooded back, Taita's eyes filled with tears. He remembered her on the day they had raised the obelisk: Lostris had been twenty, proud in her royalty and womanly glory.

'It was on this spot that Queen Lostris placed the Gold of Praise upon my shoulders,' he told Meren. 'It was heavy, but less precious to me than her favour.' They went down to the horses and rode on.

The desert enveloped them like the flames of a mighty bonfire. They could not ride during the day, so they boiled and limed the river water, then lay in any shade they could find, panting like hard-run hounds. When the sun touched the western horizon, they rode on through the night. In places the gaunt cliffs crowded the riverbank so closely that they could only ride in single file along the narrow track. They passed tumbledown huts that had once given shelter to travellers who had gone before them, but they were deserted. They found no fresh sign of any human presence until the tenth day after they had left Assoun when they came across another cluster of abandoned huts beside what had been a deep pool. One had been recently occupied: the ashes on the hearth were still fresh and crisp. As soon as Taita entered it, he sensed the faint but unmistakable taint of the witch. As his eyes adjusted to the shadows, he made out writing in hieratic script that had been scratched on the wall with a stick of charcoal.

'Eos is great. Eos cometh.' Not long ago, one of the witch's adherents had passed this way. His footprints were still in the dust of the floor at the bottom of the wall where he had stood to write the exhortation. It was almost sunrise, and the heat of the day was coming swiftly upon them. Meren ordered the column to make camp. Even the ruined huts would afford some shelter from the cruel sun. While this was happening and before the heat became unbearable, Taita cast around for other traces of the Eos worshipper. In a patch of loose earth on the stony track that led south he found hoofprints. By their set he could tell that the horse must have carried a heavy load. The tracks were heading south, towards Qebui. Taita called Meren, and asked, 'How old are these tracks?' Meren was an expert scout and tracker.

'Impossible to be certain, Magus. More than three days, less than ten.'

'Then already the Eos worshipper is far ahead of us.'

As they turned back for the shelter of the huts a pair of dark eyes watched their every move from the hills above the camp. The dark brooding gaze was that of Soe, the prophet of Eos who had bewitched Queen Mintaka. It was he who had written the inscription on the wall of the hut. Now he regretted having announced his presence.

He lay in a patch of shade thrown by the crags above him. Three days previously his horse had stepped into a cleft in the rocks on the path and broken its foreleg. Within an hour a pack of hyenas had arrived to pull down the crippled animal. While it still screamed and kicked they ripped chunks of flesh from it and devoured them. Soe had drunk the last of his water during the previous night. Stranded in this terrible place he had resigned himself to death, which could not be long delayed.

Then unexpectedly, and to his great joy, he had heard hoofs coming up the valley. Rather than rush down to greet the newcomers and beg to accompany them, he had spied upon them warily from his hiding place. He recognized the troop immediately it came into sight as a detachment of the royal cavalry. They were well equipped and superbly mounted. It was plain that they were on a special assignment, possibly on the orders of the pharaoh himself. It was even possible that they had been sent to apprehend him and drag him back to Karnak. He knew that he had been noticed at the ford of the Nile below Thebes by the magus Taita, and that the magus was a confidant of Queen Mintaka. It did not need a stretch of the imagination to realize that she had probably confided in him, and that he knew of Soe's involvement with the queen. Soe was patently guilty of sedition and treason and would stand no chance before a tribunal of Pharaoh. Those were the reasons why he had fled Karnak. Now he recognized Taita among the troopers camped below where he lay.

Soe studied the horses that were tethered among the huts on the riverbank. It was not clear which he needed most to ensure his survival: a horse or the bulging waterskins that a trooper was offloading from his pack mule. When it came to his choice of a mount, the mare that Taita had tethered outside his hut was indubitably the strongest and finest of them all. Even though she was with foal, she would be Soe's first choice, if he could reach her.

There was a great deal of activity in the camp. Horses were being fed and watered, copper pots were being carried up from the river pool and placed on the fires at which men were busy preparing food. When the meal was ready, the troopers divided into four platoons and squatted in separate circles around the communal pots. The sun was well above the horizon before they found a little shade in which to settle down. A somnolent silence fell over the camp. Soe marked the position of the sentries carefully. There were four at intervals round the periphery. He saw that his best approach would be along the dry riverbed, so he gave the sentry on that side his full attention. When he had not moved for some considerable time, Soe decided that he was dozing. He slipped down the flank of the hill, screened from the eyes of the more alert sentry on the near-side boundary. He reached the dry river course half a league below the camp and made his way quietly upstream. When he was opposite it he raised his head slowly above the top of the bank.

A sentry was sitting cross-legged only twenty paces away. His chin was on his chest and his eyes were closed. Soe ducked below the bank again, stripped off his black robe and bundled it under his arm. He tucked his sheathed dagger into his loincloth and climbed to the top of the bank. Boldly he headed for the hut behind which the grey mare was tethered. In nothing more than a loincloth and sandals he could try to pass himself off as a legionary. If he was challenged he could reply, in fluent, colloquial Egyptian, that he had gone to the riverbed to attend to his private business. However, no one challenged him. He reached the corner of the hut and ducked round it.

The mare was tethered just beyond the open doorway, and a full waterskin lay in the shade of the wall. It would be the work of a few seconds to swing it over the mare's withers. He always rode bareback and needed no saddle blanket or rope stirrups. He crept up to the mare and stroked her neck. She turned her head and sniffed his hand, then shifted restlessly, but quieted again as he murmured to her soothingly and patted her shoulder. Then he went to the waterskin. It was heavy but he lifted it and threw it over her back. He slipped the knot of her halter rope and was on the point of mounting when a voice called to him from the open doorway of the hut, 'Beware the false prophet. I was warned about you, Soe.'

Startled, he glanced over his shoulder. The magus stood in the doorway. He was naked. His body was lean and muscled like that of a much younger man, but the terrible scar of the old gelding wound showed silver in his crotch. His hair and beard were in disarray, but his eyes were bright. He raised his voice in a loud cry of alarm: 'On me, the guards! Hilto, Habari! Meren! Here, Shabako!' At once the cry was taken up and shouted across the camp.

Soe hesitated no longer. He swung up on to Windsmoke's back and urged her away. Taita threw himself into her path and seized her halter rope. The mare came to such a sudden halt that Soe was thrown on to her neck. 'Stand aside, you old fool!' he shouted angrily.

He carries a knife. Fenn's warning echoed in Taita's head, and he saw the flash of a dagger in Soe's right hand as he leant down from Windsmoke's back to slash. If he had not been forewarned Taita would have received the thrust full in the throat, where it was aimed, but he had just enough time to duck to one side. The point of the dagger caught him high in the shoulder. He stumbled backwards, blood streaming down his shoulder and flank. Soe urged the mare forward to run him down. Clutching the wound, Taita whistled sharply and Windsmoke shied again, then bucked furiously and hurled Soe headlong into the fire, knocking over the water-pot in a hissing cloud of steam. Soe crawled off the hot coals, but before he could regain his feet two burly troopers pounced on him and pinned him to the dust.

''Tis a little trick I taught the mare,' Taita told Soe quietly, and picked the dagger out of the dust where he had dropped it. He placed the point against the soft skin of Soe's temple just in front of the ear. 'Lie still or I will skewer your head like a ripe pomegranate.'

Meren rushed from the hut naked, sword in hand. He took in the situation instantly, and pressed the bronze point into the back of Soe's neck, then looked up at Taita. 'The swine has wounded you. Shall I kill him, Magus?'

'No!' Taita told him. 'This is Soe, the false prophet of the false goddess.'

'By Seth's sweaty testicles, I recognize him now. It was he who set the toads on Demeter at the ford.'

'One and the same,' Taita agreed. 'Bind him well. As soon as I have seen to this cut I desire to converse with him.'

When Taita emerged from the hut a short while later, Soe was trussed up like a pig for market and laid in the full glare of the sun. They had stripped him naked, to ensure he had no other blade concealed, and already his skin was reddening under the caress of the sun. Hilto and Shabako were standing over him with drawn swords. Meren placed a stool with a seat of leather thongs in the shade thrown by the wall of the hut, and Taita took his ease upon it. He took time to survey Soe with the vision of the Inner Eye: the man's aura was unchanged from the last time he had scried it, angry and confused.

At length Taita began to ask a series of simple questions to which he already knew the answers so that he could watch how Soe's aura reacted to either the truth or a lie.

'You are known as Soe?'

Soe glared at him in silent defiance. 'Prick him,' Taita ordered Shabako, 'in the leg and not too deeply.' Shabako delivered a finely judged stab. Soe jumped, shrieked and twisted against his bonds. There was a thin trickle of blood on his thigh.

'I shall begin again,' Taita told him. 'You are Soe?'

'Yes,' he grated, through clenched teeth. His aura burned steadily.

Truth, Taita confirmed silently.

'You are an Egyptian?'

Soe kept his mouth closed and stared at him sullenly.

Taita nodded at Shabako. 'The other leg.'

'I am,' Soe answered quickly. His aura remained unchanged. Truth.

'You preached to Queen Mintaka?'

'Yes.' The truth again.

'You have promised her that you will bring her dead children back to life?'

'No.' Soe's aura was suddenly shot through with greenish light.

The sign of a lie, Taita thought. He had the yardstick against which to measure Soe's next replies.

'Forgive my lack of hospitality, Soe. Are you thirsty?'

Soe licked his dry, cracked lips. 'Yes!' he whispered. Clearly the truth.

'Where are your manners, Colonel Meren? Bring our honoured guest some water.'

Meren grinned and went to the waterskin. He filled a wooden drinking bowl, and came back to kneel beside Soe. He held the brimming bowl to the parched lips, and Soe gulped huge mouthfuls. Coughing, gasping and panting in his eagerness, he drained the bowl. Taita gave him a few moments to regain his breath.

'So, are you scurrying back to your mistress?'

'No,' mumbled Soe. The green tinge to his aura marked the lie.

'Is her name Eos?'

'Yes.' Truth.

'Do you believe she is a goddess?'

'The only goddess. The one supreme deity.' The truth again, very much so.

'Have you come face to face with her?'

'No!' Lie.

'Has she allowed you to *gijima* her yet?' Deliberately Taita used the coarse soldier's word to provoke the man. The original meaning had been 'to run', which was what a soldier in a victorious army had to do to catch the womenfolk of the defeated enemy.

'No!' It was shouted with fury. Truth.

'Has she promised to *gijima* you when you have obeyed all her commands, and secured Egypt for her?'

'No.' It was said softly. Lie. Eos had offered him a reward for his loyalty.

'Do you know where she has her lair?'

'No.' Lie.

'Does she live near a volcano?'

'No.' Lie.

'Does she live beside a great lake in the south beyond the swamps?'

'No.' Lie.

'Is she a cannibal?'

'I do not know.' Lie.

'Does she devour human infants?'

'I do not know.' Lie again.

'Does she lure wise and powerful men into her lair, then strip them of all their knowledge and powers before she destroys them?'

'I know nothing of this.' A great and veritable lie.

'How many men has she copulated with, this whore of all the worlds? A thousand? Ten thousand?'

'Your questions are blasphemous. You will be punished for them.'

'As she punished Demeter, the magus and savant? On her behalf, did you send the toads to attack him?'

'Yes! He was an apostate, a traitor. It was a judgement he richly deserved. I will listen no longer to your filth. Kill me, if you like, but I will say no more.' Soe struggled against the ropes that held him. His breathing was hoarse and his eyes were wild. The eyes of a fanatic.

'Meren, our guest is overwrought. Let him rest awhile. Then peg him out where the morning sun can warm him. Take him outside the camp, but not so far that we cannot hear him sing when he is ready to converse once more, or when the hyenas find him.'

Meren strung the rope round his shoulders and began to drag him away. Then he paused and looked back at Taita. 'Are you certain that you have no further use for him, Magus? He has told us nothing.'

'He has told us everything,' said Taita. 'He has bared his soul.'

'Take his legs,' Meren ordered Shabako and Tonka, and between them they carried Soe away. Taita heard them hammering the pegs to hold him on the baked earth. In the middle of the afternoon Meren went out to speak to him again.

The sun had raised fat white blisters across his belly and loins; his face was swollen and inflamed.

'The mighty magus invites you to continue your discussions with him,' Meren told him. Soe tried to spit at him but could gather no saliva. His purple tongue filled his mouth, and the tip protruded between his front teeth. Meren let him lie.

The hyena pack found him a little before sunset. Even Meren, the hardened old veteran, was uneasy as their demented howling and giggling drew nearer.

'Shall I bring him in, Magus?' he asked.

Taita shook his head. 'Leave him. He has told us where to find the witch.'

'The hyenas will make it a cruel death, Magus.'

Taita sighed, and said quietly, 'The toads made Demeter's death as cruel. He is a minion of the witch. He spreads sedition through the kingdom. It is fitting that he should die, but not like this. Such cruelty will sit heavily on our consciences. It reduces us to his level of evil. Go out there and cut his throat.'

Meren came to his feet and drew his sword, then paused and cocked his head. 'Something is amiss. The hyenas are silent.'

'Quickly, Meren. Go and find out what is happening,' Taita ordered sharply.

Meren ran out into the gathering darkness. Moments later his voice echoed from the hills in a wild shout. Taita jumped up and ran after him. 'Meren, where are you?'

'Here, Magus.'

Taita found him standing on the spot where they had pegged Soe down, but he was gone. 'What happened, Meren? What did you see?'

'Witchcraft!' Meren stuttered. 'I saw—' He broke off, at a loss to describe what he had seen.

'What was it?' Taita urged. 'Tell me quickly.'

'A monstrous hyena as large as a horse, with Soe upon its back. It must have been his familiar. It galloped off into the hills, bearing him away. Shall I follow them?'

'You will not catch them,' Taita said. 'Instead you will place yourself in mortal peril. Eos possesses even greater powers than I had thought possible to have rescued Soe at such a great distance. Let him go now. We will reckon with him at some other time and place.'

They went on, night after stifling night, week after wearying week, and month after gruelling month. The knife wound in Taita's shoulder healed cleanly in the hot dry air, but the horses sickened and faltered, and the men were flagging long before they reached the second cataract. This was where Taita and Queen Lostris had rested for a season to await the renewed flood of the Nile, which would ensure sufficient depth for the galleys to surmount the cataract. Taita looked down upon the settlement they had built: the stone walls were still standing – the ruins of the crude royal palace he had built to shelter Lostris. Those were the lands where they had planted the dhurra crop, still demarcated by the furrows of the wooden ploughshare. Those were the stands of tall trees from which they had cut the timber to build chariots and repair the battered hulls of the galleys. The trees were still alive, sustained by the deep roots that reached down to the underground pools and streams. Over there was the forge that the coppersmiths had built.

'Magus, look to the pool below the cataract!' Meren had ridden up beside him and his excited cry interrupted Taita's memories. He looked in the direction Meren was pointing. Was it a trick of the early light? he wondered.

'Look at the colour of the water! It is no longer blood red. The pool is green – as green as a sweet melon.'

'It might be another ruse of the witch.' Taita doubted his eyes, but already Meren was racing down the slope, standing high in his stirrups and yelling, his men following him. Taita and Windsmoke maintained a more sedate and dignified pace to the edge of the pool, which was lined now with men, horses and mules. The animals' heads were down and they were sucking up the green water like *shadoofs*, the waterwheels of the peasant farmers, as the men scooped handfuls to pour it over their own faces and down their throats.

Windsmoke sniffed the water suspiciously, then began to drink. Taita loosened her girth rope to allow her belly to expand. Like a pig's bladder, she blew up before his eyes. He left her to it, and waded out into the pool, then sat down. The tepid water reached his chin and he closed his eyes, an ecstatic smile on his face.

'Magus!' Meren called from the bank. 'This is your doing, I am sure. You have cured the river of her foul disease. Is it not so?'

Meren's faith in him was limitless and touching. It would not do to disappoint him. Taita opened his eyes to see that a hundred men were waiting attentively for his reply. It was also prudent to build their trust in him. He smiled at Meren, then dropped his right eyelid in an enigmatic wink. Meren looked smug and the men cheered. They waded into the pool, still in sandals and shirts, and splashed sheets of water at each other, then wrestled each other's heads beneath the surface. Taita left them to their revelry and waded to the bank. By this time Windsmoke was so bloated with both water and foal that she waddled rather than walked. He took her to roll in the crisp white river sand and sat down. While he watched her he pondered the change in their fortunes and the miracle of the clear water that Meren had ascribed to him.

This is as far as the contamination has spread, he decided. From here southwards the river will be clear. Wasted and shrivelled, but clear.

They camped that morning in the shade of the grove.

'Magus, I plan to stay at this place until the horses are recovered. If we go on immediately we will begin to lose them,' Meren said.

Taita nodded. 'You are wise,' he said. 'I know this place well. I lived here for a full season during the great exodus. There are plants in the forest whose leaves the horses will eat.

They are rich in nutrients and will put fat and condition on them within days.' And Windsmoke will soon drop her foal. It will have a better chance of survival here than out in the desert, Taita thought but did not say.

Meren was speaking animatedly: 'I saw the tracks of oryx near the pool. The men will enjoy hunting them, and be grateful for the fine meat. We can dry and smoke the rest to take with us when we ride again.'

Taita stood up. 'I will go to search out fodder for the animals.'

'I will come with you. I want to see more of this little paradise.' They wandered together among the trees and Taita pointed out edible shrubs and vines. They were desert adapted and hardened to the drought conditions. Sheltered from direct sunlight by the tall trees, they were thriving. They gathered armfuls, and took them back to camp.

Taita offered samples of the wild harvest to Windsmoke. After due consideration she nibbled one of his offerings, then nuzzled him for more. Taita assembled a large foraging party and took the men into the forest to show them the edible plants and to harvest them. Meren took a second party, and they scouted at the edge of the forest for game. Two large antelopes were disturbed by the sound of axes and ran within easy arrow shot of the hunters.

When the warm carcasses were brought into camp to be butchered, Taita examined them carefully. The male carried stout horns, and had a dark, beautifully patterned hide. The female was hornless and more delicately built, her coat red brown and soft. 'I recognize these beasts,' he said. 'The males are aggressive when brought to bay. During the exodus one of our hunters was gored by a big buck. It severed the blood vessel in his groin and he bled to death before his companions could summon me. However, the flesh is delicious, the kidneys and liver in particular.'

While they were encamped at the pools Meren allowed his men to return to the diurnal pattern of activity. After they had fed the horses, he set them to build a sturdy and readily defensible stockade of logs cut in the forest to accommodate the horses and themselves. They feasted that evening on antelope meat grilled on the fire, wild spinach and herbs that Taita had selected, with rounds of dhurra bread hot off the coals. Before he retired to his mattress, Taita wandered down to the pool to study the night sky. The last vestige of the Star of Lostris had disappeared, but there were no other celestial phenomena of import. He meditated for a while, but sensed no psychic presence. Since the escape of Soe, the witch seemed to have lost contact with him.

He returned to the camp and found only the sentries still awake. In a whisper, so that he did not disturb the sleepers, he wished them a safe watch then went to his sleeping mat.

Windsmoke woke him by nuzzling his face. Sleepily he pushed away her head, but she was insistent. He sat up. 'What is it, my sweet? What ails you?' She kicked at her belly with a back foot, and gave a soft groan that alarmed him. He stood up and ran his hands over her head and neck, then down her flank. Deep in her swollen belly he felt the strong contractions of her womb. She groaned again, spread her back legs apart, raised her tail high and urinated. Then she nuzzled her flank. Taita placed one arm round her neck and led her to the far end of the stockade. He knew how important it was to keep her quiet. If she was disturbed or alarmed the contractions might stop and delay the birth. He squatted to watch over her in the moonlight. She fretted and shifted restlessly, then lay down and rolled on to her back.

'What a clever girl,' he encouraged her. She was instinctively positioning the foal correctly for birth. She came to her feet and stood with her head down. Then her belly heaved and the waters broke. She turned and licked the grass on which the fluid had spilled. Now her tail was towards him and he saw the pale opaque bulge of the birth sac appear beneath it. She heaved again, contracting strongly and regularly. Through the thin membrane he discerned the outline of a pair of tiny hoofs then, with each contraction, the fetlocks appeared. At last, to his relief, a little black muzzle peeped out between them. He would not be called on to perform a breech delivery.

'*Bak-her!*' he applauded her. 'Well done, my darling.' He restrained the urge to go to her assistance. She was doing perfectly well on her own, the contractions regular and strong.

The foal's head popped out. 'Grey like its mother,' he whispered, with pleasure. Then, abruptly, the entire sac and the foal within it were ejected. As it hit the ground the placenta parted and the sac was free. Taita was amazed. It had been the swiftest of thousands of equine births he had witnessed. Already the foal was struggling to break out of the membrane.

'Fast as a whirlwind.' Taita smiled. 'That shall be its name.' Windsmoke watched her newborn's struggles with interest. At last the membrane tore and the colt, for a colt he was, heaved himself upright and stood swaying drunkenly. He was breathing deeply from his efforts, his silvery flanks heaving.

'Good!' Taita said softly. 'Good brave boy.' Windsmoke gave her foal a hearty maternal lick of welcome that almost knocked him down again. He staggered but recovered his balance. Then she started the process in earnest: with long firm strokes of her tongue, she scrubbed off the amniotic fluid. Then she moved to place her swollen udder within easy reach. Already the milk was dripping from her waxed teats. The colt sniffed at them, then latched on to one like a limpet. He gave furious suck, and Taita stole away. His presence was no longer needed or desirable.

At daybreak the troopers came to admire mother and baby. Horsemen all, they knew better than to crowd them. At a discreet distance they pointed out to each other the new foal's shapely head and long back.

'Good deep chest,' said Shabako. 'He will be a stayer. He will run all day.'

'Front legs not splayed or pigeon-toed. He will be fast,' said Hilto.

'Hindquarters finely balanced, neither sickle-hocked nor hip-shot. Yes, fast as the wind,' said Tonka.

'What will you call him, Magus?' Meren asked.

'Whirlwind.'

'Yes,' they agreed at once. 'A good name for him.'

Within ten days Whirlwind was frolicking around his dam, butting her udder fiercely when she did not let down her milk fast enough for his appetite.

'Greedy little fellow,' Taita observed. 'Already he is strong enough to follow when we go on.'

Meren waited another few days for the rise of the full moon before he took once more to the south road. As Taita rode down the column Meren saw him looking at the water-pots and lime bags strapped to the back of each pack mule. Hurriedly he explained, 'I am certain we will have no further need of them, but . . .' He groped for an explanation.

Taita supplied it. 'They are too valuable to discard. We can sell them in Qebui.'

'Exactly what I had in mind.' Meren looked relieved. 'Not for an instant did I doubt the efficacy of your magic. I am sure that from now on we will find only good water ahead.'

So it proved. The next pool they came to was green and filled with huge catfish that had long barbels round their mouths. The shrinking pools had concentrated them in dense shoals so they were readily speared. Their flesh was bright orange and rich with fat. They made delicious eating. Among the men Taita's reputation was now carved in marble and embossed in pure gold. The four captains and their troopers were ready to follow him to the ends of the earth, which was exactly what Pharaoh had ordered them to do.

Fodder for the horses was always in short supply, but Taita had passed that way before and hunted in the surrounding country. He led them on detours from the river to hidden valleys in which grew stands of a low, leathery desert shrub that seemed dead and desiccated, but buried beneath each plant an enormous tuber was filled with water and nutrients. They were the staple diet of the oryx herds in hard times – they pawed them up with their hoofs. The troopers chopped them into chunks. At first the horses refused to touch them, but hunger soon overcame their reluctance. The men cached the water-pots and lime bags and replaced them with tubers.

They sustained the pace of the march over the ensuing months, but the weaker horses started to falter. When they broke down, the troopers despatched them with a sword blow between the ears that went deep into the skull. They left their bones to bleach in the sun. In all twenty-two died before they faced the final obstacle: the Shabluka gorge, a narrow cutting through which the Nile forced its way.

Above the gorge the Nile, in spate, was almost a mile wide. However, through the gorge it was compressed to a hundred yards from one steep rocky bank to the other. When they camped below it they saw running water for the first time since they had left Karnak. A thin stream emerged through the rocky chute and spilled into the pool below. However, it had not run more than a mile before it was sucked into the sands and vanished below them.

They ascended the Shabluka Ridge up a wild-goat track along the lip of the gorge. From the summit they looked southwards across the plains to a distant line of low blue hills. 'The Kerreri hills,' said Taita. 'They stand guard over the two Niles. Qebui is only some fifty leagues ahead.'

The course of the river was marked by groves of palm trees along each bank, and they followed the western bank towards the hills. The river flowed stronger as they drew nearer to Qebui and their spirits rose. They covered the last leg of the journey in a single day and at last stood at the confluence of the Nile.

Qebui was the outpost at the furthest limit of the Egyptian domain. The small fort housed the governor of the nome and a detachment of border guards. The town spread out along the southern bank. It was a trading post, but even at this distance they could see that many buildings were run-down and abandoned. All trade with Mother Egypt in the north had been strangled by the failure of the Nile. Few were prepared to take a caravan along the perilous road that Taita, Meren and their men had negotiated.

'This flow of water comes down from the highlands of Ethiopia.' Taita pointed to the wide, eastern river course. The water was running and they could see *shadoof* wheels turning along the far bank as they lifted the water into the irrigation channels. Wide fields of green dhurra surrounded the town.

'I expect to find good supplies of grain here to fatten the horses.' Meren smiled with pleasure.

'Yes,' Taita agreed. 'We shall have to rest now until they are fully recovered.' He patted Windsmoke's neck. She was sadly out of condition: her ribs were showing and her coat was dull. Even though Taita had shared his ration of dhurra with her, feeding her foal and the rigours of the journey had taken their toll on her.

Taita turned his attention to the eastern fork of the river. 'That is the way Queen Lostris led the exodus,' he said. 'We sailed the galleys as far as the mouth of another steep gorge which they could not surmount, anchored them there and went on with chariots and wagons. In the mountains the queen and I chose the site of Pharaoh Mamose's tomb. I designed it and concealed it most cunningly. I have no doubt it has never been discovered and desecrated. Nor will it be.' For a short while he reflected on his achievement with satisfaction, then went on, 'The Ethiopians have fine horses, but they are warriors and fiercely defend their mountain fastnesses. They have driven back two of our armies sent to subdue them and bring them into the empire. I fear that there will never be a third attempt.' He turned and pointed directly down the southern branch of the river. It was wider than the eastern fork, but it was dry, not even a trickle moving in its bed. 'That is the direction we must follow. After a few short leagues the river enters the swamp that has already swallowed two armies without trace. However, if we are fortunate we will find it much reduced. Perhaps we might find an easier way through it than the others did. With judicious use of the royal Hawk Seal we will be able to procure from the governor native guides to lead us. Come, let us cross to Qebui.'

The governor had been stranded at this outpost for the seven years of the drought. His name was Nara, and he was bent and yellowed after constant attacks of swamp-fever, but his garrison was in much better case. They were well fed with dhurra, and their horses were fat. Once Meren had shown him the royal seal and informed him of Taita's identity, Nara's hospitality was unbounded. He ushered Taita and Meren to the guesthouse in the fort and placed the best rooms at their disposal. He sent slaves to attend them and his own cooks to prepare their meals, then threw open his armoury for them to re-equip their men.

'Choose the horses you need from the remount depot. Tell my quarter-master how much dhurra and hay you require. There is no need to stint. We are well provisioned.'

When Meren inspected the men in their new quarters he found them well content. 'The rations are excellent. There are not many women in the town but those few are friendly. The horses and mules are filling their bellies with dhurra and green grass. No one has any complaint,' Hilto reported.

After his long exile Governor Nara was eager for news of the civilized world, and hungry for the company of sophisticated men. In particular Taita's learned dissertations fascinated him. Most evenings he invited him and Meren to dine with him. When Taita revealed to him their intention to ride south through the swamps, Nara looked grave.

'Nobody returns from the lands beyond the swamps. I believe implicitly that they lead to the end of the earth and those who go there are swept over the edge into the abyss.' Then, hastily, he adopted a more optimistic tone: these men bore the royal Hawk Seal and he should encourage them in their duty. 'Of course, there is no reason why you should not be the first to reach the end of the earth and return safely.

Your men are tough and you have the magus with you.' He bowed to Taita. 'What more can I do to assist you? You know you have only to ask.'

'Do you have native scouts to guide us?' Taita asked.

'Oh, yes,' Nara assured him. 'I have men who come from somewhere out there.'

'Do you know what tribe they belong to?'

'No, but they are tall, very black and tattooed with strange designs.'

'Then they are probably Shilluk,' Taita said, pleased. 'During the exodus General Lord Tanus recruited several regiments of the Shilluk. They are intelligent men and readily instructed. Although they are of cheerful disposition, they are fearsome fighters.'

'That would describe them well enough,' Governor Nara agreed. 'Whatever their tribe, they seem to know the country well. The two men I have in mind have worked with the army for some years, and have learnt a little of the Egyptian language. I will send them to you in the morning.'

In the dawn when Taita and Meren left their quarters they found two Nubians squatting against the wall of the courtyard. When they rose to their feet they towered even over Meren. Their lean frames were sheathed in flat, hard muscle, decorated with intricate patterns of ritual scarring, and their skin shone with oil or fat. They wore short skirts of animal skin, and carried long spears with barbed heads carved from bone.

'I see you. Men!' Taita greeted them in Shilluk. Men was a term of approbation, used only between warriors, and their handsome Nilotic faces lit with delight.

'I see you, ancient and wise one,' the taller man replied. Those also were terms of reverence and respect. Taita's silver beard had made a deep impression on them. 'But how is it that you speak our tongue so well?'

'Have you heard of Lion Liver?' Taita asked. The Shilluk considered the liver to be the seat of a man's courage.

'Hau! Hau!' They were astonished. It was the name that their tribe had given Lord Tanus when they served under him.

'Our grandfather spoke of Lion Liver, for we are cousins. He fought for that man in the cold mountains of the east. He told us that Lion Liver was the father of all warriors.'

'Lion Liver was my brother and my friend,' Taita told them.

'Then you are truly old, older even than our grandfather.' They were even more impressed.

'Come, let us sit in the shade and converse.' Taita led them to the enormous fig tree in the centre of the courtyard.

They squatted in the council circle, facing each other, and Taita questioned them closely. The elder cousin was their spokesman. His name was Nakonto, the Shilluk word for the short stabbing spear. 'For in battle I have slain many.' He was not boasting, but stating a fact. 'My cousin is Nontu for he is short.'

'All things are relative.' Taita smiled to himself: Nontu stood a full head taller than Meren.

'Where do you come from, Nakonto?'

'From beyond the swamps.' He indicated the south with his chin.

'Then you know the southern lands well?'

'They are our home.' For a moment he seemed wistful and nostalgic.

'Will you lead me to your home?'

'I dream every night of standing by the graves of my father and grandfather,' Nakonto said softly.

'Their spirits are calling you,' said Taita.

'You understand, old one.' Nakonto looked at him with deepening respect. 'When you leave Qebui, Nontu and I will go with you to show you the way.'

Two more full moons had shone down upon the pools of the Nile before the horses and their riders were fit to travel. On the night before their departure Taita dreamed of fishes in vast shoals, of every colour, shape and size.

You will find me hiding among the other fishes. Fenn's sweet, childish voice echoed through the dream. *I will be waiting for you.*

He woke in the dawn with feelings of happiness and soaring expectations.

When they called on him to take their leave, Governor Nara told Taita, 'I am sad to see you go, Magus. Your company has done much to lighten the monotony of my duties here at Qebui. I hope it is not long before I have the pleasure of welcoming you back. I have a parting gift for you that I think you will find most useful.' He took Taita's arm and led him out into the bright sunlight of the courtyard. There he presented him with five pack mules. Each carried two heavy sacks filled with glass beads. 'These baubles are much sought after by the primitive tribes of the interior. The men will sell their favourite wives for a handful.' He smiled. 'Although I cannot think of any reason why you would want to waste good beads on such unappealing goods as those women.'

When the column rode out from Qebui, the two Shilluk loped ahead, easily matching their speed to that of the trotting horses. They were tireless, keeping up the same pace for hour after hour. During the first two nights the men rode over wide scorched plains on the east bank of the wide dry riverbed. In the early morning of the third day when the column halted to make camp, Meren stood in his stirrups and gazed ahead.

In the slanting sunlight he made out a low green wall that stretched unbroken across their horizon.

When Taita called Nakonto, he came to stand beside Windsmoke's head.

'What you see, old one, are the first papyrus beds.'

'They are green,' Taita said.

'The swamps of the Great Sud never dry. The pools are too deep and screened from the sun by the reeds.'

'Will they block our way?'

Nakonto shrugged. 'We will reach the reed banks after one more night's march. Then we shall see if the waters have shrunk enough to let the horses pass, or if we must make a wide circle out towards the eastern hills.' He shook his head. 'That will make the way to the south much longer.'

As Nakonto had predicted, they reached the papyrus the next night. From the reed beds the men cut bundles of dried stalks and built low thatched shelters to protect themselves from the sun. Nakonto and Nontu vanished into the papyrus, and were gone for the next two days.

'Will we see them again,' Meren fretted, 'or have they run off to their village, like the wild animals they are?'

'They will return,' Taita assured him. 'I know these people well. They are loyal and trustworthy.'

In the middle of the second night Taita was roused by the challenge of the sentries, and heard Nakonto reply from the papyrus stands. Then the two Shilluk materialized out of the darkness into which they had blended so perfectly.

'The way through the swamps is open,' Nakonto reported.

In the dawn the two guides led them into the papyrus. From there onwards it was no longer possible for even Nakonto to find the way in darkness, so they were forced to travel by day. The swamps were an alien, forbidding world. Even from horseback they could not see over the tops of the fluffy seedheads of the papyrus. They had to stand in the stirrups to view the undulating green ocean that stretched away before them to the infinite horizon. Over it hovered flocks of water-fowl, and the air was filled with the sound of their wings and their plaintive calls. Occasionally large beasts crashed away unseen, rippling the tops of the reeds. They could not guess at their species. The Shilluk glanced at the tracks they left in the mud, and Taita translated their descriptions. 'That was a herd of buffalo, great black wild cattle,' or 'That was a water goat. A strange brown creature with spiral horns that lives in the water. It has long hoofs to help it swim like a water rat.'

The ground under the papyrus was mostly wet, sometimes merely damp but often the water covered the horses' fetlocks. Nevertheless the little colt, Whirlwind, was well able to keep up with his dam. Pools were hidden in the reeds: some of these were small but others were extensive lagoons. The Shilluk, even though they were unable to see over the reeds, unerringly steered around or between them. The column was never forced to turn back to find an alternative route. When it was time to make camp each evening Nakonto was able to lead them to openings in the papyrus where the ground was dry. They built their cooking fires from bundles of dried stalks, and were careful not to allow the flames to escape into the standing reeds. The horses and mules wandered through the stagnant pools to eat the grasses and plants that grew in them.

Each evening Nakonto took his spear, waded out into one of the pools and stood poised like a hunting heron. When one of the big catfish swam close enough he would skewer it cleanly and lift it struggling, tail whipping, out of the water. In the meantime Nontu plaited a loose basket of reeds and placed it over his head, his eyes visible through the gaps in the weave. Then he left the bank and submerged his entire body until only his head, disguised by the reed basket, showed above the surface. He moved with infinite patience and caution to a flock of wild duck. When he was within range he reached out beneath the surface, grabbed a bird's legs and plucked it under. It did not have a chance to squawk before he had wrung its neck. In this way he could take five or six birds from a flock before the others became suspicious and took off with loud honks and clattering wings. Most evenings the company dined on fresh fish and roasted wild duck.

Stinging insects plagued men and animals. As soon as the sun set they rose in buzzing clouds from the surface of the pools, and the troopers huddled miserably in the smoke of the campfires to avoid their onslaught. In the morning their faces were swollen and spotted with bites.

They had been travelling for twelve days before the first man showed symptoms of swamp-sickness. Soon, one after another, his comrades succumbed to it. They suffered from blinding headaches and uncontrollable shivering, even in the humid heat, and their skin was hot to the touch. But Meren would not break the march to let them recover. Each morning the stronger troopers helped the invalids to mount, then rode alongside them to hold them in their saddles. At night many babbled deliriously. In the morning dead bodies lay round the fires. On the twentieth day Captain Tonka died. They scraped a shallow grave for him in the mud, and rode on.

Some of those struck down threw off the disease, although their faces were left yellowed and they were weak and exhausted. A few, including Taita and Meren, were unaffected by the sickness.

Meren urged the fever-racked men on: 'The sooner we escape from these terrible swamps and their poisonous mists, the sooner you will recover your health.' Then he confided to Taita, 'I worry ceaselessly that should we lose the Shilluk to the swamp-sickness or they desert us, we will be helpless. We will never escape from this dreary wilderness and shall all perish here.'

'These swamps are their home. They are shielded from the diseases that abound here,' Taita assured him. 'They will stay with us to the end.'

As they travelled on southwards, vast new expanses of papyrus opened before them, then closed behind them. They seemed trapped like insects in honey, never able to break free despite their violent struggles. The papyrus imprisoned them, ingested them and suffocated them. Its bland monotony wearied and dulled their minds. Then, on the thirty-sixth day of the march, there appeared at the limit of their forward vision a cluster of dark dots.

'Are those trees?' Taita called to the Shilluk. Nakonto sprang on to Nontu's shoulders and stood to his full height, balancing easily. It was a position he often adopted when he needed to see over the reeds.

'Nay, ancient one,' he replied. 'Those are huts of the Luo.'

'Who are the Luo?'

'They are hardly men. They are animals who live in these swamps, eating fish, snakes and crocodiles. They build their hovels on poles, such as those you see. They plaster their bodies with mud, ash and other filth to keep off the insects. They are savage and wild. We kill them when we find them for they steal our cattle. They drive the beasts they have stolen from us into this fastness of theirs and eat them. They are not true men but hyenas and jackals.' He spat in contempt.

Taita knew that the Shilluk were nomadic herders. They had a deep love for their cattle, and would never kill them. Instead they carefully punctured a vein in a beast's throat, caught the blood that flowed in a calabash, and when they had sufficient they sealed the tiny wound with a handful of clay. They mixed it with cow's milk and drank it. 'That is why we are so tall and strong, such mighty warriors. That is why the swamp-sickness never affects us,' the Shilluk would explain.

They reached the Luo encampment to find that the huts sitting high on their stilts were deserted. However, there were signs of recent occupation. Some of the fish heads and scales beside the rack on which they smoked their catch were quite fresh, and had not yet been eaten by fresh-water crabs or the buzzards that perched on the roofs, and live coals still glowed in the fluffy white ash of the fires. The area beyond the encampment that the Luo had used as a latrine was littered with fresh excrement. Nakonto stood by it. 'They were here this very morning. They are still close by. Probably they are watching us from the reeds.'

They left the village and rode on for another seemingly interminable distance. Late in the afternoon Nakonto led them to an opening that was slightly higher than the surrounding mudbanks, a dry island in the wastes. They tethered the horses to wooden pegs driven into the earth, and fed them crushed dhurra meal in leather nosebags. Meanwhile Taita tended the sick troopers, and the men prepared their dinner. Soon after nightfall they were asleep around the fires. Only the sentries remained awake.

The fires had long burned out, and the troopers were deep in slumber when suddenly they were shocked awake. Pandemonium swept through the camp. There were shouts and screams, the thunder of galloping hoofs, and splashing from the pools around the island. Taita sprang up from his mat and ran to Windsmoke. She was rearing and plunging, trying to pull the peg that held her out of the ground, as most of the other horses had. Taita grabbed her halter rope and held her down. With relief he saw that the foal, shivering with terror, was still at her side.

Strange dark shapes flitted around them, prancing, screaming and ululating shrilly, poking at the horses with spears, goading them to break away. The frenzied animals plunged and fought their ropes. One of the figures charged at Taita and thrust at him with his spear. Taita knocked it aside with his staff and drove the point into his assailant's throat. The man dropped and lay still.

Meren and his captains rallied their troops and rushed in with bared swords. They managed to cut down a few attackers before the others vanished into the night.

'Follow them! Don't let them get away with the horses!' Meren bellowed.

'Do not let your men go after them in the dark,' Nakonto called urgently to Taita. 'The Luo are treacherous. They will lead them into the pools and ambush them. We must wait for the light of day before we follow.'

Taita hurried to restrain Meren, who accepted the warning reluctantly for his fighting blood was up. He called his men back.

They assessed their losses. All four sentries' throats had been cut, and another legionary had received a spear wound in the thigh. Three Luo had been killed, and another was badly wounded. He lay groaning in his blood and the vile matter that dribbled from the stab wound through his guts.

'Finish him!' Meren ordered, and one of his men decapitated the man with a swing of his battleaxe. Eighteen horses were missing.

'We cannot afford to lose so many,' Taita said.

'We won't,' Meren promised grimly. 'We will retrieve them – on Isis's teats, I swear it.'

Taita examined one of the Luo corpses in the firelight. It was the body of a short, stocky man, with a brutal ape-like face. He had a sloping forehead, thick lips and small close-set eyes. He was naked, except for a leather belt round his waist from which hung a pouch. It contained a collection of magical charms, knuckle bones and teeth, some of which were human. Around his neck, on a lanyard of plaited bark, hung a flint knife caked with the blood of one of the sentries. It was crudely fashioned, but when Taita tested the edge on the dead man's shoulder it split the skin with little pressure. The Luo's body was coated with a thick plaster of ash and river clay. On his chest and face were traced primitive designs in white clay and red ochre, spots, circles and wavy lines. He stank of woodsmoke, rotten fish and his own feral odour.

'A repulsive creature,' Meren spat.

Taita moved to attend to the wounded trooper. The spear thrust was deep and he knew it would mortify. The man would be dead within hours, but Taita showed him a reassuring face.

In the meantime Meren was picking his strongest and fittest troopers for the punitive column to follow the thieves. The rest of the party would be left to guard the baggage, the remaining horses and the sick. Before it was fully light the two

Shilluk went out into the reedbeds to find the outward spoor of the raiders. They returned before sunrise.

'The Luo dogs rounded up the runaway horses and drove them in a herd towards the south,' Nakonto reported to Taita. 'We found the bodies of two more and another who was wounded but still living. He is dead now.' Nakonto touched the hilt of the heavy bronze knife that hung from his belt. 'If your men are ready, ancient and exalted one, we will follow immediately.'

Taita would not take the grey mare on the raid: Whirlwind was still too young for hard riding, and Windsmoke had been wounded in her hindquarters by a Luo spear, fortunately not gravely. Instead he mounted his spare horse. When they rode out, Windsmoke whinnied after him, as though expressing indignation at having been passed over.

The hoofs of the eighteen stolen horses had beaten a wide road through the reedbeds. The bare footprints of the Luo overlay the tracks of the horses they were driving. The Shilluk ran easily after them, and the horsemen followed at a trot. The trail led them south all that day. When the sun set, they rested to allow the horses to recover, but when the moon rose it shed sufficient light for them to go on. They rode all night with only short breaks to rest. At dawn they made out another feature in the distance ahead. After so long in the monotonous seas of papyrus their eyes rejoiced to behold even this low dark line.

Nakonto sprang on to his cousin's shoulders and stared ahead. Then he grinned at Taita, his teeth shining like pearls in the early light of day. 'Old man, what you see is the end of the swamps. Those are trees, and they stand on dry land.'

Taita passed on this news to Meren and the troopers, who shouted, laughed and thumped each other's backs. Meren let them rest again for they had ridden hard.

From their tracks Nakonto judged that the Luo were not far ahead. As they rode forward the line of trees loomed larger and darker, but they could not make out any sign of human habitation. At last they dismounted and went forward leading their mounts, so that the riders' heads would not show above the tops of the papyrus. It was long after midday before they stopped again. Only a thin strip of papyrus screened them now, then even that ended abruptly against a low bank of pale earth. It was no more than two cubits high, and beyond it lay pastures of short green grass, and groves of tall trees. Taita recognized Kigelia sausage trees, with their massive hanging seedpods, and sycamore figs, with the yellow fruit growing directly on the fat grey trunks. Most of the other species were foreign to him.

From the cover of the groves they could clearly make out the tracks that the stolen horses' hoofs had left as they climbed the soft earth bank. However, there was no sign of the animals in the open pasture beyond. They scrutinized the tree line.

'What are those?' Meren pointed out distant movement among the trees and a fine haze of dust.

Nakonto shook his head. 'Buffalo, a small herd. No horses. Nontu and I will scout ahead. You must remain hidden here.' The two Shilluk moved forward into the papyrus and disappeared. Although Taita and Meren watched carefully they did not see them again, not even a glimpse of them crossing the open pasture.

They moved back from the edge of the papyrus, found a small patch of open, drier ground, filled the nosebags and let the horses feed while they stretched out to rest. Taita wrapped his shawl round his head, placed his staff at hand and lay back. He was very tired and his legs ached from trudging through the mud. He drifted over the edge of sleep.

'Be of good heart, Taita, I am close.' Her voice, a faint whisper, was so clear and the tone so unmistakably Fenn's that he jerked awake and sat up. He looked around quickly, expectantly, but saw only the horses, mules, the resting men and the eternal papyrus. He sank back again.

It was some time before sleep returned, but he was weary and at last he was dreaming of fishes that leapt from the waters around him and sparkled in the sunlight. Although they were myriad, none was the fish he knew was there. Then the shoals opened and he saw it. Its scales sparkled like precious stones, its butterfly tail was long and lithe, the aura that surrounded it ethereal and sublime. As he watched, it transmuted into human shape, the body of a young girl. She glided through the water, her long naked legs held together, pumping from her hips with the grace of a dolphin. The sunlight from above dappled her pale body and her long bright hair streamed out behind her. She rolled on to her back and smiled up at him through the water. Tiny silver bubbles streamed from her nostrils. 'I am close, darling Taita. Soon we will be together. Very soon.'

Before he could reply a voice and a rough touch shattered the vision. He tried to cling to the rapture, but it was torn from him. He opened his eyes and sat up.

Beside him squatted Nakonto. 'We have found the horses and the Luo jackals,' he said. 'Now comes the killing time.'

They waited until nightfall before they left the conceal-ment of the papyrus and climbed the low earth bank on to the open pasture. The horses' hoofs made almost no sound on the soft sand. Through the darkness Nakonto led them to the trees that were silhouetted against the stars. Once they were under the spreading, protecting branches, he turned parallel to the edge of the swamp. They rode in silence for only a short while before he turned into the forest, where they had to bend low on the backs of the horses to avoid the overhanging foliage. They had not gone far when, above the treetops ahead, the night sky was suffused with a rosy glow. Nakonto led them towards it. Now they could hear drums beating a frenetic rhythm. As they moved towards it, the sound grew louder, until the night throbbed like the heart of the earth. Closer still, a chorus of discordant chanting joined the pounding of the drums.

Nakonto stopped them at the edge of the forest. Taita

rode up beside Meren and they looked across an expanse of cleared ground to a large village of primitive thatch and mud-daub huts lit by the flames of four huge bonfires, sparks streaming up in torrents. Rows of smoking racks stood beyond the last huts, covered with the split carcasses of fish, whose scales glittered like a sheet of silver in the firelight. Around the bonfires dozens of human bodies twisted, leapt and spun. They were painted from scalp to heels in glaring white, decorated with weird designs in black, ochre and red mud. Taita realized they were of both sexes, all naked under their coating of white clay and ash. As they danced, they chanted in a barbaric cadence, a sound like the baying of a pack of wild animals.

Suddenly, from out of the shadows, another band of prancing and cavorting Luo dragged one of the stolen horses. All of the horsemen recognized her, a bay mare named Starling. The Luo had knotted a bark rope round her neck, and five of them were heaving on it as a dozen more shoved at her flanks and hindquarters or goaded her cruelly with pointed sticks, blood glistening from the wounds they inflicted. One of the Luo lifted a heavy wooden club in both hands, and rushed at her. He aimed a heavy blow at her head and the club cracked against her skull. She dropped instantly to kick spasmodically; her bowels voided in a liquid green rush. The painted Luo swarmed over her carcass, brandishing their flint knives. They hacked off lumps of her still twitching flesh and crammed it into their mouths. Blood dribbled down their chins to run across their painted torsos. They were a pack of wild dogs, fighting and howling over a kill. The watching troopers growled with outrage.

Meren glanced sideways at Taita, who nodded. 'Left and right wheel into extended order.' Meren gave the command, low but clear. On each flank the two columns opened like wings into an extended line. As soon as they were in position Meren called again: 'Detachment will charge! Present arms!' They cleared their swords from the sheaths. 'Forward march! Trot! Gallop! Charge!'

They swept forward in close formation, the horses running shoulder to shoulder. The Luo were in such frenzy that they did not see the troopers coming until they burst into the village. Then they tried to scatter and run, but it was too late. The horses swept over them, crushing them beneath their hoofs. The swords rose and fell, the blades thumping through bone and flesh. The two Shilluk were at the front of the charge, howling, stabbing, leaping and stabbing again.

Taita saw Nakonto send a spear clean through the body of one, so that the point stood out between the Luo's shoulder-blades. When Nakonto cleared it, it seemed to suck out with it every drop of blood from the man's body, a black spray in the firelight.

A painted woman with pendulous dugs that hung to her navel raised both arms to cover her head. Meren stood in his stirrups and hacked off one of her arms at the elbow, then swung the blade again and split her unprotected head like a ripe melon. Her mouth was still crammed with raw meat, which spewed out with her death wail. The troopers kept their tight formation, riding down the Luo, their sword arms rising and falling in a deadly rhythm. The Shilluk caught those who tried to break away. The drummers, seated before the long, hollowed-out trunks of the Kigelia tree, were in such a transport that they did not even look up. They continued beating out their frenzied rhythm with their wooden clubs until the horsemen rode over to cut them down where they sat. They fell, writhing and bleeding, on to their drums.

At the far side of the village Meren checked the charge. He looked back and saw no one still standing. The ground around Starling's carcass was covered with the painted naked bodies. A few of the wounded were trying to crawl away. Others were groaning and thrashing in the dust. The two Shilluk were running among them, stabbing and howling in murderous ecstasy.

'Help the Shilluk finish them!' Meren ordered. His men dismounted and went swiftly over the killing ground, despatching any who showed signs of life.

Taita reined in alongside Meren. He had not been in the first rank of the charge, but had followed close behind. 'I saw a few run into the huts,' he said. 'Root them out, but don't kill them all. Nakonto might glean good information from them about the country ahead.'

Meren shouted the order to his captains, who went from hut to hut, ransacking them. Two or three Luo women ran out, wailing, with young children. They were hustled into the centre of the village where the Shilluk guides shouted orders to them in their own language. They forced them to squat in rows with their hands clasped on top of their heads. The children clung to their mothers, tears gleaming on their terrified faces.

'Now we must find the surviving horses,' Meren shouted. 'They cannot have slaughtered and eaten them all. Search there first.' He pointed into the dark forest from which they had seen the butchers drag Starling to the slaughter. Hilto took his troop with him and rode into the dark. Suddenly a horse whinnied.

'They are here!' Hilto shouted happily. 'Bring torches!'

The men tore thatch from the roofs of the huts and made crude torches with it, lit them and followed Hilto into the forest. Leaving five men to guard the captured women and children, Meren and Taita followed the torch-bearers. Ahead, Hilto and his men called directions, until in the thickening light they made out the herd of stolen animals.

Taita and Meren dismounted and ran to them. 'How many are left?' Meren asked urgently.

'Eleven only. We have lost six to the jackals,' Hilto replied. The Luo had tied them all to the same tree on cruelly short ropes. They could not even stretch their necks to the ground.

'They have not been allowed to graze or drink,' Hilto shouted indignantly. 'What kind of beasts are these people?'

'Free them,' Meren ordered. Three troopers dismounted and ran to obey. But the horses were so crowded together that they had to push between them.

Suddenly a man bellowed with outrage and pain. 'Beware!

One of the Luo is hiding here. He has a spear and has wounded me.'

Suddenly there were the sounds of a scuffle, followed by a high-pitched childish scream from among the horses' legs.

'Catch him! Don't let him get away.'

'What is happening there?' Meren demanded.

'A little savage is hiding here. He is the one who speared me.'

At that a child darted out from among the horses, carrying a light assegai. A trooper tried to grab him but the child stabbed at him, and vanished into the darkness in the direction of the village. Taita had only a brief glimpse of him before he was gone, but he sensed something different about him. The Luo, even the children, were stocky and bow-legged, but this one was as slender as a papyrus stem, and his legs were elegantly straight. He ran with the grace of a frightened gazelle. Abruptly Taita realized that beneath the white clay and tribal designs, the child was female, and he was struck by an intense sensation of *déjà vu*: 'I swear to all the gods I have seen her before,' he murmured to himself.

'When I catch the little swine, I'll kill him slowly!' the wounded trooper shouted, as he came out from among the horses whence he had flushed the child. There was a spear wound in his forearm, and blood dripped from his fingertips.

'No!' Taita shouted urgently. 'It is a girl. I want her taken alive. She has run back towards the village. Surround the area and search the huts again. She will have gone to ground in one.'

Leaving a few men to deal with the recovered horses, they galloped back to the village. Meren threw a cordon round the huts, and Taita questioned Nakonto and Nontu, who were guarding the women and their children. 'Did you see a child run this way? About this height and covered, like the rest of them, with white clay?'

They shook their heads.

'Apart from these,' Nakonto indicated the wailing captives, 'we have seen no one.'

'She can't have gone far,' Meren assured Taita. 'We have the village surrounded. She cannot escape. We will find her.' He sent Habari's platoon in to carry out a hut-by-hut search. When he came back to Taita he asked, 'Why is the murderous brat important to you, Magus?'

'I am not certain, but I think she is not one of the Luo. She is different. She might even be Egyptian.'

'I doubt that, Magus. She is a savage. Naked and covered with paint.'

'Catch her,' Taita snapped.

Meren knew that tone, and hurried to take command of the search. The men went slowly and cautiously, none wanting to risk a spear thrust in his belly. By the time they were half-way through the village dawn was breaking over the forest. Taita was troubled and restless. Something gnawed at him, like a rat in the granary of his memory. There was something he must remember.

The dawn breeze veered into the south, wafting to him the stench of half-rotten fish from the smoking racks. He moved away to avoid it and the memory he was seeking rushed in.

Where else would you search for a moon fish? You will find me hiding among the other fishes. It was the voice of Fenn, speaking through the mouth of the stone image of the goddess. Was the child they were pursuing a soul caught up in the wheel of creation? The reincarnation of someone who had lived long ago?

'She promised to return,' he said aloud. 'Is it possible – or does my own longing delude me?' And then he answered himself: 'There are things that surpass the wildest imagining of mankind. Nothing is impossible.'

Taita glanced around swiftly to make certain that nobody was watching him, then moved casually to the edge of the village and walked to the smoking racks. As soon as he was out of sight his attitude changed. He stood like a dog testing the air for the scent of its quarry. His nerves jumped. She was very close, her presence almost palpable. Holding his staff at the ready to fend off a stroke from her assegai he moved forward. Every few paces he went down on one knee to try to see under or between the racks on which the layers of fish were packed densely together. At intervals bundles of firewood and drifting clouds of smoke obstructed his view. He had to circle each wood-pile as he came to it to make certain she was not hiding behind one, which slowed his progress. By now the rays of the early sun were flooding the village. Then as he crept round another wood-pile he heard a stealthy movement ahead. He peered round the corner. Nobody was there. He glanced at the ground and saw the prints of her small bare feet in the grey ash. She was aware that she was being stalked, moving just ahead of him, darting from one wood-pile to the next.

'There is no sign of the brat. She is not here,' he called, to an imaginary companion, and started back towards the village. He went noisily, tapping the racks with his staff, then doubled back in a wide circle, moving swiftly and silently.

He reached a position close to where he had last seen her footprints, and squatted behind a wood-pile to wait for her. He was alert for any movement or the faintest sound. Now that she had lost sight of him, she would become nervous and change her position again. He threw a spell of concealment round himself. Then, from behind the screen, he reached out for her, searching the ether.

'Ah!' he murmured, as he descried her. She was very close, but not moving. He sensed her fear and uncertainty: she did not know where he was. He saw that she was cowering under one of the wood-piles. Now he focused all his power on her, sending out impulses to lure her towards him.

'Magus! Where are you?' Meren called, from the direction of the village. When he received no answer, his voice rose urgently. 'Magus, do you hear me?' Then he was coming towards where Taita waited.

That's right, Taita encouraged him silently. Keep coming. You will force her to move. Ah! There she goes.

The girl was moving again. She had crawled out from under the wood and was scurrying in his direction, running ahead of Meren.

Come, little one. He tightened the tentacles of the spell round her. Come to me.

'Magus!' Meren called again, much closer. The girl appeared in front of Taita, at the corner of the wood-pile. She paused to glance back towards where Meren's voice had come from and he saw that she was quivering with terror. She looked in his direction. Her face was a hideous mask of clay, her hair built up in a mass on top of her head with a mixture of what looked like clay and acacia gum. Her eyes were so bloodshot from the smoke of the fires and the dye that had run from her hair that he could not make out the colour of the irises. Her teeth had been deliberately blackened. All of the Luo women they had captured had blackened their teeth and wore the same ugly hairstyle. Clearly, it was their primitive idea of beauty.

As she stood there, terrified, her head cocked, Taita opened his Inner Eye. Her aura sprang up around her, enveloping her in a sublimely magnificent cloak of living light, just as he had seen it in his dreams. Beneath the grotesque coating of clay and filth, this sorry, bedraggled creature was Fenn. She had returned to him, as she had promised. The emotion that swept over him was more powerful than any he had experienced in his long life. It surpassed in intensity the grief that had overwhelmed him at her death, which had ended her other life, when he had removed her viscera and wrapped her corpse in the linen bandages and laid her in the stone sarcophagus.

Now she was restored to him at the same age she had been when she had first been placed in his care all those bleak, lonely years ago. All that grief and sorrow was paid off with this single coin of joy, to which every cord, muscle and nerve in his body resonated.

The cloak of concealment he had spun round himself was disturbed by it. The child picked it up at once. She turned and stared in his direction, her bloodshot eyes enormous in the grotesque mask. She sensed his presence, but could not see him. He realized that she possessed the power. As yet her psychic gift was undeveloped and untutored, but he knew that, under his loving instruction, it would in time match his own. The rising sun shot a beam into her eyes, and their true lustre glowed in the deepest shade of green. Fenn green.

Meren was running in their direction, his footsteps pounding on the hard earth. There was only one escape route open to Fenn: down the narrow passage between the wood-pile and the smoking racks. She ran straight into Taita's arms. As they closed round her she shrieked in shock and renewed terror and dropped the assegai. Although she struggled and clawed at his eyes, Taita held her close to his chest. Her fingernails were long and ragged, black dirt was caked under them and they raised bloody welts across his forehead and cheeks. Still holding her with one arm circled round her waist, he took her arms one at a time and trapped them between their bodies. Now that she was helpless he leant close to her face and stared into her eyes, taking control of her. Instinctively she knew what he was doing and pushed forward to meet him, but just in time he divined her intention and jerked his head back sharply. Her sharp black teeth snapped shut a finger's breadth from the tip of his nose.

'Light of my eyes, I still have need of this old nose of mine. If you are hungry I will provide tastier fare.' He smiled.

At that moment Meren burst into sight, his expression of consternation and alarm. 'Magus!' he shouted. 'Do not let that filthy vixen near you. She has already tried to murder one man and now she will do you some grave injury.' He rushed towards them. 'Let me get my hands on her. I will take her to the swamp and drown her in the nearest pool.'

'Back, Meren!' Taita did not raise his voice. 'Don't touch her.'

Meren checked. 'But, Magus, she will—'

'She will do no such thing. Go, Meren. Leave us alone. We love each other. I just have to convince her of it.'

Still Meren hesitated.

'Go, I say. At once.'

Meren went.

Taita looked into Fenn's eyes and smiled reassuringly. 'Fenn, I have waited so long for you.' He was using the voice of power, but she resisted him fiercely. She spat, and bubbles of her saliva ran down his face to drip off his chin.

'You were not so strong when we first met. You were sullen and rebellious, oh, yes, indeed you were, but not as strong as you are now.' He chuckled and she blinked. No Luo had ever emitted such a sound. A spark of interest flashed for an instant in the green depths of her eyes, then she glared at him.

'You were so beautiful then, but look at you now.' His voice still carried the hypnotic inflection. 'You are a vision from the void.' He made it sound like an endearment. 'Your hair is filthy.' He stroked it but she tried to duck. It was not possible to guess the true colour of her hair under the thick clay and acacia gum, but he kept his voice calm and his smile reassuring as a stream of red lice crawled out of the clotted mass and climbed up his arm.

'By Ahura Maasda and the Truth, you stink worse than any polecat,' he told her. 'It will take a month of scrubbing to get down to your skin.' She wriggled and squirmed to be free. 'Now you are rubbing your filth on to me. I shall be in no better case than you by the time I have quietened you. We shall have to camp away from Meren and his troopers. Even rough soldiers will not withstand our combined odour.' He kept speaking: the sense of the words was unimportant, but the tone and inflection gradually lulled her. He felt her begin to relax, and the hostile light in her green eyes faded. She blinked almost sleepily, and he relaxed his grip. At that she shook herself awake, and the malevolence flared again. He had to hold her hard as she renewed her struggles.

'You are indomitable.' He let the admiration and approval sound in his voice. 'You have the heart of a warrior, and the determination of the goddess you once were.' This time she quietened more readily. The migrating lice nipped Taita under his tunic, but he ignored them and continued to talk.

'Let me tell you about yourself, Fenn. You were once my ward, as you have become again. You were the daughter of an evil man who cared little for you. To this day I cannot fathom how he sired a lovely thing like you. You were beautiful, Fenn, beyond the telling of it. Under the fleas, lice and dirt I know you are still.' Slowly her resistance faded as he related her childhood to her in loving detail, and recounted some of the funny things she had done or said. When he laughed now she looked at him with interest rather than anger. She began to blink again. This time when he relaxed his grip she did not attempt to escape but sat quietly in his lap. The sun had reached its zenith when at last he stood up. She looked up at him solemnly and he reached down to take her hand. She did not pull away.

'Come along, now. If you are not hungry, I certainly am.' He set off towards the village and she trotted at his side.

Meren had set up a temporary camp well away from the village: in the sun the Luo corpses would soon begin to rot and the area become uninhabitable. As they approached the camp, he hurried to meet them. 'I am glad to see you, Magus. I thought the vixen had done away with you,' he shouted. Fenn hid behind Taita and clung to one of his legs as Meren came up to them. 'By the wounded eye of Horus, she stinks. I can smell her from here.'

'Lower your voice,' Taita ordered. 'Ignore her. Do not look at her like that or you will undo my hard work in an instant. Go ahead of us to the camp and warn your men not to stare at her or alarm her. Have food ready for her.'

'So now we have a wild filly to break?' Meren shook his head ruefully.

'Oh, no! You underestimate the task ahead of us,' Taita assured him.

Taita and Fenn sat in the shade under the great sausage tree in the centre of the camp, and one of the men brought food. Fenn tasted the dhurra cake gingerly, but after the first mouthfuls she ate ravenously. Then she turned her attention to the cold slices of wild duck breast. She stuffed them into her mouth so rapidly that she choked and coughed.

'I can see you need instruction in manners before you are fit to dine with Pharaoh,' Taita observed, as she gnawed the duck bones with her black teeth. When she had stuffed her skinny belly to bursting point, he called for Nakonto. Like most of the men, he had been watching from a discreet distance, but he came to squat in front of them. Fenn huddled closer to Taita and stared at the huge black man with renewed suspicion.

'Ask the child her name. I am sure she speaks and understands Luo,' Taita instructed, and Nakonto spoke a few words to her. It was clear that she understood him, but her face set and her mouth closed in a hard, stubborn line. He tried for a while longer to induce her to answer him, but Fenn would not budge.

'Fetch one of the captured Luo women,' Taita told Nakonto. He left them briefly, and when he returned he was dragging with him a wailing old woman from the village.

'Ask her if she knows this girl,' Taita said.

Nakonto had to speak sharply to the woman before she would cease whining and weeping, but at last she made a lengthy statement. 'She knows her,' Nakonto translated. 'She says she is a devil. They drove her out of the village, but she lived close by in the forest, and she has brought bad witchcraft on the tribe. They believe it was she who sent you to kill their men.'

'So the child is not of her tribe?' Taita asked.

The old woman's reply was a vehement denial. 'No, she is

a stranger. One of the women found her floating in the swamps in a tiny boat made of reeds.' Nakonto described a papyrus cradle such as Egyptian peasant women wove for their infants. 'She brought the devil to the village and named her Khona Manzi, which means "the one from the waters". The woman was childless and for that reason had been rejected by her husband. She took this strange creature as her own. She dressed her ugly hair in the decent fashion, and covered her fish-white body with clay and ash to protect her from the sun and the insects, as is fitting and customary. She fed her and cared for her.' The old woman looked at Fenn with evident distaste.

'Where is this woman?' Taita asked.

'She has died of some strange disease that the devil child brought down upon her with witchcraft.'

'Is that why you drove her out of the village?'

'Not for that reason alone. She brought many other afflictions upon us. In the same season that she came into the village the waters failed and the swamp, which is our home, began to shrivel and die. It was the devil child's work.' The old woman gobbled with outrage. 'She brought sickness upon us that blinded our children, made many of our young women barren and our men impotent.'

'All this from one child?' Taita asked.

Nakonto translated the woman's reply. 'She is no ordinary child. She is a devil and a sorcerer. She led our enemies to our secret places, and caused them to triumph over us, just as she has now brought you to attack us.'

Then Fenn spoke for the first time. Her voice was filled with bitter anger.

'What does she say?' Taita asked.

'She says that the woman lies. She has done none of those things. She does not know how to make witchcraft. She loved the woman who was her mother, and she did not kill her.' The old woman replied to this with equal venom, and then the two were screeching at each other.

For a while Taita listened to them with mild amusement, then told Nakonto, 'Take the woman back to the village. She is no match for the child.'

Nakonto laughed. 'You have found a lion cub as your new pet, old one. We will all learn to fear her.'

As soon as they were gone Fenn quietened.

'Come,' Taita invited her. She recognized his meaning, if not the word, and stood up at once. As he walked away she ran after him and took his hand again. The gesture was so unaffected that Taita was deeply moved. She began to chatter naturally, so he answered her although he did not understand a word she said. He went to his saddle-bag and found the leather roll of his surgical instruments. He paused only to speak to Meren: 'Send Nontu back to fetch the rest of the men and horses out of the swamps and bring them here. Keep Nakonto with us for he is our eyes and our tongue.'

Then, with Fenn still in tow, he went down to the edge of the swamp and found a clear opening among the reeds. He waded out knee deep, then sat down in the lukewarm water. Fenn watched him from the bank with interest. When he splashed handfuls of water over his head she burst out laughing for the first time.

'Come,' he called, and she jumped into the pool without hesitation. He sat her between his knees with her back to him and poured water over her head. The mask of filth began to dissolve and run down her neck and over her shoulders. Gradually patches of pale skin started to show through, speckled with louse bites. When he tried to wash the filth out of her hair, the congealed gum defied his best efforts to dislodge it. Fenn wriggled and protested as he pulled at her scalp. 'Very well. We will deal with that later.' He stood her up and began to scrub her with handfuls of sand from the bottom of the pool. She giggled when he tickled her ribs, and tried half-heartedly to escape, but she was still giggling when he pulled her back. She was enjoying his attention. When at last he had cleaned away the superficial layers of dirt he fetched a bronze

razor from the surgical roll and started on her scalp. With the
utmost care he began to scrape away the matted hair.

She bore it stoically, even when the razor nicked her and
drew blood. He had to keep stropping the edge for her matted
hair blunted it after only a few strokes. It fell away in clumps,
and gradually he exposed her pale scalp. When at last he had
finished he laid aside the razor and studied her. 'What big ears
you have!' he exclaimed. Her bald head seemed too large for
the thin neck it was balanced upon. In contrast her eyes were
even bigger, and her ears stuck out at each side of her head
like those of a baby elephant. 'Looked at from every angle and
in any light, and giving you the benefit in any area of doubt,
you are still an ugly little thing.' She recognized the affection
in his tone and smiled at him trustingly with the blackened
teeth. He felt tears sting his eyelids, and wondered at himself.
'When did you last find a tear to shed, you old fool?' He
turned away from her and reached for the flask that contained
his special salve, a blend of oils and herbs, his sovereign cure
for all minor cuts, bruises, sores and other ailments. He
massaged it into her scalp and she leant her head against him,
closing her eyes like a kitten being petted. He kept talking to
her softly, and every now and then she opened her eyes,
looked up at his face, then closed them again. When he had
finished they climbed out of the pool, and sat together. While
the sun and the hot breeze dried their bodies, Taita selected a
pair of bronze forceps and went over every inch of her. The
herbal salve had killed most of the lice and other vermin, but
he found many still stuck to her skin. He plucked them off
her, and crushed the life out of them. To Fenn's delight, they
made a satisfying pop as they exploded in a spot of blood.
When he had removed the last one, she took the forceps from
him, and set about the insects that had changed their abode
from her to him. Her eye was sharper and her fingers were
more nimble than his as she ruffled through his silver beard
and inspected his armpits for signs of life. Then she searched
lower down. She was a savage and showed no inhibition as

she ran light fingers over the silver scar at the base of his belly where he had been castrated. Taita had always tried to conceal this mark of shame from other eyes, except those of Lostris when she was alive. Now she was alive again and he felt no embarrassment. Yet although her actions were innocent and natural, he removed her hand.

'I think we can say that, once again, we know each other well.' Taita gave his considered opinion when she had picked him clean.

'Taita!' He touched his chest. She stared at him solemnly. 'Taita.' He repeated the gesture.

She had understood. 'Taita!' She prodded his chest with a finger, then bubbled with laughter. 'Taita!'

'Fenn!' He touched the tip of her nose. 'Fenn!'

She thought that an even better joke. She shook her head vigorously, and slapped her own skinny chest. 'Khona Manzi!' she said.

'No!' Taita argued. 'Fenn!'

'Fenn?' she repeated uncertainly. 'Fenn?' Her accent was perfect, as though she had been born to speak the Egyptian language. She thought about it for a moment, then smiled and agreed, 'Fenn!'

'*Bak-her!* Clever girl, Fenn!'

'*Bak-her,*' she repeated faithfully, and slapped her chest again. 'Clever girl, Fenn.' Her precocity amazed and delighted him anew.

When they returned to the camp Meren and all the men stared at Fenn in wonder, although they had been warned not to do so.

'Sweet Isis, she is one of us,' Meren cried. 'She is not a savage at all, though she behaves like one. She is an Egyptian.' He hurried to search his saddle-bags and found a spare tunic, which he brought to Taita.

'It is almost clean,' he explained, 'and it will serve to cover her decently.'

Fenn regarded the garment as though it were a venomous serpent. She was accustomed to nakedness and tried to escape as Taita lifted it over her head. It took perseverance but at last he dressed her. The tunic was far too large, and the hem hung almost to her ankles, but the men gathered round her and loudly expressed their admiration and approval. She perked up a little.

'Woman to the core.' Taita smiled.

'Woman indeed,' Meren agreed, and went back to his saddle-bag. He found a pretty coloured ribbon and brought it to her. Meren, the lover of women, always carried a few such trifles. They facilitated his transient friendships with members of the opposite sex whom he encountered on their travels. He tied the ribbon in a bow round her waist to prevent the hem of the tunic dragging in the dirt. Fenn craned her neck to study the effect.

'Look at her preen.' They smiled. ''Tis a great pity she is so ugly.'

'That will change,' Taita promised, and thought of how beautiful she had been in the other life.

By the middle of the next morning the bodies of the dead Luo had rotted and bloated. Even at a distance the stench was so overpowering that they were forced to shift their own encampment. Before they broke camp Taita sent Nontu back into the papyrus to bring out the men and horses they had left there. Then he and Meren went to inspect the Luo women they had captured. They were still under guard at the centre of the village, roped in strings, huddled together naked and abject.

'We cannot take them with us,' Meren pointed out. 'They can be of no further use. They are such animals that they will not even serve to pleasure the men. We shall have to get rid of them. Shall I fetch some of the men to help me? It will not take long.' He loosened his sword in its scabbard.

'Let them go,' Taita ordered.

Meren looked shocked. 'That is not wise, Magus. We cannot be sure that they will not call more of their brethren out of the swamps to steal our horses and annoy us further.'

'Let them go,' Taita repeated.

When the bonds were cut from their wrists and ankles, the women did not attempt to escape. Nakonto had to make a ferocious speech, filled with dire threats, then rush at them shaking his spear and yelling war-cries before they snatched up their infants and fled wailing into the forest.

They loaded the horses and moved two leagues further along the edge of the swamp, then camped again in a grove of shady trees. The insects that rose as soon as darkness fell tormented them mercilessly.

A day later Nontu led the remaining horses and the survivors out of the swamps. Shabako, who was in charge, came to report to Taita and Meren. His news was not good: five more troopers had died since they had parted company, and all the others, including Shabako, were so sick and weak that they could hardly mount their horses unaided. The animals were hardly in better condition. The swamp grass and water plants provided little nourishment, and some had picked up stomach parasites from the stagnant pools. They were passing balls of writhing white worms and botfly larvae.

'I fear we will lose many more men and horses if we stay in this pestilential place,' Taita worried. 'The grazing is sour and rank and the horses will not recover their condition on it. Our store of dhurra is almost exhausted, hardly enough for the men, let alone the beasts. We must find more salubrious surroundings in which to recuperate.' He called Nakonto to him, and asked, 'Is there higher ground near here?'

Nakonto consulted his cousin before he replied. 'There is a range of hills many days' travel to the east. There, the grass is sweet, and in the evenings cool winds come down from the mountains. We were wont to graze our cattle there in the hot season,' he said.

'Show us the way,' Taita said.

They left early the next morning. When Taita was mounted on Windsmoke, he reached down, took Fenn's arm and swung her up behind him. From her expression he could tell that the experience had terrified her, but she wrapped both arms round his waist, pressed her face to his back and clung to him like a tick. Taita talked soothingly to her and before they had ridden a league she had begun to relax her death-grip and, from her elevated position, to look at her surroundings. Another league and she was chirruping with pleasure and interest. If he did not respond at once she drummed her little fist on his back and cried his name, 'Taita! Taita,' then pointed out whatever had caught her attention. 'What?'

'Tree,' he replied, or 'Horses,' or 'Bird. Big bird.'

'Big bird,' she repeated. She was quick, and her ear was true. It needed only one or two repetitions for her to reproduce the sound and inflection perfectly, and once she had it she did not lose it. By the third day she was stringing words into simple sentences, 'Big bird fly. Big bird fly fast.'

'Yes, yes. You're so clever, Fenn,' he told her. 'It's almost as if you are starting to remember something you once knew well but had forgotten. Now it's fast coming back to you, isn't it?'

She listened attentively, then picked out the words she had already learnt, and repeated them with a flourish: 'Yes, yes. Clever Fenn. Fast, coming fast.' Then she looked back at the foal, Whirlwind, who followed the mare: 'Little horse coming fast!'

The foal fascinated her. She found the name 'Whirlwind' difficult, so she called him Little Horse. As soon as they dismounted to make camp, she shouted, 'Come, Little Horse.' The foal seemed to enjoy her company as much as she did his. He came to her and allowed her to drape an arm round his neck and attach herself to him as though they were twins joined in the womb. She saw the men feeding dhurra to

185

the other horses, so she stole some, tried to feed it to him and was angry when he refused. 'Bad horse,' she scolded. 'Bad Little Horse.'

She had soon learnt the names of all the men, beginning with Meren who had given her the ribbon and stood high in her favour. The others competed for her attention. They saved her titbits from their frugal rations and taught her the words of their marching songs. Taita put a stop to this when she repeated some of the more salacious choruses. They found small gifts for her, bright feathers, porcupine quills and pretty stones they picked out of the sands of the dry riverbeds they crossed.

But the progress of the column was slow. Neither the men nor the horses could make a full day's march. They began late and halted early, with frequent stops. Another three troopers died of the swamp-sickness, and the others had hardly the strength to dig their graves. Among the horses Windsmoke and her foal fared best. The spear wound in the mare's hindquarters had healed cleanly and, despite the rigours of the march, she had kept her milk and was still able to feed Whirlwind.

They camped one afternoon when the horizon was turbid with dust and heat haze, but in the dawn the cool of the night had cleared the air and they could make out in the distance ahead a low blue line of hills. As they rode towards them the hills grew taller and the details more inviting. On the eighth day after they had left the swamps, they reached the foothills of a great massif. The slopes were lightly forested and scored with ravines down which tumbled streams and bounding waterfalls. Following a stream, they climbed laboriously upwards and came out at last on to a vast plateau.

There, the air was fresher and cooler. They filled their lungs with relief and pleasure, and looked about them. They saw groves of fine trees standing on grass savannahs. Herds of antelope and striped wild ponies grazed in multitudes upon the pastures. There was no sign of human presence. It was an enchanted and inviting wilderness.

Taita selected a campsite with meticulous consideration of every aspect; prevailing winds and the direction of the sun, the proximity of running water and pasture for the horses. They cut poles and thatching grass, then built comfortable living huts. They erected a zareeba, a stockade of stout poles with sharpened points, around the settlement, and divided off one end into a separate pen for the horses and mules. Each evening they brought them in from the pasture and confined them for the night, to keep them safe from marauding lions and savage humans.

On the bank of the stream, where the earth was rich and fertile, they cleared land and turned the earth. They built another sturdy fence of thornbushes and poles to keep out the grazing animals. Grain by grain, Taita sifted through the bags of dhurra seeds, picking out by their aura those that were healthy and discarding any that were diseased or damaged. They planted them in the prepared earth, and Taita built a *shadoof* to lift the water from the river to irrigate the seed beds. Within days, the first green shoots had unfurled from the soil and in a few months the grain would ripen. Meren placed a perpetual guard over the fields, troopers armed with drums to drive off the horses and any wild apes. They built guard fires around the zareeba and kept them burning night and day. Each morning the horses and mules were hobbled and turned loose upon the rich grazing. They gorged on it and swiftly regained condition.

Game was plentiful upon the plateau. Every few days Meren rode out with a party of his hunters and returned with a large bag of antelope and wild fowl. They wove fish traps from reeds, and placed them at the head of the river pools. The catch was abundant, and the men feasted each night on venison and fresh catfish. Fenn astonished them all with her appetite for meat.

Taita was familiar with most of the trees, shrubs and plants that grew on the plateau. He had encountered them during his years in the highlands of Ethiopia. He pointed out to the foraging parties those that were nutritious, and under his guidance they collected wild spinach along the banks of the river. They also dug up the roots of a euphorbiaceous plant that grew in profusion, and boiled them into a rich porridge that replaced dhurra as their staple.

In the cool, sweet airs of early morning, Taita and Fenn went into the forest to gather baskets of leaves and berries, roots and slabs of fresh wet bark that had medicinal properties. When the heat became unpleasant they returned to the camp, and boiled some of their harvest, or dried it in the sun, and pounded other items into paste or powder. With the potions they produced Taita treated the ailments of men and horses.

In particular, there was the boiled extract of the bark of a thorny shrub that was so bitter and astringent on the tongue it made the eyes smart and took the breath away. Taita administered copious draughts to those who were still suffering the symptoms of swamp-sickness. Fenn stood by and encouraged them when they gagged and gasped. 'Good Shabako. Clever Shabako.' None could resist her blandishments. They swallowed the bitter draught and kept it down. The cure was quick and complete.

From powdered bark and the seeds of a small nondescript shrub Taita compounded a laxative of such extraordinary power that Nakonto, who seemed to have rock-hard bowels, was delighted with the results. He came daily to Taita to demand his dose, and in the end Taita limited him to one every third day.

Despite her appetite Fenn remained skinny and her stomach was tight and distended. Taita prepared another potion of boiled roots, with which she assisted him. When he invited her to drink it she took a single sip, then took to her heels. She was quick, but he was ready for her. The ensuing battle of wills lasted almost two days. The men laid wagers on the outcome. In the end Taita won the day, and she drank a full dose without him having to resort to psychic persuasion, to which he was reluctant to subject her. Her sulks continued until the following day when, to her astonishment, she passed a ball of writhing white intestinal worms almost the size of her head. She was immensely proud of this achievement and took first Taita, then everybody else to admire it. They were all suitably impressed and everyone agreed loudly that Fenn was, indeed, a clever, brave girl. Within days her stomach took on more pleasing contours and her limbs filled out. Her physical development was startling: in months she had made progress that would have taken normal girls years to accomplish. To Taita, it seemed that she was growing and blossoming before his eyes.

'She is not a normal child,' he explained to himself. 'She is the reincarnation of a queen and a goddess.' If he ever felt the slightest twinge of doubt about it, he had only to open the Inner Eye and gaze upon her aura. Its splendour was divine.

'Your lovely smile would startle the horses now,' Taita told her, and she showed her once-black teeth in a wide grin. The dye had faded until her teeth were salt-white and perfect. Taita showed her how to select a green twig and chew the fibrous end into a brush to polish her new teeth and sweeten her breath. She liked the taste and never shirked the daily ritual.

Her command of the language passed from abysmal to poor, to good and, finally, to perfect. Her vocabulary burgeoned: she could choose the exact word to express her feelings or describe an object accurately. Soon she could play word games with Taita, and delighted him with her rhyming, riddling and punning.

Fenn was ravenous for learning. If her mind was not fully occupied she became bored and difficult. When it was grappling with a task he had set her, she was sweet and pliable. Almost daily Taita had to seek new challenges for her.

He made writing tablets from the clay of the riverbank and started her on a study of hieroglyphics. He laid out a *bao* board in the hard clay outside the doorway of their hut and selected coloured stones as counters. After a few days she had picked up the elementary principles, and as she advanced he taught her the Rule of Seven, then the Massing of Castles. One memorable day she vanquished Meren in three out of four straight games, to his mortification and the delight of the onlookers.

With the ashes of the saltwort bush, Taita converted into soap the fat of the game that the hunters brought in. Liberal applications removed from Fenn's body the last stubborn stains of the dyes and other nameless substances with which her adopted Luo mother had beautified her.

With further applications of Taita's sovereign salve and unrelenting persecution, the last of her vermin were rooted out. Their bites faded and finally disappeared. Her skin took on a creamy unblemished texture, shaded to lucent amber where the sun touched it. Her hair grew and at last covered her ears, becoming a shining aureate crown. Her eyes, though still green and enormous, no longer dominated her other, more delicate features but complemented and enhanced them. Before Taita's doting eyes she became as beautiful as she had been in the other life.

When he gazed upon her, or listened to her soft breathing at night on the sleeping mat beside his, his pleasure was soured by dread of what the future must bring. He was acutely aware that, in a few brief years, she would become a woman and her instincts would demand something he was unable to give her. She would be driven to look elsewhere for a man who could meet those overpowering female needs. For the second time in his life he would be forced to watch her go into the arms of another, and experience the bitter sorrow of lost love.

'The future will take care of itself. I have her for this day. I must make that suffice,' he told himself, and thrust aside his fears.

Although all about her were fascinated by her burgeoning beauty, Fenn seemed unaware of it. She repaid their adulation with unstilted grace and friendliness, but remained an unfettered spirit. She reserved her affection for Taita.

Windsmoke was just one of those who came under Fenn's spell. When Taita was preoccupied with chemistry or meditation, Fenn would go out into the pasture to find her. The mare allowed Fenn to use her mane to clamber on to her back, and then gave the child riding lessons. At first she would move no faster than a sedate walk. Despite all Fenn's urging she would not break into a trot until she felt that her rider's balance was right and her seat secure. Within weeks she had introduced Fenn to an easy canter. She ignored the hammering of small heels into her flanks, the loud exhortations and pleas to 'Hi up!' Then, one afternoon, when Taita was napping in the shade by the door of their hut, Fenn went down to the horse zareeba and swung herself on to the grey mare's back. Windsmoke walked away with her. At the gate of the zareeba Fenn poked her with a toe behind the shoulder and Windsmoke opened into a smooth, high-stepping trot. When they were in the golden fields of savannah grass Fenn asked the mare again, and she extended into a canter. Fenn was seated close up behind her withers, weight well forward, knees clamped firmly so that she was perfectly in tune with Windsmoke's every stride. Then, more in hope than expectation of the animal's co-operation, Fenn seized a handful of mane and cried, 'Come, my darling, let us away.' Under her, Windsmoke smoothly released all her speed and power, Whirlwind following closely. They swept away joyfully across the basin of open grassland.

Taita was woken by the shouts of the men: 'Run, Windsmoke, run!' And 'Ride, Fenn, ride!'

He ran to the gate just in time to see the distant trio disappear over the skyline. He was uncertain on whom he should first vent his fury.

Meren chose that moment to cry, 'By the thunderous peals of Seth's farts, she rides like a trooper!' so nominating himself the target.

Taita was still haranguing him when Windsmoke tore back across the basin with Fenn shrieking with excitement upon her back and Whirlwind at her heels. She stopped in front of Taita, and Fenn slid down and ran to him. 'Oh, Taita, did you see us? Wasn't it wonderful? Were you not proud of me?'

He glared at her. 'You are never to do something as dangerous and foolish as that again, not in all your life.' She was crestfallen. Her shoulders drooped and her eyes swam with tears. He relented stiffly: 'But you rode well enough. I am proud of you.'

'The magus means that you rode like a trooper, but we were all afraid for your safety,' Meren explained, 'but there was no cause for us to worry.' Fenn brightened immediately, and dashed away the tears with the back of her hand.

'Is that what you really meant, Taita?' she demanded.

'I suppose it was,' he admitted gruffly.

That evening Fenn sat cross-legged upon her sleeping mat and, by the light of the oil lamp, regarded Taita solemnly as he lay on his back with his beard brushed out and his hands folded on his chest, composing himself for sleep. 'You will never go away and leave me, but will always be with me, won't you, Taita?'

'Yes.' He smiled up at her. 'I will always be with you.'

'I am so glad.' She bent forward and buried her face in his silver beard. 'It is so soft,' she whispered, 'like a cloud.' Then the excitement of the day overwhelmed her and she fell asleep, sprawled across his chest.

Taita lay for a while, listening to her breathing. Such happiness cannot last, he thought. It is too intense.

They were up early the next morning. As soon as they had had breakfast, of dhurra porridge and mare's milk, they went out into the forest for herbs. When the foraging baskets were filled Taita led the way to their favourite pool in the river. They sat together on the high bank, their reflections mirrored on the surface of the pool below them.

'Look at yourself, Fenn,' he said. 'See how beautiful you have become.' She glanced down without interest, and was immediately riveted by the face that looked back at her. She knelt up, leant far out over the water, then stared and stared. At last she whispered, 'Are not my ears too large?'

'Your ears are like the petals of a flower,' he replied.

'One of my teeth is crooked.'

'Only a very little, and it makes your smile all the more intriguing.'

'My nose?'

'Is the most perfect little nose I have ever seen.'

'Really?'

'Really!'

She turned to smile at him, and he told her, 'Your smile lights the forest.'

She hugged him and her body was warm, but suddenly he felt a cold wind on his cheek although the leaves of the tree that hung over them had not stirred. He shivered, and, softly, the pulse began to beat in his eardrums. They were no longer alone.

Protectively, he held her closer, and looked over her shoulder into the pool.

There was a disturbance beneath the surface, as though a giant catfish had stirred in the depths. But the pulse in his ears beat stronger and he knew it was no fish. He concentrated his gaze and made out a tenuous shadow that seemed to undulate like the leaves of a water-lily in some deep eddy of the river. Slowly the shadow coalesced into human form, an insubstantial image of a cloaked figure, its head swathed in a voluminous cowl. He tried to see beneath the folds, but there was only shadow.

Fenn felt him stiffen and looked up into his face, then turned her head to follow the direction of his gaze. She stared down into the pool, and whispered fearfully, 'Something is there.' As she spoke the image faded, and the surface of the pool was unruffled and serene once more. 'What was it, Taita?' she asked.

'What did you see?'

'Someone was in the pool under the water.'

Taita was not surprised: he had known all along that she had the gift. It was not the first time she had given him proof.

'Did you see it clearly?' He did not want to place a suggestion in her mind.

'I saw someone under the water, dressed all in black . . . but they had no face.' She had seen all of the vision, not just fragments. The psychic genius with which she had been endowed was powerful, perhaps as powerful as his own. He would be able to work with her as he had never been able to with Meren. He could help her develop her gift and harness its force to her will.

'How did it make you feel?'

'Cold,' she whispered.

'Did you smell anything?'

'The scent of a cat – no, that of a serpent. I am not sure. But I know that it was evil.' She clung to him. 'What was it?'

'What you smelt was the scent of the witch.' He would hide nothing from her. She had the body of a child, but it contained the mind and soul of a strong, resilient woman. He did not have to shield her. Besides her gift, she had reserves of strength and experience accumulated in the other life. He had only to help her find the key to the strongroom in her mind where those treasures were stored.

'What you saw was the shadow of the witch. What you smelt was her scent.'

'Who is the witch?'

'I will tell you one day soon, but now we must return to the camp. We have pressing matters to attend to.'

The witch had found them, and Taita realized he had been lulled into remaining too long in that lovely place. His life force had built up like a wave, and she had sensed it, then smelt him out. They must move on, and swiftly.

Fortunately, the men were rested and fully recuperated. Their spirits were high. The horses were strong. The dhurra bags were filled. The swords were sharp and all the equipment had been repaired. If the witch had found them, Taita had also found her. He knew in which direction her lair lay.

Meren marshalled the men. The toll extracted by the swamps had been heavy. Almost a year and a half ago ninety-three officers and men had ridden out of the fort at Qebui. Thirty-six remained to answer the muster. The horses and mules had fared little better. Of the original three hundred, plus the gift of five pack mules, a hundred and eighty-six had survived.

No one looked back as the column pulled out of the encampment, wound down the escarpment into the plains and headed back towards the river. Fenn was no longer behind Taita on Windsmoke. After her display of her horse-handling skill she had demanded her own mount, and Taita had chosen for her a sturdy bay gelding of even disposition.

Fenn was delighted with him. 'I shall call him Goose,' she announced.

Taita looked at her enquiringly. 'Why Goose?'

'I like geese. He reminds me of a goose,' she explained loftily. He decided that the easiest course was to accept the name without further debate.

As soon as the track reached the foothills and became wide enough to allow it, she moved up and rode at Taita's side, their knees almost touching, so that they could talk.

'You promised to tell me about the witch in the water. This is a good time.'

'Yes, it is. The witch is a very old woman. She has lived since the beginning time. She is very powerful, and does wicked things.'

'What wicked things?'

'She devours newborn babes.' Fenn shuddered. 'And she lures wise men into her clutches and devours their souls. Then she casts out the husks of the bodies.'

'I would never have thought such things possible.'

'There is worse to tell, Fenn. With her powers she has stopped up the flow of the great river that is the mother of the earth, the river whose waters give life, food and drink to all peoples.'

Fenn thought about that. 'The Luo thought I had killed the river. They drove me out of their village to die of hunger in the forest, or to be eaten by wild animals.'

'They are a cruel and ignorant people,' Taita agreed.

'I am glad that you and Meren slew them,' she said matter-of-factly, and was silent again for a while. 'Why would the witch want to kill the river?'

'She wanted to break the power of our pharaoh and enslave the peoples of his kingdom.'

'What is a pharaoh, and what does "enslave" mean?' He explained, and she looked grave. 'Then she is truly wicked. Where does she live?'

'On a mountain beside a great lake in a land far to the south.' He pointed ahead.

'Is that where we are going?'

'Yes. We will try to stop her, and make the waters flow again.'

'If she lives so far away, how did she get into the pool of the river where we saw her?'

'It was not her we saw. It was her shadow.'

Fenn frowned and wrinkled her pert little nose as she wrestled with the concept. 'I do not understand.'

Taita reached into the leather pouch on his girdle and

brought out the bulb of a lily that he had brought with him for the purpose of demonstration. He handed it to her. 'You know this bulb.'

She examined it briefly. 'Of course. We have gathered many such.'

'Inside there are many layers, one within the other, and in the centre the tiny kernel.' She nodded, and he went on, 'That is how our entire universe is shaped. We are the kernel at the centre. Around us there are layers of existence we cannot see or sense – unless we have the power to do so. Do you understand?'

She nodded again, cautiously, then admitted candidly, 'No, I don't, Taita.'

'Do you dream when you are asleep, Fenn?'

'Oh, yes!' she enthused. 'Wonderful dreams! They make me laugh and feel happy. Sometimes in my dreams I can fly like a bird. I visit strange and beautiful places.' Then a haunted expression replaced the smile. 'But sometimes I have dreams that frighten me or make me feel sad.'

Taita had listened to her nightmares as she lay beside him in the night. He had never shaken her or startled her out of them but had extended his own power to calm her and bring her back gently from the dark places. 'Yes, Fenn, I know. In your sleep you leave this layer of existence and move into the next.' She smiled with comprehension, and Taita continued, 'Although most people have dreams they cannot control, some have the special gift to see beyond the tiny kernel of existence in which we are encapsulated. Some, the savants and the magi, may even have the power to travel in spirit form to wherever they choose. To see things from afar.'

'Can you do that, Taita?' He smiled enigmatically, and she burst out, 'It must be strange and wonderful. I should love to be able to do that.'

'One day perhaps you shall. You see, Fenn, you saw the shade of the witch in the pool, which means you have the power. We need only train you to use and control it.'

'So the witch had come to spy on us? She was really there?'

'Her spirit was. She was overlooking us.'

'I am frightened of her.'

'It is wise to be so. But we must not surrender to her. We must counter her with our own powers, you and I. We must oppose her and break her wicked spells. If we can, we will destroy her and this world will be a better place for it.'

'I will help you,' she declared stoutly, 'but, first, you must teach me how.'

'Your progress so far has been miraculous.' He looked upon her with unfeigned admiration. She was already developing the mind and spirit of the queen she had been in the other life. 'You are ready to learn more,' he told her. 'We will start at once.'

Her instruction began each day as they mounted and rode out side by side. It continued through the long days of travel. His first concern was to instil in her the duty of a magus, which was to employ with care and responsibility the powers with which he or she had been endowed. They must never be used lightly or frivolously, or to achieve petty or selfish ends.

Once she had understood this sacred duty, and acknowledged it with a formal vow that he made her repeat, they moved on to study the simplest forms of the magical arts. At first he was careful not to tax her powers of concentration and to set a pace that she could maintain. But he need not have worried: she was indefatigable, and her determination unbending.

First he taught her how to protect herself: to weave spells of concealment that would shield her from the eyes of others. She practised this at the end of each day, when they were secure within the makeshift stockade. She would sit quietly beside Taita and, with his assistance, attempt to work a spell of concealment. It took many nights of diligent application but at last she succeeded. Once she had cloaked herself, Taita shouted for Meren. 'Have you seen Fenn? I wish to speak to her.'

Meren looked about, and his gaze passed over the child without pause. 'She was here but a short time ago. She must have gone out to the bushes. Shall I search for her?'

'No matter. It was not important.' Meren walked away, and Fenn giggled triumphantly.

Meren whirled round and started with surprise. 'There she is! Sitting beside you!' Then he grinned. 'Clever girl, Fenn! I was never able to do that, no matter how hard I tried.'

'Now you see how, if you lose concentration, the spell shatters like glass,' Taita chided her.

Once she had learnt to shield her physical body, he could teach her to mask her mind and aura. This was more difficult. First, he had to be certain that the witch did not have them under scrutiny: until she had fully mastered the magical techniques she would be most vulnerable to interference from any malign influence while she was attempting to do it. He had to search the ether around them before they could begin the instruction, and keep his guard high.

Her first task was to understand the aura of life that surrounded every living thing. She could not see it, and would never be able to until her Inner Eye was opened. Taita was determined to take her at the first opportunity on the arduous journey to the temple of Saraswati. In the meantime he had to describe it to her. Once she had grasped the concept of the aura, he could go on to explain the Inner Eye, and the power of savants to employ it.

'Do you have the Inner Eye, Taita?'

'Yes, but so does the witch,' he replied.

'What does my aura look like?' she asked, with ingenuous female vanity.

'It is a shimmering golden light, like no other I have seen or expect to see again. It is divine.' Fenn glowed, and he went on, 'Therein lies our difficulty. If you continue to let it shine forth the witch will descry you in an instant and know what a serious threat you may pose to her.'

She thought about that. 'You say that the witch has overlooked us. In that case, has she not already descried my aura? Is it not too late to attempt to conceal it from her?'

'It is not possible even for a savant to perceive an aura by overlooking from afar. It can only be done by viewing a subject directly. We saw the witch in the water as a wraith, so she saw us in the same fashion. She could perceive our physical selves and overhear our conversation – she could even smell us as we did her – but she could not see your aura.'

'What of yours? Did you conceal it from her?'

'As savants, neither the witch nor I shed an aura.'

'Teach me the art of hiding mine,' she pleaded.

He inclined his head in agreement. 'I will, but we must be vigilant. I must be certain that she is not overlooking or listening to us.'

It was not an easy task. Fenn had to rely on him to tell her how successful her efforts were. At first her best attempts caused her aura to flicker but it soon flared up as brightly as before. They persevered, and gradually, with her most valiant efforts and his coaching, the flickering became a significant dimming. But it was weeks before she could suppress it at will to a level that was not much more striking than that of Meren or any of his troopers, and maintain it at that level of brightness for extended periods.

Nine days after leaving the encampment on the plateau, they reached the river. Although it was almost a league across from bank to bank, the Nile waters flowed no more strongly than those of the mountain stream beside which they had raised the dhurra crop. The thin trickle was almost lost in the wide expanse of dry sand and mudbanks. However, it was sufficient for their needs. They turned southwards and pushed on along the eastern bank, covering many leagues each day. Elephants had dug deep holes in the riverbed to reach the cleaner subterranean water. Men and horses drank from them.

Each day they came upon large herds of these ancient grey beasts drinking from the holes, lifting huge draughts to their mouths in their trunks and squirting them down their gaping pink throats, but at the troopers' approach they charged up the bank in a herd, flapping their ears and trumpeting before rushing into the forest.

Many of the bulls carried massive shafts of ivory. It was only with an effort that Meren controlled his hunter's heart and allowed them to escape unmolested. Now they met other men of the Shilluk tribe grazing their herds along the river-bank. Nontu was carried away on a flood of his emotions. 'Old and revered one, these people are from my own town. They have news of my family,' he told Taita. 'Two seasons ago one of my wives was taken by a crocodile when she went to draw water from the river, but the other three are well and have borne many children.' Taita knew Nontu had been at Qebui for the last eight years, and he wondered at the births. 'I left my wives in the care of my brothers,' Nontu explained blithely.

'It seems they have cared well for them,' Taita remarked drily.

Nontu went on cheerfully. 'My eldest daughter has seen her first red moon and come of child-bearing age. They tell me she has grown into a nubile girl, and the young men have offered many cattle for her as a bride price. I must return with these men, who are my kinsfolk, to the village to arrange her marriage, and to take care of the cattle.'

'I shall be saddened by our parting,' Taita told him. 'What of you, Nakonto? Will you leave us also?'

'Nay, old man. Your medicines are pleasing to my bowels. Furthermore, there is good food and good fighting to be had in your company. I prefer it to that of many wives and their squalling brats. I have grown accustomed to living without such encumbrances. I will travel on with you.'

They camped for three days beside Nontu's village, an assembly of several hundred large conical huts, beautifully thatched and laid out in a circle around the extensive cattle kraals where each night the herds were penned. There, the herdsmen milked the cows, then drew blood from one of the large veins in each beast's neck. This seemed to be their only food, as they planted no crops. The men and even the women were inordinately tall, but slender and graceful. Despite their tribal tattoos the younger women were nubile and pleasing to look upon. They gathered round the camp in giggling gaggles, ogling the troopers brazenly.

On the third day they bade farewell to Nontu, and were preparing for the departure when five troopers came in a delegation to Meren. Each led by the hand a naked Shilluk maiden, who towered over her escort.

'We wish to bring these chickens with us,' declared Shofar, the spokesman for the group.

'Do they understand your intentions?' Meren asked, to give himself time to consider the proposal.

'Nakonto has explained it to them, and they are willing.'

'What of their fathers and brothers? We do not wish to start a war.'

'We have given them a bronze dagger each, and they are happy with the bargain.'

'Can the women ride?'

'No, but they will perforce learn soon enough.'

Meren removed his leather helmet and ran his fingers through his curls, then looked to Taita for guidance. Taita shrugged, but his eyes twinkled. 'Perhaps they can be taught to cook, or at least wash our clothes,' he suggested.

'If any causes trouble, or if there is any squabbling or fighting over their favours, I will send them back to their fathers, no matter how far we have travelled,' Meren told Shofar sternly. 'Keep them under control, that is all.'

The column moved on. That evening when they went into laager, Nakonto came to report to Taita and, as had become their custom, to sit beside him for a while. 'We have made good ground today,' he said. 'After this many days more travel . . .' he showed all of his fingers twice, indicating twenty days '. . . we will leave the land of my people, and enter that of the Chima.'

'Who are they? Are they brothers to the Shilluk?'

'They are our enemies. They are short in stature and not beautiful as we are.'

'Will they let us pass?'

'Not willingly, old man.' Nakonto smiled wolfishly. 'There will be fighting. I have not had the opportunity to kill a Chima for many years.' Then he added, as a casual after-thought, 'The Chima are eaters of men.'

The routine that Meren and Taita had adopted since leaving the settlement on the high plateau was to march for four consecutive days and take a break on the fifth. On that day they repaired any damaged equipment, rested the men and horses, and sent out hunting and foraging parties to replenish their supplies. Seventeen days after they had left Nontu with his wives, they passed the last cattle post of the Shilluk, and entered territory that seemed uninhabited by anything other than large herds of antelope. Most were of species they had not encountered before. They also came across new species of trees and plants, which delighted Taita and Fenn. She had become as ardent a botanist as he was. They looked for signs of cattle or human presence, but found none.

'This is the land of the Chima,' Nakonto told Taita.

'Do you know it well?'

'No, but I know the Chima well enough. They are secretive and treacherous. They keep no cattle, which is a true sign that they are savages. They eat game meat, and they prefer that of their fellow men above all else. We must be on our guard lest we end up on their cooking fires.'

With Nakonto's warning in mind, Meren gave special attention to the construction of the zareeba each evening, and placed additional guards over the horses and mules when they let them out to graze. As they travelled further into Chima territory they came across evidence of their presence. They found hollow tree-trunks, which had been hacked open and the bees in them smoked out. Then they came across a cluster of shelters that had not been inhabited for some time. Of more recent origin were a string of footprints in the mudbanks of the river, where a party of thirty men had crossed in single file from east to west. They were only a few days old.

From the beginning the new Shilluk wives, none of whom were much older than Fenn, had been fascinated by her. They discussed the colour of her hair and her eyes among themselves and watched her every move, but kept their distance. Finally Fenn made friendly advances and soon they were conversing happily in sign language, feeling the texture of Fenn's hair, squealing with laughter together at feminine jokes and bathing naked each evening in the shallow pools of the river. Fenn appealed to Nakonto for instruction, and picked up the Shilluk language as swiftly as she had Egyptian. In ways she was still a child, and Taita was pleased that she had convivial company closer to her own age to divert her. However, he made certain that she never wandered too far with the other girls. He kept her close so that he could rush to her aid at the first unnatural chill in the air or any other inkling of an alien presence. She and Taita took to speaking in Shilluk when there was a risk of being overlooked by their adversary.

'Perhaps it is one language that even the witch will not understand, though I doubt it,' he remarked. 'At the least it is good practice for you.'

They were deep into Chima territory when, at the end of a hard day's march, they built the zareeba in a grove of tall mahogany trees. Wide pastures of grass with fluffy pink heads surrounded it. The horses favoured this grazing and herds of antelope were already feeding there. It was clear that they had never been hunted, for they were so tame and confiding that they allowed the archers to approach within easy bowshot.

Meren declared that the following day they would rest, and early in the morning he sent out four hunting parties. When Taita and Fenn set off on their customary foraging expedition, Meren insisted that Shofar and two other troopers went with them: 'There is something in the wind that makes me uneasy,' was his only explanation.

Taita preferred to have Fenn to himself but he knew not to argue when Meren smelt something in the wind. He might not be a psychic but he was a warrior and could smell trouble. They returned to camp late in the afternoon to find that only three of the hunting parties Meren had sent out had returned before them. At first they were not alarmed, expecting the last band to return at any moment, but an hour after sunset a horse belonging to one of the missing hunters galloped into camp. It was lathered with sweat, and wounded in one shoulder. Meren ordered all the troopers to stand to arms, an extra guard on the horses, and bonfires to be lit to guide the missing hunters home.

At the first flush of dawn, when it was light enough to backtrack the wounded horse, Shabako and Hilto took out a heavily armed search party. Taita left Fenn in the care of Meren, and he and Nakonto rode out with them. Within a few leagues of the camp they rode under the outspread branches of a clump of silverleaf trees and came upon a grisly scene.

Nakonto, with his tracking skills and his knowledge of the Chima's habits, knew exactly what had taken place. A large band of men had concealed themselves among the trees and lain in ambush for the hunters. Nakonto picked up an ivory bracelet that one had dropped. 'This was made by a Chima. See how crude it is – a Shilluk child could have done better,' he told Taita. He pointed out the marks on the tree-trunks where some of the Chima had climbed into the branches. 'This is the way the treacherous jackals like to fight, with stealthy cunning not courage.'

As the four Egyptian horsemen rode beneath the overhanging branches the Chima had dropped down upon them. At the same time their comrades had leapt out of hiding, and stabbed the horses. 'The Chima jackals pulled our men from their horses, probably before they could draw their weapons to defend themselves.' Nakonto pointed out the signs of the struggle. 'Here they speared them to death – see the blood on the grass.' Using plaited bark rope the Chima had hung the corpses by the heels from the low branches of the nearest silverleafs, and butchered them like antelope.

'They always eat the liver and entrails first,' Nakonto explained. 'Here is where they shook the dung from the tripes before they cooked them on the coals of the fires.'

Then they had quartered the corpses and used bark rope to tie the severed limbs on to carrying poles. The feet, cut off at the ankle joints, were still hanging from the branches. They had thrown the heads and hands on to the fires, and when they were roasted, they had chewed off the palms and sucked the flesh from the finger bones. They had split open the skulls to scoop out the baked brains with cupped fingers, then scraped off the cheeks and taken out the tongues, a great Chima delicacy. The broken skulls and small bones were scattered all around. They had not bothered with the dead horses, probably because they were unable to deal with such a heavy load of meat. Then, with the physical remains, the clothing, weapons and other equipment of the troopers they had murdered, they had set off into the west, moving fast.

'Shall we hunt them down?' Shabako demanded angrily. 'We cannot let this slaughter go unavenged.'

Nakonto was just as eager to take up the pursuit, his eyes shot with bloodlust. But after only a moment's thought Taita shook his head. 'There are thirty or forty of them and six of us. They have had a head start of almost a full day, and they will be expecting us to pursue them. They will lead us deeper into difficult territory and ambush us.' He looked around at the forest. 'Certainly they will have left men to spy on us. They are probably watching us at this moment.'

Some of the troopers drew their swords, but before they could rush among the trees and root them out, Taita stopped them. 'If we do not follow them, they will follow us, which is what we want. We will be able to lead them to a killing ground of our own choosing.' They buried the pathetic skulls with the severed feet, then returned to the zareeba.

Early the next morning they mustered into column and rode out again on the endless journey. At noon they broke the march to rest and water the horses. On Taita's orders, Nakonto slipped into the forest and made a wide circle through the trees. As stealthily as a shadow he cut the back trail of the column. The prints of three sets of bare feet were superimposed on the horse tracks. He made another wide circle to rejoin the column and report to Taita. 'Your eyes see far, old man. Three of the jackals are following us. As you foretold, the rest of the pack will not be far behind.'

That evening they sat late around the fire in the zareeba, laying plans for the morrow.

The next morning they started the march at a sharp trot. Within half a league Meren ordered the pace increased to a canter. Swiftly they opened the gap between themselves and the Chima scouts whom they knew would be following. As they rode Meren and Taita were studying the terrain they were passing through, seeking ground that they could turn to their advantage. Ahead, a small isolated hillock rose above the forest and they angled towards it. Around its eastern slope they found a smooth, well-beaten elephant road. When they followed it they saw that the hillside above was steep, covered with a dense growth of kittar thornbush. The vicious hooks and densely intertwined branches formed an impenetrable wall. On the opposite side of the road the ground was level and, at first glance, the open forest seemed to afford little cover for an ambush. However, when Taita and Meren rode out a short distance among the trees they found a wadi, a dry gully cut out by storm water, that was deep and wide enough to hide their column, men and horses. The lip of the gully was only forty yards from the elephant road, within easy bowshot. Quickly they rejoined the main column. They stayed on the elephant road for a short distance, then Meren stopped again to conceal three of his best archers beside the road.

'There are three Chima scouts following us. One for each of you,' he told them. 'Let them get close. Pick your shots. No mistakes. Quick, clean kills. You must not allow any of them to escape to warn the rest of the Chima, who are behind them.'

They left the three archers and rode on along the elephant road. After half a league they left it and made a wide circle back to the gully under the slope of the hill. They led the horses down into it, and dismounted. Fenn and the Shilluk girls held the animals, ready to bring them forward when the troopers called for them. Taita waited with Fenn, but it would take him just an instant to run to Meren's side when the time came.

The men strung their bows, and lined up below the lip of the wadi facing the elephant road. At Meren's command they squatted down, out of sight, to rest their legs and bow-arms, and to prepare themselves for combat. Only Meren and his captains watched the road, but to conceal the silhouette of their heads they stood behind clumps of grass or bushes.

They did not have long to wait before the three Chima scouts came along the road. They had been running hard to keep up with the horses. Their bodies shone with sweat, their chests heaved and their legs were dusty to the knees. Meren lifted a warning hand and none of the men stirred. The scouts passed the ambush at a rapid trot and disappeared along the road into the forest. Meren relaxed slightly. A little later the three archers he had left to take care of the scouts slipped out of the forest and dropped into the wadi. Meren looked at them questioningly. The leader grinned and pointed to fresh splashes of blood on his tunic: the scouts had been accounted for. They all settled down to await the arrival of the main body of Chima.

A short time later, from the forest on the right flank, the querulous alarm call of the grey lory, 'Kee-wey! Kee-wey!' rang out. Then a baboon barked a challenge from the top of the hill. Meren lifted a fist as a signal to his men. They nocked their arrows on the bowstrings.

The leading file of the main Chima raiding party trotted round the curve in the elephant road. As they drew closer Meren studied them carefully. They were short, stocky and bow-legged, and wore only loincloths of tanned animal skins. Even when the entire band came into view it was difficult to make an accurate head count for they were bunched in a tight formation and moving fast.

'A hundred at least, maybe more. We are in for some rich sport, I warrant you,' Meren said, with anticipation. The Chima were armed with an assortment of clubs and flint-headed spears. The bows slung across their shoulders were small and primitive. Meren judged that they would not have the draw weight to kill a man at more than thirty paces. Then his eyes narrowed: one of the leaders carried an Egyptian sword slung over his shoulder. The man behind him wore a leather helmet, but of an archaic design. It was puzzling, but there was no time to ponder it now. The head of the Chima formation came level with the white stone he had placed beside the road as a range marker. Now the entire left flank was exposed to the Egyptian archers.

Meren glanced left and right. The eyes of his men were fixed on him. He dropped his raised right hand sharply, and his archers jumped upright. As one man they drew their bows, paused to make good their aim, then loosed a silent cloud of arrows to arc high against the sky. Before the first struck home the second cloud rose into the air. The arrows fluted so softly that the Chima did not even look up. Then, with a sound like raindrops falling on the surface of a pond, they dropped among them. The Chima did not seem to realize what was happening to them. One stood gazing down, perplexed, at the shaft of the arrow protruding from between his ribs. Then his knees buckled and he crumpled to the ground. Another was staggering in small circles plucking at the arrow that had buried itself in his throat. Most of the others, even those who had received mortal wounds, did not seem to grasp that they had been hit.

When the third flight of arrows dropped among them those still on their feet panicked and bolted, screaming and howling, in every direction, like a flock of guinea-fowl scattering under the stoop of an eagle. Some ran straight towards the wadi and the archers dropped their aim. At close range none of the arrows missed their mark: they struck deep into living flesh with meaty thumps. Some went right through the torso of the primary target, and flew on to wound the man behind him. Those who tried to escape up the hill ran into the palisade of kittar thorn bushes. It stopped them in their tracks, and forced them back into the hailstorm of arrows.

'Bring up the horses!' Meren yelled. Fenn and the other girls dragged them forward by the head ropes. Taita swung on to Windsmoke's back, while Meren and his men slung their bows and mounted.

'Forward! Charge!' Meren bellowed. 'Take the blade to them.' The horsemen bounded up the side of the wadi on to the level ground and, shoulder to shoulder, charged at the disordered rabble of Chima, who saw them coming and tried to turn back up the slope. They were caught between the thorn wall and the glittering bronze circle of swords. Some made no attempt to escape. They fell to their knees and covered their heads with their arms. The horsemen stood in the stirrups to stab them. Others struggled in the thorns like fish in the folds of a net. The troopers cut them down as if they were firewood. By the time they had finished their grisly work, the slope and the ground below it were thickly strewn with bodies. Some Chima were writhing and groaning, but most lay still.

'Dismount,' Meren ordered. 'Finish the work.'

The troopers moved quickly over the field, stabbing any Chima who showed a spark of life. Meren spotted the man with the bronze sword still slung across his back. Three arrow shafts stood out of his chest. Meren stooped over him to retrieve the sword, but at that instant Taita shouted, 'Meren! Behind you!' He used the voice of power, and Meren was galvanized. He leapt up and twisted aside. The Chima lying behind him had feigned death: he had waited until Meren was off-guard, then he jumped to his feet and swung at him with a heavy flint-headed club. The blow narrowly missed Meren's head but glanced off his left shoulder. Meren pivoted in close, blocking the weapon's next swing, and drove the point of his sword clean through the Chima, transfixing him from sternum to backbone. With a wrench of his wrist, he twisted the blade to open the wound, and when he jerked it clear, a great gush of heart blood followed it.

Clutching his damaged left shoulder Meren bellowed, 'Kill them all again! Make sure of them this time.'

Remembering their comrades hanging like sheep on slaughter racks, the troopers went to work with gusto, hacking and stabbing. They found a few Chima hiding in the kittar thickets and dragged them out, squealing like pigs, to the slaughter.

Only once he was certain of them would Meren allow his men to pick over the corpses and gather up their own spent arrows for re-use. He himself was the only casualty. Bare to the waist, he sat with his back to a tree-trunk while Taita examined his shoulder. There was no bleeding, but a dark bruise was spreading over it. Taita grunted with satisfaction. 'No bones broken. In six or seven days an old dog like you will be as good as new.' He anointed the shoulder with a salve, and twisted a linen bandage into a sling to hold the arm comfortably. Then he sat beside Meren as the captains brought the spoils they had gathered from the Chima dead, and laid everything out for them to examine. There were carved wooden lice combs, crude ivory trinkets, water gourds and packets of smoked meat, some still on the bone, wrapped in green leaves and tied with bark string. Taita examined it. 'Human. Almost certainly the remains of our comrades. Bury it with respect.'

Then they turned their attention to the Chima weapons, mostly clubs and spears with heads of flint or obsidian. The knife blades were of chipped flint, the handles wrapped with strips of uncured leather. 'Rubbish! Not worth carrying away,' Meren said.

Taita nodded agreement. 'Throw it all on the fire.'

At last they examined the weapons and ornaments that were clearly not of Chima manufacture. Some had evidently been taken from the corpses of the four ambushed hunters – bronze weapons and recurve bows, leather helmets and padded jerkins, linen tunics and amulets of turquoise and lapis-lazuli. However, there were others of greater interest, well-worn old helmets and leather breastplates of a type that had not been used by Egyptian troops for decades. Then there was the sword that had almost cost Meren his life. Its blade was worn, the edges chipped and almost destroyed by rough sharpening against granite or some other rock. However, the hilt was finely worked and inlaid with silver. There were empty seatings from which precious stones had been prised or had dropped out. The engraved hieroglyphics were almost obliterated. Taita held it to the light and turned it from side to side, but he could not make out the characters. He called for Fenn: 'Use your sharp young eyes.'

She knelt beside him and pored over the engravings, then read out haltingly, 'I am Lotti, son of Lotti, Best of Ten Thousand, Companion of the Red Road, General and Commander in the guards of the divine Pharaoh Mamose. May he live for ever!'

'Lotti!' Taita exclaimed. 'I knew him well. He was second in command under Lord Aquer of the expedition that Queen Lostris sent from Ethiopia to discover the source of Mother Nile. He was a fine soldier. So, it seems that he and his men reached at least as far as this place.'

'Did Lord Aquer and all the rest die here, and were they eaten by the Chima?' Meren wondered.

'No. According to Tiptip, the little priest of Hathor with six fingers, Aquer saw the volcano and the great lake. Besides, Queen Lostris placed a thousand men under his command. I doubt the Chima could have slaughtered them all,' Taita said. 'I believe that they caught off-guard a small detachment under Lotti as they did our men. But did the Chima destroy a whole Egyptian army? I think not.' While the discussion continued, Taita was surreptitiously watching Fenn's expression. Whenever the name of Queen Lostris was mentioned she frowned, as though seeking an elusive memory that was tucked away somewhere in the depths of her mind. One day it will all return to her, every memory of her other life, he thought, but he said aloud to Meren, 'We shall probably never know the truth of Lotti's fate, but his sword is proof to me that we are indeed following the trail to the south that Lord Aquer blazed so long ago. We have spent too much time here already.' He stood up. 'How soon can we move on?'

'The men are ready,' Meren said. They were cheerful as boys just released from study, sitting in the shade and joking with the Shilluk girls, who were serving them food and passing round jars of dhurra beer. 'Look at how eager they are. A good fight is better for their morale than a night with the prettiest whore in the Upper Kingdom.' He started to laugh, then broke off to rub his injured shoulder. 'The men are ready, but the day is almost done. The horses would profit from a short rest.'

'So will that shoulder of yours,' Taita agreed.

The sharp little fight seemed to have eliminated the threat of more Chima raids. Although they saw sign of their presence over the days that followed, none was of recent origin. Even these indications gradually became infrequent and eventually ceased. They passed out of the land of the Chima and rode on into uninhabited territory. Although the Nile was still shrunken to a trickle, there had evidently been heavy rain in the surrounding countryside. The forest and savannah teemed with game, and grazing was abundant and rich. Taita had worried that, by this time, the troopers would be homesick and depressed but they remained buoyant, their spirits high.

Fenn and the Shilluks delighted the men with their girlish pranks and high jinks. Two of the girls were pregnant, and Fenn wanted to know how they had come to this happy state; when questioned, the girls dissolved into paroxysms of laughter. Fenn was intrigued and came to Taita for elucidation. He made his explanation short and vague. She pondered it for a while. 'It sounds rich sport.' She had picked up the expression from Meren.

Taita tried to look grave but he could not prevent a smile. 'So I have heard,' he conceded.

'When I am grown, I should like a baby to play with,' she told him.

'No doubt you will.'

'We could have one together. Wouldn't that be rich sport, Taita?'

'To be sure,' he agreed, with a pang, knowing it could never be. 'But in the meantime we have many other important things to do.'

Taita could not remember having been so filled with well-being since those long-ago days when he had been young and Lostris was alive. He felt quicker and more lively. He did not tire nearly as easily as he had done before. He attributed this mostly to Fenn's company.

Her studies advanced so swiftly that he was forced to find other ways to keep her mind working at or near its potential. If he allowed her to slacken for even a short while, her attention wandered. By now she spoke both Shilluk and Egyptian fluently.

If she were ever to become an adept, she must learn the arcane language of the magi, the Tenmass. No other medium encompassed the entire body of esoteric learning. However, the Tenmass was so complex and multi-faceted, and had so little association with any other human language, that only those possessed of the highest intelligence and dedication could hope to master it.

It was a challenge that brought out the best in Fenn. At first she found it was like trying to scale a wall of polished glass that gave no purchase to hand or foot. Laboriously she climbed a little way, then, to her fury, lost her grip and slithered down. She picked herself up and tried again, each time more fiercely. She never despaired, even when it seemed she was making no progress. Taita was making her face the magnitude of the task: only then would she be ready to move on.

The moment came, but still he waited until they were

alone on their sleeping mats at night. Then he placed his hand on her forehead and spoke to her quietly until she sank into a hypnotic trance. When she was fully receptive, he could begin to plant the seeds of the Tenmass in her mind. He did not use the Egyptian language as the medium of instruction, but spoke directly to her in the Tenmass. It required many such nocturnal sessions before the seeds took tenuous hold. Like an infant standing for the first time, she took a few uncertain steps, then collapsed. The next time she stood more firmly and confidently. He was careful not to tax her too hard, but at the same time to keep her moving. Aware that the strain might stale her, and bend her spirit, he saw to it that they still spent enchanted hours at the *bao* board, or in easy but sparkling conversation, or wandering together in the forest in search of rare plants or other small treasures.

Whenever they passed a likely stretch of gravel in the riverbed, he unstrapped his prospecting pan from the back of his mule and they worked the gravel. While he swirled the slurry he had picked up, Fenn used her eyes and nimble fingers to pick out lovely semi-precious stones. Many had been polished by the waters into fantastic shapes. When she had filled a bag, she showed them to Meren, who made her a bracelet with a matching anklet. One day, below a dried-up waterfall, she plucked a gold nugget the size of the first joint of her thumb from the pan. It sparkled in the sun and dazzled her. 'Fashion for me a jewel, Taita,' she demanded.

Although he had been able to hide it, Taita had felt twinges of jealousy when she wore the ornaments Meren had made for her. At my age? He smiled at his folly. Like a lovelorn swain. Nevertheless, he devoted all his art and creative genius to the task she had set him. He used the silver from the hilt of Lotti's sword to make a thin chain and a setting from which he suspended the nugget. When it was done, he worked a spell into it to give it protective qualities over its wearer, then hung it round her neck. When she looked down at her image in a river pool her eyes filled with tears. 'It is so beautiful,' she whispered, 'and it feels warm on my skin, as though it were alive.' The warmth she had detected was the emanation of the power with which he had endowed it. It became her most prized possession, and she named it the Talisman of Taita.

The further south they travelled, the lighter and more buoyant the mood of the company became. All at once it struck Taita that there was something unnatural about it. It was true that the way was not as hazardous as it had been when they were lost in the great swamps or in the lands of the Chima, but they were far from home, the road was endless and the conditions arduous. There was no reason for their optimism and light-heartedness.

In the fading light of day he was sitting beside a river pool with Fenn. She was studying the trio of the elemental symbols of the Tenmass that he had drawn on her clay tablet. Each denoted a word of power. When they were conjugated they became so portentous and charged that they could be safely absorbed only into a mind that had been prepared carefully to receive them. Taita sat close to her, ready to protect her if the shock of the conjugation produced a backlash. Across the pool a giant black and white kingfisher, with a russet chest, was hovering over the water. It dived, but Fenn's concentration on the symbols was so intense that she did not glance up at the splash as the bird struck the surface, then rose with a flutter of wings and a small silver fish clamped in its long black bill.

Taita tried to analyse his own feelings more closely. There was only one good reason he could think of for his own euphoric state of mind: his love for and delight in the child at his side. On the other hand there were compelling reasons why he should be afraid for both their sakes. He was charged with a sacred duty to protect his pharaoh and his homeland. He was travelling to a confrontation with a powerful evil force without any clear plan, a lone hare setting out to scotch a marauding leopard. All the chances were against him. Almost certainly the consequences would be dire. Why, then, was he doing so seemingly without any reckoning of the consequences?

Then he became aware that he was having difficulty in following even this simple line of reasoning. It was as though impediments were being placed deliberately in his way. He kept feeling a strong impulse to let it go and to lapse back into a complacent sense of well-being and trust in his own ability to overcome obstacles as he encountered them, without having any coherent plan. It is a dangerous and reckless state of mind, he thought, then laughed aloud as though it were a joke.

He had disrupted Fenn's concentration: she looked up and frowned. 'What is it, Taita?' she demanded. 'You warned me that it was dangerous to become distracted when I was attempting to conjugate the rational coefficients of the symbols.'

Her words brought him up sharply, and Taita realized how grievously he had erred. 'You are right. Forgive me.' She looked down again at the clay tablet in her lap. Taita tried to focus on the problem, but it remained hazy and unimportant. He bit hard into his lip, and tasted blood. The sharp pain sobered him. With an effort, he was able to concentrate.

There was something he must remember. He tried to grasp it, but it remained a shadow. He reached for it again, but it dissolved before he could catch it. Beside him Fenn stirred again and sighed. Then she looked up and set aside the clay tablet. 'I cannot concentrate. I can feel your distress. Something is blocking you.' She stared at him with those candid green eyes, then whispered, 'I can see it now. It is the witch in the pool.' Quickly she removed the nugget from round her neck and placed it in her palm. She held out both of her hands. Taita placed the Periapt of Lostris in his own palm. Then they linked hands and formed the circle of protection. Almost imperceptibly he felt the alien influence recede. The words that had troubled him jumped into his mind. He had been trying to remember the warning of Demeter: *She has already infected you with her evil. She has begun to bind you with her spells and temptations. She will twist your judgement. Soon you will begin to doubt that she is evil. She will seem to you fine, noble and as virtuous as any person who ever lived. Soon it will seem*

*that I am the evil one who has poisoned your mind against her.
When that happens she will have divided us and I will be destroyed.
You will surrender yourself to her freely and willingly. She will have
triumphed over both of us.*

They sat together in the protective circle until Taita had
thrown off the enervating influence of Eos. He was amazed
by the support Fenn rendered him. He could feel the strength
flowing from her soft little hands into his own gnarled and
knotted ones. They had shared more than one life span,
and together they had built a fortress of the spirit within walls
of marble and granite.

Darkness fell swiftly and bats flitted over the pool, wheeling
and swooping on the insects that rose from the surface of the
water. On the opposite bank of the river a hyena whooped
mournfully. Still holding Fenn's hand, Taita raised her to her
feet and led her up the bank to the zareeba.

Meren greeted them. 'I was about to send out a search party
to find you,' he called cheerfully.

Later Taita sat with him and his officers at the campfire.
They, too, were cheerful, and he could hear the laughter and
the banter from the men at the far end of the enclosure. Once
in a while Taita thought to sober them with a warning, but he
let them be: *They also are marching to the siren song of Eos,
but I will let them go happily where they must go anyway. As
long as I can hold firm, there will be time anon to recall them
to their senses.*

Each day they pushed deeper into the south, and the
determination of Meren and his men never wavered.
One evening as they built the zareeba Taita led Meren
aside and asked, 'What make you of the mood of the men? It
seems to me that they are near the end of their endurance,
eager to turn northwards for Assoun and their homes. We may
soon be faced with a mutiny.' He had said it to test the other
man, but Meren was outraged.

'They are my men and I have come to know them well. It seems you have not, Magus. There is not a mutinous hair on their heads or breath in their lungs. They are as hot for the enterprise as I am.'

'Forgive me, Meren. How could I doubt you?' Taita murmured, but he had heard echoes of the witch's voice rise from Meren's throat. It is good that I need not deal with sullen faces and surly moods on top of all else. In that Eos is making my lot easier, he consoled himself.

At that Fenn came running from the camp calling, 'Magus! Taita! Come swiftly! The baby of Li-To-Liti is bursting out of her and I cannot get it back inside!'

'Then I shall come and save the poor mite from your ministrations.' Taita scrambled to his feet and hurried with her to the encampment. With Taita kneeling beside the Shilluk girl, soothing her, the birth went swiftly. Fenn watched the process with horror. Each time Li-To-Liti squealed she started. In a pause between contractions, while the girl lay panting and drenched with sweat, Fenn said, 'It does not seem such rich sport after all. I don't think you and I should bother ourselves with it.'

Before midnight Li-To-Liti was delivered of an amber-coloured son with a cap of black curls. To Taita, the arrival of the child was some compensation for the profligate expenditure of other young lives along this bitter road. They all rejoiced with the father.

'It is a good omen,' the men told each other. 'The gods smile upon us. From now onwards our venture will prosper.'

Taita sought the counsel of Nakonto. 'What is the custom of your people? How long must the woman rest before she can go on?'

'My first wife gave birth while we were moving cattle to new pasture. It was past noon when her waters broke. I left her with her mother to do the business beside the road. They caught up with me before nightfall, which was as well, because there were lions about.'

'Your women are hardy,' Taita remarked.

Nakonto looked mildly surprised. 'They are Shilluk,' he said.

'That would explain it,' Taita agreed.

The next morning Li-To-Liti slung her infant on her hip, where it could reach the breast without her having to dismount, and was up behind her man when the column pulled out at dawn.

They continued on through well-watered, grassy countryside. The sandy earth was gentle on the animals' legs and hoofs. Taita treated any light injuries or ailments with his salves so they remained in fine condition. There were endless herds of wild antelope and buffalo so there was never any shortage of meat. Days passed with such smooth regularity that they seemed to merge into one. The leagues fell away as vast distances opened ahead.

Then, at last, an escarpment of hills appeared on the misty blue horizon ahead of them. Over the following days it loomed larger until it seemed to fill half of the sky, and they could make out the deep notch in the high ground through which the Nile flowed. They headed directly for this, knowing that it would afford the easiest passage through the mountains. Closer still, they could see each feature of the heavily wooded slopes and the elephant roads that climbed them. At last Meren could no longer contain his impatience. He left the baggage train to make its own pace and took a small party forward to reconnoitre. Naturally Fenn went with them, riding beside Taita. They entered the gorge of the river and climbed up the rugged elephant road towards the summit of the escarpment. They were only half-way up when Nakonto ran forward and dropped on one knee to examine the ground.

'What is it?' Taita called. When he received no answer he rode forward and leant out from Windsmoke to discover what had intrigued the Shilluk.

'The tracks of horses.' Nakonto pointed to a patch of soft earth. 'They are very fresh. Only one day old.'

'Mountain zebra?' Taita hazarded.

Nakonto shook his head emphatically.

'Horses carrying riders,' Fenn translated, for Meren's sake.

He was alarmed. 'Strange horsemen. Who can they be, so far from civilization? They may be hostile. We should not continue up the pass until we find out who they are.' He looked back the way they had come. On the plain below they could see the cloud of yellow dust the rest of the column had raised, still three or more leagues away. 'We must wait for the others, then go forward in strength.' Before Taita could reply a loud halloo rang down from the high ground above and echoed off the hills. It startled them all.

'We have been discovered! But, by Seth's pestilential breath, whoever they are they speak Egyptian,' Meren exclaimed. He cupped his hands round his mouth and bellowed back up the pass, 'Who are you?'

'Soldiers of the divine Pharaoh Nefer Seti!'

'Advance and be recognized,' Meren called.

They laughed with relief as three strange horsemen came clattering down to meet them. Even at a distance Meren saw that one carried the blue standard of the House of Mamose, and as they came closer still their features were clearly Egyptian. Meren started forward to meet them. As the two parties came together they dismounted and embraced rapturously.

'I am Captain Rabat,' the leader introduced himself, 'an officer in the legion of Colonel Ah-Akhton in the service of Pharaoh Nefer Seti.'

'I am Colonel Meren Cambyses, on a special duty for the same divine pharaoh.' Rabat acknowledged his superior ranking with a salute of one fist clenched across his breast. Meren went on, 'And this is the magus, Taita of Gallala.' True respect dawned in Rabat's eyes and he saluted again. Taita saw from his aura that Rabat was a man of limited intelligence, but honest and without guile.

'Your fame precedes you, Magus. Please allow me to guide you to our encampment, where you will be our honoured guest.'

Rabat had ignored Fenn for she was a child, but she was conscious of the snub. 'I don't like this Rabat,' Fenn told Taita in Shilluk. 'He is arrogant.'

Taita smiled. She had become accustomed to her favoured position. In this she reminded him strongly of Lostris when she had been sovereign of Egypt. 'He is only a rough soldier,' he consoled her, 'and beneath your consideration.' Appeased, her expression softened.

'What are your orders, Magus?' Rabat asked.

'The rest of our contingent follows with a large train of baggage.' Taita pointed at the dustcloud on the plain. 'Please send one of your men back to guide them.' Rabat despatched a man at once, then led the rest of them up the steep, rocky pathway towards the crest of the pass.

'Where is Colonel Ah-Akhton, your commander?' Taita asked, as he rode at Rabat's side.

'He died of the swamp-sickness during our advance up the river.'

'That was seven years ago?' Taita asked.

'Nay, Magus. It was nine years and two months,' Rabat corrected him, 'the term of our exile from our beloved homeland, Egypt.'

Taita realized that he had forgotten to include the time it would have taken them to reach this place since leaving Karnak. 'Who commands the army in Colonel Ah-Akhton's place?' he asked.

'Colonel Tinat Ankut.'

'Where is he?'

'He led the army southwards along the river in accordance with the command of Pharaoh. He left me here with only twenty men and some women, those with very young children who had been born during the march or those who were too sick or weak to continue.'

'Why did Colonel Tinat leave you here?'

'I was ordered to plant crops, to keep a herd of horses ready for him, and to hold a base in his rear to which he could retire, if he were forced to retreat from the wild lands to the south.'

'Have you had news of him since he marched away?'

'Some months later he sent back three men with all of his surviving horses. It seems that he had journeyed into a country to the south that is infested with a fly whose sting is fatal to horses and he had lost almost all of his herd. Since those three arrived, we have had no word of him. He and his men have been swallowed up by the wilderness. That was many long years ago. You are the first civilized men we have met in all that time.' He sounded forlorn.

'You have not thought to abandon this place and take your people back to Egypt?' Taita asked, to gauge his mettle.

'I have thought on it,' Rabat admitted, 'but my orders and my duty are to hold this post.' He hesitated, then went on, 'Besides, the man-eating Chima and the great swamps stand between us and our very Egypt.' Which is probably the most telling reason why you have remained at your post, Taita thought. As they talked they came out at the head of the pass and before them stretched a wide plateau. Almost at once they felt that the air of this high place was more pleasant than that on the plains below.

There were scattered herds of grazing cattle, and beyond them Taita was astonished to see the mud walls of a substantial military fort. It seemed out of place in this remote and savage landscape; the first sign of civilization they had come across since they had left the fort of Qebui more than two years previously. This was a lost outpost of empire of which no one in Egypt was aware.

'What is the name of this place?' Taita asked.

'Colonel Tinat called it Fort Adari.'

They rode among the grazing cattle, tall, rangy animals with huge humped shoulders and a wide spread of heavy horns. The coat of each had a distinctive colour and pattern, no two alike. They were red or white, black or yellow, with contrasting blotches and spots.

'Where did you find these cattle?' Taita asked. 'I have seen none other like them.'

'We trade them with the native tribes. They call them *zebu*. The herds provide us with milk and beef. Without them we would suffer even greater hardship than we do at present.'

Meren frowned and opened his mouth to reprimand Rabat for his lack of spirit, but Taita read his intention, and cautioned him with a quick shake of his head. Although Taita agreed with both Fenn and Meren on the fellow's worth, it would not be of any benefit to them to offend him. Almost certainly, they would need his co-operation later. The fields around the fort were planted with dhurra, melons and vegetable crops that Taita did not recognize. Rabat told them the outlandish native names, and dismounted to pick a large shiny black fruit, which he handed to Taita. 'When cooked in a stew of meat they are tasty and nutritious.'

When they reached the fort the women and children of the garrison came out through the gates to welcome them, carrying bowls of soured milk and platters of dhurra cake. Altogether there were fewer than fifty and they were a bedraggled, sorry-looking lot, although they were friendly enough. Accommodation in the fort was limited. The women offered a small windowless cell to Taita and Fenn. The floor was of packed earth, ants moved in military file along the rough-hewn walls and shiny black cockroaches scurried into cracks in the log walls. The smell of the unwashed bodies and chamber-pots of the previous occupants was pervasive. Rabat explained apologetically that Meren and the rest, officers and men alike, would have to bunk with his soldiers in the communal barracks. With expressions of gratitude and regret, Taita declined this offer of hospitality.

Taita and Meren chose a congenial site half a league beyond the fort, in a grove of shady trees on the banks of a running stream. Rabat, who was plainly relieved not to have them in the fort, honoured Meren's Hawk Seal and provided them with fresh milk, dhurra and, at regular intervals, a slaughtered ox.

'I hope we are not to stay long in this place,' Hilto remarked to Taita, on the second day. 'The mood of these people is so despondent that it will lower the morale of our men. Their spirits are high, and I would like them to remain so. Besides, all the women are married and most of our men have been celibate for too long. Soon they will want to sport with them and there will be trouble.'

'I assure you, good Hilto, that we will move on as soon as we have made the arrangements.' Taita and Meren spent the following days in close consultation with the melancholy Rabat.

'How many men went south with Colonel Tinat?' Taita wanted to know.

Like many illiterates, Rabat had a reliable memory and he replied without hesitation: 'Six hundred and twenty-three, with one hundred and forty-five women.'

'Merciful Isis, was that all who remained of the original thousand who marched from Karnak?'

'The swamps were trackless and deep,' Rabat explained. 'We were laid low with swamp-sickness. Our guides were unreliable and we were attacked by the native tribes. Our losses of men and horses were heavy. Surely you had the same experience, for you must have covered the same ground to reach Adari.'

'Yes, indeed. However, the water was lower, and our guides faultless.'

'Then you were more fortunate than ourselves.'

'You said that Colonel Tinat sent men and horses back here. How many horses were there?' Taita switched to a more agreeable subject.

'They brought back fifty-six, all fly-struck. Most died after reaching us. Only eighteen survived. Once they had delivered the horses, Colonel Tinat's men went south again to rejoin him. They took with them the porters I had recruited for them.'

'So none of Tinat's men remains with you?'

'One was so ill that I kept him here. He has survived to this day.'

'I would like to question him,' Taita told him.

'I will send for him at once.'

The sole survivor was tall but skeletally thin. Taita saw at once that his emaciated frame and thin white hair were relics of disease, rather than signs of age. Despite this he had recovered his health. He was cheerful and willing, unlike most of the other men under Rabat's command.

'I have heard of your ordeal,' Taita told him, 'and I commend your courage and zeal.'

'You are the only one who has, Magus, and I thank you for it.'

'What is your name?'

'Tolas.'

'Your rank?'

'I am a horse surgeon and a sergeant of the first water.'

'How far had you ventured south before Colonel Tinat sent you to bring back the surviving horses?'

'About twenty days' travel, Magus, perhaps two hundred leagues. Colonel Tinat was determined to travel fast – too fast. I believe this increased our loss of horses.'

'Why was he in such haste?' Taita asked.

Tolas smiled thinly. 'He did not confide in me, Magus, nor seek my counsel.'

Taita thought for a while. It seemed possible that Tinat had come under the influence of the witch, and that she had enticed him southwards. 'Then, good Tolas, tell me about the disease that attacked the horses. Captain Rabat mentioned it to me, but he gave no details. What makes you think that it was caused by these flies?'

'It broke out ten days after we first encountered the insects. The horses began to sweat excessively and their eyes filled with blood so that they became half blind. Most died within ten or fifteen days of the first symptoms occurring.'

'You are a horse surgeon. Do you know of any cure?'

Tolas hesitated, but did not answer the question. Instead he remarked, 'I saw the grey mare you ride. I have seen many tens of thousands of horses in my lifetime, but I would think that mare is as good as the best of them. You might never find another like her.'

'It is clear that you are a fine judge of horseflesh, Tolas, but why do you tell me this?'

'Because it would be a shame to sacrifice such a horse to the fly. If you are determined to go on, as I think you are, leave the mare and her foal with me until you return. I will look after her as though she were my own child.'

'I will think on it,' Taita told him. 'But to return to my question: do you know of any remedy for the fly sickness?'

'The native tribes hereabouts have a potion that they distil from wild berries. They dose their cattle with it.'

'Why did they not warn Colonel Tinat of this disease before he left Fort Adari?'

'At that time we had no contact with the tribes. It was only when I returned with the fly-ridden herd that they came forward to sell us the medicine.'

'Is it efficacious?'

'It is not infallible,' Tolas told him. 'It appears to me that it will cure six out of ten horses that have been fly-struck. But perhaps those horses I tried it on had already been too long infected.'

'What would have been your losses if you had not used it?'

'I cannot tell for certain.'

'Then guess.'

'It seems to me that some animals have a natural resistance to the sting. A very few, say, five in a hundred, will show no ill-effects. Others, perhaps thirty or forty in a hundred, will sicken but recover. The rest die. Any animal that is infected but recovers is immune to any subsequent infection.'

'How do you know this?'

'The natives know it well.'

'How many of the horses in your care have been infected but have recovered?'

'Most were too far gone before we could dose them. However, eighteen are salted,' Tolas answered promptly, then clarified, 'They are immune.'

'So, Tolas, I will need a goodly supply of this native potion. Can you procure it for me?'

'I can do better. I have had almost nine years to study the matter. Although the tribesmen are secretive and will not divulge the recipe, I have discovered for myself the plant that they use. I have spied upon them while their women are gathering it.'

'You will show it to me?'

'Of course, Magus,' Tolas agreed readily. 'But, again, I caution you that even when treated many horses will still die. Your grey mare is too fine an animal to expose to such risk.'

Taita smiled. It was apparent that Tolas had fallen in love with Windsmoke and was angling for a way to keep her with him. 'I will take into careful consideration all you have told me. But now my main concern is to learn the secret of the cure.'

'With the permission of Captain Rabat, I will take you into the forest tomorrow to gather the berries. It is a ride of several hours to reach the area where they grow.'

'Excellent.' Taita was pleased. 'Now describe for me the road to the south that you travelled with Colonel Tinat.' Tolas told them all he could remember, while Fenn made notes on a clay tablet. When he had finished Taita said, 'What you have told me, Tolas, is invaluable, but now you must describe how we will recognize the boundary of the fly territory.'

Tolas placed his forefinger on the sketch map that Fenn had drawn on the tablet. 'On about the twentieth day of the journey southwards you will come upon a pair of hills shaped like a virgin's breasts. They will be visible from several leagues off. Those hills mark the boundary. I counsel you not to take the grey mare further. You will lose her in the sad country that lies beyond.'

The next morning Captain Rabat went with them, riding beside Taita, when they set out in search of the berries. The pace was easy, and they had much opportunity to talk.

After several hours, Tolas led them into a grove of enormous wild fig trees strung out along the bank of the river, deep in the gorge. Most of the branches were draped with serpentine vines, upon which grew clusters of small purple-black berries. Fenn, Tolas and three other men, whom Tolas had brought from the fort, climbed into the trees. Each had a leather harvesting bag slung round their neck into which they packed the fruit. When they clambered down from the trees their hands were stained purple and the berries emitted a sickly, putrid odour. Fenn offered a handful to Whirlwind, but the colt refused it. Windsmoke was equally disdainful.

'It is not to their natural taste, I grant, but if you mix the berries into dhurra meal and bake it into cakes they will eat them readily enough,' Tolas said. He lit a fire and placed flat river stones in the flames. While they heated he demonstrated how to pound the fruit into a paste and mix it with the dhurra meal. 'The proportions are important. One of fruit to five of the meal. Any larger amount of the berries and the horse will refuse it, or if they eat it they will purge excessively,' he explained. When the stones were crackling hot he put handfuls of the mixture on to them and let it bake into hard cakes. He laid them aside to cool and began another batch. 'The cakes will keep without spoiling for many months, even in the worst conditions. The horses will eat them even when they are covered with green mould.'

Fenn picked one up and burnt her fingers. She passed it from hand to hand and blew on it until it cooled, then took it to Windsmoke. The mare sniffed it, fluttering her nostrils. Then she took it between her lips and rolled her eyes at Taita.

'Go on, you silly thing,' he told her sternly. 'Eat. It is good for you.'

Windsmoke crunched the cake. A few scraps fell out of her mouth, but she swallowed the rest. Then she lowered her head to pick up the pieces from the grass. Whirlwind was watching her with interest. When Fenn brought him a cake he followed her example and ate it with gusto. Then he pushed Fenn with his muzzle, demanding more.

'What dose do you give them?' Taita asked Tolas.

'It was a matter of experiment,' Tolas replied. 'As soon as they show any symptoms of being fly-struck I give them four or five cakes each day until the symptoms disappear, then continue the dose until long after they seem fully recovered.'

'What do you call the fruit?' Fenn demanded.

Tolas shrugged. 'The Ootasa have some outlandish name for it, but I have never thought to give it an Egyptian one.'

'Then I shall name it the Tolas fruit,' Fenn announced, and Tolas smiled, gratified.

The following day Taita and Fenn returned to the grove with Shofar, four troopers and the equipment they needed to bake a large quantity of Tolas cakes. They set up camp in the midst of the grove, in a clearing that overlooked the dry bed of the Nile. They stayed there for ten days, and filled twenty large leather sacks with the cakes. When they returned with purple-stained hands and ten baggage-loaded mules, they found Meren and his men eager to leave.

When they bade Rabat farewell, he told Taita dolefully, 'We shall probably never meet again in this life, Magus, but it has been a great honour for me to be allowed to render you some small service.'

'I am grateful for your willing assistance and cheerful company. Pharaoh himself will hear of it,' Taita assured him.

They struck out again southwards, with Tolas as their guide, towards the hills shaped like a virgin's breasts, and the fly country. Their time at Fort Adari had refreshed men and animals and they made good progress. Taita ordered that the hunters should keep the tails of the animal game they caught. He showed the men how to skin them, scrape flesh, salt them, then leave them to dry in the air. Meanwhile they carved wood into handles and inserted them into the tubes of dried skin in place of the bone they had removed. Finally Taita brandished one of the fly switches and told them, 'Soon you will be grateful for these. It is probably the only weapon that will discourage the fly.'

On the twentieth morning after they had left Fort Adari they made the customary early start on the day's trek. Then at a little past noon, as Tolas had predicted, the twin nipples of the hills, like the breasts of a virgin, thrust above the horizon.

'No further. Order the halt,' Taita called to Meren. He had decided before they left Fort Adari that he would not follow Tolas's advice slavishly. He had already been dosing Windsmoke and Whirlwind with the cakes and hoped that the medicine would concentrate in their blood long before they suffered the first sting. On that last evening before they entered the fly territory he took Fenn with him to the horse lines. When she saw them coming Windsmoke whickered. Taita rubbed her forehead and scratched behind her ears, then fed her a Tolas cake. Fenn did the same for Whirlwind. By now both had developed a taste for the cakes and swallowed them with appetite. Tolas had been watching from the shadows. Now he approached Taita and greeted him diffidently. 'So you are taking the grey mare and her foal with you?' he asked.

'I could not bear to leave them behind,' Taita replied.

Tolas sighed. 'I understand, Magus. Perhaps I would have done the same, for already I love them. I pray to Horus and Isis that they will survive.'

'Thank you, Tolas. We will all come together again, of that I am certain.'

Next morning they parted company. Tolas could guide them no further and turned back for Fort Adari. Nakonto was out on the point, breaking the trail, Meren and three squads marching behind him. Taita and Fenn came next, on Wind-smoke and Whirlwind. The eighteen salted horses followed in a loose herd. Shabako, with the fourth squad, brought up the rear.

They camped that evening under the hills. While they ate their dinner by the fires a pride of hunting lions began to roar on the dark plain beyond the hills, a menacing sound. Taita and Meren went to check the head ropes of the tethered horses, but the lions did not come closer and gradually their roars receded and the silence of the night settled over them.

The next morning, while the column mustered, Taita and Fenn fed the horses their Tolas cakes. Then they mounted and rode on between the twin hills. Taita had just relaxed into the rhythm of the march when suddenly he straightened and stared at Windsmoke's neck. A large dark insect had appeared on her creamy hide, close to her mane. He cupped his right hand and waited for the insect to settle, extend its sharp black proboscis and probe for the blood vessels beneath the mare's skin. The buried sting anchored it, so he was able to snatch it up in his cupped hands. It buzzed shrilly as it tried to escape but he tightened his grip and crushed its head and body. Then he held it between two fingers and showed it to Fenn. 'This is a fly that the tribes call the tsetse. It is the first of many to come,' he predicted. At the words, another fly settled on his neck and plunged its sting into the soft skin behind his ear. He winced and slapped at it. Although he caught it a hard blow, it shot away seemingly unharmed.

'Get out your fly switches,' Meren ordered, and soon they were all lashing at themselves and their mounts, like religious flagellants, trying to drive off the stinging swarms. The follow-ing days were a torment as the flies plagued them ceaselessly. They were at their worst during the heat of the day, but kept up the attack by the light of the moon and the stars, madden-ing men and horses alike.

The tails of the horses lashed continuously against their flanks and hindquarters. They tossed their heads and twitched their skins as they tried to shake off the flies that crawled into their ears and eyes.

The faces of the men swelled like some grotesque crimson fruit and their eyes became slits in the puffy flesh. The backs of their necks were lumpy and the itching was intolerable. With their fingernails they scratched raw the skin behind their ears. At night they built smudge fires of dried elephant dung and crouched, coughing and gasping, in the acrid smoke to seek respite. But as soon as they moved away for a breath of fresh air the flies arrowed in on them, driving their stings deep at the instant they landed. Their bodies were so tough that a hard blow with the palm of a hand hardly disturbed them. Even when they were knocked from their perch, they rebounded in the same movement, stinging again on some other exposed body part. The fly switches were the only effective weapon. They did not kill them, but the long tail hairs tangled legs and wings and held them so that they could be crushed between the fingers.

'There is a limit to the range of these monsters,' Taita encouraged the men. 'Nakonto knows their habits well. He says that as suddenly as we came upon them we will be free of them.'

Meren ordered forced marches and rode at the head of the column, setting a driving pace. Deprived of sleep and weakened by the venom that the flies pumped into their blood the men swayed in their saddles. When a trooper collapsed his comrades threw him over the back of his horse and rode on.

Nakonto alone was inured to the insects. His skin remained smooth and glossy, unmarked by stings. He allowed the insects to suck themselves full of his blood so that they could not fly. Then he mocked them as he tore off their wings: 'I have been stabbed by men, leopards have bitten me and lions clawed me. Who are you to annoy me? Now you can walk home to hell.'

On the tenth day after they had left the hills, they rode out of the fly country. It happened so suddenly that they were taken unawares. At one moment they were cursing and flogging at the whirling insects, then fifty paces further on the silence of the forest was no longer disturbed by the vicious whine. Within a league of passing out of the tyranny they came upon an isolated river pool. Meren took pity on the party. 'Fall out!' he roared. 'The last one into the water is a simpering virgin.'

There was a rush of naked bodies, then the forest rang with cries of relief and jubilation. When they emerged from the pool, Taita and Fenn ministered to everyone's swollen stings, smearing them with one of the magus's salves. That night the laughter and banter round the campfires was unstinted.

It was dark when Fenn knelt over Taita and shook him awake. 'Come quickly, Taita! Something terrible is happening.' She seized his hand and dragged him to the horse lines. 'It's both of them.' Fenn's voice cracked with distress. 'Windsmoke and Whirlwind together.'

When they reached the lines, the colt was down, his body heaving to the urgent tempo of his breathing. Windsmoke stood over him, licking his head with long strokes of her tongue. She reeled weakly as she tried to keep her balance. Her coat was standing on end and she was drenched with sweat: it dripped from her belly and ran down all four legs.

'Call Shofar and his troops. Tell them to hurry. Then run and ask them to fill their largest pot with hot water and bring it to me.' Taita's main concern was to get Whirlwind back on his feet and keep Windsmoke on hers. Once a horse was down it had lost the will to fight and surrendered to the disease.

Shofar and his men lifted Whirlwind and placed him on his feet, then Taita sponged him with warm water. Fenn stood at his head blowing softly into his nostrils, whispering encouragement and endearments while she persuaded him to eat one Tolas cake after another.

As soon as he had bathed the colt, Taita turned to Windsmoke. 'Be brave, my darling,' he murmured, as he wiped her down with a wet linen rag. Meren helped him to dry her vigorously with fresh cloths, and then they spread Taita's tiger-skin over her back. 'You and I will defeat this thing together.' He kept talking quietly to her, and used the voice of power whenever he spoke her name. She cocked her ears to listen to him, splayed her legs and braced herself to keep her balance. '*Bak-her*, Windsmoke. Do not give in.'

He hand-fed her the Tolas cakes, which he had dipped in honey. Even in her distress she could not resist this delicacy. Then he persuaded her to swallow a bowl of his special remedy for fever, yellow-strangler and equine distemper. He and Fenn joined hands to invoke the protection of Horus, in his form as the god of horses. Meren and his men joined in the prayers, and continued to chant them for the rest of the night. By morning, Windsmoke and her colt were still standing, but their heads were hanging and they would no longer take the cakes. They were, however, consumed by thirst, and drank eagerly from the pots of clean water that Fenn and Taita held for them. Just before noon Windsmoke raised her head and whickered to her colt, then staggered across to him and nuzzled his shoulder. He raised his head to look at her.

'He has lifted his head,' one man said excitedly.

'She stands more firmly,' another observed. 'She is fighting for herself and for her foal.'

'She has stopped sweating. The fever is breaking.'

That evening Windsmoke ate five more Tolas cakes with honey. The next morning she followed Taita down into the riverbed and rolled in the white sand. She had always favoured a particular variety of soft grass with fluffy pink seed heads that grew on the banks of the Nile, so Taita and Fenn scythed bundles of it and sorted from it the choicest stalks. On the fourth day both Windsmoke and Whirlwind filled their empty bellies with it.

'They are out of danger,' Taita pronounced, and Fenn hugged Whirlwind, then wept as though her heart had broken and would never mend.

Despite the Tolas cakes, many other horses showed symptoms of the disease. Twelve died, but Meren replaced them from the small herd of salted animals. Some men were also suffering from the effects of the fly venom: they were racked with enervating headaches, and every joint in their bodies was so stiff that they could hardly walk. It was many more days before animals and men had recovered enough to resume the march. Even then Taita and Fenn would not burden Windsmoke and Whirlwind with their weight, but rode spare horses and led them on their halter ropes. Meren reduced the length and pace of his daily marches to allow them all to recover completely. Then, over the days that followed, he increased the speed until they were moving briskly once more.

For two hundred leagues beyond the flies the land was devoid of human habitation. Then they encountered a small village of itinerant fishermen. The inhabitants fled as soon as the column of horsemen appeared. The shock of meeting these pale-skinned men with their strange bronze weapons, riding on strange hornless cattle, was too much for them. Taita examined their fish-smoking racks, and found them almost empty. The Nile no longer provided the village with her bounty. Clearly the fishermen were starving.

On the floodplains along the riverbank herds of large, robust antelope, with scimitar horns and white patches around their eyes, were feeding. The males were black, the females dark red. Meren sent out five of his mounted archers. The antelope seemed curious about the horses, and came to meet them. The first volley of arrows brought down four, and the next as many again. They laid out the carcasses on the outskirts of the village as a peace-offering, then settled down to wait. The starving villagers could not long resist and crept forward cautiously, ready to flee again at the first sign of aggression from the strangers. Once they had butchered the carcasses and had the meat grilling on a dozen smoky fires, Nakonto went forward to hail them. Their spokesman was a venerable greybeard, who replied in a squeaky treble.

Nakonto came back to report to Taita. 'These people are related to the Ootasa. Their languages are so similar that we understand each other well.'

By now the villagers were so emboldened that they came trooping back to examine the men, their weapons and horses. The unmarried girls wore only a string of beads round their waists, and almost immediately established friendships with the troopers who had no Shilluk camp-followers.

The married women brought calabashes of sour native beer to Taita, Meren and the captains, while the elder, whose name was Poto, sat proudly beside Taita and readily answered the questions Nakonto put to him.

'I know the southlands well,' he boasted. 'My father and his father before him lived on the great lakes, which were full of fish, some so large it needed four men to lift them. Their girth was thus . . .' he made a circle with his skinny old arms '. . . and their length was thus . . .' he jumped up and drew a line with his big toe in the dust, then took four full paces and drew a second line '. . . from there to there!'

'Fishermen are the same everywhere,' Taita remarked, but he made appropriate sounds of amazement. Poto seemed neglected by his tribe and, for once, had the attention of all. He was enjoying the company of his new friends.

'Why did your tribe leave such good fishing grounds?' Taita asked.

'Another stronger and more numerous people came from the east and we could not resist them. They drove us northwards along the river to this place.' He looked downcast for a moment, then brightened again. 'When I was initiated and circumcised, my father took me to the great waterfall that is the birthplace of this, our river.' He indicated the Nile on whose banks they sat. 'The waterfall is called Tungula Madzi, the Waters that Thunder.'

'Why such an unusual name?'

'The roar of the falling waters and the mighty rocks they bring crashing down can be heard from a distance of two days' march. The spray stands above the falls like a silver cloud in the sky.'

'You have looked upon such a sight as this?' Taita asked, and turned his Inner Eye upon the ancient.

'With these very eyes!' Poto cried. His aura burnt brightly, like the flame of an oil lamp before it dies from lack of fuel. He was telling the truth.

'You believe that this is the birthplace of the river?' Taita's pulse raced with excitement.

'On the ghost of my father, the falls are where the river rises.'

'What lies above and beyond them?'

'Water,' said Poto flatly. 'Nothing but water. Water to the ends of the world.'

'You saw no land beyond the falls?'

'Nothing but water.'

'You did not see a burning mountain that sends a cloud of smoke into the sky?'

'Nothing,' said Poto. 'Nothing but water.'

'Will you lead us to this waterfall?' Taita asked.

When Nakonto translated the question to him, Poto looked alarmed. 'I can never return. The people thereabouts are my enemies, and they will kill me and eat me. I cannot follow the river because, as you can see, the river is cursed and dying.'

'I will make you a gift of a full bag of glass beads if you come with us,' Taita promised. 'You will be the richest man in all your tribe.'

Poto did not hesitate. He had turned the colour of ashes and was trembling with terror. 'No! Never! Not for a hundred bags of beads. If they eat me, my soul will never pass through the flames. It will become a hyena and wander for all time in the night, eating rotting carcasses and offal.' He made as if to jump up and run, but Taita restrained him with a gentle touch, then exerted his influence to calm and reassure him. He let him drink two large swallows of beer before he spoke to him again.

'Is there another who will guide us?'

Poto shook his head vigorously. 'They are all afraid, even more than I am.'

They sat in silence for a while, then Poto began to fidget and shuffle his feet. Taita waited patiently for him to reach some difficult decision. At last he coughed, and spat a large clot of yellow mucus into the dust. 'Perhaps there is somebody,' he ventured. 'But, no, he must be dead. He was an old man when last I saw him, and that was long ago. Even then he was older than you, revered elder.' He bobbed his head respectfully at Taita. 'He is among the last of our people who remain from the time that we were a tribe of consequence.'

'Who is he? Where will I find him?' Taita asked.

'His name is Kalulu. I will show you where to find him.' Again Poto began to draw with his toe in the dust. 'If you follow the great river, which is dying, you will come at last to where it meets one of the many lakes. This is a mighty stretch of water. We call it Semliki Nianzu.' He drew it as an elliptical flattened circle.

'Is it here that we will find the waterfall that is the birthplace of the river?' Taita demanded.

'No. The river cuts through the lake like the head of a spear through the body of a fish.' He slashed his toe through the circle. 'Our river is the outlet, the inlet is on the far south bank of the lake.'

'How will I find it?'

'You will not, unless somebody like Kalulu leads you to it. He lives in the marshes, on a floating island of reeds on the lake. Near the outlet of the river.'

'How will I find him?'

'By searching diligently and by good fortune.' Poto shrugged. 'Or perhaps he will find you.' Then, almost as an afterthought, he added, 'Kalulu is a shaman of great mystical powers, but he has no legs.'

When they left the village Taita gave Poto a double handful of glass beads and the old man wept. 'You have made me rich, and my old age happy. Now I can buy two young wives to look after me.'

The Nile flowed a little more strongly as they moved south along its bank, but they could tell from the high-water line that the level was much lower than it had been in former times.

'It has shrunk twenty-fold,' Meren calculated, and Taita agreed, even though he did not say so. Sometimes Meren had to be reminded that he was not an adept, and that some matters were better left to those qualified to deal with them.

As they journeyed along the west bank, horses and men grew stronger with each day that passed. They were all fully recovered from the effects of the fly by the time they reached the lake, which was as Poto had described it to them. It was vast.

'It must be a sea, not merely a lake,' Meren declared, and Taita sent him to fetch a pitcher of water from it.

'Now taste it, my good Meren,' he ordered. Gingerly Meren took a sip, and let it run round his mouth. Then he drank the rest of the pitcher.

'Salt sea?' Taita smiled kindly.

'Nay, Magus, sweet as honey. I was mistaken, and you were right.'

The lake was so large that it seemed to create its own wind system. In the dawn the air was still and cool. What looked like smoke rose high into the air from the surface. The men discussed this animatedly.

'The water is heated by a volcano,' said one.

'No,' said another. 'The water rises like mist. It will fall again elsewhere as rain.'

'Nay, it is the fiery breath of a sea monster that lives in the waters,' Meren said with authority.

In the end they looked at Taita for the truth.

'Spiders,' said Taita, which threw them into further passionate argument.

'Spiders do not fly. He means flies – dragon flies.'

'He toys with our credibility,' said Meren. 'I know him well. He loves his little jokes.'

Two days later the wind veered and one of the cloudy up-wellings drifted over the camp. Then as it reached land it began to descend. Fenn leapt high in the air and snatched something out of it.

'Spiders!' she squealed. 'Taita is never wrong.' The cloud was formed by countless newly hatched spiders, so immature as to be almost transparent. Each had woven a gossamer sail, which it used to catch the dawn breeze and sail aloft to be transported to some new quarter of the lake.

As soon as the sun struck the surface the wind picked up, until by noon it was whipping the water to foaming frenzy. During the afternoon it subsided until, at sunset, all was calm and serene. Flights of flamingoes strung out along the horizon in wavy pink lines. Hippopotamuses wallowed like granite boulders, grunting and bellowing in the shallows, cavernous pink jaws gaping to threaten rivals with their long incisors. Mighty crocodiles stretched out on the sandbars, sunning themselves, holding their mouths wide open so that water birds could pick the scraps of flesh from between their stubby yellow fangs. The nights were still, with the stars reflected on the velvety black waters.

To the west the lake was so extensive that there was no sight of land, other than a few small islands that seemed to sail like dhows on the wind-torn surface. To the south, they could just make out the far shore of the lake. There were no high mountain peaks or volcanoes, just a blue tracing of low hills.

Poto had warned them about the ferocity of the local tribes, so they built a secure camp with branches from the thorny acacia trees that burgeoned on the shores of the lake. During the days the horses and mules grazed on the fine grasses that grew on the littoral, or waded out to feast on the water-lilies and other aquatic plants in the shallows.

'When will we set out to find Kalulu, the shaman?' Fenn demanded.

'This very evening after you have had your dinner.'

As he had promised he took her to the beach, where they gathered driftwood and built a small fire. They squatted over it and Taita took her hands in his, forming the circle of protection. 'If Kalulu is an adept, as Poto suggested, we can cast for him across the ether,' Taita told her.

'Can you do that, Taita?' Fenn asked, in awe.

'According to Poto, he lives in the marshes very close to this place, perhaps only a few leagues distant from where we are now. He is within easy call.'

'Is distance important?' Fenn asked.

Taita nodded. 'We know his name. We know his physical appearance, his amputated legs. Of course, it would be easier if we knew his spirit name, or if we possessed something of his person – a hair, nail clippings, sweat, urine or dung. However, I will teach you to cast for a subject with what we have.' Taita took a pinch of herbs from his pouch and threw them on to the fire. They flared in a cloud of pungent smoke. 'This will drive off any evil influence that may be hovering nearby,' he explained. 'Look into the flames. If Kalulu comes you will see him there.'

Still holding hands they began to sway in time to a soft humming that Taita made deep in his chest. When Fenn had cleared her mind as he had taught her, they conjured up the three symbols of power, and silently conjugated them.

'Mensaar!'

'Kydash!'

'Ncube!'

The ether sang round them. Taita cast into it.

'Kalulu, hearken! O legless one, open thine ears!' He repeated the invitation at intervals as the moon rose and travelled half-way towards its zenith.

Suddenly they felt the strike. Fenn gasped at the thrill, like a discharge of static through her fingertips. She stared into the fire, and saw the outline of a face. It looked to her like that of an ancient but eternally wise ape.

'Who calls?' The fiery lips formed the question in the Tenmass. 'Who calls on Kalulu?'

'I am Taita of Gallala.'

'If you are of the Truth, show me your spirit name.' Taita allowed it to materialize as a symbol over his head: the sign of a falcon with a broken wing. It would be mortally dangerous for him to enunciate it into the ether where it might be pounced on by a malevolent entity.

'I acknowledge you, brother in Truth,' Kalulu said.

'Reveal your own spirit name,' Taita challenged him. Slowly the outline of a crouching African hare took shape above the face in the fire. It was the mythological wise one, Kalulu the Hare, whose head and long ears were portrayed in the disc of the full moon.

'I acknowledge you, brother of the right hand. I call upon you for your help,' said Taita.

'I know where you are and I am close by. Within three days I will come to you,' Kalulu replied.

Fenn was enchanted by the art of casting for a person across the ether. 'Oh, Taita, I never dreamt it was possible. Please teach me to do it.'

'First you must learn your own spirit name.'

'I think I know it,' she replied. 'You called me by it once, did you not? Or was it a dream, Taita?'

'Dreams and reality often blend and become one, Fenn. What is the name you remember?'

'Child of the Water,' she replied diffidently. 'Lostris.'

Taita stared at her in amazement. She was unconsciously demonstrating her psychic powers as seldom before. She had managed to reach back into the other life. Excitement and elation made his breathing quicken. 'Do you know the symbol of your spirit name, Fenn?'

'No, I have never seen it,' she whispered. 'Or have I, Taita?'

'Think of it,' he instructed. 'Hold it in the forefront of your mind!' She closed her eyes, and reached instinctively for the talisman that hung at her throat. 'Do you have it in your mind?' he asked gently.

'I have it,' she whispered, and he opened his Inner Eye. Her aura was a dazzling brilliance that cloaked her from head to foot, and the symbol of her spirit name hung over her head, etched in the same celestial fire.

The shape of the nymphaea flower, the water-lily, he thought. It is complete. She has come into full bloom, like her spirit symbol. Even in childhood, she has become an adept of the first water. Aloud he said to her, 'Fenn, your mind and spirit are fully prepared. You are ready to learn everything I can teach you, and perhaps more than that.'

'Then teach me to cast upon the ether, and to reach you even when great distances separate us.'

'We will begin at once,' he said. 'I already have something of yours.'

'What is it? Where?' she asked eagerly. In reply he touched the Periapt that hung round his neck. 'Show me,' she demanded, and he opened the locket to reveal the coil of hair it contained.

'Hair,' she said, 'but not mine.' She touched it with her forefinger. 'This is the hair of an old lady. See? There are grey strands mixed with the gold.'

'You were old when I cut it from your head,' he agreed. 'You were already dead. You were lying upon the embalming table, cold and stark.'

She shuddered with delicious horror. 'Was that in the other life?' she asked. 'Tell me about it. Who was I?'

'It will take me a lifetime to tell it all,' he said, 'but let me start by saying that you were the woman I loved, even as I love you now.' She groped for his hand, blinded by tears.

'You have something of mine,' she whispered. 'Now I need something of yours.' She reached up into his beard and twisted a thick strand around her finger. 'Your beard struck me when you pursued me on the first day we met. It shines like purest silver.' She drew the small sharp bronze dagger from the sheath on her girdle, and cut the strand close to the skin, then lifted it to her nose and smelt it, as though it were a fragrant blossom. 'It is your smell, Taita, your very essence.'

'I will make you a locket to keep it in.'

She laughed with pleasure. 'Yes, I would like that. But you must have the hair of the living child to go with that of the dead woman.' She reached up, cut a lock from her head and offered it to him. He coiled it carefully and placed it in the compartment of the Periapt, on top of the lock that had lain there for more than seventy years.

'Will I always be able to summon you?' Fenn said.

'Yes, and I you,' Taita agreed, 'but first I must teach you how.'

Over the days that followed they practised the art. They started by sitting within sight of each other, but out of earshot. Within hours she was able to receive the images he placed in her mind, and respond with images of her own. When they had it perfected, they turned their backs upon each other so that they were out of eye contact. Finally Taita left her in the camp and rode several leagues west along the lakeshore in the company of Meren. From there he reached her with his first attempt.

Each time he cast, she struck more readily, and the images she presented to him were crisper and more complete. For him she wore her symbol on her forehead, and after many attempts she could change the colour of the lily to suit her fancy, from rose to lilac to scarlet.

At night, she lay close to him, for protection, on her sleeping mat, and before she fell asleep she whispered, 'Now we will never be parted again, for I can find you wherever you go.'

In the dawn, before the wind came up, they went to bathe in the lake. Before they entered the water Taita cast a spell of protection to repel crocodiles and any other monsters that might lurk in the deep. Then they plunged in. Fenn swam with the lithe grace of an otter. Her naked body flashed like polished ivory as she slipped away into the depths. He never grew accustomed to how long she could stay under water and grew alarmed as he lay on the surface staring down into the green world below. After what seemed like an eternity, he saw the pale flash of her body as she came up towards him, just as she had in his dreams. Then she burst out beside him, laughing and shaking water out of her hair. At other times he did not see her returning. The first he knew of it was when she seized his ankle and tried to pull him under.

'How did you learn to swim as you do?' he demanded.

'I am the child of the water.' She laughed at him. 'Don't you remember? I was born to swim.' When they emerged from the lake they found a place in the early sunlight to dry themselves. He sat behind her and braided her hair, weaving water-lily blossoms into the tresses. While he worked he told her about the life she had lived as Queen of Egypt, the others who had loved her and the children to whom she had given birth. Often she would exclaim, 'Oh, yes! I remember that now. I remember that I had a son, but I cannot see his face.'

'Open your mind, and I will place his image in it from my own memory of him.'

She closed her eyes and he placed his cupped hands on each side of her head, covering her ears. They were silent for a while. At last she whispered, 'Oh, what a beautiful child. His hair is golden. I see his cartouche above him. His name is Memnon.'

'That was his childhood name,' he murmured. 'When he ascended to the throne and took the double crown of the Upper and Lower Kingdoms, he became Pharaoh Tamose, the first of that name. There! Look upon him in all his power and majesty.' Taita placed the image in her mind.

She was silent for a long time. Then she said, 'So handsome and noble. Oh, Taita, I wish I could have seen my son.'

'You did, Fenn. You suckled him at your breast, and with your own hands you placed the crown upon his head.'

Again she was silent, and then she said, 'Show me yourself on the day we first met in the other life. Can you do that, Taita? Can you conjure up your own image for me?'

'I would not dare to make the attempt,' he answered quickly.

'Why not?' she asked.

'It would be dangerous,' he replied. 'You must believe me. It would be too dangerous by far.'

He knew that if he showed her that image, it would haunt her in time with unattainable dreams. He would have sown the seeds of her discontent. For when they had first met in her other life, Taita had been a slave and the most beautiful young man in Egypt. That had been his downfall. His master, Lord Intef, had been the Nomarch of Karnak and the governor of all twenty-two nomes of Upper Egypt. He had also been a pederast and insanely jealous of his slave boy. Taita fell in love with a slave girl in his master's household named Alyda. When this was reported to Lord Intef, he ordered Rasfer, his executioner, to crush Alyda's skull slowly. Taita had been forced to watch her die. Even after the deed was done Lord Intef was still not satisfied. He had ordered Rasfer to castrate the virgin Taita.

There was a further aspect to this terrible situation. Lord Intef was the father of the little girl who, years later, became Queen Lostris. He was uninterested in his daughter and had made Taita, the eunuch, her tutor and mentor. That child was now reincarnated as Fenn.

It was so complex that Taita had difficulty finding the words to explain all this to Fenn, and for the moment he was relieved of the obligation to do so by a loud hail from the direction of the camp: 'Boats coming from the east! Stand to arms.' It was Meren's voice, clearly recognizable even at this distance. They sprang up, pulled on their tunics over bodies that were still damp and hurried back towards the camp.

'There!' Fenn pointed across the green waters. It took Taita a few moments to make out the dark specks against the white horses that were already being driven up by the rising wind.

'Native war canoes! Can you count the number of rowers, Fenn?'

She shaded her eyes, stared hard, then said, 'The leading canoe has twelve on each side. The others look to be as large. Wait! The second boat is the largest by far, with twenty rowers on the nearest side.'

Meren had drawn up his men in double ranks before the gate to the stockade. They were fully armed and alert to meet any sudden exigency. They watched as the canoes beached below them. The crews disembarked and gathered round the largest vessel. A band of musicians jumped ashore and began to dance on the beach. The drummers pounded out a feral rhythm, while the trumpeters brayed on the long spiral horns of some wild antelope.

'Mask your aura,' Taita whispered to Fenn. 'We know nothing of this fellow.' He watched it fade. 'Good. Enough.' If Kalulu was a savant, to mask her aura completely would raise even deeper suspicion.

Eight bearers lifted a litter from the boat and carried it up the beach. They were sturdy young women, with muscular arms and legs, wearing loincloths that were richly embroidered with glass beads. Their breasts were anointed with clarified fat and gleamed in the sunlight. They came directly to where Taita stood, and deposited the litter before him. Then they knelt beside it, in an attitude of deep reverence.

In the middle of the litter sat a dwarf. Fenn recognized him from the image in the flames, the face of the ancient ape with protruding ears and shining bald pate. 'I am Kalulu,' he said in the Tenmass, 'and I see you, Taita of Gallala.'

'I welcome you,' Taita responded. He saw at once that Kalulu was not a savant, but he threw a powerful, intense aura. From it, Taita could tell that he was an adept and a follower of the Truth. 'Let us go where we can speak in comfort and privacy.'

Kalulu swung himself into a handstand, the stubs of his severed legs pointing to the sky, and hopped down from the litter. He walked on his hands as though they were feet, twisting his head to one side so that he could talk up into Taita's face. 'I have been expecting you, Magus. Your approach has created a sharp disturbance on the ether. I have felt your presence grow stronger as you made your way up the river.' The women came after him, carrying the empty litter.

'This way, Kalulu,' Taita invited. When they reached his quarters, the women set down the litter, then backed away until they were out of earshot. Kalulu hopped back on to it and resumed his normal head-high position, squatting on his stumps. He looked around brightly at the camp, but when Fenn knelt before him to offer him a bowl of honey mead, he concentrated his attention on her.

'Who are you, child? I saw you in the firelight,' he said in the Tenmass. She pretended not to understand and glanced at Taita.

'You may reply,' he told her. 'He is of the Truth.'

'I am Fenn, a novice to the magus.'

He looked at Taita. 'Do you vouch for her?'

'I do,' Taita replied, and the little man nodded.

'Sit beside me, Fenn, for you are beautiful.' She sat on the litter trustingly. Kalulu looked at Taita with piercing black eyes. 'Why did you call for me, Magus? What is the service you require from me?'

'I need you to take me to the place where the Nile is born.'

Kalulu showed no surprise. 'You are the one who I saw in my dreams. You are the one I have waited for. I will take you to the Red Stones. We will leave tonight when the wind drops and the waters are still. How many are in your party?'

'Thirty-eight, with Fenn and me, but we have much baggage.'

'Five more large canoes will follow me. They will be here before nightfall.'

'I have many horses,' Taita added.

'Yes.' The little dwarf nodded. 'They will swim behind the canoes. I have brought bladders of animal stomachs to support them.'

In the brief African twilight, as the last gusts of the wind died away, some of the troopers led the horses down to the shore and, in the shallow water, strapped an inflated bladder to each side of their girth ropes. While this was going on, the others loaded their equipment into the canoes. Kalulu's female bodyguards carried him on his litter to the largest canoe and placed him aboard. As the waters of the lake settled into a slick calm, they pushed out from the shore and headed into the darkness towards the great cross of stars that hung in the southern skies. Ten horses were roped behind each canoe. Fenn sat in the stern, where she could call encouragement to Windsmoke and Whirlwind as they swam behind. The ranks of rowers plied their oars and the long, narrow hulls knifed silently through the dark waters.

Taita sat beside the litter on which Kalulu lay and they conversed quietly for a while. 'What is the name of this lake?'

'Semliki Nianzu. It is one of many.'

'How is it fed?'

'Previously two great rivers ran into it, one at the western end called Semliki, the other our Nile. Both come from the south, the Semliki from the mountains, the Nile from the great waters. That is where I am taking you.'

'Is it another lake?'

'No man knows if it is truly a lake or if it is the beginning of the great void.'

'This is where our Mother Nile is born?'

'Even so,' Kalulu agreed.

'What do you call this great water?'

'We call it Nalubaale.'

'Explain our route to me, Kalulu.'

'When we reach the far shore of Semliki Nianzu we will find the southerly limb of the Nile.'

'The picture I have in my mind is that the southerly limb of the Nile is where it flows into Semliki Nianzu. The northerly limb leaves this lake and flows north towards the great swamps. This is the branch of the Nile that has brought us thus far.'

'Yes, Taita. That is the wide picture. Of course, there are other minor rivers, tributaries and lesser lakes, for this is the land of many waters, but they all flow into the Nile and run to the north.'

'But the Nile is dying,' Taita said softly.

Kalulu was silent for a while, and when he nodded a single tear ran down his wizened cheek, sparkling in the moonlight. 'Yes,' he agreed. 'The rivers that feed her have all been stoppered. Our mother is dying.'

'Kalulu, explain to me how this has happened.'

'There are no words to explain it. When we reach the Red Stones you will see for yourself. I cannot describe these events to you. Mere words fall short of such a task.'

'I will contain my impatience.'

'Impatience is a young man's vice.' The dwarf smiled, his teeth gleaming in the gloom. 'And sleep is an old man's solace.' The plash of the waters under the canoe lulled them, and after a while they slept.

Taita woke to a soft cry from the leading canoe. He roused himself and leant over the side of the vessel to splash a double handful of water into his face. Then he blinked the drops from his eyes and looked ahead. He made out the dark loom of land ahead.

At last they felt the drag of the beach under the hull as they ran aground. The rowers dropped their oars and leapt ashore to pull the canoes higher. The horses found their footing and lunged ashore, streaming water. The women lifted Kalulu in his litter and carried him up the beach.

'Your men must have breakfast now,' Kalulu told Taita, 'so

that we can march at first light. We have a long road to travel before we reach the Stones.'

They watched the rowers embark in the canoes and push off into the lake. The silhouettes of the swift craft merged into the darkness, until the white splash of oars was all that marked their position. Soon those, too, had vanished.

By firelight they ate smoked lake fish and dhurra cakes, then in the dawn they set off along the lakeshore. Within half a league they came to a dry white riverbed.

'What river was this?' Taita asked Kalulu, although he knew what the answer would be.

'This was and is the Nile,' Kalulu replied simply.

'It is completely dried up!' Taita exclaimed, as he looked across the riverbed. It was four hundred paces from bank to bank, but no water flowed between them. Instead, elephant grass, like miniature bamboo that stood twice the height of a tall man, had filled it. 'We have followed the river two thousand leagues from Egypt to this place. All the way we have found at least some water, standing pools, even trickles and rivulets, but here it is as dry as the desert.'

'The water you encountered further north was the overflow from the lake Semliki Nianzu, which ran in from its tributaries,' Kalulu explained. 'This was the Nile, the mightiest river on all the earth. Now it is nothing.'

'What has happened to it?' Taita demanded. 'What infernal power could have stopped such a vast flow?'

'It is something that defies even an imagination as all-encompassing as your own, Magus. When we reach the Red Stones you will see it all before you.'

Fenn had been translating what was said for the benefit of Meren, and now he could no longer contain himself. 'If we are to follow a dry river,' he demanded, 'where will I find water for my men and horses?'

'You will find it even as the elephants do, by digging for it,' Taita told him.

'How long will this journey take?' Meren asked.

When this had been translated, Kalulu gave him an impish smile and replied, 'Much depends on the stamina of your horses and the strength of your own legs.'

They moved fast, passing the stagnant pools of once brimming lagoons and climbing through dry, rocky gorges where waterfalls had thundered. Sixteen days later they came upon a low ridge that ran parallel to the course of the Nile. It was the first feature that had relieved the monotony of the forest for many leagues.

'On that high ground stands the town of Tamafupa, the home of my people,' Kalulu told them. 'From the heights you can see the great waters of Nalubaale.'

'Let us go there,' Taita said. They rode up through a grove of fever trees with bright yellow trunks, which covered the slope above the dry riverbed. For lack of water the trees had died back, and their branches were leafless and twisted like rheumatic limbs. They came out on top of the ridge, where Windsmoke flared her nostrils and tossed her head. Whirlwind was equally excited: he gave a series of bucks and jumps.

'You bad horse!' Fenn struck him lightly on the neck with the switch of papyrus she carried. 'Behave!' Then she called to Taita, 'What is exciting them, Magus?'

'Smell it for yourself,' he called. 'Cool and sweet as the perfume of Kigelia flowers.'

'I smell it now,' she said, 'but what is it?'

'Water!' he answered, and pointed ahead. To the south stood a silver cloud, and beneath it lay a curve of ethereal blue that stretched across the breadth of the horizon. 'Nalubaale, at last!'

A sturdy palisade of hardwood poles dominated the crest of the ridge. The gates stood open and they rode through into the abandoned village of Tamafupa. Evidently it had once been the centre of a prosperous, thriving community – the abandoned huts were palatial and magnificently thatched – but the brooding silence that hung over them was eerie. They turned back to the gates and called up the rest of the party.

In response to their halloo, Kalulu was borne up to them on his litter by the panting and perspiring bodyguards. They were all solemn and contemplative as they gathered before the gates of Tamafupa and stared at the distant blue waters.

Taita broke the silence. 'The source of our very Mother Nile.'

'The end of the earth,' Kalulu said. 'There is nothing beyond those waters but the void and the Lie.'

Taita looked back at the fortifications of Tamafupa. 'We are in dangerous country, surrounded by hostile tribes. We will use it as our stronghold until we move on,' he told Meren. 'We will leave Hilto and Shabako here with their men to make the walls secure against attack. While they attend to this, Kalulu will take us to see the mysterious Red Stones.'

In the morning they went on: the last short stage of the journey that had taken them more than two years to complete. They followed the riverbed, often riding in the middle of the wide dry dip. They came round another gentle bend and ahead of them sloped a glacis of water-worn rocks. Surmounting it, like the fortification of a great city, rose a wall of solid red granite.

'In the holy names of Horus, the son, and Osiris, the divine father!' Meren exclaimed. 'What fortress is this? Is it the citadel of some African emperor?'

'What you see are the Red Stones,' said Kalulu, quietly.

'Who placed them there?' Taita asked, as perplexed as any of his companions. 'What man or demon has done this?'

'No man,' Kalulu replied. 'This is not the work of human hands.'

'What, then?'

'Come, let me show it to you first. Then we can discuss it.'

Cautiously they approached the Red Stones. When at last they stood under the great wall of rock that blocked the course of the Nile from one bank to the other, Taita dismounted and walked slowly along the base. Fenn and Meren followed him. They paused at intervals to inspect. It was flow-shaped, like the wax of a candle.

'This rock was once molten,' Taita observed. 'It has cooled into these fantastic shapes.'

'You are correct,' Kalulu agreed. 'That is precisely how it was formed.'

'It seems impossible, but this is a single mass of solid stone. There are no joints between individual blocks.'

'There is at least one crack, Magus.' Fenn pointed ahead. Her keen eyes had spotted a narrow fissure that ran through the centre of the wall, from top to bottom. When they reached it, Taita drew his dagger and tried to work the blade into it, but it was too narrow. The blade went in only as deep as the first joint of his little finger.

'That is why my people call it the Red Stones, rather than the Red Stone,' Kalulu told them, 'for it is divided into two sections.'

Taita went down on one knee to examine the base of the wall. 'It is not built upon the old riverbed. It emerges from it as though it has grown up from the centre of the earth like some monstrous mushroom. The stone of this wall seems to differ from any other around it.'

'Again, you are right,' Kalulu told him. 'It cannot be chiselled or chipped like the rock that surrounds it. If you look closely you will see the red crystals in it that give it the name.'

Taita leant forward until the minute crystals of which the wall was composed caught the sunlight and sparkled like tiny rubies. 'There is nothing obscene or unnatural about it,' he said softly. He came back to where Kalulu sat on his litter. 'How did this thing come to be here?'

'I cannot say with any certainty, Magus, even though I was here when it happened.'

'If you witnessed it, how do you not know what happened?'

'I will explain it to you later,' said Kalulu. 'Suffice to say that many others witnessed it, as I did, yet they have fifty different legends to describe it.'

'This entire wall of stone is chimerical,' Taita pointed out. 'Perhaps seeds of the truth may be buried in the legends and fantasies.'

'That may be so.' Kalulu inclined his head in agreement. 'But let us first ascend to the summit of the wall. There is much still that you must see.' They had to retreat along the riverbed to find a place to climb out and to the top of the bank. Then they picked their way back to the base of the red-stone wall.

'I will wait for you here,' Kalulu said. 'The way up is too difficult.' He indicated the daunting climb over glassy and almost vertical rock to the summit. They left him, and cautiously climbed upwards. In some places they were forced to crawl on hands and knees, but at last they stood on the rounded top of the Red Stones. From there they looked out across the lake. Taita shaded his eyes against the sun-dazzle that danced on the surface of the water. Close by there were a number of small islets, but he could see not the faintest trace of land beyond them. He looked back the way they had come. The foreshortened figure of the dwarf was far below. Kalulu was gazing up at him.

'Has anyone ever tried to cross to the far side of the lake?' Taita called down.

'There is no far side,' Kalulu shouted back. 'There is only the void.'

The surface of the water lapped the wall only four or five cubits below their feet. Taita looked back into the riverbed and made an approximate calculation of the discrepancy in the heights on each side of the wall.

'It is holding back forty or fifty cubits' depth of water.' He made a sweeping gesture, which took in the limitless extent of the lake's surface. 'Without this wall, all that water would have spilled over the cataract into the Nile and been carried down into Egypt. Little wonder that our land has been reduced to such straits.'

'We could sweep through the surrounding country, capture a host of slaves and set them to work on it,' Meren suggested.

'What would they do?' Taita asked.

'We will tear down this barrier, and let the Nile waters flow into our very Egypt once more.'

Taita smiled and stamped one sandalled foot on the wall beneath him. 'Kalulu has told us how hard and adamantine this stone is. Look at the size of it, Meren. It is many times bigger than all three of the great pyramids of Giza placed on top of each other. If you captured every man in Africa and set them to work for the next hundred years, I doubt they could move even a small part of it.'

'We should not take that strange man's word for how hard it is. I will get my men to test the rock with fire and bronze. Remember also, Magus, the engineering skills that raised those pyramids might be used to cast them down again. I see no reason why we should not be able to carry out the same feat, for we are also Egyptians, the most advanced culture on this earth.'

'I see some small merit in your arguments, Meren,' Taita agreed. Then something beyond the far end of the wall caught his attention. He frowned. 'Is that a building on the bluff overlooking us? I will put the question to Kalulu.'

They scrambled down the slippery rockface to where the dwarf sat on his litter surrounded by his bodyguards. When Taita pointed out the ruins he nodded brightly. 'You are right, Magus. That is a temple built by men.'

'Your tribe do not build in stone, do they?'

'No, that place was built by strangers.'

'Who were these strangers, and when did they build it?' Taita demanded.

'It is almost exactly fifteen years ago that they laid the first stones.'

'What manner of men were they.' Taita asked.

Kalulu hesitated before he answered. 'They were not southern men. Their features were like yours and those men with you. They wore the same dress and carried the same weapons.'

Taita stared at him, stunned into silence. At last he said,

'You suggest that they were Egyptians. It does not seem possible. Are you sure they came from Egypt?'

'I know nothing about the land from which you have come. I have never been down the Nile even as far as the great swamps. I cannot say with any certainty, but to me they appeared to be men of your race.'

'Did you speak to them?'

'No,' Kalulu said, with feeling. 'They were secretive and spoke to no one.'

'How many were here, and where are they now?' Taita asked keenly. He seemed to be watching the little man's eyes intently, but Fenn knew he was reading his aura.

'There were more than thirty, and less than fifty. They disappeared as mysteriously as they came.'

'They disappeared after the damming of the river with the Red Stones?'

'At the same time, Magus.'

'Surpassing strange,' Taita said. 'Who inhabits the temple now?'

'It is deserted, Magus,' Kalulu replied, 'as all the land for a hundred leagues around is deserted. My tribe and all the others fled in terror at these and other strange events. Even I took shelter in the marshes. This is the first time I have returned, and I admit that I would never have done so without your protection.'

'We should visit the temple,' Taita said. 'Will you show it to us?'

'I have never been inside that building,' Kalulu said softly. 'I never will. You must not ask me to go with you.'

'Why not, Kalulu?'

'It is the site of utmost evil. The force that has brought disaster upon all of us.'

'I respect your caution. These are deep matters and should not be undertaken lightly. Return with Meren. I will go alone to the temple.' He turned to Meren. 'Spare no labours to make the camp secure. Fortify it well, and post a strong guard. When you have done that we will return to assay the hardness of the Red Stones.'

'I implore you to return to the camp before darkness falls, Magus.' Meren looked jaundiced with worry. 'If you are not back at sunset, I will come to search for you.'

As the bodyguards hefted the litter and followed Meren, Taita turned to Fenn. 'Go with Meren. Hurry to catch up with him.'

She stood to her full height, arms behind her back, mouth set obstinately. He had come to know that expression well. 'There is no spell you can weave to make me leave you,' she declared.

'When you scowl you are no longer beautiful,' he warned her mildly.

'You cannot imagine how ugly I can be,' she said. 'Try to rid yourself of me and I will show you.'

'Your threats unman me.' He could scarce prevent himself smiling. 'But stay close to me, and be ready to form the circle at the first malevolent emanation we encounter.'

They found a path that climbed the bluff. When they reached the temple they saw that the stonework was beautifully executed. The entire building was roofed with hewn timber planking, over which had been laid a thatch of river reeds that was collapsing in places. They walked slowly round the walls. The temple was laid out on a circular foundation, about fifty paces across. At five equidistant points tall granite stele had been built into the walls. 'The five points of the black magicians' pentagram,' Taita told Fenn softly. They came back to the entrance portals of the temple. The door jambs were carved with bas-reliefs of esoteric symbols.

'Can you read them?' Fenn asked.

'No,' Taita admitted. 'They are alien.' Then he looked into her eyes for any sign of fear. 'Will you enter with me?'

For answer she took his hand. 'Let us form the circle,' she suggested.

Together they stepped through the gateway into the circular

outer portico. It was paved with flat grey stones, and shafts of light beamed down through the holes in the roof. There was no opening in the inner wall. Side by side they followed the curving portico. As they drew level with each stela, they found the points of the pentagram laid out in white marble under their feet. Within each point was enclosed another mysterious symbol, a serpent, a *crux ansata*, a vulture in flight, another at roost and, last, a jackal. They stepped over a pile of loose thatching and heard a harsh hiss, then a violent rustle beneath their feet. Taita slipped an arm round Fenn's waist and lifted her clear. Behind them the hooded head of a black Egyptian cobra rose out of the tumbled reeds. It stared hard at them with tiny black marble eyes, the long tongue flickering and testing the air for their scent. Taita set Fenn down, raised his staff and pointed it at the serpent's head. 'Don't be alarmed,' he said. 'This is no apparition. It is a natural animal.' He began to move the tip of the staff rhythmically from side to side, and the cobra swayed to the motion. Gradually it was lulled, the hood deflated, and it sank back into the tangle of thatch. Taita led Fenn away down the gallery. They stopped at last in front of an ornate doorway.

'The opposed opening,' Taita told her. 'This is diametrically opposite the outer entrance. It limits the ingress and egress of alien influences to the inner sanctum.'

The doorway that faced them was shaped like a petalled flower. The jambs were covered with tiles of polished ivory, malachite and tiger's eye. The closed doors were covered with lacquered crocodile skin. Taita used his staff to lean his full weight against one door. It swung open, bronze hinges whining. The interior was lit only by a shaft of sunlight cast from a single opening in the dome of the roof. It struck the floor of the sanctum in an eruption of colour.

The floor was decorated with an elaborately designed pentagram, the pattern worked in tiles of marble and semi-precious stones. Taita recognized rose quartz and rock crystal, beryllium and rubellite. The workmanship was masterly. The heart of the design was a circle of tiles so superbly fitted together and polished that the joints were invisible. It seemed to be a single shield of gleaming ivory.

'Let us go in, Magus.' Fenn's childish treble was thrown back and forth between the rounded walls.

'Wait!' he said. 'There is a presence within, the spirit of this place. I think it is dangerous. It is what terrified Kalulu.' He pointed to the sunlight on the temple floor. 'It is almost noon. The beam is about to fall upon the heart of the pentagram. That will be the fateful moment.'

They watched the sunlight creep across the floor. It touched the lip of the ivory circle and was reflected on to the surrounding walls, its radiance enhanced tenfold. Now it seemed to advance more swiftly, until suddenly it filled the ivory disc. Immediately they heard sistrums hum and rattle. They heard the wings of bats and vultures in the air around them. White light filled the sanctum with such brilliance that they lifted their hands to shield their eyes. Through the dazzle they saw the spirit sign of Eos appear at the centre of the disc, the cat's paw picked out in fire.

The odour of the witch filled their nostrils with the redolence of wild beasts. They reeled back from the doorway, but then the sunlight passed over the ivory disc and the fiery letters were expunged. The reek of the witch abated, leaving only the smell of musty thatch and bat droppings. The sunlight faded, leaving the sanctum once more in gloom. In silence they retreated down the gallery and out into the sunlight.

'She was there,' whispered Fenn. She took a deep breath of the cool lake air, as if to cleanse her lungs.

'Her influence remains.' Taita pointed with his staff at the humped Red Stones. 'She still presides over her fiendish works.'

'Could we destroy her temple,' Fenn glanced back at the building, 'and in that way destroy her also?'

'No,' Taita told her firmly. 'Her influence is powerful within the inner sanctum of her stronghold. To challenge her there would be mortally dangerous. We will find another time and place to attack her.' He took Fenn's hand and led her away.

'We will return tomorrow to test the wall for weakness, and to learn more from Kalulu of how the Red Stones were placed across the gorge.'

M eren pointed out the central crack that divided the Red Stones. 'There is no doubt that this is the weakest point in the length of the wall. It may be a shear line.'

'Certainly that seems the best point at which to begin the experiment,' Taita agreed. 'There is no dearth of firewood.' Most of the big trees that covered the slopes of the gorge had died when their water was dammed. 'Tell the men to begin.'

They watched them spread out through the forest. Soon the sound of their axes rang down the gorge and woke the echoes from the cliffs. Once the trees were felled, they used the horses to drag them to the base of the red wall. There they cut them into lengths, which they stacked against the wall of stone so that they formed a flue through which air would be drawn to fuel the flames. It took several days to set the gigantic mound of combustibles in place. In the meantime Taita supervised the building of four separate *shadoof* wheels to raise the water from the lake to the top of the wall and spill it on to the reverse face to drench the rock once it was red hot.

When all was in readiness, Meren set fire to the stack of wood. The flames took hold and leapt upwards. In minutes the entire pile of timber was a roaring conflagration. No man could stand within a hundred yards of it without having the skin flayed from his flesh.

While they waited for the fire to subside, Taita and Fenn sat with Kalulu on the bluff above the gorge, looking across at the temple of Eos on the far side. They sheltered from the sun under a small ruined pavilion that stood on the spot. The bodyguards had repaired the roof thatch.

'While the river still ran and my tribe lived here, I was in the habit of coming to this place during the hot season of the year, when all the earth groans under the lash of the sun,' Kalulu explained. 'You can feel how the breeze comes off the lake. Furthermore, I was fascinated by the activity of the strangers in the temple across the river. I used this as a lookout from where I could spy upon them.' He pointed at the temple sitting high on the opposite bluff. 'You must visualize the scene at that time. Where the wall of red stone now stands there was a deep gorge with a series of rapids, and cascades down which descended such a volume of water that the senses were numbed by the thunder of their fall. A tall cloud of spray towered above them.' He lifted his arms high and described the hovering cloud with an eloquent, graceful gesture. 'When the wind shifted, the spray blew over us here, as cool and blessed as rain.' He smiled with pleasure at the thought. 'Thus, from here, I had the view of a vulture over all the momentous occurrences of that time.'

'You watched the temple being constructed?' Fenn asked. 'Did you know that there is much ivory and many precious stones within its precincts?'

'Indeed, my pretty child. I watched the strangers bring them in. They used hundreds of slaves as beasts of burden.'

'From which direction did they arrive?' Taita asked.

'They came from the west.' Kalulu pointed into the hazy blue distance.

'What country lies out there?' Tait asked.

The dwarf did not answer immediately. He was silent for a

while, and then he responded hesitantly: 'When I was a young man and my legs were whole and strong, I travelled there. I went in search of wisdom and learning, for I had heard of a wondrous sage who lived in that far country to the west.'

'What did you discover?'

'I beheld mountains, mighty mountains, hidden for most of the year by masses of dense cloud. When it parted, it revealed peaks that climbed to the very skies, peaks whose bald heads were shining white.'

'Did you climb to the summits?'

'No. I saw them only from a great distance.'

'Do these mountains have a name?'

'The people who live within sight of them call them the Mountains of the Moon for their tops are as bright as the full moon.'

'Tell me, my learned and revered friend, did you see any other wonders on these travels?'

'The wonders were many and legion,' Kalulu replied. 'I saw rivers that burst from the earth and boiled with steam as though from a seething cauldron. I heard the hills groan and felt them shake beneath my feet, as though some monster stirred in his deep cavern.' The memories illuminated his dark eyes. 'There was such power in this range of mountains that one of the peaks burned and smoked like a gigantic furnace.'

'A burning mountain!' Taita exclaimed. 'You saw a peak that belched fire and smoke! You discovered a volcano?'

'If that is what you call such a miracle,' the little man acceded. 'The tribes that lived within sight of it called it the Tower of Light. It was a sight that filled me with awe.'

'Did you ever find the famous sage for whom you went in search?'

'No.'

'The men who built this temple came from the Mountains of the Moon? Is that what you believe?' Taita brought him back to the original question.

'Who knows? Not I. But they came from that direction. They laboured for twenty months. First they carried in the building materials with their slaves. Then they erected the walls and covered them with timbers and thatch. My tribe provided food for them, in exchange for beads, cloth and metal tools. We did not understand the purpose of that building, but it seemed harmless and posed no threat to us.' Kalulu shook his head at the memory of their naïvety. 'I was interested in the work. I tried to ingratiate myself with the builders and learn more about what they were doing, but they turned me away in a most hostile manner. They placed guards around their camp and I could not get close. I was forced to watch their works from this vantage-point.' Kalulu lapsed into silence.

Taita encouraged him with another question. 'What happened after the temple was completed?'

'The builders and slaves departed. They marched back into the west, the way they had come. They left nine priests to serve in the temple.'

'Only nine?' Taita asked.

'Yes. I became familiar with the appearance of every one of them, at this distance, of course.'

'What makes you believe they were priests?'

'They wore religious habits, red in colour. They conducted rituals of devotion. They made sacrifices and burnt offerings.'

'Describe the rituals.' Taita was listening with great attention. 'Every detail may be important.'

'At noon every day three of the priests descended in procession to the head of the cataract. They drew water in pitchers and carried it to the temple, dancing and exulting in some strange dialect.'

'Not the Tenmass?' Taita demanded.

'No, Magus. I did not recognize it.'

'That is all that happened? Or do you remember anything else? You spoke of sacrifices.'

'They bought black goats and black fowls from us. They were very particular about the colour. They had to be pure black. They took them into the temple. I heard singing, and afterwards I saw smoke and smelt burnt flesh.'

'What else?' Taita insisted.

Kalulu thought for a moment. 'One of the priests died. I do not know why. The other eight carried his body to the lakeside. They laid it naked on the sand. Then they retreated up the slope of the bluff. From there they watched as the crocodiles came out of the lake and dragged it under the waters.' The dwarf made a gesture of finality. 'Within weeks another priest arrived at the temple.'

'Coming from the west again?' Taita hazarded.

'I know not, for I did not see him arrive. One evening there were eight, the next morning there were nine once more.'

'So the number of priests was significant. Nine. The cipher of the Lie.' Taita mused for a while then asked, 'What happened after that?'

'For more than two years the routine of the priests was maintained. Then I was aware that something of consequence was about to take place. They lit five beacon fires around the temple and kept them burning day and night for many months.'

'Five fires,' Taita said. 'At what positions did they set them?'

'There are five stele built into the outer wall. Did you remark them?' Kalulu asked.

'Yes. They form the points of a great pentagram, the mystical design over which the temple stands.'

'I have never been inside the temple. I know nothing of any pentagram. I know only that the fires were placed at the five points around the outer wall,' Kalulu told them.

'Was that all that occurred which was untoward?'

'Then another person joined the brotherhood.'

'Another priest?'

'I think not. This person was clad in black, not red. An airy black veil covered the features, so I was unable to tell with any certainty if it was male or female. However, from the shape of the figure beneath the robes and the grace of its movement I thought it might be a woman. She emerged from the temple each morning at sunrise. She prayed before each of the five fires, then returned to the temple precincts.'

'Did you ever see her face?'

'She was always veiled. She moved with an ethereal, haunting grace. The other priests treated her with the greatest reverence, prostrating themselves before her. She must have been the high priestess of their sect.'

'Did you observe any significant signs in the heavens or in nature while she inhabited the temple?'

'Indeed, Magus, there were many strange celestial signs. On the day I first saw her pray at the temple fires, the evening star reversed its track through the skies. Shortly thereafter another insignificant and unnamed star swelled up into monstrous proportion and was consumed by flames. During all her tenure in the temple strange lights of many colours danced in the northern night sky. All these omens flew in the face of nature.'

'Do you believe they were the works of the veiled woman?'

'I say only that they occurred when she arrived. It may have been mere happenstance, I do not know.'

'Was that all?' Taita asked.

Kalulu shook his head firmly. 'There was more. Nature seemed plunged into turmoil. Our crops in the field turned yellow and withered. The cattle aborted their calves. The paramount chief of our tribe was bitten by a snake and died almost at once. His senior wife gave birth to a son with two heads.'

'Dire omens.' Taita looked grave.

'There was worse to follow. The weather was disturbed. A mighty wind blew through our town on the hill, and ripped off the roofs. A fire destroyed the tribal totem hut and consumed the relics and jujus of our ancestors. Hyenas dug up the corpse of the paramount chief and devoured it.'

'This was a direct onslaught on your people, your ancestors and your religion,' Taita murmured.

'Then the earth moved and shook itself like a living beast under our feet. The waters of the lake leapt into the air, boiling white and furious. The fish shoals disappeared. The lake birds flew away towards the west. The waves crushed our canoes where they lay upon the beaches. They ripped out our fishing nets. The people begged me to intercede with the angry gods of our tribe.'

'What could you do in the face of the elements?' Taita wondered. 'They had set you a daunting task.'

'I came to this place where we now sit. I cast a spell, the most potent in my power. I evoked the shades of our ancestors to placate the gods of the lake. But they were deaf to my pleas, and blind to the suffering of my tribe. They shook these hills on which we sit as a bull elephant shakes a ngong nut tree. The earth danced so that men could not stand upright. Deep cracks opened like the jaws of hungry lions and swallowed men and women with their infants strapped upon their backs.' By now Kalulu was weeping. His tears dripped from his chin on to his naked chest. One of his bodyguards wiped them away with a linen cloth.

'While I watched, the waters of the lake began to roll and thunder upon the beaches with increasing fury. They leapt half-way up the cliff below us. The spray burst over me in torrents. I was blinded and deafened. I looked across at the temple. Through the clouds and the spray, I saw the black-robed figure standing alone before the gateway. She had her arms held out towards the tumultuous lake like a wife welcoming the return of her beloved husband from the wars.' Kalulu panted for breath and struggled to control his body. His arms jerked and danced, his head shook like that of a man with the palsy. His features convulsed as though he were in a fit.

'Peace!' Taita laid a hand on his head, and slowly the dwarf calmed and relaxed, but the tears still poured down his face. 'You need not continue if this is too painful.'

'I must tell you. Only you will understand.' He took a gulp of air, then gabbled on: 'The waters opened and dark masses pushed through the waves. At first I thought they were living monsters from the depths.' He pointed at the nearest island. 'There was no island. The lake waters were open and empty.

Then that mass of rock pushed through the surface. The island you look upon now was born like an infant squeezed from the womb of the lake.' His hand trembled wildly as he pointed at it. 'But that was not the end. Once again the waters were riven asunder. Another great mass of rock rose up from the bottom of the lake. That is it! The Red Stones! They were glowing like metal from the flames of the forge. The waters hissed and turned to steam as they were pushed aside. The stones were half molten, hardening as they emerged from the depths into the air. The clouds of steam they generated were so dense as to obscure almost everything, but when they parted I saw that the temple was untouched. Every stone of the walls was in place, the roof firm. But the black-robed figure had disappeared. The priests also had gone. I never saw any of them again. The Red Stones kept swelling, like a gigantic pregnant belly, until they were the size and shape they are now, sealing off the mouth of the Nile. The river shrivelled to nothing, while the rocks and sandbanks in its bed appeared from beneath the waters.'

Kalulu gesticulated to his bodyguards. One ran forward to support his head while another held a gourd to his lips. He swallowed noisily. The liquid had a pungent smell and seemed to calm him at once. He pushed aside the gourd and went on talking to Taita.

'I was so overcome by these cataclysmic events that I ran from this hut down the slope of the bluff.' He pointed out the route he had taken. 'I was level with that clump of trees when the ground split and I was hurled into the deep trench that opened in front of me. I tried to claw my way out, but one of my legs was broken. I had almost reached the top when, like the jaws of a man-eating monster, the earth closed on me as swiftly as it had opened. Both my legs were caught, the bones crushed to fragments. I lay there for two days before survivors from Tamafupa found me. They tried to free me but my legs were trapped between two slabs of rock. I asked them to bring me a knife and an axe. While they held me, I cut off my legs, and bound up the stumps with bark cloth. When my tribe fled from this accursed place into the marshes of Kioga they carried me with them.'

'You have lived again through all the terrible events of those days,' Taita told him. 'It has tried your strength to the limit. I have been deeply moved by all you have told me. Call your women. Let them carry you back to the safety of Tama-fupa, where you must rest.'

'What will you do, Magus?'

'Colonel Meren is ready to quench the heated rockface to find out if it will shatter. I will assist him.'

The mountain of wood stacked against the rock wall had burnt down to a pile of glowing ash. The red rock was so hot that the air around it shimmered and wavered like a desert mirage. Four gangs of men gathered around the *shadoof* wheels on top of the Red Stones. None had any experience of rock-breaking. However, Taita had explained it to them.

'Are you ready, Magus?' Meren's voice echoed up from the gorge.

'Ready!' Taita shouted back.

'Start pumping!' Meren cried.

The men seized the handles of the *shadoofs* and put their full weight behind them. Their heads bobbed up and down to the rhythm Habari beat on a native drum. The line of empty buckets dipped into the lake surface, filled, then rose to the top of the wall. There, they spilled over into the wooden trough that channelled the water over the hump of the wall to cascade down the heated rockface on the opposite side. Immediately the air was filled with dense white clouds of hissing steam that enveloped the wall and the men on top of it. Those on the handles never faltered, and water streamed over the lip. The steam billowed, and the contracting rock groaned and growled.

'Is it breaking?' Taita shouted.

At the base of the wall Meren was lost in the dense steam. His reply came back, almost drowned in the rush of water and the hiss of steam. 'I cannot see anything. Keep them pumping, Magus!'

The men on the *shadoofs* were tiring, and Taita replaced them with fresh teams. They kept the water pouring down the face, and gradually the hissing clouds of steam began to subside and disperse.

'Pump!' Meren roared. Taita changed the teams again, then gingerly approached the lip and peered over, but the curvature of the cliff hid the base of the wall. 'I am going down,' he called to the men on the pumps. 'Don't stop until I give the order.' He hurried to the path that led into the gorge and made his way down at his best speed. The steam had cleared sufficiently for him to make out the shapes of Meren and Fenn below. They had moved much closer to the wall, and were discussing the result of the experiment.

'Don't get too close to the rockface,' Taita called, but they did not seem to hear him. Water was still pouring down it and had washed the ashes into the dry riverbed.

'Ho, Meren! What success?' Taita called, as he hurried down the path. Meren looked up at him, his expression so comically mournful that Taita laughed. 'Why so glum?'

'Nothing!' Meren lamented. 'All that effort in vain.' He moved into the eddies of steam and stretched out his hand towards the rock.

'Take care!' Taita shouted. 'It is still hot.' Meren pulled his hand back, then drew his sword. He reached out with the point of the bronze blade.

Fenn had moved close to his side. 'The rock is still intact,' she cried. 'No cracks.' She and Meren were only an arm's length from the steaming face when Taita came up behind them. He saw that Fenn was correct: the red rock wall was blackened by the flames but unscathed.

Meren tapped it with the point of his sword. It sounded solid. Angrily, he raised the sword to deliver a harder blow and relieve his frustration. The steam clouds in which they were enveloped were moist and warm, but Taita felt a sudden intense contrast, an icy chill on his arms and face. Immediately he opened his Inner Eye. Through it he saw a tiny spot appear on the soot-blackened stone where Meren had struck it. It glowed red, then took on the shape of the cat's paw, symbol of Eos of the Dawn.

'Get back!' Taita ordered, and used the voice of power to reinforce the command. At the same time he lunged forward, seized Fenn's arm and flung her away. But his warning to Meren had come too late. Although Meren tried to check his stroke, the point of his sword touched the glowing spot again. With a sound like shattering glass the small area of rock directly beneath the symbol of Eos exploded outwards and a blast of splinters struck him full in the face. Although most were small fragments, they were as sharp as needles. His head snapped back, he dropped the sword and clutched at his face with both hands. Blood poured between his fingers and ran down on to his chest.

Taita ran to him and caught his arm to steady him. Fenn had been thrown to the ground, but now she scrambled up and ran to help. Between them they led Meren back from the steaming rock, found a patch of shade and sat him down.

'Stand back!' Taita ordered the men, who had followed and were now crowding forward. 'Give us room to work.' To Fenn, he said, 'Bring water.'

She ran to a gourd and brought it to him. Taita lifted Meren's hands away from his ruined face. She exclaimed with horror, but Taita cautioned her to silence with a frown.

'Am I still as beautiful?' Meren tried to grin, but his eyes were tightly closed, the lids swollen and clotted with blood.

'It's a great improvement,' Taita assured him, and began to wash away the blood. Some of the cuts were superficial, but three were deep. One ran through the bridge of his nose, the second through his upper lip, but the third and worst had pierced his right eyelid. Taita could make out a shard of stone embedded in the eye cavity.

'Fetch my medicine bag,' he ordered Fenn, who ran to where their equipment had been placed and brought back the leather satchel.

Taita opened the roll of surgical instruments and selected a pair of ivory forceps with a probe. 'Can you open your eyes?' he asked gently.

Meren made an attempt and the left lid opened a little, but although the damaged lid quivered, the right eye remained closed.

'No, Magus.' His voice was subdued.

'Is it sore?' Fenn asked timorously. 'Oh, poor Meren.' She took his hand.

'Sore? Not in the least. Your touch has made it better.'

Taita placed a square of leather between Meren's teeth. 'Bite down on that.' He closed the jaws of the forceps over the fragment of stone and, with a single firm movement, drew it out. Meren grunted and his face contorted. Taita laid aside the forceps and, with a finger on each eyelid, gently drew them apart. Behind him he heard Fenn gasp.

'Is it bad?' Meren asked.

Taita remained silent. The eyeball had burst and the bloody jelly dribbled down his cheek. Taita knew at once that Meren would never see with that eye again. Gently he prised open the lid of the other and stared into it. He saw the pupil dilate and focus normally. He held up his other hand. 'How many fingers?' he asked.

'Three,' Meren answered.

'You aren't completely blind, then,' Taita told him. Meren was a tough warrior. It was neither necessary nor advisable to shield him from the truth.

'Only half-way there?' Meren asked, his smile lopsided.

'That was why the gods gave you two eyes,' Taita said, and began to bind up the ruined one with a white linen bandage.

'I hate the witch. This is her doing,' said Fenn, and began to weep softly. 'I hate her. I hate her.'

'Make a litter for the colonel,' Taita ordered the men, who waited close at hand.

'I don't need one,' Meren protested. 'I can walk.'

'The first law of the cavalry,' Taita reminded him. 'Never walk when you can ride.'

As soon as the litter was ready they helped Meren on to it and started back to Tamafupa. They had been moving for a short time when Fenn called to Taita: 'There are strange men up there, watching us.' She pointed across the dried-up river course. On the skyline stood a small group of men. Fenn counted them swiftly. 'Five.'

They were dressed in loincloths, but their torsos were bare. They all carried spears and clubs. Two were armed with bows. The tallest among them stood at their head. He wore a headdress of red flamingo feathers. Their bearing was arrogant and hostile. Two of the men behind the chief seemed wounded or injured: they were being supported by their comrades.

'Magus, they have been in a fight,' Shofar, one of the litter-bearers, pointed out.

'Hail them!' Taita ordered. Shofar shouted and waved. None of the warriors showed any reaction. Shofar shouted again. The chief in the flamingo headdress lifted his spear in a gesture of command and immediately his men disappeared from the skyline, leaving the hillside deserted. A distant chorus of shouts broke the silence that followed their departure.

'That comes from the town.' Fenn turned quickly in that direction. 'There has been trouble.'

When they had left Taita at the Red Stones, Kalulu's bodyguards carried him down the river valley towards Tamafupa. He was in such distress that they went slowly and carefully. They halted every few hundred yards to let him drink from his gourd of medicine, to wet his face and wipe it with a damp cloth. Measured against the arc of the sun, it was almost two hours before they started the climb from the valley towards the gates of Tamafupa.

As they entered a thicket of dense kittar thorn a tall figure stepped onto the pathway. Kalulu and his women recognized him, not only by his headdress of flamingo feathers. The women lowered the litter to the ground and prostrated themselves.

'We see you, great chief,' they chorused. Kalulu struggled up on one elbow, and stared at the newcomer with trepidation. Basma was paramount chief of all the Basmara tribes that inhabited the land between Tamafupa and Kioga. Before the coming of the strangers who had built the temple and raised the Red Stones from the depths of the lake, he had been a mighty ruler. Now his tribes were scattered and his rule disrupted.

'Hail, mighty Basma,' Kalulu said respectfully. 'I am your dog.'

Basma was his bitter rival and enemy. Until this time Kalulu had been protected by his reputation and status. Even the chief of the Basmara had not dared to harm a shaman of his power and influence. However, Kalulu knew that ever since the damming of the Nile, Basma had been waiting for his opportunity.

'I have been watching you, wizard,' Basma said coldly.

'I am honoured that such a mighty chief would even notice my humble existence,' Kalulu murmured. Ten Basmara warriors stepped out of the thicket and formed up behind their chief.

'You have led these enemies of the tribe to Tamafupa. They have taken over my town.'

'They are not enemies,' Kalulu replied. 'They are our friends and allies. Their leader is a great shaman, much more learned and powerful than I am. He has been sent here to destroy the Red Stones and to make the Nile flow again.'

'What feeble lies are these, you pathetic legless thing? Those men are the same sorcerers who built the temple at the mouth of the river, the same wizards who called up the wrath of the dark spirits, who caused the lake waters to boil and the earth to burst open. They are the ones who conjured up the rocks from the depths, and blocked off the great river, which is our mother and our father.'

'That is not so.' Kalulu hopped off his litter and balanced on his stumps to confront Basma. 'Those people are our friends.'

Slowly Basma raised his spear and pointed it at the dwarf. This was a gesture of condemnation. Kalulu looked at his bodyguards. They were not members of a tribe subservient to Basma, one of the many reasons he had selected them. They came from a warrior tribe far to the north. However, when it came to a choice between himself and Basma he could not be certain in which direction their loyalty would sway. As if in answer to his unspoken question, the eight women tightened their ranks around him. Imbali, the flower, was their leader. Her body might have been carved from anthracite. Her jet skin was anointed with oil so that it glowed in the sunlight. Her arms and legs were sleek with fine flat muscle. Her breasts were high and hard, decorated with an intricate pattern of ritual scarification. Her neck was long and proud. Her eyes were fierce. She loosened the battleaxe from the loop at her waist. The others followed her example.

'Your whores will not save you now, Kalulu,' Basma sneered disdainfully. 'Kill the wizard,' he shouted at his warriors, and hurled his spear at Kalulu.

Imbali anticipated the throw. She jumped forward, swung the battleaxe in her right hand and hit the spear in mid-air, knocking it straight upwards. As it fell back she caught it neatly in her left hand and raised the point to meet the rush of warriors. The first man ran on to it, transfixing himself just below the sternum. He reeled backwards into the man coming up behind him, knocking him off balance. Then he dropped on to his back and lay kicking with the shaft of the spear standing out of his belly. Imbali leapt gracefully over his corpse, and caught the man behind him before he could recover. She swung the axe in a rising stroke that lopped off his spear-arm neatly at the elbow. She pirouetted and used the momentum to decapitate a third man as he rushed forward.

The headless corpse dropped into a sitting position, the open arteries sending up a tall fountain of bright red, then flopped over and bled into the earth.

Shielding Kalulu, Imbali and the other women fell back quickly and picked up the litter by its rawhide carrying straps. Then using it as a battering ram, they charged into the Basmara. Their war-cry was a shrill ululation as the axe blades whistled and fluted, then thudded into flesh and bone.

Basma's men rallied swiftly. They met the women with a wall of locked shields and threw their long spears at their heads. One went down, killed outright with a flint point through her throat. The others raised the litter and hammered it into the line of shields. Both sides heaved against each other. One of the Basmara dropped to his knees and stabbed up under the bottom edge of the litter into the belly of the girl at the centre of the line. She released her grip and reeled backwards. She tried to turn away but her assailant jerked his spear free and stabbed again, aiming for her kidneys. The blow went in deep and the girl screamed as the blade slipped alongside her spine crippling her instantly.

Kalulu's bodyguards retreated a few steps, filled the gap left by the wounded girl and held the litter steady. The Basmara raised their shields and, once more, charged shoulder to shoulder. As they crashed into the litter they stabbed up under the bottom edge of the shields, aiming for groins and bellies. The line of shields swayed back and forth. Two more girls went down, one hit in the upper thigh so that the femoral artery erupted. She fell back and tried to stem the bleeding by pushing her fingers into the wound to pinch the artery closed. While she was bowed over her back was exposed and a Basmara stabbed her in the spine. The spearhead found the joint between her vertebrae, and her paralysed legs gave way. The man stabbed her again, but while he was concentrating on killing her, Imbali ducked under the litter and chopped deep into his skull.

The uneven pressure on the litter slewed it round. Kalulu was left unprotected on one flank. Chief Basma seized the moment: he darted out of the wall of shields, dodged around the litter and ran at him. Kalulu saw him coming and swung himself into a handstand. With amazing agility he shot towards the shelter of the nearby thicket of kittar thorns. He had almost reached it when Basma overhauled him and stabbed him twice. 'Traitor!' the chief screamed, and the spearhead hit Kalulu in the centre of the back. With a huge effort he managed to stay balanced on his hands. He bounced along, but Basma caught up with him again. 'Witchmonger!' he yelled and thrust again, deeply through the little man's inverted crotch and into his belly. Kalulu howled and tumbled into the thicket. Basma tried to follow up his attack, but from the corner of his eye he saw Imbali rushing at him with her axe above her head. He ducked and when her blade hissed past his ear, he swerved away from her return stroke and ran. His men saw him go and followed, pelting away down the slope.

'The sorcerer is dead!' Basma shouted.

His warriors took up the chant: 'Kalulu is dead! The familiar of devils and demons is slain!'

'Leave them to run back to the bitches that whelped them.' Imbali stopped her girls chasing them. 'We must save our master.'

By the time they found him in the thicket Kalulu was curled into a ball, whimpering with pain. Tenderly they extricated him from the hooked thorn branches and placed him on his litter. At that moment a shout from further down the slope checked them.

'It is the voice of the old man.' Imbali had recognized Taita, and ululated to direct them.

Soon Taita and Fenn came into view, followed closely by the party carrying Meren on his litter.

'Kalulu, you are wounded grievously,' Taita said gently.

'Nay, Magus, not wounded.' Kalulu shook his head painfully. 'I fear I am slain.'

'Swiftly. Take him to the camp!' Taita told Imbali and her

three surviving companions. 'And you men!' He picked out four following Meren's litter. 'Your help is needed here!'

'Wait!' Kalulu seized Taita's hand to prevent him leaving. 'The man who did this is Basma, the paramount chief of Basmara.'

'Why did he attack you? You are his subject, surely?'

'Basma believes that you are of the same tribe who built the temple, and that you have come here to instigate further calamity and catastrophe. He thinks I have joined with you to destroy the land, the rivers, the lakes and to kill all the Basmara.'

'He has gone now. Your women have driven him away.' Taita tried to reassure and calm him.

Kalulu would have none of it. 'He will return.' He reached up and seized Taita's wrist as he stooped over the litter. 'You must get into the town and prepare to defend yourselves. Basma will return with all his regiments.'

'When I leave Tamafupa, I will take you with me, Kalulu. Our pursuit of the witch cannot succeed without your help.'

'I can feel the bleeding deep in my belly. I will not be going on with you.'

Before sunset Kalulu died. The four bodyguards dug an adit into the side of a large abandoned anthill outside the stockade of Tamafupa. Taita wrapped the corpse in a sheet of unbleached linen and they laid it in the damp clay tunnel. Then they sealed it with large boulders to prevent the hyenas digging it out.

'Your ancestral gods will welcome you, Shaman Kalulu, for you were of the Truth.' Taita bade him farewell.

When he turned away from the tomb, the four bodyguards stood before him, and Imbali spoke for them all in the Shilluk language. 'Our master is gone. We are far from our own land, alone. You are a mighty shaman, greater even than Kalulu. We will follow you.'

Taita looked at Nakonto. 'What do you make of these women? If I enlist them, will you take them under your command?' he asked.

Nakonto considered the question solemnly. 'I have seen them fight. I will be content to have them follow me.'

With a regal tilt of her head, Imbali acknowledged his presence and his words. 'For as long as it pleases us to do so, we will march shoulder to shoulder with this strutting Shilluk rooster, but not behind him,' she told Taita.

Her eyes were almost on a level with Nakonto's. The magnificent pair stared at each other with apparent scorn. Taita opened his Inner Eye and smiled as he saw how their auras mirrored the inclination they felt towards each other. 'Nakonto, is it agreed?' he asked.

'It is agreed.' Nakonto made another lordly gesture of acquiescence. 'For the time being.'

Fenn and the Shilluk camp-followers swept out one of the largest huts for Meren. Then Fenn burnt a handful of Taita's special herbs in the open fireplace. The aromatic smoke drove out the insects and spiders that had made the hut their home. They cut a mattress of fresh grass and laid Meren's sleeping mat upon it. He was in such pain that he could hardly raise his head to drink from the bowl that Fenn held to his lips. Taita promoted Hilto-bar-Hilto to take his place at the head of the four divisions until Meren had recovered sufficiently to assume command again.

Taita and Hilto toured the town to inspect the defences. Their first concern was to ensure that the water supply was secure. There was a deep well in the centre of the village, with a narrow circular clay staircase descending to the water, which was of good quality. Taita ordered that a party under Shofar should fill all of the gourds and waterskins in readiness for the anticipated assault by the Basmara. In the thick of the fighting, thirsty men would have no opportunity to draw from the well.

Taita's next concern was the condition of the outer stockade. They found that it was still in a reasonable state of repair, except for a few sections where termites had eaten the poles.

However, it was immediately apparent that they could not hope to hold such an extended line. Tamafupa was a big town that had once been home to a large tribe. The stockade was almost half a league in circumference. 'We will have to shorten it,' he told Hilto, 'then burn the remainder of the town to clear the approaches and enable our archers to cover the ground.'

'You have set us a daunting task, Magus,' Hilto remarked. 'We had better begin at once.'

Once Taita had marked out the new perimeter, men and women fell to. They dug out the best preserved of the stockade poles and set them up along the line Taita had surveyed. There was no time to make a permanent fortification, so they filled the gaps with branches of kittar thorn bush. They erected tall watch-towers at the four compass points of the new stockade, which commanded a good view over the valley and all the approaches.

Taita ordered bonfires to be set around the perimeter. When they were lit they would illuminate the stockade walls in the event of a night attack. Once this was done he built an inner keep round the well, their last line of defence if the Basmara regiments broke into the town. Within this inner stronghold, he stored the remaining bags of dhurra, the spare weapons and all other valuable supplies. They built stables for the remaining horses. Windsmoke and her colt were still in good condition, but many others were sick or dying after the long hard road they had travelled.

Every evening after she had fed Meren and helped Taita change the dressing over the empty socket of his right eye, Fenn went down to visit Whirlwind and take him the dhurra cakes he loved.

Taita waited for a favourable wind before he set fire to the remains of the old town that lay outside the new stockade. The thatch and wooden walls had dried and burned rapidly, the wind blowing the flames away from the new walls. By nightfall that day the old town was levelled to a smouldering field of ashes.

'Let the Basmara attack across that open ground,' Hilto observed, with satisfaction, 'and we will shock them.'

'Now you can set up markers in front of the stockade,' Taita told him. They placed cairns of white river stones at twenty, fifty and a hundred paces so that the archers could have the enemy accurately ranged as they sent in their attacks.

Taita sent Imbali with her companions and the other women to the dry river to cut reeds for arrow-making. He had brought bags of spare arrowheads from the armoury at Qebui fort, and when they had been used, he discovered an outcrop of flint in the hillside below the stockade. He showed the women how to chip the flint fragments into arrowheads. They learnt the skill quickly, then bound the heads into the reed shafts with bark twine and soaked them in water to make them tight and hard. They stacked bundles of spare arrows at salient points along the perimeter of the stockade.

Within ten days all of the preparation had been completed. The men and Imbali's women sharpened their weapons and checked their equipment for what might be the last time.

One evening as the men gathered around the fires for the evening meal, there was a sudden stir and a burst of cheering as an ill-assorted couple came into the firelight. Meren was unsteady on his feet, but supported himself with a hand on Fenn's shoulder as he came to where Taita sat with the captains. They all jumped to their feet and crowded round him, laughing and congratulating him on his swift recovery. A linen bandage covered his empty eye socket, and he was pale and thinner, but he was making an effort to walk with something of his old swagger, and countered the sallies of the officers with ribald ripostes. At last he stood before Taita and saluted him.

'Ho, Meren, bored with lying abed to be tended by all the females in camp?' Taita had spoken with a smile but he had difficulty in repressing the pang he felt when he saw the callused warrior's hand on Fenn's dainty shoulder. He knew that his jealousy would become keener as her body and beauty matured. He had experienced that corrosive emotion during her other life.

The following morning Meren was at the practice butts with the archers. At first he had difficulty in keeping his balance with only one eye to steady himself, but with fierce concentration he was at last able to master his unruly senses and train them anew. His next difficulty came in estimating the range and the hold-over of his aim. His arrows either dropped away before they reached the target or flew high above it. Grimly he persevered. Taita, who had been the champion archer in all the armies of Queen Lostris, coached him, teaching him the technique of letting fly his first arrow as a marker, and using it to correct the second, which he released immediately afterwards. Soon Meren could loose a second while the first was still in flight. Fenn and the Shilluk wives made him a leather eyepatch to cover the unsightly socket. His countenance regained its naturally healthy hue, and the remaining eye its old sparkle.

Every morning Taita sent out a mounted patrol, but they returned each evening without having discovered any sign of the Basmara regiments. Taita consulted Imbali and her women.

'We know Chief Basma well. He is a vengeful, merciless man,' Imbali told him. 'He has not forgotten us. His regiments are scattered along the hills of the Valley of the Great Rift, in the river gorges and the marshes of the lakes. It will take time for him to muster them, but in the end he will come. We can be certain of it.'

Now that the most important preparations had been completed, Taita had time for less vital work. He showed the women how to make dummy human heads with lumps of clay and grass set on top of long poles. These they painted with natural pigments, until the results were convincing when seen from a distance. They enjoyed this more than arrow-making. However, the waiting was starting to wear on their nerves.

'Even considering the distance they must cover from here to Kioga, Basmara should have arrived,' Taita told Meren, as they ate their dinner round the campfire. 'Tomorrow you and I will ride out to scout the terrain for ourselves.'

'And I shall go with you,' piped up Fenn.

'We shall see about that when the time comes,' said Taita, gruffly.

'Thank you, beloved Taita,' she said, her smile sweet and sunny.

'That was not what I meant,' he replied, but they both knew that it was.

The child was endlessly fascinating, and Taita delighted in her presence. He felt that she had become an extension of his own being.

When the patrol rode out, Fenn was between Taita and Meren. Nakonto and Imbali trotted ahead as trackers to read the signs. On her long legs Imbali could match Nakonto over the leagues. Habari and two troopers brought up the rear. For once Taita wore a sheathed sword at his waist, but carried his staff in his hand.

They rode along the crest of the hills whence they could look down the full length of the valley. On the left the terrain was rolling and heavily forested. They saw numerous large herds of elephant spread out below the ridge. Their huge grey bodies showed up clearly in every open glade, and every so often a large fruit-bearing tree was sent crashing to earth by their massive strength. When a tree was too strong to yield to the efforts of a single beast, the other bulls came to his assistance. No tree could resist their combined assault.

Since the tribes had fled from this land the elephant had not been molested, and they were unalarmed by the close proximity of humans. They did not flee at the first approach but stood their ground while the horsemen passed close by. Occasionally a cantankerous female indulged in a threatening display, but none pushed home her attack. Fenn was delighted by the antics of the calves, and plied Taita with questions about the mighty beasts and their ways.

The elephants were not the only wild animals they encountered. There were herds of antelope, and yellow baboons foraged in the open glades or swarmed nimbly to the tops of the tallest trees. One troop erupted into shrieking panic. The mothers snatched up their infants and slung them under their bellies as they bounded away in flight. The big males formed a belligerent rearguard, fluffing out their manes and uttering explosive barks of fury.

'What ails them?' Fenn demanded.

'Likely a leopard or some other predator.' As Taita spoke, a beautiful gold and black spotted cat stalked out of a patch of grass just ahead. The leopard's markings blended perfectly with the background.

'You were right again, Taita. You must know everything there is to know in this world,' Fenn told him admiringly.

They angled up the slope of the next range of hills, but before they reached the crest a vast herd of zebra thundered over the skyline. Their hoofs tore up the dry earth and lifted a cloud of pale dust high into the brazen sky. They took little notice of the horses, seemingly accepting that they were of their own species, and passed them within a few paces.

'Something must have alarmed them,' Meren said.

'Fire or men,' Taita agreed. 'Nothing else would have caused a stampede on this scale.'

'I see no smoke of a bushfire,' Meren said. 'It must be men.' They rode cautiously now, approaching the skyline at a walk.

Suddenly Fenn exclaimed again and pointed to the left. 'A child! A little black child.'

It was a naked infant of no more than three or four years. He was toddling up the slope on bowed legs, his plump little buttocks wobbling with each pace.

'I am going to pick him up,' Fenn exclaimed. She pressed Whirlwind into a trot, but Taita grabbed her rein.

'Fenn, this smells like ripe bait.'

'We cannot let him go,' Fenn protested, as the child went over the skyline and disappeared. 'He is lost, and all alone.'

'We will follow him,' Taita agreed, 'but with caution.' He did not release his hold on Whirlwind's rein as they rode on. He halted a hundred paces below the ridge.

'Come, Meren!' he ordered. They dismounted and passed their reins to Fenn.

'Stay here and hold our horses, but be ready to ride hard,' Taita told her. He and Meren went forward on foot. They used a small bush to break up the outline of their heads as they peered over the far slope of the hill. The child stood just below them, facing them with a cheerful grin on his round face. He was holding his tiny penis in both hands, piddling a yellow stream on to the sun-baked earth. It was such a homely scene that it lulled them for a moment. Meren started to grin in sympathy but Taita seized his arm. 'Look beyond!'

They stared for an instant longer, then Meren reacted. 'The Basmara impis!' he cried. 'That little devil *was* the bait.'

Not fifty paces beyond where the child stood, they squatted rank upon close-packed rank. They were armed with wooden clubs, long throwing spears and shorter, stabbing assegais, tipped with sharp flint. Their rawhide shields were slung upon their backs, and their features were daubed with coloured clay to form warlike masks. They wore headdresses of fur and feathers, ivory pins pierced their nostrils and earlobes, while bracelets and anklets of ostrich shell and ivory beads adorned their limbs.

As Taita and Meren looked at them a hum, as though from a disturbed beehive, went up from the close-packed masses. With a single concerted movement they unslung their war shields and drummed upon them with their spears. Then they burst into their battle hymn. The deep, melodious voices soared and swelled with the drumming. Then the din was pierced by a shrill blast on an antelope-horn whistle. This was the signal for the ranks to leap to their feet and, in a mass, they started up the slope.

'Back to the horses,' said Taita.

Fenn saw them coming and galloped to meet them, bringing Windsmoke and Meren's steed. They mounted swiftly and had turned the horse's heads as the first rank of Basmara warriors burst over the crest behind them. They galloped back to where Habari and the remainder of the patrol were waiting.

'Already they have sent out men to try to head us off,' Fenn called, rising in the stirrups and pointing into the forest. Now they could make out figures among the trees, racing to surround them.

'Take my stirrup rope!' Taita called to Nakonto, as he kicked his left foot free of the loop. Nakonto grabbed it.

'Meren, pick up Imbali to cover your blind side.' Meren swerved and Imbali snatched the right loop. She and Nakonto were carried along by the horses, their feet skimming the earth.

'Ride hard!' Taita shouted. 'We must break through before they encircle us.' The fastest runners among the Basmara were streaking ahead of their companions. 'Fenn, stay between Meren and me. Don't allow yourself to be separated from us.'

Four of the racing Basmara cut in directly ahead of them, closing the gap for which Taita had been aiming. They turned to face the oncoming riders, their tall shields on their backs so that their hands were free to use their weapons. Taita and Meren slipped their short recurved cavalry bows, designed to be shot from horseback, from their shoulders as they closed in. They dropped the reins on to the necks of their mounts and, guiding them with the pressure of their feet and knees, rode straight at the spearmen. A Basmara hurled his spear. He was aiming at Meren, but the range was long. Meren had time to react. With a touch of his toe he turned the bay and the spear flew past his left shoulder. He raised his bow and loosed two arrows in rapid succession. One flew high, almost an arm's length over the man's head and went on for fifty paces – at this close range the bow was massively powerful – but the second hit the Basmara in the centre of his chest and flew clean through him. It burst out between his shoulder-blades in a spray of blood. He was dead even before he hit the ground.

Out on the right the second spearman heaved back his throwing arm. He, too, was concentrating on Meren, and he was in Meren's blind zone. Meren did not see him so made no effort to defend himself. Imbali swung out on the rope stirrup and threw her axe, which cartwheeled through the air. The Basmara's weight was on his back foot – he was in the very moment of his throw, unable to dodge or duck. The axe struck him in the middle of the forehead and buried itself deep in his skull. Imbali leant down to retrieve it as they swept by. Taita shot an arrow into the body of the third spearman, who dropped the weapon he had been about to throw and tried to pull the arrow out of his belly but the barbs had bitten deep.

The fourth and last warrior stood his ground. He was poised to make his throw, the shaft of the spear resting on his right shoulder. His eyes were bloodshot with battle rage, and Taita saw that they were fastened on Fenn. She was sitting high on Whirlwind's back, a perfect target. The Basmara grimaced with the effort of launching the heavy spear at her.

Taita nocked another arrow from his quiver. 'Down, Fenn,' he commanded, in the voice of power. 'Lie flat!' She dropped forward and pressed her face into Whirlwind's mane. Taita threw up his bow, drew until the bowstring touched his nose and lips, then released the arrow. The spearman was already swinging his body into the forward stroke, but Taita's flint arrowhead hit the notch at the base of his throat and killed him instantly. However, the spear had already left his hand. Taita watched, helpless, as it flew straight at Fenn. She had her face down and did not see it coming, but Whirlwind did. As it flitted across his nose he shied violently to one side and threw up his head so that Taita lost sight of the spear for a moment. He thought that it had missed her and he felt a leap of relief. But then he heard her cry out in pain and surprise, and saw her writhe on the colt's back.

'Are you hit?' Taita shouted, but she did not reply. Then

he saw the shaft of the spear dangling down Whirlwind's flank, dragging along the ground behind him.

Taita turned Windsmoke behind the colt and saw at once that the head of the spear was lodged in Fenn's bare thigh. She had dropped the reins and was clinging with both hands to the colt's neck. She turned towards him, and Taita saw that she was ash pale, her green eyes seeming to fill half of her face as she stared at him. The shaft of the spear was bucking and kicking as it bounced along the ground, and he knew that the razor edges of the head were working brutally in her flesh, worrying and enlarging the wound. It had lodged close to the femoral artery. If it severed that great blood vessel she would be dead within minutes.

'Hold hard, my darling,' he called, and glanced over his shoulder. He saw a pack of Basmara in full pursuit after them, baying as they raced through the forest. 'We dare not stop. If we do, they will be upon us in an instant. I am coming to get you.'

Taita drew his sword and came up beside the colt. He measured his stroke carefully. The sight of the girl in such anguish seemed to restore the strength he had thought lost so many years ago. He focused his mind on the jerking spear. As he swung the heavy bronze blade he shouted a word of power: 'Kydash!'

In his grip the weapon seemed to take on a life of its own. There is a spot on the cutting edge of a well-balanced blade where all the weight and energy of the blow is concentrated. It caught the hardwood shaft precisely a finger's length above the leather bindings that secured the shank of the head and sliced through it as though it were a green twig. The shaft dropped away, and he saw the instant relief that lit Fenn's features.

'I am coming to get you,' he told her, as he slipped the blade back into its scabbard. 'Be ready.' He pushed Windsmoke in beside her colt and Fenn opened her arms to him trustingly. He slipped his own arm round her waist and lifted her across the gap. She wrapped her arms round his neck as he sat her sideways across Windsmoke's withers.

'I was so afraid, Taita,' she whispered, 'until you came. Now I know it will be all right.'

'Hold tight,' he ordered, 'or it will be all wrong.' With his teeth he tore a strip of linen from the hem of her tunic, then pressed the stub of the severed shaft flat against her upper thigh and secured it with the linen. 'Not very neat or pretty,' he told her, 'but you are the bravest girl I know, and that will hold it firmly until we get back to Tamafupa.'

The pursuing Basmara dropped back, and soon disappeared from sight among the trees. They were able to rein down to a trot, but still reached the gates of Tamafupa before the sun had made its noon.

'Stand the garrison to arms,' Taita ordered Meren. 'Those devils will be upon us before another hour has passed.' He lifted Fenn down from Windsmoke's back, carried her to the hut they shared and laid her gently on her sleeping mat.

Taita spoke reassuringly to Fenn as he washed away the clotted black blood from around the shank of the spearhead. Then he began a thorough examination of her leg. Until he was ready to operate, he would not remove the linen strip with which he had secured it.

'You were always a favourite of the gods,' he told her at last. 'The spear has missed the big artery by the breadth of your little fingernail. If we hadn't stopped the sharp edges sawing away inside you they would have ruptured it. Now, lie quietly while I mix you something to drink.' He measured a strong dose of the red sheppen powder into a ceramic bowl and topped it up with hot water from the pan that stood on the coals of the central fireplace. 'Drink this. It will make you sleepy and dull the pain.'

While the drug took effect he searched in his leather medical bag. There was a separate compartment in which he kept his silver spoons. To his knowledge only one other surgeon had ever owned a set, and he was dead. When he was ready he called Meren, who was hovering at the door of the hut. 'You know what to do,' he said.

'Of course. You know how many times I have done this before,' Meren replied.

'You have washed your hands, of course?' Taita asked.

Meren's expression changed. 'Yes,' he said doubtfully.

'When?'

'This morning, before we rode out on patrol.'

'Wash them again.'

'I see no reason for it,' Meren muttered, as he always did, but he went to the pan on the fire and filled a bowl.

'We will need another pair of hands,' Taita decided, as he held the silver cups in the flames. 'Call Imbali.'

'Imbali? She is a savage. What about one of our own men?'

'She is strong and clever,' Taita contradicted him. What was more to the point, she was female. Taita did not want another man handling Fenn's naked body. It was bad enough that he must use Meren, but not another rough soldier – and the Shilluk women were flighty creatures. 'Call Imbali,' he repeated, 'and make sure she washes her hands also.'

Although the red sheppen had sedated Fenn, she groaned and stirred when he disturbed the spearhead. Taita nodded at Meren. Between them they lifted Fenn into a sitting position, then Meren squatted behind her, folded her arms across her chest and pinioned them.

'Ready,' he said.

Taita glanced at Imbali, who was kneeling at Fenn's feet. 'Hold her legs straight. Make sure she does not move.' Imbali leant forward and gripped Fenn's ankles. Taita took a deep breath, and focused his mind. While he flexed his long, bony fingers, he reviewed every move he must make. Speed and decisiveness were the keys to success. The longer the patient suffered, the more damage was inflicted on body and spirit, and the lower the chances of recovery. Quickly he cut the linen strip that held the spearhead, and gently lifted it into the vertical. Fenn groaned again. Meren had the leather gag ready and slipped it between her teeth to prevent her biting through her tongue.

'Make sure she does not spit it out,' Taita told him. He leant closer and studied the wound. The movements of the flint had already enlarged it considerably, but not enough to allow him to introduce the silver spoons into the gash. He palpated the swollen flesh and traced the regular pulsing of the great artery. He slipped his first and second finger into the wound to stretch it open, then ran them down into the warm raw flesh until he touched the sharp points of the barbs buried there. Fenn screamed and struggled. Meren and Imbali tightened their grip. Taita stretched the wound channel a little wider. Although his movements were so quick, they were controlled and precise: within seconds he had located the points of the barbs. Fenn's flesh and muscle fibres were clinging to them. With his free hand he took up the spoons, placed them over the shank and ran them into the wound, one on each side of the spearhead. He guided them over the sharp flint to mask it so that he could draw out the spearhead without it snagging.

'You are killing me!' Fenn screamed. Meren and Imbali were using all their strength, but they could hardly hold her as she wriggled and squirmed. Twice Taita managed to guide the spoons over the barbs, but each time she twisted them loose. At the next attempt, he felt them slide into place. He closed the polished metal over the barbs, and in the same movement drew them upwards. There was a clinging suction as the bloody lips of the wound resisted the movement. With his fingertips deep in Fenn's flesh he could feel the artery thudding steadily. It seemed to reverberate through his soul. He concentrated on guiding the spoons past it. If even a sliver of the flint was protruding from the enclosing metal it might catch the artery and slice it open. Smoothly he applied more pressure. He felt the mouth of the wound begin to yield, and then, abruptly, the blood-smeared silver spoons and the flint spearhead came free. Quickly he withdrew his fingers from the wound, and pressed the gaping lips of raw flesh together. With his free hand he snatched the thick linen pad Meren handed to him and pressed it over the wound to staunch the bleeding. Fenn's head fell back. Her screams became soft moans, the tension went out of her limbs, and the rigid arch of her spine relaxed.

'Your skill never fails to astonish me,' Meren whispered. 'Each time I see you work like that I am in awe. You are the greatest surgeon who ever lived.'

'We can discuss that later,' Taita replied. 'Now you can help me to stitch her up.'

Taita was laying the final horsehair stitch when they heard a shout from the northern watch-tower. He did not look up at Meren as he tied the knot that closed the wound. 'I believe that the Basmara have arrived. You must go to your duties now. You may take Imbali with you. Thank you for your help, good Meren. If the wound does not mortify, the child will have much to thank you for too.'

After he had bandaged Fenn's leg, Taita went to the door of the hut and called for Lala, the most reliable and sensible of the Shilluk wives. She came with her naked baby on her hip. She and Fenn were close friends. They spent much time together, talking and playing with the infant. Lala burst into loud lamentations when she saw Fenn pale and blood-smeared. Taita took some time to calm her and rehearse her in her duties. Then he left her to watch over Fenn while she slept off the effects of the red sheppen.

Taita scrambled up the makeshift ladder to join Meren at the north wall of the stockade. Meren greeted him gravely and, without another word, pointed down the valley. The Basmara were advancing in three separate formations. They came at a steady trot. Their headdresses nodded and waved in the breeze of their passage, and their columns wound like long black serpents through the forest. They were singing again, a deep repetitive chant that chilled the blood of the defenders and made their skin crawl. Taita turned to look along the parapet. Their entire active strength was assembled there, and he was sobered by how few they were.

'Thirty-two of us,' he said softly, 'and at least six hundred of them.'

'Then we are evenly matched, Magus, and we are in for some rich sport, I wager,' Meren averred. Taita shook his head in mock-disbelief at such phlegm in the face of the storm that was about to break over them.

Nakonto stood with the Imbali and her women at the far end of the parapet. Taita walked over to them. As always, Imbali's noble Nilotic features were calm and remote.

'You know these people, Imbali. How will they attack?' he asked.

'First they will count our numbers and test our mettle,' she replied, without hesitation.

'How will they do that?'

'They will rush directly at the wall to make us show ourselves.'

'Will they try to set fire to the stockade?'

'No, Shaman. This is their own town. Their ancestors are buried here. They would never burn their graves.'

Taita returned to Meren's side. 'It is time for you to set up the dummies along the parapet,' he said, and Meren passed the order to the Shilluk wives. They had already placed the dummies in position below the parapet. Now they scampered along the stockade lifting them so that the false heads were visible to the Basmara over the top of the wall.

'We have seemingly doubled the strength of our garrison at a single stroke,' Taita remarked. 'It should make the Basmara treat us with a little more respect.'

They watched the formations of spearmen manoeuvre across the ash-strewn ground on which the huts had burnt. The Basmara massed their three regiments in distinct columns, captains at the front.

'Their drill is sloppy and their formations are untidy and

confused.' Meren's tone was scornful. 'This is a rabble, not an army.'

'But a large rabble, while we are a very small army,' Taita pointed out. 'Let us delay our celebrations until after the victory.'

The singing ceased, and a heavy silence fell over the field. A single figure left the Basmara ranks and advanced half-way to the stockade. He wore the tall pink flamingo headdress. He posed in front of his men to let them admire his warlike appearance, then harangued them in a high-pitched shriek, punctuating each statement with a leap high in the air and a clash of spear against war shield.

'What is he saying?' Meren was puzzled.

'I can only guess that he is not being friendly to us.' Taita smiled.

'I will encourage him with an arrow.'

'He is seventy paces beyond your longest shot.' Taita restrained him. 'We have no arrows to waste.'

They watched Basma, the paramount chief of the Basmara, strut back to his waiting regiments. This time he took up a command position behind the rear ranks. Another silence fell over the field. There was no movement. Even the wind had died away. The tension was as oppressive as the lull before a tropical thunderstorm. Then Chief Basma screeched, '*Hau! Hau!*' and his regiments started forward.

'Steady!' Meren cautioned his men. 'Let them get in close. Hold your arrows!'

The massed ranks of the Basmara swept past the outer markers and they began to chant their war-cry. The spears drummed on the shields. At every fifth pace they stamped their bare feet in unison. The rattles on their ankles clashed, and the ground jumped at the impact. The fine dust from the ashes of the burned city rose waist high around them so they seemed to wade through water. They came up to the one-hundred-pace markers. The chanting and drumming swelled into a frenzy.

'Steady!' Meren bellowed, so that his voice carried above the din. 'Hold hard!' The front rank was coming up to the fifty-pace marker. They could see every detail of the weird patterns painted on the Basmara faces. The leaders were past the markers now; and were so close that the archers on the stockade were looking down upon them.

'Nock and aim!' Meren roared. Up came the bows. They arced as the archers drew. Their eyes narrowed as they aimed along the shafts. Meren knew better than to let them hold the draw, until their arms began to judder. His next command came only a breath behind the last. At that precise moment the dense ranks reached the thirty-pace markers.

'Let fly!' he shouted, and they loosed as one man. At that range not a single arrow missed. They flew in a massed, silent cloud. It was a mark of their mettle that no two archers aimed at the same Basmara warrior. The first rank went down as though they had fallen into a pit in the earth.

'Loose at will!' Meren howled. His archers nocked the second arrow with practised dexterity. They threw up, drew and released in one movement, making it appear easy and un-hurried. The next rank of Basmara went down, and moments later, the next fell on top of them. Those that followed stumbled over growing mounds of corpses.

'Arrows here!' The cry went up along the top of the parapet, and the Shilluk women scurried forward, bowed under the bundles they carried on their shoulders. The Basmara kept coming, and the archers shot at them until at last they milled about below the stockade trying for a handhold on the poles of the wall to hoist themselves up. Some reached the top, but Nakonto, Imbali and her women were waiting for them. The battleaxes rose and fell as though they were chopping firewood. Nakonto's cries were murderous as he plied his stabbing spear.

At last a shrill piping of ivory whistles brought the carnage to an abrupt end. The regiments melted away across the ash-dusted field to where Basma waited to regroup the survivors.

Meren strode along the parapet. 'Is anyone wounded? No? Good. When you go out to pick up your arrows, watch out for those who are feigning dead. It's a favourite trick of such devils.'

They opened the gates and rushed out to gather up the arrows. The barbs of many were buried in the dead flesh and had to be chopped out with sword or axe. It was grisly work and they were soon as blood-spattered as a gang of butchers. Once they had the arrows they collected the spears of the fallen Basmara. Then they ran back into the stockade and slammed the gates.

The women brought up the waterskins with baskets of dried fish and dhurra cakes. While most of the men were still chewing, the chanting began again and their captains called them back to the parapet: 'Stand to your arms!'

The Basmara came again in a tight phalanx, but this time the leaders carried long poles they had cut in the forest. When they were shot down by the archers on the wall, the men that followed picked up the poles they had dropped and carried them forward. Fifty or more men died before the poles reached the outer wall of the stockade. The Basmara crowded forward to lift one end of a pole and prop it against the top of the wall. Immediately they swarmed up it, their short stabbing spears clamped in their teeth.

Once their weight was on the pole it was impossible for the defenders to dislodge it. They had to meet the warriors hand to hand when they reached the top of the wall. Imbali and her women stood in the line with the men, and dealt out deadly execution with their battleaxes. But the Basmara seemed impervious to their losses. They clambered over the corpses of their comrades, and rushed into the fray, eager and undaunted.

At last a small bunch had fought their way on to the parapet. It took hard and bitter fighting before the last was hurled back. However, fresh waves swarmed to take their places. Just when it seemed that the exhausted defenders were about to be overwhelmed by the sheer weight of painted bodies, the whistles shrilled again and the attackers melted away.

They drank, dressed their wounds and changed their blunted swords for new ones with keener edges, but the respite was short-lived before the cry went up once more: 'Stand to your arms! They are coming again.'

Meren's men met two more rushes before sunset, but the last was costly. Eight men and two of Imbali's companions had been speared or clubbed to death on the parapet before the Basmara were thrown back.

Few of the troopers had survived the day unscathed. Some had only light cuts or bruises. Two had broken bones from blows of the heavy Basmara clubs. Two more would not see out the night: a spear thrust through the guts and another through the lungs would carry them off before dawn. Many were too weary to eat or even to drag themselves to the shelter of the huts. As soon as they had quenched their thirst they threw themselves down on the parapet and fell asleep in their sweat-soaked armour and bloody bandages.

'We will not hold out here another day,' Meren told Taita. 'This village has become a death-trap. I had not thought the Basmara could be so tenacious. We will have to kill every one before we can get away.' He looked tired and despondent. His eye cavity was hurting – he kept lifting the patch and rubbing it with his knuckles.

Taita had seldom seen him in such a reduced state. 'We do not have enough men to hold this perimeter,' he agreed. 'We will have to pull back to the inner line.' They looked across at the final ring of defences around the well. 'We can do that under cover of night. Then we will set fire to the stockade at the first enemy charge in the morning. That will hold them for a few hours until the flames burn down.'

'And then?'

'We will keep the horses saddled, and wait for our chance to break out of the town and escape.'

'To where?'

'I will tell you when I know,' Taita promised, and stood up stiffly. 'Make sure the men holding the stockade have fire-pots. I am going to Fenn.'

She was asleep when he entered the hut. He did not want to wake her to examine her leg, but when he touched her cheek it was cool, not flushed or feverish. The wound has not mortified, he reassured himself. He sent Lala away, and lay down at Fenn's side. Before he had taken more than three breaths, he had dropped into a deep, dark sleep.

He awoke in the uncertain light of dawn. Fenn was sitting over him anxiously. 'I thought you were dead,' she exclaimed, as he opened his eyes.

'So did I.' Taita sat up. 'Let me see your leg.' He unwrapped the bandage and found the wound only slightly inflamed, but no hotter than his own hand. He leant close and sniffed at the stitches. There were no putrescent odours. 'You must get dressed. We may have to move quickly.' While he helped her into her tunic and loincloth, he told her, 'I am going to make a crutch for you, but you will have little opportunity to learn to use it. The Basmara will certainly attack again at sunrise.' Quickly he fashioned it from a light staff and a carved crosspiece, which he padded with bark cloth. She leant on it heavily as he helped her hobble out to the horse lines. Between them, they put the bridle and saddle on Whirlwind. There was a warning shout from the outer stockade.

'Stay with Whirlwind,' Taita told her. 'I will come back to find you.' He hurried to the stockade, where Meren was waiting for him.

'Fenn – how is she?' were his first words.

'She will be able to ride and is waiting with the horses,' Taita told him. 'What is happening here?'

Meren pointed across the open ground. Two hundred paces away, the Basmara regiments were mustering at the edge of the forest.

'So few,' Taita observed. 'Half as many as there were last evening.'

'Look to the south wall,' Meren told him.

Taita swivelled around to gaze in the direction of the great lake. 'So! They are doing what they should have done yesterday,' he remarked drily. 'They will make a double-pronged assault.' He pondered a moment, then asked, 'How many men are fit enough to hold a weapon this morning?'

'Three died during the night, and four of our troopers took their Shilluk whores and brats and deserted in the darkness. I doubt they will get far before the Basmara find them. That leaves sixteen of us, including Nakonto, Imbali and her tribe-sister, Aoka.'

'We have fifteen horses strong enough to carry a man and his baggage,' Taita said.

'Do we stand to meet another Basmara charge or set fire to the outer stockade and try to escape on the horses in the smoke?'

Taita did not take long to decide. 'To stay here will only delay the inevitable,' he said. 'We will take our chance on the horses and make a run for it. Warn the men of what we intend.'

Meren went down the line with the order and returned swiftly. 'They all know what to do, Magus. The fire-pots are ready. The dice of hazard are in the cup and ready for the throw.' Taita was silent, watching the enemy regiments. They heard the familiar war chant begin, the drumming of the shields and the stamp of hundreds of bare feet.

'They are coming,' said Meren softly.

'Fire the stockade,' Taita ordered. The men at the piles of dry kindling dashed on to them the smouldering contents of the fire-pots and fanned them with their sleeping mats. The flames leapt up instantly.

'Fall back!' Meren bellowed, and the survivors jumped down from the burning parapet. Some ran, while others hobbled or limped, supporting each other painfully. Watching them go, Taita felt suddenly tired, frail and old. Was it all to end here in this remote, wild corner of the earth? Was so much endeavour, suffering and death to be of no consequence? Meren was watching him. He straightened his shoulders and stood to his full height. He could not falter now: he had his duty to Meren and the remaining men, but even more so to Fenn.

'It is time to go, Magus,' Meren said gently, and took his arm to help him down the ladder. By the time they reached the horses the entire length of the outer stockade was enveloped in a roaring, leaping wall of flame. They shrank away from the fierce, blistering heat.

The troopers led out the horses. Meren went down the column assigning the mounts. Of course, Fenn would ride Whirlwind and take Imbali on her stirrup to guard her. Taita would have Windsmoke, with Nakonto hanging on to his stirrup ropes. Meren would be on his bay with Aoka covering his blind side. All the other troopers would ride their own mounts. Now that no mules were left alive the two spare horses were loaded with food and baggage. Hilto and Shabako took them on lead reins.

Under cover of the flaming stockade they mounted, facing the outer gateway. Taita raised high the golden Periapt of Lostris, and cast the spell of concealment over them, shielding them from the eyes of the enemy. He was well aware of the difficulty in cloaking such a large group of horses and men, but the primitive Basmara would be readily susceptible to the illusions he wove.

The Basmara made no effort to break through the burning stockade. Evidently they believed that their victims were trapped within and were waiting their chance to finish them. They were chanting and shouting on the far side of the blaze. Taita waited until the flames had burnt through the outer gates and sent them crashing to earth.

'Now!' he ordered. Habari and Shabako galloped into the smoke and threw loops of rope over the fallen gates. Before the fire could burn through the ropes, they dragged them aside. Now the way was open and the two men galloped back to the others.

'Keep together, the closer the better, and follow me,' Taita said. The spell's efficacy would be revealed once they were through the gates and out on the open ground beyond. The gateway was framed with fire and they had to get through quickly, before they were roasted alive.

'Forward at the gallop,' Taita ordered quietly, but he used the voice of power, which carried clearly to every man in the line. They charged to the flaming gate. The heat struck them like a wall and some of the horses balked, but their riders forced them on with spurs and whips, the heat singeing coats and manes. It scorched the men's faces too and stung their eyes before, still in a tight group, they were on open ground.

Basmara were prancing and howling all around them. Although some looked at them their eyes passed blankly over them, then lifted to the top of the burning stockade. Taita's spell was holding.

'Quietly, slowly,' Taita warned. 'Keep close together. Make no sudden movement.' He kept the Periapt held high. Beside him, Fenn followed his example. She lifted her own gold talisman and her lips moved as she recited the words he had taught her. She was assisting Taita, reinforcing the spell. They moved across the open ground until they were almost clear. The edge of the forest was less than two hundred paces ahead, and still their presence had not been detected by the tribesmen. Then Taita felt a cold draught on the back of his neck. Beside him, Fenn gasped and dropped her talisman on its chain. 'It burnt me!' she exclaimed, and stared at the red mark on her fingertips. Then she turned, with a stricken expression, to Taita. 'Something is breaking our spell.' She was right. Taita felt it tear and shred, like a perished sail in a blast of wind. They were being stripped of their concealing cloak. Another influence was working on them, and he could not deflect or divert it.

'Forward at the gallop!' he shouted, and the horses headed for the edge of the forest. A great shout went up from the Basmara legions. Every painted face turned in their direction, every eye lit with bloodlust. They swarmed towards the little band of riders from every quarter of the field.

'Run!' Taita urged Windsmoke, but she was carrying two big men. Everything seemed to happen with dreamlike slowness. Although they were pulling ahead of the warriors that followed them, another formation of spearmen was running in from the right flank.

'Come on! Fast as you can!' Taita urged. He saw that Basma was leading the race to cut them off. He bounded across their front with his spear balanced on his right shoulder, ready for a clean throw. His men were baying like hounds on a hot scent.

'Come on!' Taita yelled. He judged the angles and speeds. 'We're going to get through.'

Basma made the same calculation as the band of horsemen swept past him, thirty paces clear. Basma used the impetus of his run and the strength of his frustration to hurl the spear after them. He launched it high and it dropped towards Meren's heavily laden bay gelding.

'Meren!' Taita shouted a warning, but the spear was in his blind spot. It struck his mount just behind the saddle, hitting the spine. The bay's back legs collapsed. Meren and Aoka were thrown into a tangle on the scorched earth. The Basmara, who had been about to abandon the chase, took heart and rushed forward, led by their chief. Meren rolled to his feet and saw the faces of the other horsemen looking back at him as they were carried away by their own mounts.

'Go on!' he shouted. 'Save yourselves, for you cannot save us.' The Basmara were closing round him swiftly.

Fenn touched Whirlwind's neck and called to him: 'Whoa! Whirlwind, whoa!'

The grey colt turned like a swallow in mid-flight, and before any of them realized what had happened Fenn was racing back to where Meren stood with Aoka. For a moment he was too astonished to speak as he saw Fenn tearing back towards him, with Imbali hanging on to her stirrup and brandishing her axe. He tried to wave her back: 'Go away!' But as soon as Fenn had turned, so had Taita in the same suicidal gesture. The rest of the band was thrown into confusion. The horses reared and plunged, bumping into each other and milling about until the riders had them under control. Then they all raced back.

Now the nearest Basmara, led by their chief, were almost upon them. They hurled spears as they closed in. First Hilto's horse, then Shabako's were hit and fell heavily, throwing the men from their backs as they went down.

With a quick glance Taita assessed their changed circumstances: there were no longer enough horses to carry them all away. 'Form the defensive circle!' he shouted. 'We must stand and fight them here.'

The men who had been thrown struggled to their feet and limped towards him. Those on unwounded mounts jumped down and pulled them into the centre of the circle. The archers unslung their bows; Imbali and Aoka hefted their axes. They faced outwards. When they looked upon the massed formations of spearmen rushing to attack them they were in no doubt as to the final outcome.

'This is the last fight. Give them something to remember us by!' Meren shouted joyfully, and they met the first rush of Basmara head on. They fought with the ferocity and abandon of despair. They pushed back the attackers. But Chief Basma rallied them, leaping and screeching, and they came again with him at the head of the charge. He went for Nakonto and ducked under his guard to hit him in the thigh.

Imbali was beside him and when she saw his blood springing from the wound she flew at Basma like a lioness protecting her mate. He turned to defend himself and lifted his spear to deflect the sweep of the axe. Imbali's blow sheared the shaft as though it were a papyrus reed and went on to thump into Basma's right shoulder. He staggered back, his half-severed arm hanging at his side. Imbali jerked the blade free and struck again, this time for the head. The blade cut cleanly through the crown of flamingo feathers, and went on to split Basma's skull to his teeth. For a moment the divided eyes squinted at each other round the blade, then Imbali levered it free. The metal grated harshly against the bone as it came away, yellow brain matter oozing after it.

The Basmara saw their chief struck down and, with a despairing shout, drew back. The fighting had been hard. They had suffered heavy losses – corpses lay thickly around the little circle. The Egyptians were few, but they hesitated to rush in and end it. Taita took advantage of the pause to bolster their position. He forced the horses to lie flat, a trick that all cavalry mounts were taught. Their bodies offered some protection from the javelins of the Basmara. He placed his archers behind them and held Imbali, Aoka and Fenn with him in the centre, then took his own position at Fenn's side. He would be with her at the end, just as he had been in the other life. This time, though, he was determined to make it quicker and easier for her.

He looked at the others in the circle. Habari, Shofar and the last two troopers were all dead. Shabako and Hilto were still on their feet, but had been wounded. They had not bothered to treat their injuries, had merely staunched the bleeding by slapping a handful of dirt over it. Beyond them, Imbali was kneeling to bind up Nakonto's thigh. When she finished, she looked up at him with an expression in her eyes that was much more woman than warrior.

Meren had fallen on his face when his horse threw him. His cheek was grazed and his ruined eye was bleeding again. A tiny trickle of blood ran out from under the leather patch down the side of his nose and on to his upper lip. He licked it away as he stropped the whetting stone down the blade of his sword. Surrounded by the dense ranks of the enemy, wounded and broken as they were, there was nothing heroic about any of them.

If by some miracle I should survive this day I will write of them a battle poem that will flood the eyes of all who hear it, Taita promised himself grimly.

A single voice broke the silence with a high-pitched challenge: 'Are we old women or are we fighting impis of the Basmara?' The multitudes began again to hum, sway and stamp.

Another voice called an answer to the first question: 'We are men and we have come for the killing!'

'Kill! Bring the spear! Use the spear! Kill!' The chant went up and the ranks came forward, dancing and stamping. Imbali stood beside Nakonto, a thin, cruel smile on her lips. Hilto and Shabako smoothed back their hair and replaced their helmets. Meren wiped the blood off his lip and blinked his good eye to clear and sharpen his vision. Then he slipped his sword into its scabbard, picked up his bow and leant upon it as he watched the enemy close in. Fenn came stiffly to her feet, favouring her wounded leg. She took Taita's hand.

'Don't be afraid, little one,' he told her.

'I am not afraid,' she said, 'but I wish you had taught me to draw a bow. I could have been more use to you now.'

The ivory whistles squealed and the hordes poured down upon them. The little knot of defenders loosed a flight of arrows into them and another, then nocked and shot as fast as they could draw, but they were so few that they caused barely a ripple in the waves of prancing black bodies.

The Basmara broke into the circle, and it was hand-to-hand again. Shabako was hit in the throat and spouted blood like a harpooned whale as he died. The frail circle broke up under the rush of bodies. Imbali and Nakonto stood back to back as they hacked and thrust. Aoka fell, dead. Meren gave ground until he and Taita had Fenn between them. They might fight on a little longer, but Taita knew that soon he must give mercy to Fenn. He would follow her swiftly, and they would remain united.

Meren killed a man with a straight thrust through the heart, while at the same moment Taita struck down the man beside him.

Meren glanced at him. 'It is time, Magus, but I will do it for you if you wish,' he croaked, through a throat rough with thirst and dust.

Taita knew how Meren had come to love Fenn and how

much it would cost him to kill her. 'Nay, good Meren, though I thank you for it. The duty is mine.' Taita looked down at Fenn fondly. 'Kiss Meren farewell, my sweet, for he is your true friend.' She did so, then turned trustingly to Taita. She bowed her head and closed her eyes. Taita was glad of that: he could never have done it while those green eyes were upon him. He raised his sword, but checked the stroke before it was launched. The war chant of the Basmara had changed to a great moan of despair and terror. Their ranks broke and scattered, like a shoal of sardines before a wolf-fanged barracuda.

The little group were left standing bewildered in the circle. They were bathed in their own sweat and blood and that of their enemies. They looked at each other with incomprehension, unable to understand why they were still alive. The field was almost obscured by the clouds of dust kicked up by feet and hoofs, while thick eddies of smoke drifted down from the burning stockade. It was barely possible to see the tree line.

'Horses!' gritted Meren. 'I hear hoofs.'

'You imagine it,' said Taita, as hoarsely. 'It is not possible.'

'No, Meren is right,' piped up Fenn, and pointed towards the trees. 'Horses!'

Taita blinked in the dust and smoke, but he could not see clearly. His vision was blurred and dull. He wiped his eyes on his sleeve, then stared again. 'Cavalry?' he muttered, in disbelief.

'Egyptian cavalry,' Meren whooped. 'Crack troops! A blue pennant flying over them.' The cavalry charged through the Basmara lines, taking them on the lance, then wheeling back to finish the work with the sword. The Basmara threw down their weapons and fled in disarray.

'It cannot be,' Taita muttered. 'We are two thousand leagues from our very Egypt. How come these men to this place? It is not possible.'

'Well, I believe my eyes – or should I say my one good eye?' cried Meren gaily. 'These are our countrymen!' Within minutes the only Basmara remaining on the field were either dead or soon to be so. The guardsmen were trotting back, leaning from the saddle to lance the wounded where they lay. A trio of high-ranking officers detached themselves from the main body of cavalry and cantered towards the small party of survivors.

'The senior officer is a colonel of the Blue,' Taita said.

'He wears the Gold of Merit and the Cross of the Red Road Brotherhood,' Meren said. 'He is a warrior indeed!'

The colonel pulled up in front of Taita and raised his right hand in salute. 'I feared that we might be too late, exalted Magus, but I see that you are in good health still and I thank all the gods for that mercy.'

'You know me?' Taita was further astonished.

'All the world knows Taita of Gallala. However, I met you at the court of Queen Mintaka, after the defeat of the false pharaoh, but that was many years ago when I was a mere ensign. No wonder it has slipped from your memory.'

'Tinat? Colonel Tinat Ankut?' Taita resurrected a memory of the man's face.

The colonel smiled with gratification. 'You honour me with your recognition.'

Tinat Ankut was a handsome man, with strong, intelligent features and a level gaze. Taita viewed him through the Inner Eye and saw no taint or defect in his aura, although a sombre blue flicker in its depths betokened some deep emotional disturbance. He knew at once that Tinat was not a contented man. 'We had news of you when we passed through Fort Adari,' Taita told him, 'but the men you left there thought you had perished in the wilderness.'

'As you can see, Magus, they were mistaken.' Tinat did not smile. 'But we must leave this place. My scouts have descried many thousands more of these savages converging upon us here. I have done what I was sent to do, which was to take you under protection. We must waste no time, but leave at once.'

'Where will you take us, Colonel Tinat? How did you know

that we were here and in need of aid? Who sent you to rescue us?' Taita demanded.

'Your questions will be answered in due course, Magus, but I regret not by me. I leave Captain Onka here to care for your other needs.' He saluted again and turned his horse away.

They got the horses up. Most had been wounded, two so gravely that they had to be destroyed, but Windsmoke and Whirlwind had come through unscathed. Although they had little baggage remaining, Taita's medical equipment was heavy and bulky. They did not have enough baggage animals to carry it all so Captain Onka called for more pack horses, and Taita tended the injuries and wounds of his band and their mounts. Onka was impatient, but the work could not be hurried, and it was some time before they were ready to ride out.

When Colonel Tinat returned a squadron of his cavalry led them. Taita's band marched in the centre and was well protected. Another large column laboured behind, which included many hundreds of lamenting captives, most of them Basmara women.

'Slaves,' Meren guessed. 'Tinat combines slave-catching with saving innocent travellers.'

Taita made no comment, but considered their own position and status. Are we prisoners also, or honoured guests? he wondered. Our welcome was ambiguous. He considered putting the question to Captain Onka, but he knew it would be a wasted effort: Onka was as reticent as his commander had been.

Once they had left Tamafupa they went south, following the dry course of the Nile towards the lake. Soon they were in sight of the Red Stones and the abandoned temple on the bluff above, but at that point they left the river and headed eastwards on a track beside the lake. Taita tried to talk to Onka about the temple and the stones, but Onka had a stock reply: 'I know nothing about it, Magus. I am a common soldier and no great sage.'

After several more leagues the party climbed another bluff above the lake and looked down into a sheltered bay. Taita and Meren were astonished to see a fleet of six war galleys and several large transport barges riding at anchor on the tranquil waters only a few cubits off the white beach. The craft were of an unusual design the like of which they had never seen in Egyptian waters: they were open-decked and double-ended. It was obvious that the single long mast could be unstepped and laid flat down the length of the hull. The sharp bows and sterns were designed to drive through rough white water in the cataracts and rapids of a fast-flowing river. It was a clever design, Taita conceded. He learned later that the hulls could be broken into four separate sections to be carried round waterfalls and other obstructions.

The fleet looked handsome and businesslike, riding at anchor in the bay. The water was so pure and clear that the hulls seemed to hang suspended in air rather than water, and their shadows were clearly outlined on the bottom of the lake. Taita could even make out the shoals of large fish that cruised round them, attracted by the rubbish that the crews threw overboard.

'The design of those hulls is foreign,' Meren remarked. 'They are not Egyptian.'

'On our travels in the Orient we saw their like in the countries beyond the Indus river,' Taita agreed.

'How did such vessels come to be on this remote uncharted inland sea?'

'One thing I know for certain,' Taita remarked, 'is that there will be no profit in asking Captain Onka.'

'For he is just a common soldier and no great sage.' Meren laughed for the first time since they had left Tamafupa. They followed their guide down to the beach, where embarkation began almost immediately. The captured Basmara were put on two of the barges, the horses and Tinat's troops on to the others.

Colonel Tinat Ankut became quite animated as he studied Windsmoke and Whirlwind. 'What a magnificent pair. Clearly they are dam and foal,' he remarked to Taita. 'I have probably seen fewer than three or four to match them in my life. They have the fine legs and strong chests you see only in animals of Hittite bloodlines. I would hazard these hail from the plains of Ecbatana.'

'You have hit upon it exactly.' Taita applauded. 'I congratulate you. You are a skilled judge of horseflesh.'

Tinat mellowed still further, and he set aside quarters for Taita, Meren and Fenn aboard his galley. Once everyone was embarked, the fleet cast off from the beach and headed out into the lake. As soon as they had made their offing they turned westward along the shoreline. Tinat invited the three to share a meal with him on the open deck. In comparison to the lean fare of the years since they had left Qebui, the food that his cook provided was memorable. Freshly caught and grilled lake fish were followed by a casserole of exotic vegetables, and the amphora of red wine was of a quality that would have graced Pharaoh's own table.

As the sun sank into the waters ahead the fleet drew level with the Red Stones at the mouth of the Nile, and they pulled beneath the tall bluff on whose summit stood the temple of Eos. Tinat had drunk two bowls of wine and had become a gracious, affable host. Taita attempted to take advantage of his mood. 'What building is that?' He pointed across the water. 'It seems to be a temple or palace, but of a design such as I never saw in our very Egypt. I wonder what manner of men erected it.'

Tinat frowned. 'I have given it little thought, as I have no particular interest in architecture, but you may be right, Magus. It is probably a shrine or a temple, or possibly for storage of grain.' He shrugged. 'May I offer you more wine?' Clearly the question had annoyed him, and he was once more aloof and coolly polite. Furthermore, it was apparent that the galley crew had been instructed not to hold any conversation with them, or to answer their questions.

Day after day the fleet sailed westward along the lakeshore. At Taita's request the captain rigged a sail to give them shade and privacy. Screened from the eyes of Tinat and the crew, Taita made progress training Fenn. During the long march southwards there had been little opportunity for them to be alone. Now their secluded corner of the deck became sanctuary and schoolroom, in which he could hone her perception, concentration and intuition to a fine edge.

He introduced her to no new aspects of the esoteric arts. Instead he spent hours each day practising those she had already acquired. In particular he worked on communication through the telepathic exchange of mental images and thoughts. He was haunted by a premonition that at some time in the near future they would be separated. If this should happen, then such contact would be their lifeline. Once the connection between them was swift and sure, his next concern was to suppress the display of her aura. Only when he was satisfied that she had perfected these disciplines could they proceed to review the conjugation of the words of power.

Hours and days of practice was so demanding and exhausting that Fenn should have been mentally and spiritually drained: she was a novice in the arcane arts, a girl in body and strength. However, even when he had taken into account that she was an old soul, who had lived another life, her resilience astounded him. Her energy seemed to feed on her exertions in the same way that the water-lily, her life symbol, fed on the mud of the river bed.

Disconcertingly, she could change in a beat from serious student to spirited girl as she switched from the obscure conundrum of the conjugations to delight in the beauty of ruby-winged flamingos passing overhead. At night when she slept near him under the awning on the sleeping mats spread on the deck he wanted to snatch her up and crush her to him so tightly that not even death could tear them apart.

The galley captain spoke of sudden violent gales that swept across the lake without warning. He told of the many vessels that had been overwhelmed and now lay in the unplumbed deeps. Each evening, as night fell over the great waters, the flotilla found anchorage in a sheltered bay or cove. Only when the first rays of the rising sun opened, like the tail of a peacock, above the eastern horizon did the ships hoist their sails, run out the banks of their oars and turn their prows east once more. The extent of the great lake astounded Taita. The shoreline seemed endless.

Is it as large as the Middle Sea or the mighty Ocean of the Indies, or is it without limits or boundaries? he wondered. In spare moments he and Fenn drew maps on sheets of papyrus, or made notes of the islands they passed and the features they saw upon the shore.

'We shall take these to the geographer priests at the temple of Hathor. They know nothing of these secrets and wonders,' he told her.

A dreamy look clouded the green of her eyes. 'Oh, Magus, I long to return with you to the land of my other life. You have made me remember so many precious things. You will take me there one day, won't you?'

'Be sure of it, Fenn,' he promised.

By observations of the sun, the moon and other heavenly bodies, Taita calculated that the lakeshore was gradually inclining towards the south. 'This leads me to believe that we have reached the western limit of the lake, and that we will soon be sailing due south,' he said.

'Then in time we will reach the end of the earth and fall off it into the sky.' Fenn sounded undaunted by the prospect of such a catastrophe. 'Will we fall for ever, or will we come to rest at last in another world and another time? What do you think, Magus?'

'I hope our captain will have the sense to turn back as soon as he sees the void gaping ahead, and we will not have to tumble through time and space. I am quite content with the here and now.' Taita chuckled, delighted with the blossoming of her imagination.

That evening he examined the wound in her thigh and was gratified to find that it had healed cleanly. The skin around the horse-hair stitches was flushed an angry red, a sure sign that it was time to remove them. He snipped at the knots and pulled them out with his ivory forceps. A few drops of yellow pus oozed from the puncture marks they left. Taita sniffed it and smiled. 'Sweet and benign. I could not have hoped for a better result. See what a pretty scar it has left you, shaped like the petal of your water-lily symbol.'

She cocked her head to one side as she examined the mark, which was no bigger than the nail on her little finger. 'You are so clever, Magus. I am sure you did that by design. It is more pleasing to me than Imbali's tattoos are to her. She will be so envious!'

They sailed on through a maze of islands on which grew trees with trunks so thick and tall they seemed to be the pillars that held aloft the inverted blue bowl of the heavens. Eagles roosted upon the galleries of shaggy nests they had built in the high branches. They were magnificent birds with shining white heads and russet pinions. In flight they would emit a wild, chanting cry, then plunge into the lake and emerge with a large fish gripped in their talons.

They saw monstrous crocodiles sunning themselves on every beach, and gatherings of hippopotamus in the shallows. The rounded grey backs were as massive as granite boulders. When they sailed out into open water again, the shore turned due south, as Taita had predicted, and they ran on towards the end of the earth. They sailed past endless forests populated by great herds of black buffalo, grey elephant and enormous pig-like creatures that carried sharp horns upon their noses. They were the first of the kind they had encountered, and Taita drew sketches of them, which Fenn declared a marvel of accuracy.

'My friends the priests will hardly believe in the existence of such wondrous beasts,' Taita observed. 'Meren, might you be able to slay one of those creatures so that we could take the nose-horn back with us as a gift for Pharaoh?' Their mood had become so buoyant that they had begun to believe there would be an eventual return to their own land in the far north.

As always, Meren was eager for the chase, and leapt at the suggestion. 'If you can prevail upon Tinat and the captain to anchor for a day or two, I will go ashore with a mount and a bow.'

Taita approached Tinat with the suggestion that the horses, having been confined so long in the cramped conditions aboard the barges, would benefit greatly from a gallop, and found him surprisingly amenable.

'You are correct, Magus, and a goodly supply of fresh meat would not go amiss. With soldiers and slaves, I have many bellies to fill.'

That evening they came to a wide floodplain on the lakeshore. The open glades were alive with multitudes of game, from the grey pachyderms to the smallest, most graceful antelope. The plain was bisected by a small estuary running in from the east and debouching into the lake. It was navigable for a short distance, and provided a secure harbour for the flotilla. They landed the horses, and the men set up a camp on the riverbank. They were all delighted to have solid ground under their feet, and as they rode out the next morning the mood was festive. Tinat instructed his hunters to attack the herds of buffalo and to pick out the cows and heifers, whose flesh was more palatable than that of the old bulls – they were so tough and rank that they were almost inedible.

By now Meren and Hilto had recovered from the wounds they had received at Tamafupa. They would lead the chase after the monstrous pachyderms with nose-horns. Nakonto and Imbali would follow on foot, while Taita and Fenn would stay behind as spectators. At the last moment Colonel Tinat rode across and asked Taita, 'I would like to ride with you to watch the sport. I hope that you do not object to my presence.'

Taita was surprised. He had not expected such a friendly overture from the morose fellow. 'I would be delighted to have your company, Colonel. As you know, we are after one of those strange creatures which carries a horn upon its nose.'

By this time bands of cavalry were roving across the plain, harrying the buffalo herds with cries of excitement, riding in close to use the lance upon them. When the doughty bovines turned at bay they shot them down with volleys of arrows. Soon black carcasses were littered across the sward, and the panic-stricken herds charged willy-nilly about the plain, desperate to escape the hunters.

To avoid the confused ruck of herds and horsemen, and to discover open ground where they could hunt the pachyderm selectively, Meren crossed the little estuary and rode along the bank. The others followed him until they were out of sight of the vessels, and had the field to themselves. Ahead, they could see a number of quarry scattered across the grassland in small family groups of females and calves. However, Meren was determined to procure the horn of a patriarch, a trophy fit to present to Pharaoh.

As he led them further from the anchored ships, Taita noticed a gradual change coming over Colonel Tinat. His reserve was softening, and he even smiled at some of Fenn's chatter. 'Your ward is a bright young girl,' he remarked, 'but is she discreet?'

'She is a young girl, as you said, and is free of spite or malice.' Tinat relaxed a little more, so Taita opened his Inner Eye and assessed the man's state of mind. He is under restraint, he thought. He does not want to be seen by his officers to converse freely with me. He is afraid of somebody among his men. I have no doubt it is Captain Onka, who has probably been placed here to watch and report on his superior officer. Tinat has something to tell me, but he is fearful.

Taita reached out with his mind to Fenn, and saw her become receptive. He sent her a message in the Tenmass: 'Join Meren. Leave me alone with Tinat.'

Immediately she turned towards him and smiled. 'Please excuse me, Magus,' she said sweetly. 'I would ride with Meren a space. He has promised to build me a bow of my own.' With her knees she pushed Whirlwind into a canter, leaving Taita alone with Tinat.

The two men rode in silence until Taita said, 'From my conversation with Pharaoh Nefer Seti, I understood that his orders to you when you left Egypt all those years ago were to journey to the source of Mother Nile, then return to Karnak to report your findings.'

Tinat glanced at him sharply, but did not reply.

Taita paused delicately, then went on: 'It seems strange that you have not returned to tell him of your success and to claim from him the reward you so handsomely deserve. It puzzles me to discover that we are journeying in the diametrically opposite direction to Egypt.'

Tinat remained silent for a short while longer, then said softly, 'Pharaoh Nefer Seti is no longer my ruler. Egypt is no longer my homeland. My men and I have adopted a more beautiful, bountiful and blessed country as our own. Egypt is under a curse.'

'I would never have believed that any officer of your status could turn away from his patriotic duty,' Taita said.

'I am not the first Egyptian officer to do so. There was another, ninety years ago, who discovered this new country and never returned to Egypt. He was sent by Queen Lostris on a similar mission, to discover the headwaters of the Nile. His name was General Lord Aquer.'

'I knew him well,' Taita interjected. 'He was a good soldier, but unpredictable.'

Although Tinat looked at him askance, he did not query Taita's assertion. Instead he continued, 'Lord Aquer pioneered the settlement of Jarri, the Land of the Mountains of the Moon. His direct descendants have built it into a powerful and advanced state. I am honoured to serve them.'

Taita regarded him with the Inner Eye and saw that this

statement was untrue: far from being honoured by his service to this foreign government, Tinat was a man in turmoil. 'That is where you are taking us now, is it? To this state of Jarri?'

'Those are my orders, Magus,' Tinat agreed.

'Who is the king of this country?' Taita asked.

'We do not have one. An oligarchy of noble and wise men rules us.'

'Who chooses them?'

'They are selected for their apparent virtues.'

Again, Taita saw that Tinat did not truly believe this. 'Are you one of the oligarchs?'

'Nay, Magus, I could never warrant that honour as I am not of noble birth. I am a recent arrival in Jarri, an incomer.'

'So Jarrian society is stratified?' Taita asked. 'Divided into nobility, commoners and slaves?'

'In broad outline, that is so. Although we are known as migrants, not commoners.'

'Do you Jarrians still worship the panoply of Egyptian gods?'

'Nay, Magus, we have but one god.'

'Who is he?'

'I do not know. Only the initiates to the religion know his name. I pray that one day I am granted that boon.' Taita saw many conflicting currents running below this assertion: there was something that Tinat could not bring himself to say, even though he had escaped the surveillance of Onka to voice it.

'Tell me more of this land, so wondrous that it could pre-empt the loyalty of a man of your worth.' Taita was encouraging him to speak out.

'No words are adequate to the task,' Tinat replied, 'but we will be there soon enough, and you shall judge for yourself.' He was letting the opportunity to speak openly slip away.

'Colonel Tinat, when you rescued us from the Basmara you said something that made me believe you had been sent for that express purpose. Was I correct?'

'I have already said too much ... because I hold you in such high respect and esteem. But I must ask you not to press me. I know that you have a superior and enquiring mind, but you are entering a land that has a different code of customs and laws. At this stage you are a guest, so it will be expedient to us all if you respect the mores of your hosts.' Now Tinat was in full retreat.

'One of which is not to pry into matters that don't concern me?'

'Precisely,' Tinat said. It was a sober warning, and that was as much as he could bring himself to say.

'I have always held the view that expediency is a justification for tyranny, and the sop of serfs.'

'A dangerous view, Magus, which you should keep to yourself while you are in Jarri.' Tinat closed his mouth as if it were the visor of his bronze helmet, and Taita knew that he would learn no more now, but he was not disappointed. Indeed, he was surprised to have learnt so much.

They were interrupted by the faint cries of the hunters. Far ahead, Meren had run down a quarry worthy of his arrows.

The antediluvian monster stood at bay, snorting like a fire-breathing dragon, making short but furious rushes towards its tormentors, kicking up the dust with its great hoofs, swinging its horned nose from side to side, piggy eyes bright, ears pricked forward. Its nose-horn stood tall as a man, polished by constant honing on tree trunks and termite mounds until it gleamed like a sword.

Then Taita saw Fenn, and felt acid rise in his throat. She was flirting with the beast. Serenely confident of her own horsemanship and Whirlwind's speed, she was crossing at an oblique angle in front of the beast's nose, inviting his charge. Taita kicked his heels into Windsmoke's flanks and raced to restrain her. At the same time he sent an urgent astral impulse directly to her. He felt her parry it, with the skill of an expert swordsman, then close her mind to him. His anger and concern flared hotly. 'The little she-devil!' he muttered.

At that moment the creature's eye was drawn by Whirlwind's shining grey coat, and it accepted Fenn's challenge. It hurled itself at them, grunting, snorting and pounding the earth with its great hoofs. Fenn touched the colt's neck and they jumped into full gallop. She was twisted in the saddle to judge the distance between the point of the horn and Whirlwind's flying tail. When they drew a little too far ahead, she held Whirlwind back to let the gap close and to urge the beast on.

Despite his fear for her safety Taita could not help but admire her skill and nerve, as she led the animal in front of Meren at close range. He loosed three arrows in rapid succession, and all flew in behind the shoulder to bury their full length up to the fletching in the thick grey hide. The animal stumbled and Taita saw bloody froth spray from its mouth. At least one of Meren's arrows had pierced a lung. Fenn led the beast on, skilfully bringing it round in a circle under Meren's poised bow and forcing it to expose its other flank to him. He shot and shot again, and his arrowheads went deep, raking through the heart and both lungs.

The beast slowed as its lungs filled with blood. The lethargy of death transmuted its mighty limbs to stone. At last it stood, head hanging, blood pouring in rivulets from its open mouth and its nose. Nakonto raced in from the side and drove in the point of his spear behind its ear, slanting the blade forward to find the brain. The body dropped with such weight that it jarred the earth and raised a cloud of dust.

By the time Taita reached them they had all dismounted and were gathered around the carcass. Fenn was dancing with excitement and the others were laughing and clapping. Taita was determined to punish her defiance by sending her back to the galley in disgrace, but as he dismounted, stony-featured, she rushed to him and jumped up to throw her arms round his neck.

'Taita, did you see it all? Was it not splendid? Were you not proud of Whirlwind and me?' Then, before he could deliver himself of the harsh rebuke that scalded his lips, she pressed her lips to his ear and whispered, 'You are so kind and good to me. I do love you, darling Taita.'

He felt his anger deflate and he asked himself ruefully, who is training whom? These are the arts she perfected in the other life. I still find myself defenceless against them.

The hunters had killed more than forty large animals, so it was a few days before all the carcasses could be butchered, the meat smoked and packed aboard the barges. Only then could they board the galleys and continue the voyage southward. When Tinat was back with his officers he became aloof and unapproachable once more. Watching him with the Inner Eye, Taita saw that he was regretting their conversation and the disclosures he had made. He was fearful of the consequences of his indiscretion.

The wind veered into the north and freshened. The galleys shipped their oars and hoisted large lateen sails. White water curled under their prows and the shore flew by on the starboard side. On the fifth morning after the hunt they reached the mouth of another tributary. Coming down from the high ground to the west, it poured an enormous volume of water into the lake. Taita heard the crew talking among themselves, and the name 'Kitangule' bandied about. Clearly that was the name of the river before them. He was not surprised when the captain ordered the sail to be lowered and the oars run out once more. Their galley led the flotilla into the Kitangule and pushed against the mighty flow.

Within a few leagues they had come to a large settlement built along the riverbank. Here, there were shipyards with the unfinished hulls of two large vessels lying on the slipways. Workmen swarmed over them, and Taita pointed out the overseers to Meren. 'That accounts for the foreign design of the ships in this squadron. All must have been built in these yards, and those who built them are unmistakably from the lands beyond the Indus.'

'How came they to this place, so far from their own land?' Meren wondered.

'There is something here that attracts worthy men from afar, like bees to a garden of flowers.'

'Are we bees also, Magus? Does the same attraction entice us?'

Taita looked at him with surprise. This was an unusually perceptive idea from Meren. 'We have come here to fulfil a sacred oath made to Pharaoh,' he reminded him. 'However, now that we have arrived we must be on our guard. We must never allow ourselves to be turned into dreamers and lotus-eaters, as it seems so many of these Jarrians are.'

The flotilla sailed on up the river. Within days they had encountered the first cataracts of white water that blocked the river from bank to bank. This did not daunt Tinat and his captains, for at the foot of the torrent there was another small village, and beyond that extensive cattle stockades, which held herds of humped oxen.

Passengers, horses and slaves disembarked on to the bank. With only the crews still on board, the vessels were hitched with heavy ropes of twisted liana to teams of oxen and dragged up the chutes of fast water. Ashore, the men and horses climbed the track that ran beside the cascade until they reached higher ground. Above the cataracts the river was deep and placid, and the galleys rode lightly at anchor. All embarked again, to voyage on until they reached the next waterfall where the procedure was repeated.

Three times they came to falls too steep and furious to permit the vessels to be dragged up them. Egyptian engineering genius was evident in the extensive works that circumvented the obstacles: a zigzag series of channels had been dug alongside the falls, with locks at each end and wooden gates to lift the vessels to the next level. It took many days and much labour to bring the flotilla up the water ladders, but eventually they were in the deep, gentle flow of the main stream once more.

Since leaving the lake, the terrain they had passed through was fascinating in its magnificent diversity. For a hundred leagues or so after they had entered the Kitangule, the river ran through dense jungle. Branches almost met overhead and it seemed that no two trees were of the same species. They were festooned with lianas, other vines and flowering creepers. High in the canopy, troops of monkeys squabbled noisily in gardens of flowering orchids and fruit. Glistening monitor lizards sunned themselves on branches that overhung the river. At the approach of the boats they launched themselves into the air and fell to hit the water with a splash that showered the men at the oars.

At night when they moored along the bank, tied to the trunks of the great trees, the darkness was loud with the cries and scuffling of unseen animals, and the roars of the predators that hunted them. Some of the crew set fishing lines in the black water, the bronze hooks baited with offal. Three men on one line struggled to pull out the huge catfish that seized the bait.

Slowly the vegetation along the banks changed as they climbed up through the cataracts. The sweltering heat cooled and the air became more salubrious. Once they had negotiated the final water ladder, they found themselves in an undulating landscape of grassy glades and open forests dominated by many species of acacia – leafless and thorny; covered with soft, feathery foliage; with vast black trunks and dark boughs. The tallest were decorated with bunches of lavender fruit hanging like grapes from the high branches.

This was a fertile, well-watered land with lush sweet grass filling the glades, and dozens of streams joining the main flow of the Kitangule. The plains swarmed with herds of grazing animals, and not a day passed when they did not see prides of lions hunting or resting in the open. At night their thunderous roars were terrifying. No matter how often they heard them, the listeners' nerves jangled and their hearts raced.

At last a tall escarpment rose across the horizon, and they were aware of a murmur that grew louder as they drew closer. They came round another bend in the river, and saw before them a mighty waterfall that fell in thundering gouts of white foam from the top of a cliff into a swirling green pool at the foot.

On the beaches that surrounded it teams of oxen were standing ready to draw the boats ashore. Once again they disembarked, but this was for the last time. No device of man could lift the vessels to the top of those cliffs. In the settlement on the riverbank there were guesthouses to accommodate the officers and Taita's party while the rest of the men, horses and baggage were brought ashore. The Basmara slaves were locked into barracoons.

It was three days before Colonel Tinat was ready to continue the journey. Now all of the baggage was loaded on to pack oxen. The slaves were led out of the barracoons and roped together in long lines. The troopers and Taita's band mounted, and rode out along the base of the cliff in a long caravan. Within a league the road was climbing sharply up the escarpment in a series of hairpin bends and narrowed to a path. The gradient became so steep that they were forced to dismount and lead the horses, the heavily laden oxen and the slaves toiling behind them.

Half-way up the cliff they reached a place where a narrow rope suspension bridge crossed a deep gorge. Captain Onka took control of the crossing, allowing only a small number of pack animals and men to venture out on to the precarious structure at a time. Even with a limited load the bridge swayed and sagged alarmingly, and it was the middle of the afternoon before the caravan was across the gorge.

'Is this the only route to the top of the cliffs?' Meren asked Onka.

'There is an easier road that scales the escarpment forty leagues to the south, but it adds several days' travel to the journey.'

Once they were across the void they looked down and their view seemed to encompass the earth. From on high they surveyed golden savannahs over which the rivers crawled like dark serpents, distant blue hills and green jungles. Finally, on the misty horizon, the waters of the great lake Nalubaale along which they had sailed gleamed like molten metal.

At last they reached the border fort perched on the ridge to guard the pass, the Kitangule Gap, and the entrance to Jarri. It was dark by the time they bivouacked outside it. It rained during the night, but by morning the sun was shining benevolently. When they looked out of their shelter Taita and Fenn were presented with a sight that made all the splendours they had seen up to then seem commonplace. Below them lay a wide plateau that stretched to a distant horizon. Along it rose a range of rugged mountains so tall they must have been the abode of the gods. Three central peaks shone with the ethereal luminance of the full moon. Taita and Meren had travelled through the peaks along the Khorasan highway, but Fenn had never seen snow before. She was struck dumb by the glorious sight. At last she found her voice: 'Look! The mountains are on fire,' she cried.

From the summit of each shining mountain billowed silver clouds of smoke.

'You were seeking a single volcano, Magus,' Meren said softly, 'but you have found three.' He turned and pointed back at the distant shimmer of Lake Nalubaale on the far side of the pass. 'Fire, air, water and earth . . .'

'. . . but the lord of these is fire,' Taita finished the incantation of Eos. 'Surely that must be the stronghold of the witch.' His legs were trembling and he was overcome with emotion. They had come so far and endured such hardship to reach this place. He had to find somewhere to sit for his legs could hardly bear his weight. He found a vantage-point from which he could gaze upon the sight. Fenn sat on the rock beside him to share his emotions.

At last Captain Onka rode back from the head of the caravan to find them. 'You may linger here no longer. We must move on.'

The road descended at an easier gradient. They mounted the horses and rode down through the foothills and on to the plateau. For the rest of that day they travelled towards the mountains, through an enchanted land. They had climbed just high enough above the lake, the jungles and deserts to reach this sweet, benevolent clime. Each breath they drew seemed to charge their bodies and clear their minds. Streams of clear water ran down from the mountains. They passed cottages and farms built of stone with golden thatch, surrounded by orchards and olive groves. There were meticulously tended vineyards where the vines were heavy with ripening grapes. The fields were planted with dhurra, the vegetable gardens with melons, beans, lentils, red and green peppers, pumpkins and other vegetables that Taita did not recognize. The pastures were green, and herds of cattle, sheep and goats grazed in them. Fat pigs rooted in the forests, ducks and geese paddled in river pools, and flocks of chickens scratched in every farmyard.

'Seldom in all our travels have we come upon such rich lands,' Meren said.

As they passed, the farmers and their families came out to welcome them with bowls of sherbet and red wine. They spoke Egyptian with the accents of the Two Kingdoms. They were all well nourished and dressed in good leather and linen. The children appeared healthy, but they were strangely subdued. The women were rosy cheeked and well favoured.

'What pretty girls,' Meren remarked. 'Not an ugly one among them.'

They soon found out why the pastures were so green. Suddenly the triple peaks of the snow-decked volcanoes were hidden behind a heavy layer of cloud. Onka rode back to them and told Taita, 'You should don your capes. It will rain within the hour.'

'How do you know?' Taita asked.

'Because it rains every afternoon at this time.' He pointed ahead at the gathering clouds. 'The three peaks that dominate Jarri have many names, one of which is the Rainmakers. They are the reason why the land is so bounteous.' As he finished speaking, rain swept over them and, despite their capes, soaked them to the skin, but within a few hours the clouds had been blown aside and the sun shone once more. The land was washed clean and bright. The leaves on the trees glistened and the soil smelt of rich dhurra cake.

They came to a fork in the road. The column of slaves took the left-hand path, and as they marched away Taita heard a sergeant of the escort remark, 'They are sorely needed in the new mines at Indebbi.'

The rest of the convoy continued along the right fork. At intervals the troopers came to salute Colonel Tinat, then left the column and rode away in different directions to their home farms. In the end only Tinat and Onka, with an escort of ten troopers, remained with them. It was late afternoon when they topped a gentle rise and discovered another small village nestled below them among green trees and pastures.

'This is Mutangi,' Tinat told Taita. 'It is the local market town and magistracy. It will be your home for the time being. Quarters have been set aside for you and I am sure you will find them comfortable. You have heard it said before, but you are honoured guests in Jarri.'

The magistrate came out in person to welcome them, a man of middle age named Bilto. His full beard was tinged with silver, but he was straight and strong, his eye steady and his smile warm. Taita looked at him with the Inner Eye and saw that he was honest and well-intentioned but, like Colonel Tinat Ankut, he was neither happy nor contented. He greeted Taita with the greatest respect, but looked at him strangely, as though he was expecting something from him. One of his own wives took Hilto and the others, including Nakonto and Imbali, to a commodious stone house near the far side of the village, where slave girls were waiting to attend to them. Bilto led Taita, Fenn and Meren to a larger building across the road. 'I think you will find all you need for your comfort. Rest and refresh yourselves. Within the next few days the council of oligarchs will send for you. In the meantime I am your host, and yours to command.' Before he left them, Bilto looked again at Taita with troubled, searching eyes, but he said no more.

When they entered the house a major-domo and five house slaves were lined up to receive them. The rooms were large and airy, but the windows could be covered with leather curtains, and there were open hearths in the main rooms where fires were already burning. Although the sun was still above the horizon there was a chill in the air, so the fires would be welcome when the sun set. Fresh clothes and sandals had been laid out for them and the slaves brought jars of hot water for washing. The evening meal was served by the light of oil lamps, a rich stew of wild-boar chops, washed down with a robust red wine.

Until then they had not realized that the journey had exhausted them. Meren's eye was paining him so Taita poured a warm balm of olive oil and soothing herbs into the socket, then administered a dose of red sheppen.

The next morning they all slept late. Meren's eye had improved but still hurt.

After breakfast, Bilto took them on a tour of the village, of which he was proud, and explained how the community lived. He introduced them to the leaders and Taita found in the main that they were honest and uncomplicated. He had expected to detect some ambiguity in their psyches, as he had with Bilto and Colonel Tinat, which might be attributed to the proximity and influence of Eos, but there was nothing of significance, just the petty foibles and frailties of humanity. One was discontented with his wife, another had stolen an axe from his neighbour and was consumed with guilt, while someone else lusted for his young step-daughter.

Early in the morning of the fifth day Captain Onka returned to Mutangi to deliver a summons from the Supreme Council. They were to leave at once, he told them.

'The citadel that contains the chamber of the Supreme Council is forty leagues hence in the direction of the Mountains of the Moon. It is a ride of several hours,' Onka told Taita. The weather was fine and sunny, the air crisp and exhilarating. Fenn's cheeks were glowing and her eyes sparkling. At Taita's bidding she fell back with him to the rear of the party, where he spoke quietly to her in the Tenmass. 'This will be a crucial test,' he warned. 'I believe we are heading for the stronghold of the witch. You must suppress your aura now and keep it so until we return to Mutangi.'

'I understand, Magus, and I will do as you bid me,' she answered. Almost immediately, her expression became neutral and her eyes dulled. He saw her aura fade and its colours diminish until they were little different from those emitted by Imbali.

'No matter what stimulation or provocation you encounter, you must not allow it to flare up again. You will not know from which direction you are observed. You dare not relax for a moment.'

It was well past noon when they entered a steep-sided valley that cut into the central massif of the mountain range. No more than a league further on they reached the outer wall of the citadel. It was built of large rectangular blocks of volcanic rock that had been fitted together by skilled masons of another age. The passage of time had weathered the stone. The gates stood open: it seemed probable that they had not been closed against an enemy for many years. When they rode into the citadel they found that the buildings were grander and more substantial than anything they had seen since leaving Egypt. Indeed, the largest was strongly reminiscent of the temple of Hathor at Karnak.

Grooms were waiting to take the horses, and red-robed functionaries led them through pillared halls until they reached a small door in a loggia and went through it into an antechamber. Refreshments had been set out on the long table, bowls of fruit, cakes and jugs of red wine, but first they went into the adjoining rooms to freshen themselves after their journey. Everything had been arranged with consideration for their comfort.

When they had eaten a light meal, the council usher came to lead them into the audience chamber. It was warmed by charcoal braziers and padded mats lay on the stone floor. He asked them to seat themselves and pointed out the positions they should occupy. He placed Taita at the head of the group, with Meren and Hilto behind him. He sent Fenn to the rear rank with the others, and Taita was relieved that he had shown no special interest in her. He glanced at her out of the corner of his eye as she sat demurely beside Imbali and saw that she was restraining her aura to match that of the tall woman.

Taita returned his attention to the layout and furnishings of the chamber. It was a large room of agreeable proportions. In front of where he sat, there was a raised stone platform on which stood three stools. They were of a design he had seen in the palaces of Babylon, but they were not inlaid with ivory and semi-precious stones. The wall behind them was covered with a painted leather screen, which hung from the high ceiling to the stone paving and was adorned with patterns in earthy colours. When Taita studied them he saw that they were not esoteric or arcane symbols but merely decorative.

There was the sound of hobnailed sandals on the stone floor. A file of armed guards entered from a side door and arranged themselves at the base of the platform, grounding the butts of their spears. The robed usher returned and addressed the company in sonorous tones: 'Pray show respect for the noble lords of the Supreme Council.' All followed Taita's example and leant forward to touch the ground with their foreheads.

Three men came from behind the leather screen. There could be no doubt that they were the oligarchs. They wore tunics of yellow, scarlet and pale blue, and plain silver crowns on their heads. Their manner was stately and dignified. Taita scried their auras and found them diverse and complex. They were men of force and character, but the most impressive was the man in the blue robe who took the central stool. There were depths and nuances to his character, some of which Taita found puzzling and disturbing.

The man made a gesture for them to relax, and Taita straightened.

'Greetings, Magus Taita of Gallala. We welcome you to Jarri, the land of the Mountains of the Moon,' said the blue-robed leader.

'Greetings, Oligarch Lord Aquer of the Supreme Council,' Taita replied.

Aquer blinked and inclined his head. 'You know me?'

'I knew your grandfather well,' Taita explained. 'He was younger than you are now when last I saw him, but your features are cast in his exact mould.'

'Then much that I hear about you is true. You are a Long Liver and a sage,' Aquer acknowledged. 'You will make a shining contribution to our community. Would you be kind enough to introduce to us your companions, whom we know less well?'

Taita called them forward by name. Meren was the first and went to stand before the platform. 'This is Colonel Meren Cambyses, bearer of the Gold of Valour and Companion of the Red Road.' The council studied him in silence. Suddenly Taita became aware that something unusual was afoot. He diverted his attention from the three oligarchs to the leather screen behind them. He scried for some hidden presence but there was none. It was as though the area behind the screen was a void. This alone was enough to alert him. Some psychic force was cloaking that part of the chamber.

Eos is here! he thought. She throws no aura, and has concealed herself behind a screen more impenetrable than leather. She is watching us. The shock was so intense that he had to fight to keep himself under control: she was the ultimate predator, and would smell blood or weakness.

At last Aquer spoke again: 'How did you lose your eye, Colonel Cambyses?'

'Such things happen to a soldier. There are many hazards in our lives.'

'We will deal with that in due course,' Aquer said.

Taita could make little of such an enigmatic statement. 'Please return to your place, Colonel.' The interview had been cursory, but Taita knew they had extracted all the information they required from Meren.

Next Taita called Hilto. The oligarchs took an even shorter time to consider him. Taita saw Hilto's aura burning honest and unremarkable, except for the fluttering ribbons of blue light at its edges, which betrayed his agitation. The oligarchs sent him back to his seat. They treated Imbali and Nakonto in much the same manner.

At last Taita called Fenn. 'My lords, this is an orphan of war on whom I took pity. I have made her my ward and named her Fenn. I know little about her. Never having had a child of my own, I have grown fond of her.'

Standing before the Supreme Council, Fenn looked like an abandoned waif. She hung her head and shifted her weight shyly from one foot to the other. It was as though she could not bring herself to look directly at her inquisitors. Anxiously, Taita watched her with the Inner Eye. Her aura remained subdued, and she was playing perfectly the role he had set for her. After another pause Aquer asked, 'Who was your father, girl?'

'Sir, I knew him not.' There was no flicker of falsehood in her aura.

'Your mother?'

'Neither do I remember her, sir.'

'Where were you born?'

'Sir, forgive me, but I do not know.'

Taita noted how well she was holding herself in check.

'Come here,' Aquer ordered. Timidly she hopped up on to the platform and went to him. He took her arm and drew her closer to his stool. 'How old are you, Fenn?'

'You will think me stupid, but I know not.' Aquer turned her, slipped his hand into the top of her tunic and felt her chest under the linen.

'There is already something.' He chuckled. 'There will soon be much more.' Fenn's aura glowed softly pink and Taita feared she was about to lose her self-control. Then he realized she was displaying only the shame that any young girl would experience on being handled in a manner she did not understand. He had more difficulty with keeping his own anger in check. However, he sensed that this little scene was a test: Aquer was attempting to goad a reaction from either Fenn or Taita. Taita remained stony-faced but he thought: In the time of reckoning you shall pay in full for that, Lord Aquer.

The oligarch continued to fondle Fenn. 'I am sure you will grow to be a young woman of rare beauty. If you are fortunate you may be chosen for great honour and distinction here in Jarri,' he said. He pinched one of her small round buttocks and laughed again. 'Run along now, little one. We shall consider it again in a year or two.'

He dismissed them, but asked Taita to remain. When the others had left the room, Aquer said politely, 'It is necessary that we of the council confer privily, Magus. Please pardon us while we withdraw. We shall not leave you long alone.'

When they returned the three oligarchs were more relaxed and friendly, and remained respectful.

'Tell me what you know of my grandfather,' Lord Aquer invited. 'He died before I was born.'

'He was a loyal and respected member of the court of Regent Queen Lostris during the period of the exodus and the Hyksos invasion of the Two Kingdoms. Her Majesty entrusted him with many important tasks. He discovered the road that cuts across the great bight of the Nile. It is still used, and saves several hundred leagues of the journey between Assoun and Qebui. The queen bestowed honours upon him for this and his other accomplishments.'

'I still have the Gold of Honour I inherited from him.'

'The queen trusted him to the extent that she chose him

to lead an army of two thousand men south from Qebui to discover and chart the Nile to its source. Only one man returned, demented with fever and the hardships he had encountered. Nothing was ever heard of the rest of the army, or the wives and other women who accompanied them. It was presumed that they had been swallowed up in the vastness of Africa.'

'The survivors of my grandfather's legion who won through and finally reached Jarri were our ancestors.'

'They were the pioneers who built this little nation?' Taita asked.

'They made an invaluable contribution,' Aquer agreed. 'However, there were others who had been here long before them. People have been in Jarri since the beginning time. We honour them as the Founders.' He turned to the man who sat at his right hand. 'This is Lord Caithor. He is able to trace his direct line back through twenty-five generations.'

'Then it is only right that you should honour him.' Taita bowed towards the silver-bearded oligarch. 'But I know that others have joined you since the time of your grandfather.'

'You are referring to Colonel Tinat Ankut and his legion. Of course, you are already acquainted with him.'

'Indeed, the good colonel rescued me and my party from the Basmara savages at Tamafupa,' Taita agreed.

'Tinat Ankut's men and their women have made a welcome addition to our community. Our land is large and we are few. We need them here. They are of our blood, so they have assimilated smoothly into our society. Many of their young people have married ours.'

'Of course, they worship the same panoply of gods,' Taita said delicately, 'headed by the holy trinity of Osiris, Isis and Horus.'

He watched Aquer's aura flare angrily, then saw him bring his temper under control. When he spoke his response was mild: 'The subject of our religion is one we will cover in more depth later. At this stage, suffice it to say that new countries are protected by new gods, or even by a single god.'

'A single god?' Taita feigned surprise.

Aquer did not rise to the lure. Instead he reverted to the previous subject: 'Apart from Colonel Tinat Ankut's legion, there have been many thousands of immigrants from far across the earth who, over the centuries, have made their way over great distances to Jarri. All, without exception, have been men and women of worth. We have been able to welcome sages and surgeons, alchemists and engineers, geologists and miners, botanists and farmers, architects and stone-masons, shipbuilders and others with special skills.'

'Your nation seems to have been built on firm foundations,' Taita said.

Aquer paused for a moment, then seemed to change tack. 'Your companion, Meren Cambyses. It seems to us that you have a great affection for him.'

'He has been with me since he was a stripling,' Taita replied. 'He is more than a son to me.'

'His damaged eye has been troubling him sorely, has it not?' Aquer went on.

'It has not healed as cleanly as I had wished,' Taita agreed.

'I am sure that, with your skills, you are aware that your *protégé* is dying,' Aquer said. 'The eye is mortifying. In time it will kill him . . . unless it is treated.'

Taita was taken aback. He had not divined this impending disaster from Meren's aura, but somehow he could not doubt what Aquer had said. Perhaps he himself had known it all along but had shunned such an unpalatable truth. Yet, how could Aquer have known something that he did not? He saw from his aura that the man had no special skills or insights. He was neither sage, seer nor shaman. Of course, he left the chamber, but not to confer with the other oligarchs. He has been with another, Taita thought. He gathered himself and replied, 'No, my lord. I have some little skill as a surgeon but I did not suspect the injury was so grave.'

'We of the Supreme Council have agreed to accord to you and your *protégé* a special privilege. This boon is not granted to many, not even to worthy and eminent members of our own nobility. We do this as a mark of our deep respect and goodwill towards you. It will also be a demonstration to you of the advanced state of our society, our science and learning. Perhaps it might persuade you to remain with us in Jarri. Meren Cambyses will be taken to the sanatorium in the Cloud Gardens. This may take a little time to arrange because the medications to treat his condition must be prepared. When this has been done, you, Magus, may accompany him to observe his treatment. When you return from the sanatorium we will be pleased to meet you again and discuss your views.'

As soon as they returned to Mutangi, Taita examined Meren's eye and his general condition. The conclusions were troubling. There seemed to be a deep-seated infection in the wound cavity, which would account for the repeated pain, bleeding and suppuration. When Taita pressed firmly on the area round the wound, Meren bore it stoically, but the pain caused his aura to flicker like a flame in the wind. Taita told him that the oligarchs were planning to treat him.

'You care for me and my injuries. I do not trust these renegade Egyptians, traitors to our land and Pharaoh. If anybody is to cure me, it will be you,' Meren declared. As much as Taita tried to persuade him, he remained determined.

Bilto and the other villagers were hospitable and friendly, and Taita's party found themselves drawn into the daily life of the community. The children seemed fascinated by Fenn, and soon she had made three friends with whom she seemed happy. At first she spent much time with them, hunting for mushrooms in the forest, or learning their songs, dances and games. They could teach her nothing about *bao*, and she was soon the village champion. When she was not with the children, she was often at the stables grooming and training Whirlwind. Hilto was instructing her in archery and had carved her a bow of her own. One afternoon, after she had spent an hour chatting and laughing with Imbali, she came to Taita and asked, 'Imbali says that all men have a dangling thing between their legs, which, like a kitten or a puppy, has a life of its own. If it likes you, it changes shape and size. Why don't you have one, Taita?'

Taita was at a loss for an appropriate reply. Although he had never attempted to hide it from her, she was not yet of an age at which he could discuss with her his mutilation. That time would come all too soon. He thought of remonstrating with Imbali, then decided against it. As the only female in their band, she was as good an instructress as any. He smoothed over the moment with a noncommittal reply, but afterwards he felt a keener awareness of his own inadequacy. He began to take pains to keep his body covered from her sight. Even when they swam together in the stream beyond the village he did not remove his tunic. He had believed himself resigned to his imperfect physical state, but that was changing each day.

It could not be much longer before Onka arrived to escort Meren to the mysterious sanatorium in the Cloud Gardens, and Taita exerted all his powers of persuasion to make him agree to undergo the treatment, but Meren was capable of immutable obstinacy and stood firm against all blandishments.

Then one evening Taita was awakened by the sound of soft groans from Meren's chamber. He lit the lamp and went through to find him doubled over on his sleeping mat with his face buried in his hands. Gently Taita lifted away his hands. One side of his face was horribly swollen, the empty eye socket a tight slit, and his skin was burning. Taita applied hot poultices and soothing ointments, but by morning the old injury was little improved. It seemed more than coincidence that Onka arrived before noon that same day.

Taita reasoned with Meren: 'Old friend, there seems nothing that I can do to cure you. Your choice is to endure this suffering, which I now believe will lead before too long to your death, or you can allow the Jarrian surgeons to try where I have failed you.'

Meren was so weak and feverish that he resisted no longer. Imbali and Fenn helped him to dress, then packed a small bag of his possessions. The men led him out and helped him into the saddle. Taita bade Fenn a hasty farewell, and commended her to the care of Hilto, Nakonto and Imbali before he mounted Windsmoke. They left Mutangi on the road to the west. Fenn ran beside Windsmoke for half a league, then stopped beside the road and waved them out of sight.

Once again they headed towards the triple peaks of the volcanoes but before they reached the citadel they took a fork that led in a more northerly direction. Finally they entered a narrow pass into the mountains, and climbed up it to a height from which they could look down on the citadel far to the south. From this distance the council hall where they had met the oligarchs seemed tiny. They went on up the mountain path. The air grew colder and the wind moaned sadly along the cliffs. Higher they climbed, and higher still. White hoar-frost formed on their beards and eyebrows. They huddled into their capes and continued to climb upwards. By now Meren was swaying drunkenly in the saddle. Taita and Onka rode on each side to support him and prevent him falling.

Suddenly the mouth of a tunnel appeared in the cliff face ahead behind gates of heavy wooden beams. As they approached, the gates swung open ponderously to allow them through. From a distance they saw that there were guards at the entrance. Taita was so concerned by Meren's condition that, at first, he paid them little heed. As they drew closer he saw that they were of short stature, barely half as tall as a normal man but with massively developed chests and long, swinging arms that reached almost to the ground. Their stance was hunchbacked and bow-legged. Suddenly he realized that they were not humans but large apes. What he had taken to be brown uniform coats were pelts of shaggy fur. Their foreheads sloped almost straight back above beetling eyebrows, and their jaws were so over-developed that their lips did not close fully over their fangs. They returned his scrutiny with a close-set implacable stare. Quickly Taita opened the Inner Eye and saw that their auras were rudimentary and bestial, their murderous instincts balanced on a knife edge of restraint.

'Do not look into their eyes,' Onka warned. 'Do not provoke them. They are powerful, dangerous creatures, and single-minded in their guard duties. They can rip a man to pieces as you would dismember the carcass of a roasted quail.' He led them into the mouth of the tunnel and immediately the heavy gates boomed shut behind them. Flaming torches were set in brackets on the walls and the hoofs of the horses clattered on the rocky footing. The tunnel was only wide enough to allow two horses to pass side by side, and the riders were forced to stoop in the saddle so that the roof cleared their heads. The rock around them was murmurous with the sounds of running subterranean rivers and seething lava pipes. They had no means of measuring the passage of time or the distance they travelled, but at last they were aware of a nimbus of natural light ahead. It grew stronger and they approached another gate similar to the first that had sealed the tunnel entrance. This gate also swung open before they reached it, to reveal another contingent of apes. They rode past them, blinking in the brilliant sunshine.

It took some time for their eyes to adjust, and then they looked around in wonder and awe. They were in an enormous volcanic crater, so wide that it would have taken even a swift horse half a day to traverse it, from one vertical wall to the other. Not even a nimble mountain ibex could have climbed those lava walls. The bottom of the crater was a concave green shield. In its centre lay a small lake of milky sapphire-tinted water. Tendrils of steam drifted over the surface. A flake of ice melted from Taita's eyebrow and tapped his cheek as it fell. He blinked, and realized that the air in the crater was as balmy as that of an island in a tropical sea. They shed their leather capes and even Meren's condition seemed to improve in the warmer air.

'It is the water from the furnaces of the earth that heat this place. There is no cruel winter here.' With a sweep of his arms Onka encompassed the hauntingly lovely forest that surrounded them. 'Do you see the trees and plants that flourish all around? You will find them nowhere else in the world.'

They rode on along the well-defined pathway, with Onka pointing out the remarkable features of the crater. 'Look at the colours of the cliffs,' he invited Taita, who craned his neck to gaze up at the mighty walls. They were not grey or black, the natural colours of volcanic rock, but covered with a motley of soft blue and ruddy gold streaked with azure. 'What seem to be multicoloured rocks are mosses as long and thick as the hair of a beautiful woman,' Onka told him.

Taita dropped his gaze from the cliffs, and looked over the forests in the basin below. 'Those are pine trees,' he exclaimed, at the towering green spears that pierced the thickets of golden bamboo, 'and gigantic lobelias.' Incandescent blooms were suspended from the thick fleshy stems. 'I would hazard that those are some strange type of euphorbia, and the thickets covered with blossoms of pink and feathery silver are proteas. The tall trees beyond are aromatic cedars, and the smaller ones are tamarind and Khaya mahogany.' I wish Fenn were here to enjoy them with me, he thought.

The mist from the heated water of the lake wafted like smoke among the mossy branches. They turned to follow a stream, but before they had gone more than a few hundred paces they heard splashing, women's voices and laughter. They came out into a clearing to see three women swimming and disporting themselves in the steaming blue waters of the pool below. In silence the women watched the men ride by. They were young and dark-skinned, their long wet hair jet black. Taita thought that they were most likely from the lands across the eastern ocean. They seemed oblivious of their nakedness.

All three were with child, and leant back from the hips to balance the weight of their bulging bellies.

As they rode on Taita asked, 'How many families live in this place? Where are the husbands of those women?'

'They may work in the sanatorium, perhaps even as surgeons.' Onka evinced little interest. 'We should be able to see it when we come out on to the lakeshore over there.'

Seen from across the smoky sapphire waters the sanatorium was a complex of low unobtrusive stone buildings. It was evident that the stone blocks of the walls had been quarried from the cliffs. They had not been lime-washed, but remained their natural dark grey. They were surrounded by trim green lawns on which flocks of wild geese grazed. Waterfowl of twenty different varieties bobbed on the lake, while storks and herons waded in the shallows. As they rode round the gravelly beach Taita noticed a few large crocodiles floating like logs in the blue water.

They left the beach and crossed the lawns to enter the courtyard of the main building through a handsome colonnade covered with flowering creepers. Grooms were waiting to take the horses, and four sturdy male attendants lifted Meren from the saddle and laid him on a litter. When they carried him into the building Taita walked beside him. 'You are in good hands now,' he comforted Meren, but the ride up the mountain in the wind and cold had taken its toll and Meren was hovering on the edge of consciousness.

The attendants took him to a large, sparsely furnished room with a wide doorway that overlooked the lake. The walls and ceiling were tiled with pale yellow marble. They lifted him on to a padded mattress in the middle of the white marble floor, undressed him and took away his soiled clothing. Then they sponged him with hot water from a copper pipe that ran into a basin built into a corner of the room. It had a sulphurous odour, and Taita realized that it came up from one of the hot springs. The marble floor under their feet was pleasantly warm and he guessed that the same water ran in conduits beneath it. The warmth of the room and the water seemed to soothe Meren. The attendants dried him with linen towels, then one held a bowl to his lips and made him drink an infusion of herbs that smelt of pine. They withdrew and left Taita sitting beside his mattress. Soon Meren lapsed into a sleep so deep that Taita knew it had been induced by the potion.

This was the first chance he had had to inspect their new surroundings. When he looked towards the corner of the wall adjacent to the washroom door he detected a human aura emanating from behind it. Without seeming to do so he focused closely on it, and realized there was a concealed peep-hole in the wall and they were observed through it. He would warn Meren as soon as he was awake. He looked away as though he was unaware of the watcher.

A short while later a man and a woman entered the room, dressed in clean white knee-length tunics. Although they wore no necklaces or bracelets of magic beads and carved figurines and carried none of the other accoutrements of the arcane arts, Taita recognized them as surgeons. They greeted him politely by name and introduced themselves.

'I am Hannah,' said the woman.

'And I am Gibba,' said the man.

Immediately they began their examination of the patient. At first they ignored his bandaged head and considered instead the palms of his hands and the soles of his feet. They palpated his belly and chest. Hannah scratched the skin of his back with the point of a sharp stick to study the nature of the welt it raised.

Only when they had satisfied themselves did they move to his head. Gibba took it between his bare knees and held it firmly. They peered into Meren's throat, ears and nostrils. Then they unwrapped the bandage with which Taita had covered the eye. Although it was now soiled with dried blood and pus, Hannah remarked with approval on the skill with which it had been applied. She nodded at Taita to express her admiration of his art.

They now concentrated on the empty eye socket, using a

pair of silver dilators to hold the eyelids apart. Hannah ran
the tip of her finger into the cavity and palpated it firmly.
Meren moaned and tried to roll away his head, but Gibba held
it steady between his knees. At last they stood up. Hannah
bowed to Taita, her fingertips held together and touching her
lips. 'Please excuse us for a short while. We must discuss the
patient's condition.'

They went out through the open doorway on to the lawn,
where they paced together, immersed in talk. Through the
doorway, Taita studied their auras. Gibba's had the shimmering gleam of a sword blade held in the sunlight, and Taita saw
that his high intelligence was cold and dispassionate.

When he studied Hannah, he saw at once that she was a
Long Liver. Her accumulated experience was immense, and
her skills were legion. He realized that her medical ability
probably surpassed his own, yet she lacked compassion. Her
aura was sterile and astringent. He saw from it that in her
devotion to her calling she was single-minded and would not
be constrained by kindness or mercy.

When the pair returned to the sickroom it seemed natural
that Hannah should speak for them. 'We must operate at
once, before the effects of the sedative dissipate,' she said.

The four muscular attendants returned and squatted over
Meren's arms and legs. Hannah laid out a tray of silver surgical
instruments.

Gibba swabbed Meren's eye socket and the surrounding
skin with an aromatic herbal solution, and then, with two
fingers, spread the eyelids wide and placed the silver dilators
between them. Hannah chose a scalpel with a narrow, pointed
blade and poised it above the pit of the socket. With the
forefinger of her left hand she felt the back as though she was
trying to find some precise spot in the inflamed lining, then
used it to guide the scalpel to the point she had selected.
Carefully she probed the flesh. Blood welled around the metal,
and Gibba mopped it away with a swab held in the cleft at
the end of an ivory rod. Hannah cut deeper until half of the
blade was buried. Suddenly green pus erupted from the wound

she had opened. It squirted up in a thin fountain and sprayed against the tiled ceiling of the sickroom. Meren screamed, and his whole body bucked and heaved so that the men who held him needed all their strength to prevent him tearing himself out of their grasp.

Hannah dropped the scalpel on to the tray and clapped a cotton pad over the eye socket. The smell of the pus that dripped from the ceiling was rank and fetid. Meren collapsed under the weight of the men above him. Quickly Hannah removed the pad from his eye and slid the open jaws of a pair of bronze forceps into the incision. Taita heard the points scrape on something buried in the wound. Hannah closed the jaws until she had a firm grip on it, then drew back gently and firmly. With another gush of watery green pus the foreign object popped out. She held it up with the forceps and examined it closely. 'I do not know what it is, do you?' She looked at Taita, who held out his cupped hand. She dropped the thing into it.

He stood up and crossed the room to examine it by the light from the open doorway. It was heavy for its size, a sliver the size of a pine kernel. Between his finger and thumb he rubbed away the blood and pus that coated it. 'A splinter of the Red Stones!' he exclaimed.

'You recognize it?' Hannah asked.

'A piece of stone. I cannot understand how I overlooked it. I found all the other fragments.'

'Don't blame yourself, Magus. It was deeply buried. Without the infection to guide us, we might not have found it either.' Hannah and Gibba were cleaning the socket and stuffing wadding into it. Meren had lapsed into unconsciousness. The burly attendants relaxed their hold on him.

'He will rest more easily now,' Hannah said, 'but it will be some days before the wound has drained and we can replace the eye. Until then he must rest quietly.'

Although he had never seen it done, Taita had heard that the surgeons of the Indies could replace a missing eye with an artificial one made of marble or glass, skilfully painted to

344

resemble the original. Although not a perfect substitute, it was less unsightly than a glaring empty socket.

He thanked the surgeons and their assistants as they left. Other attendants cleaned the pus from the ceiling and marble floor, then replaced the soiled bedding. At last another middle-aged woman came to watch over Meren until he recovered consciousness, and Taita left him in her care to escape from the sickroom for a while. He walked across the lawns to the beach and found a stone bench on which to rest.

He felt tired and depressed by the long, difficult journey up the mountain, and the strain of watching the operation. He took the sliver of red stone from the pouch on his belt, and studied it again. It appeared commonplace but he was aware that this was deceptive. The tiny red crystals sparkled and seemed to emit a warm glow that repelled him. He stood up, walked to the water's edge and drew back his arm to toss the fragment into the lake. But before he could do so there was a weighty disturbance in the depths as though a monster lurked there. He jumped back in alarm. At the same moment a cold wind fanned the back of his neck. He shivered and glanced round, but saw nothing alarming. The gust had passed as swiftly as it had come, and the still air was soft and warm once more.

He looked back at the water as a ring of ripples spread across the surface. Then he remembered the crocodiles they had seen earlier. He looked at the fragment of red stone in his hand. It seemed innocuous, but he had felt the cold wind and he was uneasy. He dropped the stone into his pouch and started back across the lawn.

In the middle he paused again. With all the other distractions, this was the first opportunity he had had to study the front of the sanatorium. The block that contained Meren's room was at one end of the main complex. He could see five other larger blocks. Each was separated from its neighbours by a terrace over which a pergola supported vines with bunches of grapes. In this crater everything seemed fecund and fruitful. He felt certain that the buildings contained many extraordinary scientific marvels that had been discovered and developed here over the centuries. He would take the first opportunity to explore them thoroughly.

Suddenly he was distracted by feminine voices. When he looked back he saw the three dark-skinned girls they had encountered earlier, returning along the beach. They were fully clothed and wore crowns of wild flowers in their hair. They still seemed full of high spirits. He wondered if during their picnic in the forest they had imbibed a little too deeply of the good wine of Jarri. They ignored him and went on down the beach until they were opposite the last block of buildings. Then they turned across the lawns and disappeared inside. Their unrestrained behaviour intrigued him. He wanted to speak to them: they might help him understand what was happening in this strange little world.

However, the sun was already disappearing and the clouds were gathering. A light drizzle began to fall. It was cold on his upturned face. If he was to speak to the women, he must hurry. He set off after them. Half-way across the lawns his steps slowed, and his interest in them wavered. They are of no consequence, he thought. I should rather be with Meren. He stopped and looked up at the sky. The sun had gone behind the crater wall. It was almost dark. The thought of speaking to the women, which had seemed imperative only a short time before, slipped from his mind as though it had been erased. He turned away from the building and hurried to Meren's sickroom. Meren sat up when Taita entered and smiled wanly.

'How do you feel?' Taita asked.

'Perhaps you were right, Magus. These people seem to have helped me. There is little pain, and I am feeling stronger. Tell me what they did to me.'

Taita opened his pouch and showed him the stone fragment. 'They removed that from inside your head. It had mortified and was the cause of your troubles.'

Meren reached out to take the stone, then jerked his hand back. 'So small, but so evil. That foul thing has taken my eye.

I want nothing to do with it. In the name of Horus, throw it away, far away.' But Taita slipped it back into his pouch.

A servant brought them their evening meal. The food was delicious, and they ate with appetite and enjoyment. They ended the meal with a bowl of some hot beverage, which helped them to sleep soundly. Early the next morning, Hannah and Gibba returned. When they lifted the dressing from Meren's eye they were pleased to see that the swelling and inflammation had subsided.

'We will be able to proceed in three days' time,' Hannah told them. 'By then the wound will have settled but it will still be sufficiently open to accept the seeding.'

'Seeding?' Taita asked. 'Learned sister, I do not understand the procedure you are describing. I thought you were planning to replace the missing eye with one made of glass or stone. What are the seeds you speak of now?'

'I may not discuss the details with you, Brother Magus. Only adepts of the Guild of the Cloud Gardens are privy to this special knowledge.'

'It is natural that I am disappointed not to learn more, for I am impressed with the skills you have demonstrated. This new discovery sounds even more exciting. I look forward at least to observing the end results of your new procedure.'

Hannah frowned slightly as she replied, 'It is not correct to describe this as a new procedure, Brother Magus. It has required the dedicated labours of five generations of surgeons here at the Cloud Gardens to bring it so far. Even now it is not yet perfected, but each day brings us closer to our goal. However, I am certain that it will not be long before you may join our Guild and take part with us in this work. I am certain also that your contribution will be unique and invaluable. Of course, if there is anything else you wish to know that is not forbidden to those outside the Inner Circle, I will be happy to discuss it with you.'

'Indeed, there is something that I would like to ask.' The thought of the girls he had first seen by the pool in the forest, then again as they returned along the beach to the sanatorium in the rain, had been lurking in the back of his mind. This seemed a good opportunity to learn more about them. But before the question reached his lips it started to fade. He made an effort to hold on to it. 'I was going to ask you . . .' He rubbed his temples as he tried to recall the question. Something about the women . . . He tried to grasp it, but it blew away like morning mist at the rise of the sun. He sighed with annoyance at his foolishness. 'Forgive me, I have forgotten what it was.'

'Then it could not have been of any great importance. It will probably come back to you later,' Hannah said, as she rose to her feet. 'On a different subject, Magus, I have heard that you are a botanist and herbalist of great learning. We are proud of our gardens. If you would like to visit them, I would be delighted to act as your guide.'

Taita passed most of the following days exploring the Cloud Gardens with Hannah. He expected to be shown much of interest, but his hopes were exceeded a hundredfold. The gardens, which extended over half the area of the crater, were filled with a vast multitude of plant species from every climatic region on earth.

'Our gardeners have gathered them over the centuries,' Hannah explained. 'They have had all that time to develop their skills and understand the needs of every species. The waters that bubble up in the springs are laden with riches, and we have constructed special barns in which we are able to manage the climate.'

'There must be more to it than that.' Taita was not completely satisfied. 'It does not explain how giant lobelia and tree-heaths, which are plants of the high mountains, can grow beside teak and mahogany, trees of the tropical jungles.'

'You are perceptive, Brother,' Hannah conceded, 'and correct. There is more to it than warmth, sunlight and nutrients. When you enter the Guild you will begin to realize the magnitude of the marvels we have here in Jarri. But you must not expect instant enlightenment. We are discussing a thousand-year accumulation of knowledge and wisdom. Nothing so precious can be obtained in a day.' She swung round to face him. 'Do you know how long I have lived in this life, Magus?'

'I can see that you are a Long Liver,' he replied.

'As are you, Brother,' she replied, 'but I was already old on the day you were born, and I am still a novice to the Mysteries. I have enjoyed your company, these last few days. We often allow ourselves to become isolated in the rarefied intellectual climes of the Cloud Gardens, so talking to you has been a tonic as efficacious as any of our herbal preparations. However, we must go back now. I must make the final arrangements for tomorrow's procedure.'

They parted at the gates to the garden. It was still early in the afternoon and Taita made his way round the lake at a leisurely pace. From one spot there was a particularly splendid vista across the full length of the crater. When he came to it, he sat on a fallen tree-trunk and opened his mind. Like an antelope sniffing the air for the scent of the leopard, he searched the ether for any trace of a malicious presence. There was none that he could discern. It was tranquil, yet he knew this might be an illusion: he must be close to the witch's lair, for all the psychic signs and auguries pointed to her presence. This hidden crater would make her a perfect stronghold. The many wonders he had already discovered here might be the product of her magic. Hannah had hinted at it less than an hour ago when she had said, 'There is more to it than warmth, sunlight and nutrients.'

In the eye of his mind he saw Eos sitting patiently at the centre of her web like a monstrous black spider, waiting for the faintest quiver on the gossamer strands before she sprang at her prey. He knew that those invisible meshes were spread for him, that he was already trapped among them.

Until now he had been testing the ether passively and quietly. He had been tempted to make a cast for Fenn, but he knew that if he did so he might invite the witch in her place.

He could not put Fenn in such danger, and he was about to close his mind, when he was struck by a tidal wave of psychic turmoil that made him cry out and clutch his temples. He reeled and almost lost his seat on the log.

Somewhere close to where he sat a tragedy was being played out. It was difficult for his mind to accept such sorrow and suffering, such utter evil, as rushed across the ether to him almost overwhelming him. He struggled against it, like a drowning swimmer fighting a riptide in the open ocean. He thought he was going under, but then the turmoil abated. He was left with a dark sadness that such a terrible event had touched him and he had been helpless to intervene.

It was a long time before he recovered sufficiently to stand up and set off along the path towards the clinic. As he came out on to the beach he saw another disturbance taking place near the middle of the lake. This time he could be certain that it was physical reality he was witnessing. He saw the scaly backs of a pack of crocodiles breaking the surface, their tails slashing in the air. They seemed to be feeding on carrion, fighting over it in a frenzy of greed. He stopped to watch them, and saw a bull crocodile breach clear out of the water. With a shake of its head, it tossed a chunk of raw meat high into the air. As it fell back, the beast seized it once more and, with a swirl, disappeared below the surface.

Taita watched until it was almost dark then, deeply troubled, walked back across the lawns.

Meren woke as soon as he entered the room. He seemed refreshed and unaffected by Taita's sombre mood. As they shared the evening meal, he joked with morbid humour about the operation Hannah was planning for the following day. He referred to himself as 'the cyclops, about to be given an eye of glass'.

Hannah and Gibba came to their room early the next morning with their team of assistants. After they had examined Meren's eye socket, they pronounced him ready to take the next step. Gibba prepared a draught of the herbal opiate while Hannah laid out her tray of instruments, then came to sit on the mat beside Meren. From time to time she drew up the lid of his good eye and studied the dilation of the pupil. At last she was satisfied that the drug had taken effect and he was resting peacefully. She nodded to Gibba.

He rose and left the room, to return a short while later with a tiny alabaster pot. He carried it as though it were the holiest of relics. He waited until the four attendants had restrained Meren by his ankles and wrists, then set down the pot close to Hannah's right hand. Once again he took Meren's head between his knees, opened the lids of his missing eye and set the silver dilators in place.

'Thank you, Dr Gibba,' Hannah said, and began to rock lightly and rhythmically on her haunches. In time to her movements, she and Gibba began a chanted incantation. Taita recognized a few words, which seemed to have the same root as some verbs in the Tenmass. He guessed that it might be a higher, more evolved form of the language.

When they reached the end, Hannah took up a scalpel from her tray, passed the blade through the flame of the oil lamp, then made a quick hatching of shallow parallel incisions in the inner lining of the eye cavity. Taita was reminded of a plasterer preparing the surface of a wall to receive an application of wet clay. There was a weeping of blood from the light cuts but she sprinkled on a few drops, from a phial, which stopped it at once. Gibba swabbed away the clotted blood.

'Not only does this salve staunch the bleeding, but it provides a bonding glue for the seeding,' Hannah explained.

With the same deferential care as Gibba had shown earlier, Hannah lifted the lid off the alabaster pot. Craning for a better view, Taita saw that the pot contained a minute amount of pale yellow translucent jelly, hardly enough to cover his little fingernail. With a small silver spoon Hannah scooped it up and, with infinite care, applied it to the incisions in Meren's eye socket.

'We are ready to close the eye, Dr Gibba,' she said softly. Gibba withdrew the dilators, then pinched the lids shut between thumb and forefinger. Hannah took up a thin silver needle threaded with a fine strand prepared from a sheep's intestine. With deft fingers she placed three stitches in the lids. While Gibba held Meren's head she bandaged it with the same intricate pattern of intertwined linen strips that was used by the embalmers at the Egyptian funereal temples. She left openings for Meren's nostrils and mouth. Then she sat back on her haunches with an air of satisfaction. 'Thank you, Dr Gibba. As usual your assistance has been invaluable.'

'Is that all?' Taita asked. 'Is the operation complete?'

'If there is no mortification or other complication, I will remove the stitches in twelve days' time,' Hannah replied. 'Our main concern until then will be to protect the eye from light and interference by the patient. He will experience a great deal of discomfort during this period. There will be sensations of burning and itching so intense that they cannot be readily alleviated by sedatives. Although he might control himself while he is awake, in his sleep he will try to rub the eye. He must be watched day and night by trained attendants, and his hands will be bound. He must be moved to a windowless, dark cell to avoid light aggravating the pain and preventing the seeding from germinating. It will be a difficult time for your *protégé* and he will need your help to come through it.'

'Why is it necessary to close both his eyes, even the one that is unharmed?'

'If he moves the healthy eye to focus on objects it perceives, the new one will respond in sympathy. We must keep it as quiescent as possible.'

Despite Hannah's warning, Meren experienced little discomfort for the first three days after the seeding of his eye. His greatest hardship was being deprived of sight, and the subsequent boredom. Taita tried to entertain him with reminiscences of the many adventures they had shared over the years, the places they had visited and the men and women they had known. They discussed what effect the drought of the Nile was having on their homeland, the suffering inflicted on the people and how Nefer Seti and the queen were dealing with the calamity. They spoke about their home at Gallala and what they might find there when they returned from their odyssey. These were all subjects they had covered many times before, but the sound of Taita's voice soothed Meren.

He was woken on the fourth day by sharp pains lancing through the socket. They were as regular as the beat of his heart and so painful that he gasped with each stab and reached instinctively to his eye with both hands. Taita sent the attendant to find Hannah. She came at once and unwound the bandage. 'No mortification,' she said immediately, and began to replace the old bandage with a fresh one. 'This is the result we hoped for. The seeding has grafted and is beginning to take root.'

'You use the same terms as a gardener,' Taita said.

'That is what we are: gardeners of men,' she replied.

Meren did not sleep for the next three days. As the pain intensified he moaned and tossed on his mattress. He would not eat, and was able to drink only a few bowlfuls of water each day. When at last sleep overcame him he lay on his back, arms strapped to his sides with strips of leather, and snored through the mouth hole in his bandages. He slept for a night and a day.

When he awoke the itching began. 'It feels as though fire ants are crawling in my eye.' He groaned and tried to rub his face against the rough stone wall of the cell. The attendant had to call two of his colleagues to restrain him, for Meren was a powerful man. With lack of food and sleep, though, the flesh seemed to melt from his body. His ribs showed clearly through the skin of his chest, and his belly shrank until it seemed to rest against his backbone.

Over the years he and Taita had become so close that Taita suffered with him. The only time he could escape from the cell was when Meren fell into short and restless bouts of sleep. Then he could leave him in the care of an attendant and wander in the botanical gardens.

Taita found a peculiar quality of peace in these gardens that drew him back time after time. They were not laid out in any particular order: rather, they were a maze of avenues and pathways, some of which were heavily overgrown. Each twist or turning led to fresh vistas of delight. In the warm sweet airs, the mingled scents of the blooms were heady and intoxicating. The grounds were so extensive that he encountered only a few of the gardeners who tended this paradise. At his appearance they slipped away, more like wraiths than humans. On each visit he discovered delightful new arbours and shaded walks that he had overlooked before, but when he tried to find his way back to them on his next visit they had disappeared and been replaced with others no less lovely and enticing. It was a garden of exquisite surprises.

On the tenth day after the seeding Meren seemed easier. Hannah rebandaged the eye, and declared herself pleased. 'As soon as the pain ceases completely I will be able to remove the stitches from the eyelid and review the progress he has made.'

Meren passed another peaceful night and woke with a fine appetite for his breakfast, and a resuscitated sense of humour. It was Taita rather than the patient who felt depleted and drained. Even though his eyes were still covered, Meren seemed to sense Taita's condition, his need to rest and be alone. Taita was often surprised by the flashes of intuition his usually bluff and uncomplicated companion displayed, and was moved when Meren said, 'You have played nursemaid to me long enough, Magus. Leave me alone to piddle the mattress if I need to. Go and rest. I am sure you must look dreadful.'

Taita took up his staff, and hitched the skirts of his tunic under his girdle and set off for the upper section of the gardens furthest from the sanatorium. He found this the most attractive area. He was not sure why, except that it was the wildest, most untended part of the crater. Huge boulders had broken off the rock wall and tumbled down to stand like ruined monuments to ancient kings and heroes. Over them, plants climbed and twisted in flowering profusion. He picked his way along a track he had thought he knew well, but at the point that it turned sharply between two of the great boulders he noticed for the first time that another well-defined path continued straight on towards the soaring cliff of the crater wall. He was sure that it had not been there on his last visit, but he had become accustomed to the gardens' illusory features and followed it without hesitation. Within a short distance he heard running water somewhere to his right. He followed the sound and at last pushed his way through a screen of greenery to discover another hidden nook. He stepped into the little clearing and looked around curiously. A tiny stream issued from the mouth of a grotto, ran down over a series of lichen-covered ledges and into a pool.

It was all so charming and restful that Taita eased himself on to a patch of soft grass and, with a sigh, leant back against the trunk of a fallen tree. For a while he gazed down into the dark waters. Deep in the pool he picked out the shadow of a large fish, half concealed by a rock shelf and the ferns that overhung the water. Its tail waved hypnotically, like a flag in a lazy wind. Watching it, he realized how tired he was, and closed his eyes. He did not know how long he had slept before he was awakened by soft music.

The musician sat on a stone ledge at the far side of the pool, a boy of three or four, an imp with a mop of curls that bounced on his cheeks when he moved his head in time to the tune he was blowing on a reed flute. His skin was tanned to gold, and his features were angelic, while his little limbs were perfectly rounded and plump. He was beautiful, but when Taita gazed at him with the Inner Eye he saw no aura surrounding him.

'What is your name?' Taita asked.

The imp let the flute drop from his lips to dangle on the cord round his neck. 'I have many names,' he replied. His voice was childlike and lisping, lovelier even than the enchanted music he had played.

'If you cannot give me a name, then tell me who you are,' Taita insisted.

'I am many,' said the imp. 'I am legion.'

'Then I know who you are. You are not the cat, but the mark of her paw,' Taita said. He would not say her name aloud, but he guessed that this cherub was a manifestation of Eos.

'And I know who you are, Taita the Eunuch.'

Taita's expression remained inscrutable, but the gibe pierced the shell that protected his core like an arrow of ice. The child came to his feet with the grace of a fawn rising from its forest bed. He stood facing Taita and lifted the flute to his lips again. He played a softly lilting note, then took the reed from his lips. 'Some call you Taita the Magus, but half a man can never be more than half a Magus.' He played a silvery trill. The beauty of the music could not alleviate the agony his words had inflicted. He dropped the pipe again and pointed down into the dark pool. 'What do you see there, Taita the Deformed? Do you recognize that image, Taita-who-is-neither-man-nor-woman?'

As he was bidden Taita stared down into the dark waters. He saw the image of a young man appear from the depths, his hair thick and lustrous, his brow wide and deep, his eyes alive with wisdom and humour, understanding and compassion. It was the countenance of a scholar and an artist. He was tall with long, clean limbs. His torso was lightly muscled. His bearing was poised and graceful. His groin was clothed by a short skirt of bleached white linen. It was the body of an athlete and warrior.

'Do you recognize this man?' the imp insisted.

'Yes,' Taita whispered huskily, his voice almost failing.

'It is you,' said the imp. 'You as you once were, so many long years ago.'

'Yes,' Taita murmured.

'Now see yourself as you have become,' said the infernal child. The back of the young Taita bowed, and his limbs became thin and stick-like. The fine muscle turned stringy, and his belly pouted. His hair faded to grey and became long, straight and sparse, the white teeth yellow and crooked. Deep lines appeared in his cheeks, and the skin beneath his chin sagged into folds. The eyes lost their sparkle. Although the image was a caricature, reality was only slightly exaggerated.

Then, suddenly, the loincloth was stripped away, as if by a gust of wind, and the groin exposed. A thin fringe of frizzy grey pubic hair surrounded the glaring pink, puckered cicatrice left by the cut of the castrating knife and the red-hot cauterizing rod. Taita moaned softly.

'Do you recognize yourself as you are now?' asked the imp. Strangely, his tone was filled with infinite compassion.

The pity wounded Taita more than the mockery. 'Why do you show me these things?' he asked.

'I come to warn you. If your life was lonely and barren before, it will soon become a thousand times worse. Once again you will know love and longing, but those passions can never be requited. You will burn in the hell of an impossible love.' Taita had no words to deny him, for already the agony the imp threatened had taken its grip. This, he knew, was just a foretaste of what must follow and he groaned.

'The time will come when you pray for death to release you from the agony,' the imp went on remorselessly, 'but think on this, Taita the Long Liver. How long is your suffering to last before death gives you surcease?'

In the pool the image of the ancient figure faded, and that

of the beautiful, vigorous youth replaced it. He smiled up at Taita from the dark water, teeth shining, eyes sparkling.

'What has been taken away, I can give back to you,' said the child, and his voice was the purring of a kitten. The silken cloth dropped from around the youth's waist to reveal perfectly formed genitalia, majestic and weighty.

'I can give you back your manhood. I can make you as whole again as the image I set before you.' Taita could not tear his gaze away from it. As he stared at it, the phallus of the phantom youth swelled and lengthened. Taita was filled with longings he had never entertained in all his life. They were so grossly prurient that he knew they could not have sprung from his own mind but had been placed there by the diabolical imp. He tried to tread them down, but they oozed back like the slime of a cesspool.

The beautiful child lifted one small hand and pointed at Taita's groin. 'Anything is possible, Taita, if only you believe in me.'

Suddenly Taita felt a powerful sensation in his crotch. He had no idea what was happening to him – until he realized that the sensations experienced by the phantom youth were being mirrored in his own body. He felt the weight of that magnificent phallus tugging at his guts. When he watched it stiffen and arc like a drawn war bow, he felt the tension stretch his own nerves to breaking point. When he saw the youth's glans engorge with blood, turning a dark, angry red, it resonated in every fibre of his own body. A copious ejaculation gushed from the gaping cleft and he felt the exquisite agony of each scalding jet. His back arched involuntarily and his lips drew back in rictus as he clenched his teeth. A hoarse cry burst from his throat. His whole body jerked and trembled like that of a man seized by the palsy, then he sagged back on the grass, panting as though he had run a league, his strength spent.

'Had you forgotten? Had you suppressed the memory of the ultimate pinnacle of physical delight? What you have just experienced is only a grain of sand compared to the mountain that I can give to you,' said the child, and ran to the edge of the stone step. He poised there and looked across at Taita for the last time. 'Think on it, Taita. It is yours if you dare stretch out your hand to me.' He dived cleanly into the pool.

Taita saw his pale body flash as he shot down into the depths and disappeared. He could not summon the strength to rise to his feet again until the sun had made half its transit of the sky.

It was late in the afternoon when he reached the sanatorium. He found Meren sitting in his darkened cell with his nurse. His pleasure when he heard Taita's voice was pathetic to witness, and Taita felt guilty to have left him so long alone in the cell with the darkness and doubts that must be consuming him.

'The woman came again while you were away,' Meren cried. 'She says that tomorrow she will remove the bandages completely. I can hardly contain myself that long.'

Taita was still so overwrought by memories of the afternoon's events that he knew he would not be able to sleep that night. After they had eaten the evening meal he asked the male nurse if he could find a lute he might borrow.

'Dr Gibba is a lute player,' the fellow replied. 'Shall I refer your request to him?'

He went off and returned some little time later with the instrument. There had been a time when Taita's voice had been the joy of all who heard him sing, and it was still tuneful and true. He sang until Meren's chin dropped on to his chest and he began to snore. Even then Taita went on strumming softly, until he found his fingers picking out the haunting melody that the imp had played on his flute. He stopped playing and put away the lute.

He lay down on the mattress on the opposite side of the cell from Meren and composed himself, but sleep eluded him. In the darkness his mind ran on, then took flight like a wild horse he could not control. The images and sensations that the imp had grafted into his mind crowded back so vividly that he had to escape them. He took his cloak, slipped from the cell and went out on to the lawns, which were bathed in brilliant moonlight, to walk along the edge of the lake. He felt the ice on his cheeks, but this time it was his own tears and not some alien presence that had chilled him.

'Taita who is neither man nor woman.' He repeated the imp's gibe and wiped his eyes on the fold of his woollen cloak. 'Am I to be imprisoned in this ancient maimed body for all eternity?' he wondered. 'Eos's temptations are as great a torment as any physical torture. Horus, Isis and Osiris, give me the strength to resist them.'

'We do not need your nurses today,' Hannah said, as she knelt beside Meren and trimmed the wick of the one small oil lamp that was the cell's only illumination. 'We will not inflict more pain on you. Instead we hope to compensate you for that which you have already suffered.' She set aside the lamp. It threw a soft light on to Meren's bandaged head. 'Are you ready, Dr Gibba?' While Gibba supported Meren's head she unpicked the knot in the bandage and peeled it away. Then she handed the lamp to Taita. 'Please direct the light on to his eye.'

Taita held a polished silver disc behind the flame to reflect a beam on to Meren's face. Hannah leant closer to examine the stitches that closed his eyelids. 'Good,' she said comfortably. 'I can see no vice in the way it has healed. I believe it is now safe to remove the stitches. Please hold the light steady.'

She snipped the stitches and, with forceps, drew the gut threads from the needle punctures. The lids were glued together with dried mucus and blood. Gently she washed it away with a cloth dipped in warm aromatic water.

'Please try to open your eye now, Colonel Cambyses,' she

instructed. The eyelid quivered, then flickered open. Taita felt his heart thump louder and more rapidly as he looked into the eye socket, which was no longer an empty pit.

'In the name of the holy triumvirate, Osiris, Isis and Horus,' Taita whispered, 'you have regrown a perfect new eye!'

'Not yet perfect,' Hannah demurred. 'It is but half-way grown and is still much smaller than the other. The pupil is cloudy.' She took the silver disc from Gibba and deflected the beam directly into the immature eye. 'On the other hand, see how the pupil contracts. It has already started to function correctly.' She covered Meren's good eye with the cotton pad. 'Tell us what you can see, Colonel,' she ordered.

'A bright light,' he replied.

Hannah passed her hand in front of his face with her fingers splayed open. 'Tell us what you see now.'

'Shadows,' he said doubtfully, but then he went on, firmly now, 'No, wait! I see fingers. The outline of five fingers.'

It was the first time Taita had seen Hannah smile and, in the yellow lamplight, she looked younger and gentler. 'Nay, good Meren,' he said. 'This day you have seen more than fingers. You have seen a miracle.'

'I must bandage the eye again.' Hannah was brisk and businesslike once more. 'It will be many more days before it is able to withstand the light of day.'

The image of the imp in the grotto haunted Taita. He experienced a compulsion that grew more powerful each day to return to the gardens and wait for him beside the hidden pool. In the forefront of his mind he knew that this urge was not his own: it came directly from Eos.

Once I enter her territory I am powerless. She possesses every advantage. She is the great black cat and I am her mouse, he thought.

Then his inner voice answered: What then, Taita? Did you

not come to Jarri to struggle against her? What became of your grand design? Now that you have found her, will you slink away cravenly?

He sought another excuse for his cowardice: If only I could find a shield to deflect her malicious darts.

He tried to find distraction from these haunting fears and temptations by helping Meren to gain full use of his immature eye. At first Hannah removed the bandages for only a few hours, and even then she did not allow him to experience daylight but kept him indoors.

The lens of the eye was still cloudy and the colour of the iris was also pale and milky. It did not work in unison with the good eye but wandered at random. Taita helped him focus it: he held the Periapt of Lostris in front of Meren and moved it from side to side, up and down, nearer and further away.

At first the new eye tired quickly. It watered and the lid blinked involuntarily. It grew bloodshot and itchy. Meren complained that images remained blurred and distorted.

Taita discussed this with Hannah: 'The eye is of a different colour from the original. It does not match in size or motion. You said once that you were a gardener of men. Perhaps the eye you have grafted is of another strain.'

'Nay, Magus. The new eye is grown from the same root stock as the original. We have replaced limbs that have been cut away in battle. They do not appear fully fledged. Like your protégé's eye, they begin like seedlings and gradually attain their mature form. The human body has the ability to shape and develop itself over time to match the original. A blue eye is not replaced with a brown one. A hand is not replaced with a foot. There exists in each of us some life force that is able to replicate itself. Have you not wondered at how a child may resemble its parents?' She paused and looked into his eyes intently. 'In the same way an amputated arm is replaced with a perfect copy of the missing limb. A castrated penis would regrow in identical shape and size to the one that was destroyed.' Taita stared at her, aghast. She had turned the discussion back upon him in a cruel and wounding fashion.

She is speaking of my own imperfection, he thought. She knows about the mutilation I have suffered. He sprang to his feet and hurried from the room. Blindly he stumbled to the lakeside and knelt on the beach. He felt helpless and defeated. At last, when the tears no longer stung and his vision cleared, he looked up at the cliffs that towered above the gardens. He felt Eos nearby. He was too weary and sick at heart to fight on.

You have won, he thought. The battle is over before it was joined. I will submit to you. Then he felt her influence changing. It seemed no longer completely evil and malign, but kindly and benevolent. He felt as though she was offering him release from pain and emotional strife. He wanted to go up into the gardens and surrender to her, cast himself upon her mercy. He struggled to his feet and was struck by the incongruity of his thoughts and actions. He straightened his back and lifted his chin. 'Nay!' he whispered aloud. 'This is not surrender. You have not yet won the battle. You have taken only the first skirmish.' He reached for the Periapt of Lostris and felt strength flow into him. 'She has taken Meren's eye. She has taken my manly parts. She has all the advantage over us. If only I had something of hers to use against her, a weapon with which to counterattack. When I have found one I will go against her again.' He glanced at the tops of the tall flowering trees of her gardens below the painted cliffs, and before he could stop himself he had taken a step in that direction. With an effort he turned away. 'Not yet. I am not ready.'

His tread was firmer as he returned to the sanatorium. He found that Hannah had moved Meren from the darkened cell to their more spacious and comfortable former quarters. Meren sprang up as soon as he entered and seized the sleeve of his tunic. 'I read a full scroll of hieroglyphics that the woman set for me,' he exclaimed, bursting with pride at his latest achievement. Even now he could not bring himself to use Hannah's name or title. 'Tomorrow she will remove the bandage for ever. Then I will astonish you with how the colour has come to match the other, and how nimbly it moves. By the sweet breath of Isis, I declare I will soon be able to judge the flight of my arrows as accurately as I ever did.' His loquacity was a sure sign of his excitement. 'Then we shall escape this infernal place. I hate it here. There is something foul and detestable about it, and the people in it.'

'But see what they have done for you,' Taita pointed out.

Meren looked slightly abashed. 'I give most of the credit to you, Magus. It was you who brought me here, and saw me through this trial.'

That night, Meren stretched himself out on his mattress and, like a child, dropped into sleep. His snores were boisterous and carefree. Taita had grown so accustomed to them over the decades that to him they were a lullaby.

He closed his eyes, and the dreams that the hellish imp had placed in his mind returned. He tried to force himself back into consciousness, but they were too compelling. He could not break free. He could smell the perfume of warm, feminine flesh, feel silken swells and hollows rubbing against him, hear sweet voices heavy with desire whispering lascivious invitations. He felt wicked fingers touching and stroking, quick tongues licking, soft mouths sucking and hot, secret openings engulfing. The impossible sensations in his missing parts rose up like a tempest. They hovered at the brink, then faded away. He wanted them to return, his whole body craved release, but it stayed beyond his reach, racking and tormenting him.

'Let me be!' With a violent effort he tore himself free, and woke to find himself wet with sweat, his breath roaring harshly in his ears.

A shaft of moonlight slanted in through the high window in the opposite wall. He stood up shakily, went to the water jug and drank deeply. As he did so, his eyes fell upon his girdle and pouch where he had laid them as he prepared for sleep. The moonlight was falling directly upon the pouch. It was almost as though some outside influence was directing his attention to it. He picked it up and unfastened the drawstring, reached in and touched something so warm that it seemed to be alive. It moved beneath his fingertips. He jerked away his hand. By now he was fully awake. He held the mouth of the pouch open and turned it so that the moonbeam lit the interior. Something glowed in the bottom. He stared at it and watched the glow take an ethereal shape. It was the sign of the five-padded cat's paw.

With care Taita reached once more into the pouch and brought out the tiny fragment of red rock that Hannah had removed from Meren's eye socket. It still felt warm and glowed, but the cat's paw had disappeared. He clasped it firmly in his hand. Immediately the disturbance of the dreams subsided.

He went to the oil lamp in the corner of the room and turned up the wick. By its light he studied the tiny fragment of stone. The ruby sparkle of the crystals seemed to be alive. Gradually it dawned on him that the stone contained a tiny part of the essence of Eos. When she had driven the splinter into Meren's eye she must have endowed it with a trace of her magic.

I came so close to throwing it into the lake. Now I know for certain that something was waiting to receive it. He remembered the monstrous swirl he had seen beneath the surface of the water. Whether or not it was crocodile or fish, in reality that thing was another of her manifestations. It seems that she places great importance on this insignificant fragment. I shall accord it the same respect.

Taita opened the locket lid of the Periapt and placed the little ruby stone in the nest of hair he had taken from Lostris in both her lives. He felt stronger and more confident. Now I am better armed to go out against the witch.

In the morning his courage and resolve were undiminished. No sooner had they broken their fast than Hannah arrived to inspect Meren's new eye. The colour of the iris had darkened and almost matched the original. When Meren focused on her finger as it moved from side to side or up and down both eyes tracked in unison.

After she had gone, Meren took up his bow and the embossed leather quiver of arrows, and went with Taita to the open field beside the lake. Taita set up a target, a painted disc on a short pole, then stood to one side as Meren selected a new string for his bow, then rolled an arrow between his palms to test its symmetry and balance.

'Ready!' he called, and addressed the target. He drew and loosed. Even though the breeze coming across the lake moved it perceptibly in flight, the arrow struck less than a thumb's length from the centre.

'Allow for the wind,' Taita called. He had coached Meren in archery since the younger man had run the Red Road with Nefer Seti. Meren nodded in acknowledgement, then drew and loosed a second arrow. This one struck dead centre.

'Turn your back,' Taita ordered, and Meren obeyed. Taita brought the target twenty paces closer. 'Now turn and loose instantly.'

Moving lightly on his feet for such a big man, Meren obeyed. He had recovered the balance and poise he had lost when his eye was blinded. The arrow swung slightly with the breeze, but he had allowed for that in his aim. His elevation was perfect. Again the arrow slammed into the bull's eye. They practised for the rest of the morning. Gradually Taita moved the target out to two hundred paces. Even at that range Meren placed three out of four arrows in an area the size of a man's chest. When they stopped to eat the simple meal that an attendant brought them, Taita said, 'That is enough for one day. Let your arm and your eye rest. There is a matter I must attend to.'

He picked up his staff, made certain the Periapt of Lostris was hanging on its gold chain at his throat and set off briskly for the upper gates of the garden. He retraced his steps to the imp's grotto. The closer he came to it, the more intense his feelings of eager anticipation became. They were so unwarranted that he knew he was still being led by outside influences. He was mildly surprised to reach the grotto again so readily. In this garden of surprises he had expected to find it hidden from him, but all was as he had last seen it.

He settled down on the grassy bank and waited for he knew not what. All seemed peaceful and natural. He heard the chittering of a golden sunbird and looked up to see it hovering before a scarlet blossom and delicately probing its long, curved bill into the trumpet of petals to suck out the nectar. Then it darted away like a flash of sunlight. Taita waited, composing himself and marshalling his resources to meet whatever was coming his way.

He heard a regular tapping sound that was familiar, although he could not place it immediately. It came from the pathway behind him. He turned in that direction. The tapping ceased but after a short while it began again.

A tall, stooped figure came down the pathway carrying a long staff. The sound of it on the stony path was what Taita had heard. The man had a long silver beard, but although he was stooped and ancient, he moved with the alacrity of a much younger man. He seemed not to notice Taita sitting quietly at the edge of the pool but followed the bank round in the opposite direction. When he reached the far side he sat down. Only then did he lift his head and look directly at Taita, who stared at him silently. He felt the blood drain from his face and grasped the Periapt in his clenched fist, struck dumb with astonishment. The two looked deep into each other's eyes, and each saw his identical twin stare back at him.

'Who are you?' Taita whispered at last.

'I am you,' said the stranger, in a voice Taita recognized as his own.

'No,' Taita burst out. 'I am one, and you are legion. You bear the black mark of the cat's paw. I am touched with the white mark of the Truth. You are the fantasy created by Eos of the Dawn. I am the reality.'

'You confound us both with your obstinacy, for we are one and the same,' said the old man across the pool. 'What you deny me you deny yourself. I come to show you the treasure that could be ours.'

'I will not look,' Taita said, 'for I have already seen the poisonous images you create.'

'You dare not say no, for in doing so you deny your very self,' said his reflection. 'What I will show you has never before been looked upon by mortal man. Gaze into the pool, you who are myself.'

Taita stared down into the dark water. 'There is nothing there,' he said.

'Everything is there,' said the other Taita. 'Everything we have ever truly wanted, you and I. Open our Inner Eye and let us gaze upon it together.' Taita did so, and a shadowy vista appeared before him. It was as though he looked across a wide desert of barren dunes.

'That desert is our existence without knowledge of the Truth,' said the other Taita. 'Without the Truth all is sterile and monotonous. But look beyond the desert, my hungry soul.'

Taita obeyed. On the horizon he saw a mighty beacon, a divine light, a mountain cut from a single pure diamond.

'That is the mountain that all the seers and magi strive towards. They do so in vain. No mortal man can attain the divine light. It is the mountain of all knowledge and wisdom.'

'It is beautiful,' whispered Taita.

'We look upon it at a great distance. Mortal mind cannot imagine the beauty when you stand upon the summit.' Taita saw that the old man was weeping with joy and reverence. 'We can stand upon that pinnacle together, my other self. We can have what no man has ever had before. There is no greater prize.'

Taita stood up and walked slowly to the edge of the pool. He gazed down upon the vision and felt a longing that surpassed any he had ever known. It was no shameful craving, no base physical desire. It was something as clean, noble and pure as the diamond mountain.

'I know your feelings,' said his double, 'for they are mine exactly.' He stood up. 'Look upon the frail and ancient body that encases and imprisons us. Compare it to the perfect form that was once ours, and can be ours again. Look down into the water and behold what none has seen before us, nor will see again. All this is being offered to us. Is it not sacrilege to refuse such gifts?' He pointed at the vision of the diamond mountain. 'See how it fades. Will we ever look upon it again? The choice is ours, yours and mine.' The vision of the shining mountain dissolved into the dark water, leaving Taita bereft and empty.

His mirror image stood up and came round the pool towards him. He opened his arms to embrace Taita, who felt a shiver of revulsion. Despite himself he lifted his arms to return the fraternal gesture. Before they touched a blue spark crackled between them, and Taita felt a shock, like a discharge of static electricity, as his other self vanished into him, and they became one.

The glory of the diamond mountain he had looked upon remained with him long after he had left the magical pool and gone down through the gardens.

Meren was waiting for him at the lower gates. 'I have been searching for you these last few hours,' he rushed to meet Taita, 'but there is aught very strange about this place. There are a thousand paths but they all lead back to this spot.'

'Why did you come to look for me?' It was fruitless to try to explain to Meren the complexities of the witch's garden.

'Colonel Tinat Ankut arrived at the clinic a short while ago. No sign of Captain Onka, I am pleased to say. I had no chance to talk to the good colonel, not that I would have achieved a great deal by doing so. He never has much to say.'

'Did he come alone?'

'No, there were others, an escort of six troopers and about ten women.'

'What kind of women?'

'I only saw them from afar – I was on this side of the lake. There was nothing unusual about them. They seemed young, but they did not sit comfortably on their mounts. I thought I should warn you of his arrival.'

'You did right, of course, but I can always rely on you for that.'

'What ails you? You wear a strange expression – that dazed half-smile and those dreaming eyes. What mischief have you been at, Magus?'

'These gardens are very beautiful,' Taita said.

'I suppose they are pretty in a repellent way.' Meren grinned with embarrassment. 'I cannot explain it, but I do not like it here.'

'Then let us be gone,' said Taita.

When they reached their quarters in the sanatorium an attendant was waiting for them. 'I have an invitation for you from Dr Hannah. As it will soon be time for you to leave the Cloud Gardens, she would like you to dine with her this evening.'

'Kindly tell her that we are pleased to accept.'

'I will come to fetch you a little before sunset.'

The sun had just sunk below the clifftops when the attendant returned. He led them through a series of courtyards and covered galleries. They met others hurrying along the galleries, but they passed without exchanging greetings. Taita recognized some as attendants who had been with them during Meren's treatment.

Why have I not noticed how extensive these buildings are until now? Why have I not felt any inclination to explore them before? he wondered. Hannah had told them that the gardens and clinic had been built over many centuries, so it was no wonder that they were so large, but why had they not excited his curiosity? Then he remembered how he had tried to follow the three girls into one of the blocks, but had lacked the will to continue.

They have no need for gates or guards, he realized. They can prevent strangers entering where they are not welcome by placing mental barriers to exclude them – as they did to me, and as they did to Meren when he came to find me.

They passed a small group of young women sitting quietly beside a fountain in one of the courtyards. One was playing a lute and two others were waving sistrums. The rest were singing in sweet sad harmony.

'Those are some of the women I saw this afternoon,' Meren whispered. Although the sun had already gone behind the cliffs, the air was still warm and balmy and the women were lightly dressed.

'They are all with child,' Taita murmured.

'Like those we met on our first day in the crater,' Meren agreed. For a moment it seemed to Taita that there should be something significant in that, but before he could grasp the idea they had crossed the courtyard and reached a portico on the far side.

'I will leave you here,' said their guide, 'but I shall return to fetch you after you have dined. The doctor is waiting for you with her other guests. Please enter. She is expecting you.'

They entered a large and artistically furnished room, lit by tiny glass lamps floating in toy ships on an ornamental pool in the centre. Splendid floral displays hung in baskets from the walls or grew in ceramic and earthenware pots arranged on the mosaic floor.

Hannah came across the room to them. She took them each by a hand and led them to the other guests, who lounged on low couches or sat cross-legged on piles of cushions. Gibba was there, with three other doctors, two men and another woman. They looked very young to hold such eminent positions and to be privy to such extraordinary medical wonders as existed in the Cloud Gardens. The other guest was Colonel

Tinat. He rose as Taita approached his couch and saluted him with grave respect. He did not smile, but Taita had not expected it.

'You and Colonel Cambyses are to go down the mountain in a few days' time,' Hannah explained to Taita. 'Colonel Tinat has come to be your escort and guide.'

'It will be my pleasure and honour,' Tinat assured Taita.

The other surgeons clustered round Meren to examine his new eye and marvel at it. 'I know of your other achievements, Dr Hannah,' said the woman, 'but surely this is the first eye that you have successfully replaced.'

'There were others, but they were before your time,' Hannah corrected her. 'I feel confident now that we can look forward to succeeding with any part of the human body. The gallant colonels who are our guests here this evening will vouch for that.' The three surgeons turned towards Tinat.

'You also, Colonel?' asked the younger woman. In reply, Tinat held up his right hand and flexed the fingers.

'The first was chopped off by a savage warrior wielding an axe. This one comes from the skills of Dr Hannah.' He saluted her with the hand. The other surgeons came to examine it with as much interest as they had Meren's eye.

'Is there no limitation on the body parts that you are able to regrow?' a male surgeon wanted to know.

'Yes. First, the operation has to be approved and sanctioned by the oligarchs of the Supreme Council. Second, the remaining parts have to continue to function. We would not be able to replace a head or a heart, for without those parts the rest of the body would die before we could seed it.'

Taita found the evening most enjoyable. The conversation of the surgeons touched on many medical wonders that he had not heard spoken of previously. Once their reserve had been softened by a bowl or two of the wonderful wine of the Cloud Gardens vineyards, Meren and Tinat entertained them with accounts of the strange things they had seen on their campaigns and travels. After the meal Gibba played the lute and Taita sang.

When the attendant came to take Taita and Meren back to their quarters, Tinat walked part of the way with them.

'When do you plan to take us down the mountain, Colonel?' Taita asked.

'It will not be for a few days yet. There are other matters I must attend to before we leave. I shall give you plenty of warning of our departure.'

'Have you seen my ward, the girl Fenn, since we left Mutangi?' Taita asked. 'I miss her sorely.'

'She seems equally attached to you. I passed through the village on my way here. She saw me and ran after my horse to enquire after you. When I told her that I was on my way to fetch you she was much excited. She charged me to give you her respects and duty. She seemed in the best of health and spirits. She is a lovely girl, and you must be proud of her.'

'She is,' Taita agreed, 'and I am.'

That night Taita's dreams were complex and many-tiered, in most cases peopled by men and women he had known. But others were strangers, yet their images were so meticulously etched that it seemed they were creatures of flesh and blood, not woven in fantasy and gossamer. The dreams were linked by the same thread: through all of them he was carried along by the expectation of something marvellous that was about to take place – he was searching for a fabulous treasure that was almost within his grasp.

He woke in the first silver glimmer of day to a sense of elation for which he could find no reason. He left Meren snoring and went out on to the lawns, which were pearled with dew. The sun had just gilded the cliffs. Without further thought, except to check that the Periapt was still suspended from its chain round his neck, he set off for the upper gardens once more.

As he entered the gardens his sense of well-being became stronger. He did not lean upon his staff but shouldered it and struck out with long, determined strides. The pathway to the grotto of the imp was not obscured. When he reached it he found the nook deserted. Once he had determined that he was alone, he quartered the ground swiftly, looking for some trace of a living being. No other person had been there. Even the ground over which his other self had walked, although damp and soft, showed no tracks of human feet. Nothing made sense. It was becoming increasingly difficult for him to trust his own sanity, and to accept the evidence of his mind and senses. The witch was leading him to the borders of madness.

Gradually he became aware of music: the silvery slither of sistrums and the staccato tapping of a finger drum. He clasped the Periapt tightly and turned slowly to face the mouth of the grotto, half in dread and half in defiance of what he might see.

A solemn ceremonial procession issued from the mouth of the cave and paced down the moss-covered ledges. Four weird creatures bore on their shoulders a palanquin of gold and ivory. The first bearer was the ibis-headed Thoth, the god of learning. The second was Anuke, the goddess of war, magnificent in golden armour and armed with bow and arrows. The third was Heh, the god of infinity and long life, his visage green as an emerald, his eyes shining yellow; he carried the Palm Fronds of a Million Years. The last was Min, the god of virility and fertility, who wore a crown of vulture feathers; his phallus was fully erect and rose from his loins like a marble column.

Upon the palanquin stood a splendid figure twice the height of any mortal man. Its skirt was cloth-of-gold. Its bracelets and anklets were of purest gold, its breastplate was of gold set with lapis-lazuli, turquoise and carnelians and on its head rested the double crown of Egypt, with the heads of the royal cobra and vulture at the brow. Crossed over its jewelled pectorals the figure held the symbolic flails of power.

'Hail, Pharaoh Tamose!' Taita greeted him. 'I am Taita, who eviscerated your earthly body and attended you during the ninety days of mourning. I wrapped the bandages of mummification about your corpse and laid you in your golden sarcophagus.'

'I see and acknowledge you, Taita of Gallala, you who were once less than Pharaoh, but who shall be mightier than any pharaoh who has ever lived.'

'You were pharaoh of all Egypt, the greatest kingdom that ever was. There could never be another mightier than you.'

'Approach the pool, Taita. Gaze into it and see what fate awaits you.'

Taita stepped to the edge and looked down into the water. For a moment he swayed with vertigo. He seemed to be standing on the pinnacle of the highest mountain on earth. The oceans, deserts and lesser mountain ranges were spread far below him.

'Behold all the kingdoms of the earth,' said the image of the pharaoh. 'Behold all the cities and temples, green lands, forests and pastures. Behold the mines and quarries from which slaves bring forth the precious metals and glittering stones. Behold the treasuries and arsenals wherein are stored the accumulations of the ages. These shall all be yours to possess and rule.' Pharaoh waved the golden flails, and the scene changed beneath Taita's gaze.

Mighty armies marched across the plains. The horsetail plumes surmounting the bronze helmets of the warriors frothed like sea spume. The armour, the blades and the spearheads glittered like the stars of the heavens. The warhorses reared and plunged in the traces of the chariots. The mailed tread of marching feet and the rumble of wheels shook the earth. The rear ranks of this vast array were cloaked in the dust of their advance so it seemed there was no limit to their multitudes.

'These are the armies you shall command,' cried Pharaoh. Again he waved the jewelled flails, and the scene changed again.

Taita beheld a vista of all the oceans and seas. Across this mighty main sailed squadrons of warships. There were galleys and biremes with double banks of oars, their sails embellished with paintings of dragons and boars, lions, monsters and mythical creatures. The pounding of the drums set the beat for the oarsmen, and the waters creamed and curled before the long bronze beaks of their fighting rams. The numbers of warships were so vast that they covered the oceans from horizon to far horizon.

'Behold, Taita! These are the navies you shall command. No man or nation will prevail against you. You will have power and dominion over all the earth and its peoples.' Pharaoh pointed the flails directly at him. His voice seemed to fill the air and stun the senses, like the thunder of the heavens.

'These things are within your grasp, Taita of Gallala.' Pharaoh stooped and, with the flail, touched Min's shoulder. The god's great phallus twitched. 'You shall have indefatigable virility and potency.'

Then he touched the shoulder of Heh, the god of infinity and long life; he waved the Palm Fronds of a Million Years. 'You shall be blessed with youth eternal in a body whole and perfect.'

Then he touched Thoth, the god of wisdom and all learning, who opened his long, curved beak and uttered a harsh, resounding cry. 'You shall be given the key to all wisdom, learning and knowledge.'

When Pharaoh touched the last divine figure, Anuke clashed her sword against her shield. 'You shall triumph in war, and hold dominion over earth, sea and heaven. The wealth of all nations shall be yours to command, and their peoples will bow down before you. All these are being offered to you, Taita of Gallala. You have but to reach out your hand and seize them.'

The golden image of Pharaoh stood tall and regarded Taita with a straight, burning gaze. Then, with solemn majesty, the bearers carried the palanquin back into the dark recesses of the grotto. The vision faded and disappeared.

Taita sank down upon the grass and whispered, 'No more. I can suffer no more temptations. They are part of the great Lie, but no mortal man can resist them. Against all reason my mind longs to accept them as the Truth. They arouse hunger and craving in me that will destroy my senses and deprave my eternal soul.'

When at last he left the grotto and went down, he found Meren waiting for him at the garden gates: 'I tried to find you, Magus. I had a premonition that you were in danger and might need my help, but I lost my way in these jungles.'

'All is well, Meren. You have no need for concern, although I value your help above all other.'

'The woman doctor is asking for you. I know not what she wants of you, but it is my instinct that we should not trust her too far or too deeply.'

'I shall bear your advice in mind. However, good Meren, thus far she has not treated you unkindly, has she?'

'Perchance there is more to her kindness than we are aware of.'

Hannah came to the point as soon as they had exchanged greetings.

'Colonel Tinat Ankut has delivered to me a decree from the Supreme Council signed by Lord Aquer. I apologize for any inconvenience or embarrassment that this may cause you, but I am commanded to conduct an examination of your person and to furnish the Council immediately with a full report. This may take some time. I would be most obliged, therefore, if you would accompany me to my rooms so that we may begin at once.'

Taita was surprised by Hannah's peremptory tone, until he realized that a decree from the Supreme Council would have the same force and urgency in Jarri as a pharaonic order under the Hawk Seal in Karnak.

'Of course, Doctor. I shall be pleased to comply with the decree.'

Hannah's spacious rooms were in one of the most distant blocks of the sanatorium, tiled with pale limestone. They were austere and free of clutter. Two rows of large glass containers were set out along a bank of stone shelves against the far wall. In each one, a human foetus floated in a clear liquid that was evidently some kind of preservative. On the lower shelf the nine specimen foetuses were arranged according to the age at which they had been taken from the womb. The smallest was no more than a pale tadpole and the largest just short of full term.

On the upper shelf all of the foetuses were grossly deformed, some with more than two eyes, others with missing limbs and one with grotesque twin heads. Taita had never seen such a collection. Even as a surgeon, accustomed to the sight of mutilated and distorted human flesh, he was repelled by this explicit display of pathetic relics.

'She must have a special interest in child-bearing,' he thought, as he recalled the unusually large number of pregnant women he had seen since he had been at the Cloud Gardens. The rest of the room was dominated by a large examination table, hewn from a single block of limestone. Taita realized that Hannah probably used it for operations and deliveries, because grooves were chiselled into the stone top and a drain hole at the foot channelled fluids into a bowl placed on the floor below.

Hannah began the examination by asking Taita for samples of his urine and stools. He was only a little taken aback. He had met a surgeon in Ecbatana who had had a morbid fascination with the excretory processes, but he had not expected one of Hannah's status to show similar interest. Nevertheless he allowed himself to be led to a cubicle where one of her assistants provided him with a large bowl and a jug of water with which to wash himself once he had satisfied her request.

When he returned to Hannah, she examined his output, then asked him to lie face up on her table. Once he was at full length, she transferred her interest from the contents of his bowels to his nose, eyes, ears and mouth. Her assistant used a polished silver disc to direct the beam from an oil lamp into them. Then she placed her ear against his chest and listened intently to his breathing and the beating of his heart.

'You have the heart and lungs of a young man. No wonder you are a Long Liver. If only we were all allowed to partake of the Font.' She was talking more to herself than to him.

'The Font?' he asked.

'No matter.' She realized her lapse and glossed over it. 'Take no notice of an old woman's idle chatter.' She did not look up, but continued her examination.

Taita opened his Inner Eye, and saw that the fringes of her aura were distorted, a sign that she regretted mentioning the Font. Then he saw the distortion clear, and her aura harden as she closed her mind to further questions he might ask about it. Clearly it must be one of the deeper secrets of the Guild. He would bide his time.

Hannah completed her examination of his chest, then stood back and looked squarely into his eyes. 'Now I must examine the injuries to your manhood,' she said.

Instinctively Taita reached down with both hands to protect himself.

'Magus, you are a man entire in your mind and soul. Your flesh is damaged. I believe I may be able to repair it. I have been ordered to do so by an authority I dare not gainsay. You can oppose me, in which case I shall be forced to call for my assistants and, if necessary, for Colonel Tinat Ankut and his men to assist me. Or you can make it easier for both of us.' Still Taita hesitated. She went on quietly, 'I have nothing but the deepest respect for you. I have no wish to humiliate you. On the contrary, I wish to shield you from humiliation. Nothing would give me deeper satisfaction than to be able to repair your injuries so that you may command the respect of all the earth for the perfection of your body as well as that of your mind.'

He knew that yet another temptation had been placed before him, but there seemed no way in which he could resist it. In any case, if he co-operated it might carry him one step closer to Eos. He closed his eyes and raised his hands from his groin. He crossed his arms over his chest and lay quiescent. He felt her lift the skirts of his tunic and touch him lightly. Unbidden, the lascivious images that the imp had placed in his mind returned. He clenched his teeth to prevent himself groaning.

'I have finished,' said Hannah. 'Thank you for your courage. I will send my report to the Council with Colonel Tinat Ankut when you leave us tomorrow.'

Tomorrow, he thought. He knew he should have been relieved and happy to be escaping from this hell that masqueraded as paradise. Instead, he experienced the opposite emotion. He did not want to leave, and he looked forward eagerly to being allowed to return. Eos was still playing shadow games with his mind.

It would be another hour before the sun showed above the wall of the crater, but Colonel Tinat and his escort were waiting in the stableyard when Taita and Meren came out of their quarters, Meren carrying their bags. He slung his on to the bay, then went to Windsmoke and strapped Taita's behind her saddle. When Taita came to her, the mare whinnied a greeting and nodded vigorously. Taita patted her neck. 'I have missed you also, but they must have been feeding you too much dhurra,' he admonished her. 'Either that or you are in foal again.'

They mounted and followed Tinat's troop out through the colonnade and across the lawns to the lake's beach. Taita turned in the saddle and looked back as they reached the point where the path entered the forest. The sanatorium buildings seemed deserted: there was no sign of life except the plumes of steam rising from the vents of the flues that carried the hot waters from the springs under the floors. He had expected that Hannah might come to see them off, and was mildly disappointed. They had shared unusual experiences over the previous weeks. He respected her learning and dedication to her calling, and he had begun to like her. He faced forward again and followed the escort into the woods.

Tinat rode ahead with the vanguard. He had spoken to Taita just once since they had left the clinic, to exchange a brusque, formal greeting.

Taita felt his unnatural desire to remain in the Cloud Gardens recede as they approached the entrance to the tunnel through the crater wall that led into the outer world. He thought of being reunited with Fenn, and his spirits soared. Meren was whistling his favourite marching song, a monotonous, tuneless sound, but a sure sign of his good humour. Taita had grown accustomed to it over the thousands of leagues that he had listened to it and it no longer irritated him.

As the gates of the tunnel appeared, Tinat fell back and rode beside him. 'You should don your cloaks now. It will be cold in the tunnel and freezing on the far side. We must keep together when we reach the entrance. Do not straggle. The apes are unpredictable and can be dangerous.'

'Who controls them?' Taita asked.

'I do not know. There was never a human being in sight when I came this way before.' Taita studied his aura and saw that he was telling the truth.

He avoided the brutish stares of the apes as they drew level. One hopped forward and sniffed his foot, and Windsmoke skittered nervously. The other two bobbed their heads aggressively but allowed them to pass. Nevertheless, Taita sensed how close they were to violence and how easily provoked to attack. If they did so there was nothing he could do to restrain them.

Taita stooped forward in his saddle as they entered the mouth of the tunnel and the hood of his cloak brushed against the rock. As before, the tunnel seemed endless, but eventually they heard the dismal howl of the wind and saw fitful grey light ahead.

They emerged into the austere, magnificent grandeur of the mountains, so different from the beautiful serenity of the Cloud Gardens. The apes crowded round them, but reluctantly they shuffled and hopped aside to let them pass. They rode out on to the pathway and into the scourge of the wind. They huddled in their leather cloaks, and the horses lowered their heads to plod into the gale. Their tails streamed out behind them, their breathing steamed in the icy air and their hoofs slithered on the ice.

Tinat was still beside Taita and now he leant towards him until his lips were level with Taita's ear. 'I have not been able to speak to you before this, but now the gale will cover our voices,' he said. 'I do not know which of my men has been set to spy on me. It goes without saying that we can trust nobody at the sanatorium, from Hannah herself downwards. They are all spies for the oligarchs.'

From under the leather hood Taita studied him closely. 'I know that something troubles you, Colonel, and I think by now that you have learnt to trust me.'

'I am troubled that you should look upon me as a renegade Egyptian, a traitor to my pharaoh and my country.'

'Is that not an accurate description?'

'It is not. I long with all my soul to escape this haunted place and the great evil that has sunk its roots deep into the land and the souls of its inhabitants.'

'That is not what you told me before.'

'No. That was when Onka was close at hand. It was not possible for me to tell you all that is in my heart. This time I have been able to escape from under his eye. He has a woman who is one of us. She placed something in his wine to discourage him from acting as your guide back to Mutangi. I volunteered in his place.'

'What role does Onka play?'

'He is one of the high-ranked spies of the Supreme Council. He has been set to watch over all of us, but you in particular. They are fully aware of your importance. Although you might not know it, you have been deliberately enticed to Jarri.'

'For what reason?'

'That I cannot tell you, for I do not know. I have been here less than ten years, but I have observed many men of special worth and talent come to this land as though by pure chance. But the oligarchs knew they were coming. Just as they knew you were coming. You are not the first of these whom I have been sent to meet. Can you imagine how many of these superior men and women have been brought to Jarri in this manner over the centuries?'

'There seem to be many layers in this society,' Taita said. 'You speak of them and us as though we are separate bands. Who are they, and who are we? Are we not all Egyptians? Do you include me in your band or am I one of them?'

Tinat replied simply, 'I count you as one of us because I now know enough about you to believe that you are a good and just man. I perceive that you are gifted. You are a man of power. I believe that you may be the saviour sent to put an end to the pervasive evil that directs the oligarchs and controls all things in Jarri. I hope that, if any man can, you will destroy the greatest evil of all ages.'

'What is it?' Taita asked.

'It is the reason I was sent here originally. Why you were sent after me,' Tinat replied. 'I think you understand what I refer to.'

'Tell me,' Taita insisted.

Tinat nodded. 'You do well not to trust me yet. The reason that Pharaoh Nefer Seti sent you south was to seek out and bring down the barriers that have been placed across the rivers that feed our Mother Nile so that she may run down once more to Egypt, revive and renew our nation. Then it is your purpose to destroy the one who raised those barriers.'

'I retract what I said of you before. You are a loyal soldier and a patriot. Our cause is one and it is just. How should we proceed? What do you propose?'

'Our first concern must be to identify our enemy.'

'The oligarchs?' Taita suggested, testing his understanding of the quest.

'The oligarchs do not stand alone. They are straw men, puppets, who strut and puff on the stage of the Supreme Council. There is aught that stands behind them. An unseen thing or person. They carry out its dictates, and the worship of this nameless power is the religion of Jarri.'

'Do you have any conception of what this thing may be? Is it a god, or do you believe it is mortal?'

'I am a soldier. I know how to fight men and armies. I do not understand this other dark presence. You are the magus. You understand the other world. It is my fervent hope that you will command us, that you will guide and counsel us. Without somebody like you we are not warriors but lost children.'

'Why have you not risen up against the oligarchs and seized power from them?'

'Because it has been done before, two hundred and twelve years ago. There was a rebellion in Jarri. In the first days it was successful. The oligarchs were seized and executed. Then a terrible plague swept the land. The victims died in agony, bleeding from their mouths, ears, noses and the secret openings of their bodies. It was a disease that selected only the liberators and spared those who were loyal to the Supreme Council and worshipped the secret godhead.'

'How do you know this?'

'The history of the rebellion is engraved on the walls of the council chamber as a warning to all the citizens of Jarri,' Tinat replied. 'No, Magus, I am fully aware of the power we seek to bring down, and the risk we shall run. I have thought on it without ceasing since I found you at Tamafupa. Our only hope of success will be if you can hold the dark power in check while we destroy the oligarchs and their human supporters. I know not if you will be able to destroy the evil thing itself, but I pray to all the gods of Egypt that, with your wisdom and magical skills, you will be sufficient to protect us from its wrath long enough for us to escape from Jarri. I pray also that you can use those powers to shatter the barriers that the thing has placed across the tributaries of the Nile.'

'We tried once to destroy the wall of the Red Stones, Meren and I. In the attempt Meren lost his eye.'

'That was because you treated the demolition as a physical

problem. At that stage you had not realized its deeper, more sinister implications. We know that our chance of success is infinitesimally small, but my followers and I are prepared to lay down our lives for it. Will you make the attempt? Will you lead us?'

'That is why I came to Jarri,' said Taita. 'If we are to have that smallest chance, there is much work ahead of us. As you have pointed out, it will not be easy to escape detection. We must take full advantage of this rare opportunity to be alone and unobserved. First, you must tell me everything I should know of your preparations up to this time. How many men and women are with you? What dispositions have you made? Then I will tell you my own observations and conclusions.'

'That is a sensible course of action.'

In order to draw out the journey to its limit and thus give themselves every possible moment alone, Taita feigned weakness and exhaustion. He demanded frequent stops to rest and even when he was on her back he held Windsmoke at her slowest pace. Tinat, who had evidently prepared for this conference, provided him with a full report of his plans and the battle order of his forces.

When he had finished Taita told him, 'It seems to me that you are not strong enough to take on the task of overthrowing the oligarchs, let alone pitting yourselves against the power behind them. From your own report most of your loyalists are imprisoned or enslaved in the mines and quarries. How many will be fit to travel, let alone fight, when you free them?'

'Certainly we could not muster the forces to win a pitched battle against the oligarchs, then capture and hold the entire country. That was never my plan. I thought to capture the oligarchs by some subterfuge or ruse, then hold them hostage for the release of our compatriots from captivity and our safe passage out of Jarri. I know that this is the barest outline of a plan, one that, without your help, is bound to end in failure and death.'

Taita called Meren to ride in their company. 'Meren, as you know, is my trusted companion, a brave and clever warrior. I would like you to accept him as your second in command.'

Tinat did not hesitate. 'I accept your recommendation.'

As they rode on down the steep pathway the three discussed the basic battle plan, enlarging upon it and trying to find ways to strengthen it. The time passed too swiftly and soon the buildings and roofs of the citadel came into view far below. They stopped the horses and dismounted to divest themselves of their heavy leather cloaks and other mountain clothing.

'We have little more time to talk,' Taita said to Tinat. 'You and Meren know what you must do. Now I shall explain what I plan. Colonel Tinat, all that you have told me so far has the ring of truth, and coincides with everything I have observed and discovered. I was informed by a seer and magus much greater than myself of the dark presence about which you spoke. This "goddess" is neither divine nor immortal but of such immense antiquity that she has been able to accumulate powers far beyond any possessed before by a mortal being. She has taken the name of Eos, the Daughter of the Dawn, and has a monstrous, remorseless appetite for power. All this I learnt from the magus Demeter, who was as well known to Meren as to me.' Taita glanced at his companion for confirmation.

Meren nodded. 'He was indeed a great man, but I must contradict you, Magus. He was no greater than you.'

Taita smiled indulgently at the compliment. 'Loyal Meren, I hope you never discover my true defects. However, to continue, Demeter had encountered Eos face to face. Despite his power and wisdom, she almost destroyed him at their first encounter, and succeeded at the next. Meren and I witnessed the manner of his death, but he survived long enough to pass on to me vital information about Eos. He explained that her purpose in damming the Nile is to reduce Egypt to such a parlous state that the populace will welcome her as their saviour. That would enable her to usurp the throne of the Two Kingdoms. With all the power and wealth of Egypt behind her, she would launch herself upon the other nations of the earth like a falcon upon a flock of sparrows. Her ultimate design is to subjugate them all to her sway.'

Tinat had listened raptly to this point, but now he interjected: 'Where did Demeter encounter the Eos creature? Was it here in Jarri?'

'No, it was in a distant land where she once lived in the caverns of a volcano. It appears that she fled from there to this place. She needs to draw her vital forces from underground fires and boiling rivers. Demeter's clues led me to Jarri.' All three turned in their saddles to look back at the tall plumed peaks.

Tinat spoke at last: 'There are three great volcanoes here. Which is her home?'

'The Cloud Gardens are her stronghold,' Taita replied.

'How can you be certain?'

'She disclosed herself to me while I was there.'

'You saw her?' Meren exclaimed.

'Not Eos herself, but she appeared to me in some of her many manifestations.'

'She did not attack you as she did Demeter, the magus of whom you spoke?' asked Tinat.

'No, because she wants something from me. When she has it she will destroy me without hesitation. But until then I am safe – or as safe as anything can be when it is near to her.'

'What is it that she wants from you?' Tinat demanded. 'She seems already to have almost everything.'

'She wants learning and wisdom that I have and she does not.'

'I do not understand. Are you saying she wants you to teach her?'

'She is like a vampire bat, but instead of blood, she sucks the essence and soul from her victims. She has done so with thousands of seers and magi over the centuries. You told me of those you brought to Jarri, Colonel Tinat. What became of them once you had delivered them?'

'Captain Onka led them up the mountains, along this

pathway. I do not know what happened to them after that. Perhaps they are somewhere in the Cloud Gardens, living in the sanatorium. Perhaps they are working with Dr Hannah.'

'You may be right, but I do not think so. I believe they were stripped of their wisdom and learning by the witch.'

Tinat stared at him with horror. When he asked his next question it was in a different tone – one of fear: 'Then what became of them, do you think, Magus?'

'You have seen the crocodiles in the lake? You have observed their gigantic size?'

'Yes,' said Tinat, in the same small voice.

'I believe that answers your question.'

Tinat was silent for a while, then asked, 'Would you risk that fate, Magus?'

'It is the only way I will come close to her. I must be able to look upon her person, not upon one of her manifestations. Then she might unwittingly give me my chance. She might underestimate me and lower her guard.'

'What happens to my people if you fail?'

'You must all flee from Jarri. If you remain, it will mean certain death for you.'

'Death will be preferable to a lifetime of slavery,' said Tinat, with his customary gravity. 'So, you are determined to return to the Cloud Gardens?'

'Yes. I must go back into the witch's den.'

'How will you achieve it?'

'By order of the Supreme Council. I believe that Eos will command them to send me to her. She hungers for my soul.'

As they descended the last slopes of the mountain they saw a larger group of horsemen coming towards them. When the two parties were separated by less than a few hundred paces one of the strange riders spurred forward at a canter. As he drew closer, Meren exclaimed, 'It is Onka.'

'Your new eye serves you as well as the old one,' Taita remarked, and he looked upon the approaching horseman with the Inner Eye. Onka's aura was aflame, seething like the cauldron of an active volcano.

'The captain is angry,' said Taita.

'I have given him good reason,' admitted Tinat. 'You and I will be unable to speak to each other in private again. However, if you need to send a message to me, you can do so through Bilto, the magistrate of Mutangi. He is one of us. But now we have the company of Captain Onka.'

Onka reined in just ahead of them, forcing them to a halt. 'Colonel Tinat, I am grateful to you for taking over my duties.' He did not salute his superior, and his sarcasm came close to insubordination.

'I see you are fully recovered from your indisposition,' Tinat replied.

'The Supreme Council are less grateful to you than I am. You exceeded your orders in taking over the escort of the magus.'

'I shall be happy to answer to Lord Aquer.'

'You may be required to do so. In the meantime he has ordered you to place the Magus, Taita of Gallala, in my charge. You are also to hand Dr Hannah's report to me. I shall take it to him. You are then further ordered to guide these other travellers to the Cloud Gardens without delay.' He indicated the group following him. 'Once you have delivered them to Dr Hannah you are to return at once.' Tinat took the papyrus scroll of Hannah's report from his pouch and gave it to Onka. They saluted each other stiffly. Tinat nodded a chilly farewell to Taita and Meren, then rode off down the path to take his place at the head of the second column and retrace his tracks up the mountain.

At last Onka turned to Taita. 'Greetings, revered Magus. Hail, Colonel Cambyses. I see that the operation on your eye was successful. My felicitations. I have been ordered to take you to your quarters at Mutangi. You are to wait there until sent for by the Supreme Council. Their summons should not be more than a few days in coming.' Onka's aura was still blazing with anger. He kicked his horse into a trot and they rode on down the mountain.

Neither Tinat nor Onka acknowledged each other as the two parties passed, one ascending, the other descending the mountain. Taita, too, ignored Colonel Tinat but looked instead at the members of the party he was leading up to the Cloud Gardens. There were six troopers in full uniform, three in the van and the other three in the rear. Between them rode five young women, all comely and all with child. They smiled at Meren and Taita as they passed, but none spoke.

They were still half a league from Mutangi when a small figure on a large grey colt burst out of the woods and tore across the green fields towards them, her long blonde hair streaming out behind her like a banner in the wind.

'Here comes trouble, and as usual she is in good voice,' laughed Meren. Even at this distance they could hear Fenn squealing with excitement.

'That is a sight to warm the heart,' Taita said, his gaze fond and tender.

Fenn reined in beside him and launched herself across the gap. 'Catch me!' she cried breathlessly.

Taita was almost taken unawares by the onslaught, but he recovered his balance and she locked both arms round his neck, pressing her cheek to his.

'You are getting too big for those tricks. You could have injured us both,' Taita protested, but held her as tightly as she was hugging him.

'I thought you would never come back. I have been so bored.'

'You have had all the village children for company,' Taita pointed out mildly.

'They are children and therefore childish.' Still clinging to Taita, she looked across at Meren. 'I missed you too, good Meren. You will be amazed at how Hilto has taught me to shoot. We shall have an archery contest, you and I, for an enormous prize—' She broke off and stared at him with astonishment. 'Your eye!' she cried. 'They have mended your eye! You look so handsome again.'

'And you are bigger and even more beautiful than you were when last I saw you,' Meren replied.

'Oh, silly Meren!' She laughed, and once more Taita felt the twinge of jealousy.

When they reached the village, Hilto, Nakonto and Imbali were just as happy to welcome them back. As a home-coming gift Bilto had sent five large jugs of excellent wine and a fat sheep. Hilto and Nakonto slaughtered it, while Imbali and Fenn prepared dhurra and vegetables. Later, they feasted round the fire for half the night, celebrating their reunion. It was all so homely and familiar after the weird otherworld of the Cloud Gardens that, for the moment, the menace of Eos seemed remote and insubstantial.

At last they left the fire and retired to their sleeping chambers. Taita and Fenn were alone for the first time since he and Meren had left her.

'Oh, Taita, I was so worried. I expected you to cast for me and I could hardly sleep for fear that I might miss you if you did.'

'I am sorry I caused you distress, little one. I have been to a strange place where strange things happen. You know the good reasons why I was silent.'

'Good reasons are just as hard to bear as bad ones,' she said, with precocious feminine logic. He chuckled and watched as she pulled off her tunic and washed herself, then rinsed her mouth with water from the large earthenware jug. She was maturing with such extraordinary rapidity that he felt another pang.

Fenn stood up, dried herself on the tunic, then threw it over the lintel to air. She came to lie beside him on the mat, slipped an arm around his chest and snuggled close. 'It's so cold and lonely when you are gone,' she murmured.

This time I may not be forced to give her up to another, he thought. Perhaps there is a chance that Hannah can transform me into a full man. Perhaps one day Fenn and I may become man and woman who know and love each other, not only in spirit but also in body.' He imagined her in her magnificent womanhood and himself as youthful and virile, as he had appeared in the image that the imp had shown him in the pool. If the gods are kind and we both attain that happy state, what a wondrous couple we would make. He stroked her hair and said aloud, 'Now I must tell you all that I have discovered. Are you listening or are you half asleep already?'

She sat up and looked at him sternly. 'Of course I am listening. How cruel you are! I always listen when you talk.'

'Well, lie down again and keep listening.' He paused. When he went on, his tone was no longer light. 'I have found the witch's lair.'

'Tell me about it – all of it. Keep nothing from me.'

So he told her about the Cloud Gardens and the magical grotto. He described the sanatorium and the work Hannah was doing there. He told her the details of the operation on Meren's eye. Then he hesitated, but at last he summoned the courage to tell her of the operation Hannah planned for him.

Fenn was quiet for such a long time that he thought she had fallen asleep, but then she sat up again and stared at him solemnly. 'You mean she will give you a dangling thing, like the one Imbali told me about, the thing that can change shape and size?'

'Yes.' He could not help but smile at the description, and for a moment she looked bemused. Then she smiled like an angel, but the outer corners of her green eyes slanted upwards wickedly. 'I would love us to have one of those. It sounds like such rich sport, much better than a puppy.'

Taita laughed at the way she had claimed joint ownership, but his guilt was as keen as a razor's edge. The imp of the grotto had put the devils into his mind, but Taita found himself imagining things that were best kept locked away and never spoken of. In the time Fenn had been with him she had developed much faster than a normal child would. But she was not a normal child: she was the reincarnation of a great queen, not governed by the natural order of this world. As swiftly as her body was altering, their relationship was also changing. His love for her was strengthening by the day, but it was no longer solely the love of a father for a daughter. When she looked at him in that new way, her green eyes slanted like those of a Persian cat, she was no longer a girl: the woman lay just below the innocent surface, a butterfly in its chrysalis. The first cracks were appearing in the shell and soon it would burst open for the butterfly to fly free. For the first time since they had been together, the witch in her Cloud Gardens was out of both their minds, and they were occupied with each other to the exclusion of all else.

Over the ensuing days, while they waited for the summons from the Supreme Council, they fell back into their old ways. Taita and Fenn studied from early morning until after the midday meal. In the afternoons they exercised at archery or rode out with Meren and the others to hunt the giant forest hogs that abounded in the surrounding woods. Nakonto and Imbali acted as hounds and went on foot into the densest thickets, armed only with spear and axe to flush the animals into the open. Hilto took them with the lance and Meren sharpened his new eye with the bow, then finished off the wounded beasts with the sword. They sought out the huge old boars, which were ferocious, fearless and could rip a man to shreds with their tusks. The sows, even though they were smaller, had sharper tusks and were just as aggressive as the boars – they were also better eating. Taita kept Fenn with him, holding her in check when she wanted to race forward on Whirlwind and try her little bow on one of the great boars. They were short-necked and barrel-chested, their hides so thick and tough that they stopped or turned all but the heaviest arrows. Their humped backs, bristling with black manes, were level with Whirlwind's stirrup. With a toss of the head they could lay a man's thigh open to the bone, and sever the femoral artery.

Nevertheless, when a fat sow came grunting and snorting out of the thickets, Hilto and Meren drew back and shouted, 'This one is for you, Fenn!'

With a quick appraisal of the quarry, Taita decided to let her ride. He had shown her how to come in at an angle from behind the animal, leaning out from the saddle to draw her short recurved cavalry bow until the string touched her lips. 'The first arrow is the one that counts,' he had said. 'Go in close and send it to the heart.'

As the sow felt the strike she turned in a single stride and lowered her head for the charge, sharp white tusks protruding from the sides of her jaws. Fenn pivoted Whirlwind neatly and led the sow's charge, drawing her out so that the arrowhead could work deeper into her chest, its cutting edges slicing through arteries, lungs and heart. Taita and the others cheered her lustily.

'Now the Persian shot!' Taita shouted. He had learnt it from the horsemen of the great plains of Ecbatana, and taught it to her. Adroitly, she reversed her grip on the bow stock, holding it in her right hand, and drew with her forward hand so that the arrow was aimed back over her shoulder. Then, with her knees, she controlled Whirlwind, slowing him to let the sow close in to a certain range. Without turning in the saddle she sent arrow after arrow thumping into the sow's chest and throat. The beast never gave up, but kept fighting until it collapsed in full stride and died. Fenn wheeled Whirlwind and, flushed and laughing with excitement, rode back to claim the tail and ears as trophies.

The sun was not far above the horizon when Taita called, 'Enough for one day! The horses are tired and so should the rest of you be. Back to Mutangi.' They were more than two leagues from the village and the path wound through thick forest. The shadows of the trees fell across it and the light was sombre. They were strung out in single file, Taita and Fenn in the fore, Nakonto and Imbali bringing up the rear, leading the pack horses, with the carcasses of the five hogs they had killed strapped over their backs.

Suddenly they were all startled by a series of terrified screams from the forest on the right of the path. They reined in the horses and hefted their weapons. A girl ran into the path just ahead. Her tunic was muddy and torn, her knees were grazed and her feet bare and bleeding from the thorns and rocks. Her hair was thick and black, tangled with twigs and leaves, and her eyes were huge, dark and lit with terror. Even in her present state she was beautiful. Her skin was moon pale, and her body lithe and shapely. She saw the horses and turned, like a swallow in flight, towards them. 'Help me!' she screamed. 'Don't let them get me!' Meren spurred forward to meet her.

'Beware!' the girl shrieked. 'They are close behind me!'

At that moment two huge shaggy shapes burst out of the forest, running on all fours. Briefly Meren thought they were wild boar, then realized they were propelling themselves on long arms, knuckling the ground with each bounding stride. They were overhauling the girl.

'Apes!' Meren yelled, as he nocked an arrow and urged the bay to the top of its speed, racing to intercept the leader before it could catch the girl. He drew the bow to full stretch and let fly. The arrow caught the animal high in the chest. It roared and reached up to snap the shaft as though it were a straw, hurling the butt away in the same movement. It barely broke stride and bounded forward again only yards behind her.

Meren shot another arrow and hit the beast close to where the stump of the first arrow protruded from its hairy torso.

Now Hilto was galloping forward to help. He shot and hit the leading creature again. It was so close behind the girl that when it bellowed her legs buckled under her. It reached out to grab her, but Meren drove the bay between them and leant out to seize her round the waist and swing her up in front of his saddle. Then he spurred the bay away. The ape bounded after him, shrieking with the pain of its wounds, and fury at having been deprived of its prey. The second ape was close behind its mate, gaining ground swiftly.

Hilto couched his long lance and galloped to head it off. The ape saw him coming and turned to meet him. As they closed, Hilto lowered the lance head and the ape sprang at him, launching itself high in the air. Hilto caught it on the lance, sending the bronze head through the centre of its chest, right up to the cruciform guard on the shaft, which prevented it penetrating deeper than a cubit. The ape squealed as Hilto used his weight and the momentum of the charge to pin it to the earth.

The first ape, although mortally wounded, was using the last of its strength to chase down Meren and the girl. Meren was holding her, so he was unable to nock an arrow, and the animal was gaining on them. Before Taita realized what she was about, Fenn turned Whirlwind and raced off to help.

'Come back! Be careful!' Taita yelled after her, in vain. With the stumps of the broken arrows in its chest and blood splattering from the wounds, the ape sprang high and landed on the rump of Meren's horse. Its jaws were wide open, its head thrust forward to sink its long yellow fangs into the back of Meren's neck. He turned to meet the attack. Still holding the girl in the crook of his left arm, he used his right hand to thrust the stock of his bow into the ape's open mouth and force its head backwards. The ape locked its jaws on the wood, chewing splinters out of it.

'Be careful!' Taita yelled again, as Fenn rode in beside Meren with her little bow at full draw. 'Don't hit Meren!' She gave no sign of having heard him, and as soon as she had the right angle, she let fly. The range was less than two arms' span. The arrow hit the ape in the side of its neck, severing both of the great carotid arteries, half of its length emerging on the other side of its neck. It was a perfect shot.

The ape released Meren's bow and tumbled backwards over the bay's rump. It rolled in the forest mulch, squealing with rage and plucking at the arrow with both hands. Imbali darted in, lifted her axe high and swung down, splitting the thick bone of the skull as though it were eggshell. Nakonto left the pack horses, which took to their heels, and rushed past her to where Hilto was still holding down the other on the end of his lance. He stabbed down with his short assegai, twice through the throat, and the ape uttered one last roar before it died.

Fenn was still keeping pace with Meren's bay, but now they slowed. Meren was holding the girl tenderly to his chest. Her face was buried in his neck and she was sobbing wildly. He patted her back, murmuring reassurance. 'It's all over, my beauty. No need to weep, sweetling. You are safe now. I will take care of you.' His attempts to express concern and sympathy were spoiled somewhat by his self-satisfied grin.

Fenn wheeled back on one side of him, and Taita rode up on the other. 'Young lady, I am not sure which is the greater danger to you, the wild ape or the man who rescued you from it,' he remarked. With one last sob, the girl looked up, but she kept her arm round Meren's neck and he made no effort to dislodge her. Her nose was running and her eyes were streaming. They all studied her with interest.

Tears notwithstanding, Taita decided, she is a beauty. Then he asked her, in a kindly tone, 'What were you doing alone in the forest when you were set upon by those beasts?'

'I escaped and the trogs came after me.' The girl hiccuped.

'Trogs?' Meren asked.

Her dark eyes went back to his face. 'That is what they are called. They are horrible things. We are all terrified of them.'

'Your reply has flushed out a flock of questions. But let us find an answer to the first one. Where were you going?' Taita intervened. The girl tore her eyes from Meren and looked at Taita. 'I was coming to find you, Magus. I need your help. You are the only one who can save me.'

'That raises another flock of questions. Shall we begin with a simple one? What is your name, child?'

'I am called Sidudu, Magus,' she said, and shivered violently.

'You are cold, Sidudu,' Taita said. 'No more questions until we have you home.' Taita turned to Meren and kept his expression serious as he asked, 'Is the lady causing you inconvenience or discomfort? Do you think you will be able to carry her as far as the village, or shall we put her down and make her walk?'

'I can abide with any suffering she may cause me,' Meren replied, equally seriously.

'Then I believe we have finished our business here. Let us go on.'

It was dark when they entered the village. The houses were mostly in darkness and nobody seemed to notice their passing. By the time they dismounted in the stableyard Sidudu had made a remarkable recovery. Nevertheless Meren was taking no risks and carried her into the main living room. While Fenn and Imbali lit the lamps and reheated a pot of rich game stew on the hearth, Taita examined Sidudu's injuries. They were all superficial grazes, scrapes and embedded thorns. He dug the last out of her pretty calf and smeared ointment over the wound, sat back and studied her. He saw a maelstrom of fear and hatred. She was a confused, unhappy child, but beneath the turmoil of suffering her aura was clear and pure. She was essentially a sweet, innocent creature forced prematurely to face the world's evils and wickedness.

'Come, child,' he said. 'You must eat, drink and sleep before we talk any more.' She ate the stew and dhurra bread that Fenn brought to her, and when she had wiped the bowl with the last crust of bread and popped it into her mouth, Taita reminded her, 'You said that you were coming to find me.'

'Yes, Magus,' she whispered.

'Why?' he asked.

'May I talk to you alone, where nobody else can hear us?' she asked shyly, and glanced involuntarily at Meren.

'Of course. We shall go to my chamber.' Taita picked up one of the oil lamps. 'Follow me.' He led her to the room that he and Fenn shared, sat on his mat and indicated Fenn's to her. Sididu folded her legs under her and arranged her torn skirts modestly. 'Now tell me,' he invited.

'Everybody in Jarri says you are a famous surgeon and skilled with all manner of herbs and potions.'

'I am not sure who "everybody" is, but I am indeed a surgeon.'

'I want you to give me something to flush the infant from my womb,' she whispered.

Taita was taken aback. He had not expected anything like that. It took him some moments to decide how to reply. At last he asked gently, 'How old are you, Sididu?'

'I am sixteen, Magus.'

'I thought you were younger,' he said, 'but no matter. Who is the father of the child you are carrying? Do you love him?'

Her reply was bitter and vehement: 'I don't love him. I hate him and wish he was dead,' she blurted out.

He stared at her while he composed his next question. 'If you hate him so, why did you lie with him?'

'I did not wish it, Magus. I had no choice. He is a cruel, cold man. He beats me, and mounts me so violently when he is in wine that he tears me and makes me bleed.'

'Why do you not leave him?' he asked.

'I have tried, but he sends the trogs to fetch me back. Then he beats me again. I hoped that he would beat me until I lost the brat he put inside me, but he is careful not to hit me in the belly.'

'Who is he? What is his name?'

'You promise to tell nobody?' She hesitated, then went on in a rush, 'Not even the good man who saved my life and carried me in from the forest? I don't want him to despise me.'

'Meren? Of course I will not tell him. But you have no need to worry. No one would ever despise you. You are a good, brave girl.'

'The man's name is Onka – Captain Onka. You know him, I think. He told me about you.' She seized Taita's hand. 'Please help me!' She shook it in her desperation. 'Please, Magus! I beg you! Please help me! If I don't rid myself of the baby they will kill me. I don't want to die for Onka's bastard.'

Taita began to make sense of the situation. If Sidudu was Onka's woman, she was the one of whom Colonel Tinat had spoken, the one who had doctored Onka's food to keep him out of the way so that Tinat could escort Taita down from the Cloud Gardens. She was one of them and she must be protected. 'I must examine you first, but I will do my best. Would you object if I called Fenn, my ward, to be with us?'

'The pretty blonde girl who shot the trog off Meren's back? I like her. Please call her.'

Fenn came at once. As soon as Taita had explained what was required of her, she sat down beside Sidudu and took her hand. 'The magus is the finest surgeon on earth,' she said. 'You need have no fear.'

'Lie back and lift your tunic,' Taita instructed her, and when she obeyed, he worked quickly but thoroughly. 'Are these bruises from the beatings Onka gave you?' he asked.

'Yes, Magus,' she replied.

'I will kill him for you,' Fenn offered. 'I never liked Onka, but now I hate him.'

'When the time comes I will kill him myself,' Sidudu squeezed her hand, 'but thank you, Fenn. I hope you will be my friend.'

'We are friends already,' Fenn told her.

Taita finished his examination. 'Already he could discern the faint aura of the unborn child, shot through with the black evil of its father.

Sidudu sat up and smoothed down her clothing. 'There is a baby, isn't there, Magus?' Her smile faded and she looked woebegone again.

'In the circumstances, I am sad to have to say, yes.'

'I have missed my last two moons.'

'The only good thing in this business is that you have not gone too far. So early in your term, it will not be difficult for us to dislodge the foetus.' He stood up and crossed the room to where his medical bag stood. 'I shall give you a potion. It is very strong and will make you vomit and purge your bowels, but it will bring down the other thing at the same time.' He measured a dose of green powder from a stoppered phial into an earthenware bowl, then added boiling water. 'Drink it as soon as it cools, and you must try to keep it down,' he told her.

They sat with her as she forced herself to swallow it, a mouthful at a time, gagging at the bitter taste. When she had finished she sat for a while, panting and heaving spasmodically. At last she grew quieter. 'I shall be all right now,' she whispered hoarsely.

'You must sleep here with us tonight,' Fenn told her firmly. 'You might need our help.'

Sidudu's groans woke them at the darkest hour of the night. Fenn sprang from her mat and lit the oil lamp. Then she helped Sidudu to her feet and led her, doubled over with cramps, to the nightsoil pot in the small adjacent room. They reached it just before Sidudu voided, with a spluttering liquid rush. Her cramps and pains grew more intense as the hours passed and she strained over the pot. Fenn stayed at her side, massaging her belly when the cramps were at their height, sponging her sweating face and chest after each bout passed. Just after the moon set Sidudu was convulsed with a spasm more powerful than all those that had gone before. At its height she cried out wildly, 'Oh, help me, Mother Isis! Forgive me for what I have done.' She fell back, spent, and the foetus made a pathetic mound of bloody jelly in the bottom of the pot. With fresh water and a linen cloth, Fenn cleaned and dried Sidudu's body. Then she helped her to her feet and led her back to the sleeping mat. Taita gathered up the foetus from the pot, washed it carefully, then wrapped it in a fresh linen headcloth. It had not developed far enough to tell whether it had been a boy or a girl. He carried it out into the stableyard, called Meren to help him and they lifted a paving slab in the corner of the yard. They scooped a hollow in the earth beneath it, then Taita laid the bundle in it.

When Meren had replaced the slab Taita said quietly, 'Mother Isis, take this soul into your care. It was conceived in pain and hatred. It perished in shame and suffering. It was not meant for this life. Holy Mother, we pray you, treat the little one more kindly in its next life.'

When he returned to the chamber, Fenn looked up at him enquiringly. 'It is gone,' he said. 'The bleeding will soon staunch, and Sidudu will be well in a few days. She has nothing more to fear.'

'Except the awful man who beats her,' Fenn reminded him.

'Indeed. But she is not the only one: we must all fear Captain Onka.' He knelt by the sleeping mat and studied Sidudu's exhausted face. She was sleeping soundly. 'Stay with her, Fenn, but let her sleep as long as she can. I have matters to attend to.'

As soon as he had left the chamber, Taita sent for Nakonto and Imbali. 'Go back to where we killed the apes. Hide the carcasses in the forest, then find the pack horses and dispose of the hogs. Pick up the spent arrows and cover any signs we were there. Come back when you have finished.' After they had left, he told Meren and Hilto, 'Colonel Tinat said that his agent in Mutangi is the headman, Bilto. He will take any message to Tinat. Go to Bilto secretly. Tell him to let Tinat know that we have the girl Sidudu with us—' He was about to go on when they heard many horses galloping down the lane that ran past the front of the house. Loud hectoring shouts rang through the village, then the sound of blows, the wail of women and the whimpering of children.

'Too late, I fear,' Taita said. 'The soldiers are already here. I have no doubt that they are searching for Sidudu.'

'We must hide her.' Meren jumped to his feet. At that moment they heard hobnailed sandals on the paving of the stableyard, followed by pounding on the door. Meren half drew his sword from its scabbard.

'In the name of the Supreme Council, open up!' It was Onka's angry voice.

'Put up your blade,' Taita told Meren quietly. 'Open the door and let them in.'

'But what of Sidudu?' Meren looked towards the door of the inner chamber, his expression distraught.

'We must trust to Fenn's good sense,' Taita replied. 'Open the door before Onka becomes truly suspicious.' Meren crossed the room and lifted the bar. Onka burst in.

'Ah, Captain Onka!' Taita greeted him. 'To what good fortune do we owe the unexpected pleasure of your company?'

With an effort Onka regained his composure. 'I beg your understanding, Magus, but we are searching for a missing girl. She is disturbed and may be raving.'

'What is her age and appearance?'

'She is young and pretty. Have you seen her?'

'I regret I have not.' Taita looked enquiringly at Meren. 'Have you seen anybody matching that description, Colonel?'

'I have not.' Meren was not the best of liars and Onka peered into his face suspiciously. 'You might have waited until morning before disturbing the magus and his household,' Meren blustered.

'I apologize once more,' said Onka, without any attempt to appear sincere, 'but the matter is urgent and cannot wait until morning. May I search this house?'

'I see that you will do so, whatever I say.' Taita smiled. 'But do it swiftly, then let us be in peace.'

Onka strode to the door of the inner chamber and threw it open, then marched in.

Taita followed him and stood in the doorway. Onka went to the pile of sleeping mats and fur blankets in the middle of the floor. He turned them over with the point of his sword. There was nobody beneath them. He glared around the room, then crossed quickly to the cubicle and peered into the nightsoil pot. He grimaced, then returned to the sleeping chamber, and looked around it again, more carefully than before.

Meren stepped into the doorway behind Taita. 'It's empty!' he exclaimed.

'You sound surprised.' Onka rounded on him.

'Not at all.' Meren recovered himself. 'I was merely confirming what the magus has already told you.'

Onka stared at him for a moment, then switched his attention back to Taita. 'You are aware that I am only doing my duty, Magus. Once I have searched the rest of the house, I have been ordered to conduct you to the citadel where the oligarchs will receive you. Please be ready to leave immediately.'

'Very well. At this hour of the night it is not convenient, but I will bow to the dictates of the Supreme Council.'

Onka pushed past Meren, who followed him.

As soon as they were gone Taita opened his Inner Eye. Immediately he picked up the shimmer of two separate auras in the far corner of the chamber. As he concentrated on them the shapes of Fenn and Sidudu appeared. Fenn was holding the girl protectively in the crook of her left arm. With the other hand she held the gold nugget of the Talisman of Taita. She had suppressed her aura to a pale glow. Sidudu's danced and flamed with terror, but in spite of that Fenn had been able to cloak them with her spell of concealment. Taita gazed into Fenn's eyes and sent her an astral impulse: 'You have done well. Remain as you are. When it is safe to do so I will send Meren to you. He will take you to a better place than this.'

Fenn's eyes opened wider as she received the message, then narrowed again as she replied: 'I will do as you tell me. I heard Onka say that the Council have summoned you. I shall hold vigil for you while we are apart.'

For a few moments longer, Taita held her eyes. He exerted all his powers to conceal from her his fears for her safety, and instead to convey to her his love and protection. She smiled trustingly and her aura took on its usual fire and beauty. With the talisman in her right hand she made the circular sign of benediction towards him.

'Stay concealed,' he repeated, and left the chamber.

Meren was waiting alone in the living room, but Taita could hear Onka and his men rampaging at the back of the house. 'Listen well, Meren.' Taita stood close to him and spoke quietly. 'Fenn and Sidudu are still in my chamber.' Meren opened his mouth to speak but Taita raised his hand to caution him to silence. 'Fenn has cast a spell of concealment over them. When Onka and I have left for the citadel to answer the summons of the oligarchs, you may go to them. You must pass a message through Bilto to Tinat. Tell him how precarious the position of the girls has become. He must find a more secure hiding-place for them while I am away, which may be a long time. I believe that the oligarchs intend to send me back at once to the Cloud Gardens.' Meren looked worried. 'I will only make astral contact with Fenn in case of dire urgency, or when our purpose has been achieved. In the meantime, you and Tinat must continue to make preparations for our flight from Jarri. Do you understand?'

'Yes, Magus.'

'There is one other matter, good Meren. There is every chance that I will not prevail against Eos. She may destroy me as she has done all the others she has sucked into her thrall. If that happens I shall warn Fenn before it is over. You must not attempt to rescue me. You must take Fenn with the others of our band and fly from Jarri. Try to find your way back to Karnak and warn Pharaoh of what has happened.'

'Yes, Magus.'

'Guard Fenn with your life. Do not let her fall alive into the clutches of Eos. You understand what I mean by that?'

'I do, Magus. I will pray to Horus and the trinity that it will not be necessary, but I will defend Fenn and Sidudu to the end.'

Taita smiled. 'Yes, my old and trusted friend. Sidudu may be the one for whom you have waited so long.'

'She reminds me so strongly of the Princess Merykara when first I fell in love with her,' Meren said simply.

'You deserve all the joy Sidudu can bring you and more,' Taita whispered. 'But hush now. Here comes Onka.'

Onka stormed into the room. He was making no attempt to conceal his annoyance.

'Did you find her?' Taita asked.

'You know I did not.' Onka went back to the doorway of the bedchamber and stood there for a while, glowering suspiciously into the empty room. Then, with an angry shake of his head, he came back to Taita. 'We must leave at once for the citadel.'

'I will need warm clothing if the oligarchs send me to the Cloud Gardens.'

'It will be provided,' Onka told him. 'Come.'

Taita clasped Meren's upper arm in farewell. 'Be firm in resolve and steadfast in courage,' he said softly, then followed Onka out into the stableyard. One of Onka's men was holding a bay mare, saddled for the road. Taita stopped short. 'Where is my mare, Windsmoke?' he demanded.

'The grooms tell me that she is lame and cannot be ridden,' Onka replied.

'I must see to her before we leave.'

'That is not possible. My orders are to escort you to the citadel without delay.'

Taita argued a little longer, but it was to no avail. He looked back despairingly at Meren.

'I will care for Windsmoke, Magus. You need not fret.'

Taita mounted the strange horse, and they rode out through the gate.

It was the middle of the following morning when they reached the palace of the oligarchs. Once again, Taita was taken to the antechamber. There was a basin of hot water in which he refreshed himself while one of the palace servants held a clean linen towel for him. The same servant gave him a meal of spiced chicken and a bowl of red wine.

Then the usher came to lead him through into the Supreme Council's chamber. With the utmost respect, the man settled him on a woollen mat at the front of the room just below the dais. Taita looked carefully about him, then concentrated on the leather screen. He could detect no trace of Eos. He relaxed and composed himself, for he expected a long wait.

However, a short time later, the guards filed in and took up their positions below the dais. The usher announced the entrance of the oligarchs: 'Pray show respect for the honourable lords of the Supreme Council.'

Taita made his obeisance but watched the oligarchs from under his eyelashes as they filed in from behind the screen. Once again they were led by Lord Aquer. Taita was surprised that there were only two: Lord Caithor was missing. Aquer and his companion seated themselves on their stools and left the third unoccupied.

Aquer smiled. 'You are welcome. Please be at ease, Magus. You are among your peers.'

Taita was surprised by this, but tried not to show it. He straightened and leant back against the cushions. 'You are gracious, Lord Aquer,' he said.

Aquer smiled again, then addressed the usher and the commander of the palace guards: 'We wish to be alone. Please leave us and do not return until you are summoned. Make certain that no stranger listens at the doors.'

The guards thumped the butts of their spears upon the floor, then filed out. The usher followed them, walking backwards with his whole body doubled over in a low bow.

As soon as they were gone and the great doors were closed Aquer spoke again: 'At our last meeting I did not formally introduce you to the noble Lord Ek-Tang.' Taita and the councillor exchanged a seated bow.

Ek-Tang was a short, portly man of indeterminate age and Asiatic features. His eyes were coal black and inscrutable.

Lord Aquer went on: 'We have excellent reports from the surgeons of the Cloud Gardens. We have been told that the operation on Colonel Cambyses' eye was a complete success.'

'It was an amazing achievement,' Taita agreed. 'He has regained the full sight of the eye. Not only that, but the organ is completely natural in appearance. It cannot be differentiated from its twin in any way.'

'Our surgeons are the most advanced on earth, but their greatest achievement is yet to come,' Aquer told him.

Taita inclined his head in enquiry but remained silent.

'We shall return to that later,' said Aquer, with a mysterious air, evidently designed to intrigue Taita. Then, abruptly, he changed the subject. 'You will notice that Lord Caithor is not here,' he said.

'Indeed, my lord. I was surprised by his absence.'

'He was an old man, and wearied by the weight of years. Tragically he passed away in his sleep ten days ago. His end was peaceful and without suffering.'

'We should all be so fortunate,' said Taita, 'but I mourn his passing with you.'

'You are a man of compassion,' said Aquer, 'but the fact remains that there is now an empty seat on the Supreme Council. We have conferred at length and prayed most earnestly for guidance from the one true goddess, whose name will soon be disclosed to you.'

Taita bowed in acknowledgement of this favour.

Aquer went on: 'We have reached the conclusion that one man is eminently suited for election to the Council in Lord Caithor's place. That man is you, Taita of Gallala.'

Again Taita bowed, but this time he was truly speechless.

Aquer continued genially, 'It is the decree of the Supreme

Council that you are to be ennobled, with the title Lord Taita.' Again Taita bowed. 'There is, however, one impediment to your election. It is customary for members of the Council to be whole and healthy. You, Lord Taita, through no fault of your own, have suffered a grievous injury that disqualifies you from this position. However, that need not be final. Your *protégé*, Colonel Cambyses, was sent to the Cloud Gardens for treatment but not on the merits of his case. Access to these extraordinary procedures is usually reserved for the most worthy members of our society. It is difficult to place a value on the immense cost of the treatments. You will learn more of this later. Officers of low or intermediate military rank do not usually qualify. Cambyses was chosen to convince you of the possibilities that exist. Without this demonstration, you would certainly have been sceptical and would most likely have declined to participate.'

'What you say is indubitably true. However, I am glad for the sake of Meren Cambyses that he was chosen.'

'As are we all,' Aquer agreed unconvincingly. 'That is no longer relevant. What is, though, is that you have been examined by the surgeons and, as a nobleman and elected member of the Supreme Council, you are entitled to preferential treatment. The surgeons of the Cloud Gardens have been warned of your imminent arrival. Their preparations to receive you are well advanced, which accounts for the delay in informing you. It takes time to make such preparations, but now the seeds have been harvested. The surgeons await your arrival. Are you prepared to take the opportunity that you are offered?'

Taita closed his eyes and pressed his fingertips into his eyelids while he thought. Our entire enterprise depends upon this, he reminded himself. There is no other way in which I can get within striking range of Eos. However, the board is laid out in the witch's favour. My chances of success are as thin as a silken thread. The end cannot be foreseen, but must be taken at hazard. The only certainty is that all is steeped in the poison of the witch, therefore it will be not only evil but surpassing perilous. He massaged his closed eyes as he wrestled with his conscience. Am I justifying a baser motive? If I do this thing will it be for Pharaoh and Egypt, or for Taita the man and his own selfish desires? he asked of himself, with cruel self-appraisal. Then he replied, with equally cruel honesty, For both. It will be for the Truth against the Lie, but it will also be for myself and Fenn. I long to know what it is to be a full man. I long for the power to love her with a passion that threatens to consume my very soul.

He lowered his hands and opened his eyes. 'I am ready,' he said.

'It was wise of you to consider your reply so carefully, but I am pleased with your decision. You will be our honoured guest at our palace for this night. In the morning you will commence your journey up the mountain and into a new life.'

The storm was raging as they set out next morning. As they climbed the pathway the temperature fell remorselessly. Swathed in his leather cloak Taita followed the shape of Onka's horse, which was almost obliterated by the swirling snow and the shimmering clouds of ice crystals that were blown across the track. The journey seemed much longer than before, but at last they saw the entrance to the tunnel appear out of the blizzard. Even the trogs that guarded the tunnel crouched down against the wind and blinked at Taita as he passed, their eyelashes laden with ice. With relief he followed Onka into the tunnel and out of the tempest.

They passed through the mountain and emerged from the dank darkness and the guttering light of the torches into the warm sunshine. They rode past the trogs outside the tunnel, and saw the splendour of the Cloud Gardens spread below them. Taita felt his spirits lift as they always did in the enchanted crater. They took the now familiar path through the forest and on the far side came out on the beach of the steaming azure lake. The crocodiles were lying on the sand-banks, sunning themselves. It was the first time Taita had seen them out of the water and he was astounded: they were even larger than he had thought. At the approach of the horses the crocodiles lifted themselves on bowed legs and waddled to the water's edge, then launched themselves into the lake, sliding gracefully below the surface.

When they rode into the stableyard servants and grooms were waiting to welcome them. The grooms took the horses and the major-domo conducted Taita to the rooms he had shared with Meren. Once again fresh clothing was laid out for him, a wood fire burned in the hearth and large jugs of hot water stood ready.

'I hope you will find everything convenient and to your liking, revered Magus. Of course, if there is anything you lack, you have only to ring.' He gestured towards the bell pull that hung beside the door. 'Dr Hannah has invited you to dine with her in her private quarters this evening.' The major-domo moved backwards towards the door, bowing deeply at every second pace. 'I will come to take you to her at the setting of the sun.'

Once Taita had bathed he lay down to rest, but he was unable to sleep. Again he was imbued with restless excitement and an undirected sense of anticipation. As before, he realized the sensation came not from within himself but an exterior source. He tried to compose himself, but with little success. When the major-domo came for him, Taita was dressed in a fresh tunic and waiting for him.

Dr Hannah came to the door to welcome him into her rooms as though he were an old friend. News of his ennoble-ment had reached her and she greeted him as 'Lord Taita'. One of her first concerns was to ask after Meren, and she was delighted when Taita told her of his continued excellent progress. There were three other dinner guests. Dr Gibba was one and, like Hannah, he greeted Taita affably. The other two were strangers.

'This is Dr Assem,' Hannah said. 'He is a distinguished member of our Guild. He specializes in the use of herb and vegetable substances in surgery and medicine.'

Assem was a small, sprightly man with a lively, intelligent face. Taita saw from his aura that he was a Long Liver of vast knowledge, but not a savant.

'May I also introduce Dr Rei? She is an expert on reknitting damaged or severed nerves and sinews. She understands more than any other living surgeon about the bony structures of the human body, particularly the skull and teeth, the vertebrae of the spine and the bones of the hands and feet. Dr Assem and Dr Rei will assist with your surgery.'

Rei had rugged, almost masculine features, and large, powerful hands. Taita saw that she was clever and single-minded in the pursuit of her profession.

Once they had settled round the board, the company was convivial, and the conversation fascinating. Taita revelled in the interplay of their superior intelligence. Although the servant kept the bowls fully charged, they were all abstemious and none did more than sip their wine.

At one stage the conversation turned to the ethics of their profession. Rei hailed from a far-eastern kingdom. She described how the Qin emperor had handed over to his surgeons the captives he had taken in battle. He had encouraged them to use the prisoners for live dissection and experiment. All the company agreed that the emperor must have been a man of vision and understanding.

'The vast majority of human beings are only one cut above domestic animals,' Hannah added. 'A good ruler will make every effort to see that they are provided with all the necessities of life and many of its comforts, depending on the means at his disposal. However, he should not allow himself to be persuaded that the life of each individual is sacrosanct, to be preserved at all costs. As a general must not hesitate to send his men to certain death if the battle is to be won, so an emperor should be prepared to dispense life or death according to the needs of the state, not by some artificial standard of so-called humanity.'

'I agree entirely, but I would go further still,' said Rei. 'The value of the individual should be taken into account when the decision is made. A slave or a brutish soldier cannot be weighed against a sage or a scientist whose knowledge may have taken centuries to accumulate. The slave, the soldier and the idiot are born to die. If they can do so for good reason, then so much the better. However, the sage and the scientist whose value to society is incalculably higher should be preserved.'

'I agree with you, Dr Rei. Knowledge and learning are our greatest treasures, far outweighing all the gold and silver of this earth,' said Assem. 'Our intelligence and our ability to reason and remember lift us above the other animals, above even the masses of lower humanity who lack those attributes. What are your views, Lord Taita?'

'There is no clear or obvious solution,' Taita answered carefully. 'We could debate the matter endlessly. But I believe that what is in the common good must be preserved, even if it means cold-blooded sacrifice. I have commanded men in battle. I know how bitter the decision to send them to their death can be. But I did not hesitate to order it when the freedom or welfare of all was at stake.' He had told them not what he believed but what he knew they wanted to hear. They had listened attentively, then relaxed and their attitude towards him seemed easier and more open. It was as though he had shown his credentials and they had lowered a barrier to allow him into their fellowship.

Despite the good food and wine they did not sit for long. Gibba was the first to come to his feet. 'We must rise early on the morrow,' he reminded them, and they all stood to thank Hannah and take their leave.

Before she allowed Taita to depart she said, 'I wanted you to meet them because they will assist me tomorrow. Your injuries are much more extensive than that of your *protégé*

413

and, what is more, they have consolidated over the years. There will be considerably more work for us, and we need the extra hands and experience. Furthermore we will not be able to work in your quarters, as we did with Colonel Cambyses. The operation will be carried out in the rooms where I made my initial examination.' She took his arm and led him to the door. 'The other surgeons will join me tomorrow morning to conduct the final examination and plan our surgical strategy. I wish you a peaceful night, Lord Taita.'

The major-domo was waiting to show Taita back to his quarters, and Taita followed him without taking account of their route through the complex of passages and galleries. He was thinking about the conversations in which he had participated that evening when his reverie was interrupted by the sound of weeping. He stopped to listen. It came from not far away, and there was no doubt that it was a woman's. She sounded as though she was in the extremes of despair. When the major-domo realized that Taita had paused and was no longer following him closely, he turned back.

'Who is that woman?' Taita asked.

'Those are the cells of the house slaves. Perhaps one has been punished for her faults.' The man shrugged with indifference. 'Please don't concern yourself, Lord Taita. We should go on.'

Taita saw that there was no point in pursuing the matter. The man's aura showed that he was intractable, and that he was simply following the orders of his superiors.

'Lead on,' Taita agreed, but from there he noted their route carefully. After he has left me, I will return to investigate, he decided. However, his interest in the weeping woman faded rapidly, and before they reached his quarters it had been obliterated from his mind. He lay down on his sleeping mat and fell almost immediately into an easy, untroubled sleep.

T he major-domo came for him as soon as he had break-
fasted. He led Taita to Hannah's rooms, where he
found all four surgeons awaiting his arrival. They began
at once. It was strange for Taita not to be consulted and
instead to be treated like a piece of insensate meat on a
butcher's slab.

They began with the preliminary examination, not neglect-
ing the product of his digestive processes, the smell of his
breath, the condition of his skin and the soles of his feet. Dr
Rei opened his mouth and looked at his tongue, gums and
teeth. 'Lord Taita's teeth are much worn and corroded, Dr
Hannah, the roots badly mortified. They must be causing him
pain. Is that not so, my lord?' Taita's grunt was noncommittal,
and Rei went on, 'Very soon they will constitute a serious
threat to his health and eventually his life. They should be
removed as soon as possible and the gums seeded afresh.'

Hannah agreed at once. 'I have taken such eventualities
into account and made arrangements to harvest more essence
than we will need for the regrowth of the damaged area in the
groin. There will be sufficient for you to use on his gums.'

At last they arrived at the site of his injuries. They hovered
over his lower body, pressing and touching the area of the
cicatrice. Rei measured it with a pair of calipers, and made
notes on a papyrus scroll in small, beautifully drawn hieroglyphics. While they worked they discussed the mutilated area
in dispassionate detail.

'All the scar tissue will have to be dissected out. We must
get down to the raw flesh and the open blood vessels so that
the seeding will have a firm foundation on which to grow,'
Hannah explained, then turned to Rei. 'Will you trace the
major nerves and determine their residual viability for us?'

Rei used a bronze needle to trace the nerve endings. It was
torture to submit to her probe. Quickly Taita controlled his
mind to filter out the pain. Rei realized what he was doing and

415

told him sternly, 'I admire your ability to suppress pain, Lord Taita, as it will stand you in good stead later. However, during my examination you must let it through. If you continue to block it, I will be unable to discover which part of your flesh is dead and must be removed, and which is alive for us to build upon.'

She used black dye to draw lines and symbols on his lower body to guide Hannah's scalpel. By the time she had set it aside, Taita was bleeding from hundreds of tiny painful needle pricks, and was pale and sweating from the torment she had inflicted. While he recovered, the four surgeons discussed her conclusions.

'It is as well that we have on hand more than the usual quantity of seeding. The area we will have to recover is larger than I first calculated. Taking into account the amount needed for the new teeth, we shall require all that I have harvested,' Hannah told them.

'That is indeed so. The open area will be extensive, and will take much longer to heal than any reconstruction we have attempted previously. By what means can we ensure the passage of urine and faeces from the site without contaminating the wound?' asked Gibba.

'The anus will not be involved, and will continue to function in its accustomed manner. However, I intend to place a copper tube in the urethra. Initially this will convey the urine, but as soon as the seeding begins to stabilize and cover the open wound, it will be removed to allow normal regrowth of the organ.'

Although Taita was the subject, he managed to maintain an objective interest in the discussion and even made contributions that the others welcomed. When every facet of the procedure had been covered in exhaustive detail, Assem referred to him one last time: 'I have herbs that can be used to suppress pain, but perhaps they will not be necessary. While Dr Rei was examining you, I was amazed by your technique of pain control. Will you be able to use it during the operation, or should I employ my potions?'

'I am sure that they are most effective, but I would prefer to control the pain myself,' Taita told him.

'I shall observe your technique with the utmost attention.'

It was the middle of the afternoon before Hannah brought the conference to a conclusion, and Taita was allowed to return to his quarters. Before he left her, Hannah said, 'Dr Assem has arranged for a herbal potion to be left beside your bed in a green glass phial. Drink it in a full bowl of warm water. It will purge your bladder and bowels in preparation for the operation. Please do not drink or eat anything more tonight or tomorrow morning. In the morning I would like to begin as soon as the light is good enough. We must give ourselves ample time. We cannot be sure what unexpected difficulties we may encounter. It is essential that we finish during daylight hours. Oil lamps will give insufficient light for our needs.'

'I will be ready,' Taita assured her.

When Taita arrived at Hannah's room the next morning, her team of surgeons was assembled and ready to begin. Two nursing attendants, whom he recognized from his previous visit with Meren, helped him to undress. When he was naked they lifted him up on to the stone table and made him lie on his back. The stone was hard and cool under him, but the air was pleasantly warm, heated by the hot-water ducts beneath the floor. All four doctors were bare to the waist, and wore only white linen loincloths. Hannah's and Rei's breasts and upper bodies were firm and rounded as those of young women, and their skin was smooth and unwrinkled. He supposed that they had availed themselves of their arcane skills to keep themselves in that condition, and smiled faintly at the eternal vanity of the female. Then he considered himself: Lying here waiting for the knife, am I any less vain than they? He stopped smiling, and took one last look round the room. He saw that on another table close at hand a large selection of silver, copper and bronze surgical instruments had been laid out. Among them he was surprised to see at least fifty gleaming scalpels lying in neat lines on the white marble.

Hannah saw his interest. 'I like to work with sharp knives,' she explained, 'for your comfort as well as my own.' She indicated two technicians sitting at another worktable in the far corner of the room. 'Those men are skilled cutlers. They will resharpen each scalpel as soon as its edge becomes dull. You will be grateful to them before the day is done.' She turned to her assistants. 'If all is in readiness we can proceed.'

The two male nurses swabbed Taita's lower body with a pungent-smelling liquid. At the same time the surgeons washed their hands and forearms in a bowl of the same fluid. Dr Rei came to Taita's side. The markings she had made the previous day had faded until they were barely visible. Now she renewed them, then stood back to make way for Hannah.

'I am about to make the first incision. Lord Taita, will you please compose yourself to resist the pain?' she said.

Taita grasped the Periapt of Lostris, which lay upon his naked chest. He filled his mind with a soft mist, and let the circle of their faces above him recede until they were vague outlines.

Hannah's voice reverberated strangely in his ears, seeming to come from a distance: 'Are you prepared?' she asked.

'I am. You may begin.' He felt a tugging sensation as she made the first incision, and as she went deeper he felt the first pain, but it was not unbearable. He let himself drop a level until he was just aware of her touch and the bite of her scalpel. He could hear their voices. Time passed. Once or twice the pain flared brightly as Hannah worked in a sensitive area, but Taita dropped a little deeper. When the pain receded he let himself rise to just below the surface, and listened to their discussions, which enabled him to follow their progress.

'Very well,' said Hannah, with obvious satisfaction. 'We

have removed all the scar tissue, and we are ready to insert the catheter. Can you hear me, Lord Taita?'

'Yes,' Taita whispered, his voice echoing in his ears.

'Everything is going even better than I had hoped. I am placing the tube now.'

Taita felt it being worked into him, a mildly uncomfortable sensation that he did not need to suppress.

Already fresh urine is flowing from your bladder,' said Hannah. 'All is in readiness. You may relax, while we wait for the seedings to be brought from the laboratory.'

There followed a long silence. Taita let himself drift deeper until he was only just conscious of his surroundings. The silence continued, but he felt no sense of alarm or urgency. Then, gradually, he became aware of an alien presence in the room. He heard a voice that he knew was Hannah's, but it was very different now: soft, trembling with fear or some other strong emotion. 'This is the essence,' she said.

Taita brought himself to the level of bearable pain. He opened his eyes to slits so that he was looking through the screen of his own eyelashes. He saw Hannah's hands above him. They were cupped round an alabaster pot similar to that which had held the seeding for Meren's eye but much larger. Hannah lowered it from his line of vision and Taita heard the light scraping sound of a spoon against the alabaster as Hannah scooped out some of the contents. Moments later he felt a sensation of cold in the area of the open wound in his groin, and a light touch as the seeding was spread over it. This was followed by an acute stinging sensation in the same area. He masked it, then something else caught his half-open eyes.

He realized, for the first time, that a strange figure stood against the far wall. It had appeared without a sound, a tall but statuesque shape, veiled from head to floor in filmy black silk. The only movement was a light undulation as the person's chest rose and fell with each breath. The bosom beneath the veil was proudly feminine, perfect in size and shape.

Taita was possessed by an overpowering sense of awe and

fear. He opened his Inner Eye and saw that the veiled figure threw no aura. He was certain that it was Eos, not one of her shadowy manifestations but Eos, with whom he had come to do battle.

He wanted to sit up and challenge her, but as soon as he tried to rise from his trance to full consciousness the pain soared and drove him back. He wanted to speak, but no words rose to his tongue. He could only stare at her. Then he felt the softest touch on his temples, like that of teasing fairy fingers. He knew it was not Hannah: Eos was trying to enter his mind and take out his thoughts. Swiftly he raised his mental barriers to frustrate her. The fairy touch withdrew: Eos had sensed his resistance and, like a skilled swordsman, had given ground. He imagined her poised for the riposte. She had made her first delicate test of his defences. He knew he should have felt threatened and intimidated by her presence, repelled by her wickedness, the great weight of her evil, but instead he felt a strong, unnatural attraction to her. Demeter had warned him of her beauty and the effect it had on all men who gazed upon it, and he tried to keep his guard high, but he found that he still longed to look upon her fateful beauty.

At that moment Hannah moved to the foot of the table and blocked his view. He wanted to shout at her to stand aside, but now that Eos was not directly in his eye his self-control reasserted itself. It was a valuable discovery. He had learnt that if he looked upon her she was irresistible. If he turned away his eyes the attraction, although powerful, could be denied. He lay staring quietly at the ceiling, and allowed the pain to rise to the pitch at which it acted as a counter to the animal craving she aroused in him. Hannah was bandaging the open wound now and he concentrated on the touch of her hands and the feel of the linen strips being laid upon his body. When she had finished Hannah came back to his side. Taita looked at the far wall, but Eos was gone. Only the faintest psychic trace of her remained, a haunting sweetness that hung in the air like a precious perfume.

Dr Rei took Hannah's place at the head of the table,

opened his mouth and placed wooden wedges between his jaws. He felt her settle the forceps over the first of his teeth and masked the pain before she began the extraction. Rei was expert: she pulled out his teeth in rapid succession. Then Taita felt the sting of the seeding being placed in the open wounds, and the prick of the needle as she closed the wounds with sutures.

Gently the two male nurses lifted Taita down from the stone table and laid him on a light litter. Hannah walked beside him as they carried him to his quarters. When they reached his room she saw him safely transferred from the litter to his sleeping mat. Then she made the arrangements for his comfort and care.

At last she knelt on the floor beside him. 'One of the nurses will remain at your side night and day. They will send for me the moment they detect any adverse change in your condition. If there is anything you need you have only to let them know. I will call upon you morning and evening to change the dressings on your wound and to observe your progress,' she told him. 'I do not have to warn you of what lies ahead. You were present during the grafting of the seedings into the eye socket of your *protégé*. You will remember the pain and discomfort he endured. You know, too, of the usual sequence of events – three days relatively free of pain, six days of agony, and relief on the tenth. However, because your wound is so much larger than that of Colonel Cambyses, your pain will be more intense. You will need all your skills to keep it under control.'

Once again Hannah's predictions proved accurate. The first three days passed with only minor discomfort; a dull ache in the pit of his stomach and a burning sensation when he passed water. His mouth hurt more. It was difficult to prevent himself worrying with his tongue the stitches that Rei had placed in his gums. He could eat no solid food, and took only a light broth of mashed vegetables. He could walk only with the greatest difficulty. They had provided him with a pair of crutches, but he needed the help of a nurse to reach the washroom when he needed to use the nightsoil pot.

When Hannah came to change his dressing he looked down as she worked, and he saw that a soft sticky scab covered the wound. It looked like the resin that oozes from a cut or blaze made in the bark of the gum-arabic tree. Hannah was careful not to disturb it, and to prevent it from adhering to the linen bandages she coated it with a greasy ointment that Dr Assem had provided.

On the fourth morning he awoke in the grip of an agony so deep that he screamed involuntarily before he could exert his mental powers to check the pain. The nurses rushed to his side and sent immediately for Dr Hannah. By the time she appeared he had rallied his forces and reduced it to the extent that he could speak intelligibly.

'It is bad,' Hannah said, 'but you knew it would be.'

'It is far beyond anything I have ever known. It feels as though a crucible of molten lead has been poured over my belly,' he whispered.

'I can call Dr Assem to administer a potion.'

'No,' he replied. 'I will come to terms with it alone.'

'Six more days,' she warned him. 'Maybe longer.'

'I shall survive.' The agony was dread and constant. It filled his existence to the exclusion of all else. He did not think of Eos, or even of Fenn. The pain was all.

He managed with great effort to hold it off during waking hours, but as soon as sleep overcame him his defences slipped and it returned in full force. He came awake, whimpering and moaning with its intensity. He lived with the temptation to yield and send for Assem with his narcotics, but resisted with all his mental and physical strength. The danger of letting himself be carried into a stupor outweighed the pain. His resolve was all the shield he had left against Eos and the Lie.

On the sixth day the pain faded, only to be replaced at once by the itching, which was almost more difficult to resist than the pain. He wanted to rip off the dressings and tear at his flesh with his fingernails. The only relief he had was when Hannah came to change the dressings. Once she had removed the soiled bandages she bathed him with a warm herbal solution that was soothing and comforting.

By this time the huge scab that covered his lower belly and crotch had turned as hard and black as the skin of a great crocodile of the azure lake. These periods of surcease were brief. No sooner had Hannah bound him up with fresh linen strips than the itching returned in full force. It drove him to the borders of sanity. There seemed no end to it. He lost track of the days.

At one stage Rei came to him. While the nurses prised apart his jaws she removed the stitches from his gums. He had forgotten about them in the overwhelming anguish of the main wound. However, the faint relief afforded him by their removal was sufficient to stiffen his resolve.

When he awoke one morning he felt such a rush of relief that he moaned. The pain and the itching were gone. The peace that followed was so blessed that he fell into a deep, healing sleep that lasted a day and a night. When he woke again he found Hannah kneeling beside his sleeping mat. While he was asleep she had unwrapped his bandages. He was so exhausted that he had not even been conscious of what she was doing. As he raised his head she smiled at him with proprietary pride.

'Mortification is always the greatest danger, but there is no sign of it. Your body is not heated with fever. The seed graft has taken across the whole area. You have crossed the sea of pain and reached the far shore,' she told him. 'Considering the depth and extent of your wound, your courage and fortitude have been exemplary, although I expected no less of you. Now I can remove the catheter.'

The copper tube slipped out easily, and again the relief was a delight. He was surprised by how weak and wasted the ordeal had left him. Hannah and the nurses had to help him to sit up. He looked down at his body. It had been lean before but now it was skeletally thin. The flesh had melted away until every rib showed.

'The scab is beginning to come away,' Hannah told him. 'Look how it is lifting and sloughing off around its borders. See the healing beneath it.' With a forefinger she traced the demarcating line along which the old and new skin met. The two blended together flawlessly. The old skin was crinkled with age like crêpe cloth, the hair growing upon it wispy and grey. The narrow strip of exposed new skin was as smooth and firm as polished ivory. A fine down grew upon it, becoming denser in a line extending downwards from his navel. It was the first fluffy promise of the luxuriant bush of pubic hair it would become. In the middle of the scab crust was the aperture from which Hannah had removed the copper catheter. Hannah covered it with another thick layer of Dr Assem's herbal ointment.

'The ointment will soften and help to lift away the dry scab without damaging the new tissue beneath it,' she explained, as she bandaged him again.

Before she had finished Dr Rei came into the room and knelt beside Taita's head. She slipped her finger into his mouth. 'Is anything happening in here?' she asked. Her manner was relaxed and friendly, in contrast to her formerly serious and professional mien.

Taita's voice was muffled by her finger. 'I can feel something growing. There are hard lumps below the surface of my gums, which are tender when you touch them.'

'Teething pains.' Rei chuckled. 'You are passing through your second infancy, my lord Taita.' She ran her finger to the back of his mouth, and laughed again. 'Yes, a full set, including your wisdom teeth. They will show themselves within days. Then you can eat more substantial fare than pap and broth.'

Within a week Rei returned. She brought with her a mirror of burnished silver. Its surface was so true that the image it presented to Taita of the interior of his mouth was only slightly distorted. 'Like a string of pearls from the Arabian

Sea,' she said, as Taita gazed for the first time at his new teeth. 'Probably more regular and pleasingly shaped than the first crop you grew so long ago.' Before she left, she said, 'Please accept the mirror as my gift. I warrant you will have more to admire with it before too long.'

The moon had waxed and waned once more before the last flakes of the scab at the base of Taita's belly crumbled away. By now he was eating normally and regaining the flesh he had lost. He spent several hours each day exercising with his long staff in a series of movements that he had designed to build up his suppleness and strength. Dr Assem had prescribed a diet that included large quantities of herbs and vegetables. All these measures were proving most beneficial. The hollows in his cheeks filled out, his colour was healthier, and it seemed to him that the muscles that replaced those he had lost were firmer and stronger. Soon he was able to discard his crutches and walk around the lakeshore without having to stop and rest. However, Hannah would not allow him to leave the sanatorium unaccompanied, and one of the male nurses went with him. As he regained his strength, the constant surveillance and restriction became more difficult to endure. He was increasingly bored and restless, demanding of Hannah, 'When will you allow me to leave my cell and return to the world?'

'The oligarchs have cautioned me to keep you here until you are fully recovered. However, your days need not be wasted. Let me show you something that will help you pass the time.' She conducted him to the sanatorium's library, which stood in the forest at some distance from the main complex. It was a large building that comprised a series of enormous interconnected rooms. On all four walls of each one stone shelves reached from floor to ceiling, stacked with papyrus scrolls and clay tablets.

'On our shelves we have more than ten thousand works and as many scientific studies,' Hannah told him, with pride. 'Most are unique. No other copies exist. It would take a normal lifetime to read even half.' Taita walked slowly through the rooms, picking up a scroll or tablet at random and glancing at its contents. The entrance to the final room was closed with a heavy bronze grating. He looked askance at Hannah.

'Unfortunately, my lord, entrance to that particular room, and to the editions kept in it, is restricted to members of the Guild,' she said.

'I understand,' Taita assured her, then looked back at the rooms through which they had come. 'This must be the greatest treasury of knowledge that civilized man has ever assembled.'

'I agree with your estimation, my lord. You will find much to fascinate you and stimulate your mind, and perhaps even open for you new avenues of philosophical thought.'

'I shall certainly avail myself of the opportunity.' Over the following weeks Taita spent many hours each day in the library. Only when the light through the high windows grew too dim for easy reading did he make his way back to his quarters in the main building.

One morning when he had finished his breakfast he was surprised and a little irritated to find a stranger waiting outside his door. 'Who are you?' he demanded impatiently. He was anxious to get to the library and finish reading the scroll on astral travel and communication, which had engaged his full attention over the preceding days. 'Speak up, fellow.'

'I am here on the orders of Dr Hannah.' The little man kept bowing and smirking. 'I am your barber.'

'I have no need of your doubtless excellent services,' said Taita, brusquely, and tried to push past him.

The barber stepped in front of him. 'Please, my lord. Dr Hannah was most insistent. It will go hard for me if you refuse.'

Taita hesitated. For longer than he cared to remember he had taken no particular interest in his appearance. Now he ran his fingers through the long hair and silver beard that hung almost as far as his waist. He kept them washed and combed, but apart from that he allowed them to grow in wild but comfortable disarray. In truth, until he had received the recent gift from Dr Rei he had not even possessed a mirror. He looked at the barber dubiously. 'I fear that, unless you are an alchemist, there is little you can do to transmute this dross into gold.'

'Please, my lord, at least let me try. If I do not, Dr Hannah will be displeased.'

The little barber's agitation was comical. He must be terrified of the formidable Hannah. Taita sighed and acquiesced with as good grace as he could muster. 'Oh, very well, but be sharp about it.'

The barber led him out on to the terrace where he had already placed a stool in the sunshine. His instruments were at hand. After the first few minutes Taita found his ministrations quite soothing and he relaxed. While the barber snipped and combed, Taita turned his mind to the scroll that waited for him in the library and reviewed the sections that he had read the previous day. He decided that the author's grasp of his subject was fragmentary and that he should provide the missing material himself, as soon as he had the opportunity. Then his thoughts turned to Fenn. He missed her sorely. He wondered how she was faring and what had become of Sidudu. He took no notice of the abundant clippings of grey hair that fell like autumn leaves on to the paving stones.

At last the little barber interrupted his thoughts by holding up a large bronze mirror in front of his eyes. 'I hope my work pleases you.'

Taita blinked. His image was wavering and distorted by the uneven surface of the metal, then suddenly it came into focus, and he was startled by what he saw. He hardly recognized the face that stared back at him haughtily. It appeared far younger than he knew it was. The barber had trimmed his hair to shoulder length and tied it back behind his head with a leather thong. He had clipped his beard short and square.

'Your skull has a fine shape,' said the barber. 'You have a wide, deep brow. Yours is the head of a philosopher. The fashion in which I have swept your hair back shows off its nobility to best advantage. Before, your beard masked the strength of your jaw. Cropping it shorter, as I have done, enhances and emphasizes it.'

In his youth Taita had been pleased with his appearance – perhaps too pleased. At the time it had compensated a little for the loss of his manhood. Now he saw that, even after all this time, he had not entirely lost his looks.

Fenn will be surprised, he thought, and smiled with pleasure. In the mirror his new teeth gleamed and the expression in his eyes quickened. 'You have done well,' he conceded. 'I would not have thought it possible to make so much of such unpromising material.'

When Hannah called upon him that evening, she studied his features thoughtfully. 'Long ago I decided that dalliance consumed time that might otherwise have been applied to more rewarding and productive business,' she told him. 'However, I can see why some women might consider you handsome, my lord. With your permission, and in the interest of scientific knowledge, I should like to invite some carefully selected members of the Guild to meet you and to be apprised of what you have been able to achieve.'

'What you and your colleagues have been able to achieve,' Taita corrected her. 'I owe you that courtesy at the very least.'

Some days later he was conducted back to Hannah's operating room to find that it had been rearranged as an impromptu lecture theatre. A semicircle of stools was set out in front of the stone table. Eight men and women were already seated, including Gibba, Rei and Assem.

Hannah led Taita back to the table and asked him to sit facing the small audience. Apart from the surgeons who had attended him from the beginning, Taita had met none of the others. This was strange when he considered how long he had been at the Cloud Gardens. The sanatorium must cover a greater area than he had realized, or perhaps other departments were detached from the main buildings and tucked away, like the library, in the forest. However, the most likely possibility was that much of the Cloud Gardens was still concealed from him by the dark arts of Eos. Like a child's puzzle, boxes were hidden within boxes.

One of the new faces was a woman's. The others were men, but all appeared to be distinguished and dignified scientists. Their attitude was attentive and serious. After she had introduced Taita, in the most flattering terms, Hannah went on to outline the treatment he had undergone. Rei described how she had removed Taita's worn or rotten teeth, and seeded the cavities in his gums. After that she invited each guest in turn to come forward and examine the new ones. Taita sat stoically through the examinations and answered the questions they levelled at him. When they had returned to their stools Hannah came to stand beside him again.

She described Taita's castration and the extent of the injuries inflicted upon him. Her listeners were horrified. The woman surgeon was particularly moved and expressed her sympathy eloquently.

'Thank you for your concern,' Taita replied, 'but it happened a long time ago. Over the years the memory has faded. The human mind has a trick of burying what is most painful to recall.' They nodded and murmured agreement.

Hannah went on to describe the preliminary tests she had carried out, and the preparations she had made for the surgery.

Taita expected that at this stage of her lecture she might describe the harvesting and preparation of the seedings for grafting. He had been kept ignorant of this and was most anxious to have it explained. He was disappointed that she made no effort to do so. He presumed that her audience were fully informed, and had probably employed the same techniques in their own work. In any event Hannah went on to an account of the surgery, describing how she had dissected out the scar tissue to form a foundation on which the graft could be set. Her audience asked many searching, erudite questions, which she answered at length. Finally she told them, 'As you are all well aware, Lord Taita is a magus of the highest level, and is also an eminent surgeon and scientific observer in his own right. The reconstruction of his organs of procreation was an unusually intimate and sensitive experience for him. I have no need to tell you that he was subjected to a great deal of pain. All of this was a gross imposition on the dignity and privacy of such an extraordinary person. Despite this, he has agreed to allow us to examine and evaluate the results. I am sure we all realize that this was not an easy decision for him to make. We should be grateful for this opportunity.'

At last she turned to Taita. 'With your permission, Lord Taita.'

Taita nodded and stretched out on the table top. Gibba came to stand on the opposite side of the table from Hannah. Between them they lifted the skirts of Taita's tunic. 'You may come forward to obtain a better view,' Hannah told the onlookers. They left their stools and formed a circle round the table.

Taita had become so accustomed to being pored over that he felt no particular embarrassment under their scrutiny. He raised himself on his elbows and looked down his body as Hannah resumed her lecture.

'You will observe how the new skin has covered the wound. It has the suppleness and elasticity that one would expect to find in a pubertal male. In contrast please note the hair on the pubes, which is well advanced. It has grown with extraordinary rapidity.' She laid her hand on the area she was discussing. 'This whole fleshy promontory comprises the mons pubis. If you feel it you will discern how the cushion of flesh has already formed over the pelvic bone. You will observe that the general development approximates that of a ten-year-old male. This has been achieved in the weeks since the surgery was performed. Now observe the penis. The prepuce is well formed, not too tight as it is in many young boys.' She took the foreskin and drew it back carefully. Taita's glans penis emerged from its hood of loose skin. It was little larger than a ripe acorn, soft and glossy pink. Hannah went on, 'Please note the opening of the urethra. We formed this by inserting a catheter during the operation. When we removed it the aperture was round, but now you will see that it has become a characteristic slit.' Hannah slid the foreskin back.

She turned her attention to the scrotum below the immature shaft. 'The sac is developing normally but with the usual extraordinary rapidity we have noted in all our other seedings.' She squeezed it gently. 'There! It already contains the immature testicles.' She looked across the table at the lone female visitor. 'Dr Lusulu, would you care to examine them for yourself?'

'Thank you, Dr Hannah,' the woman said. She seemed to be in the region of thirty-five years, but when Taita studied her aura he saw that this was deceptive and that she was much older. Her demure attitude did not accurately depict her true nature, which contained a lascivious streak. She took his scrotum and deftly located the two little orbs it contained. She rolled them thoughtfully between her fingers. 'Yes,' she said at last. 'They seem perfectly formed. Do you have any sensation there, Lord Taita?'

'Yes.' His voice was husky.

The woman continued to touch him as she studied his face. 'You must not be embarrassed, my lord. You must learn to enjoy the manly parts that Dr Hannah has returned to you, to delight in and glory in them.' She moved her fingers up to the shaft of his penis. 'Do you have sensation here yet?' She began to move her fingers up and down the shaft. 'Can you feel how I am manipulating you?'

'Very distinctly,' Taita replied, his voice huskier still. This new feeling far exceeded any that he had experienced before. In the short time since the small appendage had made its appearance he had treated it with caution and reserve. He had handled it only when he was forced to do so, in response to the demands of hygiene and nature. Even then his touch had been clumsy and inept, certainly lacking the dexterity and expertise that Dr Lusulu was demonstrating.

'What dimensions do you expect the organs to attain when they are fully developed?' Dr Lusulu asked Hannah.

'We can be no more certain of that than we could be in the case of a child. However, I expect that they will eventually be a close copy of the original organs.'

'How very interesting,' Dr Lusulu murmured. 'Do you think it might be possible at some future time to grow organs and parts that are superior to the original? For example, to replace a clubbed foot or a cleft palate with a perfect specimen, an abnormally small penis with a larger one? Is that impossible?'

'Impossible? No, Doctor, nothing is impossible until you prove it to be so. Even if I never achieve my goals, those who follow me might do so.'

Their discussion lasted a little longer, then Lusulu broke off and transferred her attention to Taita. She was still stroking his parts, and now she looked pleased. 'Oh, very good,' she said. 'The member is functional. The patient is nearing full erection. That really is proof of your skills, Dr Hannah. Do you think he will be able to reach orgasm yet? Or is it too soon for that advance?' By now the shaft in her hand had more than doubled its dimensions and the prepuce was fully retracted. Both women studied it with full attention.

Hannah considered the question seriously, then replied, 'I think that orgasm may already be possible, but it will be some time before ejaculation is achieved.'

'Perhaps we should put it to the test. What do you think, Doctor?'

They were conducting the discussion in cool impersonal tones. However, the unfamiliar sensations that Dr Lusulu was creating with her simple hand movements were so pervasive that Taita was thrown into a state of confusion. He had no idea where or how it would end. For someone who was accustomed to being in full control of himself and all those about him, it was an alarming prospect. He reached down and removed her hand. 'Thank you, Doctor,' he said. 'We are all impressed by Dr Hannah's surgical brilliance. I certainly am. Nevertheless, I feel that the test that you are suggesting might better be conducted in a less public environment.' He straightened the skirts of his tunic and sat up.

Dr Lusulu smiled at him and said, 'I wish you much joy.' From the look in her eyes it was plain that she did not subscribe to the philosophy on dalliance that Dr Hannah professed.

N ow that Taita had access to the great library, the days passed quickly. As Hannah had remarked, a lifetime would be too short to take in all of the knowledge that was stored there. Oddly, he mustered no interest in the locked and barred room. Like the weeping woman in the night and many other unexplained occurrences, the thought simply receded into the mists of his memory.

When he was not studying, he spent much time in discussion with Hannah, Rei and Assem. They took turns to guide him through some of the other laboratories where they were engaged in a number of extraordinary projects.

'Do you recall Dr Lusulu's question regarding replacing bodily parts with improved versions?' Hannah asked. 'Well, let us consider a soldier with legs that can carry him at the speed of a horse. What if we could grow him more than one pair of arms? A pair to fire a bow, a second to wield a battleaxe, the third to swing a sword and the last to carry a shield. Nothing could stand against such a warrior.'

'A slave with four strong arms and extremely short legs could be sent into the most confined stopes in the mines to shovel out the gold ore in great quantities,' said Rei. 'How much better if his intelligence was reduced to that of an ox, so that he was inured to hardship and would work in the harshest conditions without complaint? Dr Assem has grown herbs that will achieve that mental effect. In time Dr Hannah and I might be able to create the physical improvements.'

'No doubt you saw the trained apes that stand guard at the

entrance to the tunnel that leads into these gardens,' Hannah said.

'Yes, I have seen them, and heard them referred to as trogs,' Taita replied.

Hannah looked a little annoyed. 'A term coined by the common people. The name we use is troglodyte. They were originally derived from a species of arboreal apes that inhabit the great forests in the south. Over the centuries that we have bred them in captivity we have been able, by surgical procedure and the use of certain herbs, to enhance their intelligence and aggression to the level at which they are most useful to us. By similar techniques we have been able to manipulate them until they respond completely to the will of the person who controls them. Of course, their minds are rudimentary and brutish, which makes them much more susceptible than humans to manipulation. However, we are experimenting with the same techniques on some of our slaves and captives. We have had exciting results. Once you are a member of the Guild I will be pleased to show them to you.'

Taita was sickened by these revelations. They are discussing putting together creatures that are no longer men, but aberrant monstrosities, he thought, but he was careful not to express his horror. These people are tainted with the evil of Eos. Their brilliance has been perverted and corrupted by her poison. How I miss the company of decent, honest men, like Meren and Nakonto. How I long for the fresh bright innocence of Fenn.

Some time later when they were returning from the library, he raised again with Hannah the subject of when he would be allowed to leave the Cloud Gardens and return to Mutangi, even for a short time. 'My companions must be much distressed by my continued absence. I should like to reassure them of my safety and well-being. Then I would be happy indeed to return here to begin my initiation into the Guild.'

'Unfortunately, my lord, the decision does not rest with me,' she replied. 'It seems that the Supreme Council wishes you to remain in the Cloud Gardens until you have been fully initiated.' She smiled at him. 'Be not downcast, my lord. This should not be longer than another year. I assure you, we will do all in our power to make the time you spend with us as fruitful and productive as possible.'

The prospect of another year without being able to see Fenn or Meren appalled Taita, but he took consolation from the thought that the witch would not wait that long before she made her decisive move in the game she was playing with him.

His grafted parts continued to grow with amazing rapidity. He remembered Dr Lusulu's advice: 'You must learn to enjoy the manly parts that Doctor Hannah has returned to you. You must learn to delight in them, to glory in them.' Alone on his sleeping mat in the night he began to explore himself. The sensations aroused by his own touch were so intense that they intruded into his dreams. The lascivious devils that the imp of the grotto had set loose in his mind became more insistent and demanding. The dreams were at once shocking and fascinating. In them he was visited by a beautiful houri. She displayed her womanly parts shamelessly to him, and he saw that they were as perfectly formed as an orchid. The woman smell and taste of her was sweeter than any fruit.

For the first time in almost a century he felt his loins erupt. It was a sensation so powerful that it went far beyond ecstasy or even agony. He awoke panting and shaking, as though in fever. He was drenched in sweat and his own bodily fluids. It seemed an age before he could return from the far borders of his imagination to which the dream woman had transported him.

He rose and lit the oil lamp. He found the silver mirror that Rei had given him and went back to kneel on the mat. By the light of the lamp he gazed with awe at the reflection of his genitalia. They were still tumescent, and as the imp had shown him in the waters of the pool: perfectly formed, majestic and weighty.

Now I understand the urges that govern all natural men. I have become one of them. This thing that I have been given is the beloved enemy, a beast with two faces. If I can control it, it will bring me all the joy and delights that Lusulu spoke of. If it controls me, it will destroy me as surely as Eos plans to do.

When he returned to the library later that morning, he found it difficult at first to concentrate on the scroll that he unrolled on the low worktable in front of him. He was very much aware of a glow in the pit of his belly, and the presence under the skirts of his tunic.

It is as though another person has come to share my life, a spoilt brat who endlessly demands attention. He felt an indulgent proprietary affection for it. This is going to be a contest, a trial of wills to decide which of us is in command, he thought. But a mind like his, which had been honed to such perfection that it could suppress high levels of pain, an intelligence that had been trained to assimilate vast quantities of information, was able to deal with this much lesser distraction. He returned his full attention to the scroll. Soon he was so absorbed in it that he was only vaguely aware of his immediate surroundings.

The atmosphere in the library was quiet and studious. Although patrons were sitting at worktables in the adjoining rooms, he had this one to himself. It was as if the others had been warned to keep at a respectful distance. Occasionally the librarians passed through the room in which he sat, carrying baskets of scrolls to replace them on the shelves. Taita took little notice of them. He heard the grille that barred the forbidden room being opened, and glanced up in time to see a librarian going through the open gate, a woman of middle age and unremarkable appearance. He thought nothing of it and went on with his reading. A little later he heard the grille open again. The same woman came out and locked it behind her. She walked quietly down the room, then paused unexpectedly beside Taita's table. He looked up enquiringly. She laid a scroll on the table top. 'You are mistaken, I fear,' Taita told her. 'I did not ask for this.'

'You should have,' said the woman, so softly that he could barely catch the words. She extended the little finger of her right hand, then touched her lower lip with it.

Taita started. It was the recognition signal that Colonel Tinat had shown him. The woman was one of his people. Without another word she walked on, leaving the scroll on his table. Taita wanted to call after her, but restrained himself and watched her leave the room. He went on reading his own scroll until he was certain that he was alone and unobserved, then rolled it up and set it aside. In its place he opened the one that the librarian had brought him. It was untitled and the author was not named. Then he recognized the hand that had formed the unusually small and artistically drawn hieroglyphics.

'Dr Rei,' he whispered, and read on quickly. The subject that she was addressing was the replacement of human body parts by the process of seeding and grafting. His eyes skipped down the sheet of papyrus. He was intimately familiar with everything that Rei had written: her coverage of the subject was impressively detailed and lucid, but he found nothing new until he was almost half-way through the scroll. Then Rei began to describe how the seedings were harvested and prepared for application to the wound site. The chapter was headed: 'Selecting and cultivating the seedings'. As his eye ran on, the enormity of what she was so coldly enumerating crashed down on him like an avalanche. His mind numb with shock, he went back to the beginning of the chapter and reread it, this time very slowly, returning time and again to those sections that were beyond rational belief.

The donor should be young and healthy. She should have demonstrated at least five menstrual periods. Neither she nor her immediate family should have any history of serious disease. Her appearance should be pleasing. For reasons of management she should be obedient and tractable. If any difficulty is encountered in this area, the use of calming drugs is recommended. They should be administered with care so as not to contaminate the end product. There is a list of recommended drugs in the appendix at the end of this thesis. Diet is also important. It should be low in red meat and milk products, which heat the blood.

There was much more in this vein. Then he reached the next chapter, headed simply 'Breeding'.

As with the donor, the impregnators should be young and healthy, without defect or blemish. Under the present system they are usually selected as a reward for some service to the state. Often this is for military accomplishment. Care must be exercised to prevent any establishing emotional ties with the donor. They should be rotated at brief intervals. As soon as the donor's pregnancy is confirmed she must be denied any further contact with her impregnator.

Taita looked up sightlessly at the shelf of tablets directly in front of him. He remembered the stark terror of little Sidudu. He recalled vividly her pathetic plea: 'Please, Magus! I beg you! Please help me! If I don't rid myself of the baby they will kill me. I don't want to die for Onka's bastard.'

Sidudu the runaway had been one of the donors. Not a wife or mother, but a donor. Onka was one of her impregnators. Not her husband, lover or mate, but her impregnator. Taita's horror mounted steadily, but he forced himself to read on. The next section was headed 'Harvesting'. Some phrases seemed to leap at him from the text.

The harvesting must take place between the twentieth and twenty-fourth week of pregnancy.

The foetus must be removed intact and entire from the womb. Natural birth should not be allowed to take place as this has proved to be detrimental to the quality of the seedings.

As the chance of the donor surviving after the removal of the foetus is remote, her life should be terminated immediately. The surgeon should usually take measures to prevent unnecessary suffering. The preferred method is to place the donor under restraint. Her limbs are pinioned and she is gagged to prevent her screams alarming the other donors. The foetus is then removed swiftly by frontal section of the abdomen. Immediately this has been carried out the donor's life should be terminated by strangulation. The ligature is kept in place until the heart has stopped beating and her flesh has cooled.

Taita hurried on to the next chapter, entitled 'The foetus'. His heart was beating so rapidly that he could hear it resonating in his eardrums.

The sex of the foetus appears to be unimportant, although it seems logical and desirable that it should be the same as that of the recipient. The foetus should be healthy and well formed with no detectable deformity or defect. If it does not conform to these criteria it should be discarded. For these reasons it is advisable to have more than one donor available. If the area to be grafted is extensive there should be a choice of at least three donors available. Five would be a more desirable number.

Taita rocked back. Three donors. He remembered the three girls in the waterfall on the day of their first arrival. They had been brought as sacrificial lambs to provide a new eye for Meren. Five donors. He remembered the five girls whom Onka had been bringing up the mountain when they met him on the pathway. Had they all died of strangulation in the approved manner? Had it been one of them he had heard weeping in the night? Had she known what was about to happen to her and the babe in her womb? Was that why she had wept? He jumped up from the table, rushed out of the building and into the forest. As soon as he was hidden among the trees he doubled over and retched painfully, vomiting his shame and guilt. He leant against the trunk of one of the trees and stared down at the bulge beneath his tunic.

'Is this the reason why those innocents were slaughtered?' He drew the small knife from the sheath on his girdle. 'I will hack it off and force it down Hannah's throat. I will choke her with it!' he raged. 'It is a poisonous gift that will bring me only guilt and torment.'

His hand was shaking so violently that the knife slipped from his fingers. He covered his eyes with both hands. 'I hate it – I hate myself!' he whispered. His mind was filled with violent and confused images. He remembered the frenzied feasting of the crocodiles in the azure lake. He heard the weeping of women and the wailing of infants, the sounds of sorrow and despair.

Then the confusion cleared and he heard again the voice of Demeter the savant: *This Eos is the minion of the Lie. She is the consummate impostor, the usurper, the deceiver, the thief, the devourer of infants.*

'She is the devourer of infants,' he repeated. 'She is the one who orders and directs these atrocities. I must turn my hatred for myself upon her. She is the one I truly hate. She is the one I have come to destroy. Perhaps by grafting this thing upon me she has unwittingly given me the instrument of her own destruction.' He lifted his hands from his eyes and stared at them. They were no longer trembling.

'Screw up your courage and resolve, Taita of Gallala,' he whispered. 'The skirmishing is over. The battle royal is about to begin.'

He left the forest and made his way back to the library to retrieve Dr Rei's scroll. He knew he must read and remember every detail. He must know how they desecrated the bodies of the little ones to create the vile seedings. He must make sure that the sacrifice of the infants was never forgotten. He went to the worktable where he had left the scroll, but it was gone.

By the time he reached his own rooms in the sanatorium the sun had gone behind the crater wall. The servants had lit oil lamps, and the bowl that contained his evening meal was warming over the glowing charcoal in the copper brazier. After he had eaten sparingly, then brewed and drunk a bowl of the coffee grown by Dr Assem, he settled himself cross-legged on the sleeping mat and composed himself for meditation. This was his nightly routine, and the watcher at the hidden peep-hole would find nothing unusual in it.

At last he doused the oil lamp and the room was plunged into darkness. Within a short time the aura of the man behind the peep-hole faded as he left his station for the night. Taita waited a little longer, then relit the lamp, but turned down the wick until it was only a soft glow. He held the Periapt in his cupped hands and concentrated on the mental image of Lostris, who had become Fenn. He opened the locket and took out the locks of her hair, the old and the new. His love for her was the central redoubt upon which his defences against Eos hinged. Holding the curls to his lips he affirmed that love.

'Shield me, my love,' he prayed. 'Give me strength.' He felt the power that flowed from the soft hair warm his soul, then laid it back in the locket, and took out the fragment of red stone they had removed from Meren's eye. He placed it in the palm of his hand and concentrated upon it.

'It is cold and hard,' he whispered, 'as is my hatred of Eos.' Love was the shield, hatred the sword. He affirmed both. Then he placed the stone in the locket with the hair and hung the Periapt round his neck. He blew out the lamp and lay down, but sleep would not come.

Disjointed memories of Fenn haunted him. He remembered her laughing and crying. He remembered her smiling and teasing. He remembered her serious expression as she studied some problem he had set for her. He remembered her body lying warm and soft beside him in the night, the gentle sigh of her breathing and the beat of her heart against his.

I must see her once more. It may be the last time. He sat up on his mat. I dare not cast for her, but I can overlook her. These two astral manoeuvres were similar but in essence very different. To cast was to shout to her across the ether, when an unwelcome listener might detect the disturbance. To overlook was to spy upon her secretly, like the watcher at the peep-hole. Only a savant and seer, like Eos, might be able to detect it, as he had detected the watcher. However, he had refrained from any astral activity for so long now that the witch might no longer be on the alert.

I must see Fenn. I must take the chance.

He held the Periapt in his right hand. The locks of hair were part of Fenn and would guide him to her. He pressed the Periapt to his forehead and closed his eyes. He began to rock from side to side. The locket in his right hand seemed to take on some strange life of its own. Taita felt it pulsing softly in rhythm to his own heartbeat. He opened his mind and let the currents of existence enter freely, swirling round him like a great river. His spirit broke free of his body and he soared aloft as though he were borne on the wings of a gigantic bird. Far below, he saw fleeting, confused images of the forests and plains. He saw what looked like an army on the march, but as he drew closer he saw it was a slow-moving column of refugees, hundreds of men, women and children trudging along a dusty road, or packed into cumbersome ox-carts. There were soldiers with them, and men on horseback. But Fenn was not among the multitude.

He moved on, his spirit soul ranging wide, holding the amulet as his lodestone, searching until the tiny cluster of buildings at Mutangi appeared in the distance ahead. As he drew closer, he realized with mounting alarm that the village was in ruins, blackened and charred. The astral memory of a massacre hung like fog over the village. He sifted through the traces but, with surging relief, found that neither Fenn nor any others of his band were among the dead. They must have escaped from Mutangi before it had been destroyed.

He let his spirit soul range wider until he detected a pale glimmer of her presence in the foothills of the Mountains of the Moon, far to the west of the village. He followed the gleam and at last hovered above a narrow valley, hidden in the forests that covered the lower slopes of the mountains.

She is down there. He searched closer until he discovered a picket of horses. Windsmoke was among them, and so was Whirlwind. Just beyond the horses, firelight glowed from the narrow entrance to a cave. Nakonto sat above the entrance with Imbali beside him. Taita allowed his spirit soul to drift inside.

There she is. He picked out the form of Fenn stretched on a sleeping mat beside the small fire. Sidudu lay on one side of her, Meren beside Sidudu, then Hilto. Taita was so close to Fenn that he could hear her breathing. He saw that she had laid out her weapons close at hand. All the other members of the small party were also fully armed. Fenn was lying on her back. She wore only a linen loincloth and was bare to the waist. He gazed upon her tenderly. Since last he had seen her, her body had become even more womanly. Her breasts were larger and rounder, the nipples still tiny, but alert and darker pink now. The last vestiges of puppy fat had melted from her belly. The hollows and swells of her flesh were shadowed and highlighted by the low flames of the fire. In repose her countenance was lovely beyond his fondest memories. Taita realized with astonishment that she must now be at least sixteen. The years he had spent with her had passed so quickly.

The pattern of her breathing changed and slowly she opened her eyes. They were green in the glow from the hearth fire but darkened as she sensed his presence. She raised herself on one elbow, and he could feel her making ready to cast for him. They were close to the Cloud Gardens. He must stop her before she betrayed her position to the hostile thing up there on the mountain. He let his spirit sign appear in the air before her eyes. She started up as she realized he was watching her. She stared directly at the sign and he commanded her to remain silent. She smiled and nodded.

She formed her own spirit sign in reply to his, the delicate tracing of the water-lily bloom entwined with his falcon in a lover's embrace. He stayed with her a moment more. The contact had been fleeting, but to tarry longer might be deadly. He placed a single last message in her mind: 'I will return to you soon, very soon.' Then he began to withdraw.

She felt him going and the smile died on her lips. She held out a hand as if to hold him back, but he dared not stay.

With a start he jerked back into his own body, and found himself sitting cross-legged on the sleeping mat in his room at the Cloud Gardens. The sorrow of parting from her, after so brief a contact, was a heavy weight on him.

Over the months that followed he wrestled with his new flesh. Because he had always been a horseman, he treated it as if it were an unbroken colt, bending it to his will by force and persuasion. Since his youth he had made many more arduous demands upon his body than the one he was making now. He schooled and disciplined himself mercilessly. First he practised breathing techniques, which gave him extraordinary stamina and powers of concentration. Then he was ready to master his newly grown parts. Within a short time he was able, without manual stimulation, to remain fully tumescent from dusk to dawn. He schooled himself until he was able to withhold his seed indefinitely or to spend it at the precise moment of his choosing.

Demeter had described what he had experienced when Eos had had him in her power and their 'infernal coupling'. Taita knew that he would soon be the victim of her carnal invasion, and if he were to survive he must learn to resist. All his preparations for the struggle seemed futile. He was matching himself against one of the most voracious predators of the ages, yet he was a virgin.

I need a woman to help me arm myself, he decided. Preferably one who is vastly experienced.

Since their first meeting, he had seen Dr Lusulu on more than one occasion in the library. Like him, she seemed to spend much of her spare time in study. They had exchanged brief salutations, but although she seemed ready to take their friendship further, he had not encouraged it. Now he looked out for her and one morning he came across her, sitting at a worktable in one of the library rooms.

'The peace of the goddess upon you,' he greeted her quietly. He had heard Hannah and Rei use the same phrase. Lusulu looked up and smiled warmly. Her aura flared with fiery zigzag lines, her colour rose and her eyes glowed. When she was aroused, she was a handsome woman.

'Peace on you, my lord,' she replied. 'I am much taken by the new cut of your beard. It suits you most admirably.' They spoke for a few minutes, then Taita took his leave and went to his own table. He did not look in her direction again until much later when he heard her roll the scrolls she was studying and stand up. Her sandals slapped lightly on the stone floor as she crossed the room. Now he glanced up and their eyes met. She inclined her head towards the door and smiled again. He followed her out into the forest. She was walking away slowly along the path towards the sanatorium. He caught her up before she had gone another hundred yards. They chatted together, and at last she asked, 'I often wonder about your recovery from the procedure that Dr Hannah performed on you. Has it gone as well as it started off?'

'Indeed, yes,' he assured her. 'Do you recall that you discussed with Dr Hannah my ability to ejaculate?'

He saw her aura light when he used the evocative word, and her voice was slightly hoarse as she replied, 'Yes.'

'Well, I can assure you that it is now happening regularly. As a surgeon and a scientist, you might have some professional interest in a demonstration.'

They kept up the pretence of being colleagues until they entered his rooms. He took a moment to cover the peep-hole in the corner with his cloak, then came back to where she stood.

'I will need your assistance once again,' he said, as he took off his tunic.

'Of course,' she agreed, and came to him readily. She reached down for him and, after a few deft strokes, she said, 'You have grown a great deal since our first meeting.' Then, a little later, she asked, 'My lord, may I ask if you have ever known a woman before?'

'Alas!' He shook his head mournfully. 'I would not know how to begin.'

'Then let me instruct you.'

Naked she was even more handsome than when she was clothed. She had wide hips, large resilient breasts and big dark nipples. When she lay on her back on his sleeping mat, spread her thighs and guided him into her he was taken off-guard by the heat and the clinging oleaginous embrace of her secret flesh. He came perilously close to spending himself before they had begun in earnest. With a huge effort he regained control of himself and his body. Now he was able to profit from all his practice and self-training. He blocked out his own sensations and concentrated on reading her aura in the way a mariner reads a chart of the oceans. He used it to divine her needs and wants before she became aware of them. He made her cry out and whimper. He made her screech like a condemned woman on a torture table. She spasmed and her whole body convulsed. She pleaded with him to stop, then begged him never to stop. 'You are killing me,' she sobbed at last. 'In the holy name of the goddess, I can go on no longer.' But he went on and on.

She was weakening, unable to meet his thrusts. Her face was wet with tears and sweat. Dark shadows of fear fell across her eyes. 'You are a devil,' she whispered. 'You are the devil himself.'

'I am the devil that you, Hannah and others like you have created.'

She was ready at last. There was no resistance left in her. He held her down, pinning her deeply. Her body and mind were open to him. He covered her mouth with his, forcing her lips open, then arched his back and, like a pearl diver taking a long last breath before plunging below the surface, he drew it all out, her strength, her wisdom and her knowledge, her triumphs and defeats, her fear and her deeply buried guilt. He took everything she had and left her empty on the mat. Her breathing was quick and shallow, her skin pale and translucent as wax. Her eyes stared ahead unblinking, but saw nothing. He sat beside her through the rest of that night, reading her memories, learning her secrets, truly coming to know her.

The dawn light was filtering into the room when at last she stirred and rolled her head from side to side. 'Who am I?' she whispered weakly. 'Where am I? What has happened to me? I can remember nothing.'

'You are a person named Lusulu, but you have wrought great evil in your life. You were tormented by guilt. I have taken it and all else from you. But there is nothing of yours that I wish to keep. I am giving it back to you, especially the guilt. In the end it will kill you, and you so richly deserve that death.'

As he spread her again and knelt over her, she tried to fight him off but she did not have the strength. As he entered her for the second time she screamed, but the scream burbled in her throat and did not reach her lips. When he was deep in her, he took another deep breath and strained. He expelled it all back into her in a single long ejaculation. After he had finished, he uncoupled from her and went to bathe himself.

When he came back into the sleeping chamber she was pulling on her tunic. She gave him one look of stark terror, and he saw that her aura was shredded. She stumbled to the door, pulled it open and scuttled into the passage. The sound of her running feet receded.

He felt the first twinge of pity for her, but he recalled all her heinous crimes and it fell away. Then he thought: But she has made retribution in small part by teaching me how I must deal with her mistress, the great witch.

D ay after day and week after week, he waited patiently for the invitation from Eos that he knew must come. Then, one morning, he awoke with the familiar sense of well-being and expectation. 'The witch is summoning me to her lair,' he told himself. On the terrace overlooking the lake he ate a frugal breakfast of dates and figs as he watched the sun break through the morning mist and clothe the walls of the crater with golden light. Apart from the servants he saw nobody: not Hannah, Rei, or Assem. He was relieved by this: he did not trust himself to come face to face with one of them so soon after the revelations contained in the scroll from the secret room. Nobody accosted him or attempted to restrain him when he left the building and set out for the gates of the upper gardens.

He walked slowly, taking his time to assemble and review his forces. The only reliable intelligence he had about Eos was the description Demeter had given him. He was able to run over it word for word as he walked. So complete were his powers of recall that it was as if the old man was speaking to him again.

If she is threatened she can change her appearance as a chameleon does, Demeter's voice said in his ears, and Taita remembered the manifestations he had encountered at the grotto: the imp, the pharaoh, the gods and goddesses and his own self.

Yet vanity is among her multitudinous vices. You cannot imagine the beauty she is able to assume. It stuns the senses and negates reason. When she takes on this aspect no man can resist her wiles. The sight of her reduces even the most noble soul to the level of a beast. Taita cast his mind back to his sighting of Eos in the operating room at the sanatorium. He had not glimpsed her face through the black veil, but such was her beauty that even unseen it had flooded the room.

Despite all my training as an adept I was not able to restrain my basest instincts. Demeter spoke again, and Taita hearkened to him. *I lost the ability and the inclination to reckon consequences. For me, in that moment, nothing but her existed. I was consumed by lust. She toyed with me, like the winds of autumn with a dead leaf. To me it seemed she gave me everything, every delight contained in this world. She gave me her body.* Taita heard again his tormented groans as he went on: *Even now the memory drives me to the brink of madness. Each rise and swell, enchanted opening and fragrant cleft . . . I did not try to resist her, for no mortal man could do so.*

Will I be able to do so? Taita wondered.

Then Demeter's most dire warning echoed in his head: *Taita, you remarked that the original Eos was an insatiable nymphomaniac, and that is so, but this other Eos outstrips her in appetite. When she kisses, she sucks out the vital juices of her lover, as you or I might suck out the juices from a ripe orange. When she takes a man between her thighs in that exquisite but infernal coupling she draws out of him his very substance. She takes from him his soul. His substance is the ambrosia that nourishes her. She is as some monstrous vampire that feeds on human blood. She chooses only superior beings as her victims, men and women of Good Mind, servants of the Truth, a magus of illustrious reputation or a gifted seer. Once she detects her victim, she runs him down as relentlessly as a wolf harries a deer.*

As she has done to me. Taita reflected.

She is omnivorous. Those were the words of Demeter who had known her as no living man ever could. *No matter age or appearance, physical frailty or imperfection. It is not their flesh that feeds her appetites, but their souls. She devours young and old, men and women. Once she has them in her thrall, wrapped in her silken web, she draws from them their accumulated store of learning, wisdom and experience. She sucks it out through their mouths with her accursed kisses. She draws it out from their loins in her loathsome embrace. She leaves only a desiccated husk.*

The witch's minions, Hannah, Rei and Assem, had regenerated Taita's missing organs for one reason only; to enable Eos to destroy him, body, mind and soul. He crushed down the terror that threatened to rise like a tidal wave and sweep him away.

I am ready for her, as ready as I can ever be. But will that be enough?

The gates to the gardens were wide open, but as he stood in front of them a hush fell over the crater. The soft wind died away. A pair of bulbul shrikes that had been calling a duet to each other fell silent. The high branches of the trees froze and remained as motionless as a painting against the blue canopy of the sky. For a moment longer he listened to the silence, then he stepped through the gates.

The earth moved under his feet. It trembled, the branches of the trees quivering in sympathy. The tremble became a harsh juddering. He heard rock groan under his feet. A section of the crater wall split away and fell with a roar into the forest below. The earth tipped under him like the deck of a ship caught in a gale. He almost lost his balance and reached out to grab one of the gate's bars to prevent himself being cast down. The wind rose again, but it came from the direction of the imp's grotto. It swept over the tops of the trees and swirled round him in a vortex of dead leaves. It was as cold as the hand of a corpse.

Eos is trying to intimidate me. She is the mistress of the volcanoes. She commands the earthquakes and the lava rivers that flow up from hell. She is showing me how puny I am in the face of her might, he thought. Then he shouted aloud, 'Hear me, Eos! I accept your challenge.'

The trembling of the earth ceased, and once again the mysterious hush fell over the crater. Now the pathway lay clear and inviting before him. When at last he passed through the gap between the tall boulders he heard ahead the chortling of the waters that flowed out of the grotto. He pushed his way through the screen of greenery and stepped into the clearing beside the pool. All was as he remembered it. He took his customary seat on the grass with his back to the fallen tree-trunk, and waited.

The first warning he received of her approach was an icy breeze that tickled the back of his neck, and he felt the hair rise on his forearms. He watched the opening of the grotto and saw a fine silver mist billow from it. Then a dark figure appeared through the mist, coming down the lichen-covered ledges towards him with stately grace. It was the veiled woman he had last seen in Hannah's rooms, dressed in the same voluminous, translucent robe of black silk.

Eos stepped out of the silver mist, and he saw that her feet were bare. Her toes peeped out from under the hem of her robe, the only part of her that was visible. They were wet and shining from the spring water that spilled over them, small and perfectly shaped, as though carved by a great artist from creamy ivory. Her toenails were pearly bright. Those feet were the only part of her body he had ever laid eyes on, and they were exquisitely erotic. He could not tear his gaze from them. He felt his manhood swell, and stilled it with an effort.

If she can affect me thus with a glimpse of her toes, what chance have I of resisting her if she reveals the rest of herself?

At last he was able to lift his eyes. He tried to see beyond her veil but it was impenetrable. Then he felt the touch of her regard as though a butterfly had landed upon his skin. She spoke, and he caught his breath. He had never heard a sound to match the music of her voice. It was as silvery as the chiming of crystal bells. It shivered the foundations of his soul.

'I have waited through the aeons for you to come to me,' said Eos, and although he knew that she embodied the great Lie, he could not help but believe her.

Fenn and Meren had kept Sidudu hidden for many long months after Taita had been taken away by Captain Onka to the Cloud Gardens. At first she had been so enfeebled by her ordeal that she was confused and distraught. Meren and Fenn were gentle and soon she became pathetically reliant upon them. One or other had to stay with her at all times. Slowly she rallied and her confidence began to return. At last she was able to describe her experiences and to tell them of the Temple of Love.

'It is dedicated to the one true goddess,' she explained. 'All the temple virgins are chosen from the incomers, never the noble families. Each arriving family must offer up one of their daughters, and it brings great honour and privilege on those whose daughters are chosen. All the people in our village held a festival of praise to the goddess and dressed me in the finest robes, placed a crown of flowers on my head and took me to the temple. My father and mother went with me, laughing and weeping with joy. They gave me to the mother superior and left me there. I never saw them again.'

'Who chose you for the service of the goddess?' Fenn asked her.

'They told us it was the oligarchs,' she replied.

'Tell us about the Temple of Love,' Meren said. She was silent for a while as she thought about it. Then she went on, speaking softly and hesitantly: 'It was very beautiful. There were many other girls when first I arrived. The priestesses were kind to us. We were given lovely clothes and delicious food. They explained that when we had proved ourselves to be worthy we would go up into the mountain of the goddess and be exalted by her.'

'You were happy?' Fenn asked.

'At first I was. Of course I missed my mother and father, but each morning they gave us a delicious sherbet to drink that filled us with joy and high spirits. We laughed, sang and danced.'

'Then what happened?' Meren asked.

She turned away her face and spoke so softly that he could hardly hear her. 'The men came to visit us. We thought they were to be our friends. We danced with them.' Sidudu began to weep silently. 'I am ashamed to tell you more.'

They were silent, and Fenn took her hand. 'We are your true friends, Sidudu,' she said. 'You can speak to us. You can tell us everything.'

The girl let out a heart-wrenching sob and threw her arms round Fenn's neck. 'The priestesses ordered us to have congress with the men who visited us.'

'Which men were they?' Meren asked grimly.

'The first was Lord Aquer. He was horrible. After him there were others, many others, then Onka.'

'You need tell us no more.' Fenn stroked her hair.

'Yes! I must! The memory is a fire inside me. I cannot keep it from you.' Sidudu took a deep, shuddering breath. 'Once a month a woman doctor named Hannah came to examine us. On each occasion she chose one or more of the girls. They were taken away to the mountain to be exalted by the goddess. They never returned to the temple.' She stopped speaking again, and Fenn passed her a square of linen on which to blow her nose. When she had finished, Sidudu folded the cloth carefully and went on: 'One of the other girls became my dearest friend. Her name was Litane. She was very gentle and lovely, but she missed her mother and hated what we had to do with the men. One night she ran away from the temple. She told me she was going and I tried to stop her, but she was determined. The next morning the priestesses laid her dead body on the altar. As a caution, they made each of us walk past it. They told us that the trogs had caught her in the forest. Lying on the altar, Litane was no longer lovely.'

They let her cry for a while, and then Meren said, 'Tell us about Onka.'

'Onka is a nobleman. Lord Aquer is his uncle. He is also Aquer's chief spy-master. For all these reasons, he has special privileges. He was taken with me. Because of his position he was allowed to see me more than once. Then they allowed him to take me away from the temple to live with him as his house slave. I was a reward for the services he had performed for the state. When he was drunk he beat me. It gave him pleasure to hurt me. It made his eyes sparkle and he smiled when he was doing it. One day while Onka was away on military duty a woman came secretly to see me. She told me that she worked in a great library in the Cloud Gardens. She told me what happened to the girls from the temple who were taken up into the mountain. They were not exalted by the goddess. Their babies were cut from their wombs before they were born and given as food to the goddess. That is why the goddess is known secretly as the Devourer of Infants.'

'What happened to the girls who bore the infants?'

'They disappeared,' Sidudu said simply. She sobbed again. 'I loved some of those girls who have gone. There are others in the temple whom I also love. They, too, will go up the mountain when there is a baby inside them.'

'Calm yourself, Sidudu,' Fenn whispered. 'This is all too dreadful to be told.'

'No, Fenn, let the poor girl speak,' Meren intervened. 'What she says fires me with rage. The Jarrians are monsters. My anger arms me against them.'

'So you will help me to save my friends, Meren?' Sidudu looked at him with more than trust in her large dark eyes.

'I will do whatever you ask of me,' he answered at once. 'But tell me more of Onka. He will be the first to know my vengeance.'

'I thought he would protect me. I thought that if I stayed with him I would never be sent to the mountain. But one day, not long ago, Dr Hannah came to examine me. I was not expecting her, but I knew what her visit meant. When she had finished she said nothing, but I saw her look at Onka and nod. It was enough. I knew then that when the baby inside me grew larger I would be taken up the mountain. A few days later I had another visitor. She came to see me in secret while Onka was with Colonel Tinat at Tamafupa. She was the wife of Bilto. She asked me to work with the incomers who were planning an escape from Jarri. I agreed, of course, and when they asked me to do so I gave a potion to Onka that made him sick. After that Onka suspected me. He treated me even more cruelly, and I knew that soon he would send me back to the temple. Then I heard that the magus was in Mutangi. I thought he would be able to take away Onka's baby, and I decided to risk everything to find him. I ran away, but the trogs came after me. That is when you rescued me.'

'It is a terrible story,' Fenn said. 'You have suffered much.'

'Yes, but not as much as the girls who are still in the temple,' Sidudu reminded them.

'We will rescue them,' Meren blurted out impulsively. 'When we escape from Jarri those girls will go with us, I swear it!'

'Oh, Meren, you are so brave and noble.'

Thereafter Sidudu made a swift recovery. She and Fenn grew closer each day. All the others liked her, Hilto, Nakonto and Imbali, but Meren more so than all the rest. With the help of Bilto and the other villagers of Mutangi, they were able to escape from the house during the day and spend time in the forest. Meren and Hilto continued to train Fenn in archery, and soon they invited Sidudu to join in. Meren made her a bow, which he matched carefully to her strength and the span of her arms. Although small and slim, Sidudu was surprisingly strong, and showed a natural aptitude with the bow. Meren set up a target for them in a clearing in the woods, and the girls shot against each other in friendly rivalry.

'Pretend that the mark is Onka's head,' Fenn told her, and after that Sidudu seldom missed. Her arms strengthened and developed so swiftly that soon Meren had to build her another bow with a heavier draw weight. After much devoted practice she was able to send out an arrow to the mark at two hundred paces.

Meren, Hilto and Nakonto were all inveterate gamblers and laid wagers on the girls when they shot against each other. They urged on their favourite, and haggled over the allowances given to Sidudu. Because Fenn had been using the bow for so much longer than Sidudu, they made her shoot from longer range. At first this was agreed at fifty paces, but gradually it became shorter as Sidudu's skill increased.

One morning they were holding another tournament in the clearing, Meren and Sidudu teamed against Hilto and Fenn. The competition was keen and the banter raucous when out from among the trees rode a stranger on an unfamiliar horse. He was dressed like a field worker, but he rode like a warrior. At a quiet word from Meren they nocked fresh arrows and stood ready to defend themselves. When the stranger saw their intention he reined in his mount and pulled aside the head-cloth that covered his face.

'By Seth's dung-smeared buttocks!' Meren exclaimed. 'It's Tinat.' He hurried forward to greet him. 'Colonel, something is amiss. What is it? Tell me at once.'

'I am pleased to have found you,' Tinat told him. 'I have come to warn you that we are in great danger. The oligarchs have issued a summons for all of us to appear before them. Onka and his men are hunting for us everywhere. At this very moment they are searching every house in Mutangi.'

'What does this mean?' Meren asked.

'Only one thing,' Tinat told him morosely. 'We have come under suspicion. I believe Onka has denounced me as a traitor. Which, of course, by Jarrian standards, I am. He found the bodies of the trogs you killed when you rescued Sidudu, which infuriated him because now he is certain that you are hiding her.'

'What proof has he?'

'He needs none. He is closely related to Lord Aquer. His

word is enough to condemn us all,' Tinat replied. 'The judgement of the oligarchs is certain. We will be interrogated under torture. If we survive that, we will be sent to the quarries or the mines . . . or worse.'

'So now we are all fugitives.' Meren did not seem worried by the prospect. 'At least the pretence is over.'

'Yes,' Tinat agreed. 'We are outlaws. You cannot return to Mutangi.'

'Of course not,' Meren said. 'There is nothing there that we need. We have the horses and our weapons. We must take to the forests. While we wait for Taita to return from the Cloud Gardens we will make the final preparations for our flight from this accursed place back to our very Egypt.'

'We must leave at once,' Tinat concurred. 'We are much too close to Mutangi. There are many places in the remote hills where we can hide. If we keep moving, Onka will be hard put to catch up with us.' They mounted and rode eastwards. By late afternoon they had covered twenty leagues. As they climbed into the foothills of the range of mountains below the Kitangule Gap a herd of large grey antelope with long spiral horns and huge ears broke cover and ran across their front. Immediately they unslung their bows and gave chase. Fenn, on Whirlwind, was the first to catch up with them and her arrow brought down a fat, hornless female.

'Enough!' Meren cried. 'There is plenty of meat on it to last us for days.' They allowed the rest of the herd to escape and dismounted to butcher the carcass. As the sun set, Sidudu led them to a stream of clear sweet water. They bivouacked beside it and grilled antelope chops over embers for dinner.

As they gnawed the bones, Tinat reported to Meren on the most recent disposition of the forces loyal to the rebel cause. 'My own regiment is the Red Standard, and all the officers and men will come over to us when I call them to arms. I can also rely on two divisions of the Yellow Standard, which is commanded by my colleague Colonel Sangat. He is one of us. Then there are three divisions of troops who are responsible for guarding the prisoners and captives working in the stopes of the mines. They have had first-hand experience of the brutality and inhumanity with which the captives are treated. They await my orders. As soon as we begin the struggle they will release their charges, arm them and bring them by forced march to join us.' They went on to discuss the mustering point, and eventually decided that each unit must make independently for the Kitangule Gap, where they would all come together.

'What force will the Jarrians be able to deploy against us?' Meren asked.

'Although they will outnumber us ten to one, it will take the oligarchs many days to muster their troops and march against us. As long as we can achieve initial surprise and a head start on the pursuit our forces will be of sufficient strength to fight a rearguard action as far as the boatyards at the head of the Kitangule river. When we get there we will seize the craft we need. Once we are on the river it will be an easy run downstream to the great Nalubaale lake.' He paused and looked shrewdly at Meren. 'We can be ready to leave within ten days.'

'We cannot leave without the Magus Taita,' Meren said quickly.

'Taita is one man,' Tinat pointed out. 'Hundreds of our own people are in danger.'

'You will not succeed without him,' Meren said. 'Without his powers you and all your people will be doomed.'

Tinat thought about it, frowning morosely and pulling at a strand of his bristling beard. Then he seemed to reach a decision. 'We cannot wait for him for ever. What if he is already dead? I cannot take the risk.'

'Colonel Tinat!' Fenn burst out. 'Will you wait for Taita until the rise of the harvest moon?'

Tinat stared at her, then nodded curtly. 'But no longer. If the magus does not come down from the mountain before then, we can be sure he never will.'

'Thank you, Colonel. I admire your courage and good sense.' Fenn smiled sweetly at him. He mumbled with embarrassment and looked into the flames. She went on remorse-lessly, 'Do you know about the girls in the Temple of Love, Colonel?'

'Of course I know there are temple maidens, but what of it?'

Fenn turned to Sidudu. 'Tell him what you told us.'

Tinat listened with mounting horror to Sidudu's account. By the time she had finished, his expression was bleak. 'I had no inkling that atrocities such as these were being perpe-trated on our young women. Of course I knew that some of the girls were being taken to the Cloud Gardens. Indeed, I escorted some, but they went willingly. I had no idea that they were being sacrificed to the goddess, or that cannibal rites were being conducted on the mountain.'

'Colonel, we have to take them with us. We cannot leave them to the Jarrians,' Meren broke in. 'I have already sworn an oath that I will do everything in my power to set them free and take them with us when we escape from Jarri.'

'Here and now I make that same oath,' Tinat growled. 'I swear in the name of all the gods that I will not leave this land until we have freed those young women.'

'If we must wait until the harvest moon how many more will be sent up the mountain before then?' Fenn asked.

The men were silenced by her question.

'If we act too soon, we will lose the element of surprise. The Jarrians will immediately unleash all their forces upon us. What do you propose, Fenn?' It was Tinat who had spoken.

'Only the girls with child are sent up the mountain,' Fenn pointed out.

'From my own observation I know that is true,' Tinat admitted. 'But how does that help us? We cannot prevent them conceiving if they are being treated as playthings by many men.'

'Perhaps we cannot prevent it, as you say, but we can halt the growth of an infant.'

'How?' Meren demanded.

'As Taita did for Sidudu, with a potion that induces

miscarriage.' The men thought about what Fenn had said, until Meren spoke again.

'Taita's medical bag is in the house at Mutangi. We cannot return to fetch it.'

'I know which herbs he used to make the potion. I helped him gather them.'

'How will you get these medicines to the women?' Tinat asked. 'They are guarded by trogs.'

'Sidudu and I will take them to the temple and explain to the girls how to use them.'

'But the trogs and the priestesses – how will you avoid them?'

'In the same way that we hid Sidudu from Onka,' Fenn replied.

'A spell of concealment!' Meren exclaimed.

'I don't understand,' Tinat said. 'What are you talking about?'

'Fenn is the magus's initiate,' Meren explained. 'He has taught her some of the esoteric arts and she is far advanced in these skills. She is able to hide herself and others behind a cloak of invisibility.'

'I don't believe it is possible,' Tinat declared.

'Then I will demonstrate it to you,' Fenn told him. 'Please leave the fire and wait beyond that clump of trees until Meren calls you back.' Frowning and grumbling, Tinat stood up and strode into the darkness. Within minutes Meren hailed him and Tinat returned to find him alone.

'Very well, Colonel Cambyses. Where are they?' Tinat growled.

'Within ten paces of you,' Meren told him. Tinat grunted and walked slowly round the fire, peering left and right until he came back to where he had started from.

'Nothing,' he said. 'Now tell me where they are hiding.'

'Directly in front of you.' Meren pointed.

Tinat stared hard, then shook his head. 'I see nothing—' he began, then reeled back and let out a shout of astonishment. 'Osiris and Horus, this is witchcraft!' The two girls sat exactly where he had last seen them. They were holding hands and smiling at him.

'Yes, Colonel, but only a small act. The trogs will be much easier to deceive than you were,' Fenn told him, 'for they are brutes of limited intelligence, while you are a trained warrior with a superior mind.' Tinat was disarmed by the compliment.

She really is a witch. Tinat is no match for her. Meren smiled inwardly. If she set her mind to it, she could make him stand on his head and whistle through his arse.

They could not approach the Temple of Love too closely on horseback. Unlike Taita, Fenn's skills were not sufficient to conceal a large party of horses and men. They left the horses with Meren and Nakonto, hidden in a dense stand of trees, and the two girls went forward alone on foot. Sidudu was carrying four small linen bags of herbs tied round her waist under her skirt.

They climbed up through the forest until they reached a crest of higher ground and could look down into the valley beyond. The temple stood at the far end. It was built of yellow sandstone, a large, gracious building, surrounded by lawns and pools of water on which floated the leaves of a gigantic water-lily. There was the faint sound of revelry, and they saw a gathering of women on the bank of the largest pool. Some were sitting in a circle, singing and clapping, while others danced to the music.

'We did that every day at this time,' Sidudu whispered. 'They are waiting for the men to visit them.'

'Do you recognize any of them?' Fenn asked.

'I am not sure. We are too far away for me to tell.' Sidudu shaded her eyes. 'Wait! The girl on her own at this side of the pool – do you see her? That is my friend Jinga.'

Fenn studied a willowy girl who was walking along the

bank of the pool. She was dressed in a short chiton. Her arms and long legs were bare, and there were yellow flowers in her hair. 'How reliable is she?' Fenn asked.

'She is a little older than most of the others, the most sensible of them all. They look up to her.'

'We will go down to speak to her,' Fenn said, but Sidudu seized her arm.

'Look!' she said, her voice shaking. Just below where they crouched on the ridge a file of shaggy black shapes emerged from the trees. They lolloped along on all fours, knuckling the ground with their hands. 'Trogs!'

The great apes were circling the periphery of the temple grounds, but keeping out of sight of the women on the lawns. Every few paces one sniffed at the ground with dilated nostrils, searching for the scent of strangers or runaways from the temple.

'Can you mask our scent?' Sidudu asked. 'The trogs have a keen sense of smell.'

'No,' Fenn admitted. 'We must let them pass before we go down to the girls.' The trogs were moving rapidly and disappeared back among the trees.

'Now!' said Fenn. 'Quickly!' She reached for Sidudu's hand. 'Remember, don't speak, and don't run or break contact with me. Move slowly and carefully.'

Fenn cast the spell over them, then led Sidudu down the slope. Sidudu's friend, Jinga, was still alone, sitting under a willow tree, throwing crumbs of dhurra cake to a shoal of fish in the water below her. The pair knelt beside her and softly Fenn lifted the spell of concealment from Sidudu. She herself remained cloaked so that Jinga was not startled by a strange face. The girl was so preoccupied with the swirling fish that, for a while, she was not aware of Sidudu. Then she started and half rose to her feet.

Sidudu restrained her with a hand on her arm. 'Jinga, don't be afraid.'

The girl stared at her, then smiled. 'I didn't see you, Sidudu.

462

Where have you been? I missed you so much. You have grown even more beautiful.'

'You also, Jinga.' Sidudu kissed her. 'But we have little time to talk. There is so much I must tell you.' She studied the girl's face and, with dismay, saw that the pupils of her eyes were dilated from a potion she had been given. 'You must listen carefully to what I say.' Sidudu spoke slowly as though to a very young child.

Jinga's eyes focused more clearly as she began to understand the enormity of what Sidudu was telling her. At last she whispered, 'They are murdering our sisters? It cannot be true.'

'It is, Jinga, you must believe me. But there is something we can do to prevent it.' Quickly she explained about the herbs, how to prepare and administer them. 'They only take the girls who are with child up the mountain. The medicine brought down my infant. You must give it to anyone who is in danger.' Sidudu lifted her skirt and untied the bags of herbs from round her waist. 'Hide these well. Don't let the priestesses find them. As soon as Dr Hannah chooses a girl to go up the mountain to be exalted by the goddess, you must give her a potion. This is all that can save them.'

'I have already been chosen,' Jinga whispered. 'The doctor came four days ago and told me I was soon to meet the goddess.'

'Oh, my poor Jinga! Then you must take it this very night, as soon as you are alone,' Sidudu told her. She embraced her friend again. 'I cannot stay with you longer, but soon I will return with a band of good men to rescue you. We will take you and the others away to a new land where we will be safe. Warn them to be ready to leave.' She released Jinga. 'Hide the herbs well. They will save your life. Now go, and don't look back.'

As soon as Jinga had turned her back Fenn spread the cloak of concealment over Sidudu. Jinga had gone no more than twenty paces before she glanced over her shoulder. Her face paled as she saw that Sidudu had vanished. With a visible effort she braced herself and walked away across the lawns towards the temple.

Fenn and Sidudu started back through the forest. Half-way up the hill Fenn stepped off the path and stood perfectly still. She dared not speak, but squeezed Sidudu's hand firmly to caution her to keep the spell intact. Barely breathing the two girls watched a pair of huge black trogs shamble down the path towards them. The apes were swinging their heads from side to side as they searched the bushes that flanked the track, their eyes moving quickly beneath beetling brows. The male was the larger of the pair, but the female following him seemed more alert and aggressive. They drew level with the girls and, for a moment, it seemed they would pass by. Then the female stopped abruptly, lifted her snout, flaring the wide nostrils and snuffling noisily at the air. The male followed her example and both of them began to grunt softly but eagerly. The male gaped to display a vicious set of fangs, then gnashed them shut. They were so close that Fenn smelt the stench of his breath. She felt Sidudu's hand tremble in hers and squeezed her fingers again to encourage her.

Both trogs hopped forward cautiously towards where they stood, still testing the air. The female lowered her head and sniffed the ground over which the girls had passed. She shuffled towards them slowly, following their scent. Sidudu was shaking with terror and Fenn could sense the panic rising in her to the point when it must boil over. She drew deeply upon her training and sent out waves of psychic strength to steady her, but by now the ape's questing snout was only inches from the toe of Sidudu's sandal. Sidudu urinated with terror. Her water ran down her legs and the trog grunted again as she smelt it. The ape gathered herself to spring forward, but at that moment a small antelope rustled the bushes as it fled, and the male trog let out a ferocious bellow and bounded away in pursuit. Immediately the female went after him, passing so close to Sidudu that she almost brushed against her. As the apes crashed away through the undergrowth, Sidudu sagged against Fenn and might have fallen to the ground if Fenn had

not grabbed her. Holding her close, Fenn led her slowly up to
the crest of the hill, taking care not to break the spell of
concealment until they were out of sight of the temple. Then
they ran to where Meren and Nakonto were waiting with the
horses.

They never slept two nights in the same bivouac.
Between them Tinat and Sidudu knew all the back
ways and hidden tracks through the forest, so they
moved swiftly and secretly, avoiding well-travelled paths,
covering much ground between one camp and the next.

They went from village to village, meeting local magistrates
and headmen who were sympathizers. All were incomers, and
most of the villagers were loyal to them. They provided food
and safe houses for the fugitives. They kept watch for Jarrian
patrols and warned of their approach.

In each village Meren and Tinat held a war council.

'We are going back to our very Egypt!' they would tell the
magistrates and headmen. 'Have your people ready to march
on the night of the harvest moon.'

Tinat would look round the circle of faces that glowed with
elation and excitement in the firelight. He pointed to the
chart he had unrolled and spread before him. 'This will be
the route you must follow. Arm your menfolk with what
weapons you have to hand. Your womenfolk must gather
food, warm clothing and blankets for their families, but bring
nothing that you cannot carry. It will be a long, hard march.
Your first assembly point will be here.' He indicated the place
on the chart. 'Move swiftly to it. There will be scouts waiting
for you. They will have more weapons for your men, and they
will guide you to the Kitangule Gap. That will be the main
mustering ground for all our people. Be discreet and circum-
spect. Tell only those you can trust of our plans. You know
from bitter experience that the spies of the oligarchs are
everywhere. Do not move before the appointed time, unless

you receive direct orders from either Colonel Cambyses or me.' Before sunrise they rode on. The commanders of the outlying garrisons and military forts were almost solidly Tinat's men. They listened to his orders, made few suggestions and asked fewer questions. 'Send us the order to march. We will be ready,' they told him.

The three main mines were in the south-eastern foothills of the mountains. In the largest, thousands of slaves and prisoners toiled on the stopes, digging out the rich silver ore. The commander of the guards was one of Tinat's men. He was able to spirit Tinat and Meren, dressed as labourers, into the slave barracoons and prison compounds. The inmates had organized themselves into secret cells and elected their leaders. Tinat knew most of the leaders well: before their arrest and incarceration they had been his friends and comrades. They listened to his orders with joy.

'Wait for the harvest moon,' he told them. 'The guards are with us. At the appointed time they will open the gates and set you free.'

The other mines were smaller. One produced copper and zinc, the alloy needed to turn copper into bronze. The smallest of all was the richest. Here the slaves worked a thick seam of gold-bearing quartz, so rich that lumps of pure gold gleamed in the light of the miners' lamps.

'We have fifteen wagonloads of pure gold stored in the smelter,' the chief engineer told Tinat.

'Leave it!' Meren ordered brusquely.

Tinat nodded. 'Yes! Leave the gold.'

'But it is a vast treasure!' the engineer protested.

'Freedom is an even greater treasure,' Meren said. 'Leave the gold. It will slow us down, and we can find better use for the wagons. They will carry the women, children and any men who are too frail or sick to walk.'

It was still twenty days short of the harvest moon when the oligarchs struck. Many thousands were already privy to the planned exodus so a bright flame was burning throughout Jarri. It was inevitable that the spies would pick up its smoke. The oligarchs sent Captain Onka with two hundred men to Mutangi, the village from which the rumours had emanated.

They surrounded it at night and captured all the inhabitants. Onka interrogated them one at a time in the village council hut. He used the lash and the branding iron. Although eight men died during the questioning, and many more were blinded and maimed, he learned little. Then he started on the women. Bilto's youngest wife was the mother of twins, a girl and a boy aged four. When she resisted Onka's questions, he forced her to watch while he decapitated her son. Then he threw the boy's severed head at her feet, and picked up his sister by a handful of her curls. He dangled her screaming and wriggling before her mother's face. 'You know that I will not stop with just one of your brats,' he told the woman and pricked the little girl's cheek with his dagger. She shrieked afresh with pain, and the mother broke down. She told Onka everything she knew, and that was a great deal.

Onka ordered his men to drive all the villagers, including Bilto, his wife and their surviving daughter, into the thatched council hut. They barred the doors and windows, then set fire to the thatch. While the screams were still ringing from the burning building, Onka mounted and rode like a fury for the citadel to report to the oligarchs.

Two of the villagers had been hunting in the hills. From afar they witnessed the massacre and went to warn Tinat and Meren that they had been betrayed. They ran all the way to where the band was hiding, a distance of almost twenty leagues.

Tinat listened to what the two men told him, and did not

hesitate. 'We cannot wait for the harvest moon. We must march at once.'

'Taita!' Fenn cried out, in agony of spirit. 'You promised to wait for him.'

'You know that I cannot,' Tinat replied. 'Even Colonel Cambyses must agree that I dare not do so.'

Reluctantly Meren nodded. 'Colonel Tinat is right. He cannot wait. He must take the people and fly. Taita himself wanted it.'

'I will not go with you,' Fenn cried out. 'I will wait until Taita comes.'

'I will stay too,' Meren told her, 'but the others must leave at once.'

Sidudu reached for Fenn's hand. 'You and Meren are my friends. I will not go.'

'You are brave girls,' said Tinat, 'but will you go again to the Temple of Love and bring out our young women?'

'Of course!' Fenn exclaimed.

'How many men will you need to go with you?' asked Tinat.

'Ten will suffice,' Meren told him. 'We will also need spare horses for the temple girls. We will bring them to you at the first river crossing on the road to Kitangule. Then we will come back to wait for Taita.'

They rode for most of the night. Fenn and Sidudu led, but Meren followed close behind on Windsmoke. In the early light of dawn, before sunrise, they breasted the top of the hills and looked down on the Temple of Love, nestled in the valley below.

'What is the morning routine in the temple?' Fenn asked.

'Before sunrise the priestesses take the girls to the temple to pray to the goddess. After that they go to the refectory for breakfast.'

'So they should be in the temple now?' Meren asked.

'Almost certainly,' Sidudu affirmed.

'What of the trogs?'

'I am not sure, but I think they will be patrolling the temple grounds and the woods.'

'Are any of the priestesses kind to the girls? Are there any good women among them?'

'None!' said Sidudu bitterly. 'They are all cruel and merciless. They treat us like caged animals. They force us to submit to the men who come, and some of the priestesses use us for their own foul pleasures.'

Fenn looked across at Meren. 'What shall we do with them?'

'We kill any who get in our way.'

They drew their swords and rode down in a tight group, making no attempt to conceal their approach. The trogs were nowhere to be seen, and Sidudu led them directly to the temple, which stood detached from the main building. They raced towards it and pulled up the horses in front of the wooden doors. Meren jumped down and tried the latch, but it was barred from the inside.

'On me!' he shouted to the men who followed him, and they formed up in phalanx. At his next order they lifted their shields and charged the door, which burst open. The girls were huddled on the floor of the nave with four black-robed priestesses standing guard. One was a tall, middle-aged woman with a hard, pockmarked face. She lifted the golden talisman she held in her right hand and pointed it at Meren.

'Beware!' Sidudu shouted. 'That is Nongai and she is a powerful sorceress. She can blast you with her magic.'

Fenn already had an arrow nocked to her bow and did not hesitate. She drew and released it in a single fluid movement. The arrow hummed down the length of the nave and struck Nongai in the centre of her chest. The talisman spun out of her hand and she crumpled on to the stone floor. The other three priestesses scattered like a flock of crows. Fenn shot two more arrows and brought down all but the last, who reached the small door behind the altar. As she wrenched it open

Sidudu shot an arrow between her shoulder-blades. The woman slid down the wall leaving a trail of blood on the stonework. Most of the temple maidens were screaming. The others had pulled their chitons over their heads and were cowering in a terrified group.

'Speak to them, Sidudu,' Meren ordered. 'Quieten them.'

Sidudu ran to the girls, and pulled some to their feet.

'It's I, Sidudu. You have nothing to fear. These are good men, and they have come to save you.' She saw Jinga among them. 'Help me, Jinga! Help me bring them to their senses!'

'Take them out to the horses, and get them mounted,' Meren told Fenn. 'We can expect an attack from the trogs at any moment.'

They dragged the girls out through the doorway. Some were still weeping and wailing and had to be thrown up bodily on to the saddles. Meren was ruthless with them, and Fenn slapped one across the face as she shouted at her: 'Get up, you foolish creature, or we will leave you to the trogs.'

At last they were all mounted, and Meren shouted, 'Forward at the gallop!' and touched Windsmoke's flanks with his heels. He had two girls up behind him, clinging to him and each other. Nakonto and Imbali hung on Fenn's stirrup ropes and she carried them along with her. Sidudu had Jinga behind her and one of the other girls seated in front. All the other horses carried at least three girls. Heavily laden, they galloped in a tight group back across the temple lawns, heading for the hills and the road to Kitangule.

As they entered the track through the forest, the trogs were waiting for them. Five of the huge apes had climbed into the trees and they dropped out of the branches on to the horses as they passed below. At the same time other apes came bellowing and roaring out of the undergrowth. They leapt up at the riders or snapped with their powerful jaws at the legs of the horses.

Nakonto had a short stabbing spear in his right hand and killed three of the brutes with as many quick blows. Imbali's axe hissed and hummed through the air as she cut down two more. Meren and Hilto hacked and thrust with their swords, and the troopers who followed spurred their horses into the fight. But the trogs were fearless and single-minded and the fight was ferocious. Even when they were gravely wounded or dying the apes tried to drag themselves back into the fray. Two set upon Windsmoke and tried to savage her hindquarters. The grey mare aimed two mighty kicks. The first crushed the skull of one and the second caught the other under the jaw and snapped its neck cleanly.

One of the temple maidens was dragged down from behind Hilto's saddle and her throat was ripped out by a single bite before Hilto could smash in the brute's skull. By the time Nakonto had speared the last trog many of the horses had been bitten: one had been so gravely savaged that Imbali had to despatch it with an axe stroke through the crest of its skull.

They formed up again, rode out of the valley, and when they reached the fork in the track they turned eastwards towards the mountains and the Kitangule Gap. They rode through the night, and early the next morning they saw a dustcloud rising above the plain ahead of them. Before noon they had caught up with the tail of a long dense column of refugees. Tinat was riding with the rearguard, and as soon as he saw them coming he galloped back to meet them. 'Well met, Colonel Cambyses!' he shouted. 'I see you have saved our girls.'

'Those who have survived,' Meren agreed, 'but they have had a hard time of it, and are near the end of their tether.'

'We will find places for them on the wagons,' Tinat said. 'But what of you and your party? Will you come out of Jarri with us, or are you determined to go back to find the old magus?'

'You already know what our answer must be, Colonel Tinat,' Fenn replied, before Meren could speak.

'Then I must bid you farewell. Thank you for your courage and for what you have done for us. I fear we might never meet again, but your friendship has done me great honour.'

'Colonel Tinat, sir, you are the eternal optimist.' Fenn

smiled at him. 'I warrant you shall not be rid of us that easily.' She pushed Whirlwind up beside his mount and planted a kiss on his whiskery cheek. 'When we meet again in Egypt I shall kiss the other,' she told him, and turned Whirlwind back, leaving Tinat staring after her in pleasurable confusion.

They were reduced to a tiny band now, only three women and three men. For once Nakonto and Imbali had chosen to ride rather than run, and each led a spare horse.

'Where are we going?' Fenn asked Meren, as she rode beside him.

'As close to the mountains as is safe,' Meren answered. 'When Taita comes we must be able to join him swiftly.' He turned to Sidudu, who rode at his other side. 'Do you know of a place near to the mountain where we can hide?'

She thought for only a moment. 'Yes,' she replied. 'There is a valley where I used to go with my father to collect mushrooms when they came into season. We camped in a cave that few know of.'

Soon the shining white peaks of the three volcanoes rose above the western horizon. They skirted round the village of Mutangi, and looked down on the burnt-out ruins from the low hills where they had hunted the wild hog. The smell of ashes and charred bodies wafted up to them. No one said much as they turned away and went on westwards towards the mountains.

The valley to which Sidudu took them was tucked away in the foothills. It was so well concealed by trees and the folds of the land that it was not visible until they were looking down into it. There was good grazing for the horses and a tiny spring that supplied sufficient water for their needs. The cave was dry and warm. Sidudu's family had left a pair of battered old cooking pots and other utensils in a crevice at the back, with a large pile of firewood. The women cooked the evening meal, and they all gathered round the fire to eat.

'We will be comfortable enough here,' Fenn said, 'but how far are we from the citadel and the road that leads up to the Cloud Gardens?'

'Six or seven leagues to the north,' Sidudu answered.

'Good!' said Meren, through a mouthful of venison stew. 'Far enough to be unobtrusive but close enough to reach Taita swiftly when he comes down.'

'I am pleased that you said *when* and not *if*,' Fenn observed quietly.

There was silence for a while, except for the clinking of spoons in the copper bowls.

'How will we know when he comes?' Sidudu asked. 'Will we have to keep watch for him on the road?' They all looked at Fenn.

'There will be no need for that,' Fenn replied. 'I will know when he comes. He will warn me.'

They had been continually on the move, riding and fighting, for many months. In all that time this was their first chance for a full night's sleep, broken only by their turns on sentry duty. Fenn and Sidudu took the midnight watch and when the great cross of stars in the south dipped towards the horizon they stumbled half asleep into the cave to wake Nakonto and Imbali for the dog watch. Then they fell on to their sleeping mats and dropped into oblivion.

Before dawn the next morning Fenn shook Meren awake. He started up so violently that he woke the others – and when he saw the tears on Fenn's cheeks he reached for his sword. 'What is it, Fenn? What is amiss?'

'Nothing!' Fenn cried. Now he looked properly at her face, and realized she was weeping for joy. 'Everything is perfect. Taita is alive. He came to me in the night.'

'Did you see him?' Meren seized her arm and shook her in agitation. 'Where is he now? Where has he gone?'

'He came to overlook me while I was asleep. When I awoke

he showed me his spirit sign and told me, *I will return to you soon, very soon.*'

Sidudu leapt up from her mat and embraced Fenn. 'Oh, I am so happy for you, and for the rest of us.'

'Now everything will be all right,' Fenn said. 'Taita is coming back and we will be safe.'

'I have waited through the aeons for you to come to me,' said Eos, and although he knew that she embodied the great Lie, Taita could not help but believe her. She turned and walked back into the mouth of the grotto. Taita did not try to resist. He knew that he could do nothing but follow her. Despite all the defences he had raised against her enchantments, there was nothing he wanted to do more at that moment than follow wherever she might lead.

Beyond the entrance the tunnel narrowed until the lichen-covered rock brushed his shoulders. The spring water was icy as it burbled over his feet and splashed the hem of his tunic. Eos glided ahead. Under the black silk her hips moved with the undulating motion of a swaying cobra. She left the stream and went up a narrow stone ramp. At the top the tunnel widened and became a roomy passageway. The walls were covered with lapis-lazuli tiles carved in bas-relief, depicting human forms, and beasts both real and fabulous. The floor was inlaid with tiger's eye, and the roof with rose quartz. Large rock crystals the size of a man's head were set on brackets on the wall. As Eos approached each in turn they emitted a mysterious orange glow that illuminated the passage ahead. As they moved on, the crystals faded into darkness. Once or twice Taita glimpsed the shaggy black shapes of apes as they moved away into the shadows and disappeared. Silently Eos's small bare feet flitted over the golden tiles. They fascinated him, and he found it difficult to take his eyes off them. As she moved on she left a delicate perfume on the air. He savoured it with intense pleasure and recognized it as the scent of sun lilies.

At last they reached a commodious chamber of elegant proportions. Here the walls were of green malachite. Shafts in the high ceiling must have reached up to the earth's surface for the sunlight spilled down through them and was reflected from the walls in a glowing emerald effusion. The furniture of the room was of carved ivory, and the central pieces were two low couches. Eos went to one and seated herself, folding her legs under her and spreading her cloak so that even her feet were concealed. She gestured to the couch facing her. 'Please be at your ease. You are my honoured and beloved guest, Taita,' she said, in the Tenmass.

He went to the couch and sat opposite her. It was covered with an embroidered silk mattress.

'I am Eos,' she said.

'Why did you call me "beloved"? This is our first meeting. You do not know me at all.'

'Ah, Taita, I know you as well as you know yourself. Perhaps even better.'

Her laughter was sweeter on his ears than any music he had ever listened to. He tried to close his mind to it. 'Even though your words defy reason, somehow I cannot doubt them. I accept that you know me, but I know nothing of you, except your name,' he replied.

'Taita, we must be honest with each other. I will speak only the truth to you. You must do the same for me. Your last statement was a lie. You know much about me, and you have formed opinions that are, alas, mostly erroneous. It is my purpose to enlighten you, and to correct your misconceptions.'

'Tell me where I have erred.'

'You believe I am your enemy.'

Taita remained silent.

'I am your friend,' Eos went on. 'The dearest and sweetest friend you will ever have.'

Taita inclined his head gravely, but again made no reply.

He found he wanted desperately to believe her. It took all his determination to keep his shield high.

After a beat, Eos continued, 'You imagine that I will lie to you, that I have already lied to you as you have lied to me,' she said.

He was relieved that he threw no aura for her to read: his emotions were seething.

'I have spoken only the truth to you. The images I showed you in the grotto were the truth. There was no element of deceit in them,' she told him.

'They were forceful images,' he said, his tone neutral and noncommittal.

'They were all true. All I have promised is in my power to give to you.'

'Why of all mankind have you chosen me?'

'All mankind?' she exclaimed, with scorn. 'All mankind is no more important to me than the individual termites in a colony. They are creatures of instinct, not of reason or wisdom, for they do not live long enough to acquire those virtues.'

'I have known wise men of learning, compassion and humanity,' he contradicted her.

'You make that judgement from the observations of your own short existence,' she said.

'I have lived long,' he said.

'But you will not live much longer,' she told him. 'Your time is nearly done.'

'You are direct, Eos.'

'As I have already promised, I will speak only the truth to you. The human body is an imperfect vehicle and life is ephemeral. A man lives too short a span to acquire true wisdom and understanding. By human standards you are a Long Liver, one hundred and fifty-six years by my reckoning. To me, that is not much longer than a butterfly lives, or the blooming of a night-flowering cactus, born at dusk and perishing before dawn. The physical vehicle in which your spirit soul rides will soon fail you.' Suddenly she thrust her right

476

hand from beneath the black silk cloak and made a sign of benediction.

If her feet were lovely, her hand was exquisite. His breathing checked and he felt the hair on his forearms rise as he watched its graceful gestures.

'But for you it need not be so,' Eos said softly.

'You have not answered my question, Eos. Why me?'

'In the short time that you have lived you have achieved much. If I extend your life eternally you will become a giant of intellect.'

'That does not explain all of it. I am old and ugly.'

'I have already renewed part of your body,' she pointed out. He laughed bitterly. 'So, now I am an ugly old man with a young and beautiful cock.'

She laughed with him, that thrilling sound. 'So elegantly phrased.' She drew her hand back under the cloak, leaving him bereft. Then she went on, 'In the grotto I showed you an image of yourself as a young man. You were beautiful, and you can be again.'

'You can have any beautiful young man you choose. I do not doubt that you have already done so,' he challenged.

She answered at once, fairly and honestly: 'Ten thousand times or more, but despite their beauty they were ants.'

'Will I be any different?'

'Yes, Taita – yes.'

'In what way?'

'Your mind,' she said. 'Carnal passion alone soon palls. A superlative intellect is endlessly alluring. A great mind growing stronger with time in a fine body eternally youthful: these are godlike attributes. Taita, you are the perfect companion and mate I have longed for down the ages.'

Hour after hour they discoursed. Although he knew that her genius was cold and malevolent, it was still fascinating and seductive. He felt charged with energy, physical and intellectual. Eventually, to his annoyance, he felt the need to absent himself, but before he could voice it she told him, 'There are quarters set aside for you. Pass through that doorway at your right hand and follow the passage to the end.'

The room to which she had directed him was large and imposing, but he hardly noticed his surroundings for his mind was alight. He felt no fatigue. In a cubicle he found an ornately carved stool with a latrine bucket set beneath it and relieved himself. In the corner, scented warm water ran from a spout into a basin of rock crystal. As soon as he had washed he hurried back to the green chamber, hoping that Eos would still be there. The sunlight no longer glowed through the shafts in the roof. Night had fallen but the rock crystals on the walls glowed with a warm light. Eos sat as he had last seen her, and as he settled himself opposite her, she said, 'There is food and drink for you.' With that lovely hand she indicated the ivory table beside him. During his absence silver dishes and a chalice had been set upon it. He felt no hunger, but the fruit and sherbet looked delicious. He ate and drank sparingly, then returned eagerly to their conversation: 'You speak easily of eternal life?'

'The dream of all men, from pharaohs to serfs,' she agreed. 'They long for eternal life in an imagined paradise. Even the old people who lived before I was born painted images of that dream on the walls of their caves.'

'Is it possible to fulfil it?' Taita asked.

'I sit before you as living proof that it is.'

'How old are you, Eos?'

'I was already old when I watched Pharaoh Cheops raise the great pyramid at Giza.'

'How is this possible?'

'Have you heard of the Font?' she asked.

'It is a myth that has come down to us from antiquity,' he replied.

'It is no myth, Taita. The Font exists.'

'What is it? Where is it?'

'It is the Blue River of all life, the essential force that drives our universe.'

'Is it truly a river or a fountain? And why "Blue"? Can you describe it for me?'

'There are no words, not even in the Tenmass, that adequately describe its might and beauty. When we have become one, I will take you to it. We will bathe side by side in the Blue, and you shall come forth in all the splendour of youth.'

'Where is it? Is it in the sky or in the earth?'

'It moves from one place to another. As the seas shift and the mountains rise and fall, so the Font moves with them.'

'Where is it now?'

'Not far from where we sit,' said Eos, 'but be patient. In time I will lead you to it.'

She lied. Of course she lied. She was the Lie. Even if the Font existed, he knew she would lead no other person to it, but still the false promise intrigued him.

'I see you doubt me still,' Eos said softly. 'To demonstrate my utmost good faith, I will allow you to take another person with you to the Font, to share in its blessing. Someone whom you count dear. Is there such a person?'

Fenn! Instantly he cloaked the thought so that even she could not read it. Eos had set a trap, and he had almost blundered into it. 'There is no such person,' he answered.

'Once when I overlooked you, you sat beside a pool in the wilderness. I saw a child with you, a pretty child with pale hair.'

'Ah, yes,' he agreed. 'I forget even her name, for she was one of those you call termites. She was a companion of the moment only.'

'You do not wish to take her with you to the Font?'

'There is no reason why I should.' Eos was silent, but he could feel the softest touch on his temples, like that of teasing fairy fingers. He knew that Eos was unconvinced by what he had said and was trying to enter his head, trying to reach into his mind and steal his thoughts. With a psychic effort he blocked her entrance, and immediately she withdrew.

'You are tired, Taita. You must sleep awhile.'

'I am not tired in the least,' he replied, and it was true: he felt vital and fresh.

'We have so much to discuss that we are like runners at the start of a long race. We must pace ourselves. After all, we are destined to become companions for all eternity. There is no need to hasten. Time is our plaything, not our adversary.' Eos rose from her couch and, without another word, slipped through a doorway in the back wall that he had not noticed before.

Although he had felt no fatigue, when he stretched out on the padded silken sleeping mat in his chamber Taita fell into deep sleep. He woke to find a shaft of sunlight playing down through the opening in the ceiling. He felt wonderfully alive.

His soiled clothing had disappeared and a fresh tunic had been laid out for him with a new pair of sandals beside his leather cloak. A meal had been placed on the ivory table near his head. He bathed, ate and dressed. The tunic Eos had provided was of a delicate material that caressed his skin, while the sandals were worked from the skin of a new-born goat and embossed with gold leaf. They fitted perfectly.

He returned to Eos's green room to find it deserted. Only her perfume lingered. He crossed to the doorway through which she had gone the previous night. The long passage beyond led him out into the sunlight. Once his eyes had adjusted he found that he was in another volcanic crater, not as large as the Cloud Gardens but more lovely by far. Yet he had no eyes for the luxuriant forests and orchards that covered the floor of the crater in profusion: directly in front of him spread a green lawn with a small marble pavilion above a pool in the middle, a rill of bright water cascading into it. Although the stream was clear, the surface of the pool was black and shiny as polished jet.

Eos sat on the marble bench in the pavilion. Her head was bare, but she faced away from him so that only her hair was visible. He moved quietly towards her, hoping to come on her unawares and catch a glimpse of her face. Her hair rippled down to her waist. It was as dark as the water of the pool, but ineffably more lustrous. As he drew closer to her he saw that the soft reflections of the sunlight glowed in the tresses like the glint of precious rubies. He longed to touch it, but as he reached out, Eos lifted the veil over her head, covering herself, denying him even the briefest glimpse of her face. Then she turned to him. 'Take your place beside me, for that is where you belong.'

They sat in silence for a while. Taita was angry and frustrated: he longed to see her face. She seemed to sense his mood and laid her hand on his arm. Her touch thrilled him, but he steeled himself and asked, 'We have spoken much of physical appearance, Eos. Do you suffer from some blemish? Is that why you hide yourself behind the veil? Are you ashamed of the way you look?'

He had tried to provoke her as she had him. But her voice was sweet and calm as she replied: 'I am the most beautiful person, man or woman, who has ever walked the earth.'

'Then why do you hide that beauty?'

'Because it can blind the eyes and unhinge the minds of men who look upon it.'

'Must I take your boast on trust?'

'It is no boast, Taita. It is the truth.'

'Will you never reveal this beauty to me?'

'You will look upon my beauty when you are ready to do so, when you realize the consequences and are prepared to accept them.' Her hand still lay upon his arm. 'Do you not see how my lightest touch disturbs you? I can feel the beating of your heart through the tips of my fingers.' She withdrew her hand, leaving his senses in turmoil. It took him a while to bring them under control. 'Let us speak of other matters. There are many questions you have for me, and I have given you my undertaking to answer them truthfully,' she said.

Taita's voice sounded a little breathless as he took up her invitation. 'You have placed barriers across the headwaters of the Nile. What was your purpose in doing so?'

'My reasons were twofold. First, it was an invitation to you to come to me. You were unable to resist it, and now you sit beside me.'

He thought on it deeply, then asked, 'What was the other reason?'

'I was preparing a gift for you.'

'A gift?' he exclaimed.

'A betrothal gift. Once we are joined in spirit and flesh, I will give to you the Two Kingdoms of Egypt.'

'Only after you have destroyed them? What perverse and savage gift is this?'

'When you wear the double crown and we sit side by side on the throne of Egypt, I will restore the Nile and its waters to our kingdom . . . the first of our many kingdoms.'

'In the meantime it is only the termites of humanity who suffer?' Taita asked.

'Already you begin to think and act like the lord of all creation, whom you will soon become. I showed it to you in the images beside the grotto in the Cloud Gardens. Dominion over all the nations, eternal life, youth and beauty, and the wisdom and learning of the ages, which is the diamond mountain.'

'The greatest prize of all,' Taita said. 'I call it the Truth.'

'It shall be yours.'

'I still doubt that you offer me this without demanding some commensurate price from me.'

'Oh, I have already spoken of that. In return for what I offer, I demand your eternal love and devotion.'

'You have existed so long without a companion, why do you wish one now?'

'I have been overtaken by the tedium of eternity, a staleness of spirit and the aching boredom of lacking someone with whom to share these wonders.'

'That is all the price you ask of me? I have had a glimpse of your mighty intellect. If your beauty matches your mind, it is a trivial price to pay.' Her lies were disguised by truths. He pretended to believe them. They were like the commanders of two armies arrayed against each other. This was the skirmishing and manoeuvring that preceded the battle. He was afraid, not so much for himself as for Egypt and Fenn, the two things dearest to him, both in deadly danger.

They spent the days that followed beside the black pool and most of the nights in Eos's green chamber. Gradually she exposed more of her physical form to him while keeping her spirit soul concealed. Her discourse grew daily more absorbing. Occasionally she would lean forward to pick up a morsel of fruit from the silver tray and artlessly let her sleeve fall back to reveal her forearm. Or she would shift position on her ivory couch and let the skirt of her black robe expose a knee. The shape of her calf was sublime. He should have become conditioned to the perfection of her limbs, but he had not. He dreaded the moment when her entire body would be revealed. He doubted his ability to resist its enchantment.

The days and nights sped by with startling rapidity. The carnal and astral tensions built up between them until they were almost unbearable. She touched him, taking his hand when she wanted to emphasize a point. Once she clasped it to her bosom and he had to exert all of his self-control not to groan at the pain in his groin as he felt the warm elasticity of her breast.

Her perfume never changed: it was always the scent of sun lilies. However, she changed her raiment morning and evening. Always it was long and voluminous, barely hinting at the swells and curves of her body beneath the delicate fabrics. Sometimes she was serene, at other times restless: then she circled his couch with the graceful menace of a man-eating tigress. Once she knelt in front of him and brazenly slipped her hand up his thigh under his tunic while continuing her erudite discourse, her fingers stopping just short of his manhood and withdrawing as she felt it swell. At other times she reverted to the black robes and kept herself completely hidden, not allowing even her toes to show.

One morning they were in her green chamber and Eos was wearing a robe of diaphanous white silk. She had never worn white before. In the midst of their conversation she rose unexpectedly to her small bare feet and came to stand before him. The white veil she was wearing floated about her like a cloud. The pink and ivory tones of her skin shone through the material as the light played on her. Seen through the silk, her image was ethereal. Her moon-pale belly was as sleek as that of a hunting greyhound, with a mysterious triangular shadow at its base. Her breasts were indefinite creamy orbs, tipped with strawberry aureoles.

'Do you truly wish me to unveil myself, my lord?' she asked.

He was so taken by surprise that he could not reply at once. Eventually he said, 'It seems that I have waited all my life for the moment that you do so.'

'I want you to have all of me. I will hold nothing back from you. I set no conditions on you. I expect nothing from you in return but your love.' She threw back the silken sleeves and held up her bare arms. They were slim, rounded and firm. She took the hem of her veil between those tapering fingers and began to lift it from her face. She paused at her chin. Her neck was long and graceful.

'Be very sure that you wish to look upon my face. I have warned you what the consequences may be. My beauty has enslaved all before you who have looked upon it. Will you be able to resist it?'

'Even if it destroys me I must do so,' he whispered. He knew that this was the fateful moment when they joined battle.

'So be it,' she said, and raised her veil with infinitely tantalizing deliberation. Her chin was rounded and dimpled. Her lips were full and curved, charged with red blood to the colour of ripe cherries. She licked her lips. Her tongue was tapered and it curled at the tip like that of a yawning kitten.

It left a glistening trace of saliva on her lips, then drew back between small, lustrous teeth. Her nose was narrow and straight but flared slightly at the tip. Her cheekbones were set high, and her forehead was wide and deep. Her arched brows formed a perfect frame for her eyes, which were dark jewels that seemed to dispel the shadows with their glory. They looked deep into Taita's soul. Each separate part of her countenance was perfect. Taken as a whole, it was incomparably lovely.

'Do I please you, my lord?' she asked, as she swirled the veil off her head and let it float down to the green malachite tiles. Her hair tumbled over her shoulders in a sable cascade shot through with ruby lights. It hung to her waist, springing and curling, vibrant with life of its own.

'You do not answer me,' she said. 'Do I displease you?'

'My mind cannot encompass your beauty,' he said, in a voice that shook. 'There are no words that can describe even a tenth part of it. Having looked upon it, I understand how it may burn a man to ash as though he were caught up in a raging forest fire. It terrifies me, but I am unable to resist it.'

She glided closer to him, and the perfume of sun lilies enveloped him. She stood over him until he was forced to turn his face up to hers. She stooped slowly and placed her lips on his, warm and soft. Her curling kitten tongue slipped deep into his mouth. For a fleeting moment it twined round his own, and then it was gone, but the taste of her filled his mouth like the juice of some wondrous fruit.

She whirled away across the malachite tiles. Her translucent robe billowed round her as she arched her back and pirouetted until the back of her head almost touched the bulge of her buttocks, her hair brushing the tiles. Her feet danced until they blurred with speed. His eyes could not follow them. Then they stopped and she stood on tiptoe, still as a statue, only her hair swinging round her.

'There is more, my lord.' Her voice took on a deep, throbbing intensity he had not heard before. 'There is much more. Or have you seen enough?'

'If I gaze upon you for a thousand years, I will never see enough.'

With a toss of her head she threw her hair off her shoulders, and stared at him with those smouldering eyes. 'You stand on the lip of the volcano,' she warned him. 'Even at this late stage it is possible for you to draw back. Once you take the plunge there will be no return. For you the universe will change for ever. The price will be high – higher than you can imagine. Are you prepared to pay it?'

'I am ready.'

She slipped off the robe over one shoulder. Its curve was perfectly harmonious with that of the long, delicate neck. She let the robe fall lower, and one breast strained to be free. She released both. Round, full and womanly, they swung against each other. She let the robe drop until it caught on the curve of her hips. Her belly was as smooth as a field of newly fallen snow. A fiery ruby glowed in the pit of her navel. She undulated her hips and the robe slipped down her slender thighs to garland her ankles.

She stepped out of it and came naked to him, with that long gliding stride. Once again she leant over him and put an arm round the back of his neck. With the other hand she cupped one of her breasts, drew his face towards her and eased the nipple into his mouth. 'Take suck, my lord,' she whispered in his ear.

As he drew on it like an infant, the nipple swelled between his lips and it began to exude a thick creamy fluid. Taita relished it, until she pushed his head away and drew it out from between his lips. 'Be not so greedy,' she admonished him. 'My body has many delights for you to savour. You must not satiate yourself too soon.'

She stepped back and ran both hands down her belly with a smoothing motion. His eyes followed them slavishly. She moved her feet apart and bent her knees, spreading her thighs. He watched her hand burrow between them, deep into the cloud of dark hair. Then she brought it out again and held up a forefinger. It was glossy with a pellucid dampness. 'See how I long for you,' she whispered huskily, as she touched the tip of her wet finger with her thumb. When she parted them, a gelatinous thread stretched between them. 'This is the true ambrosia that all men crave.' She came to him. 'Open your mouth, my lord.' She slid her finger between his lips, and the heady scent of her sex pervaded his senses. She reached down with her free hand under the hem of his tunic and took hold of his manroot. Already it was as hard as ironstone, but in her cunning fingers it stretched harder and longer still.

He looked deep into her eyes and saw in them a stark, predatory hunger that had not been there a moment before. He knew that it was not for what she held in her hand but his very soul that she lusted. Now she placed both hands upon him, lifted him to his feet and led him to the couch. She knelt before him, loosened the straps of his sandals and slipped them off his feet. She lifted her head and nuzzled him, taking him between her lips and sucking voraciously. As she stood up again she lifted his tunic over his head, then pushed him back on to the couch. She stepped over him with one leg as though she was mounting a steed, then crouched over him to guide him into her secret depths.

He uttered a deep groan as the pleasure became so intense it was transmuted into agony. She froze immobile over him. The muscles deep inside her pulsed and contracted, tightening as inexorably on him as the coils of a python round its prey. She locked him in a union so powerful that neither could break from it. Her eyes gazed into his, filled with the triumphant glare of a warrior about to make the killing stroke. 'You belong to me.' Her voice was the hiss of a serpent. 'Everything you are is mine.' No more dissembling, she had stripped off her disguise to reveal her true colours.

He felt her carnal invasion begin. It was as though a barbaric horde had besieged the citadel of his soul and was battering down the walls. He rallied all his powers to resist her, closing his gates to deny her entrance, hurling her back from the breach. The look in her eyes changed to consternation as she realized he had enticed her into an ambush.

Then her expression became murderous, and she surged back into the attack.

They struggled against each other, at first evenly matched. He moved his body to one side, and when she threw her weight across to counter him, he rolled with her off the couch. Locked together they crashed on to the malachite floor, but she was under him and bore the brunt of his weight. Just for an instant the grip of the muscles deep within her slackened at the shock. He used the lapse to drive himself further inside, trying to reach her centre. She tightened instantly, holding him out. They strained against each other silently, pitting all their forces, holding each other in precarious equilibrium.

He felt her summon her reserves and gathered his own in readiness. Then she launched herself against him in a psychic avalanche. She was forcing a breach in his defences, breaking through into the secret places of his soul. He could feel his body yielding to her. Once again, gloating triumph lit her eyes. He reached down and closed his fist over the Periapt of Lostris that still hung at his throat. In his mind he conjugated the word of power: Mensaar! His manroot leapt with the impulse, and she cried out incoherently as she felt it. 'Kydash! Ncube!' he shouted. A bolt of psychic power flashed from the Periapt. Like a lightning strike, it flung Eos from the breach in his soul. Once again they held each other at bay, their strength evenly matched. Locked in each other's flesh they lay as still as figures carved in ivory.

The oil in the lamps burnt low, the flames guttered and went out. The only light in the chamber came through the shaft high in the roof above. That light faded as the sun set behind the mountains, and left them in darkness to continue the battle. All through the night they were braced against each other in the hellish coupling, his manroot buried inside her, her muscles clamped on it remorselessly, no longer organs of procreation and pleasure but deadly weapons.

When the dawn light seeped through the shaft in the roof, it found them still locked together. As the light strengthened, he could see into her eyes. In their depths he discerned the first flutter of panic, like the wings of a trapped bird beating against the bars of its cage. She tried to shutter them from him, but he held her eyes as she held his sex. Both were far past the borders of exhaustion. There was nothing left in either but the will to hold out. She had locked her long legs round his hips, and her arms round his back. He clasped her buttocks in one hand, pulling them on to him. His right hand, still clutching the Periapt of Lostris, was clenched at the small of her back. Very carefully, so that he did not alert her, he eased open the lid of the locket with his thumbnail and the chip of red stone fell into his palm.

He pressed the stone against her spine, and felt it grow hot as it turned its power back on to her. She screamed, a long despairing wail, and struggled weakly, pumping her sex like bellows in a desperate effort to expel him. He timed his thrusts to her spasms. Each time she relaxed he drove in deeper. He reached the final barrier and, with one last mighty effort, pierced it.

She collapsed under him, moaning and gibbering. He covered her mouth with his own and thrust his tongue down her throat, stifling her cries. He rampaged through the inner sanctum of her being, tearing open the coffers in which her knowledge and power were locked away and draining the contents. As he did so, his own strength flooded back, multiplied a hundredfold by what he took from her.

He stared into her unspeakably lovely face, into those magnificent eyes, and saw them change. Her mouth gaped, drooling silver ropes of saliva. Her eyes turned opaque and dull as pebbles. Like a lump of wax held close to a flame, her nose broadened and coarsened. Her glowing skin faded to sallow yellow, became desiccated and as rough as the scaly hide of a reptile. It puckered into deep creases at the corners of her lips and eyes. The vibrant curls fell out of her hair, leaving it straight and flecked with dry skin from her scalp.

Taita was still buried inside her, drawing in the torrent of astral and psychic substance that flowed from her, like the waters of a burst dam. There was such a vast quantity that the flood continued hour after hour. The ray of sunlight from the shaft in the ceiling had crept across the malachite tiles and reached the centre mark of noon before Taita felt the flow weaken and shrivel. At last it dried up completely. He had taken all there was. Eos was drained and empty.

Taita allowed his manroot to deflate and slither out of her. He rolled off her and stood up. His sex was swollen, bruised and rubbed raw in places. He suppressed the pain and went to the silver jug of water on the table beside her couch. He drank deeply, then sat on the edge of her couch, watching her as she lay on the floor.

She breathed harshly through her open mouth. Her eyes were fixed in a blind stare on the roof of the chamber as her body began to swell. Like a corpse left in the sun, her belly ballooned as though filling with the gases of decay. The slim arms and legs bloated. The flesh puffed, soft and shapeless as a bladder of butter. Taita watched as her flesh billowed until her limbs disappeared in the pasty white folds. Only her head remained, tiny in comparison with the rest of her.

Gradually her swollen body filled half of the chamber. Taita jumped off the couch and backed against the wall to give her space to expand. She had taken on the shape of a queen termite lying in her royal cell in the centre of a mound. She was trapped within her own flesh, able to move only her head, the rest of her pinned down by her own grossness. She would never be able to escape from this cavern. Even if the trogs returned to help her, they could never drag her through the narrow rock passages and tunnels into the open air.

A dreadful stench permeated the cavern. A thick, oily fluid oozed from the pores of Eos's skin and ran down her carcass, each drop pale green with the sheen of putrescence. The nauseating odour clogged Taita's throat and smothered his lungs. It was the smell of rotting corpses: the victims of her murderous appetites, the unborn babes she had torn from the womb and the young mothers who had carried them; the bodies of those who had perished in the famines, droughts and plagues she had bred and loosed upon the nations; the warriors who had died in the wars she had incited and commanded; the innocents she had condemned to the gallows and the garotte; the slaves who had perished in her quarries and mines. It was compounded by the fetor of an immense evil that issued from her mouth with every rasping breath she exhaled. Even Taita's control of his senses wavered under its miasma. Keeping as far from her as the confines of the cavern would allow, he moved along the wall towards the mouth of the tunnel.

An ominous sound brought him up short. It was as though a gigantic porcupine was rattling its quills in warning. Eos's grotesque head rolled towards him and her eyes focused upon his face. Her features were ravaged so no trace of her beauty remained. Her eyes were deep, dark pits. Her lips had retracted to expose her teeth, like those of a skull. Her features were ineffably ugly, the true mirror of her twisted soul. She spoke in a croak, harsh as the cawing of carrion crows: 'I shall persist,' she said.

He reeled back at the rankness of her breath, then braced himself and looked steadily into her eyes: 'The Lie will always persist, but so will the Truth. There will never be an end to the struggle,' he replied.

She closed her eyes and spoke no more. Only her breathing rumbled in her throat.

Taita found his cloak, then slipped through the green chamber into the passage that led to the outer air. As he came out into her secret garden, the sunlight was striking the top of the cliff but it left the depths of the crater in shadow. He looked around carefully for any evidence of Eos's trogs, searching for their auras, but there was none. He knew that, with her destruction, they had been deprived of a guiding intelligence. They had crept mindlessly into the tunnels and passages of the mountain to die.

The air was cold and clean. He breathed it deeply with relief, washing the stench of Eos from his lungs as he went to the pavilion beside the black pool. He took his seat on the bench where he had sat with her when she was still young and beautiful. He pulled the leather cloak round his shoulders. He expected to find himself exhausted and wasted by his ordeal but elation filled his being. He felt strong and indefatigable.

At first this bewildered him, until he understood that he was charged with the power and energy he had taken from the witch. His mind soared and expanded as he began to explore the mountainous accumulations of knowledge and experience that now filled him. He could look back over the millennium that Eos had existed, back to the beginning time. Every detail was fresh. He was able to fathom her lusts and desires as though they were his own. He was amazed by the depths of her cruelty and depravity. He had not understood the nature of true and utter evil until now when it had been clearly revealed to him. There was so much to learn from her that he knew it would take him a natural lifetime to examine even a small part of it.

The knowledge was seductive in a vile and loathsome way, and he knew at once that he must condition himself to resist its addictive fascination, lest it corrupt him too. There was dire danger that the grasp of so much evil might turn him into a monster of her like. He was humbled by the thought that the cognizance he had wrested from the witch, added to his own arsenal, had made him now the most powerful man on earth.

He rallied his powers and began to lock away the vast body of foul matter in the deep warehouses of his memory, so that he would not be haunted and sullied by it but could retrieve any part as he required it.

In addition to the evil, he had now in his possession an equal or greater quantity of wholesome learning which might be infinitely beneficial to himself and humanity. He had taken from her the keys to the natural mysteries of ocean, earth and heaven; of life and death; of destruction and regeneration. All this he held in the forefront of his mind where he could explore and master it.

The sun had set and night had passed before he had assembled and rearranged all this in his mind. Only then was he conscious of his creature needs: he had not eaten for days, and although he had drunk, he was thirsty. He now knew the layout of the witch's lair as if he had lived in it for as long as she had. He left the crater and went back into the rocky warren, finding his way unerringly into the storerooms, pantries and kitchens from which the trogs had served Eos. He ate sparingly of the best fruits and cheeses and drank a cup of wine. Then, refreshed, he returned to the pavilion. Now his foremost concern was to make contact with Fenn.

He composed himself and made his first cast across the ether, calling to her clearly and openly. At once he realized he had underestimated the power of the witch. His efforts to reach Fenn were blocked and turned back by some residual force that emanated from her. Even in her enfeebled condition, she had managed to spin around herself and her warren a protective shield. He abandoned the effort, and devoted himself to finding a means of escape from the mountains. He searched the memory of Eos and he made discoveries that staggered him, taxing his powers of belief to the utmost.

He left the pavilion again, and went back into the rock tunnel that led to Eos's green chamber. Immediately the stench of corruption filled his nostrils. If anything, it had become even stronger and more noisome. He covered his nose and mouth with the hem of his tunic, and choked back waves of nausea. Eos's body almost entirely filled the cavern now, bloated with its own putrid gas. Taita saw that she was in the midst of a metamorphosis from human to insect. The green fluid that oozed from her pores and coated her body was hardening into a glistening shell. She was sealing herself into a cocoon. Only her head was still exposed. The ruined tresses of her hair had fallen out and littered the green tiles. Her eyes were closed. Her hoarse breathing made the foul air tremble. She had thrown herself into a profound hibernation, a suspended form of life that he knew could last indefinitely.

Is there some way in which I can destroy her as she lies

helpless? he wondered, and searched his newly acquired knowledge for the means to do so. There is none, he concluded. She is not immortal, but she was created in the flames of the volcano and she can perish only in those flames. Aloud he said, 'Hail and farewell, Eos! May you slumber for ten thousand years that the earth will be, for a little space, rid of you.' He stooped and picked up one of the coils of her hair. He twisted it into a thick braid, then placed it carefully in the pouch on his belt.

There was just sufficient room to allow him to pass between her and the glittering malachite wall, then reach the far end of the chamber. There he found, as he had already known he would, the hidden doorway. It was so cunningly carved into the mirror-like wall that its reflection tricked the eye. Only when he reached out his hand to touch what had seemed solid green rock did the opening become apparent. It was only just wide enough to allow him to enter.

Beyond, he found himself in a narrow passage. As he moved down it, the light faded into darkness. He went on confidently, holding one hand out in front of him until he touched the wall where the passage turned at right angles. Here he reached up into the darkness and found the stone shelf. He felt the warmth of the clay fire-pot on the back of his hand. This guided him to the rope handle of the pot, and he brought it down. There was a faint glow in the bottom, which he blew gently into flame. By its light he found a stack of rush torches. He lit one, placed the fire-pot with two extra torches in the basket that stood ready on the stone shelf, then went on along the narrow tunnel.

It was descending at a steep angle so he used the rope that was strung along the right-hand wall to steady himself and maintain his balance. At last the passage opened into a small bare chamber. The roof was so low that he had to bend almost double under it. In the centre of the floor he saw a dark opening that looked like the mouth of a well. He held the torch over it and peered down. The feeble light was swallowed by the darkness.

Taita picked up a shard of broken pottery from the floor, and dropped it into the shaft. He counted while he waited for it to strike the bottom. After fifty, there had been no sound of it hitting the rock below. The pit was bottomless. Directly in front of him a sturdy bronze hook had been driven into the roof of the cave. From this a rope of plaited leather strips dangled into the pit. The roof above him was blackened by the smoke of the torches that Eos had held aloft as she had passed this way on her innumerable visits to the cave. She had possessed the strength and agility to descend the rope with her torch between her teeth.

Taita removed his sandals and dropped them into the basket. Then he wedged his torch into a crack in the side wall, so that it would afford him a little light during his descent. He slung the handle of the basket over his shoulder, reached for the rope and swung himself out over the pit. At intervals the rope was knotted, which provided a precarious hold for his hands and bare feet. He began to clamber downwards, moving his feet first, then his hands. He knew how long and arduous the descent would be and he paced himself carefully, pausing regularly to rest and breathe deeply.

Before long his muscles were quivering and his limbs weakening. He forced himself to go on. The light of the torch he had left in the chamber above was now a mere glimmer. He climbed down and down into utter darkness but, from Eos's memory, he knew the way. The muscles in his right calf spasmed with cramp and the pain was crippling, but he closed his mind to it. His hands were numbed claws. He knew that one was bleeding from under the nails for droplets of blood fell into his upturned face. He forced his fingers to open and close on the rope.

Down he went and still down until, at last, he knew he could go no further. He hung motionless in the darkness, bathed in sweat, unable to attempt another change of grip on the swaying rope. The darkness suffocated him. He felt his hand, slippery with blood, slide as his fingers began to open.

'Mensaar!' He conjugated the words of power. 'Kydash!

Ncube!' At once his legs steadied and his grip firmed. Still he could not force his worn-out body to reach downwards for the next knot.

'Taita! My darling Taita! Answer me!' Fenn's voice was as clear and sweet in his ears as if she hung beside him in the darkness. Her soul sign, the delicate outline of the water-lily bloom, glowed before his eyes. She was with him again. He had passed beyond the point where the enfeebled witch could block their astral contact.

'Fenn!' He sent a desperate cry across the ether.

'Oh, thank the benevolent Mother Isis,' Fenn called back. 'I thought I was too late. I sense you are in desperate straits. I am joining all my forces with yours, as you taught me.'

He felt his shaking legs still and harden. He lifted his feet off the knot and, hanging on his arms, reached down with his toes. The drop beneath sucked at him as he revolved on the rope.

'Be strong, Taita. I am with you,' Fenn exhorted.

His feet found the next knot, and he slid his hands down to take another grip. He had been counting, so he knew there were still twenty knots before he reached the end of the rope.

'Go on, Taita! For both our sakes, you must go on! Without you I am nothing. You must endure,' Fenn urged.

He felt her strength come to him in warm, astral waves. 'Nineteen . . . Eighteen . . .' He counted the remaining knots as they passed through his bloody hands.

'You have the strength and the determination,' she whispered in his mind. 'I am beside you. I am part of you. Do this thing for us. For the love I have for you. You are my father and my friend. I came back for you and you alone. Don't leave me now.'

'Nine . . . Eight . . . Seven . . .' Taita counted.

'You are growing stronger,' she said softly, 'I can feel it. We will come through together.'

'Three . . . Two . . . One . . .' He counted and stretched down with one leg, groping with his toes for the rope. There was nothing under his foot but space. He had reached the end of the rope. He drew a deep breath, let go with both hands and fell with a rush that stopped his breath. Then, abruptly, he struck the bottom with both feet. His legs gave way and he sprawled, like a fledgling fallen from the nest. He lay on his belly, face down, sobbing with exhaustion and relief, too weak even to sit up.

'Are you safe, Taita? Are you still there? Do you hear me?'

'I hear you,' he answered, as he sat up. 'I am safe for the moment. Without you it would have been different. Your strength has armed me. I must go on now. Listen for my call. Surely I will need you again.'

'Remember, I love you,' she called, as her presence faded, and he was alone in the darkness once more. He fumbled in the basket and brought out the clay fire-pot. He blew the embers to life and lit a fresh torch. He held it high, and by its light examined his immediate surroundings.

He was on a narrow wooden catwalk, built against the sheer wall on his left and secured to it by rows of bronze bolts driven into holes drilled in the rock. On his other side yawned the dark void. The feeble light of the torch could not fathom the extent of it. He crept to the edge of the catwalk and looked over it. Under him stretched endless darkness and he knew that he was suspended above a chasm that reached into the very bowels of the earth, those nether regions from which Eos had sprung.

He rested a little longer. His thirst was raging, but there was nothing to drink. He quelled the longing with the force of his mind and drove the weariness from his limbs, then he took his sandals from the basket and fastened them on to his feet, which had been rubbed raw by the rope. At last he got to his feet and hobbled along the narrow catwalk. The drop on his left-hand side was unprotected by any balustrade, and the darkness beneath drew him with a hypnotic attraction that was difficult to resist. He went slowly and cautiously, placing each step with care.

He saw in his mind's eye how Eos had run lightly along this same catwalk like a child through an open meadow, and how she had swarmed up the knotted rope on her return to her warren high above, holding the flaming torch in her strong white teeth. He knew that, by contrast, he had barely the strength to negotiate the level footing beneath him.

Beneath his feet the wooden planking gave way to rough-hewn rock. He had reached a ledge in the rock face. It was barely wide enough to afford him a foothold, and slanted downwards so sharply that he had to cling to the wall to steady himself.

The ledge seemed endless. It took all his self-control to stop himself panicking. He had descended several hundred cubits down the ledge before he reached a deep fissure. He stepped through it into another tunnel. Here he was forced to rest again. He placed the torch in a slot that had been carved into the rock, the wall above it blackened by the smoke of countless other flames. His face sank into his cupped hands and he closed his eyes, breathing deeply until the racing of his heart slowed. Now the torch was guttering and smoking as it burnt out. He lit the last from the dying flame and went on down the tunnel. It was descending even more steeply than the open ledge he had just left. Finally it became a rocky staircase that spiralled on downwards. Over the centuries the steps had been worn by Eos's bare feet until they were smooth and concave.

He knew that the interior of the mountain was a honeycomb of ancient volcanic pipes and fissures. The rock was hot to the touch, heated by the bubbling lava at its heart. The air became as sulphurous and stifling as the fumes from a charcoal forge.

At last Taita reached the fork in the tunnel he had been expecting. The main chute went straight on downwards, while the lesser branch turned off at a sharp angle. Taita did not hesitate but turned into the narrower opening. The footing was rough but almost level. He followed the tunnel through several twists and turns until finally he stepped out into another cavern, lit by a ruddy furnace-like glow. Even this fluctuating light could not penetrate to the furthest reaches of the immense space. He looked down, and saw that he stood on the brink of another deep crater. Far below him boiled a lake of fiery lava. Its surface bubbled and swirled, shooting up fountains of molten rock and sparks. The heat struck his face so fiercely that he raised his hands to ward it off.

From the surface high above the burning lava sucked in gales of wind. They roared, howled and tugged at his clothing so that he staggered before he could brace himself to resist them. Before him a spur of rock stretched out across the bubbling cauldron. It sagged in the middle, like a suspended rope bridge, and was so narrow that two men could not have walked across it side by side. He tucked the skirts of his tunic under his girdle and stepped out on to it. The wind that roared through the cavern was not constant. It gusted, then dropped. It swirled viciously, at times reversing its direction without warning. It sucked him backwards, then all at once propelled him forward again. More than once it unbalanced him and made him totter at the brink, windmilling his arms to regain his balance. At last it forced him to his hands and knees. He crawled on, and when the stronger squalls howled over him he flattened himself against the bridge and clung to it. All the time the lava bubbled and seethed below.

At last he saw the far side of the cavern ahead, another precipitous rock wall. He crawled towards it, until he saw, to his horror, that the last section of the rocky spur had crumbled away and fallen into the fiery cauldron below. There was a gap between the end of the spur and the far wall of the cavern as wide as three strides of a tall man. He went to the edge and looked across this gap. There was a small opening in the facing wall.

From Eos's memory he knew that she had not passed this way for hundreds of years. On her last visit the spur had been entire. This last section must have crumbled away only relatively recently. Eos had been unaware of it, and that was why he had not expected to be confronted by this obstacle.

He crawled back a short way, knelt up and kicked off his sandals, then shrugged the handle of the basket off his shoulder and discarded it. The sandals and the basket fell over the edge and plummeted into the lava lake. He knew he did not have the strength to go back, so he must go forward. He closed his eyes and regulated his breathing, then gathered the last of his physical strength and bolstered it with all his mental and psychic powers. Then he came up into a crouch like a marathon runner at the start of a race. He waited for a lull in the furious winds that swept over the spur. Then, in the momentary stillness, he drove himself forward along the narrow path, leaning forward and stepping high. He leapt out into space, and knew in that instant he would fall short. The cauldron waited below to receive him.

Then the wind was shrieking again. It had changed direction and doubled its fury. It came from directly behind him. It swept under the skirts of his tunic, billowed them and flung him forward. But not quite far enough. His lower body slammed into the cliff and he just caught hold of the lip of the opening. He hung there, his legs dangling over the drop, all his weight hanging on his arms. He tried to pull himself up high enough to hook one elbow over the lip, but could raise himself only a little way before he fell back at full stretch of his arms. Frantically he kicked and groped with his bare feet for a foothold on the cliff, but the rock was smooth.

A fountain of burning lava erupted from the cauldron below him. Before it fell back, particles of molten magma splattered his bare legs and feet. The pain was unbearable and he screeched in agony.

'Taita!' Fenn had sensed his pain and called to him across the ether.

'Help me,' he sobbed.

'I am with you,' she replied. 'With all our might – now!'

The pain was a goad. He strained upwards until he felt the sinews of his arms popping, and gradually, achingly slowly, he drew himself up until his eyes were level with the lip, but then he could rise no further. He felt his arms giving way.

'Fenn, help me!' he cried again.

'Together! Now!' He felt the surge of her strength. He drew himself up slowly until at last he could throw one arm over the lip. He hung on it for a moment, then heard her cry again.

'Together again, Taita. Now!'

He heaved upwards and threw out his other arm. It found purchase. With both arms holding his courage returned. He ignored the pain of his burnt legs, heaved upwards and the top half of his body flopped over the lip. Kicking and panting, he dragged himself into the mouth of the opening. He lay there for a long time until he had recovered the strength to sit up. Then he looked down at his legs and saw the burns. He pulled off the lumps of lava that were still adhering to the soles of his feet, and lumps of his flesh came away with them. Upon his calves, blisters filled with transparent fluid were ballooning. He was crippled by pain but, using the wall as support, he dragged himself to his feet. Then he staggered on down the tunnel. The soles of his feet were raw, and he left bloody footprints on the rock. The glow from the fiery cauldron behind him lit his way.

The tunnel ran straight for a short distance then began to descend and the ruddy light faded. In its last glimmer he made out a half-consumed torch jammed into a crack in the rock. It had been there since Eos's last visit so long ago. He had no means of igniting it, he thought. Then he remembered the power he had taken from the witch and stretched out his hand towards it, pointing his forefinger at the charred end and focusing on it his psychic force.

A glowing spot appeared at the head of the dead torch. A thin spiral of smoke rose from it, and then, abruptly, it burst into flame and burnt up brightly. He took it down from the crack and, holding it high, hobbled on as fast as his scalded feet would carry him. He came to the head of another inclined shaft. This was also stepped, but the rock was not worn, the marks of the masons' chisels still fresh. He started down it, but the steps seemed endless and he had to stop repeatedly to rest. In one such interval he became conscious of a low susurration, a trembling in the air and in the rock upon which he sat. The sound was not constant but rose and fell intermittently, like the slow beating of a gigantic pulse.

He knew what it was.

Eagerly now, he came to his feet and started downwards again. As he went, the sound became stronger and clearer. Down again and still down Taita went, and the sound swelled, his excitement, too, until it was strong enough to dull the pain in his legs. The sound of the mighty pulse reached the peak of its volume. The rock walls shook. He dragged himself forward, then stopped, astounded. He had acquired the memory of this place from Eos but the tunnel had come to a dead end. Slowly, painfully, he went forward and stood before the wall.

It seemed to be of natural rough stone. There were no cracks or openings in it, but in its centre, level with his eyes, three signs had been carved. The first was so old and eroded by the sulphurous gas of the lava cauldron that it was illegible, its antiquity unfathomable. The second was only slightly fresher, and when he studied it more closely he saw that it was the outline of a tiny pyramid, the soul sign of a priest or a holy man. The third was the most recent but, nevertheless, many centuries old. It was the cat's-paw outline of Eos's spirit sign.

The engravings were the signatures of those who had visited this place before him. Since the beginning time, only three others had found their way here. He touched the stone and found it cold, a marked contrast to the hellish craters and flaming lava that he had passed along the way.

'This is the gateway to the Font for which men have searched down the ages,' he whispered, in deep reverence. He laid his hand upon the cat's-paw symbol, which grew warm to his touch. He waited for a lull in the great pulse of the earth, then uttered the three words of power he had taken from the witch: her secret conjugation known to no other.

'Tashkalon! Ascartow! Silondela!'

The rock groaned and began to move under his hand. He pressed harder, and there was a harsh, grinding noise as the entire wall rolled ponderously aside, like a turning millstone. Behind it lay another short flight of stairs, then a bend in the tunnel from which came a roar like that of a wounded lion. No longer muffled by the stone door the full thunder of the earth pulse burst round him. Before he could brace himself, he was driven back a pace by its power. The tunnel ahead was lit by a weird blue light, which grew stronger in harmony with the great pulse, then faded as the sound receded.

Taita stepped through the portals. Two more torches were set into slots in the walls on each side. He lit them, and when they were burning brightly, he limped on slowly down the passage towards the source. He was filled with a sense of awe far greater than he had ever known, even in the holy sanctums at the temples of the great deities of Egypt. He turned the corner at the end of the passage and stood at the top of another short stone staircase. At the bottom he could make out a smooth floor of white sand.

Filled with trepidation, he went down the steps and found himself standing in what appeared to be the dry bed of a great subterranean river. He knew that, soon, the sound and light would burst out of the dark tunnel. What would be the consequences if he were to allow the mystical waters of the river of life to pour over him?

To live for ever might be a curse rather than a blessing. After the first aeons of time had passed, they might be followed by paralysing boredom and staleness from which there would be no escape. Would conscience and morality become eroded by time? Would high principles and decency fade until they were replaced by the perverse evil and wickedness in which Eos had indulged?

His nerve failed and he turned to flee. But he had hesitated too long. Austere blue light filled the tunnel. Even if he had wished to, he could no longer escape it. He turned to face the tunnel and braced himself to receive the approaching thunder. From the mouth of the subterranean river burst a radiance that had no apparent source. Only when it swirled round his bare feet did he realized that it was neither gaseous nor liquid. It was as light as air but at the same time dense and weighty. It was icy cold on his skin, but it warmed the flesh beneath.

This was the elixir of life eternal.

Swiftly it grew to a flood that rose to his waist. Had it been water its weight would have swept him off his feet and carried him down the river course into the depths of the earth. Instead it buoyed him up in its soft embrace. The thunder filled his head and the blue tide rose to his shoulders. He felt weightless and free, light as thistledown. He drew a last deep breath and shut his eyes as the tide rushed over his head. He could still see the blue radiance through his closed eyelids, and the thunder filled his ears.

He felt the Blueness seeping into his lower body openings, filling him. He opened his eyes and it washed over them. He exhaled the breath he was holding, then drew the next. He felt the blue elixir flow into his nostrils, down his throat and into his lungs. He opened his mouth and gulped in the Blueness. His heart pumped strongly as the Blueness filtered from his lungs into his blood and was carried to every part of his body. He felt it tingling in his fingertips and toes. His weariness fell away and he felt stronger than he could ever remember. His mind sparkled with a crystalline brilliance.

The Blueness warmed his tired and aged flesh, soothing and renewing it. The pain in his legs and feet was gone. The raw, burned skin was healing. He felt his sinews stiffen and his bones harden. His spine straightened and his muscles firmed. His mind was recharged with the wonder and optimism of the youth he had lost so long ago, but the innocence was tempered by the infinite store of wisdom and experience he now possessed.

Then, softly, the Blueness began to recede. The thunder abated and he heard it race away down the tunnel. He stood alone in the silent riverbed and looked down at himself. He raised one foot at a time. The burns on his calves and the soles of his feet were healed. The skin was smooth and unflawed. The muscles of his legs stood out hard and proud.

His legs wanted to run. He turned and bounded up the staircase towards the rolling stone gate. He took the rough-hewn steps three or four at a time. His legs hurled him up effortlessly. His feet never stumbled. He paused briefly at the portal of the chamber. He snatched down the torches from their brackets, and turned back to shout the words of power. The rock gate rumbled shut. He saw that another signature was now engraved in the stone beside the other three, the symbol of the wounded falcon: his own spirit sign. He turned away and went on up the steep staircase. He heard the eternal thunder of the Font behind him as he climbed, and the mighty heartbeat of the earth was echoed in his chest.

He felt no need to pause for rest: his breathing was quick and light, his bare feet flew over the stone. Up he went, and the sound of the Font diminished until soon he heard it no more. The ascent seemed shorter than the descent had been. Before he expected it, he saw the furnace glow of the cauldron ahead. Once again he looked down into the seething lava lake. He paused only long enough to measure with his eye the broken gap in the rock spur. Once so deadly and intimidating, now it seemed insignificant. He backed off half a dozen paces, then sped forward. Holding the flaming torch high he jumped out from the mouth of the tunnel and flew across the gap. He landed in perfect balance three full paces beyond the fracture. Even though at the moment another furious gust struck him his balance was true: he did not waver.

He launched himself along the narrow rock causeway, running lightly where previously he had been forced to crawl. Though the wind clawed at him and whipped the skirt of his tunic round his legs he never slowed his pace. He ducked his head under the stone roof of the tunnel at the end of the causeway and went on, following the twists and turns, not stopping until he reached the fork of the tunnel and stepped out into the main branch.

Even here he did not feel any need to linger. His breathing was deep but even, his legs as strong as cedarwood baulks. Nevertheless he jammed the torches upright into natural cracks in the wall, hiked up his tunic and sat on a stone step. He lifted his skirt as high as his waist and admired his legs. He ran his hands over the smooth skin: the muscles beneath it were full, each clearly defined. He touched them, and they were hard and resilient. Then he noticed his hands. The skin on the back was that of a man in his prime. The dark foxing blotches of age had disappeared. His arms were like his legs, hard and shapely. He raised his hands to his face and explored it with his fingertips. His beard felt thicker, the skin on his throat and under his eyes taut and devoid of wrinkles. He ran his fingers through his hair, which was dense and springing again.

He laughed aloud with pleasure at the thought of how his features must have altered. He wished he had brought with him the mirror that had been given him. He had not felt the satisfaction of justified vanity for a century at least.

'I am young again!' he shouted, as he jumped to his feet and took up the torches.

Before he had gone much further, he came to a seep where sweet water ran from a crack and dripped down the wall of the tunnel into a natural stone basin. He drank, then went on. Even as he ran, his mind was filled with Fenn. It was so many months now since he had last seen her and he wondered how much more her appearance had altered since he had overlooked her. During the two brief contacts he had made with her earlier that day he had sensed a sea-change in her.

Of course she has changed, but not as much as I have. We will astonish each other when next we meet. She is a young woman now. What will she make of me? He felt heady in anticipation of their meeting.

He had lost all sense of the passage of time. He did not know whether it was night or day, but he went on. At last he reached a point where the tunnel descended another steep flight of steps. When he reached the bottom he found the way forward closed off by a heavy leather curtain, decorated with mystic symbols and characters. He doused the torches, then moved closer to it. A soft ray of light showed through a chink in the leather. He listened intently, his hearing immeasurably sharper and clearer than it had been before he had entered the Font. Now he heard nothing. Cautiously he opened the chink in the curtain a little wider and peered through. He was looking into a small but magnificently furnished room. He searched quickly for any sign of life but he found no aura. He opened the curtain wider and stepped through.

This was Eos's boudoir. The walls and roof were covered with tiles of ivory, each carved with beautifully executed designs that had been painted with jewel-like colours. The effect was gay and enchanting. Four oil lamps were suspended from the ceiling on bronze chains. The light they threw was mellowy. Against the far wall a silk-covered couch was piled with cushions and a low ebony table stood in the centre of the floor. On it were set bowls of fruit, honey cakes and other sweetmeats, with a small crystal jug of red wine, its stopper in the shape of a golden dolphin. On another table lay a pile of papyrus scrolls and an astrological model of the heavens, depicting the tracks of the sun, the moon and the planets, fashioned in fine gold. The floor was covered with multiple layers of silk carpets.

He went directly to the central table and selected a bunch of grapes from a bowl. He had eaten nothing since he had left the witch's warren, and now he had the appetite of a young man. Once he had devoured half of the bowl's contents, he crossed to a second door in the wall beside the couch. It was screened by another richly decorated leather curtain, the twin to the one through which he had entered. He listened beside it but heard nothing, then slipped through the division in the curtains into a smaller anteroom. Here, a stool was set beside the far wall in which a peep-hole had been drilled. Taita went to it and stooped to peer through.

He found that he was looking into the Supreme Council

chamber of the oligarchs. This was the spy-hole Eos used whenever she came down from the high mountain to preside over and direct the Council's proceedings. The chamber was the one in which Taita had first met Aquer, Ek-Tang and Caithor. Now it was deserted and in semi-darkness. The high window at the back framed a square of the night sky, which included part of the constellation of Centaurus. From its angle to the horizon he made a rough estimate of the time. It was past midnight, and the palace was quiet. He returned to Eos's boudoir and ate the rest of the fruit. Then he stretched out upon the couch, spun a web of concealment to protect him while he slept, closed his eyes and was almost immediately asleep.

He was awoken by voices coming from the Supreme Council chamber. The intervening walls should have muffled them, but his hearing was so enhanced that he could recognize Lord Aquer's.

Taita rose quickly from the couch and went to Eos's spy-hole. He looked through it. Eight warriors in full battledress were kneeling before the dais in attitudes of subservience and respect. The two oligarchs faced them. Lord Aquer was on his feet haranguing the men who knelt before him.

'What do you mean, they have escaped? I ordered you to capture them and bring them to me. Now you say that they have eluded you. Explain yourself.'

'We have two thousand men in the field. They will not be at liberty much longer.' The speaker was Captain Onka. He was cringing on his knees before Aquer's wrath.

'Two thousand?' Aquer demanded. 'Where are the rest of our troops? I commanded you to call up the entire army to deal with this insurrection. I will take the field at the head of the force. I will find the traitor Tinat Ankut and all his fellow conspirators. All of them, do you hear? Especially the new-comer Meren Cambyses and the strangers he has brought with him to Jarri. I will personally oversee their torture and execution. I will make an example of them that will never be forgotten!' He glared at his officers but none dared speak or even look at him.

'When I have dealt with the ringleaders, I will unleash my vengeance on every incomer in Jarri,' Aquer ranted. 'They are traitors. By order of this Council their property is confiscated by the goddess and the state. The men will be sent to the mines – we are short of slaves. I want older women, and children over the age of twelve years, placed in the slave pens. The younger children without exception are to be put to the sword. Any desirable girls will go to the farms for the breeding programme. How long will it take you to muster the remainder of our regiments, Colonel Onka?'

Taita realized that Onka must have been promoted to command the regiment that had formerly been Tinat's.

'We will be ready to ride before noon today, great lord,' Onka replied.

Taita listened in consternation. Everything in Jarri had changed during his sojourn in the mountains. Now his first concern was for Fenn and Meren. Perhaps they were already in Onka's hands. He must make contact with Fenn immediately to reassure himself of her safety, but it was vitally important, too, that he make the most of this opportunity to eavesdrop on Aquer's plans.

He stayed at the peep-hole while Aquer continued to issue orders. He was an experienced commander and it seemed that his tactics would be effective. However, Taita could make his own plans to counteract them. At last Aquer dismissed his colonels, and the two oligarchs were left alone in the hall. Aquer threw himself angrily on his stool.

'We are surrounded by fools and poltroons,' he complained. 'How was this insurrection allowed to flourish under our very noses?'

'I smell the odour of the putative magus, Taita of Gallala, in this,' Ek-Tang answered. 'I have no doubt that he has instigated this outrage. He comes directly from Egypt and

Nefer Seti. No sooner do we welcome him into Jarri than the country is plunged into the first rebellion in two hundred years.'

'Two hundred and twelve years,' Aquer corrected him.

'Two hundred and twelve,' Ek-Tang agreed, his voice crackling with irritation, 'but such pedantry serves no good purpose. What is to be done about the rabble-rouser?'

'You know that Taita was the special guest of the goddess and that he has gone to meet her on the mountains. Those who are summoned by Eos never return. We need spare no further thought for him. You will never see him again. Those he brought with him to Jarri will soon be arraigned—' Aquer broke off and his angry expression cleared. He smiled with anticipation. 'His ward, the girl he called Fenn, will receive my special concern.' Taita saw his aura throw off sparks of lust.

'Is she old enough?' Ek-Tang asked.

'For me, they are always old enough.' Aquer made an expressive gesture.

'Each of us has his own tastes,' Ek-Tang conceded. 'It is as well that we do not all enjoy the same amusements.' The two oligarchs rose and, arm in arm, left the hall. Taita returned to the witch's boudoir and barred the door before he made the first cast for Fenn. Almost immediately her sign appeared in his mind's eye, and he heard her sweet voice ring in his head: 'I am here.'

'I cast for you earlier. Are you in danger?'

'We are all in danger,' she replied, 'but for the moment we are safe. The land is in turmoil. Where are you, Taita?'

'I have escaped from the mountain and I am hidden near the Supreme Council chamber.'

Even over the ether her surprise was clear. 'Oh, Taita, you never fail to amaze and delight me.'

'When we meet I will have much more for your delight,' he promised. 'Are you or Meren able to come to me or must I find you?'

'We are hidden too, but only five or six leagues from where you are,' Fenn replied. 'Tell us where we must meet you.'

'To the north of the citadel a narrow valley is carved into the foothills. It is not far from the mountain road, about three leagues from the palace. The entrance is marked by a distinctive grove of acacia trees on the hillside above it. Seen from far off, it is shaped like the head of a horse. This is the place,' he told her, and transmitted an image of the grove to her across the ether.

'I see it clearly,' she replied. 'Sidudu will recognize it. If she does not I will cast for you again. Go to the valley quickly, Taita. We have but little time left to flee this wicked place and the wrath of the Jarrians.'

Swiftly Taita searched the boudoir for a weapon or some form of disguise, but found neither. He was still bare-footed and dressed in the simple tunic, which was filthy with dust and soot and scorched by drops of burning magma. He went quickly to the outer door and let himself through into the empty audience hall. He had a clear memory of the route he must follow to reach the entrance through which Tinat had brought him on his first visit to the citadel. He stepped out into the corridor to find it deserted. When the oligarchs had left, they must have dismissed the guards. He made for the rear of the building and had almost reached the tall double doors to the rear courtyard when a loud voice halted him.

'You there! Stand and give account of yourself.'

In his haste Taita had neglected to spin about himself a spell of concealment. He turned back with a friendly smile. 'I am confused by the size of this place, and I would be glad of your assistance in finding my way out.'

The man who had accosted him was one of the citadel guards, a burly middle-aged sergeant in full uniform. He had drawn his sword and was striding towards Taita with a belligerent scowl.

'Who are you?' he shouted again. 'You have the look of a dirty, thieving rascal to me.'

'Peace, friend.' Still smiling, Taita held up both hands in a placatory gesture. 'I carry an urgent message for Colonel Onka.'

'The Colonel has left already.' The sergeant held out his left hand. 'Give the message to me, if you are not lying and you truly have one. I will see it gets to him.'

Taita pretended to grope in his pouch, but as the man came closer, he seized his wrist and pulled him off balance. Instinctively the sergeant pulled back with all his weight. Instead of resisting Taita went with him and used the impetus to crash with both elbows into his chest. With a shout of surprise the man lost his balance and went over backwards. Quick as a leopard, Taita landed on top of him and drove the ball of his right hand up under his chin. The vertebrae of the sergeant's neck parted with a loud crack, killing him instantly.

Taita knelt beside him and began to untie his helmet, intending to use his uniform as a disguise, but before he could get the helmet off his head there was another shout and two more guards rushed down the corridor towards him with drawn swords. Taita prised the blade out of the dead man's hand, and sprang to his feet to face his attackers.

He hefted the sword in his right hand. It was a heavy infantry model but it felt familiar and comfortable in his grip. Many years ago he had written the manual of arms for Pharaoh's regiments, and swordsmanship was one of his passionate interests. Since then age had taken from him the force of his right arm, but now it was restored to him, as was his agility and fleetness of foot. He parried the thrust of the first assailant and ducked under the cut of the second. Keeping low, he slashed at the back of the man's ankle, neatly severing his Achilles tendon. Then he jumped up and pirouetted unexpectedly between the two before either could recover. The unwounded man turned to follow him, but as he did so he opened his flank and Taita stabbed deep in his armpit, sliding the point of his blade between the ribs. With a twist of his wrist, he turned it in the wound, opening it wide and freeing it from the suction of wet flesh. His victim dropped to his knees coughing up gouts of blood from pierced lungs. Taita spun away to face the trooper he had crippled.

The man's eyes filled with terror and he tried to back away but his maimed foot flopped nervelessly, and he almost fell. Taita feinted for his face and, when he raised his guard to protect his eyes, sent a thrust into his belly, cleared his blade and jumped back. The man dropped his weapon and fell to his knees. Taita stepped forward again and stabbed down into the back of his neck, under the rim of his helmet. The trooper dropped face down and lay still.

Taita jumped over the two corpses and went to the first man he had killed. Unlike the others, his uniform was not bloodstained. Swiftly he stripped off the man's sandals and laced them on to his own bare feet. They were a tolerable fit. He strapped the sword belt and scabbard round his waist, then took the helmet and cloak and pulled them on as he ran for the rear doors of the citadel. He slowed to a walk as he reached them and spread the scarlet cloak to cover his torn, soiled tunic. As he marched towards the doors he sent out an impulse to lull the minds of the sentries who guarded them. They glanced at him with little interest as he passed between them and went down the marble steps into the courtyard.

The parade-ground was bustling with the men and horses of Onka's regiment preparing for campaign. Taita saw Onka himself strutting about and shouting orders to his captains. He mingled with the throng and passed close to Onka as he made his way towards the stables. Although Onka glanced in his direction he showed no sign of recognition.

Taita reached the stableyard without being accosted. Here, there was the same furious activity. The farriers were reshoeing the horses, the armourers were busy at the grindstones sharpening arrowheads and blades, and the grooms were saddling the officers' mounts. Taita thought of attempting to steal a horse from the lines, but he realized there was almost no hope of that plan succeeding. Instead he made his way towards the back wall of the palace compound.

The stench guided him to the latrines tucked behind the

buildings. When he found them he looked around carefully to make sure he was unobserved. A sentry was patrolling the top of the walls above him, so he waited for the diversion he knew must come. It was not long before he heard angry shouts from the direction of the citadel. Whistles bleated and a drumbeat signalled the call to arms. The three bodies he had left in the passage had been discovered, and the attention of the garrison was focused on the citadel. The sentry rushed to the far end of the parapet from where he stared out over the parade-ground to find the reason for the alarm. His back was turned.

Taita swung himself up on to the flat roof of the latrines. From there the top of the wall was within reach. He took a run and leapt for the lip of the parapet, then he pulled himself up with both arms until he could throw a leg over. He rolled across the top of the wall and dropped over the far side. It was a long fall, but he rode the shock of landing with braced legs and glanced round swiftly. The sentry was still gazing away from him. The edge of the forest was close by and he darted across the open ground into the trees. Here he took a minute to orient himself, then began the steep climb into the foothills, using the cover of gullies, long grass and shrubs to hide himself from a chance watcher below. When he reached the crest of the hill he peered over it cautiously. The road that led up to the Cloud Gardens was just beneath him. It was deserted. He ran down, crossed it quickly and took cover in a patch of scrub. From there he could see across to the horse's head grove of trees on the next promontory. He bounded down the scree slope into the valley, the loose stones rolling under his feet, and reached the bottom without losing his balance. He trotted along the base of the hill and came to an opening. The valley sides were steep and he went a short distance into it, then turned and climbed to a vantage-point from where he could watch the entrance and settled down to wait.

The sun reached its zenith, then began to drop towards the horizon. He saw dust on the road across the valley. It looked as though a large troop of cavalry was riding hard towards the east. An hour or so passed, and then he heard the faint sound of hoofs coming closer. He sat up, alert. A small band of riders appeared below him and stopped.

Sidudu was at the front, mounted on a chestnut pony. She pointed up the valley towards where Taita was hiding. Meren spurred past her and took the lead. The party came on at a trot, Meren followed closely by a lovely young woman on a grey colt. Her long legs were bare and her blonde hair was tumbled by the wind on to her shoulders. She was slim, the set of her shoulders proud. Even from this distance Taita could see her breasts standing out under the bleached linen of her tunic. The wind flicked aside her golden curls to reveal her face, and Taita drew a sharp breath. It was Fenn, but a different Fenn from the girl he had known and loved. This was a confident, poised young woman in the first flower of her beauty.

Fenn was riding her grey colt and she had Windsmoke on a lead rein behind her. Hilto rode at her right hand. Nakonto and Imbali followed them closely, both mounted and sitting their horses well – they had learnt new skills in the many months he had been away. Taita left the ledge on which he squatted and scrambled down the cliff. He jumped out and dropped down the last steep pitch. The scarlet cloak opened round him like a pair of wings, but the visor of the leather helmet obscured the top half of his face. He landed in the path directly before Meren.

With the reflexes of a trained warrior, Meren saw the Jarrian uniform and rode at him with an intimidating yell, drawing his sword and swinging it high. Taita had only just enough time to straighten and draw his own weapon. Meren leant from the saddle and hacked at his head. Taita turned the blow with his blade and jumped aside. Meren pulled his horse down on its haunches and dragged its head round. Then he came back at the charge. Taita ripped the helmet off his head and threw it aside. 'Meren! It is Taita,' he yelled.

'You lie! You are nothing like the magus!' Meren did not check his charge. He leant out from the saddle and levelled his blade, sighting along it at the centre of Taita's chest. At the last moment Taita swayed aside and the point of the sword grazed his shoulder as Meren swept past.

Taita shouted at Fenn as she rode forward. 'Fenn! It is me. Taita.'

'No! No! You are not Taita! What have you done with him?' she screamed. Meren was gathering his mount under him, bringing its head round for his next attack. Nakonto had his throwing spear resting on his shoulder and was ready to hurl it as soon as he had a clear view past Meren. Imbali jumped down from her horse and hefted her battleaxe as she ran forward. Hilto followed her with drawn sword. Both Fenn and Sidudu were nocking arrows to their bows.

Fenn's eyes glittered like emeralds in her anger. 'You have done away with him, you villain!' she yelled. 'You shall have an arrow through your black heart.'

'Fenn! Behold my spirit sign!' Taita called urgently, in the Tenmass. Her chin jerked up. Then she saw the sign of the wounded falcon floating above his head and blanched with shock. 'Nay! Nay! It is him! It is Taita! Put up your sword, I tell you! Put it up, Meren!' Meren swerved, then reined his mount back.

Fenn sprang down from Whirlwind and raced to Taita. She flung both her arms round his neck and sobbed brokenheartedly. 'Oh! Oh! Oh! I thought you were dead. I thought they had killed you.'

Taita held her tightly to his chest, her body lithe and hard against his. The sweet smell of her filled his nostrils and made his senses swim. His heart swelled in his chest so that he was unable to speak. They held each other with a silent intensity, while the others stared at them in bewilderment. Hilto tried to maintain his usual phlegmatic air, but he was unsuccessful. Nakonto and Imbali were mute with the fear of witchcraft, both spitting to left and right, making the sign against evil spirits.

'It's not him,' Meren was repeating. 'I know the magus better than any man alive. This young buck is not him.'

After a long while Fenn drew back and held Taita at arm's

length. She studied his face raptly, then stared into his eyes. 'My eyes tell me it is not you, but my heart sings that it is. Yes, it is you. It is verily you. But, my lord, how have you become so young and surpassingly beautiful?' She stood on tiptoe to kiss his lips. At this the others burst out laughing.

Meren jumped down from the saddle and rushed to join them. He pulled Taita out of Fenn's embrace and wrapped him in a bear-hug of his own. 'I still cannot believe it! It is not possible!' He laughed. 'But I give testimony that you wield a pretty sword, Magus, else I would have run you through.' They crowded round him excitedly.

Sidudu came to kneel before him. 'I owe you so much, Magus. I am so glad to see you safe. Before you were beautiful of spirit, but now you are beautiful in the flesh too.'

Even Nakonto and Imbali at last conquered their superstitious dread and came to touch him in awe.

Hilto exclaimed loudly, 'I did not doubt for a second that you would come back to us. I knew it was you the instant I laid eyes on you.' No one took any notice of this blatant falsehood.

Meren demanded answers to twenty different questions and Fenn clung to his right arm and gazed into his face with shining eyes.

At last Taita recalled them to stark reality: 'There will be time for this later. All you need to know now is that Eos can harm neither us nor our very Egypt again.' He whistled for Windsmoke, who rolled her eyes at him coquettishly and came to nuzzle his neck. 'You at least recognize me, my darling.' He hugged her round the neck, then looked again to Meren. 'Where is Tinat?'

'Magus, he is already on the march for the Kitangule river. The Jarrians have discovered our plans. We must ride at once.'

By the time they had left the valley and started towards the plain, the sun was setting. It was dark when they entered the forest and, once again, Sidudu was their guide. Taita checked her heading by the stars and found that her knowledge of the land and her sense of direction were infallible. He could devote all of his attention to Fenn and Meren. The three rode side by side with Taita in the middle, their stirrups touching, while Fenn and Meren described to him all that had transpired while they were apart.

Then Taita told them, 'While I was in the palace I was able to eavesdrop on Aquer's battle council. He is taking command of the army himself. His scouts have reported the movement of the main body of our people along the road towards the east. He has deduced that Tinat is trying to reach the shipyards at the head of the Kitangule river and seize the boats there, for he knows that our only escape from Jarri is down that river. Tell me where exactly Tinat is now and how many are with him.'

'He has about nine hundred people, but many of the men are sick and weak from the treatment to which they were subjected in the mines. He has only a few more than three hundred who can fight. The rest are women and children.'

'Three hundred!' Taita exclaimed. 'Aquer has five thousand trained warriors. If he catches Tinat it will go hard with him.'

'Worse, Tinat is short of horses. Some of the children are very young. With them and all the sick, he is moving slowly.'

'He must send a small band of fighting men ahead with all speed to seize the boats. In the meantime we must delay Aquer,' Taita said grimly.

'Tinat hopes to give him pause at the Kitangule Gap. Fifty men can hold an army there, at least until the women and the sick are on the boats,' said Meren.

'Don't forget that Aquer has scouts who know the country as well as Sidudu does,' Taita reminded him. 'They will certainly know of the other route to bypass the gap and reach the boatyards. Instead of waiting for him to come at us, we should strike at him before he expects it.' Meren had glanced at Sidudu as Taita mentioned her name. Even in the moonlight his expression was doting. Poor Meren, the famous philanderer, is smitten, Taita thought, and smiled inwardly, but he said, 'We will need more men than we have now if we are to hold Aquer. I will stay to watch the road for him.

Meren, you must take Fenn with you and ride as fast as you can to find Tinat—'

'I will not leave you!' Fenn cried. 'I have come so close to losing you that I will never leave you again.'

'I am not a messenger, Magus. You owe me more respect than to treat me as one. Like Fenn, I will stay with you. Send Hilto,' Meren declared.

Taita made a gesture of resignation. 'Will no one take an order from me without argument?' he demanded of the night sky.

'Probably not,' Fenn answered primly, 'but you might try speaking gently to Hilto.'

Taita capitulated and called Hilto forward. 'Ride ahead at first light as fast as your horse will carry you. Find Colonel Tinat Ankut and say that I have sent you. Tell him that Aquer knows we are aiming for the Kitangule river, and is in hot pursuit. Tinat must send a small detachment of fighting men ahead to seize the boats at the headwaters of the river before the Jarrians can destroy them. Tell him his plan to hold the Kitangule Gap until all our people have been embarked is a good one, but he must send me twenty of his best men. This is desperately urgent. Hilto, you must lead the men he gives you back along the east road towards Mutangi until you find us. Go now! At once!' Hilto saluted and, without another word, cantered away.

'What we need is an ambuscade where we can wait for Aquer.' Taita turned back to Meren. 'You know precisely the kind of place we are looking for. Ask Sidudu if she knows of one.' Meren spurred forward to Sidudu, who listened intently to his request.

'I know just such a place,' she said, as soon as he had finished speaking.

'You are such a clever girl,' Meren told her proudly, and for a moment the two of them were lost in each other's eyes.

'Come, then, Sidudu,' Taita called. 'Show us if you are truly as clever as Meren declares you are.'

Sidudu led them off the track they had been following and turned towards the great starry cross in the southern sky.

Within an hour's ride she had reined in at the top of a low, wooded hill and, in the moonlight, pointed down at the valley that opened before them.

'There is the ford of the Ishasa river. You can see the glint of the water. The road that Lord Aquer must follow to reach the Kitangule Gap crosses there. The water is deep so their horses will have to swim. From the top of the cliff we can shower arrows and rocks on them once they enter the water. They will have to ride forty leagues downstream to find another ford.'

Taita studied the crossing carefully, and nodded. 'I doubt that we will find a better place.'

'I told you,' said Meren. 'She has a warrior's eye for good ground.'

'You carry a bow, Sidudu.' Taita nodded at the weapon that hung over her shoulder. 'Can you use it?'

'Fenn taught me,' Sidudu replied simply.

'During your absence Sidudu has become an expert archer,' Meren confirmed.

'It seems there is no end to the virtues of this young paragon,' Taita said. 'We are fortunate to have her with us.'

They swam the horses through the ford, whose current was strong. Once they reached the eastern bank they saw that the path followed a narrow, rocky defile between the cliffs. It was only wide enough for horses to pass in single file. Taita and Meren climbed it and from there surveyed the ground below.

'Yes,' Taita said. 'This will do.'

Before he allowed them to rest, he went over his plans for the ambush and made each in turn repeat the role he had assigned to them. Only then did he allow them to unsaddle and hobble the horses, fill their nosebags with crushed dhurra meal and turn them loose.

It was a cold camp because Taita would not allow a fire. They ate dhurra cakes and slices of cold roast goat's meat dipped in a fiery pepper sauce. As soon as they had finished Nakonta took his spears and went to stand sentry at the ford. Imbali followed him.

'She is now his woman,' Fenn whispered to Taita.

'That comes as no surprise, but I trust that Nakonto will keep at least one eye on the ford,' Taita remarked drily.

'They are in love,' said Fenn. 'Magus, you have no romance in your soul.' She went to untie her bedroll from the back of Whirlwind's saddle, selected a sleeping spot in the lee of a rocky outcrop well away from the others and spread her sleeping mat on the ground with a fur kaross.

Then she came back to Taita. 'Come.' She took his hand and led him to the mat, helped him out of his tunic, balled it up and held it to her nose. 'It smells very strong,' she remarked. 'I will wash it as soon as I have the chance.' She knelt beside him on the mat and covered him with the kaross, then took off her own tunic. Her body was very pale and slim in the light of the moon. She slipped under the kaross beside him and pressed her body to his.

'I am so glad that you have come back to me,' she whispered, and sighed. After a while she stirred and whispered again, 'Taita.'

'Yes?'

'There is a little stranger with us.'

'You must sleep now. It will soon be morning.'

'I will, in a moment.' She was silent again for a long while as she explored his altered body. Then she said softly, 'Taita, where did he come from? How did it happen?'

'Miraculously. In the same way as my appearance was changed. I will explain it all later. Now we must sleep. There will be many other opportunities for you and the little stranger to become better acquainted.'

'May I hold him, Taita?'

'You are already doing so,' he pointed out.

She was quiet again for a while. Then she whispered, 'He is not so little, and he is growing bigger and bigger.' A little later she added happily, 'It seems to me that he is already a friend, no longer a stranger. So now there are three of us. You, me and him.' Still holding him, she fell fast asleep. It took Taita much longer to do the same.

It seemed only minutes later that Nakonto woke him. 'What is it?' Taita sat up.

'Cavalry on the road from the west.'

'Have they crossed the river?'

'No. They are bivouacked on the far side. I think that they did not want to chance a crossing in the dark.'

'Rouse the others and saddle up, but do it quietly,' Taita ordered.

In the faintest glimmer of dawn Taita lay on his belly on the rim of the cliff overlooking the ford. The two girls were at either side of him. On the far bank of the river the Jarrian bivouac was stirring, the troopers throwing wood on the watch fires. The smell of roasting meat drifted to where the three lay. Now the light was strong enough for Taita to count heads. There were about thirty men in the troop. Some were at the cooking fires, others at the horse lines tending their mounts. A few were squatting among the bushes at their private business. Soon it was light enough to make out the features of some.

'There is Onka,' Sidudu whispered fiercely. 'Oh, how I hate that face.'

'Truly I understand your feelings,' Fenn whispered back. 'We will seek the first chance to deal with him.'

'I pray for it.'

'There is Aquer, and that is Ek-Tang with him.' Taita pointed them out. The two oligarchs were standing a little apart from the others. They were drinking from bowls that steamed in the cool morning air. 'They have not been able to contain themselves. They have rushed ahead of their regiments. They will start to cross the ford soon, and when they do so they will give us an opportunity. If they don't, we will shadow them until Hilto brings up our reinforcements.'

'I could put an arrow through Aquer from here.' Fenn narrowed her eyes.

'The range is long and the dawn wind treacherous, my darling.' Taita laid a restraining hand on her arm. 'If we give them warning, the advantage passes to them.' They watched as Onka selected four of his men and gave them curt orders, at the same time gesticulating towards the ford. The men ran to their horses and mounted, then trotted to the river and plunged in. Taita signalled their movements to Meren.

The four horses were swimming before they were half-way across, struggling against the current and lunging forward again as they felt ground under their hoofs. They came out with water streaming from their coats and the equipment. The scouts looked around carefully before they started up the narrow defile. Meren and his men kept hidden and let them through. On the far bank the rest of Onka's troops were drawn up in three ranks, standing at the heads of their mounts. They all waited.

At last there was a clatter of hoofs and one of the scouts galloped back down the defile to the riverbank. He stopped there and waved his arms over his head. 'All is clear this side!' he shouted. Onka called out an order to his men, who mounted and began to move down towards the ford in single file. Onka remained with the rearguard, where he could better control the crossing, but Taita was surprised to see that Aquer and Ek-Tang were in the forefront. He had not expected that. He had thought they would take position in the middle of the column where they were protected by the men around them.

'I think we have them.' His voice was tight with excitement. He signalled to Meren to be ready. At the head of the column the two oligarchs spurred their mounts into the river. Half-way across they began to swim, and the file lost its tight formation as the current pushed them downstream.

'Get ready!' Taita warned the two girls. 'Let the oligarchs and these three riders behind them reach the bank, then shoot any others who try to follow. At least for a short while, until Onka can regroup his men we will have the oligarchs cut off from the main body and at our mercy.'

The current was strong, and large spaces opened in the column.

'Nock your arrows!' Taita ordered quietly. The girls reached into the quivers on their backs. Aquer's horse found the bottom and scrambled up the bank. Ek-Tang followed, with three troopers bunched behind him. Then there was a gap in the line and the rest of the column was still scattered across the river.

'Now!' Taita shouted. 'Shoot the riders coming up behind the leaders.'

Fenn and Sidudu sprang to their feet and drew the long recurved bows. The range was short, almost point-blank. They loosed and the two arrows flew silently downwards. Both struck home. A trooper reeled in the saddle and screamed as Sidudu's flint arrowhead buried itself in his stomach. The man behind him took Fenn's in the throat. He threw up both hands and toppled backwards into the water with a splash. Their horses turned and collided with those that followed them, throwing the rest of the column into confusion. Aquer and Ek-Tang spurred forward into the defile.

'Oh, yes! Fine practice.' Taita applauded the girls. 'Have at them until I give the order to break and run.' He left them and ran down the pathway into the defile.

Meren let the oligarchs enter the mouth of the defile, then he and the two Shilluk jumped out of the bushes behind them. Imbali ran at Ek-Tang and swung her axe. With that single stroke she severed the oligarch's left leg above the knee. Ek-Tang shouted and tried to urge his mount forward, but with one leg gone he lost his balance and fell sideways, clutching at the horse's mane to save himself. Bright arterial blood pumped from the stump of his leg. Imbali ran after him and swung again. Ek-Tang's head jumped off his shoulder and rolled on to the rocky pathway. His nerveless fingers clung to the horse's mane for a few moments longer, then fell open. He flopped sideways to the ground.

With a yell the trooper who was following Ek-Tang rode down on Imbali. Nakonto flung his spear. It struck the trooper in the middle of his back and transfixed him. The spearhead stood out an arm's length from his chest. He dropped his sword and tumbled out of the saddle. Meren ran up beside the last trooper in the line. The man saw him coming and tried to free his sword from the scabbard, but before he could get the blade clear Meren had leapt up and thrust him through the ribs. He hit the ground with his shoulders and the back of his head. Before he could rise Meren finished him off with another thrust in the throat, then turned in pursuit of Aquer. The oligarch saw him coming, dug his spurs into his mount and tore away up the defile, with Meren and Imbali running after him, but they could not gain on him.

From above Taita saw Aquer break away. He turned off the path and ran along the edge of the cliff above him, stopped and poised on the lip of the cliff. As Aquer's horse raced below him, he dropped on to the oligarch's back, so heavily that Aquer lost the reins and was almost thrown from the saddle. Taita whipped one arm around his neck and began to throttle him. Aquer fumbled his dagger from the sheath and tried to stab back over his shoulder into Taita's face. With his free hand, Taita seized his wrist and they wrestled for the advantage.

Thrown off balance by the shifting weight on its back, the horse crashed into the wall of the defile and reared on its hind legs. Locked together, Taita and Aquer were thrown back over its hindquarters. Aquer was on top as they hit the ground, and his full weight slammed into Taita. The shock broke his grip on Aquer's throat and dagger hand. Before he could recover, Aquer had twisted round and thrust for Taita's throat with the dagger. Taita grabbed his wrist again and held him off. Aquer put his full weight behind the dagger but could make no impression. Taita now had the abundant strength of a young man and Aquer was long past his physical prime. Aquer's arm began to tremble with the strain and his expression turned to dismay. Taita smiled up at him. 'Eos is no more,' he said. Aquer flinched. His arm gave way and Taita rolled over on top of him.

'You lie,' Aquer cried. 'She is the goddess, the only true goddess.'

'Then call upon your only true goddess now, Lord Aquer. Tell her that Taita of Gallala is about to kill you.'

Aquer's eyes flew wide with consternation. 'You lie again,' he gasped. 'You are not Taita. Taita was an old man, but by now he is dead.'

'You are mistaken. It is Eos who is dead, and you who will be soon.' Still smiling, Taita tightened his grip on Aquer's wrists until he felt the bone begin to give. Aquer squealed and the dagger fell from his fingers. Taita sat up and twisted him round, pinning him so that he was helpless.

At that moment Meren ran up. 'Shall I finish him?'

'No.' Taita stopped him. 'Where is Sidudu? She is the one he has most sinned against.' He saw the two girls racing down the pathway from the top of the cliff. They came up to where Taita was holding Aquer.

'Taita, we must fly! Onka has rallied his men and they are coming back across the ford in force!' Fenn cried. 'Finish this swine and let us ride.'

Taita looked past her at Sidudu. 'This is the man who gave you to Onka,' he told her. 'He is the one who sent your friends up the mountain. Vengeance is yours.'

Sidudu hesitated.

'Take this dagger.' Meren picked up Aquer's fallen weapon and handed it to her.

Fenn ran forward and ripped Aquer's helmet from his head. She seized a double handful of his hair and dragged his head backwards, exposing his throat. 'For yourself and for all the other girls he sent to the mountain,' she said. 'Cut his throat, Sidudu.'

Sidudu's expression hardened with determination.

Aquer saw death in her eyes and he struggled and whimpered, 'No! Please, listen to me. You are only a child. Such a heinous deed will scar your mind for ever.' His voice was broken and almost incoherent. 'You don't understand, I am anointed by the goddess. I had to do what she commanded. You cannot do this to me.'

'I do understand,' Sidudu answered him, 'and I can do it.' She stepped up to him, and Aquer began to squeal. She laid the blade against the stretched skin of his neck just under his ear and drew it down in a long, deep stroke. The flesh opened and the great artery in the depths of the wound erupted. The breath whistled from his severed windpipe. His legs kicked spasmodically. His eyes rolled back in their sockets. His tongue protruded and he blubbered strings of blood and spittle.

Taita pushed him away and he rolled over to lie, like a slaughtered pig, face down in the spreading puddle of his own blood. Sidudu dropped the dagger and jumped back, staring down at the dying oligarch.

Meren stepped up behind her and placed an arm round her shoulders. 'It is done, and it was well done,' he said softly. 'Waste no pity on him. Now we must go.'

As they ran to their horses they heard the shouts of Onka's men at the ford behind them. They mounted and dashed up the defile, with Taita and Windsmoke in the lead. They came out on top of the hills and paused to look down on a wide level plain of grassland that stretched ahead. In the blue distance they made out another line of hills, the peaks rugged and sharp.

Sidudu pointed to a break in their silhouette. 'There is the Kitangule Gap where we are to meet Colonel Tinat.'

'How far is it?' Meren asked.

'Twenty leagues, perhaps a little more,' Sidudu answered. They turned and looked back to the ford.

At the head of his squadron Onka flogged his horse up the riverbank and shouted with anger when he saw the corpses of the oligarchs but came on all the faster.

'Twenty leagues! Then we have a merry race ahead of us,' Meren said.

They put the horses to the slope and flew down towards the plain. They reached it as Onka's men came boiling over the skyline of the hill behind them. With a chorus of savage yells they started down, the white ostrich plumes on Onka's helmet distinguishing him from his men.

'No need to linger here,' called Taita. 'Let us be gone.'

Within half a league it became apparent that the bay filly Sidudu rode could not keep up with the other horses. They had to moderate their pace to hers. Meren and Fenn dropped back beside her.

'Courage!' Fenn called. 'We will not leave you.'

'I can feel my horse weakening,' Sidudu cried.

'Have no fear,' Meren told her. 'When she is blown, I will take you up behind me.'

'No!' Fenn was emphatic. 'You are too heavy, Meren. The extra weight would kill your mount. Whirlwind can carry both of us with ease. I will take her.'

Taita rose in the stirrups and looked back. The pursuit was spreading out as the faster horses pulled ahead, the slower ones dropping back. Onka's plumed helmet was conspicuous in the centre of the leading rank of three Jarrian horsemen. He was pushing hard, closing the gap steadily. As he urged Wind-smoke onwards, Taita looked at the mountains ahead. He could now see the notch that marked the gap, but it was so distant that they could not hope to reach it before Onka was upon them. Then something else caught his eye. There was a fine smear of pale dust on the plain ahead. His heartbeat quick-ened, but he tried to control it. No time for false hope now. It is almost certainly a herd of gazelle or zebra. But as he thought it he saw under the dustcloud a bright flash of sunlight reflected off metal. 'Armed men!' he muttered. 'But are they Jarrian, or is it Hilto returning with the reinforcements?' Before he could decide, there was a faint shout from behind. He recognized Onka's voice.

'I see you, you traitorous bitch! When I catch you I will rip out your womb. Then I will roast it and force it down your throat.'

'Close your ears to his filth,' Fenn urged Sidudu, but tears ran down Sidudu's face and splattered the front of her tunic.

'I hate him!' she said. 'I hate him with all my soul.'

Behind them, Onka's voice was clearer and closer as he yelled, 'After you have dined, I will have you in the way you most hated. The last thing you will remember will be me inside your bowels. Even in hell you will never forget me.' Sidudu let out a racking sob.

'You must not hearken to him. Close your ears and your mind,' Meren urged.

'I wish I had died before you heard that,' she sobbed.

'It means nothing. I love you. I will not let the swine harm you again.'

At that moment Sidudu's filly stepped with its off fore into a mongoose burrow that was hidden in the long grass. The bone snapped like the breaking of a dry branch and her horse somersaulted. Sidudu was thrown headlong. At once Meren and Fenn wheeled back for her.

'Get ready, Sidudu. I will pick you up,' Fenn called, but Sidudu rolled to her feet and turned to look back at the pursuit. By now Onka was well ahead of the men who followed him. He was leaning forward eagerly, pushing his horse to its top speed, bearing down on Sidudu.

'Prepare to meet your constant lover! he shouted.

Sidudu unslung the bow from her shoulder and reached for an arrow.

Onka laughed with delight. 'I see you have a toy to amuse yourself. I have something better for you to play with before you die!'

He had never seen her shoot. She took her stance and brought up the bow. He was close enough now to see her face clearly. His mocking laughter died as he recognized the deadly anger in her eyes. She drew the fletching back to her lips. He sawed his horse's head round and tried to turn away. Sidudu loosed her arrow. It took him in the ribs and he dropped his sword to try with both hands to pluck it out, but the barbed head was buried deep. His horse pranced in a circle, fighting against the curb. Sidudu shot again. He was turned away from her, and the arrow struck low in the centre of his back. It went deep and skewered his kidneys, inflicting a mortal, agonizing wound. He twisted to reach for the arrow. She shot again, hitting him in the chest, cutting through both lungs. He uttered a sound that was half groan and half sigh, then fell backwards as his horse lunged under him. One of Onka's feet caught in the stirrup and his horse broke into a gallop, towing him away, the back of his head bouncing over the earth as the frantic animal kicked back with both hind legs at his corpse.

Sidudu slung her bow over her shoulder and turned to meet Fenn as she galloped up. Fenn reached down, Sidudu jumped up and they linked arms. Fenn used Whirlwind's speed and impetus to swing her up over the hindquarters. Seated, Sidudu wrapped both arms round her friend's waist, and Fenn spun Whirlwind round.

The next three Jarrians were close upon them, howling with anger at the killing of Onka. Meren met them head on. He cut one man down, and the others broke away rather than risk a collision. They circled him, waiting for an opening, but his blade danced in a glittering arc they could not penetrate. By this time Taita and the two Shilluk had taken in his predicament and were coming at full tilt to support him.

'Nobly done!' Taita shouted to Fenn, as they passed each other. 'Now ride for the Gap. We will cover your retreat.'

'I cannot leave you, Taita,' Fenn protested.

'I will be close behind you!' he shouted over his shoulder, then plunged into the fray. He hacked one of the Jarrians from the saddle, and the other found himself heavily out-numbered, the rest of his squadron still far behind. He tried to defend himself, but Nakonto thrust his long spear into his side and Imbali swung her axe into his raised sword arm, severing it above the wrist. He broke away and galloped to meet his comrades, swaying in the saddle.

'Let him go!' Taita ordered. 'Follow Fenn.' With the rest of the Jarrian squadron coming up behind them, they raced away. Taita gazed ahead: the band of strange horsemen was much closer now. They were heading directly towards each other.

'If they are Jarrians we will fort the horses and stand to meet them,' Taita shouted. They would form the animals in a circle, dismounting behind them, and use their bodies as a defensive wall.

Taita watched the newcomers intently. His eyesight was so

acute now that he recognized the leading rider even before Meren or Fenn could. 'Hilto!' he cried. 'It is Hilto.'

'By the sweet breath of Isis, you're right!' Meren shouted. 'By the look of it, he has brought half of Tinat's regiment with him.' They slowed to a trot as they waited for Hilto to come up. This confused the pursuing Jarrians, who had thought the interlopers were a detachment of their own forces. They halted uncertainly.

'By the wounded eye of Horus, you are welcome, Hilto, old friend,' Meren greeted him. 'As you see, we have left a few of the rascals for you to test your blades upon.'

'Your kindness is overwhelming, my colonel.' Hilto laughed. 'We will make the most of it. We do not need your help. Ride on to where Colonel Tinat Ankut awaits you at the Kitangule Gap. It will not be long before we are free to follow you.'

Hilto galloped on with Tinat's men in a tight group behind him. He gave the order and they extended their line into battle formation. He led them in the charge straight at the milling Jarrians. They crashed into them and sundered their ranks. Then they chased them back in rout across the plain the way they had come, cutting them down as they overhauled the winded horses.

Taita led his own band on towards the blue hills. As they caught up with the two girls on Whirlwind, Meren reined in beside them. 'You shot like a demon,' he told Sidudu.

'Onka brought out the demon in me,' she told him.

'Methinks you have paid off all your debts in gold coinage. Now you and your demon can sleep peacefully at night.'

'Yes, Meren,' she answered demurely. 'But I never wanted to be a warrior – it was forced upon me. Now I would rather be a wife and mother.'

'A most laudable aspiration. I am certain you will find a good man to share it with you.'

'I hope so, Colonel Cambyses.' She looked at him from under lowered eyelashes. 'A short while ago you spoke to me of love . . .'

'Whirlwind is already tiring under the great weight Fenn is forcing him to carry,' Meren said seriously. 'I have room for you behind me. Will you not come across to me?'

'With the greatest pleasure, Colonel.' She held out her arms to him. He swung her across effortlessly and placed her behind his saddle. She circled his waist with both arms, and laid her head between his shoulder-blades. Meren could feel her trembling against him, and occasionally her body heaved with a sob before she could choke it back. His heart ached. He wanted to protect and look after her for as long as they should live. He rode on after Taita and Fenn, with Nakonto and Imbali bringing up the rear.

Before they reached the foothills, Hilto and his squadron caught up with them. Hilto came forward to report to Meren. 'We killed seven and took their horses,' he said. 'The rest would not stand to fight. I let them go rather than follow them. I could not be sure what enemy force might be coming behind them.'

'You did well, Hilto.'

'Shall I bring one of the captured horses for little Sidudu to ride?'

'No, thank you. You have done enough for the present. She is quite safe where she is. I am sure there will be need for more horses when we catch up with Tinat. Keep them until then.'

As they climbed the track through the foothills towards the Gap they met the tail end of the long procession of refugees. Most were on foot, although those who were too sick or weak to walk were being pushed in two-wheeled handcarts or carried on litters by their families or comrades. Fathers had small children on their shoulders and some of the women had infants strapped to their backs. Most recognized Meren and called to him as he passed, 'The blessings of all the gods upon you, Meren Cambyses. You have released us from bitter durance. Our children will be free.'

The young girls they had released from the breeding pens ran beside Fenn and Sidudu, trying to touch them. Some were weeping with the strength of their emotion. 'You have saved us from the mountain of no return. We love you for your compassion and your courage. Thank you, Sidudu. The blessings of all the gods on you, Fenn.'

None recognized Taita, although the women gazed with interest at the young man with the penetrating gaze and commanding presence as he rode by. Fenn was acutely aware of their interest and moved closer to him in a proprietary fashion. With these lets and delays their ascent of the hills was slow and the sun was setting before they reached the crest and stood once again in the Kitangule Gap.

Tinat had seen them coming, from the watch-tower of the border fort. He clambered down the ladder and strode out through the gate to meet them. He saluted Meren, embraced Fenn and Sidudu, then stared at Taita. 'Who is this?' he asked. 'I do not trust him, for he is too pretty by a long way.'

'You may trust him with your life,' Meren said. 'The truth is that you already know him well. I will explain later, though it is not likely you will believe me when I do.'

'You vouch for him, Colonel Meren?'

'With all my heart,' said Meren.

'And with all of mine,' said Fenn.

'And mine,' said Sidudu.

'Mine also,' said Hilto.

Tinat shrugged and frowned. 'I find myself in the minority, yet still I reserve my final judgement.'

'Once again I am grateful to you, Colonel Tinat,' Taita said quietly. 'As I was at Tamafupa when you rescued us from the Basmara.'

'You were not among those I found at Tamafupa,' said Tinat.

'Ah, you have forgotten.' Taita shook his head. 'Then

surely you recall escorting Meren and me down from the Cloud Gardens after his eye surgery. That was the first time you revealed your true loyalty and your longing to return to our very Egypt. Do you recall how we discussed Eos and her powers?'

Tinat stared at Taita, and his stern expression crumbled. 'Lord Taita! Magus! Did you not perish on the mountain in the Cloud Gardens? Surely this cannot be you!'

'Most surely it can and is,' Taita smiled, 'although I admit to certain changes in my appearance.'

'You have become a young man! It is a miracle that defies belief, yet your voice and eyes convince me that it is true.' He ran forward and took Taita's hand in a powerful grip. 'What has become of Eos and her oligarchs?'

'The oligarchs are dead, and Eos no longer threatens us. That is enough for now. How stand your present circumstances?'

'We surprised the Jarrian garrison here. There were only twenty men and none escaped. We threw their corpses into the gorge. See? The vultures have already found them.' Tinat pointed up at the carrion birds circling in the sky above. 'I have sent a hundred men to seize the boatyard at the headwaters of the Kitangule river, and to secure the vessels lying there.'

'You have done good work,' Taita commended him. 'Now you must go down to the boatyard and take command there. Assemble the vessels, and as our people arrive embark them and send them down the river, with a good pilot to guide them. The whole flotilla will muster again on the shores of Lake Nalubaale, at the place where we disembarked to hunt the beast with the nose horn.'

'I remember it well.'

'On your way down the mountain, leave a gang of twenty good axemen at the bridge over the gorge. They will cut down the bridge and let it drop into the gorge after the last of our people have passed over.'

'What will you do?'

'Meren and I will wait here at the fort with some of the men you sent with Hilto. We will delay the Jarrian pursuit until the bridge is down.'

'As you command, Lord Taita.' Tinat hurried away, shouting for his captains.

Taita turned back to Meren. 'Send Hilto, the two Shilluk and as many men as we can spare back down the path to give assistance to our refugees. They must hurry them. Look! The main Jarrian army is not far behind us.' He pointed back down the mountain the way they had come up. In the distance, far out on the plain, they could see the dustclouds, as red as spilt blood in the setting sun, that the Jarrian chariots and the marching legions had raised.

Taita took Fenn with him to make a rapid inspection of the small fort and the defences in the throat of the Gap and he found them rudimentary, the walls low and in poor repair. However, the arsenal and the quarter-master's store were well stocked, as were the kitchen and larder.

'We will not hold the enemy here very long,' he told Fenn. 'Speed is our best defence.' They gazed down at the straggling column of refugees.

'They will need food and drink to give them strength to carry on. Find willing younger women to help you and Sidudu hand out food to them as they pass, whatever you can find, especially those with young children. Then send them on down the track to the boatyards. Keep them moving. Don't let them rest or they will die here.'

Meren hurried back to join them. He and Taita climbed the ladder to the top of the watch-tower. From there, Taita pointed out a ledge higher up the scree slope that overlooked the head of the path. 'Assemble all the men you can spare and take them up there. Tell them to gather large rocks and · pile them on the ledge. We will roll them down on the Jarrians as they come up the path.' Meren scrambled back down the ladder and went for his men, while Taita hastened

535

to join Fenn beside the path. While she selected women to prepare food, he picked out the able-bodied men and sent them to work with Meren on the ledge.

Gradually they made order from the confusion. The pace of the retreat quickened. With food and drink in their bellies the people took new heart. As they passed him, Taita exchanged banter with the men and made weary women smile and hoist their infants higher on their shoulders. Everyone plodded on with renewed determination. As evening fell, the laughter of Fenn's helpers sweetened the night, and the light of the torches that Hilto's rearguard carried marked the tail of the column.

'By the grace of Isis, it looks as though we shall get them all through,' said Fenn, as they picked out the tall figure of Hilto in the torchlight, and heard his deep voice urging the column along.

Taita ran down to meet him. 'You have done well, good Hilto,' he greeted him. 'Have you seen the Jarrian vanguard?'

'Nothing since sunset when we made out their dust. But they cannot be far behind.' Hilto was carrying a young child on each shoulder and his men were similarly burdened.

'Go on with all speed,' Taita ordered, and ran on down the empty track until he was alone and the noise of the retreating column was muted by distance. He stopped to listen and heard a faint murmur below him. He fell to his knees and pressed his ear to the rock. The sound was sharper. 'Chariots and marching men.' He jumped to his feet. 'They are coming up fast.' He raced back to where Hilto was shepherding the tail of the column. Almost the last in the line was a woman with a child strapped to her back. She dragged two others behind her, snivelling and whining.

'I am tired. My feet are hurting.'

'Can we rest now? Can we go home?'

'You *are* going home,' Taita said, then picked up both children and settled them on his shoulders. 'Hold tight,' he told them and reached out his free hand to the mother.

'Come, now. We shall soon have you at the top.' He strode on upwards, pulling the woman after him.

'Here we are.' He set the children down as they reached the top of the pass. 'These two pretty girls will give you something good to eat.' He pushed them towards Fenn and Sidudu, then smiled at the mother, who was worn out and wan with worry. 'You will be safe now.'

'I don't know who you are, but you are a good man.'

He left them and went back to join Hilto. Together, they saw the last of the refugees over the top of the pass and started them down the far side. By now dawn was breaking. Taita looked up to where Meren stood on the ledge at the top of the scree slope. Meren waved, his men crouched among the piles of loose rock they had gathered.

'Go to the top of the watch-tower,' Taita ordered Fenn and Sidudu. 'I will join you presently.' For a moment it seemed that Fenn might argue but she turned away without a word.

Soon Taita heard the chariot wheels grinding up towards the fort. He walked a short way down the track to meet them, intending to divert the attention of the Jarrians from Meren's men on the ledge above. Suddenly the first vehicle appeared round the bend of the narrow track not far below him. As it climbed towards him, others appeared behind it. A dozen foot soldiers ran beside each vehicle, clinging to the sides as they were towed up the steep pathway. There were eight chariots in all, and behind the last came a mass of infantry.

Taita made no attempt to conceal himself, and a shout rang out from the leading chariot. The driver cracked his whip and the chariot bounced over the rough surface as it speeded up. Taita did not move. A spearman hurled a javelin at him, but Taita did not flinch. He watched the weapon fall five or six paces short of where he stood and clatter on the rocks. He let them come on again. The next javelin might have hit him, but he dodged aside and it flew past his shoulder. He heard Fenn cry from the tower, 'Come back, Taita. You are placing yourself at hazard.' He ignored her warning and watched the chariots. At last they were all fully committed: there was no space for them to turn and flee. He waved up at Meren. 'Now!' he shouted, and the echoes flung his voice along the cliffs: 'Now! Now! Now!'

Meren's men bent to the task. The first rocks rolled over the ledge and bounced down the steep slope. They loosened others and set off a rumbling rockslide. The charioteers heard it coming and, with startled cries, abandoned their vehicles and ran for safety. But there was no shelter in the narrow pass from the tide of rock. It crashed into the stranded chariots, sweeping them and the men off the path and into the gorge below. When the rock stopped sliding, the track was blocked with piles of debris.

'No chariots will be able to use that road for a while, and even men on foot will have difficulty getting over these obstacles,' Taita said to himself, with satisfaction. 'It should hold them for the rest of the morning.' He signalled Meren to bring his men down to the fort. By the time he had climbed to the top of the tower, the last of the refugees had long disappeared down the track on the reverse slope.

Fenn was so relieved to see him that she embraced him fiercely. 'You are very dear to me, my lord,' she whispered. 'My heart stops beating when I see javelins flying about your head.'

'If you have such high regard for me, then the least you should do is feed me before the rest of the Jarrian army arrives.'

'You have become so masterful since you returned from the mountain. It pleases me, my lord.' She laughed and disappeared to the kitchens. When she returned they leant on the parapet and ate eggs with dhurra cake. They watched the Jarrian commander send a detachment of fifty men up the slope to seize the ledge from which Meren and his men had hurled the rocks. He was standing in the middle of the track, just out of long bowshot, below them. He was tall and lean, and wore the ostrich plumes of a colonel on the crest of his helmet.

'I don't like the look of him in the least,' Taita remarked.

The man had swarthy features, a hard, jutting chin and a large, hooked nose. 'Do you recognize him, Sidudu?'

'I do, Magus. He is a hard and merciless man, hated by us all.'

'His name?'

'Colonel Soklosh.'

'Colonel Snake,' Taita translated. 'He bears more than a passing resemblance to his namesake.'

As soon as he had control of the ledge, Soklosh sent his skirmishers forward to clear the rock-strewn path before the fort, and to test the mettle of the defenders.

'Send them a few arrows,' Taita told Fenn. Quickly the two girls unslung their bows. Sidudu's arrow passed so close over the head of one Jarrian that he ducked and ran. Fenn hit another in the calf. He hopped about on the uninjured leg howling like a wolf, until his comrades held him down and snapped off the arrow shaft short. Then they retreated down the track, two supporting the wounded man between them. After that there was a long pause before a dense phalanx of armoured men jogged around the bend, and came up the track towards the fort.

'I think it is time for me to go down,' said Meren, and slid from the ladder to the parapet. As the next wave of enemy infantry came into bowshot range, he called to Hilto: 'Stand by!'

'Massed volleys!' Hilto called. His men sheathed their swords, and unslung their bows. 'Level! Take aim! Let fly!'

The volley of arrows rose against the early-morning sky, dark as a swarm of locusts. It fell upon the Jarrians, the arrowheads clattering on bronze armour. A few went down, but the others closed ranks, lifted their shields over their heads to form a canopy and came on at a trot. Again and again Hilto's men fired their volleys but under the canopy of shields the Jarrians were undeterred. They reached the foot of the wall. The front rank braced themselves against the stonework, and the second clambered on to their shoulders to form a pyramid. The third rank used them as a ladder to reach the top of the wall. Hilto's men hurled them back, hacking with swords and thrusting with spears. Others climbed up in their place, blades clanging and rasping against each other. Men shouted, cursed and screamed in pain. A small group of Jarrians forced their way on to the parapet, but before they could exploit their advantage, Meren, Nakonto and Imbali fell upon them. They cut down most and shoved the rest off the top.

On the tower, Fenn and Sidudu stood at each side of Taita, choosing their targets with care, picking off the Jarrian captains as they tried to regroup their men at the base of the wall. When the assault faltered and failed, their arrows hastened the Jarrians back down the track. The enemy left their dead at the base of the wall but dragged the wounded away with them.

Soklosh launched two more attacks before noon. Meren's men beat back the first as readily as they had the chariots. However, in the next, the Jarrians came in three separate detachments, carrying with them hastily constructed assault ladders.

Simultaneously they struck at both ends of the wall and in the centre. The defenders were already thinly stretched, but now Meren was forced to split them into even smaller units to meet the triple-pronged attack. It was desperate fighting, and Taita climbed down to join in. He left the girls in the tower with bundles of arrows they had found in the arsenal. For the rest of the morning the battle raged at the top of the wall. When at last they had thrown back the Jarrians, Meren's men were in poor shape. They had lost twelve men killed, and another ten were too badly wounded to carry on the fight. Most of the others were at least lightly wounded and all were close to exhaustion. From down the track they heard Soklosh and his captains shouting commands as they mustered a fresh attack.

'I doubt we can hold them much longer.' Meren glanced along the parapet at his men, who sat in small groups, drinking from the waterskins that Fenn and Sidudu had brought them, sharpening their chipped and blunted blades, binding their wounds or simply resting, their faces blank and eyes dull.

'Are you ready to set fire to the buildings?' Taita asked.

'The torches are already burning,' Meren affirmed. Only the foundations of the wall were of stone: everything else, including the main building and watch-tower, was built of timber. The wood was old and desiccated and would burn readily. The conflagration would seal off the head of the pass until the flames subsided sufficiently to allow the Jarrians through.

Taita left Meren and went to the far end of the parapet. He crouched in a corner and pulled his cloak over his head.

The men watched him curiously.

'What is he doing?' asked one.

'He is sleeping,' answered another.

'He is a religious man. He is praying.'

'We need his prayers,' remarked a fourth.

Fenn knew what he was attempting and stood close to him, screening him with her own body and adding her psychic force to his.

After such fierce fighting, it took much effort for Taita to compose himself, but at last he broke free of his body and his astral self soared above the mountain peaks. He overlooked the battlefield and saw the massed Jarrian army, three thousand men or more thronging the track from the plain. He saw the next assault forming just below the fort but still out of sight of the walls. Then he passed over the mountain tops and looked down to the Kitangule river, and the distant blue of the lake.

He saw Tinat's men in the boatyards at the head of the river. They had overpowered the garrison, and were assembling and launching the boats down the slipways into the swift flow of the river. Already the first refugees were embarking and the men were taking their places on the rowing benches. But hundreds more were still trudging down the mountain path. He sank closer to earth and hung above the deep gorge that split the flank of the mountain. The suspension bridge that crossed it seemed tiny and insubstantial against the massif of grey rock. The last of the refugees were venturing out on to its frail timbers to make the perilous transit of the gorge. Tinat's men were helping the weak and elderly, and his axemen stood ready to cut away the bridge pylons and let the timbers fall into the dark void beneath. Taita jerked back and swiftly regained full control of his body, then uncovered his head and sprang to his feet.

'What did you discover, Taita?' Fenn asked quietly.

'Most of our people have crossed the gorge,' he replied. 'If we leave the fort now the rest should be over the bridge by the time we get down to them. Fenn, you and Sidudu will make ready the horses.'

He left her to it, and strode down the parapet to Meren. 'Rally the men. Set fire to the walls and take to the path before the next Jarrian attack develops.'

The men's spirits rose when they understood that the fight was over. Within a short time they were marching out of the rear gates of the fort in tight order, carrying their weapons and the wounded. Taita stayed back to supervise the lighting of the fires. The Jarrian garrison had used rushes as a floor covering and sleeping mats. Now they were stacked along the base of the walls. Meren's men had sprinkled them liberally with lamp oil from the quarter-master's stores. When the lighted torches were thrown on to them the flames shot up immediately. The wooden walls caught fire with such ferocity that Taita and the torchmen were forced to run for the gates.

Fenn was already mounted on Whirlwind, holding Windsmoke for him to mount. They trotted down the track together, following the last platoon, which was headed by Meren and Hilto.

When they reached the suspension bridge they were dismayed to find that at least a hundred refugees had still to make the crossing. Meren forced his way through the throng to find out the reason for the delay. Five old but vociferous women were refusing to venture out on to the narrow planks that crossed the deep gorge. They were lying flat in the middle of the path, screaming with terror and kicking anyone who came near them.

'You want us to die!' they howled.

'Leave us here. Let the Jarrians kill us, rather than throw us into the pit.' Their terror was contagious. Those coming up behind them were hanging back now, and holding up the rest of the column. Meren seized the ringleader round the waist and threw her over one shoulder. 'Come, now.' She tried to scratch his face and bite his ear, but her crooked black teeth made no impression on the bronze visor of his helmet. He ran with her on to the narrow way, the planking trembling beneath them, the drop on each side seeming bottomless. The old woman wailed with fresh voice and Meren realized suddently that his back was wet. He roared with laughter. 'It has been hot work. Thank you for cooling me.' He reached the far side and set her down. She made one last effort to claw out his eyes, then collapsed in a whimpering heap on the path. He left her and ran back to pick up the others, but Hilto and three of his men were already coming across the gorge, each with an old woman struggling and screaming on his back. Behind them, the traffic was flowing once more over the bridge. However, the delay had cost them dear. Meren pushed his way back through the throng until he found Taita at the tail of the column.

'The flames at the fort will not hold Soklosh much longer. He will be on us again before we can get them all across. We dare not begin to cut away the supports until the very last of our people is over,' he told Taita.

'Three men could hold an army on this narrow path,' Taita said.

'Hilto and we two?' Meren stared at him. 'By the festering sores on Seth's buttocks, Magus, I had forgotten how things have changed. You now have the strongest and craftiest sword arm of any.'

'This day we shall have a chance to put that statement to the test,' Taita assured him, 'but make certain that we have good stout fellows behind us to fill the gap if one of us should fall.'

There were still fifty or more refugees waiting their turn to cross the bridge when they heard Soklosh's men behind them: the tramp of their feet, the rattle of their weapons on shield and scabbard.

Taita, Meren and Hilto took up station, shoulder to shoulder, across the path. Taita was in the centre, with Hilto on his left and Meren on the outer verge with the cliff face dropping away below him. Nakonto and ten picked men waited behind them, ready to jump forward if they were needed. A little further down the track, Fenn and Sidudu sat their horses, holding Taita's and Meren's on lead reins. They had unslung their bows and had them at the ready. Sitting high in their saddles they had a clear view over the heads of Taita and the others.

The foremost rank of the Jarrian brigade came round the bend in the pathway and halted abruptly when they saw the three men confronting them. The ranks following bunched behind them, and there was momentary confusion until they had recovered their formation. Then they stared in silence at the three defenders. It lasted only as long as it took the Jarrians to realize the strength of the opposition. Then the burly sergeant in the leading rank pointed at them with his sword, threw back his head and bellowed with laughter.

'Three against three thousand! Ho! Ha!' He choked with laughter. 'Oh! I am dirtying myself with fright.' He began to thump the blade of his sword against his shield. The men around him took up the beat, a menacing staccato rhythm. The Jarrians came on, stamping and banging their shields. Fenn watched them over the fletching of the arrow she held at full draw. Just before the Jarrians launched themselves into the attack she whispered from the side of her mouth, without taking her eye or aim from the face of the bearded sergeant that showed over the top of his shield, 'I have the one in the middle. You take the one on your side.'

'I have him in my eye,' Sidudu murmured.

'Shoot him!' Fenn snapped, and they let fly together. The two arrows fluted over Taita's head. One took the Jarrian sergeant cleanly in the eye: he went over backwards and his armoured weight crashed into the two men behind him, bringing them down. Sidudu's shot hit the man beside him in the mouth. Two of his teeth snapped off and the arrowhead buried itself in the back of his throat. The troopers behind them shouted with anger, jumped over the corpses and rushed upon Taita and his two companions. Both sides were now so closely engaged that the girls dared not fire another arrow for fear of hitting their own.

However, only three Jarrians at a time could reach the head of the line. Taita ducked under the blow of the man who came at him and, with a low sweep of the blade, cut his legs out from under him. As he dropped, Taita sent a thrust through the lacing of his breastplate into his heart. Hilto parried the blade of his man, then killed him with his riposte, which flew through the gap below the visor of his helmet. The three squared up and retreated two paces.

Three more Jarrians jumped over their dead comrades and rushed at them. One struck at Meren, who parried, seized his opponent's sword wrist and swung him out over the edge of the cliff to fall, shrieking, to the rocks far below. The man who came next at Taita lifted his sword with both hands and aimed at his head, as though he were cutting firewood. Taita caught the blow on his blade, then stepped up close and drove the dagger he held in his left hand into the fellow's belly, and pushed him staggering back into his own ranks. Meren maimed another and, as he was falling, kicked him in the head to send him reeling backwards over the cliff. Hilto split the helmet of the next Jarrian with a blow that cut through the bronze crest and went on deeply into his skull. The force of the blow was more than the blade could withstand. It snapped off short and left Hilto with the hilt.

'A sword! Give me a fresh blade,' he shouted desperately, but before those behind him could pass it to him he was attacked again. Hilto hurled the hilt at the face of the Jarrian but he ducked and deflected it with the visor of his helmet as he thrust at Hilto. The blow went home but Hilto seized him round the waist in a bear-hug and dragged him back into his own lines. The men behind him killed the Jarrian as he struggled to free himself from Hilto's grip. But Hilto was hard hit and would fight no more that day. He leant heavily on the comrade who led him back to the bridge, and Nakonto stepped into his place in the line beside Taita. He had a stabbing spear in each hand and wielded them with such speed and dexterity that the bronze heads merged into a blur of dancing light. Leaving a trail of dead and dying Jarrians on the pathway, the three backed away towards the bridgehead, matching the pace of their retreat to that of the tail end of the refugee column.

At last Fenn shouted, 'They are all across!' Her ringing tones carried clearly above the din of the battle. Taita killed the man he was fighting with a parry and riposte to the throat before he glanced back. The bridge was clear.

'Order the axeman to lay on with a will. Bring down the bridge!' he called to Fenn, and heard her repeat the order as he turned back to meet the next enemy. Over their heads he could see the ostrich plumes in the crest of Soklosh's helmet and heard his harsh cries urging on his men. But the Jarrians had seen the slaughter of their comrades, and the ground under their feet was red and muddy with blood. The track was cluttered with corpses, and their ardour was waning. Taita had time enough to look back again. He could hear the thudding of the axes on the guy lines and the bridge timbers. However, the two mounted girls had not yet crossed the gorge. With them, a small group of men stood ready to fill any gap in the line.

'Go back!' Taita shouted at them. 'All of you, go back!' They hesitated, reluctant to leave so few to face the foe. 'Go back, I tell you. You can do no more here.'

'Back!' roared Meren. 'Give us space. When we come it will be fast.'

The girls swung the horses round and their hoofs clattered on the planks of the bridge. The other men followed them across the gorge and reached the far side. Nakonto, Meren and Taita, still facing the Jarrian host, backed slowly out on to the bridge and took their stand in the centre, with the deep drop on either side. The cliffs resounded to the thudding of axes as men hacked away at the main supports.

Three of the enemy rushed out on to the bridge. The planking trembled under their tread. They clashed their shields against those of the three in the centre. Hacking and thrusting, both sides balanced on the swaying catwalk. When the first Jarrian rank was cut down, others ran out to take their places, slipping in the blood puddles and tripping over the corpses of their comrades. Others crowded on to the narrow bridge behind them. Blades clanged on blades. Men fell, then slithered off the sides of the bridge and dropped wailing into the void. All the time the axe strokes boomed against the timbers, and shouts started the echoes anew.

Suddenly the bridge shuddered, like a dog trying to shake off its fleas. One side dropped and hung askew. Twenty Jarrians were hurled, screaming, into the gorge. Taita and Meren fell to their knees to keep their balance on the swaying deck. Only Nakonto stayed upright.

'Come back, Taita!' Fenn cried, and all those round her took up the cry. 'Come back! The bridge goes down! Come back!'

'Back!' Taita roared at Meren, who jumped up and ran, balancing like an acrobat. 'Go back!' he ordered Nakonto, but the Shilluk's eyes were glazed red with battle lust. They were fixed upon the enemy and he did not seem to hear Taita's voice. Taita hit him a resounding blow across the back with the flat of his sword. 'Get back! The fighting is over!' He seized his arm and thrust him towards the far end.

Nakonto shook his head as though waking from a trance and ran after Meren. Taita followed a few yards behind him. Meren reached the end of the bridge and sprang on to the rocky path, but at that moment there was a crack like a whiplash as one of the main guy ropes that held the bridge parted. The catwalk heaved and sagged at a sharper angle, before it caught again. Those Jarrians who still had a footing could no longer maintain it. One after another they slid towards the edge and dropped off. Nakonto reached solid ground a moment before the bridge sagged again.

Taita was still on it when it tilted violently. He slid towards the edge and, to save himself, flung aside his sword and threw himself flat. There were narrow gaps between the lashings of the planking. Clawing with hooked fingers, he found a handhold. The bridge shuddered again and fell until it hung vertically down the cliff face. Taita's feet dangled over the gorge as he hung on by his fingertips. He groped for a foothold, but the toes of his sandals were too bulky to squeeze into the narrow gaps in the planking. He drew himself up by the main strength of his arms.

An arrow thumped into the plank closest to his head. The Jarrians on the opposite side of the gorge were shooting at him, and he could not defend himself. He drew himself up hand over hand. Each time he changed his grip he hung on one hand and groped with the other for the planking above. The bridge was twisted so that each successive gap between the planks was narrower than the preceding one. At last he reached a point where he could not force his fingers into the next opening and hung there helplessly. The next arrow struck so close that it pegged the skirt of his tunic to the wood.

'Taita!' It was Fenn's voice and he craned his neck to look up. Her face was ten feet above him. She was lying on her stomach peering over the edge. 'Oh, sweet Isis, I thought you had fallen.' Her voice trembled. 'Hold hard for just a little longer.' She was gone. Another arrow thumped into the timbers close to his left ear.

'Here, take hold of this.' The looped end of a halter rope dropped beside him. He reached for it with one hand and slipped it over his head, then worked the bight of the loop under his armpit.

'Are you ready?' Fenn's eyes were huge with fear. 'The other end is knotted to Whirlwind's saddle. We'll pull you up.' Her head disappeared again. With a jerk the rope came up tight. As he went up, he fended himself off the dangling bridge with his feet and hands. More arrows slammed into the timbers but although he could hear the Jarrians clamouring for his blood, like a pack of dogs beneath a treed leopard, not one of their arrows touched him.

As he came level with the path the strong hands of Meren and Nakonto reached out to haul him to safety. He regained his feet, and Fenn dropped Whirlwind's reins to run back to him. She embraced him silently with tears of relief streaming down her cheeks.

All that night they kept the column of refugees moving down the track, and in the early light of dawn they shepherded the last on to the bank of the Kitangule river. Tinat was waiting for them at the gates of the boatyard stockade, and came quickly to meet Taita. 'I am glad to see you safe, Magus, but I am sorry to have missed the fighting. I have reports that it was hot and heavy. What news of the Jarrian pursuit?'

'The bridge over the gorge is down, but that will not hold them for long. Sidudu says there is an easier road down the escarpment forty leagues further to the south. We can be sure that Soklosh knows about it, and that he will take his men that way. He will be moving a great deal faster than we were able to. We can expect him to join us again soon.'

'The southern road is the main entry port into Jarri. Of course Soklosh must know of it.'

'I have left pickets upon the road to watch for him and to warn us of his approach,' Taita told him. 'We must get these people on to the boats at once.' First they loaded the horses, then the remaining refugees.

Before the last were aboard the pickets galloped into the boatyards. 'The Jarrians' leading cohorts will be upon us within the hour.'

Meren and his men chivvied the last group of refugees

down the jetty and into the boats. As soon as each vessel was filled the rowers pulled out into the mainstream of the river and turned the bows down the current. Fenn and Sidudu carried Hilto's litter on to the last boat in the flotilla. Twenty remained empty on the slipways so Taita remained ashore with a few men to see to their destruction. They threw lighted torches into them and when the timbers were blazing fiercely they pushed them into the river where they burned swiftly to the waterline. The lookouts on the walls of the stockade that surrounded the boatyard sounded the alarm on kudu-horn trumpets. 'The enemy is in sight!'

There was a final scramble for the boats. Taita and Meren jumped on to the deck where the two girls were waiting anxiously for them. Meren took the helm and the rowers pulled away from the dock. They were still within bowshot of the bank when the leading squadron of the Jarrian vanguard galloped into the boatyard. They dismounted and crowded the bank to loose volleys of arrows, some of which pegged into the deck but nobody was hit.

Meren swung the bows to catch the current of the wide Kitangule, which was in spate and bore them away, sweeping them round the first bend. He leant on the long steering oar as they gazed back at the high cliffs of the Jarrian massif. Perhaps they should have been ecstatic as they took their leave of the kingdom of Eos but, rather, they were silent and sober.

Taita and Fenn stood apart from the others. Fenn broke the silence at last. She spoke low, for Taita's ears alone: 'So we have failed in our quest. We have escaped, but the witch survives and the Nile flows no longer.'

'The game is not yet played out. The pieces are still on the board,' Taita told her.

'I do not take your meaning, my lord. We are flying from Jarri, deserting the battlefield and leaving the witch alive. You have nothing to take back to Egypt and Pharaoh but these miserable fugitives and our own poor selves. Egypt is still doomed.'

'Nay, that is not all I take back with me. I have all the wisdom and astral power of Eos.'

'How will that profit you or Pharaoh if Egypt dies of drought?'

'Perhaps I will be able to use the witch's memories to unravel her mysteries and designs.'

'Do you already hold the key to her magic?' she asked hopefully, watching his face.

'This I do not know. I have taken from her a mountain and an ocean of knowledge and experience. My inner mind and consciousness are awash with it. There is so much that, like a dog with too many bones, I have had to bury most of it. Perhaps some is so deeply buried that I will never retrieve it. At best it will take time and effort to assimilate it all. I will need your assistance. Our minds have become so attuned that only you can help me with this task.'

'You do me honour, Magus,' she said simply.

The Jarrian cohorts pursued them for several leagues downstream, riding hard along the track that followed the riverbank, until swamps and thick jungle forced them to abandon the chase. The flotilla raced along on the current, which was swollen with the rain that had fallen on the Mountains of the Moon, leaving the enemy far behind.

Before nightfall that day the leading vessels of the squadron reached the first of the rapids that had so impeded their voyage upriver so many months before. Now the white water sent them hurtling down the chutes, the banks blurring past on each side. At the tail of the rapids when they stormed ashore below the stockade walls of the small Jarrian garrison, they discovered that the soldiers had fled as soon as they realized that the flotilla was hostile. The barracks was deserted, but the storerooms were well stocked with weapons, tools and stores. They loaded the pick of the supplies on to the barges and pressed on eastwards. A mere ten days after embarking, they sailed out through the mouth of the Kitangule into the vast blue expanses of the Lake Nalubaale and turned northwards, following the shore round towards the hills of Tamafupa.

By this time the voyage had settled into a routine. Taita had claimed a corner of the deck just forward of the rowing benches for himself and Fenn. He had spread a matting sail over it for shade and privacy. They spent most of their days sitting close together on a sleeping mat, holding hands and gazing into each other's eyes while he whispered to her in the Tenmass. It was the only language that was adequate to convey to her all the new information with which his mind brimmed.

As Taita murmured to her he became acutely aware of how her mind and her astral soul were expanding. She was giving back to him almost as much as she was taking, and the experience strengthened and enriched them. Also, far from exhausting them, their intense, unremitting mental activity enlivened them.

Each evening the flotilla anchored before sunset, and most of those aboard went ashore for the night, leaving only an anchor watch aboard. Usually Taita and Fenn took advantage of the last hours of daylight to wander along the shore and the fringes of the forest, gathering roots, herbs and wild fruit. When they had sufficient for their dinner and for any medicines they required, they returned to their shelter, which was set apart from the rest of the encampment. On some evenings they invited Meren and Sidudu to share the meal they had concocted, but often they kept their own company and continued with their studies far into the night.

When at last they lay down on their sleeping mat and pulled the fur kaross over themselves Taita took her in his arms. She cuddled against him and, without the least sign of self-consciousness, reached down and took him in an affectionate but unskilled grip. Often her last drowsy words before she fell asleep were not to Taita himself but to the part of him that she held. 'Ho, my sweet mannikin, I like playing with you but you must lie down to sleep now, or you will keep us awake all night.'

Taita wanted her desperately. He longed for her with all his newfound manhood, but in many ways he was as innocent and untutored as she was. His only carnal experience had been the brutal warfare of the Cloud Gardens, in which he had been forced to use his body as a weapon of destruction, not as a vehicle of love. It had had not the remotest relationship to the bittersweet emotion he felt now, which grew more poignant each day.

When she fondled him he was consumed with an overpowering desire to express his love in the same intimate manner, but instinct warned him that although she stood at the very portals of womanhood, she was not yet ready to take the final step across the threshold.

We have a lifetime, perhaps many, ahead of us, he consoled himself, and determinedly composed himself to sleep.

T he men on the rowing benches were bound for a lost motherland, so they pulled with a will. The familiar lakeshore streamed past, and the leagues dropped away behind the flotilla, until at last the hills of Tamafupa rose from the blue lake ahead. They crowded the rails of the boats and stared at them in awed silence. This place was fraught with evil, and even the bravest were filled with dread. As they rounded the headland of the bay and saw before them the Red Stones that dammed the mouth of the Nile, Fenn moved closer to Taita and took his hand for comfort. 'They are still there. I had hoped they had fallen with their mistress.'

Taita made no reply. Instead he called to Meren, at the helm, 'Steer for the top of the bay.'

They camped on the white beach. There was no celebration that night. Instead the mood was subdued and uncertain. There was no Nile on which to continue the voyage, or enough horses to carry them all back to Egypt.

In the morning Taita ordered the boats to be dragged up on to the beach and dismantled. No one had expected this, and even Meren looked at him askance, but none thought to question his orders. Once the baggage and equipment had been unloaded, the dowel pins were knocked out of their slots and the hulls were broken down into their separate sections.

'Transport everyone and everything, boats and baggage and people, up to the village where Kalulu, the legless shaman, lived on the crest of the headland.'

'But that is high above the river,' Meren reminded him, puzzled.

He shuffled his feet and stood awkwardly as Taita turned an enigmatic gaze upon him. 'It is also high above the great lake,' he said at last.

'Is that important, Magus?'

'It may be.'

'I shall see to it at once.'

It took six days of back-breaking effort to carry everything up into the hills. When at last they had stacked the sections of hull on the open ground in the centre of the blackened ruins of Kalulu's village, Taita let them rest. He and Fenn placed their own shelter on the forward slope of the hills, overlooking the dry bed of the Nile and the impervious rock barrage at its mouth. In the dawn, they sat under the plaited reed awning and looked out over the lake, a vast expanse of blue water that reflected the images of the clouds in the sky above. They had an uninterrupted view of the dam and the tiny temple of Eos on the bluff above it.

On the third morning Taita said, 'Fenn, we are prepared. We have mustered our forces. Now we must wait for the full moon.'

'That is four days hence,' she said.

'There is one more sally we can make against the witch before then.'

'I am ready for whatever you decide, Magus.'

'Eos has thrown an astral barricade around herself.'

'That was why we could not contact each other while you were in her lair.'

'I intend to test her defences for the last time. It will be dangerous, of course, but you and I must combine our powers and make another attempt to pierce her shield and overlook her in her stronghold.' They went down to the lakeshore again. They washed their clothing, then bathed in the limpid waters. It was a ritual cleansing: evil flourishes in dirt and foul matter. While their naked bodies dried in the sunlight, Taita combed her hair and plaited the wet tresses. She attended to his crisp new beard. They scrubbed their teeth with green twigs, then picked bunches of aromatic leaves which they took back up the hills to the encampment. When they reached their shelter Fenn built up the smouldering embers of their fire and Taita sprinkled the leaves into the flames. Then they sat cross-legged, hand in hand, to inhale the cleansing, stimulating smoke.

It was the first time they had attempted astral travel together, but this transfer into the astral plane went smoothly. Linked in spirit, they rose high above the lake and glided westward over the forests. They found the land of Jarri covered with thick cloud: only the peaks of the Mountains of the Moon rose out of it and the snows upon them shone with an austere radiance. The hidden crater of the Cloud Gardens nestled in their icy embrace. They sank down towards the witch's stronghold, but as they drew closer the ether became turbid and oppressive, as though they swam through a cesspit. Its weight and density resisted their passage. Linked as one they strove forward against its debilitating influence. At last, after immense spiritual exertion, they had forced their way down to the green chamber in the witch's lair.

Eos's massive cocoon lay where Taita had last seen it, but now the protective carapace was fully formed, green and lustrous, shining with an adamantine glitter. Taita had achieved his purpose: he had brought Fenn to look upon the veritable form of Eos, not merely one of her shadowy manifestations. Now, when the time came, they would be able to combine all their force and concentrate it upon her.

They drew back from the Cloud Gardens, over the mountains, the forests and the lake, back into their physical bodies. Taita was still holding her hands. As she came alive again, he looked at her through his Inner Eye. Her aura smouldered like molten metal pouring from the furnace, heated by her fear and anger.

'That thing!' She clung to him. 'Oh, Taita, it was horrible beyond my wildest imagining. That carapace seems to contain all the evil and malice of the universe.' Her face was ashen and her skin cold.

'You have looked upon the enemy. Now you must steel yourself, my love,' he told her. 'You must call upon all your courage and strength.' He held her to him. 'I need you with me. I cannot prevail against her without you.'

Fenn's face hardened with determination. 'I will not fail you, Taita.'

'I have never thought for a moment that you might.' Over the next few days he employed all of his esoteric art to bolster in her the spiritual powers that the sight of Eos had shaken.

'Tomorrow night the moon will be full, the most propitious phase of its cycle. We are ready and the time is ripe.' But Taita was awakened at dawn by Fenn's sobs and moans. He stroked her face and whispered in her ear, 'Wake up, my darling. It is only a dream. I am here beside you.'

'Hold me, Taita. I had such a terrible dream. I dreamt that Eos struck at me with her magic. She drove her dagger into my belly. The blade was glowing hot.' She groaned again. 'Oh, I can still feel the pain. It was not a dream. It is true. I am wounded and the pain is bitter.'

Taita's heart leapt with alarm. 'Let me feel your stomach.' He pushed her down gently, drew the kaross as far as her knees and laid his hand upon her flat white belly.

'The pain is not all, Taita,' she whispered. 'I am bleeding from the wound she has inflicted.'

'Bleeding? Where is the wound?'

'Here!' She spread her thighs and pushed his hand lower. 'The blood is pouring through the cleft between my legs.'

'Has this not happened to you before – at your age?'

'Never,' she replied. 'This is the very first time.'

'Oh, my sweetest heart.' He took her tenderly in his arms.

'It is not what you think. That comes not from Eos. It is a gift
and blessing from the gods of the Truth. I wonder that Imbali
did not mention it. You have become a full woman.'

'I do not understand, Taita.' She was still afraid.

'This is your moon blood, the proud emblem of your
womanhood.'

Taita realized that the rigours of the journey, the depriva-
tion and hardship she had suffered, must have delayed her
natural development.

'But why the pain?'

'Pain is the lot of woman. In pain she is born and in pain
she gives forth life. It was ever so.'

'Why now? Why am I struck down at the very time you
need me so?' she lamented.

'Fenn, you must rejoice in your womanhood. The gods have
armed you. The first moon blood of a virgin is the most potent
talisman in all nature. Neither the witch nor all the host of
the Lie can prevail against you on this day when you have
come of age.' They rose from the mat and Taita showed her
how to fold a square of linen into a pad filled with dried herbs
to soak up the discharge. They washed again and drank a little
lake water, but took no food.

'The lion and his lioness hunt better on a hungry stomach,'
he told her. They left their shelter, and walked through the
main encampment. In anxious silence the people watched
them pass. Something in their manner and mien warned that
some fateful business was afoot.

Only Meren came forward to meet them. 'Do you need my
help, Magus?'

'Good Meren, you were ever faithful but we are bound
whither you cannot follow.'

Meren went down on one knee in front of him. 'Then give
me your blessing, I beseech you.'

Taita placed his hand on his head. 'You have it in full
measure,' he said, then he and Fenn walked out of the
encampment and down the hillside towards the lake. The air
was sultry and still, all the earth hushed. No animal moved or

called. No bird flew. The sky was a bright, aching blue, with only one tiny cloud hanging far out over the lake. As Taita watched, it changed gradually into the shape of a cat's paw.

'Even in her cocoon the witch has sensed the threat we pose to her and she moves against us,' he told Fenn softly. She leant closer to him, and they went on until they stood at last on the heights of the bluff. They gazed down on the Red Stones, the mighty barrier that choked the mouth of the infant Nile.

'Is there any force commanded by man or nature that can shift something of that magnitude?' Fenn wondered aloud.

'It was raised by the force of the Lie. Perchance it can be brought down by the power of the Truth,' he answered her, and as one they turned their eyes towards the temple of Eos.

'Are you ready?' he asked and she nodded. 'Then we must go to confront Eos in her temple.'

'What will happen if we enter there, Magus?'

'That I do not know. We must expect the worst, and prepare for it.' Taita took another moment to look down once more upon the surface of the lake. It was smooth and glassy. High above it sailed the little cloud, still in the shape of the cat's paw. Holding hands, they stepped on to the paved pathway that led up towards the domed roof of the temple. Immediately a tiny wind stirred the sullen air. It was cold upon their cheeks, cold as the fingers of a dead man. It scuttled across the lake, scratching the polished surface, then dropped away again. They walked on upwards. Before they were half-way to the crest, the wind came again. Whistling softly, it smeared the little cloud across the horizon and furrowed the lake with dark blue streaks.

The sound of the wind rose sharply. Then it hurled itself upon them. It shrieked as it tore at their clothing and ripped at Taita's beard. They staggered before it, clutching each other for support. The surface of the lake was lashed into dancing white waves. The trees along the shore swayed, their branches whipping. Painfully they climbed on until at last they stood before the main doors of the temple, which were wide open, one sagging on its hinges, the other banging and flapping. Suddenly the howling wind seized both and slammed them shut with such force that the rendering round the jambs cracked and crumbled.

Taita reached up to his throat and closed his hand over the Periapt of Lostris, which hung there on its golden chain. Fenn grasped the gold nugget of the Talisman of Taita. Then, with his free hand, Taita reached into his pouch and brought from it the thick braid of Eos's hair. He held it high, and the earth moved beneath them, shuddering with such agitation that one of the closed doors was torn from its hinges and crashed down at their feet. They stepped over it and went through the opening into the circular portico of the temple. Here, the air was thick and viscous with evil. It was difficult to wade through it, as though they were struggling in the mud of a deep morass. Taita took Fenn's arm to steady her, and guided her along the passageway to the opposite side of the temple. At last they stood before the flower-shaped doorway, its jambs tiled with polished ivory, malachite and tiger's eye. The crocodile-skin door was closed. Taita struck the centre with the rope of Eos's hair. The door opened slowly, its hinges squealing.

The splendour of the interior was undiminished, the emblems in the great pentagram glowing with marble and semi-precious stones. But their eyes were drawn irresistibly to the ivory shield at the centre. The ray of sunlight that fell through the aperture in the roof moved slowly but inexorably towards the heart of the pentagram. It would soon be noon.

The wind moaned and wailed round the outer walls of the temple, shaking the thatching and the roof timbers. They stood transfixed and watched the beam of sunlight. When it entered the ivory circle the power of the Lie would reach its peak.

A draught of icy air blew in through the ceiling aperture. It hissed like a cobra and fluttered like the wings of bats and vultures in the air around them. The beam of sunlight touched the ivory circle. Blinding white light filled the sanctum but they did not shrink from it or shield their eyes. They concentrated on the fiery spirit sign of Eos that appeared in the centre of the ivory disc. As the stench of the witch filled the air Taita stepped forward and held aloft the braid of her hair.

'Tashkalon!' he shouted, and hurled the hair into the ivory circle. 'Ascartow! Silondela!' He had turned Eos's words of power back upon her. The wind dropped abruptly and a frozen silence gripped the temple.

Fenn stepped up beside Taita and lifted the hem of her tunic. She tore the linen pad from between her legs and threw it on top of Eos's hair in the ivory circle. 'Tashkalon! Ascartow! Silondela!' she repeated, in a sweet clear voice. The temple rocked on its foundations and a deep rumble rose from the earth. A section of the facing wall buckled outwards, then collapsed in a pile of rubble and plaster dust. Behind them one of the roof rafters cracked and fell into the outer portico, bringing down with it a mass of rotten thatch.

With a thunderous roar the floor of the temple was torn open. A deep crevice split the pentagram down the centre, ripping through the ivory circle, and running through the paving between them, isolating them from each other. There was no bottom to the crevice. It seemed to reach down into the bowels of the earth.

'Taita!' Fenn screamed. They were divided, and she could feel the strength she had drawn from him guttering and fading like the flame of a lamp running out of oil. She tottered on the lip of the crevice, which sucked at her voraciously.

'Taita, I am falling. Save me!' She tried to turn away from the lip, her arms flailing and her back arched as she was drawn towards it.

He had not realized the full strength of the astral forces they had built between them and he sprang out across the fatal pit to land lightly at her side. He seized her before she toppled into the crevice, swept her up in his arms and ran with her to the flower-shaped doorway. He held her close to his heart, recharging the force that Eos had taken from her.

He left the inner sanctum and raced along the portico towards the outer doors of the temple. A massive roof timber crashed to the ground in front of them, narrowly missing them. He jumped over it and ran on. It was like being on the deck of a small ship in a hurricane. All around him more deep fissures opened in the floor. He leapt over them. The earth heaved and quaked. Another section of the outer wall just ahead tumbled down into a pile of loose debris but he bounded over the rubble and burst out into the open air.

Still there was no respite from the primordial chaos of the elements. Staggering to keep his balance on the heaving earth, Taita looked about in wild amazement. The lake was gone. Where the pale lucid blue waters had lain there was now a vast empty basin in which stranded shoals of fish flapped, crocodiles writhed and ponderous hippopotamus tried to find their footing on the mud. The red rock barrier was nakedly revealed, its magnitude defying the imagination.

Abruptly the upheaval ceased, replaced by an eerie still-ness. All of creation seemed frozen. There was no sound or movement. Taita placed Fenn carefully on her feet, but she clung to him still as she stared out over the empty lake. 'What is happening to the world?' she breathed, through pale dry lips.

'It was an earthquake of cataclysmic proportions.'

'I give thanks to Hathor and Isis that it has passed.'

'It is not over. Those were merely the first shocks. Now there is a lull before the full force breaks.'

'What has happened to the waters of the lake?'

'They have been sucked away by the shifting crust of the earth,' he told her, then held up a hand. 'Listen!' There was a rushing sound like that of a mighty wind. 'The waters are returning!' He pointed across the empty basin.

On the horizon rose a blue mountain of water laced with creamy spume that advanced upon the land with ponderous, stately might. One after another it overwhelmed the outer islands and came on, rearing higher into the sky as it approached the shore. It was still several leagues distant, but already its crest seemed to tower above the height of the bluff on which they stood.

'It will sweep us away! We will be drowned! We must run!'

'There is nowhere for us to run to,' he told her. 'Stand firm beside me.'

She sensed him throwing a spell of protection round them, and immediately joined her own psychic forces to his.

Another gargantuan convulsion racked the earth, so violent that they were thrown to their knees, but they clung together and gazed at the approaching wave. There was a sound like all the thunder of the heavens, so loud that it dulled their hearing.

The red rock barrier was split through from its foundations to its summit. Its entire surface was crazed with a network of deep cracks. The huge wave rose high above it and crashed into it in a smother of foam and leaping wave crests. The mighty rock pier was submerged beneath it. Then there was a roar as the fragments of red rock tumbled over each other and were carried on by the force of the tidal wave into the empty bed of the Nile. They were swept along the riverbed as though they were of no more consequence than beach pebbles. The waters of the lake continued to pour through the breach in a thunderous green spout. The riverbed was neither deep nor wide enough to contain such a volume so the waters burst from its banks and reached as high as the topmost branches of the trees on either side. They were uprooted and toppled into the flow, to be borne downstream like driftwood. Dense clouds of spray towered into the sky above the tumultuous cauldron, catching the sunlight and spinning it into marvellous rainbows that arched across the river.

The crest of the tidal wave surged up the bluff towards where they crouched beside the ruins of the temple. It seemed that it would engulf them also and carry them away in the torrent, but its strength dissipated before it reached them. The residue of its might swirled round the shattered walls of the temple, and reached as high as their knees before it faltered. They linked arms and braced themselves. Although the waters dragged at them, together they were able to resist being swept into the lake.

Slowly the elements regained their composure, the tremors of the earth subsided and the waters of the lake stilled. Only the Nile thundered on, green, wide and smoking with spray towards Egypt in the north.

'The river is reborn,' Fenn whispered, 'just as you are, Magus. The Nile is renewed and made young again.'

It seemed that they would never tire of the magnificent spectacle. They stood for hour upon hour gazing down on it in wonder and awe. Then, on an impulse, Fenn turned in the circle of his arms and looked towards the west. She started so violently that Taita was alarmed. 'What is it, Fenn?'

'Look!' she cried, her voice shaking with excitement. 'The land of Jarri is burning!' Mighty clouds of smoke were rising over the horizon, boiling upwards into the heavens, grey and menacing, gradually blotting out the sun and plunging all the earth into sombre shadow. 'What is it, Taita? What is taking place in the kingdom of the witch?'

'I cannot hazard a guess,' Taita admitted. 'This thing is too vast to admit of reason or belief.'

'Might we not attempt to overlook the land of Jarri once again, and try to fathom the cause and consequences of this holocaust?'

'We must do so at once,' he agreed. 'Let us prepare ourselves.' They sat together on the barren hillside above the thundering river, linked their hands and launched themselves in unison into the astral plane. They soared on high and glided towards the mighty cloud and the land spread beneath it.

Looking down upon it they saw that it was ruined: the villages blazed and the fields were devastated by poisonous smoke and falling ash. They saw people running from it with their hair and clothing on fire. They heard women wailing and children screaming as they perished. They drew closer to the Mountains of the Moon, and saw that the peaks were blown away. From the craters that had split them asunder poured rivers of fiery lava. One spilled down on to the citadel of the oligarchs, submerging it with fire and ash until it seemed that it had never existed.

In the midst of all this destruction only the valley of the Cloud Gardens seemed untouched. But then they saw the peaks that towered above them heave and sway. While they watched, another volcanic eruption blew away half of the mountain. Massive buttresses of black rock were hurled into the heavens. The Cloud Gardens were obliterated. Where once they had stood another yawning crater spewed forth fresh rivers of lava.

'The witch! What of her?'

Taita drew her with him into the very heart of the furnace. Their astral beings were impervious to the raging temperatures that would instantly have reduced their physical bodies to puffs of steam. Down they sank through the passages of Eos's lair, which Taita remembered so well, until they reached the chamber in which her cocoon lay. Already the green malachite walls were glowing, the tiles popping and shattering with the heat.

Wisps of smoke rose from the carapace. The glistening surface began to blacken and crack. Slowly it twisted and writhed, then suddenly it split open and from it poured a glutinous yellow fluid, which bubbled and boiled as it cooked. The stench was overpowering. Then the carapace burst into flames and burnt to a powdery ash. The last of the foul liquid boiled away, leaving a black stain on the glowing malachite tiles. The roof of the cavern burst open, and burning lava forced its way through the cracks to flood the witch's chamber.

Taita and Fenn drew back and rose above the mountains. Below, the destruction was complete. Jarri had disappeared beneath the ash and the lava. When at last they dropped back across the ether into their physical bodies they were at first too moved by all they had seen and experienced to speak or even move. Still holding hands, they stared at each other. Then Fenn's eyes filled with tears and she began to weep silently.

'It is over,' Taita told her soothingly.

'Eos is dead?' Fenn begged. 'Tell me it was not an illusion. Please, Taita, tell me that what I saw in the vision was the truth.'

'It was the truth. She died in the only way that was possible for her, consumed in the flames of the volcano from which she had risen.' Fenn crawled into his lap and he put his arms round her. Now that the danger had passed her strength had evaporated. She was a frightened child again. They sat for the rest of the day gazing down upon the green Nile. Then, as the sun set behind the towering smoke and dustclouds that still filled the western half of the heavens, Taita stood up and carried her back up the hill path to the village.

The people saw them coming and rushed to meet them, the children squealing with excitement and the women ululating with joy. Meren raced ahead of the crowd to be the first to greet them. Taita set Fenn down and opened his arms to welcome him.

'Magus! We feared for your lives,' Meren bellowed, while he was still fifty paces away. 'I should have had more faith in you. I should have known that your magic would prevail. The Nile flows again!' He seized Taita in a fervent embrace. 'You have restored life to it and to our motherland.' He reached out with his other arm and pulled Fenn to him. 'None of us will ever understand the extent of the miracle that the two of you have brought to pass, but a hundred generations of Egyptians will thank you for it.' Then they were surrounded by the exultant throng and borne up to the hilltop. The singing and laughter, the dancing and rejoicing lasted all that night.

It was many weeks before the Nile had dropped sufficiently to be contained once more between its banks. Even then it was wreathed in silver spray, and the roaring flood continued to grind great chunks of the red rock along the bottom. It sounded as though a giant was gnashing his teeth in rage. Nevertheless, Taita gave the order for the boats to be carried down the hill and reassembled on the bank.

'If you had not made us bring them to the top, that wave would have smashed them to kindling,' Meren admitted. 'I argued with you then, and I ask your forgiveness and understanding for that, Magus.'

'They are freely given.' Taita smiled. 'But the truth is that, over the years, I have become inured to you jibbing like an unbroken horse at any piece of good sense I offer you.'

Once the boats were reassembled on the riverbank, they left Kalulu's old village on the heights to set up a new encampment in a pleasant wooded site closer to where the boats lay. Here they waited for the Nile to drop to a level at which it could be safely navigated. The mood in the camp was still festive. The knowledge that they were safe from further pursuit by the Jarrian army and that they need no longer fear the malignant power of Eos was a constant source of joy to everyone. It was enhanced by the realization that they would soon be embarking upon the final leg of the long journey back to the motherland they loved so well and had missed so keenly.

An enormous female hippopotamus, one of a herd that inhabited Lake Nalubaale, ventured too close to the newly opened mouth of the Nile and was caught in the current. Even her great strength was insufficient to save her from being swept down the rapids. Her body was ripped and torn as she was thrown against the rocks. Mortally wounded, she dragged herself ashore just below the encampment. Fifty men armed with spears, javelins and axes rushed down upon her and the dying beast was unable to flee. Once they had despatched her, they butchered her carcass where it lay.

That night, pieces of her flesh wrapped in the luscious white belly fat were grilled upon the coals of fifty separate fires and, once again, the people feasted and danced the night through. Although they had all gorged themselves, there remained plenty to salt and smoke; it would feed them for several weeks. In addition to this, the river teemed with catfish that were stunned and disoriented by the raging waters and easily harpooned from the bank, some were heavier than a full-grown man. They still had several tons of the dhurra they had taken from the Jarrian granaries so Taita agreed that some might be fermented to make beer. By the time the river had dropped to a level that allowed them to take to their oars, they were all strong, rested and eager for the voyage to recommence. Even Hilto was almost recovered from his wound and able to take his place on a rowing bench.

The Nile had changed from the sullen trickle they had known on the journey towards the land of Jarri. Every bend, every shoal and reef came as a surprise, so Taita could take no chances with a night run. In the evenings they moored to the bank and built a secure stockade of thorn bushes on the shore. After a long day confined between the narrow decks, the horses were turned loose to graze until nightfall. Meren led out a hunting party to bring in what game they could find. As soon as it was dark, men and animals were brought into the safety of the stockade: lions roared and leopards sawed around the thorn-bush walls, attracted by the scent of the horses and the fresh game meat.

With so many humans and animals to provide shelter for, the stockade was crowded. However, because of the respect and affection in which they were held, there was always a small but private enclosure for Taita and Fenn. When they were alone in their haven their talk turned often to their homeland. Although in her other life Fenn had once worn the double crown of the Upper and Lower Kingdoms, all she knew of Egypt now she had gleaned from Taita. She was hungry for every detail of the land and its peoples, their religion, art and customs. In particular, she longed for descriptions of the children she had borne so long ago, and their descendants who ruled now.

'Tell me about Pharaoh Nefer Seti.'

'You already know everything that there is to know,' he protested.

'Tell me again,' she insisted. 'I long for the day I meet him face to face. Do you think he will know that I was once his grandmother?'

'I will be astonished if he does. You are much less than half his age, so young and beautiful that he might even fall in love with you,' he teased her.

'That would never do,' she replied primly. 'First, it would be incest, but far more important, I belong to you.'

'Do you, Fenn? Do you truly belong to me?'

She opened her eyes wide with surprise. 'For a magus and a savant, sometimes you can be obtuse, Taita. Of course I belong to you. I promised you that in the other life. You told me so yourself.'

'What do you know of incest?' He changed the subject. 'Who told you about it?'

'Imbali,' she replied. 'She tells me the things that you don't.'

'And what did she have to say on the subject?'

'Incest is when people who are related by blood *gijima* each other,' she replied evenly.

He caught his breath to hear the coarse word on her innocent lips. '*Gijima?*' he asked cautiously. 'What does that mean?'

'You know what it means, Taita,' she said, with a long-suffering air. 'You and I *gijima* each other all the time.'

He caught his breath again, but this time held it. 'How do we do that?'

'You know very well. We hold hands and kiss each other. That is how people *gijima*.' He exhaled in a sigh of relief, at which she realized he was holding something back. 'Well, it is, isn't it?'

'I suppose so, or at least part of it.'

Now her suspicions were thoroughly aroused and she was unusually quiet for the rest of the evening. He knew that she would not easily be fobbed off.

The next night they camped above a waterfall they remembered from their journey upstream. Then the river had been almost dry, but now its position was marked by the tall column of spray that rose high above the forest. While the shore party cut the thorn bushes to build the stockade and make camp, Taita and Fenn mounted Windsmoke and Whirlwind and followed a game trail along the riverbank that was deeply scored with the tracks of buffalo and elephant and littered with piles of their dung. They carried their bows at the ready and went forward cautiously, expecting at every turn of the trail to run into a herd of one species or the other. However, although they heard elephant trumpeting and breaking branches in the forest nearby, they reached the top of the falls without glimpsing them. They hobbled the horses and let them graze, while they went forward on foot.

Taita thought of this section of the river when it had been a mere trickle in the depths of the narrow rocky gorge. Now the waters were white and foaming, leaping from rock to black rock as they flowed between the high banks. Ahead the unseen falls thundered and spray drizzled on their upturned faces.

When they came out at last on the headland above the main falls, the Nile had been compressed from a width of two hundred paces to a mere twenty. Below, the torrent plunged through brilliant arches of rainbows hundreds of cubits down into the foaming gorge.

'This is the last waterfall before we come to the cataracts of Egypt,' he said. 'The last barrier in our path.' He lost himself in the splendour of the spectacle.

Fenn seemed equally entranced by it, but in fact she was engrossed in other thoughts. With a half-smile on her lips and a dreamy look in her eyes, she leant against his shoulder. When at last she spoke, it was in a husky whisper that was almost, but not quite, lost in the thunder of the Nile waters. 'Yesterday I spoke to Imbali again about how people *gijima* each other.' She slanted those green eyes at him. 'She told me all about it. Of course I had seen horses and dogs doing it, but I'd never thought that we would do the same thing.'

Taita was at a loss for an adequate response. 'We must go back now,' he said. 'The sun is setting and we should not be on the path after dark when there are lions abroad. We shall discuss this later.'

They saddled the horses and started back along the riverbank. Usually the flow of their conversation was endless, each idea leading on to the next. But for once neither had anything to say and they followed the game trail in silence. Every time he glanced at her surreptitiously she was still smiling.

When they rode into the stockade the women were busy at the cooking fires and the men were gathered in small groups, talking and drinking beer, resting aching muscles after their long day at the oars. Meren hurried to meet them as they dismounted. 'I was about to send out a search party to find you.'

'We were scouting the trail,' Taita told him, as they dismounted and handed the horses to the grooms. 'Tomorrow we will have to dismantle the boats to carry them round the falls. The track down is steep, so there is much hard work ahead.'

'I have called all the captains and headmen into council to discuss that very matter. We were waiting for your return to camp.'

'I will bring your dinner to you,' Fenn told Taita, and slipped away to join the women at the cooking fires.

Taita took his place at the head of the gathering. He had

instituted these meetings not only to plan specific actions but also to give each an opportunity to raise any subject of interest or importance to the group. It was also a court of justice and discipline before which miscreants could be called to answer for their sins.

Before the conference began, Fenn brought him a bowl of stew and a cup of beer. As she left him she whispered, 'I will keep the lamp burning and wait up for you. We have much of importance to discuss, you and I.'

Intrigued by this, Taita hurried the meeting along. As soon as they had agreed on how they would transport the boats, he left Meren and Tinat to deal with a few matters of lesser consequence. As he passed the women at the fires they called goodnight, then giggled among themselves as if at some delicious secret. Meren had placed their hut at the far end of the enclosure behind a screen of freshly cut thatching grass. When Taita stooped through the open doorway he found that Fenn had indeed left the oil lamp burning, and was already under the kaross on their sleeping mat. She was still wide awake. She sat up and let the fur fall to her waist. Her breasts shone softly in the lamplight. Since her first moon they had become fuller and more shapely. The nipples peeped out cheerily, and their areolas had taken on a deeper shade of pink.

'You have come sooner than I expected,' she said softly. 'Throw your tunic into the corner. I will wash it tomorrow. Now come to bed.' He bent over the lamp to blow out the flame, but she stopped him. 'No, let it burn. I like to watch you.' He came to where she lay and stretched out on the mat beside her. She remained sitting, and leant over him to study his face.

'You wanted to tell me something,' he prompted her.

'You are so beautiful,' she whispered, and brushed the hair off his forehead with her fingers. 'Sometimes when I look at your face I am so happy I feel like crying.' She traced the curves of his eyebrows and then his lips. 'You are perfect.'

'Is that the secret?'

'Part of it,' she said, and ran her fingers down his throat and the muscles of his chest. Then, suddenly, she took one of his nipples between her thumb and forefinger and pinched it. She purred with laughter when he gasped.

'You have not too much there, my lord.' She took one of her own breasts in her hand. 'I, on the other hand, have enough for both of us.' They made a serious assessment of the discrepancy in sizes, then Fenn went on, 'This evening I watched Revi feeding her baby while we sat by the fire. He is a greedy little piglet. Revi says that it feels nice when he suckles.' She leant closer to him and proffered her breast, touching his lips with the nipple. 'Shall we pretend you are my baby? I want to know what it feels like.'

Then it was her turn to gasp. 'Ah! Ah! I never thought it would be like that. It makes something in my belly clench.' She was silent for a while, then gave a throaty little chuckle. 'Oh! Our mannikin has woken.' She reached for him. Her fingers, with practice, were becoming more cunning and skilful. 'I have been thinking about him ever since I spoke to Imbali this evening while you were in council. Do you know what she told me?' His mouth was still busy, so his reply was muffled. She pushed his head away from her breast. 'You will never believe what she told me.'

'Is this the secret you were keeping for me?' He smiled up at her.

'Yes, it is.'

'Tell me, then. I am all agog.'

'It's so rude, I have to whisper it.' She cupped both hands round his ear, but her voice was breathless and broken with giggles. 'It isn't possible, is it?' she asked. 'Just look at how big our mannikin is. He could never fit. I am sure Imbali was teasing me.'

Taita considered the question at length, then replied carefully, 'There is only one way to be certain, and that is to put it to the test.'

She stopped laughing and studied his face carefully. 'Now you are teasing me too.'

'No, I am serious. It would be unfair to accuse Imbali of making up stories if we don't have any proof that she is.' He reached down and ran his fingers over her belly and into the clump of soft curls at the base. She rolled on to her back and craned forward to give his hand her full attention. 'I hadn't thought of it that way. You are right, of course. Imbali is my dear friend. I don't want to be unfair to her.' She moved her legs slightly apart compliantly. Her eyes opened wider and she asked, 'What are you doing down there?'

'Trying to find out if your flower is large enough.'

'My flower? Is that what you call it? Imbali calls it something else.'

'I am sure she does,' Taita said. 'However, if we think about it, it is shaped just like a flower. Give me your finger and let me show you. These are the petals and at the top here is the stamen.' As a botanist, she accepted this description without demur.

'And I thought it was just for making water,' she said, and then was silent a little longer. At last she lay back, closed her eyes and gave a gentle sigh. 'I feel wet all over. Am I bleeding again, Taita?'

'No, it is not blood.'

They lapsed back into silence until Fenn suggested timidly, 'Do you think we should try that with your mannikin rather than just your fingers?'

'Would you like to?'

'Yes, I think I would like that very much.' She sat up quickly and gazed at his manroot with fascination. 'It is impossible, but he seems to have doubled in size. I am a bit frightened of him. You may have to perform some of your magic to get him inside me.'

So close was the bond that they had built up between them that he could feel the sensations she was experiencing as though they were his own. By reading her aura as they went along, he could anticipate her needs before she became aware of them. He paced her perfectly, never too fast or too slow. When she realized he would not hurt her she relaxed and followed his lead in total trust. With all the skills he had perfected in the Cloud Gardens, he played her body as though it was a sensitive musical instrument. Time and again he brought her to the very brink, then held her back, until at last he knew the exact moment when she was ready. Together they soared higher and impossibly higher. In the end she screamed as they plummeted back to earth, 'Oh, save me, sweet Isis. I am dying. Help me, Hathor. Help me!' Taita's own voice blended with hers, his cry as wild and unrestrained.

Meren heard their cries and sprang to his feet, dropping the beer pot he was holding. The contents splashed into the fire, sending up a cloud of steam and ash. He snatched his sword from its scabbard and, his features contorted in a warlike scowl, ran towards Taita's hut. Nakonto was almost as swift: he bounded after Meren with a stabbing spear in each fist. Before they were half-way across the enclosure, Sidudu and Imbali barred their way resolutely.

'Stand aside!' Meren shouted. 'They are in trouble. We must go to them.'

'Get back, Meren Cambyses!' Sidudu pounded on his broad chest with her small fists. 'They do not need your help. You will get no thanks from either of them.'

'Nakonto, you ignorant Shilluk!' Imbali yelled at her man. 'Put up your spears. Have you learnt nothing in all your stupid life? Leave them alone!'

The two warriors stopped in confusion and stared at the women who confronted them. Then they glanced at each other shamefacedly. 'Surely not . . . ?' Meren started. 'Not the Magus and Fenn—' He broke off lamely.

'Surely yes,' Sidudu answered him. 'That is exactly what they are at.' She took his arm firmly and led him back to his stool beside the fire. 'I will refill your beer pot for you.'

'Taita and Fenn?' Bemused, he shook his head. 'Who would have thought it?'

'Everybody except you,' she said. 'It seems that you know nothing of women and what they need.' She felt him bridle, and laid a hand on his arm to placate him. 'Oh, you know very well what a man needs. I am sure you are the greatest expert in all of Egypt on that subject.'

He subsided slowly and thought about what she had said. 'I expect you are right, Sidudu,' he admitted at last. 'Certainly I do not know what you need. If only I did I would give it to you with all my heart.'

'I know you would, dear Meren. You have been kind and gentle with me. I understand how dearly your restraint has cost you.'

'I love you, Sidudu. Since the first instant that you ran out of the forest pursued by the trogs, I have loved you.'

'I know that.' She moved closer to him. 'I explained to you. I told you much of what happened to me in Jarri, but there were other things that I could not bring myself to tell you. That monster Onka . . .' She trailed off, then said quietly, 'He left wounds.'

'Will those wounds ever heal?' he asked. 'I will wait for that all my life.'

'It will not be necessary. With your help, they have healed cleanly, without so much as a scar.' She hung her head shyly. 'Perhaps you will allow me to bring my sleeping mat to your hut tonight . . .'

'We do not need two mats.' His face in the firelight was adorned with a wide grin. 'The one I have is large enough. Certainly there is space for a little thing like you.' He stood up and lifted her to her feet. As they left the circle of firelight, Imbali and Nakonto watched them go.

'These children!' Imbali said, in an indulgent and motherly tone. 'It has not been easy to make them see what lies before their eyes, but now my work is done. Both in a single night! I am well pleased with myself.'

'Do not concern yourself with those others so that you neglect what lies closer to hand, woman,' Nakonto told her sternly.

'Ah, I was mistaken. My work is not yet done.' She laughed.

'Come with me, great chief of the Shilluk. I will sharpen your spear for you. You will sleep all the better for it.' She stood up, and laughed again. 'And so will I.'

A road beaten by countless generations of elephant wound down the escarpment of the rift valley, but it was narrow and they were forced to spend much time and labour widening it before they could carry the boats to the lower reaches of the river below the Kaba-lega falls. At last they relaunched the flotilla and rowed into the centre of the flow. The current was swift and sped them northwards, but it was also treacherous. In as many days they lost five boats on the fangs of the submerged rocks. Three men were drowned and six of the horses with them. Almost all of the other boats were battered and scarred by the time they came out into the open waters of Semliki Nianzu lake. Even in the short time since the Nile had begun to flow again, its waters had been replenished dramatically. They were no longer shallow and muddy and sparkled blue in the sunlight. Across the wide waters to the north the vague blue outline of the far shore was just visible, but to the west there was no glimpse of land.

There were many new villages along the near shore that had not been there when last they passed this way. It was obvious that they had recently been inhabited, for freshly caught catfish were laid out on the smoking racks and hot embers glowed in the fireplaces, but the people had fled at the approach of the flotilla.

'I know this tribe. They are timid fishermen and will not threaten us,' Imbali told Taita. 'These are dangerous times and they are surrounded by warlike tribes, which is why they have run away.'

Taita ordered that the boats be dragged ashore for repairs to their hulls. He left Tinat and Meren in charge of the encampment. He and Fenn took Nakonto and Imbali with them to act as interpreters and set off in one of the undamaged boats towards the western end of the lake and the mouth of the Semliki river. Taita was determined to find out if this other large tributary of the Nile was flowing again, or if it was still dammed by the malevolent influence of Eos. When they reached Karnak he must be able to inform Pharaoh of all these matters, which were essential to the welfare of Egypt.

The wind stood fair from the east and they were able to hoist the lateen sail to aid the efforts of the crew on the rowing benches. With a bow wave curling under the prow they bore away along a shoreline of white beaches and rocky headlands, with a rampart of blue mountains on the horizon. On the fifth day they reached the mouth of a broad, swift river discharging into the lake from the south.

'Is this the Semliki?' Taita demanded of Imbali.

'I have never ventured so far east before. I cannot tell,' she answered.

'I must be certain of it. We must find some of the people who live here.' The inhabitants of the villages along the banks had also fled as soon as they saw the boat, but at last they spotted a decrepit dugout canoe far out in the lake. The two old men on board were so busy that they did not see the boat until it was upon them. Then they abandoned their net and tried to make a dash for the beach, but they had no chance of outrunning the galley. They gave up in despair and resigned themselves to the cooking pot.

Once the two greybeards had realized they were not to be eaten, they became garrulous with relief. When Imbali questioned them, they confirmed readily that this river was indeed the Semliki and that until very recently it had been dry. They described the miraculous manner of its resuscitation. At a time when the earth and the mountains shivered and rocked and the lake waters were tossed by waves as high as the skies, the river had come down in full spate and was now running as high as it had done many years ago. Taita rewarded them with a gift of beads and copper spearheads, then sent the two old fishermen on their way, astonished by the extent of their good fortune.

'Our work here is done,' Taita told Fenn. 'Now we can return to Egypt.'

When they arrived back at the encampment at the mouth of the Nile, they found that Meren and Tinat had completed the repairs to the damaged hulls and the flotilla was seaworthy once more. Taita waited for the rise of the noon wind before he gave the order to weigh anchor. Hoisting the lateen sails and running out the oars, they bore away across the open waters of the lake. With the wind on their best point of sailing they reached the northern shore before sunset and sailed into the branch of the Nile that was augmented with the waters of the two mighty lakes, Nalubaale and Semliki Nianzu. It took them northwards through the territory they had traversed on their journey south.

The next impediment to their voyage was the deadly belt of tsetse fly. They had long ago used up the last of the Tolas cakes, that sovereign cure for the horse sickness, so as soon as the first fly flitted from the near bank to land on the deck of the leading boat, Taita ordered a change of course and took the flotilla into the centre of the river. They ran down in line astern, and it soon became clear that his instinct had been accurate. The fly would not cross open water to reach the boats in the middle, so they sailed on unmolested. At nightfall Taita would not allow any of the boats to approach the bank, let alone land upon it, and they sailed on in darkness, lit by a gibbous moon.

For two more days and three nights they kept strictly to the middle of the current. At last they made out in the distance the hills shaped like a virgin's breasts, which marked the northern boundary of the fly belt. Still Taita would not place the horses at risk, and they sailed on for many more leagues before he ordered the first tentative approach to the bank. To his relief they found no sign of the fly, and the run to Fort Adari was clear.

Colonel Tinat was particularly anxious to discover what had become of the garrison he had left at the fort almost eleven years previously. It was his duty, he felt, to rescue the exiles and take them back to their homeland. When the flotilla was level with the hills on which the fort stood, they moored the boats to the bank and offloaded the horses.

It was good to be released for a while from the tedium of river travel and to have good horses under them again, so Taita, Fenn and Tinat were in high spirits as they rode with a group of mounted men through the pass and were able to look down on the grassy plateau that surrounded the fort.

'Do you remember Tolas, the horse surgeon?' Fenn asked. 'I look forward to seeing him again. He taught me so much.'

'He was a wonder with horses,' Taita agreed. 'He coveted Windsmoke, and could certainly recognize a good mount when he saw one.' He patted the mare's neck and she twitched her ears back to listen to his voice. 'He wanted to steal you from me, didn't he?' She blew through her nose, and nodded. 'You would probably have gone with him willingly, too, you unfaithful old strumpet.'

They rode on towards the fort, but before they had gone much further they had the first inkling that something was seriously wrong. There were no horses or cattle in the pastures, no smoke rose from within the walls and no banners flew above the parapets.

'Where are all my people?' Tinat fretted. 'Rabat is a reliable man. I expected him to have spotted us by now ... if he is still here.' They trotted on anxiously, until Taita exclaimed, 'The walls are in a sad state of repair. The whole place seems deserted.'

'The watch-tower has been damaged by fire,' Tinat observed, and they urged the horses into a canter.

When they reached the gates of the fort they found them standing open. They paused at the entrance and looked through into the interior. The walls were blackened by fire. Tinat rose in the stirrups and hailed the deserted parapet in a stentorian bellow. He received no reply and they drew their weapons, but they were many months too late to be of assistance to the garrison. When they rode through the gates, they found their pathetic remains scattered around the cooking fires in the central courtyard.

'Chima!' Taita said, as they looked down at the evidence of the cannibal banquet. To get at the marrow, the Chima had roasted the long bones of the arms and legs on the open fires, then cracked them open between large stones. The shattered fragments were scattered all about. They had treated the severed heads of their victims in the same way, throwing them into the flames until they were scorched and blackened, then chopping them open as though they were boiled ostrich eggs. Taita imagined them sitting in a ring, passing round the open skulls, scooping out the half-cooked brains with their fingers and cramming them into their mouths.

Taita made an approximate count of the skulls. 'It seems that none of the garrison escaped. The Chima had them all, men, women and children.'

There were no words to express their horror and revulsion.

'Look!' Fenn whispered. 'That must have been a tiny baby. The skull is not much larger than a ripe pomegranate.' Her eyes were bright with tears.

'Gather up the remains,' Taita ordered. 'We must bury them before we go back to the boats.'

They dug a small communal grave outside the walls, for there was little to lay to rest.

'We have still to pass through the land of the Chima.' Tinat's face was cold and set. 'If the gods are kind they will allow me a chance to settle the score with those murderous dogs.'

Before they left they searched the fort and the forest around it, hoping for some sign of survivors, but there was none. 'They must have been taken unawares,' Tinat said. 'There is no evidence of any fighting.'

They rode back to the river in sombre silence, and on the following day resumed the journey. When they reached the territory of the Chima, Taita ordered two small detachments of mounted scouts to be landed, one on either bank.

'Ride ahead and keep a sharp eye open. We will stay well behind you so that we do not alarm the Chima. If you find any sign of them you must ride back at once to give us warning.'

On the fourth day Tinat was granted his wish. They rounded another wide bend of the river and saw Hilto, with his scouts, waving to them from the bank. Hilto jumped aboard as the leading boat grounded and hurried to salute Taita. 'Magus, there is a large village of Chima on the riverbank not far ahead. Two or three hundred of the savages are gathered there.'

'Did any spot you?' Taita demanded.

'No. They suspect nothing amiss,' Hilto replied.

'Good.' Taita summoned Tinat and Meren from the other boats and quickly explained his plan of attack. 'It was the men under Colonel Tinat's command who were massacred, so he has the right and obligation to vengeance. Colonel, this evening you will take a strong force ashore – to avoid being seen by the Chima you must make a night march. Under cover of darkness, take up a position between the village and the edge of the forest. At first light we will bring the boats to the village, then flush the Chima from their huts with a blast on the trumpets and a volley or two of arrows. They will almost certainly bolt for the trees and will be looking over their shoulders when they run into your men. Have you any questions?'

'It is a good, simple plan,' Meren said, and Tinat nodded agreement.

Taita went on, 'As soon as the Chima run, Meren and I will land the rest of our men and go after them. We should be able to catch them between us in a pincer movement. Now, remember what we found inside the walls of Fort Adari. We will take no slaves or captives. Kill every last one.'

At dusk Hilto, who had studied the location and layout of the village, led Tinat's column down the riverbank. The boats remained moored to the bank for the night. Taita and Fenn spread their sleeping mat on the foredeck and lay gazing up at the night sky. Fenn loved to listen to his discourse on the heavenly bodies, the legends and myths of the constellations. But in the end she always came back to the same subject: 'Tell me again about my own star, Magus, the Star of Lostris that I became after my death in the other life. But start at the beginning. Tell me how I died and how you embalmed me and decorated my tomb.' She allowed him to omit not a single detail. As she always did, she wept quietly when he reached the part of the story where he cut the lock of her hair, then made the Periapt of Lostris. She reached across and cupped the talisman in her palm. 'Did you always believe that I would come back to you?' she asked.

'Always. Every night I watched for the rise of your star and waited for the time when it would disappear from the firmament. I knew that that would be the sign that you were returning to me.'

'You must have been very sad and lonely.'

'Without you my life was an empty desert,' he said, and she wept again.

'Oh, my Taita, that is the most sad and beautiful story ever told. Please make love to me now. I ache for you with all my body and all my soul. I want to feel you inside me, touching my core. We must never be parted from each other again.'

With the dawn light and the river mist drifting across the water, the flotilla pulled downstream in line ahead. The oars were muffled and the silence was eerie. The archers lined the gunwales with their arrows nocked. Thatched roofs appeared out of the mist, and Taita signalled to Meren at the helm to steer in closer to the bank. From the shore a dog whined and barked, but apart from that the silence was complete. The mist stirred with the morning breeze, then drew aside like a veil to reveal the crowded squalor of the Chima village.

Taita lifted his sword high, then brought it down sharply.

It was the signal, and the trumpeters blew a ringing blast on their curling kudu horns. At the sound, hundreds of naked Chima came out of the huts to gape at the oncoming boats. A wail of despair went up, and in wild panic they scattered and ran. Few had armed themselves and most were still more than half asleep, stumbling and falling about like drunkards as they ran for the shelter of the trees. Taita raised his sword arm again and as he dropped it the archers let a cloud of arrows fly into them. Taita saw an arrow transfix an infant strapped to the back of a running woman, then kill the mother cleanly.

'Take us to the bank!' As the prow touched the shoreline he led the rush.

Spearmen and axemen raced after the routed Chima. From ahead there rose another wail of terror and despair as they ran into Hilto's ambush. The swords of Tinat's men thumped into living flesh, and made a wet sucking sound as they were pulled free. A naked Chima ran back towards Taita with one of his arms lopped off at the elbow. He was squealing shrilly as the blood from the stump sprayed over his own body, painting him a glistening scarlet. Taita cut him down with a stroke that took away the top half of his skull. Then he killed the naked woman who followed him with a single thrust between her dangling dugs. In the rage of battle he felt no pity or remorse. The next man held up his bare hands in a despairing attempt to divert the blade. Taita cut him down with as little compunction as he would have crushed a tsetse fly crawling on his skin.

Trapped between the two lines of armed men, the Chima darted about like a shoal of fish in a net. Retribution was cold and ruthless, the slaughter furious and sanguinary. A few of the Chima managed to break through the closing ring of bronze and reach the river. But the archers were waiting for those who did, and so were the crocodiles.

'Did any escape?' Taita demanded of Tinat, when they met in the middle of the field strewn with the dead and dying.

'I saw some run back into the huts. Shall we go after them?'

'No. By now they will have armed themselves, and will be

as dangerous as cornered leopards. I will not risk any more of our people. Put fire into the thatch of the huts and smoke them out.'

By the time the sun had risen above the trees it was all over. Two of Tinat's men had been lightly wounded, but the Chima were annihilated. They left the corpses lying where they had fallen for the hyenas to deal with, and were back on board, sailing northwards again, before the sun had made its noon.

'Now only the swamps of the Great Sud stand in our way,' Taita told Fenn, as they sat together on the foredeck, 'the swamps in which I found you. You were a little wild savage, running with a tribe of them.'

'It all seems so long ago,' she murmured. 'The memory is pale and faded. I remember my other life more clearly than that one. I hope we do not encounter any of the bestial Luo. I would like to forget it all completely.' She tossed her head to throw the dancing golden tresses back over her shoulder. 'Let us talk of more pleasant things,' she suggested. 'Did you know that Imbali has a baby growing inside her?'

'Ah! So that is it. I have seen Nakonto looking at her in a peculiar way. But how do you know that this is so?'

'Imbali told me. She is very proud. She says the babe will be a great warrior, like Nakonto.'

'What if it should be a girl?'

'No doubt it will be a great warrior like Imbali.' She laughed.

'It is good tidings for them, but sad for us.'

'Why sad?' she demanded.

'I fear we shall soon lose them. Now that he is to be a father, Nakonto's days as a roving warrior are numbered. He will want to take Imbali and his child back to his own village. That will be soon, for we are nearing the land of the Shilluk.'

The terrain along the banks changed its nature as they left behind the forests and the elephant country to enter a wide savannah dotted with flat-topped acacia trees. Towering giraffe, with reticulated white markings on their coffee-coloured bodies, fed on the high branches and below them, grazing on the sweet savannah grasses, herds of antelope, kob, topi, eland, mingled with herds of fat striped zebra. The resuscitated Nile had brought them flocking back to partake of her bounty.

Two days' further sailing, and they sighted a herd of several hundred humped cattle, with long swept-back horns, grazing close to the edge of the reed banks. Young boys were herding them. 'I doubt not that they are Shilluk,' Taita told Fenn. 'Nakonto has come home.'

'How can you be sure of it?'

'See how tall and slender they are, and the manner in which they stand, like roosting storks, balanced on one long leg with the other foot resting on the calf. They can be none other than Shilluk.'

Nakonto had seen them too, and his usually aloof, disdainful manner evaporated. He broke into a stamping, prancing war-dance that shook the deck, and hallooed in a high-pitched tone that carried clearly over the reeds. Imbali laughed at his antics, clapped her hands and ululated to encourage him to greater efforts.

The herders heard someone calling to them in their own language from the boat, and ran to the bank to stare at the visitors in amazement. Nakonto recognized two and hailed them across the water: 'Sikunela! Timbai!'

The lads responded with astonishment: 'Stranger, who are you?'

'I am no stranger. I am your uncle Nakonto, the famous spearman!' he shouted back.

The boys whooped with excitement, and raced away to the village to call their elders. Before long several hundred Shilluk were gathered on the riverbank, gabbling at Nakonto in amazement. Then came Nontu the Short, all four and a half cubits of him, followed by his wives and their multitudinous offspring.

Nakonto and Nontu embraced rapturously. Then Nontu

shouted instructions at the women, who trooped away to the village. They returned presently balancing on their heads enormous pots of bubbling beer.

The celebration on the riverbank lasted several days, but at last Nakonto came to Taita. 'I have travelled far with you, great one who is no longer ancient,' he said. 'It has been good, especially the fighting, but this is the end of our road together. You are returning to your own people, and I must go back to mine.'

'This I understand. You have found a good woman who can put up with your ways, and you wish to see your sons grow as tall as you. Perchance you can teach them to handle a stabbing spear with the same skill as their father.'

'This is true, old father who is younger than me. But how will you find your way back through the great swamps without me to guide you?'

'You will choose two young men of your tribe who are now as you were when I met you, hungry for fighting and adventure. You will send them with me to show me the way.' Nakonto chose two of his nephews to guide them through the Great Sud.

'They are very young.' Taita looked them over. 'Will they know the channels?'

'Does a baby know how to find its mother's teat?' Nakonto laughed. 'Go now. I shall think of you often as I grow older, and always it will be with pleasure.'

'Take as many beads from the ship's stores as will buy you five hundred head of fine cattle.' A Shilluk measured his wealth in terms of the cattle he owned and the sons he had fathered. 'Take also a hundred bronze spearheads so that your sons will always be well armed.'

'I praise you and Fenn, your woman with hair like sunlight dancing on the waters of the Nile.'

Imbali and Fenn embraced and both women wept. Nakonto and Imbali followed the flotilla for half of the morning, running along the riverbank, keeping pace with the leading boat, waving, dancing and shouting farewell. At last they halted, and Fenn and Taita stood together in the stern to watch their tall figures grow small with distance.

As the first dreary vista of the papyrus banks appeared ahead, stretching away to a boundless horizon, Nakonto's nephews took their place in the bows, and as they entered the watery wilderness they signalled the turns and twists of the narrow channel to Meren on the steering oar.

With the Nile running high, the great swamp was water and more water, with no dry landings, so they were bound to the boats day after day. But the wind that had driven them northwards remained constant and true, filling the lateen sails and driving down the swarms of stinging insects that rose from the reeds. Fenn thought often about the unnatural compliancy of that wind. At last she decided that Taita was exerting the extraordinary powers he had inherited from Eos to make even the elements sway to his will.

In these conditions, the journey through the watery wastes was not unendurable. There were few demands on Taita and he was able to leave the navigation to Meren and Nakonto's nephews, and all other matters to Tinat. He and Fenn passed most of the days and nights in their own private space on the foredeck. The subjects that dominated most of their conversations were, first, Taita's confrontation with Eos and, second, his discovery of the Font and its miraculous properties. Fenn never tired of his descriptions of Eos.

'Was she the most beautiful woman you have ever seen?'

'No, Fenn. You are the most beautiful.'

'Do you say so to still my busy tongue or do you truly mean it?'

'You are my little fish, and your beauty is that of the golden dorado, the loveliest creature in all the oceans.'

'And Eos? What of her? Was she not beautiful, also?'

'She was very beautiful, but in the same way that a great

killer shark is beautiful. She possessed a sinister and terrifying beauty.'

'When she joined her body to yours, was it the same with her as it is with me?'

'It was as different as death is from life. With her it was cold and brutal. With you it is warm, filled with love and compassion. With her I was locked into savage warfare. With you it is a meeting and blending of our separate spirits into some mystic whole that is infinitely greater than its parts.'

'Oh, Taita, I want so much to believe you. I know and understand why you had to go to Eos and join with her, but still I am consumed with jealousy. Imbali told me that men can take pleasure with many women. Did she not pleasure you?'

'There are no words to express how I loathed her infernal embrace. I was frightened and repelled by every word she uttered, every touch of her hands and body. She soiled and corrupted me so that I believed I would never be clean again.'

'When I listen to you speak so, I am no longer jealous. I am left only with a feeling of great compassion for what you suffered. Will you ever find surcease?'

'I was washed clean in the Blueness of the Font. The burdens of age, guilt and sin were lifted from me.'

'Tell me about the Font again. What did you feel as you were enveloped in the Blue?' Once again he described the miracle of his transmutation. When he had finished she was silent for a space, and then she said, 'The Font has been destroyed in the eruptions of the volcanoes, in the same way that Eos herself was.'

'It is the pulsing artery of the earth. It is the divine power of nature, which quickens and controls all life. It can never be destroyed, for if that ever happened, all creation would perish too.'

'If it still exists, then what has become of it? Where has it gone?'

'It was sucked back into the core of the earth, just as the seas are sucked away by the tides and the moon.'

'Has it been placed for ever beyond the reach of mankind?'

'I believe not. I believe that in time it must surface again. Perhaps it has already done so in some remote part of the earth.'

'Where, Taita? Where will it reappear?'

'I know only what Eos knew. It will be closely associated with a large volcano and within proximity of a vast body of water. Fire, earth, air and water, the four elements.'

'Will any man rediscover the Font?'

'It was driven deep into the earth when the volcano of Etna in the far north erupted. At that time, it was where Eos had her lair. She was driven out by the fires. She wandered for over a hundred years in search of the place where the Blue River had come to the surface again. She found it in the Mountains of the Moon. Now it has been driven under again.'

'How long will you remain young, Taita?'

'This I cannot tell with any certainty. Eos remained young for over a thousand years. I know it from her boasts, and from the certain knowledge I took from her.'

'And now that you have bathed in the Font, you will do the same,' she said. 'You will live for a thousand years.'

That night she woke him, whimpering and crying with nightmares. Then she called his name: 'Taita, wait for me! Come back! Don't leave me.' Taita stroked her cheeks and kissed her eyelids to wake her gently. When she realized it had been a dream she clung to him. 'Is it you, Taita? Is it truly you? You have not left me?'

'I will never leave you,' he reassured her.

'You will.' Her voice was still blurred with tears.

'Never,' he repeated. 'It took me so long to find you again. Tell me about your silly dream, Fenn. Were you being chased by trogs or Chima?'

She did not reply at once, still struggling to regain control of herself. At last she whispered, 'It was not a silly dream.'

'Tell me about it.'

'In the dream I had grown old. My hair was thin and white

– I could see it hanging in front of my eyes. My skin was wrinkled and my hands were bony claws. My back was bowed and my feet were swollen and painful. I hobbled behind you, but you were walking so fast that I could not keep up. I was falling back and you were going to some place where I could not follow.' She was becoming agitated again. 'I called your name, but you did not hear me.' She began to sob.

'It was only a dream.' He held her tightly in the circle of his arms, but she shook her head vehemently.

'It was a vision of the future. You strode ahead without looking back. You were tall and straight, your legs strong. Your hair was thick and lustrous.' She reached up, took a handful and twisted it between her fingers. 'Just as it is now.'

'My sweet, you must not distress yourself. You, too, are young and beautiful.'

'Perhaps now. But you will stay so, and I will grow old and die. I will lose you again. I don't want to turn into some cold star. I want to stay with you.'

With all the wisdom of the ages at his command, he could find no words with which to comfort her. At last he made love to her again. She gave herself into his embrace with a kind of desperate fervour, as though she were trying to become one with him, to unite their physical bodies as well as their spirits so that they could never be torn apart, not even by death. At last, just before dawn, exhausted by love and despair, she slept.

From time to time they sailed past long-deserted Luo villages. The huts sagged miserably on their pole foundations, on the point of toppling into the rising waters. 'When the waters rise they are driven to seek drier land at the peripheries of the Great Sud,' Fenn explained. 'They will only return to their fishing when the waters fall again.'

'It is as well,' Taita said. 'If we were to meet them we would surely be forced to fight them, and we have been delayed long enough on this voyage. Our people are eager to see their homes.'

'As I am,' Fenn agreed, 'although for me it will be the first time in this life.'

That night Fenn was haunted again by her nightmares. He woke her, rescuing her from the dark terrors of her mind, stroking and kissing her until she lay quietly in his arms. But still she trembled as though in fever and her heart drummed against his chest like the hoofbeats of a running horse.

'Was it the same dream?' he asked softly.

'Yes, but worse,' she whispered back. 'This time my eyesight was misty with age and you were so far ahead that I could only just make out your dark shape disappearing into the haze.' They were both quiet, until Fenn spoke again. 'I don't want to lose you, but I know I must not squander the loving years that the gods have granted us in futile longing and regret. I must be strong and happy. I must savour every minute of our time together. I must share my happiness with you. We must never talk about this terrible parting again, not until it happens.' She was quiet for a minute longer. Then she said, so low that he could barely make out the words: 'Not until it happens, as it surely must.'

'No, my beloved Fenn,' he answered. 'It is not inevitable. We will not be parted again, ever.' She became still in his arms, barely breathing as she listened. 'I know what we must do to avert it.'

'Tell me!' she demanded. He explained. She listened quietly, but as soon as he had finished she asked a hundred questions. When he had answered them, she said, 'It might take a lifetime.' She was daunted by the scope of the vision he had laid out before her.

'Or it might take just a few short years,' he said.

'Oh, Taita, I can hardly contain myself. When can we begin?'

'There remains much to do before we can repair the terrible

damage that Eos inflicted on our very Egypt. As soon as we have done that, we can begin.'

'I shall count the days until that time.'

Day after day, the wind held fair and the rowers pulled with a will, singing over the oars, their high spirits abounding, their arms and backs indefatigable as Nakonto's nephews guided them unerringly through the channels. Each day at noon Taita climbed to the top of the mast to scan the country ahead. Long before he expected it, he picked out, far ahead, the shapes of the first trees above the interminable papyrus. Under the keels of the galleys the Nile grew deeper, and the reed beds on either side opened out. At last they burst out of the Great Sud, and ahead lay the prodigious plains through which the Nile ran like a long green python until it disappeared into the dusty haze of distance.

They moored the galleys under the steep-cut bank. While Tinat and his men were setting up the first camp on dry land for many a long day, they unloaded the horses. A league away across the dusty plain a herd of eight giraffes was browsing in a clump of flat-topped acacia trees.

'We have had no fresh meat since we left the Shilluk,' Taita told Tinat. 'Everyone will be pleased to eat something other than catfish. I purpose to take out a hunting party. Once they have finished building the zareeba, let the people rest and disport themselves.'

Taita, Meren and the two girls strung their bows, mounted and set off in pursuit of the long-necked dappled beasts. The horses were as glad as their riders to be ashore: they stretched out their necks and whisked their tails as they tore across the open ground. The giraffes saw them coming from far off, forsook the protection of the acacia trees and broke into a ponderous rocking gallop across the plain. Their long tails with tufted black tips curled back over their haunches, and their legs on each side swung forward together so that they appeared to be moving away only slowly. However, the hunters had to push the horses to their top speed to overhaul them. As they came up behind them they rode into the dust-cloud thrown up by the giraffes' hoofs and were forced to slit their eyes to prevent them being blinded. Taita picked out a half-grown bull calf lagging near the rear of the herd whose flesh would be sufficient to feed the entire party and, just as important, tender and succulent.

'That's the one we want!' he shouted, as he pointed it out to the others. As they closed with the animal Taita drew and shot his first arrow into the back of its leg, aiming to sever the great tendon and cripple it. The giraffe staggered and almost fell, but regained its balance and ploughed on, but at a hampered pace, heavily favouring the wounded limb. Taita signalled to the others. They split into two pairs and pressed in on each side of the animal. From a range of only a few yards they shot arrow after arrow into its heaving chest. They were trying to drive through into its heart and lungs, but the skin was as tough as a war shield and the vital organs lay deep inside. Bleeding heavily, the beast ran on, swishing its tail and uttering a soft grunt of pain as each arrowhead thumped into it.

The riders edged their mounts closer and closer to shorten the range and make their arrows tell more effectively. Sidudu was slightly behind Meren and he had not noticed how recklessly she was riding in on the quarry until he glanced over his shoulder.

'Too close!' he yelled at her. 'Sheer away, Sidudu!' But the warning came too late: the giraffe bucked and lashed out at her with its back leg, a mighty kick that made her mount shy. Sidudu lost her seat and was thrown over its head. She fell heavily and rolled in a cloud of dust almost under the giraffe's hoofs. It loosed a second kick at her that would have shattered her skull had it landed square, but instead it flew over her head. When at last she stopped rolling and sliding she lay deathly still on the ground. Meren turned his own horse back immediately, and jumped down.

As he ran to where she lay, she sat up groggily and gave an uncertain laugh. 'The ground is harder than it looks.' Gingerly she felt her temples. 'And my head is softer than I thought.'

Neither Taita nor Fenn had seen her fall and raced on after the giraffe. 'Our arrows are not penetrating deep enough to kill him,' Taita shouted across at her. 'I must bring him down with the sword.'

'Don't risk your neck,' Fenn shouted anxiously, but he ignored the warning and kicked his feet free of the stirrups.

'Take Windsmoke's head,' he told her, and tossed the reins to her. Then he drew the sword from the scabbard that hung between his shoulder-blades and vaulted to the ground. He used the momentum of the mare's gallop to throw himself forward so that for a brief space he was able to match the speed of the giraffe. With each pace its huge rear hoof swung higher than his head and he ducked under it. But as the giraffe planted its nearest hoof and placed its weight upon it, the tendon stood out proud beneath the dappled skin as it came under pressure. It was as thick as Taita's wrist.

On the run he took a double-handed grip on the sword hilt and swung the blade hard, aiming to sever the tendon just above the hock. He caught it, and it parted with a rubbery snapping sound. The leg collapsed, and the giraffe went down, sliding on its haunches. It tried to heave itself upright again but the leg was crippled. Instead it overbalanced and rolled on to its side. For a moment its neck was stretched out along the ground and within his reach. Taita sprang forward and stabbed the point into the back, neatly parting the joint in the vertebrae. Then he jumped back as the giraffe kicked again convulsively. Then all four of its legs stiffened and were still. Its eyelids quivered and the lashes meshed shut over the huge eyes.

As Taita stood over the carcass, Fenn rode up to him, leading Windsmoke. 'You were so quick.' Her voice was filled with awe. 'Like a peregrine on a pigeon.' She jumped down and ran to him, her hair in a wind tangle, her lovely face flushed with the thrill of the chase.

'And you are so lovely you astonish my eyes each time I look at you.' He held her at arm's length to study her face. 'How could you believe for a moment that I would ever leave you?'

'We will speak more of this later, but here come Meren and Sidudu.'

Meren had recaptured Sidudu's horse, and she was mounted again. As she came nearer they saw that her bodice was ripped so that her breasts bounced free. She was coated with dust and there were twigs in her hair. One cheek was grazed but she was smiling. 'Ho, Fenn,' she shouted. 'Was that not rich sport?'

The four rode to the nearest clump of acacia trees and dismounted in the shade to rest the horses. They passed the waterskin round, and when they had slaked their thirst, Sidudu slipped her tunic over her shoulders and stood naked to allow Taita to assess her injuries. It did not take long.

'Put on your tunic again, Sidudu. You have broken no bones,' he assured her. 'All you need is a bathe in the river. Your bruises will fade in a few days. Now Fenn and I have something of great moment to discuss with you and Meren.' This was the true reason that Taita had taken the pair out hunting. He wanted them alone so that he could inform them of his plans.

The sun had passed its noon before he allowed Meren and Sidudu to return to the river where the flotilla waited for them. By then their mood had changed: they were worried and unhappy.

'Promise that you will not go away for all time.' Sidudu embraced Fenn fervently. 'To me, you are dearer than any sister could ever be. I could not bear to lose you.'

'Although you will not see us, Taita and I will be with you. It is just a small magic. You have seen it done many times before,' Fenn assured her.

Then Meren spoke out: 'I trust your good sense, Magus, although it seems that there is a great deal less of that than there once was. I remember a time when it was you who always cautioned me to prudence. Now it is I who must play nursemaid to you. It is strange how reckless a man becomes when something dangles between his legs.'

Taita laughed. 'A wise observation, good Meren. But do not worry yourself unduly. Fenn and I know what we are about. Go back to the boats and play your part.'

Meren and Sidudu rode off towards the river, but kept turning in their saddles to look back anxiously. They waved farewell a dozen times before they were out of sight.

'Now we must set the scene for our disappearance,' Taita told Fenn, and they went to fetch their rolled sleeping mats which were tied behind the saddles. In the bedrolls they had brought with them fresh clothing. They stripped off their dusty, sweat-stained tunics and stood for a moment to enjoy the breeze upon their naked bodies. Taita stooped to pick up his clean tunic, but Fenn stopped him. 'There is no great hurry, my lord. It will be some time before the others return to search for us. We should take advantage of this moment, and that we are unencumbered by our clothing.'

'When Meren reports our demise to Tinat, the whole company will race here to find our remains. They might arrive to find us very much alive.'

Fenn reached down between his legs. 'Do you recall what Meren said about this? How it makes a man reckless? Well, I propose that we be reckless together.'

'When you hold me like that, you could lead me anywhere, and I would make no protest.'

She smiled slyly and sank down on her knees before him.

'What are you doing now?' he demanded. 'This is something you never learnt from me.'

'Imbali gave me precise instructions. But hush now, my lord, I will not be able to reply to any more questions. My mouth will be otherwise engaged.'

They cut the matter fine, and were only just able to complete setting the stage for their subterfuge before they saw the dust of galloping horses approaching from the direction of the river. They moved back into the grove of acacias and sat quietly together at the base of a tree. They held each other's hands and wove round themselves a spell of concealment.

The hammering of hoofs grew louder until Tinat and Meren appeared out of the dustcloud, riding hard at the head of a large band of armed men. As soon as they saw Windsmoke and Whirlwind grazing at the edge of the grove, they swerved towards them and came up only twenty paces from where Taita and Fenn were sitting.

'Oh, by the guts and liver of Seth!' Meren cried. 'See the blood upon the saddles! It is even as I told you. The djinni have seized them and carried them away.'

The dark stains were giraffe blood, but Tinat was not to know that. 'By the coupling of Isis and Osiris, this is a tragic business.' He swung down from the saddle. 'Search the area for any sign of the magus and his consort.'

Within a short time they had discovered Taita's ripped, bloodstained tunic. Meren held it in both hands and buried his face in it. 'Taita has been taken from us. I am a son without a father,' he sobbed.

'I fear that good Meren is overplaying his part,' Taita whispered to Fenn.

'I never suspected such talent in him,' she agreed. 'He would be superb as Horus in the temple pageant.'

'How can we go back to Pharaoh and tell him that we allowed Taita to be taken?' Tinat lamented. 'We must at least find his body.'

'I told you, Colonel Tinat. I saw them both taken up into the sky by the djinni,' Meren tried to dissuade him.

Tinat, though, was dogged and determined: 'Nonetheless we must continue our search. We must comb every inch of the grove,' he insisted. Once again, the men spread out in an extended line and advanced through the trees.

Meren and Tinat were in the lead and Meren walked within arm's length of where they sat. His face was set in a formidable frown and he muttered to himself under his breath: 'Come now, Tinat, don't be so pigheaded. Let us go back to the boats and leave the magus to his tricks.'

At that moment there was a shout as a searcher found Fenn's bloodstained tunic. Meren hurried to him and they heard him arguing with Tinat, trying to persuade him to abandon the search. Presented with the evidence of the bloody garments Tinat at last gave in. They took Windsmoke and Whirlwind and rode back to the carcass of the giraffe to butcher it and carry away the meat to the boats. Taita and Fenn stood up, picked up their weapons and wandered away towards the north, angling back to meet the Nile again far downstream.

'I do so love being alone with you,' Fenn said dreamily. 'Shall we stop and rest again under the shade of that tree?'

'It seems I have awakened in you the sleeping dragon.'

'I have discovered that my little dragon never sleeps,' she assured him. 'She is always wide awake and ready to play. I hope she does not weary you, my lord?'

Taita led her to the trees. 'It will be pleasantly diverting to see who will first weary whom,' said he.

The entire company were plunged into mourning when they heard the dire tidings of Taita's disappearance. The next day when they had reloaded the horses and set off again downstream, they went like a procession of funeral barges. Not only had they lost the magus, but Fenn, too, was gone. Her beauty and winsome ways had been talismans of good fortune to all the company. The younger women like Sidudu, especially those she had set free from the breeding farms, worshipped her.

'Though I know it is not true, even I feel bereft without her,' Sidudu whispered to Meren. 'Why is Taita playing this cruel trick?'

'He must make a new life for himself and for Fenn. Few of those who knew him when he was ancient and silver-haired will understand his magical transformation. They will see in his rebirth some malevolent act of black witchcraft. He and Fenn will become objects of fear and loathing.'

'So they will go to some place where we will not be able to follow them.'

'I cannot comfort you for I fear that it will be so.' He placed his arm round her shoulders. 'From here on, you and I must make our own way. We must find strength and purpose in each other.'

'But what will happen to them? Where will they go?' Sidudu persisted.

'Taita seeks a wisdom that you and I cannot understand. All his life has been a quest. Now that his life has become eternal, so the quest also.' He thought about what he had said, then went on, in what was for him a rare flash of insight: 'That could be either a great blessing or a great burden.'

'Will we never set eyes upon them again? Please tell me that it will not be so.'

'We will see them again before they go. Of that we can be certain. They would never treat us so cruelly. But one day soon they will be gone.'

While Meren was speaking he was watching the near bank as it slid by, looking out for the sign that Taita had promised he would leave. At last he saw a bright prick of light from the bank, a reflection of sunlight off polished metal. He shaded his eyes and peered ahead. 'There it is!' He steered in towards the bank. The rowers shipped their oars. Meren jumped the gap between the deck and dry land and ran to the sword that stood on end, its point buried in the earth. He drew it out and brandished it over his head. 'Taita's sword!' he called to Tinat in the following galley. 'This is an omen!'

Tinat sent a shore party across to him, and they searched the bank for half a league in either direction, but found no further sign of human presence.

Taita is a crafty old fox, Meren thought. He has played this charade to such perfection that even I find myself almost taken in by it. He smiled to himself, but kept a solemn mien as he told the men, 'It is futile to continue the search. These affairs are beyond our understanding. If Taita, the magus, has succumbed, what chance do we stand? We must go back to the flotilla before we ourselves are overwhelmed.' They obeyed with alacrity, consumed by superstitious dread, and eager to take refuge in the galleys. As soon as all were safely embarked, Meren gave the order to continue the voyage. The rowers took their seats on the benches and pulled for a league in silence.

Hilto was at the stroke oar in the bows. Suddenly he lifted his head and began to sing. His voice was rough but powerful, the voice that had commanded men over the din of battle. It rang out across the silent river:

> 'Hail, thou dread goddess, Hag-en-Sa, whose years stretch
> into eternity.
> Hail, thou who art the keeper of the first pylon.
> Thou abidest in the uttermost parts of the earth. Thou
> diest each day at the setting of the sun.
> In the dawn thou art renewed. Each day thou arisest with
> thy youth renewed as the bloom of the Lotus.
> Taita possesses the words of power.
> Let him pass the first pylon!'

It was a chapter from the Book of the Dead, a lament for a king. At once the company took up the chant and sang the refrain:

> 'Let him go where we may not follow.
> Let him know the mysteries of the dark places.
> He hath become the wise serpent of the mighty God
> Horus.'

Hilto sang the next verse:

> 'Hail, Seth, the destroyer of worlds.
> Hail, Mighty One of Souls, thou divine soul who
> inspireth great dread.
> Let the spirit-soul of Taita pass the second pylon.
> He possesses words of power.
> Let Taita make his way to the Lotus Throne of Osiris,
> behind which stand Isis and Hathor.'

The others came in together with some of the women singing a descant:

> 'Let him go where we may not follow.
> Let him know the mysteries of the dark places.
> Let him pass!
> Let him pass!'

Standing in the stern of the leading boat, gripping the steering oar, Meren sang with them. Beside him, Sidudu's voice quivered and almost broke under the weight of her emotion as she reached the higher notes.

Meren felt a light touch upon his muscled right arm that rested on the steering oar. He started with surprise and looked about. Nobody was there, yet the touch had been distinct. He had learnt enough while he had been a novice in the service of Taita not to stare directly at the source, so he turned his gaze aside and saw a vague shape appear in the periphery of his vision. When he focused upon it, it disappeared.

'Magus, are you here?' he whispered, so that his lips did not move.

The voice that answered him was just as airy: 'I am with you, and Fenn stands beside Sidudu.'

As they had planned, they had come on board while the galley was moored to the bank at the spot where Taita had planted the sword. Meren tried not to show his relief and joy in any way that the others might see. He switched his gaze and saw at the opposite edge of his vision another airy shape appear close beside Sidudu.

'Fenn stands at your left hand,' he warned Sidudu, who looked round in astonishment. 'No, you cannot see her. Ask her to touch you.' As Sidudu felt the brush of Fenn's invisible fingers on her cheek her smile became radiant.

When they moored in the late afternoon to set up the zareeba on the bank, Meren addressed the assembled throng: 'We will set up a shrine on the foredeck of the leading galley in the place they favoured while they were with us. It will be a refuge where the spirit-souls of Taita and Fenn can rest during the ninety days while they are trapped in this plane of existence, the period before they may pass the first pylon on the road to the underworld.'

They rigged a screen of reed matting round the small space, and laid out the sleeping mats and possessions of the missing pair. Each evening Sidudu placed an offering of food, beer and water behind it, and by morning they had been consumed. The company was much encouraged to know that the spirit-soul of the magus still watched over them, and the mood in the flotilla lightened. Men smiled and laughed once more, but they kept well clear of the shrine on the foredeck.

They came again to Qebui, the Place of the North Wind, where the river on which they had travelled such an enormous distance joined the other mighty stream rushing down from the mountains in the east to become the true Nile. Qebui was little changed since they had last seen it, except that the irrigated fields surrounding the town were more extensive, and herds of horses and cattle grazed on the green pastures closer to the mud walls of the town. The sudden appearance of a large fleet of strange ships threw the garrison and the townsfolk into consternation and dismay. Only when Meren showed himself on the prow of the leading vessel and called out his friendly intentions did Governor Nara recognize him.

'It is Colonel Meren Cambyses!' he shouted, to the captain of his archers. 'Do not fire upon them.'

Nara embraced Meren warmly as soon as he stepped ashore. 'We had long given up hope of your return so, in the name of Pharaoh Nefer Seti, we bid you the warmest possible welcome.' Nara had never met Tinat. The expedition led by General Lotti had passed through Qebui long before he had assumed the position of governor. Of course he knew of the expedition, and accepted Meren's explanation of Tinat's status as its surviving commander. But while they were conversing on the riverbank Nara kept looking to the moored boats as though he was expecting someone else to appear. At last he could contain himself no longer and burst out, 'Forgive me, good colonels, but I must know what has become of the mighty magus, Taita of Gallala, that extraordinary man.'

'The story I have to tell you is so strange and marvellous as to defy all imagination and belief. But, first, I must bring all my people ashore and see to their needs. They have been in exile for many years and have made a long, difficult and dangerous journey to reach this outpost of the empire. As soon as this duty is done, I will make a full and formal report to you, which you will, of course, relay to Pharaoh's court in Karnak.'

'I beg your forgiveness.' Nara's innate good manners reasserted themselves. 'I have been wanting in my hospitality. You must bring them ashore at once, then refresh and restore yourselves before I press you further on the story of your travels.'

That evening, in the assembly hall of the fort, Nara held a banquet of welcome for Meren, Tinat and their senior captains. It was also attended by his own staff and the notables of the town. When they had eaten and drunk, Nara rose to address them, and made a fulsome speech of welcome. He ended by begging Meren to relate to the assembled guests the story of their sojourn in the foreign lands to the south. 'You are the first to return from those mysterious uncharted regions. Tell us what you discovered there. Tell us if you reached the place were our Mother Nile is born. Tell us how it happened that her waters dried up, then came to flow again in such sudden abundance. But tell us, above all, what has become of the magus, Taita of Gallala.'

Meren spoke first. He described all that had befallen them since they had last passed that way so long ago. He told them of how they had reached the headwaters of the Nile at Tamafupa and found the Red Stones impeding the flow of the river. He went on to relate how they had been rescued by Tinat and taken by him to the kingdom of Jarri, where they had gone before the Supreme Council of the oligarchs.

'Now I will call upon Colonel Tinat Ankut to relate the fate of the expedition led by General Lord Lotti, how he and his surviving men reached Jarri, and the conditions they found there.' Meren gave the floor to Tinat.

As was his style, Tinat's account was terse and without embellishment. In blunt soldier's terms, he described the original establishment of the Jarrian government by Lord Aquer in the reign of Queen Lostris. Then he told of how it had been turned into a ruthless tyranny by the mysterious sorceress Eos. He ended his recitation with the stark statement, 'It was this sorceress, Eos, who used her black magic to erect the rock barrier across the tributaries of the Nile. Her purpose was to subdue Egypt and bring it under her thrall.' Pandemonium broke out as the listeners expressed their indignation and shouted questions.

Nara jumped to his feet to intervene but it took him some time to quieten them. 'I call upon Colonel Meren to take up the tale again. Please hold your questions until he has finished, for I am sure he will provide the answers to many of your concerns.'

Meren was a far more eloquent speaker than Tinat, and they listened in fascination as he described how the magus, Taita of Gallala, had entered the stronghold of Eos to confront her: 'He went alone and unarmed, but for his spiritual powers. No one will ever know of the titanic struggle that must have taken place when those two adepts of the mysteries were locked in supernatural conflict. All we know is that, at the end, Taita triumphed over her. Eos was destroyed and her evil kingdom with her. The barriers she had erected across our Mother Nile were brought down so that now her waters run again. You have only to look out at the river as it flows past this town of Qebui to see how it has been revived by Taita's powers. With the help of Colonel Tinat our people who had been kept captive in Jarri all these years were released. They sit with you this evening.'

'Let them stand forth!' Governor Nara cried. 'Let us look upon their faces so that we may welcome our brothers and sisters back to our motherland.' One after another the captains and other officers of Tinat's regiment came to their feet, gave name and rank, then ended with the declaration 'I attest to the truth of all you have heard this evening from our revered leaders Colonel Meren Cambyses and Colonel Tinat Ankut.'

When they had finished Nara spoke again: 'We have heard many wonders related this evening, sufficient to fill us with awe. However, I know I speak for all present when I ask one more question that burns in my mind.' He paused dramatically. 'Tell us, Colonel Cambyses, what has become of the magus, Taita? Why is he no longer at the head of your company?'

Meren's expression was solemn. For some time he stood in silence as though at a loss to explain it. Then he sighed heavily. 'It is indeed my most sad and painful duty to have to tell you that the magus is no longer with us. He has disappeared mysteriously. Colonel Tinat and I have searched diligently for him at the site where he vanished, but to no avail.' He paused again, then shook his head. 'Although we were unable to find his body, we discovered his clothing and horse. His tunic was stained with his blood and so was his saddle. We can only attribute his disappearance to some malevolent supernatural occurrence, and conclude that the magus is dead.'

A groan of despair greeted his words.

Governor Nara sat still, his face pale and sad. At last, when the noise in the hall abated and all looked to him, he came to his feet. He began to speak but his voice failed him. He rallied himself and began again.

'These are tragic tidings. Taita of Gallala was a mighty man and a good one. I will send the news of his demise to Pharaoh Nefer Seti with a heavy heart. In my capacity as governor of the nome of Qebui I shall cause to be erected on the banks of the river a monument to the achievement of Taita of Gallala in restoring the flow of the life-bringing waters of Mother Nile to us.' He was about to say more, but shook his head and turned away. When he left the banquet hall, the guests followed him out in small groups and dispersed into the night.

Five days later the population of the town and the voyagers from the south assembled again on the spit of land that stood at the confluence of the two branches of the Nile. The monument that Governor Nara had erected there was a column hewn from a single block of blue granite. On it was carved an inscription in beautifully executed hieroglyphics. The masons had worked day and night to have it ready for this day.

This stone was erected in the name of Pharaoh Nefer Seti in the twenty-sixth year of his reign over the Two Kingdoms, may he be blessed with life eternal!

From this point departed the revered magus, Taita of Gallala, on his historic adventure to reach the headwaters of Mother Nile and to restore the flow of her blessed waters for the benefit of the Egyptian empire and all its citizens.

By virtue of his spiritual power he succeeded in this dangerous enterprise. May he be praised unstintingly!

Tragically he perished in the wilderness. Although he will never return to our very Egypt, his memory and our gratitude to him, like this granite stela, will abide for ten thousand years.

It is I, Nara Tok, governor of the nome of Qebui in the name of Pharaoh Nefer Seti, the Great One beloved of the gods, who have written these words to his praise.

Gathered around the granite monument in the early-morning sunlight, they sang praises to Horus and Hathor, and beseeched them to take the spirit-soul of Taita into their safe-keeping. Then Meren and Tinat led the company to the waiting boats. They embarked and set off again in convoy on the last long leg of the return, another two thousand leagues through the six great cataracts and into the fertile lands of Egypt.

With the Nile running so high, the cataracts were long white chutes of tumultuous water. However, the Jarrian boats were designed for precisely these conditions, and Meren was a skilled river pilot. Unseen, Taita stood at his elbow to guide him when he faltered. Between them they brought the flotilla through without loss or serious damage.

Between the fifth and second cataracts the river meandered out into the western desert in a huge loop that added almost a thousand leagues to the journey. The relay riders that Governor Nara had sent ahead of them had a lead of five days, and were able to cut across the bight of the river, taking the direct overland caravan route. The despatches they carried were read by the governor of the nome of Assoun many days before the flotilla descended the first cataract into the valley of Egypt. From that point on the voyage became a triumphal progress.

On both sides the land was inundated with the life-bringing water. The peasants had returned to their villages to work the fields and already their crops were green and flourishing. The population rushed to the banks as the boats sailed past, waving palm fronds. They threw jasmine blossoms into the current to float down with the flotilla. They wept with joy, shouting praise and adulation to the heroes returning from the dark, mysterious southern reaches of the earth.

At each city they came to the travellers were welcomed ashore by the governor, the nobles and the priests and led in joyous procession to the temple. They were feasted, fêted and showered with flower petals.

Taita and Fenn went ashore with them. Fenn was seeing the land she had once ruled for the first time in her present life. No one in Egypt would have recognized either her or Taita in their present form, so Taita dispensed with the spell of concealment behind which they had hidden for so long. Nevertheless they covered their faces with their headcloths, so that only their eyes showed, and mingled freely with the crowds.

Fenn's eyes shone with wonder and joy as she listened to Taita describing and explaining all that she saw about her. Until then her memories of her other life had been hazy and fragmentary, and even they had been restored to her by Taita.

However, now that she stood at last upon the soil of her native land, everything rushed back to her. Faces, words and deeds from a century before were as clear in her mind as though only a few short years had intervened.

At Kom Ombo they beached the boats below the massive walls of the temple complex. Gigantic images of the gods and goddesses were chiselled into the sandstone blocks. While the high priestess and her entourage came down to the riverbank to welcome the travellers, Taita led Fenn through the deserted corridors of the temple of Hathor to the dim, cool inner sanctuary.

'This is where I first looked upon the image of your spirit-soul in your present form,' he told her.

'Yes! I remember it well,' she whispered. 'I remember this place so clearly. I remember swimming down to you through the sacred pool. I remember the words we exchanged.' She paused as though rehearsing them in her mind before she spoke again: *'Fie on you that you do not know me, for I am Fenn,'* she repeated, in a sweet childlike treble that wrung his heart.

'That was exactly the tone you used,' he told her.

'Do you recall how you replied to me?' He shook his head. He remembered clearly but he wanted to hear her say it.

'You said . . .' She changed her voice to mimick his. *'I knew you all along. You are exactly as you were when first I met you. I could never forget your eyes. They were then, and still are, the greenest and prettiest in all Egypt.'*

Taita laughed softly. 'How like a woman! You never forget a compliment.'

'Certainly not such a handsome one,' she agreed. 'I brought you a gift. Do you recall what it was?'

'A handful of lime,' he answered at once. 'A gift beyond price.'

'You can pay me now. My price is a kiss,' she said. 'Or as many kisses as you deem fair.'

'Ten thousand is the figure that springs to my mind.'

'I accept your offer, my lord. I will take the first hundred at once. The rest you may pay me in increments.'

T he closer they drew to Karnak, the slower their progress became, impeded by the joyous population. Finally, royal messengers arrived, riding hard upriver from Pharaoh's palace. They carried orders to the commander of the flotilla to make all haste and present himself at the court of Karnak forthwith.

'Nefer Seti, your grandson, was never a patient boy,' Taita told Fenn, who laughed excitedly.

'How I long to see him! I am delighted that he has ordered Meren to hasten. How old will Nefer Seti be now?'

'Perhaps fifty-four years, and Mintaka, his queen and principal wife, is not much younger. It will be interesting to see what you make of her, for in character she is much like you, wild and headstrong. When aroused, she is almost as ferocious as you are.'

'I am not sure if you mean that as a compliment to us or an insult,' Fenn responded, 'but of one thing I am certain. I shall like her, this mother of my great-grandchildren.'

'I divine that she is in turmoil. She is still held in the coils of Eos and her false prophet, Soe. Although Eos is destroyed and her powers dissipated, Soe still has her in his clutches. To set her free will be our last sacred duty. After that you and I will pursue our own dreams.'

So they came to Karnak, that city of a hundred gates and countless splendours, all of which had been restored by the returning waters. The crowds there were denser and more boisterous than any they had met so far. They poured through the city gates, and the sound of drums, horns and shouting made the air throb.

On the royal wharf stood a welcoming committee of priests, nobles and army generals, clad in their robes of office and accompanied by entourages who were almost as splendidly attired.

As soon as Meren and Tinat stepped ashore, the horns blew a ringing fanfare, and a great shout of acclaim went up from the multitudes. The grand vizier led them to the pair of splendid chariots that stood ready for them. Both vehicles were covered with gold leaf and precious stones so that they sparkled and shone in the bright sunlight. They were drawn by perfectly matched teams of horses from Pharaoh's own stables, one milky white, the other ebony black.

Meren and Tinat sprang up on to the footplates and whipped up the teams. They drove wheel to wheel in the royal way, between the ranks of stone sphinxes, two heroic figures in their warlike armour and accoutrements. An escort of mounted cavalry preceded them, and a company of the Royal Guard ran behind. The voice of the crowd burst over them like a tempest.

Far behind, Taita and Fenn followed in their disguise, making their way on foot through the surging, shifting throng until they reached the palace gates. Here they paused, joined hands and shrouded themselves in the spell of concealment to pass between the palace guards into the great royal audience hall. They stood aloof from the dense press of courtiers and dignitaries that filled the space.

On the raised dais at the far end, Pharaoh Nefer Seti and his queen sat side by side on their ivory thrones. Pharaoh wore the blue war crown, Khepresh: it was a tall headdress with flanged sidepieces adorned with discs of pure gold and, on the brow of the helmet, the uraeus, the entwined heads of the cobra and the vulture, the symbols of the Upper and Lower Kingdoms. Pharaoh wore no cosmetics and his torso was bare, showing the scars of fifty battles, but the muscles of his chest and arms were still sleek and hard. Taita examined his aura and saw that it was brave in endeavour and steadfast in duty. Beside him, Queen Mintaka also wore the uraeus, but her hair was streaked with silver, and her features were etched with the marks of mourning and sorrow for her children. Her aura was confused and forlorn, riven by doubt and guilt. Her misery was deep and desolate.

Before the royal thrones Colonel Meren Cambyses and Colonel Tinat Ankut were spreadeagled face down in loyal obeisance. Pharaoh rose to his feet and lifted one hand. A deep hush fell over the assembly. When he spoke, his voice echoed among the tall sandstone pillars that rose from their plinths to the high, painted ceiling.

'Be it known through both of my kingdoms and throughout all my foreign dominions that Meren Cambyses and Tinat Ankut have found great favour in my eyes.' He paused and his grand vizier, Tentek, knelt before him and offered a silver tray on which lay a scroll of papyrus. Pharaoh took and unrolled it. He read from the parchment, in a ringing voice, 'By these presents, let all men know that I have elevated Lord Tinat Ankut to the nobility, and donated to his dignity one river unit of fertile land along the banks of the Nile below Esna.' A river unit comprised ten square leagues, an enormous extent of arable land. In one stroke Tinat had become a wealthy man, but there was more. Nefer Seti went on, 'From henceforth Lord Tinat Ankut shall be ranked a field general in my army of the Upper Kingdom. He shall have command of the Phat Legion. All this by my grace and magnanimity.'

'Pharaoh is merciful!' shouted the congregation in one voice.

'Arise, Lord Tinat Ankut, and embrace me.' Tinat stood to kiss Pharaoh's bare right shoulder, and Nefer Seti placed the deeds to his new estate in his right hand.

Then he turned to Meren, who still lay prostrate before him. Tentek offered him a second silver tray. Pharaoh took from it another scroll and displayed it to the gathering. 'By these presents, let all men know that I have elevated Lord Meren Cambyses to the nobility, and donated to his dignity three river units of fertile land along the banks of the Nile above Assuit. From henceforth Lord Meren shall be ranked marshal general of the army of the Lower Kingdom. Furthermore I bestow upon him as a mark of my special favour the Gold of Praise and the Gold of Valour. Arise, Lord Meren.'

When Meren stood before him, Pharaoh placed the heavy gold chains of Praise and Valour over his shoulders. 'Embrace me, Lord Marshal Meren Cambyses!' he said, and kissed Meren's cheek.

With his lips close to Pharaoh's ear, Meren whispered urgently, 'I have news of Taita, which is for your ears only.'

Pharaoh's grip on Meren's shoulder tightened momentarily, and he replied softly, 'Tentek will bring you to my presence directly.'

While the entire assembly prostrated themselves, Pharaoh took his queen by the hand and led her from the hall. They passed only a few paces from where Taita and Fenn stood unseen. Meren waited until Tentek reappeared and spoke quietly to him. 'Pharaoh bids you to his presence. Follow me, my lord marshal.' As Meren passed, Taita took Fenn's hand and they fell in behind him.

Tentek ushered Meren into the royal presence, but when Meren would have made another obeisance Nefer Seti came to him and embraced him warmly. 'My dear friend and companion of the Red Road, it is so good to have you back. I only wish you had brought with you the magus. His death has struck me to the heart.' Then he held Meren at arm's length and gazed into his face. 'You were never good at concealing your emotions. What is it that disturbs you now? Tell me.'

'Your eyes are as sharp as ever. They miss nothing. I have tidings that I shall relate to you,' Meren replied, 'but before I do I must caution you to prepare yourself for a great shock. What I have to tell you is so strange and wonderful that when I was first presented with it my mind could not encompass it.'

'Come now, my lord.' Nefer Seti smote him a blow between the shoulder-blades that made him stagger. 'Speak!'

Meren drew a deep breath and blurted out, 'Taita lives.'

Nefer Seti stopped laughing and stared at him in astonishment. Then his features darkened in a scowl. 'Jest with me at your peril, my lord marshal,' he said coldly.

'I speak the truth, mighty King of Kings.' In this mood Nefer Seti struck terror into the bravest heart.

'If this is the truth, and for the good of your soul, Meren Cambyses, it had better be, then tell me where Taita is now.'

'One more thing I must tell you, O majestic and magnanimous one. Taita is much altered in appearance. You may not recognize him at first.'

'Enough!' Nefer Seti's voice rose. 'Tell me where he is.'

'In this very chamber.' Meren's voice cracked. 'Standing close to us.' Then, under his breath, he added, 'At least, I hope he is.'

Nefer Seti placed his right hand on the hilt of his dagger. 'You trespass on my good nature, Meren Cambyses.'

Meren looked wildly around the empty chamber and his voice was pitiful as he spoke to the empty air: 'Magus, O mighty Magus! Reveal yourself, I beseech you! I stand in peril of Pharaoh's wrath!' Then he let out a cry of relief. 'Behold, Majesty!' He pointed across the room to a tall statue carved from black granite.

'That is the statue of Taita, carved by the master sculptor Osh,' Nefer Seti said, in fury. 'I keep it here to remind me of the magus, but it is only stone, not my beloved Taita in the flesh.'

'Nay, Pharaoh. Look not at the statue but to its right-hand side.'

Where Meren pointed a shimmering and transparent cloud appeared, like a desert mirage. Pharaoh blinked as he stared at it. 'There is aught there. It is light as air. Is it a djinni? A ghost?'

The mirage became denser, and slowly took solid shape. 'It is a man!' Nefer Seti exclaimed. 'A veritable man!' He stared in astonishment. 'But it is not Taita. This is a youth, a comely youth, not my Taita. Surely he must be a magician that he is able to mask himself in a spell of concealment.'

'It is magic,' Meren agreed, 'but of the whitest and noblest kind. A magic wrought by Taita himself. This is Taita.'

'Nay!' Nefer Seti shook his head. 'I know not this person, if he is indeed a living person.'

'Your Grace, this is the magus made young and whole again.'

Even Nefer Seti was speechless. All he could do was shake his head. Taita stood quietly, smiling at him, a warm, loving smile.

'Look to the statue,' Meren pleaded. 'Osh carved it when the magus was already an old man, but even now that he is young again the resemblance is unmistakable. Look to the depth and width of the brow, the shape of the nose and the ears, but above all look to the eyes.'

'Yes . . . perhaps I can see some resemblance,' Nefer Seti murmured dubiously. Then his tone became firm and challenging: 'Ho, phantom! If you are indeed Taita, you must be able to tell me something known only to the two of us.'

'That is so, Pharaoh,' Taita agreed. 'I could tell you many such things, but one comes instantly to my mind. Do you remember when you were still Prince Nefer Memnon and not Pharaoh of the Two Kingdoms, when you were my student and ward and my pet name for you was Mem?'

Pharaoh nodded. 'I remember well.' His voice had dropped to a husky whisper and his gaze softened. 'But many others could have known such a thing.'

'I can tell you more, Mem. I can tell you how when you were a boy we set pigeon decoys beside the pool of Gebel Nagara in the wilderness and waited twenty days for the royal falcon, your godbird, to come to them.'

'My godbird never came to the decoys,' said Nefer Seti, and Taita saw by the flickering of his aura that he was laying a trap to test him.

'Your falcon came,' Taita contradicted him. 'The lovely falcon that was proof of your royal right to the double crown of Egypt.'

'We captured him,' Nefer Seti said triumphantly.

'Nay, Mem. The falcon refused the decoy and flew away.'

'We abandoned the hunt.'

'Nay again, Mem. Your memory fails you. We followed the bird deeper into the wilderness.'

'Ah, yes! To the bitter Lake Natron.'

'Nay yet again. You and I went to the mountain of Bir Umm Masara. While I held you on the rope, you climbed to the falcon's eyrie high in the eastern face of the mountain to take down the chicks.' By now Nefer Seti was staring at him with bright eyes. 'When you reached the nest you found that the cobra had been there before you. The birds were dead, killed by the venomous bite of the serpent.'

'Oh, Magus, none but you could have known these things. Forgive me for not acknowledging you. All my life you were my guide and mentor, and now I have denied you.' Nefer Seti was stricken with remorse. He strode across the room and enfolded Taita in his powerful arms. When at last they drew apart, he could not take his eyes off Taita's face. 'The transformation in you defies my powers of comprehension. Tell me how this came about.'

'There is much to tell,' Taita agreed. 'But before that there are other matters we needs must deal with. First, there is somebody I would present to you.' Taita held out his hand and, once again, the air shimmered, then solidified into the shape of a young woman. She also smiled at Nefer Seti.

'As you have done so often before, you confound me with your magic,' Nefer Seti said. 'Who is this creature? Why have you brought her to me?'

'Her name is Fenn and she is an adept of the right-hand path.'

'She is too young for that.'

'She has lived other lives.'

'She is surpassing beautiful.' He looked at her with the eye of a lusty man. 'Yet there is something hauntingly familiar about her. Her eyes . . . I know those eyes.' He searched for the memory. 'They remind me of someone I once knew well.'

'Pharaoh, Fenn is my consort.'

'Your consort? How can that be? You are a—' He checked his tongue. 'Forgive me, Magus. I intended no slight nor injury to your dignity.'

'It is true, Pharaoh, that I was once a eunuch, but now I am a man, whole and complete. Fenn is my woman.'

'So much has changed,' Nefer Seti protested. 'No sooner do I solve one riddle than you present me with another—' He broke off, still staring at Fenn. 'Those eyes. Those green eyes. My father! Those are the eyes of my father. Is it possible that Fenn is of my own royal blood?'

'Come, Mem!' Taita chided him gently. 'First, you complain of the mysteries I lay before you, and then you demand I heap more upon you. Let me tell you simply that Fenn stands in your direct line. Your blood is her blood, but far back in time.'

'You said that she has lived other lives. Was it in one of those other lives?'

'Even so,' Taita agreed.

'Explain it to me!' Pharaoh commanded.

'Later we will have time for that. However, you and Egypt are still under threat. You already know of the witch, Eos, who stopped the waters of Mother Nile.'

'Is it true that you destroyed her in her lair?'

'The witch is no more, but one of her minions is still at large. His name is Soe. He is a dangerous man.'

'Soe! I know of a man by that name. Mintaka spoke of him. He is a preacher, the apostle of a new goddess.'

'Spelt backwards his name is Eos. His goddess was the sorceress. His purpose was to destroy you and your bloodline, and to usurp the double throne of Egypt for the witch.'

Nefer Seti's expression was horror-struck. 'This Soe had the ear of Mintaka, my principal wife. She believes in him. He converted her to his new religion.'

'Why did you not intervene?'

'I humoured her. Mintaka was demented with grief for our dead babies. Soe gave her comfort. I saw no harm in it.'

'There was great harm in it,' Taita said. 'Harm to you and

to Egypt. Soe is still a terrible threat. He is the last adherent of the witch, the last remaining vestige of her presence on this earth. He is part of the Great Lie.'

'What must I do, Taita? As soon as the Nile began to flow again, Soe disappeared. We do not know what has become of him.'

'Before anything else, I must capture him and bring him to you. Queen Mintaka is so deeply in his thrall that she believes all he tells her. She would have given you over to him. She will not believe evil of him, unless the confession of that evil comes from the mouth of Soe himself.'

'What do you need from me, Taita?' Nefer Seti asked.

'You must take Queen Mintaka away. I need to have the freedom of the Palace of Memnon on the west bank. Take her to Assuit to make sacrifice at the temple of Hathor. Tell her that the goddess appeared to you in a vision and demanded this of you both for the sake of your dear babes, Prince Khaba and his little sister Unas, who are now in the underworld.'

'It is true that I have felt the need to make sacrifice to Hathor. The queen and I will leave by royal barge in five days' time, on the night of the new moon. What else do you require of me?'

'I need Lord Meren and a hundred of your best fighting men. Meren must carry your Hawk Seal, which gives him your unbridled authority.'

'He shall have these things.'

No sooner had the royal couple embarked on their barge and sailed away than Meren and Taita, with the escort of guardsmen, crossed the Nile to the west bank. They rode up the hills to Mintaka's abode, the Palace of Memnon, and arrived with the dawn.

The household was taken by surprise. The palace vizier, with a detachment of the household guards at his back, tried ineffectually to oppose their entry. The palace guards, though, were soft from a life of good eating and high living. Nervously they eyed the hundred hard warriors that faced them.

Meren held up the Hawk Seal: 'We are carrying out the orders of Pharaoh Nefer Seti. Stand aside and let us pass!'

'He bears the Hawk Seal.' The vizier capitulated and turned to the captain of the palace guards. 'Take your men back to their barracks and keep them there until I send you word.'

Meren and Taita marched into the entrance portico of the palace, their nailed sandals ringing on the marble slabs. Taita was no longer covered by the spell of concealment. Instead he wore a breastplate of crocodile skin and a matching helmet, the visor drawn down to cover his features. He cut a formidable and menacing figure. The palace servants and Mintaka's maids fled before him.

'Where do we begin the search, Magus?' Meren asked. 'Is the creature still hiding here?'

'Soe is here.'

'You are so certain.'

'The foul reek of Eos is heavy in the air,' Taita told him.

Meren sniffed loudly.

'I can smell nothing.'

'Keep ten of your men with us. Place the rest to cover all the doors and gates. Soe has the ability to change his physical shape and form so nobody must leave this palace, neither man, nor woman, nor animal,' Taita told him. Meren relayed his orders and the men marched away to their posts.

Purposefully Taita moved through the huge, magnificently appointed rooms, Meren and his detachment following closely, swords drawn. At intervals Taita stopped and seemed to test the air, like a hunting hound following the scent of his quarry.

They came at last to the queen's inner garden, a spacious atrium surrounded by high sandstone walls and open to the cloudless blue sky. It was laid out around avenues of flowering trees with a central fountain, surrounded by marble benches strewn with silken cushions. Lutes and other musical instruments lay where they had been abandoned by Mintaka's hand-maidens at the approach of the soldiers, and the lingering perfume of nubile young women mingled with that of orange blossom.

At the far end of the atrium stood a small arbour of trellised vines. Without hesitation, Taita crossed to it, his step quick and sure. On a tall pink marble plinth in the centre stood a statue carved from the same material. Someone had laid bouquets of sun lilies at its foot, and their scent was cloying on the air. It dulled the senses, like some powerful opiate.

'The flowers of the witch,' Taita whispered. 'I remember the odour so clearly.' Then he studied the statue on the plinth. Life-sized, it was in the shape of a veiled woman, the folds of her mantle enveloping her from the top of her head to her ankles. The dainty feet below the hem were carved with such skill that they seemed made of warm flesh rather than cold, lifeless stone.

'The feet of the witch,' Taita said. 'This is the shrine at which Queen Mintaka worships her.' In Taita's nostrils the odour of evil was more pungent now than the heavy scent of the lilies. 'Lord Meren, have your men cast down this statue,' Taita said quietly.

Even the indomitable Meren was awed by the ghastly influence of the witch that filled her shrine. He gave the order in a subdued tone.

The soldiers sheathed their swords and put their shoulders to the statue. They were brawny men and strong, but it resisted their efforts to topple it.

'Tashkalon!' cried Taita, once again turning Eos's word of power against her. The statue moved, marble squealing on marble, like the cry of a lost soul. It startled the soldiers, who jumped back in alarm.

'Ascartow!' Taita pointed his sword at the figure of Eos, which began slowly to topple forward.

'Silondela!' he shouted, and the statue fell full length to the paving stones and shattered into fragments. Only the dainty feet remained intact. Taita stepped forward and touched each one with the point of his sword. Slowly they cracked and crumbled to piles of pink dust. The bunches of sun lilies on the plinth withered until they were black and dry.

Slowly Taita circled the base of the plinth. Every few paces he tapped the marble. The sound was firm and solid until he reached the back wall. Here the marble emitted a dull, hollow echo. Taita stepped back and studied it. Then he moved forward and placed the heel of his hand in the top right corner and applied a steady pressure. There was the sharp sound of some internal lever moving and the entire panel swung open like a trapdoor.

In the silence that followed they all stared into the dark square opening that was revealed in the back of the plinth. It was just large enough for a man to pass through.

'The hiding place of the false priest of Eos,' Taita said. 'Bring the torches from the brackets in the audience hall.' The soldiers hurried to obey. When they returned, Taita took one and held it into the opening. By the torchlight he saw that a flight of stone steps descended into the darkness. Without hesitation he stooped through the opening and started down them. There were thirteen and at the bottom they levelled out into a tunnel that was wide and high enough for a tall man to walk along without stooping. The floor was of plain sandstone tiles. The walls were unadorned with paintings or engravings.

'Keep close behind me,' Taita told Meren, as he strode down the tunnel. The air was stale and old, heavy with the odour of damp earth and long-buried dead things. Twice Taita came to forks in the tunnel, but each time he made an instinctive choice without pausing to consider. At last a glimmer of light appeared ahead of him. He went on resolutely.

He passed through a kitchen which contained large amphorae of oil, water and wine. There were wooden bins of dhurra bread and baskets of fruit and vegetables. Legs of smoked meat hung from hooks in the roof. In the centre of the room a thin spiral of smoke twisted up from the ashes on the hearth and disappeared into a ventilation hole in the roof. A half-eaten meal lay with a jug and bowl of red wine on the low wooden table. A small oil lamp threw shadows into the corners. Taita crossed the kitchen to the doorway in the opposite wall. He looked through it into a cell, which was dimly lit by a single lamp.

Some articles of clothing, a tunic, a cloak and a pair of sandals, were thrown carelessly into a corner. A sleeping mat was spread in the middle of the floor, with a kaross made of jackal pelts on top. Taita took a corner of the kaross and jerked it aside. A small child lay under it, of no more than two, an appealing little boy whose eyes were large and inquisitive as he stared up at Taita.

Taita reached down and placed his hand on the child's bald head. There was a sizzling sound and the sharp reek of scorched flesh. The brat screamed and twisted away from Taita's touch. Imprinted on his pate was a raw red brand, not the outline of Taita's hand but the cat's paw of Eos.

'You have wounded the little fellow,' blurted Meren, his voice softening with pity.

'It is no infant,' Taita answered. 'It is the last evil branch and twig of the sorceress. This is her spirit sign emblazoned on its head.' He reached out to touch the creature again, but it shrieked and cowered away from him. He seized it by the ankles and held it upside down, struggling and twisting in his grip. 'Unmask yourself, Soe. The witch, your mistress, has been consumed in the subterranean flames of the earth. None of her powers will avail you any longer.' He hurled the child on to the sleeping mat, where it lay whimpering.

Taita made a pass over it with his right hand, stripping away Soe's deception. The infant changed size and shape slowly until it was revealed as the witch's emissary, Soe, his eyes blazing and features contorted with malevolence and hatred.

'Do you recognize him now?' Taita asked Meren.

'By Seth's foul breath, it is Soe who set the toads upon Demeter. I last saw this devil's spawn riding off into the night on the back of the hyena, his familiar.'

'Bind him!' Taita ordered. 'He goes to Karnak to face the justice of Pharaoh.'

The morning after the royal return to Karnak from Assuit, Queen Mintaka sat beside Pharaoh in the private audience chamber of the palace. The bright sun was streaming in through the high windows. It was not flattering to her: she looked drawn and exhausted. It seemed to Meren that she had aged many years since he had last seen her only a few days before.

Pharaoh sat on a higher throne than his queen. Crossed over his chest he held the golden flails, the symbols of justice and punishment. On his head was the tall red and white crown of the Two Kingdoms, known as the Mighty One, Pschent. A pair of scribes sat at either side of the throne to record his deliberations.

Pharaoh Nefer Seti acknowledged Meren. 'Have you succeeded in the task I set you, Lord Marshal?'

'I have, mighty Pharaoh. Your enemy is in my custody.'

'I expected no less of you. Nevertheless, I am well pleased. You may bring him before me to answer my questions.'

Meren banged the butt of his spear three times on the floor. Immediately there was the tramp of nailed sandals and an escort of ten guardsmen filed into the room. Queen Mintaka regarded them with lacklustre gaze until she recognized the prisoner in their midst.

Soe was barefooted and naked, except for a white linen breech clout. Heavy bronze chains shackled his wrists and ankles. His face was haggard, but his chin was lifted high in defiance. Mintaka gasped and sprang to her feet, staring at him in consternation and dismay. 'Pharaoh, this is a mighty and powerful prophet, a servant of the nameless goddess. He is no enemy! We cannot treat him thus.'

Pharaoh turned his head slowly and stared at her. 'If he is not my enemy, why did you wish to hide him from me?' he asked.

Mintaka faltered and covered her mouth with a hand. She sank down upon her throne, her face ashen and her eyes stricken.

Pharaoh turned back to Soe. 'State your name!' he ordered the captive.

Soe glared at him. 'I acknowledge no authority above that of the nameless goddess,' he declared.

'The one you speak of is no longer nameless. Her name was Eos, and she was never a goddess.'

'Beware!' Soe shouted. 'You blaspheme! The wrath of the goddess is swift and certain.'

Pharaoh ignored this outburst. 'Did you conspire with this sorceress to dam the Mother Nile?'

'I answer only to the goddess,' Soe snarled.

'Did you, in concert with this sorceress, use supernatural powers to inflict the plagues upon this very Egypt? Was your purpose to topple me from the throne?'

'You are no true king!' Soe shouted. 'You are a usurper and an apostate! Eos is the ruler of the earth and of all its nations!'

'Did you strike down my children, prince and princess of the blood royal?'

'They were not of the royal blood,' Soe asserted. 'They were commoners. The goddess alone is of royal blood.'

'Did you use your evil influence to turn my queen aside from the path of honour? Did you convince her that she should help you to place the sorceress on my throne?'

'It is not your throne. It is the rightful throne of Eos.'

'Did you promise my queen to restore our children to life?' Pharaoh demanded, in a voice as cold and sharp as a sword blade.

'The tomb never yields up its fruit,' Soe replied.

'So you lied. Ten thousand lies! You lied and you murdered and you spread sedition and despair throughout my empire.'

'In the service of Eos, lies are things of beauty, murder is a noble act. I spread no sedition. I spread the truth.'

'Soe, you are condemned from your own mouth.'

'You cannot harm me. I am protected by my goddess.'

'Eos is destroyed. Your goddess is no more,' Pharaoh intoned gravely. He turned back to Mintaka. 'My queen, have you heard enough?'

Mintaka was sobbing quietly. She was so overcome that she was unable to speak, but she nodded, then covered her face in shame.

At last Pharaoh looked directly at two figures who were standing quietly at the back of the hall. The visor of Taita's helmet was closed and Fenn's face was covered with a veil. Only her green eyes showed.

'Tell us how Eos was destroyed,' Pharaoh ordered.

'Mighty one, she was consumed by fire,' said Taita.

'So it is fitting that her creature should share her fate.'

'It would be a merciful death, better than he deserves, better than the death he dealt out to the innocent.'

Pharaoh nodded thoughtfully, then turned back to Mintaka. 'I am minded to give you an opportunity to redeem yourself in my sight, and in the sight of the gods of Egypt.'

Mintaka threw herself at his feet. 'I did not understand what I was doing. He promised that the Nile would flow again and our children would be restored to us, if only you would acknowledge the goddess. I believed him.'

'All this I understand.' Pharaoh raised Mintaka to her feet. 'The penance I impose upon you is that your own royal hand will set the torch to the execution fire in which Soe and the last trace of the sorceress will be expunged from my domains.'

Mintaka swayed on her feet and her expression was one of utter despair. Then she seemed to rally herself. 'I am Pharaoh's loyal wife and subject. To obey his command is my duty. I shall set the fire under Soe, in whom once I believed.'

'Lord Meren, take this miserable creature down into the

courtyard where the stake awaits him. Queen Mintaka will go with you.'

The escort marched Soe down the marble staircase and into the courtyard. Meren followed them down, with Mintaka leaning heavily on his arm.

'Stand by me, Magus,' Pharaoh commanded Taita. 'You will bear witness to the fate of our enemy.' Together they went to the balcony that overlooked the courtyard.

A tall pile, built of logs and bundles of dried papyrus, stood at the centre of the courtyard below them. It had been soaked with lamp oil. A wooden ladder reached up to the scaffold that surmounted the pyre. Two brawny executioners were waiting at the foot. They took Soe from his guards and dragged him up, for his legs could barely support him, then roped him to the stake. They descended the ladder, leaving him alone on the summit. Meren went to the burning brazier beside the doorway into the courtyard. He dipped a tar-soaked torch into the flames, carried it to Mintaka and placed it in her hand. He left her at the foot of the execution pyre.

Mintaka looked up at Pharaoh on the balcony above her. Her expression was pitiful. He nodded to her. She hesitated a moment longer, then hurled the burning torch on to the bundles of oil-soaked papyrus. She staggered back as a sheet of fire shot up the side of the pyre. The flames and black smoke boiled up higher than the roof of the palace. In the heart of the flames, Soe shouted to the cloudless sky, 'Hear me, Eos, the only true goddess! Your faithful servant calls to you. Lift me out of the fire. Show your power and holy might to this petty pharaoh and all the world!' Then his voice was drowned by the crackling of the conflagration. Soe sagged forward on his bonds as the smoke and heat enveloped him, and the leaping flames screened him. For an instant they parted to reveal his form, blackened and twisted, no longer human, still hanging from the stake. Then the pyre collapsed in upon itself and he was consumed in the centre of the fire.

Meren drew Mintaka back to the safety of the stairway and led her up to the royal audience hall. She had become a frail old woman, stripped of her dignity and beauty. She went to Pharaoh and knelt before him. 'My lord husband, I beg your forgiveness,' she whispered. 'I was a stupid woman, and there is no excuse for what I did.'

'You are forgiven,' said Nefer Seti, then he seemed at a loss as to what he should do next. He made as if to lift her to her feet, but then stepped back. He knew that such condescension ill-befitted a divine pharaoh and glanced across at Taita, seeking his guidance. Taita touched Fenn's arm. She nodded and lifted her veil, revealing her golden beauty, then crossed the floor and stooped over Mintaka. 'Come, my queen,' she said, and took Mintaka's arm.

The queen looked up at her. 'Who are you?' she quavered.

'I am one who cares for you deeply,' Fenn replied, and lifted her up.

Mintaka stared into her green eyes, then suddenly she sobbed, 'I sense that you are good and wise beyond your years,' and went into Fenn's embrace. Holding her close, Fenn led her from the chamber.

'Who is that young woman?' Nefer Seti asked Taita. 'I can wait no longer to know. Tell me at once, Magus. That is my royal command.'

'Pharaoh, she is the reincarnation of your grandmother, Queen Lostris,' Taita replied, 'the woman I once loved and now love again.'

Meren's new estates extended for thirty leagues along the bank of Mother Nile. At the centre stood one of the royal palaces and a magnificent temple dedicated to the falcon god Horus. Both buildings formed part of the royal gift. Three hundred tenant farmers tilled the fertile fields, which were irrigated from the river. They tithed a fifth part of their crops to their new landlord, Lord Marshal Meren Cambyses. A hundred and fifty serfs and two hundred slaves, captives of Pharaoh's wars, worked in the palace or on the private part of the estate.

Meren named the estate Karim Ek-Horus, the Vineyards of Horus. In the spring of that year when the crops were planted, and the earth was bountiful, Pharaoh came downriver from Karnak with all his royal suite to attend the nuptials of Lord Meren and his bride.

Meren and Sidudu came together on the riverbank. Meren was dressed in all the regalia of a marshal of the army, with ostrich plumes in his helmet, the gold chains of Valour and Praise on his bare chest. Sidudu had jasmine blossoms in her hair, and her dress was a cloud of white silk from far Cathay. They broke the jars of Nile water and kissed while all the people shouted with joy and besought the gods' blessing.

The festivities lasted ten days and nights. Meren wanted to fill the palace fountains with wine, but from the moment she became his wife Sidudu forbade such extravagance. Meren was startled by how readily she had assumed the mantle of control over his household, but Taita comforted him: 'She will make you the best possible wife. Her frugality is proof of that. An extravagant wife is a scorpion in her husband's bed.'

Each day Nefer Seti sat with Taita and Meren for hours, listening avidly to the saga of their journey to the Mountains of the Moon. When the tale was told in all its detail, he commanded them to repeat it. Sidudu, Fenn and Mintaka sat with them. Under Fenn's influence the queen's nature had changed. She had shed the weight of her sorrow and guilt and was once again serene and aglow with happiness. It was clear to all that she had been fully reinstated in her husband's favour.

One part of the story fascinated them, particularly Nefer Seti. He returned to it again and again. 'Tell me once more about the Font,' he demanded of Taita. 'Make certain you leave out no single detail. Begin with the account of how you crossed the bridge of stone over the burning lava lake.'

When Taita reached the end of the tale, he was still not

satisfied: 'Describe the taste of the Blueness as you drew it into your mouth'; 'Why did it not suffocate you like water in your lungs when you breathed it?'; 'Was it cold or hot?'; 'How long after you emerged from the Font did you become aware of its marvellous effects?'; 'You say the lava burns upon your legs were healed at once, and your strength returned to all your limbs. Is that truly so?'; 'Now the Font has been destroyed by the eruptions of the volcano, has it been drowned in the burning lava? What a terrible loss that would be. Has it been placed for ever beyond our grasp?'

'The Font, like the life-giving force it bestows, is eternal. As long as life on this earth exists, so also must the Font,' Taita replied.

'Down the years the philosophers, have dreamed of this magical Font, and all my ancestors sought it. Eternal life and eternal youth, what matchless treasures are these?' Pharaoh's eyes were bright with an almost religious fervour. Suddenly he exclaimed, 'Find it for me, Taita. I do not command it but I implore you. I have only twenty or thirty years of my allotted time remaining to me. Go forth, Taita, and find the Font again.'

Taita did not have to look at Fenn. Her voice rang clearly in his head: 'My darling Taita, I add my supplications to those of your king. Take me with you. Let us go out into all the earth until we come to the place where the Font is hidden. Let me bathe in the Blue so that I may stand beside you, in love with you through all eternity.'

'Pharaoh.' Taita looked into his eager eyes. 'As you command, so must I obey.'

'If you succeed, your rewards will be without limit. I will heap upon you all the treasures and honours this world contains.'

'What I have now is sufficient. I have youth and the wisdom of the ages. I have the love of my king and my woman. I do this out of love for you both.'

Taita rode Windsmoke and Fenn was on Whirlwind. Each led a fully laden packhorse. They wore Bedouin garb and carried bow and sword. Meren and Sidudu rode with them as far as the crest of the eastern hills above the estate of Karim Ek-Horus. Here they parted. Sidudu and Fenn shared a sisterly tear, while Meren embraced Taita and kissed his cheek.

'Poor Magus! What will you do without me to care for you?' His voice was rough. 'I warrant you will not be a day out of my sight before you are in some pretty piece of trouble.' Then he turned to Fenn. 'Take care of him and bring him back to us one day.'

Taita and Fenn mounted and rode down the backslope of the hills. They halted half-way and looked back at the two small figures on the heights above them. Meren and Sidudu waved one last time, then turned their horses and vanished over the skyline.

'Where are we going?' Fenn asked.

'First we must cross a sea, great plains and then a high mountain range.'

'After that, whither?'

'Into a deep jungle to the temple of Saraswati, the goddess of wisdom and regeneration.'

'What will we find there?'

'A wise woman who will open your Inner Eye so that you will be able to help me discern the path to the sacred Font more clearly.'

'How long will our journey be?'

'Our journey will be without end, together through all time,' Taita told her.

Fenn laughed with joy. 'Then, my lord, we must begin at once.'

Side by side they spurred the horses and rode out into the unknown.

Visit **www.panmacmillan.com** to read more about all our books and to buy them. You will also find features, author interviews and news of any author events, and you can sign up for e-newsletters so that you're always first to hear about our new releases.